Also by Josephine Cox

QUEENIE'S STORY
Her Father's Sins
Let Loose the Tigers

THE EMMA GRADY TRILOGY
Outcast
Alley Urchin
Vagabonds

Angels Cry Sometimes
Take This Woman
Whistledown Woman
Don't Cry Alone
Jessica's Girl
Nobody's Darling
Born to Serve
More than Riches
A Little Badness
Living a Lie
The Devil You Know
A Time for Us
Cradle of Thorns
Miss You Forever
Love Me or Leave Me
Tomorrow the World
The Gilded Cage
Somewhere, Someday
Rainbow Days
Looking Back
Let It Shine

The Woman Who Left
Jinnie

Bad Boy Jack
The Beachcomber
Lovers and Liars
Live the Dream

The Journey
Journey's End
The Loner
Songbird
Born Bad
Divorced and Deadly

JOSEPHINE COX

Blood Brothers

HARPER

Harper
An imprint of HarperCollins*Publishers*
77–85 Fulham Palace Road,
Hammersmith, London W6 8JB

www.harpercollins.co.uk

This paperback edition 2010
3

First published in Great Britain by
HarperCollins 2010

A catalogue record for this book is
available from the British Library

ISBN: 978-0-00-730145-4

Set in Baskerville by Palimpsest Book Production Limited
Falkirk, Stirlingshire

Printed and bound in Great Britain by
Clays Ltd, St Ives plc

This book is for my Ken, as always

Second Dedication

Writing is often a lonely thing, but I find great joy in being part of the story, where the characters are like family; some you love, some you fear, and some you see as being very close like a friend or relative.

When a book is finished and the characters are launched onto an unsuspecting world, you wonder how the story and its people might be received.

I am always humbled and deeply moved by the opinions of people who interview me and by the way the world seems to have taken my stories to heart.

The letters from readers are a joy, and I want to thank you lovely people of all ages and genders, who talk to me through their correspondence, and who live the stories through reading, as passionately as I live the stories when writing them.

I want to say thank you to all my readers, for taking the time to write to me in your thousands!

And to apologise for being late with my reply. You will always get one, I promise – love and best wishes to you all. Jo x

PART ONE

~

Bedfordshire – England
May 1952

Blood Brothers

CHAPTER ONE

G ENTLY CRADLING THE injured bird, he stood on the high ground, his quiet gaze drawn to the field below.

Up there, in the windswept heights, he cut a fine figure of a man. He was not broad of shoulder, nor thick with muscle, but there was something about him, a certain strength and solitude, and the tall, proud manner in which he stood.

He was a man of integrity. He knew when to speak his mind and when to keep his silence. He also knew when to walk away.

A year ago, he had done exactly that, yet against his better instincts, he had answered his brother's letter and made his way back. Even now he felt uneasy in this familiar place, with his family less than a mile away, and Alice just a few steps from where he now stood.

It seemed he had been away forever. A year ago he left this haven to travel far and wide to search for a quietness of heart that might allow him to build a new life and move on. Yet all he ever found was loneliness.

Out here, in the wide open skies and with only the wild creatures for company, he was at home.

When he was away, this was what he missed. This . . . and a woman who was not his, and never could be.

Now that he was so close to home, he still wasn't sure

he had done the right thing. 'It might have been better if I'd stayed away . . .'

Deep down he had always known it would not be easy, seeing her again. Yet now, here he was and she was just a heartbeat away. Thankfully, she had not yet seen him.

He whispered her name, '*Alice.*' Her name was oddly comforting on his lips, '*Alice.*'

After a while he moved into the spinney where he kept watch, secure in the knowledge that she could not see him.

Discreetly, he continued to watch her through the branches of the ancient trees. He shared her joy as she raced across the field, her green skirt billowing in the breeze, her long chestnut-coloured hair playing over her shoulders. Behind her the lambs followed like children, calling and skipping as she led them, like a pied piper, down to the water's edge.

His thoughtful brown eyes followed her every step. She was the reason he had turned his back on friends and family, and yet it was not her fault, for she had done nothing wrong.

While he was away he had come to realise that whatever he did, wherever he went, she would be there; like the blood that coursed through his veins.

He saw her now; small, strappy shoes clutched in one hand, her skirt held high as she paddled barefoot through the cool-running stream. He blinked at the sun in the skies; he felt the warmth on his face, and for one magic moment the world stood still.

Oblivious to his presence, she rested herself on a boulder, her two arms stretched out and her head back, as she raised her face to the heavens. She made no move to collect the hem of her skirt as it dipped into the water. Instead she stretched out her bare legs to let the cool, frothing water trickle over her skin.

When a stray lamb drew close enough to nuzzle her neck, she tenderly reached out to caress its tiny face.

In this green and glorious landscape, wrapped in silence and surrounded by nature's beauty, she seemed at one with all creation.

For a fleeting moment, when she seemed to lift her gaze his way, he feared she had seen him, yet he made no move. In truth, he could not tear himself away. He had to see her, to fill his senses with her simple beauty. Little more than a year ago she had unknowingly opened his heart and crept inside, and now she was etched there for all time.

It pained him to realise that soon he must turn away and be gone from here. This time, never to return.

For now though, the moment, and the woman, were his. Up here, above the hubbub and maelstrom of ordinary life, time did not exist. It was just the two of them, and that was how it should be. She belonged only to him.

Content, he closed his eyes and let the feelings flow through him. He wished the world might stand still for this one, precious moment. Or maybe even forever.

The guilt was never far away: for his was a love both forbidden and wicked.

He spent every waking moment wanting her. She was the last thought on his mind when he went to sleep, and the first thought on his mind when he woke.

She had caused him such turmoil.

That was what she did to him.

Fearful, the injured bird fluttered in his arms, desperate to escape. 'Ssh!' He looked down into those piercing dark eyes that twinkled up at him. 'She's much like you,' he whispered. 'Wild as the wind; part of the earth itself.'

Acutely aware of the need to tend the bird's injury, he was loath to tear himself away. So he lingered awhile, watching as she waded ankle-deep through the water and on to the far bank. Behind her, the lambs continued to graze on the moist grass.

'She's away to the farmhouse!' Drawing the small creature nearer to his chest, he carefully folded its damaged wing into the palm of his hand. 'We'd best make our way there too.' He stroked its feathers with the tip of his thumb, 'Let's hope we can get you flying again.'

Carrying the bird gently he took the shortest route: down the hill and across the stream, carefully negotiating the stones and boulders as he went.

Soon he caught sight of Alice, running through the long grass, her voice lifted in song. It made him smile.

He continued on, to the farmhouse; the place where he grew up.

The place where he first met Alice.

The anger was like a fist inside him, '. . . yearning after a woman who's already promised to your brother is a dangerous thing,' he murmured.

Though what he felt for Alice was more than a yearning. It was a raging fire that, try as he might, he could not put out.

With the farmhouse in sight, he grew anxious; remembering why he was here. He was sobered by the knowledge that in just a few short days he would stand at the altar, where Alice and his brother would be pronounced man and wife.

It was a prospect he would rather not dwell on.

~

'I wonder if he's on his way?'

Bustling about in the cosy farmhouse kitchen, Nancy Arnold walked over to the window. A small, round woman of fifty years and more, she had the cheekiest, chubbiest face, pretty dark eyes wrinkled with laughter-lines, and a long thick plait of dark brown hair, lightly peppered with grey.

She was a woman of high standards; a woman who stood no nonsense and took no prisoners. Yet she was the kindest, most understanding woman on earth. When the neighbours suffered ill-health or encountered trouble she was the first to lend a helping hand. And when attending a merry occasion, she could outsing and outdance any man or woman; her manner and laughter were so infectious her husband Tom claimed she was shaking the ground with her terrible screeching! Her laughter filled his heart, and he loved her more with every passing year.

'Stop wittering, woman!' he grumbled at her now. 'Sit yer busy backside down an' give us a bit o' quiet!' Peering over his newspaper, he firmly chided. 'Your son will be 'ere when he gets 'ere, and all yer fussing and fretting won't get him here any the sooner!' Having lived in the countryside all his life, Tom had learned to take things as they came.

'Aw, Tom, I'm that worried.'

She turned to look at him. 'We should have had word by now. The wedding's on Saturday. It's Monday already; less than a week to go, and we've heard not a whisper from him. What if he can't get 'ere? What if he's had an accident on the way . . . oh dearie me!'

'Hey!' Crumpling the newspaper to his knee, Tom wagged a finger at her. 'We'll have none o' that kind of talk! Why don't yer make us a nice cup of tea, eh? Happen it'll calm yer nerves.'

'The only thing that'll calm my nerves is the sight of our Joe coming through that door.'

'Mebbe, but watching out for him every two minutes won't bring him 'ere any the quicker.' With his large frame, thick, beard and piercing blue eyes, Tom Arnold was a man of fierce appearance, though like his wife, he had a soft heart.

In no time at all the kettle was whistling on the hob, and Nancy had brewed a pot of tea. She got out the tray, along with two mugs, into which she spooned a generous helping of sugar, then a drop of milk for Tom, and a good measure for herself. After that she took a small plate from the cupboard and sliding four ginger-snaps on to it, she rearranged the whole lot on the tray, before waddling over to the table. 'There y'are then!' She plonked the tray unceremoniously before him. 'So, is there anything else you want?'

'Nope, except for you to sit still. Yer making my nerves bad. First yer at the window, then yer at the door, then yer upstairs at the window again. Then yer 'ere and now yer there, and soon yer off somewheres else. In and out, up and down, making me that dizzy I can't settle to read my blessed paper. Why can't you sit down, drink your tea and be patient?'

'Don't be like that.' Already on her way to the window again, she looked at him in a way that usually melted his heart. But not this time. This time he was desperate to pick out his horses for today's race. 'I know I'm a fidget, but I can't help it,' she complained. 'I'm on edge d'you see?'

She paused, feeling as though she had the weight of the world on her mind. 'Tom?'

He groaned. 'What now?'

'I really am worried.'

'Well you shouldn't be!' Frustrated, he rolled his eyes to heaven. 'Like I said, our Joe will turn up. In any case, as long as he gets here before Saturday morning, it'll be fine. Stop panicking, woman!'

'It's not just about Joe being late,' she replied quietly. 'There's something else . . .'

'Something else?' Now, he was interested. 'Come on then. Let's have it!'

Nancy had not planned to say anything, but it was on her mind and she needed reassurance. 'Has it never puzzled you why our Joe took off like he did,' she asked. 'I mean . . . one minute he was 'ere, and then he were gone, just like that, without any explanation.'

'I did wonder at the time, but I can't say I've lost any sleep over it. Besides, young men are notoriously unpredictable, so don't worry about it. Anyway, I'm sure he had his reasons.'

That was not good enough for Nancy. 'The way I see it, if he could go off on a whim like that at the drop of a hat, without any explanation, who's to say he'll not have another whim and decide to stay away?'

'Because his brother tracked him down a month back and asked him to be his best man, that's why! Like I say, Joe won't let his brother down, and well you know it.'

'He didn't write back straightaway though, did he? It was a whole month before Frank got a reply.'

'Yes, but that's only because like all other young men, Joe is not a letter writer.'

'What if he doesn't *want* to be best man at his brother's wedding?'

'Don't be daft, woman!' Tom put his newspaper aside. 'What the devil's got into you, Nancy?'

'I just wondered, that's all.'

'About what?'

Nancy shrugged her shoulders. 'I'm not really sure. It's just that when Joe left I got the feeling he was upset about something. You remember a couple of nights before he left, Joe was introduced to Alice? Oh, he smiled and gave her a kiss and everything seemed fine. Only, after that, he was too quiet for my liking.'

She recalled it only too well. 'He hardly said two words over dinner, then he went to bed early.'

'That's because he'd been working out in the field all

day, doing the work of three men. Me and the farmhand were away at the market with the calves, and as you recall, Frank had hurt his back. On top of that, it was the hottest day of summer. Joe was drenched with sweat and completely done-in when he finally got home. Frank was all excited because he'd brought Alice home and straight-away she was thrust under Joe's nose. He was even made to welcome her with a kiss, and him being so shy an' all!' Tom gave a hearty chuckle, 'I can't say I'm surprised he had little to say for himself!'

'But it wasn't like Joe to be so quiet,' Nancy insisted. 'The following morning I got up early, determined to find out what was troubling him. When I came down, he was already packed and gone, leaving only a scrap of a letter by the kettle to say he was off to see the world.'

'He wrote and put your mind at rest though, didn't he?' She shook her head. 'He's always put duty first before,' Tom replied reassuringly.

'From what I recall about his letter, Joe seemed happy enough,' Tom reminded her. 'He was making good money working the fairground, and he'd palled up with another lad. So, when the boss offered them the chance to go to Europe with the fair, they jumped at it!' He chuckled. 'I don't mind telling yer . . . if I'd been offered the same chance when I were Joe's age, I'd have been gone like a shot!'

'So, you think the only reason he left was because he wanted to see the world?' Nancy asked.

'That's *exactly* what I think, yes.' Tom was not a natural liar, but he had to put Nancy's mind to rest.

The last thing he wanted to do was alarm her with his own suspicions about why Joe left.

In fact his thoughts on the matter were so unsettling, he had never once shared them with Nancy.

Nancy was like a dog with a bone. 'Are you sure he

didn't say anything to you?' she persisted. 'About why he was rushing away, or where he was headed?'

'He said nothing to me, but like I'm telling you, it's likely he wanted to see what the big wide world had to offer before he settled down.'

Tom thought of his own life and how his world had only ever been this farm, rented from the landowner by his grandfather and father before him. 'I remember when *I* were twenty-five,' he remarked thoughtfully. 'I were still working the land morning 'til night, seven days a week.'

'Ah, yes, but that was then and this is now,' Nancy reminded him. 'Times change, don't forget that.'

'I'm not likely to, because here I am, an old man plagued with aching bones and a nagging wife. I've two grown sons: one of 'em's fled the nest, and the other's straining at the leash to get wed. I've a heap o' responsibility weighing me down, an' after all these years' hard work, I haven't even managed to buy a house to call our own!'

Nancy was taken aback by his outburst. 'In all the years we've been married, I've never once heard you talk like that.' It worried her. 'Are you saying you regret your life?'

'Absolutely not!' Giving her a reassuring wink, Tom reached out and kissed her on the mouth, before revealing sincerely, 'I don't regret a single minute of it, and as for you and my boys, you *are* my life. That's what it's all been about and still is. And there isn't a day passes that I don't give thanks.'

Feeling emotional, Nancy told him passionately, 'You're such a good man, Tom.' She gave him a look that only a woman in love could give. 'Since you first asked me to dance at the village hall, I felt proud to be with you. I always will.'

'Thank you, sweetheart.' He smiled into those pretty brown eyes. 'I'm proud of you an' all, and I'm proud of our two sons. Different though they may be, they're both good, fine fellows.'

'Tom?' There was something else playing on her mind.

'What now, sweetheart?' He so wanted to get back to his horses.

'Don't take this the wrong way, but I was wondering, what d'you think to Alice? Do you really think her and Frank will be happy together?'

'Mmm . . .' He chose his words carefully. 'If I'm honest, I reckon she might be a bit young. She's not yet twenty, and Frank is nearly seven years older. That said, she thinks the world of our Frank, and he adores her. So what do a few years matter, eh?'

'So, you really think she's the right one for our son?'

Remembering what he had witnessed that night a year ago, Tom chose his words carefully. 'Well now, I don't have a crystal ball, but I would say Alice has the true makings of a farmer's wife.'

He paused, remembering how calm and helpful Alice had been when they had had a bad incident with a month-old foal. 'D'you recall how that young postman ran to tell us how Alice was in trouble and needed help? Youngsters from the town had smashed part of the fence down at the far field, and one of the foals had got caught up in it?'

Nancy recalled it vividly. 'Its mother was running crazy, and wouldn't let anyone near.'

He reminded her, 'I reckon that mad mare would have killed anyone who went near her young 'un. The vet couldn't get anywhere near until Alice calmed the mare long enough for him to tend the foal.'

Nancy remembered it well. 'She's certainly got a way with animals. She's not afraid of hard work neither. All in all, I think you're right. Young Alice will fit in with the family very nicely.'

She added reluctantly, 'I'm not sure Joe approves of her though.'

Tom was surprised. 'What put that idea into yer head?'

'I might be wrong,' she replied thoughtfully, 'only I got the feeling that he would rather she wasn't here, that's all.'

Tom was quick to dispel her fears. 'Honestly, Nancy. Fancy thinking our Joe would take a dislike to a girl who wouldn't harm a fly! I expect he had his head so full of adventure, he didn't even notice her!'

Nancy seemed relieved. 'Yes, that must have been it. Forget what I said.'

Tom watched her as she ambled across the room. Leaning her elbows on the window sill, she gave a soft laugh. 'Hey! Wouldn't it be something if he turned up with a girl on his arm?'

'I shouldn't think our Joe will bring a woman home just yet,' he told Nancy now. He then muttered under his breath, 'Why would he do that, when the girl he fancies is right here?'

Tom had long suspected that was why Joe had gone away: because he had fallen for his brother's woman, and he couldn't deal with it. Neither could Tom, for it was a terrible, shameful thing.

All the same, Tom understood how sometimes love grabs you when you least expect it, and no one could control who they fall in love with.

He didn't blame Joe. He didn't blame anyone; though he had secretly admired his son for doing the right thing in putting a distance between himself and Alice.

He felt a sense of unease. 'I hope to God our Joe's over her. If not, it could really put the cat among the pigeons!' he whispered to himself.

'What was that you said?' Nancy swung round.

'What?' Pretending he was deep in his newspaper, Tom looked up, '*I* didn't say anything!'

'I thought you said something about a cat among the pigeons?'

'Naw. Yer must be getting old. Hearing voices in yer head now is it?'

Sighing, Nancy ambled back to her chair. 'I'm all wound up,' she said, 'I'll be all right when Joe gets here.'

As Nancy sipped her tea, Tom took a moment to look at her. As a girl she was much like Alice: the same long brown hair and inquisitive mind. She hadn't changed that much, he thought. Yes, she was plumper, and the dark hair was sprinkled with grey, but when she smiled, the years flew away, and it was the girl he saw.

Laying his hand on hers, he kissed her tenderly on the cheek, and never said a word. He didn't have to, because she knew already.

'You're an old softie, that's what you are.' She smiled up at him, 'And you're right about our sons. They *are* different; I've always thought Joe took after you, and Frank is more in the nature of your father. He'll see a lamb all caught up and rescue it, but it's not the lamb he's rescuing, it's the money it'll fetch at market.'

'Well o'course! He's a farmer, and that's how *any* farmer would think, even though he's not altogether conscious of it.'

'I know that, but what I'm saying is, Joe would rescue the same lamb yes, but only because it pains him to see it caught up. The money it might bring at market wouldn't even enter his head.'

Tom nodded. 'Aye well, there yer have it. You see, our Frank has the same attitude as my own father, and there is nothing wrong with that! It shows he's a hard-headed businessman. He sees everything in black and white, while Joe takes time to see the shades and the colours.'

'Oh, and you don't?' She smiled knowingly.

'Give over, woman. I've no time for all that!'

Embarrassed, he grabbed his newspaper and hid behind it. 'I need some new specs,' he grumbled. 'The print on the pages gets smaller by the minute!'

Gently, Nancy drew the newspaper away. 'You don't fool me, Tom Arnold.' She knew him like she knew herself.

Feigning anger, he wagged a finger. 'Look! It's hard enough to keep a family going if the crops are ruined or you lose an animal. Survival! That's the thing, and don't you be mekking any more of it!'

Snatching his newspaper he again buried his head in it. 'Go on! Away to the window and watch for Joe!'

As she prepared to move away, he caught her by the arm. 'I hope you know how much I love you, and how lucky I am to have yer,' he declared stoutly.

'Right, well just you remember that when you're yelling at me.'

Her comment made him smile. 'When have I ever yelled at you?'

'Hmm. Have you got all day?'

Chuckling, he folded the newspaper and laid it on the arm of the chair,

A few minutes later, after returning from her disappointing vigil at the window, she came to sit beside him. 'It'll be so good to have our Joe home.'

Having settled herself into the chair, she sipped her lukewarm tea, while at the same time observing the state of the painted walls. 'How long is it since these walls were painted?' she asked.

'Long time.' Tom peeked over his newspaper. 'Six or seven years . . . maybe more.'

Tom had to agree the place was looking the worse for wear, but he would never admit it.

'Folks might think it all a bit jaded, that's all I'm saying,' Nancy pointed out.

'What folks think is no concern of ours.' Tom declared.

'You need to remember, this place doesn't belong to us. I'm sure that tight-fisted landlord won't be shelling out money if he can help it, and *we* certainly can't afford to redecorate. Not with the wedding coming up an' all.'

'Ah, well, not to worry, eh?' Nancy was a sensible woman, and right now she had more important things on her mind. 'Let's just hope nobody comes back here after the celebration.' She gave him a cheeky wink. 'If they do, they'll have to accept us as we are. As long as the wedding goes without a hitch, it doesn't really matter.'

'There won't be any hitches,' he promised cheerfully. 'Not with you in charge, and half the village wanting to help.'

Nancy gave no reply to that, although she knew from experience that things could go so easily wrong. In her usual forthright manner, she had learned to take nothing for granted.

She proudly informed him, 'Everything has been well organised. Flowers are arranged and paid for. The band is booked, and the suits for you and the boys are hanging in the closet; though Joe's might need a tweak here and there, depending on whether he's changed his shape since we last saw him.'

Tom was duly impressed. 'Sounds to me like you've thought of everything.'

'I hope so. I've gone over the menu for the meal, and now there's just the wedding-cake. Seeing as I'm baking it, the cost is half what it would have been if I'd ordered one.'

She gave a little scowl. 'It's as well I'm doing the cake, because even Alice had to admit that her mother is a terrible cook. Apparently, she can't even produce a proper Yorkshire pud!'

Tom chuckled. 'There y'are y'see. It's just as well you're available then, isn't it?'

In fact, Nancy felt well pleased with herself. 'Mind you, Alice's mother played her part in helping Alice choose the flowers. Though she wasn't able to make Alice change her mind about having wild flowers in amongst the tulips and such. To be honest I reckon a mixture of colourful wild flowers will look absolutely gorgeous!'

There was one other thing. 'In the end though Alice didn't get much of a say in the wedding dress, she did manage to lose the idea of frills and bows like her mother wanted. Instead the dress will be sewn with daisies and forget-me-nots . . . all made out of silk and satin.'

Tom smiled in agreement. 'Alice is a simple country girl at heart,' he said softly. 'She won't have her head turned by expense and fancy, and I'm proud of that! If you ask me, she'll walk down the aisle looking like a million dollars!'

Nancy's thoughts had already turned again to her youngest son. 'Everything is ready now.' She glanced anxiously towards the window. 'All we need is for Joe to show his face.'

Having had enough of the cold tea, she was quickly away, watching at the window again. 'He'll not show while you're watching,' Tom groaned. 'Anyway, I thought you had umpteen jobs to get done?'

'They can wait.' She ran her finger over the smeared window. 'Tom Arnold!' Swinging round she confronted him. 'You promised faithfully you would clean the windows, and they've not even been touched!'

'Sorry, love. I'll do it later.' Shame-faced, he buried his head in his newspaper. 'Just give me a few minutes, and I'll get on with it . . . soon as I've chosen the winning horses.'

Minutes passed, and still there was no sign of Joe. 'You're right again,' she muttered. 'A watched kettle never boils.'

Just then she caught sight of Alice. 'Oh, look!' Pointing as though Tom could see from across the room, she told him, 'There's Alice. For a minute I thought it might be our Joe coming out of the barn.'

'Give over, woman! If he *is* on his way back, he'd hardly make the barn his first stop, now would he?'

Returning to his newspaper, he blocked his ears to Nancy's running commentary. 'No doubt she's off to collect the early apples. They're keepers d'you see? If you leave them too late the insects burrow in, and they're not worth tuppence. But pick them before they ripen and they'll come up a treat after a few weeks in the barn.'

'Don't teach your grandmother to suck eggs.' Tom had to put her right. 'I were collecting keeper-apples when you were still in nappies.'

'Oh, dear me I forgot!' She gave him a derisory glance. 'There's nothing *you* can teach me about farming is there, eh?'

'Nope.'

'So, what about the potatoes last season? I suggested we get the potato crop in before the rains came, and you argued that the weather would be absolutely fine for at least another week. Two days later the skies burst open and it poured for days. So thanks to you we lost half the crop.'

He suffered her teasing for the next few minutes, while intermittently nodding and grunting, as though he was paying attention. If she paused he'd look up and say, 'Really . . . well fancy that!'

'I feel awful now.' Nancy returned to the wedding. 'I promised Alice I'd give her a hand with bringing the apples in, but there's been so much on my mind I completely forgot.'

'She won't mind.'

In spite of his concerns with regard to Joe, he truly

believed that in Alice, Frank had found himself the makings of a fine wife.

~

Alice had just placed the last of the keepers into the basket when she saw Joe going into the barn. She called out after him. Collecting the basket, she ran out of the orchard and along the shingle path to the big barn.

At the doorway she peered inside, and there was Joe, tenderly stroking the injured bird. 'We'll get you right,' he told it softly. 'You'll soon be able to spread your wings and soar through the skies where you belong.'

Suddenly aware of someone watching him, he turned quickly. 'Hello, Joe,' she said softly. Putting the basket to the ground, Alice came forward, her face bright with a smile. 'I wasn't sure it was you at first. I only ever saw you the once, and then you were gone. That was a year ago now, wasn't it?' She remembered their first meeting, how quiet and shy he seemed, and how each time she glanced up, he was looking at her. There was something about Frank's younger brother that made her nervous. For a long time after he left, she found herself missing him.

For a moment, Joe didn't say anything. Instead he thought of that fateful day when Frank brought her home, and how he couldn't take his eyes off her. And yes, it may have been a year ago, but to him it was like only yesterday.

So many times of late he had hoped that when he saw her again things might be different, but they weren't. The feelings he had then were still there, haunting him. The very sight of her made his heart beat faster, and his throat was so dry he could hardly breathe.

'Alice!' He felt foolish, not really knowing what to say. 'I'm sorry. I didn't see you there.'

Closing the distance between them, she smiled up at

him. 'That's because you were so intent on comforting the bird.'

Reaching out, she stroked the bird along its velvet, feathery neck. 'He's a *falcon*, isn't he?'

'That's right,' Joe confirmed. 'I don't think he's long out of the nest. Maybe he hasn't yet learned the art of diving for his prey.'

'What's wrong with him?' Whenever a creature was hurt, Alice felt it deeply. Sometimes, when she was worried or feeling lonely, the creatures gave her a great sense of peace and timelessness.

Even as a child, she had always felt far safer with animals than with any human – including her parents.

She thought of her mother, always arguing and fighting, thinking only of herself. She was a cold person, cold and selfish. Yet she could not hate her, nor could she love her. That was her deepest regret.

'Is he badly hurt?' She turned her attention to the falcon.

'His wing is damaged, but I think he'll be okay,' Joe assured her.

Alice glanced along the run of stables where the two work-horses had their heads over the doors and were looking out. 'You could put him in the empty stable.'

Joe had already seen that possibility. 'I'll need to protect him from the cats and foxes.' He looked about him. 'There should be an old cage in here. It used to belong to my pet rabbit when I was a boy.'

'I know it!' Excited, she ran the full length of the barn and there, behind some old corn barrels, she located it: a small, wooden box with a door at the side. 'Here it is!' Pulling it out, she stood it on the barrel. 'It doesn't look broken or anything.' She continued to examine it as Joe made his way down.

'It's perfect!' Placing the fluttering bird in Alice's safe

hands, Joe quickly filled the cage with a bed of hay, then he rummaged about until he found a suitable piece of cane, which he used for a splint. Skilfully shaving off the sharp edges, he then snapped off a length of bale twine and while Alice held the bird close, he secured the splint along the falcon's damaged wing. 'That should hold.'

Collecting the bird from Alice, he placed it in the cage and secured the door. He then searched for something to fill with water. 'This'll do!' After unscrewing the deep lid from the top of an old storage jar, he went to the side of the barn where he washed it out under the tap, then he filled the container with water and placed it inside the cage near to the falcon.

'Oh look!' Alice was thrilled when the injured bird shuffled slowly along and, stretching out to reach the water, took a drink.

'That's good!' Joe was relieved. 'He'll be fine now. I'm just wondering . . . maybe he'd be safer inside the house until his wing is mended?'

'No!' Alice rejected the idea. 'I know he might be safer,' she agreed, 'but he would be so unhappy. He should never be put inside. Make him safe out here, where he won't be too afraid. Please, Joe?'

When Joe looked down into those strong, blue eyes, he was deeply moved. 'You're absolutely right,' he told her. 'I wasn't thinking.'

Quickly, he created a large harness out of a length of steel strapping. That done, he then secured it round the cage, and strung the cage from the rafters. 'That way, it'll be even more difficult for the foxes and cats to get at him.'

Together they went out of the barn and into the bright sunlight. There was something unique between them: a friendship born from shared experience.

Or something else, which was destined to have far-reaching and tragic consequences.

Inside the farmhouse, Tom was at the end of his tether. 'Will you come away from that damned window. You're making me nervous, to-ing and fro-ing, grumbling and muttering!'

He gave her an ultimatum. 'Either you find something else to do, other than stand at the window fretting, or I'm off out down the pub to find a bit o' peace . . .'

Nancy was past listening, because now she was hopping up and down on the spot, shouting at the top of her voice. 'He's here!' With a screech of delight, she was out the door, leaving Tom with a parting rebuke, 'I said he'd be here and I was right!'

Ambling to the door he watched as she ran headlong into Joe's open arms. 'That's put a smile on her face.' He observed Joe's tall, capable figure, and that easy manner he had, and he felt proud. 'Your mother's missed you, son,' he whispered. 'We all have.'

He remained at the door for a moment, a smile on his face as he watched Joe swing his mother round in a hug. 'It's damned good to see you, Joe,' he nodded his head. 'When all's said and done, it's only right that you should be here to stand beside your brother.'

He began his way down the path, his gaze intent on Joe and Alice as they talked and laughed together.

Seeing them so close and natural had a deep, unsettling effect on him. Instinctively, he glanced towards the fields, looking for his eldest son; relieved to see that Frank was nowhere in sight, because if he had been, he would not have failed to see the magnetism between these two.

As he got nearer to the little group, Tom continued to chatter to himself, his voice a mingling of sadness and anger. 'I'm no fool, Joe. Don't think I didn't see how you were, the first time you saw Alice. I'm sure you didn't mean it to happen. I know you would never do anything to hurt your brother. That's why you put a distance between yourself and Alice, but I can see now, you still have feelings for her.'

His voice hardened. 'Remember, son . . . Alice and Frank are to be wed on Saturday, and you'll be there to hand over the ring. In the eyes of the Lord and all that's legal, they'll be man and wife, and like it or not, you'll be expected to give them your blessing.'

There was nothing more he wanted than to have all his family together. But thankfully, that was not about to happen. Besides, with two men, living under the same roof and wanting the same woman? His old heart sank. That would be a recipe for trouble, and no mistake!

'Tom!' Alice came running up the path to meet him. 'Look! Joe's here!' Taking him by the hand, they approached Nancy and Joe, Alice all the while chattering excitedly. 'I knew he wouldn't let us down.'

Thrilled that at long last he was here to be Frank's best man at their wedding, Alice reached up to kiss him on the cheek. 'I forgot to thank you, Joe.'

'Joe found an injured falcon,' she informed them. 'He's made it safe in his old rabbit hutch.'

Joe was quick to hug his dad. 'It's really good to see you and Mum,' he said fondly. 'You're both looking well.'

'So are you, son, and I'll want to know all about your travels later on.' For now, he was interested in Joe's find. 'What's all this about an injured falcon?'

'Looks like a young one,' Joe explained. 'We've put a splint on its wing and bedded it down with a dish of water.' He glanced towards the barn, 'Given a few days I reckon it'll be just fine.'

Tom grinned. 'You haven't changed, son,' he said fondly. 'You always did have a soft spot for anything injured.'

Glancing at his parents, Joe thought they hadn't aged a day since he last saw them. 'Look, Dad . . . Mum, I'm sorry I couldn't make it earlier . . .' he apologised. 'Only . . . I had things to do . . .'

'We understand, Joe love, and it's all right. All that matters is that you're home for the wedding,' Nancy said warmly.

'I'm glad to be here,' Joe answered, though having seen Alice again, he suddenly wasn't so sure.

Just a short while ago, he had started to feel more confident about being here. Until Alice had kissed him. With the warmth of her lips still burning his face, he realised more than ever how coming back here was a bad mistake.

But it was too late now. For all sorts of reasons.

Not a man for hugging, Tom gave his son a fond pat on the back. 'Come on in, son. You can tell us what you've been up to.'

As the two of them went ahead, Nancy and Alice followed just a few steps behind.

Once inside the farmhouse, there was a real air of excitement. 'Shall I go and get Frank?' Alice asked eagerly. 'He's setting out the fencing posts in the top field.'

Tom thought that was a good idea. 'Although, that fence needs finishing, but I expect you'd best run off and fetch him. No doubt he'll be keen to see his brother. Matter o' fact, he might want to take him into Bedford.' He noticed how Joe had only a canvas bag, which was strung over his shoulder and appeared to be half empty. 'Happen Joe might need to buy a new shirt or two?'

Nancy was having none of it, 'Frank is not taking him anywhere! At least not yet. Joe's only just arrived. He must be worn out and hungry. Let him rest while I get us all something to eat.'

Turning to Alice, she informed her, 'Oh, and by the way, Frank isn't in the top field. I saw him earlier on. By the manner of his route, I imagine he was away to plough the rough area down by the brook.'

Alice thanked her. 'I won't be long,' she promised. 'I'll tell him he's to come home, and that we're all taking time out for something to eat . . . is that all right?'

Nancy smiled. 'That's it. Oh, and don't you forget what I said . . . no paddling in the brook. You might frighten the ducks.'

At that Alice laughed. 'They don't mind me,' she said.

While Joe was watching the two women, Tom noticed how Joe's gaze was instinctively drawn to Alice. Just before, when Alice thanked Joe with that innocent little kiss on the cheek, Tom sensed it had unsettled him.

It was nothing glaringly obvious, and it didn't seem to have attracted anyone's notice as such. Even Alice herself had not realised the effects of that grateful little kiss.

Tom had felt it though; just like before when Joe was first introduced to Alice. There was a kind of undercurrent; a strong, palpable presence that wrapped the two of them together and excluded everyone else from the room.

It was a dangerous thing, and one that deeply worried him.

It was painfully obvious to Tom that his youngest son still harboured strong feelings for his brother's woman. If anything, his absence had only fuelled the need in him.

He was grateful that for the moment at least, both Alice and Nancy had failed to sense anything untoward.

The truth was, he didn't really know how to deal with it, other than sending his son away; right now, with the wedding so near and everyone excitedly looking forward to it, that was no easy option. Besides, he didn't have the heart to do such a thing.

All he could do was keep a close eye on things, because

one thing was certain. Here was a worrying situation, which could easily escalate out of hand.

Emotions were powerful things. They could cripple a man.

And sometimes, however hard that man might try, it was hard to keep control.

CHAPTER TWO

CALLING AS SHE ran, Alice went like the wind over the rise and on down to the brook. 'Frank!' She could see him in the distance, but he was too far away to hear her.

Quickly she ran towards him, her feet hardly touching the ground as she sped along. 'Frank! Joe's here!' Her cries were lost to the elements.

Reaching the brook, she tore off her shoes and, holding them one in each hand, splashed her way through the cool water. When the water deepened, she climbed out to run the rest of the way, quickly closing the distance between her and Frank.

'Frank!' Unaware of her approach, he was intent on trying to start the tractor.

'Frank, Joe's here!' She continued to shout his name.

Suddenly Frank turned and saw her. He saw how the wind had whipped up the red in her cheeks and he saw how anxious she seemed. 'Alice!' He went at the run towards her. 'Why are you here? What's happened?' When, breathless and soaked to the waist, she ran into his arms, he feared the worst. 'Alice! What's wrong?' His concern heightened when she was unable to catch her breath and speak.

'He's here!' Gasping, she laughed up at him. 'I've been sent to fetch you!'

Holding her at arm's length, Frank demanded, '*Who's* here? *Who* sent you to fetch me?'

'Nancy! Your mother!!' Having taken a long, deep breath she laughed out loud. '*Joe's here!* He arrived just now; Nancy said I was to come and get you.'

When Frank didn't respond, Alice asked worriedly, 'Aren't you pleased? I though you *wanted* Joe for your best man. Wasn't that why you tracked him down, so you could ask him?'

'Well o'course!' Reassuring her, Frank drew Alice to him. 'There's nobody more thrilled than me to have him home for the wedding.' Though now he was actually here, Frank was not so sure.

Pushing Alice away he took note of her flushed face, and the manner in which her wet dress clung to every curve. He felt a surge of anger. 'For God's sake . . . look at you! You're soaked to the skin!' For some inexplicable reason he resented her excitement at Joe's arrival.

Grabbing his coat from the tractor, he threw it roughly round her shoulders. 'What's the matter with you?' he demanded. 'What have I told you about going in the brook? Why didn't you send Jimmy down to find me?'

'I didn't know where Jimmy was.' Her spirit deflated by his surly attitude, Alice spoke quietly. 'I haven't seen him.'

Seeing how her smile had fallen away, Frank was quick to apologise. 'Sorry, Alice . . . it's just that I hoped to get this work finished, and now I've got trouble with the damned tractor.'

Alice shrugged. 'It's all right, I understand.' All the same, she was surprised at his sudden mood change.

'I sent Jimmy to the barn to see if he could start the old tractor and fetch it down,' he explained. 'Oh, I know the old banger's about had its day, but if he can start it, we might just manage to get this job done.' His voice hardened. 'That was over an hour ago, and he's *still* not back!'

He glanced about. 'Where the hell is he? You know what? I'm beginning to think he's not up to farm work. I swear if he doesn't soon buck up his ideas, I'll kick his lazy arse out of it! I gave him a warning a couple of days ago, when I found him asleep in the hedgerow, and now you say he can't be found, eh? Well, this is the last straw!'

'I didn't say he can't be found,' Alice corrected him, 'I said I hadn't seen him.'

'Same thing!'

Just then, from somewhere in the distance, they heard the sound of an engine spluttering and coughing. 'Would you believe it!' Frank stretched his neck to see. Pointing to the plume of dark smoke rising through the air, he laughed out loud. 'Well, I'm damned! He managed to get her going!'

Alice wasn't sure if the time was right to remind him, but she did anyway. 'What about Joe? He's come back like you asked him, and Nancy said for you to come home, because she's making us all a bite to eat.'

'I can't leave now!' He scowled. 'Surely you can see that?'

'So, what will I tell her?'

Frank grew impatient. 'Tell her whatever you like.' He started running towards the tractor. 'Joe won't mind,' he shouted. 'He'll not be going anywhere.'

Throwing off his jacket, Alice ran after him, but having just dashed all the way there and with a wet skirt lapping round her legs, she could hardly keep up. 'Can't you get Jimmy to hold the fort for an hour?' she called back.

Coming to a halt, Frank waited for her to catch up. 'Get Jimmy to hold the fort . . . that idiot?' He shook his head in disbelief. 'Use your common sense! Just tell them

I can't come back right now. If we don't get on, the tractor might stop and if that happens, we're buggered!'

He gave her a dismissive kiss on the mouth, before running on up the hill. 'Don't push her too hard, you damned fool!' she heard him yelling at Jimmy. 'It's been a while since she were started up!'

He waited for Jimmy to get alongside. 'Took you long enough, didn't it?' Frank grumbled. 'Get down from there!'

Jimmy climbed down. It was not a graceful thing to see, for Jimmy Slater was a man of slow habit. Thick-built, he was not the most intelligent man on earth, nor the prettiest.

With his hair receding from a high forehead, he had a long, thick pony-tail which hung partway down his back. His bottom lip was wet and drooping and his big lolloping eyes were unnerving if they caught you in their sights.

'I never thought I'd get it started.' Covered from head to toe in patches of grease and oil, Jimmy Slater looked a comical figure.

After saying hello to Jimmy, Alice took her leave. 'I'm sure I don't know what's got into him,' she muttered as she went. 'I've never seen him in such a bad mood.' But knowing how important it was to get the ploughing done, she put it out of her mind.

All the same, by the time she arrived at the farmhouse, Alice was unusually low in spirit. 'He's right about Jimmy though,' she admitted as she came up the path. 'He *is* a bit of a daydream at times. I don't suppose you can blame Frank for not trusting him with the ploughing.'

She said the very same when Nancy asked where Frank was. 'Frank will be along soon as he can.' She relayed Frank's message word for word.

Nancy was more concerned about Alice. 'I don't need

to ask how you got soaked,' she tutted. 'Away upstairs and into some of my old dry clothes before you catch your death o' cold!'

Alice apologised. 'I got soaked because I went the quickest way, and I went the quickest way because I needed to find Frank,' Alice explained.

'You should never wade through the brook,' Nancy warned. 'There are sharp stones and bits of debris lying at the bottom. You could have hurt yourself.'

'Leave the girl be!' Tom chipped in. He thought there were times when Nancy could be a bit too sharp. 'Alice is a grown woman, about to be wed for goodness' sake. Don't treat her like a naughty child.'

Having only Alice's welfare at heart, Nancy was mortified. 'Oh, I'm sorry, Alice. Sometimes I let my tongue run away with me.'

Alice gave her a hug, 'It's really nice that you worry about me,' she said gently. 'I'll go and get changed.'

Out the corner of her eye she could see Joe standing by the window, a cup of steaming tea in his hand and a mischievous look on his face. When their eyes met, he gave a reassuring smile.

Returning the smile, Alice made her way towards the stairs.

A short while later Alice returned, washed and dried; her hair tied back in a ribbon, and looking fresh in a pale cream-coloured dress with floral collar and wide belt. 'Oh, Alice! You look pretty as a picture! I remember that dress from when I was young.' Nancy ushered her to the table. 'Now then, I've made you a cup of honey and hot milk. You're to drink it straight down and no arguments, 'cause it'll keep the chills away!'

Outside, Tom and Joe were deep in conversation. Settling Alice at the table, Nancy drew Alice's gaze to where the two men were sitting under the beech tree.

'Tom's eager to know what our Joe's been up to, and Joe needs to know that we're all right.'

A look of pride lit her homely features. 'Joe's been a fine son to us,' she confided. 'Oh, it's not to say our Frank isn't also a good lad, because of course he is. Only they have a different way of dealing with things.'

Curious, Alice asked her, 'How do you mean?'

Nancy had a heart full of love for both her sons, but she was careful in her reply. 'They're different in nature, that's all,' she answered cagily.

'In what way?' Alice asked curiously.

Nancy thought about that. 'Well now, let me see.' She parked herself in the chair opposite Alice. 'They're both hard-working, and they've each got their good points,' she emphasised. 'But y'see, Joe is more a thinker than Frank; although I'm not altogether sure his dad would agree. What I mean is that our Joe will examine a problem from all angles before he makes a decision, while Frank is more impatient and impulsive. He'll only see what he wants to see. He'll often dive in at the deep end without weighing up the consequences first.'

She laughed. 'He was the same as a boy . . . put the fear of God in me at times, he did!'

Almost oblivious to Alice's presence, she began to reminisce. 'I recall when Tom had his new fork-lift delivered. Joe was only a toddler, while Frank was coming up to his sixth birthday. I was in the kitchen and I'd put young Joe outside in the wooden playpen . . . lovely thing it was. His dad made it for him.'

She hesitated, her face drawn up in a deep frown. 'When I wasn't looking, Frank carried his brother to the truck and tied him on to the forks. 'Course little Joe thought it was all a game. When I saw what had happened, I ran out. By the time I got there, Frank was already in the driving seat, trying to start the engine.'

She gave a great heavy sigh. 'It nearly gave me a heart attack!'

Having learned a little about the mechanics on a farm, Alice was horrified. 'If Frank had started the engine and the forks had gone up, Joe could have been badly injured!' She knew that much.

Nancy agreed, though she had never seen it as a deliberately cruel prank, more as Frank's little game to amuse his baby brother.

She said so now. 'Of course, Frank didn't realise that Joe could have been injured,' she said. 'But his father was horrified. He gave Frank a bit of a spanking and put him to bed.'

Nancy chuckled. 'He went wild, kicking and yelling, and wanting to come down. But his father said he was to stay there until he realised that what he had done was dangerous. Later on Frank apologised, and nothing like that ever happened again. Like I say . . . Frank's a fine man but as a boy, he did have a bit of a temper.' She could have said more. Instead, she turned her mind to other things.

Taking hold of Alice's hand, she wrapped her two hands around it. 'You'll be so good for him, Alice,' she said quietly. 'You have a calming nature, and I've never known anyone to be so kind of heart. Oh! and you have such spirit, for a little thing!'

She looked down into Alice's remarkable dark-blue eyes and she was convinced that here was a young woman who would be a match for Frank; not in a bullish way, but with her quiet, loving nature.

'I'm so glad he met you,' she told Alice. 'There's no one else I'd rather see him spend his life with.'

Afraid she might have said too much, Nancy was quick to assure Alice. 'Frank adores the ground you walk on, did you know that?'

'Yes, I know that,' Alice said. 'And I think the world of him too.'

Relieved, Nancy went on. 'He'll make a fine husband, like he's been a fine son. To tell the truth, me and his dad don't know what we'd have done without him this past year, what with Joe having gone away so sudden.'

'Joe's back now though,' Alice pointed out. 'Maybe he won't ever go away again.'

'I'm glad he's back,' Nancy admitted. 'But to be honest, I'm not altogether sure he'll stay.'

'Why's that?'

'Because Joe has the wanderlust.' Nancy would have been overjoyed if Joe made up his mind to stay home, and she confided as much in Alice. 'We can but hope though, eh?'

Alice nodded in heartfelt agreement. She had known Joe for only a few hours, yet she felt like she had known him all her life.

Having opened up old memories, Nancy continued to sing Frank's praises. 'You'll never want for a roof over your head with Frank to look after you. He has the makings of a good husband.'

'And will *Joe* make some woman a good husband?' Alice wondered aloud.

Nancy was quick to assure her. 'Either one of my sons would protect his woman with his life, but unlike Frank, I don't reckon a roof over his head would be our Joe's first consideration.'

'Really?' Somehow, Alice was not surprised.

'Yes, really! Y'see, whereas Frank would need the security of four walls and a roof round him, our Joe would never see that as a priority. I reckon as long as he's got the sky above, the land under his feet and the open road before him, he'll be content enough.'

'So, is that where he's been this past year . . . on the open road?'

Nancy fell silent for a moment. 'Who knows? Not to worry though, because he was always a quiet soul. I expect he'll confide in us when he's good and ready.'

Just then, Tom returned from the garden. 'Our Joe's gone to give Frank a helping hand,' he informed them. 'Since falling off my horse some time back, I find it difficult walking all that way across the fields. It takes an effort just going upstairs at night. But Frank will be glad of Joe's help, I'm sure.'

Nancy nodded. 'Me and Alice were about to get dinner on the table,' she said. 'So you've at least an hour before you're needed. Why don't you go and rest your gammy leg while you've got the chance?'

Tom didn't need telling twice. 'Good idea!' Coming to the table, he collected his newspaper and went away.

Nancy groaned. 'He spends more time with his precious four-legged nags than he does with me! I swear . . . if there was a fire and he had the chance to save one thing, it would be his blessed newspaper!'

Nattering to herself, she turned away and set about making the dinner.

Before she even got started, Alice was right beside her. 'I'll do the potatoes if you want?' she told Nancy, and Nancy was only too pleased to be rid of the tedious task. 'Good girl!' she said. 'You do that, while I make a start on the apple pie.'

Through the kitchen window she could see Joe disappearing over the headland. 'I do hope he decides to stay,' she murmured to herself, 'I've missed him so.'

She had fully enjoyed her little chat with Alice, though she wondered if she had imparted a little too much. All the same, she had said nothing that should worry Alice. It was true! Frank *did* adore the ground Alice walked on, and according to what Alice had told her, she felt the very same towards Frank. It was a comforting thought.

All she wanted now was for her youngest son to stay with the family. Once Frank and Alice were wed, and moved out, this delightful farmhouse would be a lonely place; especially with Tom always hiding behind his blessed newspaper!

She looked out the window again. There was no sign of Joe at all now.

~

Joe took the long road, up the rise and down alongside the brook to the bottom field. He had no wish to soak himself by paddling through the brook. He thought of Alice and smiled. 'No doubt Alice would have gone straight through the water.'

He saw himself in Alice; a free spirit. No one should ever shackle her, he thought. No one should ever deaden her spirit and break her heart, and most of all, no one should ever change what and who she was. That would be unforgiveable.

In his mind he went over the events of the past year. He thought of how his own spirit had been broken; though here and now, among the fields and trees with only the soothing sound of nature in his ears, at long last he was beginning to heal.

Pausing in his stride, he glanced up at the shifting skies. 'You helped me,' he murmured, as though to some unseen presence. 'You helped me stay strong, when life became impossible.'

This past year there had been many bad times when he was close to despair. But day by day he had forced himself to look forward. He thought of his family, and especially Alice, and somehow, through those dark days and nights, he had managed to survive.

Thankfully it was over now, and this beautiful place

where he had grown from boy to man, was slowly reaching out, to strengthen his faith, and purpose. Giving him the ability to rise above anything that life might test him with.

He rested a moment, up there at the top of the world. He felt such peace, and a sense of joy that he had not felt for a long time.

Back there, when he had sat with his father and talked of days gone by, Joe had come dangerously close to confiding in him. There was one moment of madness when he felt the need to open his heart and reveal the truth. But he couldn't. It would have destroyed his father, who was a man of principle; a simple, uncomplicated man, who would never understand.

Joe was glad he had resisted the need to confide his secret, because to do that would be to relieve his own guilt, and that was no reason to hurt someone you loved.

As he rounded the spinney, he heard what sounded like a cry for help, and then angry shouting that grew louder as he came near. 'Who the devil's that!' Taking off at the run, he came to a clearing where he saw Frank standing over someone or something on the ground. Holding what looked like a chain, he was lashing out like a madman. 'Frank!' He was horrified when he realised it was Jimmy on the ground, crouched on his knees with his two arms crossed over his head, while Frank swung the chain at him, again and again.

Horrified, Joe broke into a run. 'Frank . . . what the hell d'you think you're doing!'

Frank took no notice. Instead, he lashed out again and again, screaming and shouting like someone demented.

'Stop it, Frank!' Joe was almost on him. 'DON'T BE A DAMNED FOOL! LAY OFF HIM, FRANK . . . FOR GOD'S SAKE LEAVE HIM BE!'

Launching himself at Frank, he threw him aside. 'What's wrong with you, have you gone mad?'

With difficulty he managed to keep his brother away while helping Jimmy up off the ground. Bloodied, and crying like a baby, Jimmy clung to Joe. 'He went crazy . . . tried to kill me!' When Frank made a threatening move towards him, Jimmy cowered away. 'It weren't my fault! Don't let him get near me.'

Each time Frank made a move towards Jimmy, Joe came between them. 'What's this all about?' he asked Jimmy. 'You said it wasn't your fault? What did you mean?'

'I tried to mend it, but the chain came off in my hands. It weren't my fault. The tractor's old and knackered. It wants breaking for spares, that's all it's good for!'

With blood running down his arm and an open gash across his cheek, he was shaking, his eyes wide with terror. 'It weren't my fault,' he kept saying. 'It weren't my fault.'

When Frank started towards him again, Joe took Jimmy out of his reach. Behind him Frank began pacing back and forwards like a trapped animal.

Relieved that Jimmy had managed to protect himself from serious injury, Joe told him worriedly, 'You need to get those cuts seen to. I'll help you. Just hang on a minute . . . I need to have a quick word with Frank.'

Jimmy shook his head. 'I'm all right. I don't need no help!' He glanced nervously at Frank, who was now leaning forward on the tractor, thumping his clenched fists against the engine cover. 'It's *him* as needs help!' Jimmy cursed. 'Bloody lunatic, that's what he is!'

'Leave him to me,' Joe calmly advised. 'And listen, Jimmy, I'd appreciate it if you didn't let Mum or Dad find out about this.'

Jimmy frowned. 'Don't worry! I'm not likely to go about telling everybody how I cowered on the ground while Frank Arnold gave me a thrashing!'

He cast a hateful glance towards Frank. 'You should watch him, Joe! I'm sorry, I know he's your brother an' all, but . . .' he dropped his voice to a whisper, '. . . sometimes, it's like he's not right in the head.'

Joe gave him a gentle but firm warning. 'It's not wise to say those things, Jimmy.'

Jimmy nodded. He had got the message.

Realising how things could easily kick off again, Joe told him, 'If you're sure you don't need me, it might be best if you go now, and get that gash seen to.' That was the one injury that worried him. The rest seemed superficial, but the gash was deep and long. 'Look! I'd rather make sure you get back; if you'll just wait on a minute, I need to have a quick word with Frank.'

He saw how Frank was deeply agitated.

He knew the signs.

'Thanks all the same, but I'd rather go on my own.' Jimmy ran his fingers along the gash. 'Look! It's already stopped bleeding.'

Joe conceded, 'All right, but mind how you go. Oh, and it might be best if you stay away altogether, for now. I'll come and find you when things have calmed down.'

'What about me wages?' Jimmy demanded. 'I'm due a week's wages? I can't live without no money, can I?'

Joe turned to Frank. 'He's right! Give him his wages.'

Frank rounded on him, 'LIKE HELL I WILL! JUST GET THE USELESS BASTARD OUT OF MY SIGHT, BEFORE I FINISH HIM OFF.'

Jimmy yelled back, 'I TOLD YOU THE TRACTOR WERE FINISHED, BUT YOU WOULDN'T LISTEN!'

When Frank came at a run towards them, Joe gave Jimmy a shove. 'Get out of here! I'll see to your wages. Go on . . . go!'

As Jimmy went, half-limping, half-running, Frank's angry voice followed him. 'You'll get no wages from me.

You're finished. D'you hear? If I clap eyes on you again, I'll shoot you on sight!'

Once out of Frank's reach, Jimmy gave as good as he got. 'You're a bloody lunatic, Frank Arnold! You want locking up!'

Frank retaliated with a warning blast from his shotgun, the shock of which sent the birds soaring from the trees. 'See that? it'll be you next time!'

Laughing out loud, Frank swung round to face his brother. 'I bet that put the fear of God in him, eh?'

Joe wasn't laughing. 'You hurt him bad, Frank. If I hadn't come along, you might even have finished him off. Is that what you planned, Frank. To kill him?'

Frank showed no remorse. 'What the hell good is he, eh?' he demanded. 'He can never do a single thing right! He's completely buggered the job.'

Joe studied his brother for a brief moment. He was no stranger to Frank's rage. He had seen it many times before, when they were younger.

Beneath Joe's steady gaze, Frank grew uncomfortable. 'What the devil are you staring at?'

'*You.*' Joe was unmoved. 'I'm staring at you, Frank. And I don't like what I see.'

'What's that supposed to mean?'

'It means you should learn to control your temper, before it gets you in real trouble.'

Frank gave a loud laugh. 'What. Like this y'mean?' Raising the shotgun, he levelled it at his brother.

Joe stood firm. 'I thought you might have got all the nastiness out of your system by now,' he said quietly. 'I can see I was wrong. If anything, you're worse than you ever were.'

Keeping the shotgun level, Frank took a step closer. 'I don't know what you're talking about!' He knew *exactly* what Joe was talking about, and it unnerved him.

'I could shoot you here and now. I could say it was an accident . . . that you ran at me, and the gun just went off.'

Opening his arms, Joe invited. 'Go on then, Frank. Shoot me. You can explain it any way you like to Mum and Dad, but in the end you'll be found out. I could have told Mum years ago what you were like, but I didn't, because you were my brother, and I loved you. I even kept quiet when you tried to drown me in the brook just because I accidentally dislodged your keep net. They never knew that. And they never will, at least not from me.'

'They'd never believe you.'

'Maybe not, but you and I know what you did, and one day, when you think they're not looking and your temper gets the better of you . . . that's when they'll see you for what you really are.'

'You'd better shut your mouth, Joe!'

Undeterred, Joe went on, 'They might even begin to ask questions, about how when you were twelve, you took their beloved dog for a walk. You told them it ran off, but some time later they found it, clumsily buried in a shallow grave down the spinney. They said he must have disturbed intruders making for the big house, but I never believed that. I've always had my suspicions.'

Frank said nothing, but the guilt was written all over his face.

'It *was* you, wasn't it, Frank? Mum and Dad believed the story about the intruders. But they knew how jealous you were of that little dog, and it wouldn't take much for them to realise what might have happened. Oh, and what about that girl from the village? She came to do the housework when Mum was laid up with a sprained ankle. What happened to the girl, Frank? Why was she there one minute, and gone the next?'

It was a question he had always wanted to ask, and now

was the time. 'What did you do to her, Frank? When I saw her in the village a week later, she wouldn't even talk to me.'

His voice dropped to a whisper. 'You frightened her, didn't you, Frank? You must have done something really bad to make her run away like that.'

'I didn't do *anything*! She was a real scaredy cat, frightened of everything! I didn't do anything to make her run away.'

'Right. So, when you go back and tell everyone that you accidentally shot and killed me, what will you do when Jimmy finds the courage to tell it like it really was?'

He glanced towards the rise. 'For all we know, he might even be up there . . . spying on us. In any case, if you killed me, there are bound to be questions: lots of difficult questions, Frank. So go on, shoot me. If that's what you really want.'

Realising that for the moment Joe had him exactly where he wanted him, Frank slowly lowered the gun to his side. 'You should be ashamed,' he snarled. 'You care nothing about Mum and Dad. First chance you got, you cleared off . . . left me to do all the work round this place. You took off without a single thought for anybody! A couple of months, that's what you said when you left. If I hadn't traced you to that pub, you might *never* have come back.'

'That was clever of you . . . contacting the pubs.'

'I always get what I want.'

'So, why did you trace me, Frank?'

'You already know why! I wanted you to be my best man.'

'That's not enough, Frank. I know you! Me being your best man is neither here nor there as far as you're concerned. There must be another reason why you wanted me back.'

'All right! There was, yes. I wanted you to see how I've changed; how I've found someone to love me. Most of all, I needed to show you how I've kept this place going without you.'

His face darkened. 'You left me here to rot. You can't even begin to know what it's been like!'

Frantically pacing up and down with the gun by his side, he ran his two hands through his hair. 'After Dad hurt his leg and couldn't do it anymore, it was up to me. Hard, back-breaking work, seven days a week, through all the seasons, morning 'til night, with no proper life of my own.'

His features softened. 'Then, one day at the Bedford market, I met Alice. She liked me straight off, so we started going out, whenever I could snatch an hour here or an evening there. For the first time ever, I began to see what life could really be like, and now we're getting wed. I wanted you to come back and be my best man, because I wanted you to see that I've got the best girl in the world.'

Throwing out his arms, he laughed crazily. 'I got myself a life, Joe! So now you see, I'm no different from anybody else. I had to show you how it's me and not you, who makes Mum and Dad proud. I'm able to knuckle down, keep the farm going, and soon I'll be wed and then I'll give them the grandchildren they've always wanted. *I'll* be the man, Joe! That's all I wanted you to know. *I will be the man!*'

Joe felt a surge of guilt. 'I'm sorry I wasn't here, Frank. You've done well.' But he knew Frank too well to accept it was that simple.

He gave a long slow smile. 'All the same, you'll need to do more than *be the man* if you hope to convince me that you've changed.'

'But I have changed!'

Joe knew different. 'What do you think people would say if they'd seen you beating Jimmy?'

'Oh, that's very clever, Joe. Especially when it's you that's in the wrong, not me!' Frank hit back. 'Mum and Dad will never forgive you for staying away all this time. For months after you went Mum watched out the window, waiting for you to come home, but you never did! You'd rather be off round the country, enjoying yourself, without a second thought for any of us back here!'

He shook his fist. 'They missed you, Joe! *I* missed you! Where were you, Joe? Why did you stay away for so long?'

Joe took a deep breath. 'I thought about Mum and Dad; believe it or not, I even thought about you! I missed this place, and I missed my life here. I did think about all of you. Every single day.'

'Liar! You must have known we were worried. You could have written!'

'It wasn't possible.' Joe had his reasons.

'How could it not be possible?'

Knowing the severity of what he was about to disclose, Joe took a moment to compose himself. '*I was in prison, Frank*. If I'd written, it would have been on prison notepaper and you would have known, and I didn't want that.'

Joe's admission hit Frank like a bolt from the blue. '*Prison?*' He took a step back. 'You were in prison?' He was shocked to the core.

Joe quietly explained, 'I was locked away for eight months, and that's the reason I couldn't contact you. The reason why I could not come home.'

The shock of Joe being in prison, had rendered Frank speechless. *Joe*, who would rather cut off his hand than commit a crime. *Joe*, who had never harmed anyone or stolen anything in his entire life. 'I don't believe it!'

Taking a moment to think it through, he gave a cynical

laugh. 'Oh, *now* I see it! You're lying, aren't you? You're *lying*, to cover up the truth, that you didn't give a sod about us!'

'No, Frank.' Joe looked him in the eye, 'Only weeks after I left here, I got caught up in a fight down London way; a man was badly hurt. I was in the wrong place at the wrong time, that's all. The three culprits ran off and I was the one who got arrested. Nothing I said made any difference. They gave me eight months' custodial sentence. I served the time and when I came out it was next to impossible to find work. I did odd jobs anywhere I could find, then I started working the pubs; the odd day here and there, for a pittance and a bed in the cellar.'

He told Frank, 'One night I wandered into the Oak Tree pub and got talking to the landlord. He said his regular barman had to take a fortnight off, and asked me if I'd like to give it a go . . . that there was a room and regular meals going as part of the wage. So naturally I jumped at the chance. I'm glad I did, because I got your letter, and that was my way back.'

'Oak Tree?' Frank recognised the name of the pub. 'That's right! That's where I traced you to.'

'So that's how it was, Frank. Through no fault of mine, I spent the best part of a year in prison, and that's God's honest truth!'

Instead of reacting with compassion, Frank took pleasure in taunting him, 'Locked up in prison, eh? Joe Arnold . . . the man who values his freedom like no one else I know . . . can't even sleep unless the window's wide open.'

He laughed. 'How did you survive, Joe . . . with four small walls closing in on you; hordes of convicts crushing your space. No open windows, or fresh air, and eyes watching you everywhere you went? I've heard how prison can cripple a spirit or send you crazy. Is that how it was, Joe? *Has* it sent you crazy?'

Joe remembered every minute of it, and though prison had not altogether crippled his soul, it had scarred him deeply. With Frank's every vicious word the memories came flooding back; awful memories he would rather forget. And now for his own evil pleasure, Frank was bringing them alive in his mind. 'Bastard!'

Frank didn't see it coming. When Joe's clenched fist set him reeling backwards, he lay on the ground for a moment, tenderly nursing his jaw. 'Oh, so you *did* learn something in that place, eh?'

'Oh, yes, I learned something. I learned that you had to look after yourself or go under, and I was not about to go under, Frank, not then, and not now.'

Laughing, Frank scrambled up. 'If you think you're a better man than I am, then you're a bigger fool than I took you for,' he snarled. 'I mean . . . look at you . . . an ex-con! Joe Arnold, ever the good son . . . locked up in prison and surrounded by thugs and criminals.'

Nursing his jaw, he laughed insanely. 'You know what, Joe . . . that's the most *useful* piece of information I've had in a long time.'

Realising how Frank meant to use the information, Joe already regretted having divulged his secret.

'Just think about it, Joe. If that got out, imagine how it would shame the family. Whatever would people say? It could even finish us if the customers went elsewhere for their hay and meat. Oh, and I can't even imagine what it would do to Mum and Dad when I tell them.'

Joe was incensed. 'Even *you* wouldn't do a cruel thing like that!'

'I would, if you forced my hand.'

'You really are scum, aren't you?' He suspected what Frank had in mind, and he was right.

'All I'm saying, Joe, is that there's no need for any nastiness. All you have to do is forget the silly ideas you've got in your head about me; and I'll keep my mouth shut about your scummy little secret.'

Disgusted, Joe turned away. Frank called after him, 'I mean it! I won't even have to shout it out loud. I'll just whisper the word round the village . . . Joe Arnold's just out of prison!' That's all I need to do, Joe! A little whisper in the right ear, and the gossips will do the rest.'

Ignoring his rantings and with a need to think, Joe made for the tractor, where he feverishly set to work. Behind him, Frank sat leisurely on a fallen tree trunk and smoked a cigarette. 'You think it over,' he told Joe confidently. 'In the end though, you'll see I'm right. If you want to save Mum and Dad a lot of grief, it's the only way.'

Working like a man possessed, Joe had fitted the chain in no time. When the engine started, Frank shouted excitedly, 'Oh, well done, Joe! I may be a better farmer than you, but you always were the better mechanic, I'll give you that!'

Paying him no heed, Joe wiped his hands on the oil rag and began his way up field. 'Dammit! I should never have told him,' he muttered angrily. 'I should have known!'

'It's a deal then is it?' Frank called after him. 'Keep your mouth shut, and your secret will be safe enough with me!'

Joe gave no answer.

The truth was, he would never have risked hurting his parents by revealing what he knew about Frank's evil doings. But Frank could not know that. Instead, Frank had judged Joe by his own standards by resorting to blackmail.

'I was a fool for trusting you,' Joe cursed himself. 'You've got me where you want me, Frank, and it's no more than I deserve.'

It was another harsh lesson he had learned.

~

'What's keeping them now?' Nancy and Alice had the dinner almost ready, 'Just the gravy to make and we can serve it up,' she told Alice.

Alice placed the condiments in the centre of the table. 'Do you want me to go and see where the boys are?'

'You'll do no such thing, my girl!' Tom chided. 'Another five minutes an' it'll be dark as nookers-knockers out there. You and Nancy take it easy, while I go and see if they're on their way.'

He was gone no longer than five minutes before he was back. 'Brrr!' He kept his jacket on. 'It's blowing a bit chilly out there now.'

'Well . . .' Nancy wanted to know. 'Did you see them?'

'Nope. Though I'm certain they'll be here soon.'

Sniffing the aroma of freshly cooked beef, he sighed. 'Can't we make a start? It'd be a shame to let the meat spoil.'

Nancy gave him one of her frosty looks. 'A few more minutes, then we'll see,' she told him sternly.

He ambled back to his chair. 'Yer always were a bossy woman,' he muttered.

'What was that?' Nancy put her hands on her hips. 'Are you calling me bossy?'

'I am, and you are. So there!'

Smiling to herself, Nancy got back to her gravy. 'You have to keep these men in their place,' she told Alice, who was enjoying their harmless banter, 'otherwise they'll begin to think they're in charge and that will never do.'

Tom continued to moan, 'No consideration! There's

me famished, and them two messing about doing goodness knows what. No consideration at all . . . keeping us
all waiting for our dinner like this.'

'I'll just pop out and see if they're about,' Alice
suggested, and before anyone could stop her, she had her
coat on and was out the kitchen door. 'Don't go no further
than the gate!' Nancy declared. 'If there's no sign of them
we'll sit down and start before the meal's spoiled.'

Tom thanked her with a chuckle. 'Good idea!'

Addressing Tom haughtily she assured him, 'It's not
for your sake, matey. It's for me and Alice.'

'What's that supposed to mean?'

'It means . . . I know how you get the wind on an empty
stomach.' She frowned, '. . . and that's not a pleasant thing
to witness!'

~

Having sat by the brook for an age, Joe was already on
his way back. He had to check the falcon, so he made
straight for the barn.

Once inside he lit the tilly lamp and carried it to the
stable. 'So, how are you, fella?' Closing the stable door
behind him, he then set about untying the straps that
held the cage in position.

Outside, Alice was halfway along the path when she saw
the light go on in the barn. 'I expect that's Joe!' she
realised. 'He'll be checking the falcon.' Setting off at a
run, she headed for the barn.

First she peeped through the window but when the
straw-stack hampered her view, she went softly to the door,
where she slipped quietly inside.

Alice stayed in the shadows, quietly observing him as
he lifted the bird out of the cage, all the while speaking
tenderly to it, 'Well now, you seem to have bucked up a

bit. And look at this . . . you're even trying to move your wing. Oh, yes! I reckon we'll have you up and away in no time at all.'

Coming out of the shadows, Alice stepped forward. 'Hello, Joe.'

'Alice! I didn't see you come in.' Though he was very glad to see her.

'Is he getting stronger?' Alice peered at the bird, now fluttering in the palm of Joe's hand. 'He looks like he wants to get away.' She thought the falcon was a magnificent thing, with his deep, bright eyes and feathers smooth as silk.

'He knows his wing is healing,' Joe said, '. . . so now he's growing anxious to leave. Look.' He gently worked the wing back and forth. 'I don't think it's broken after all,' he said, '. . . but he's lost a feather or two, and the muscle is weakened. Seems to me he might have flown into a telegraph pole, or got caught up somewhere. Either way, he seems to have rallied a bit with having the rest, and by the look of it, he's had a good drink from the container.'

Alice saw how tenderly Joe examined the bird, lifting and moving the wing and all the while talking softly to him.

'Can I hold him?'

'Keep the wing out straight,' he reminded her. 'The splint is not as tight as it was, what with him moving about.'

Carefully, he placed the falcon in her cupped hands. 'Watch he doesn't peck,' he warned, 'he's getting a bit full of himself now he's feeling better.'

He was amazed when straightaway the bird settled neatly into her hands, and calmly lay there. 'You've worn him out,' she smiled up at Joe, then concentrated on stroking the bird's head with the tip of her finger. 'Lovely thing, aren't you?' she murmured. 'You want to be out there, don't you . . . riding on the breeze and when it's time to stop, you'll be up there in the tall trees, observing everything from your lofty perch.'

After a moment or two, she returned him to Joe. 'Best let him rest now, eh?'

When she placed the falcon into Joe's grasp, her hands brushed his and Joe's heart turned over. She was so close to him; he could smell the fragrance in her hair, and her skin was soft as silk. Alice was so lovely, all he wanted to do was take her into his arms and fold her to him.

With the longing came the guilt, 'Did Mum send you to look for me?' He thought it amazing, how he could sound so casual, when his head was spinning with excitement.

Alice nodded. 'Dinner's all ready. Your mother wondered where you and Frank had got to.'

'We had to finish off,' he told her. 'I should think Frank will be along any minute.'

'And what about you, Joe?' she asked. 'How long will you be?'

'Not long. I'll make sure the falcon's settled first. It'll only take a few minutes. You'd best go now though, or they'll be wondering where you are.'

Alice stepped back. 'See you in a few minutes then?'

She went out of the barn and along the path, where the only light to show her the way was the light from the farmhouse kitchen.

When she almost there, she heard footsteps behind her. A quick glance told her it was Frank. For some reason, she felt she couldn't face him just yet. She needed time to herself . . . just a minute or two, and then she'd be all right.

Leaning into the shadows she let him pass without him suspecting that she was even there.

After he'd gone into the farmhouse, she held her hands

out before her. They were trembling. 'What's wrong with me?' she thought. Just now when she placed the falcon into Joe's palms, the touch of his bare skin against hers had quickened her heart.

'It was the *bird*,' she told herself, 'He's so wild and beautiful. Yes! That's what it was. Holding the falcon was exciting! How many people ever get to do that?'

Being there in the barn with Joe, and sharing the excitement of the falcon, had somehow unsettled her.

Suddenly the door was flung open and there was Frank. 'Oh!' Laughing, she fell into his arms. 'Frank! Oh, I'm so glad you're back,' she said breathlessly. 'We wondered where you were.' She clung fast to him, almost as though she were fleeing from something.

'Woa!' Taken aback by the way she threw herself into his arms, Frank held her at arm's length. 'I was about to come looking for you. Mum said you'd gone to stand at the gate, so you must have been invisible when I came by just now.'

'I was in the barn.'

'In the barn? What were you doing in the barn?' He smiled proudly. 'Looking for me, were you?'

'No, well yes . . . I mean, I *was* looking for you, but then I saw Joe go into the barn, and I asked him where you were and he said you should be back soon, and then I saw the falcon.' When she realised she was gabbling, she took a breath. 'Oh, Frank, the falcon is so beautiful!'

Frank noticed how excited she was, and he began to wonder. 'Oh, yes, the falcon. I was told about that. So, is it doing all right, or what?'

'Joe thinks he's doing just fine,' Alice informed him eagerly. 'At first Joe thought his wing might be broken, but it's only damaged. Anyway, Joe says he might be able to fly away soon.'

'That's good news. So! You were in the barn, were you?

I'm surprised you didn't see me go by.' All he could think was that she had mentioned Joe's name three times in less than a minute.

'I expect I didn't see you because I was holding the falcon, but then I gave it back to Joe and came to the house to see if you'd got here yet.'

Tickling her under the chin, Frank smiled broadly. 'Well, I'm here, and you're here, and it's good that the bird is repairing.' Deliberately holding his smile, he teased. 'Though I'm not sure I like the idea of you being in the barn with *a strange man.*' He emphasised the last two words by widening his eyes and pretending to frighten her.

Alice laughed. 'Joe is not a strange man. He's your brother.' Again, she recalled how she was drawn to Joe on that first meeting.

Keeping up the pretence, Frank kissed her long and slow on the mouth. 'You're right. So he is!'

When he saw the light go out in the barn, he ushered her inside. 'Come on. We'd best get back inside before Mum throws the entire dinner out the window!' Keeping her extra close, he escorted her into the kitchen.

He had a great deal to think about, because now it seemed he had a new and unexpected worry. This growing friendship between Alice and Joe had to be nipped in the bud.

Already irritated by Alice's obvious excitement, Frank vowed that if he ever suspected Joe of making a play for his future wife, it would be the last thing Joe ever did!

∼

'Oh, here you are at last!' In the kitchen, Nancy was already dishing up the food. 'Where's our Joe?' Stretching her neck, she looked towards the door.

'He'll be here in a minute,' Alice volunteered. 'He's just bedding the falcon down for the night.'

'How *is* the bird?' Tom asked eagerly, still chomping at the bit for his evening meal.

Before Alice could answer, Frank chipped in. 'Joe reckons it's almost ready to take off.'

Tom was pleased about that. 'Ah well, he always did have a way with stray creatures, did Joe.'

'Off upstairs, Frank. You need to wash and change before dinner,' Nancy ordered.

'Oh, I was hoping to beg a cuppa before I go up and change.'

'You'd best make it yourself, 'cause me and Alice have the dinner to serve,' Nancy reminded him. 'Oh, and try not to get under our feet.'

Frank took offence at being ordered about like a little boy. Smiling to himself, he wondered what his parents would say if they knew Joe had been in prison. The very thought of it made him feel good.

While Frank got himself a mug of tea, Alice and Nancy went about setting the table.

Tom got his fingers rapped for picking at the peas, while Nancy saw to the gravy and juggled dishes of steaming, juicy vegetables, she assailed everyone with stories of Joe and his boyish escapades. 'D'you recall the time Joe scampered up that huge old tree to rescue that ginger cat?'

She chuckled. 'The cat jumped down and left Joe stranded. We had to get the big ladders out and help him down. As if that wasn't enough, the very next morning he found a badger caught in a trap.'

Stealing a carrot, Tom picked up the story. 'Ten year old he were, and would you believe he turned up here with the badger still in the damned trap! The badger's leg was almost off, and it was half crazed.'

While Nancy checked there were enough places set at the table for Alice's parents, Tom went on, 'I gave Joe a right talking to. I mean . . . as we all know, badgers are bad-tempered at the best of times, and this big divil was in terrible pain. Snapping and snarling like a mad dog it was. I don't mind telling you, it's a miracle he didn't have Joe's fingers off at the bone!'

Out the corner of her eye Nancy caught Tom dibbing into the peas. 'Get your mucky fingers outta them peas!' Catching him across the knuckles with the ladle, she gave him one of her frosty stares. It was enough to send him scurrying for his raggedy old newspaper again.

When the telephone rang right beside him he almost leaped out of his chair. 'Noisy damned thing. I wish we'd never had it put in!' Tom hated all things new.

'Don't be so miserable!' Nancy chided. 'It's bad enough you made us wait till everyone else in the village had one, before you gave in. Anyway, you can't deny it's been handy.'

With the telephone still ringing and no one seeming prepared to answer it, Alice grabbed a tea towel and wiped her hands. 'I'll get it!' she said, and was across the room in no time at all.

Snatching up the receiver, she said, 'Hello? This is Brook Farm, who's that please?'

She listened for a moment or two, quietly answering in between, 'What's happened? Yes, we've just got dinner on the table. Oh, I'm sorry. Tomorrow? I will, Father. Yes, if that's what you want, all right, but what's happened?'

There was another pause while she paid attention to what her father was telling her, then, 'Oh, I see. Yes, all right. I'll tell them, yes. No, they'll understand I'm sure. Well, I don't know, but don't worry. I just hope everything's all right when you get there. Give them my love. No, Father, it's okay. Yes, I know. I expect so. Yes, I will. Bye then.'

As Alice replaced the receiver, Nancy was curious. 'That was a strange conversation,' she commented. 'I take it that was your father?'

Even Nancy would never dream of addressing the dignified Ronald Jacobs as Alice's dad. 'So, what did he have to say then?'

'I'm sorry, Nancy.' Coming back to the table, she began taking up two of the place sets. 'I'm really sorry,' she said disheartened, 'they said to give you their apologies but they won't be able to come tonight after all.'

'Oh, that's a shame.' In truth, having already once met Alice's mother, she was greatly relieved. 'A problem, is there?'

'They've gone to Hampshire to see Uncle Larry. Apparently he needs to see them urgently.'

'Oh, dear. I hope everything is all right.'

'I expect it is really,' Alice promised. 'It's Uncle Larry again. He's not ill or anything, but it seems he and Aunt Sheila have had another of their awful rows. This time though, it's more serious than before.'

'Really?' Nancy was curious.

Alice paused, before going on to explain, 'They're always having rows and fights . . . I remember one time when my parents were away on business and I was taken to stay with my aunt and uncle.'

She had never forgotten. 'It was awful! I woke up and there was all this screaming and yelling, so I crept down and sat on the stairs and I saw them . . . going mad at each other they were. Then Aunt Sheila threw a shoe at my uncle and it knocked him clean out. She's got this vicious temper, you see.'

Tom and Nancy were shocked. 'I'm not sure you should be telling us all this, luv.' Nancy had never heard the like.

Alice confided, 'This time it sounds bad. Father didn't go into too much detail, but from the little he said, I understand that they had a really bad fight, and Aunt Sheila packed her bags left. And now, Uncle Larry is in a bit of a state.'

After Nancy reassured her, Alice continued, 'Father says it's all gone a bit too far this time, and that it was all to do with Uncle Larry seeing another woman.'

'Hmm!' Nancy squared her shoulders. 'If any man of mine played about with other women, I would never leave!'

'Aw, you must really love me then?' Tom teased.

'Not that much,' she retaliated. 'Like I said . . . *I* wouldn't leave, but *you'd* be out that door on the end o' my toe!' She gave Tom another derisory glance.

'Don't you look at me like that!' Tom was indignant. 'For one thing, I have never played about in my life, and for another, I'm a burnt-out, balding man with weak eyes and a gammy leg. Who in their right mind would want to be lumbered with *me*?'

'Are you saying I'm not in my right mind, Tom Arnold?' Nancy squared up for a fight.

Recognising the danger, Tom tried to make light of it. 'Well, if the cap fits . . . an' all that.' He might have gone on, but with a well-aimed, wet tea towel landing over his mouth, he found it difficult to speak.

Snatching away the tea towel, Nancy wagged a finger at him. 'The sad thing is, I'm stuck with you, whether I like it or not. As for your weak eyes that's because you're forever staring at the small print on the racing page.' She gave Alice a cheeky wink.

'Sorry, luv. You know full well, I wouldn't swap you for the world.'

When Tom saw her quietly smiling, he reached over to hug her. 'How could I not keep you,' he chuckled. 'You make the best apple pie a man could ever want.'

Alice thought they were a delight to watch.

She had never experienced such a family as this, and

she told them so. 'Mother is so fussy. Everything has to be in its place with every plate, cup and table cloth matching.' She loved the way Nancy set out her table, with multi-coloured plates, old earthenware serving bowls and a blue table cloth, which she proudly confessed to making herself out of an old curtain. It was so perfect no one would ever have known.

This was a happy table, she thought. A real family.

The pleasure of sitting round a table with this family had proved to be a new experience to Alice. 'We're not allowed to even *speak* at meal times,' she revealed, to everyone's surprise, 'let alone tease and laugh with each other.'

Frank joked, 'What with that and your mad relatives, I didn't realise what I was letting myself in for.'

Alice laughed at that.

Draining the last dregs of his tea, Frank placed the mug in the sink. 'Why do we have to wait for Joe anyway?'

After the showdown with Joe he was not in the best of moods. 'If he can't get here like the rest of us, let's just start without him. After all, if he wants to spend his time with that flea-ridden bird, that's up to him. The rest of us don't have to eat a cold dinner, do we, eh?'

Believing that to be unfair, Alice protested, 'We can't start without him, Frank. It's his first night back. Besides, he's bound to be here soon.'

Nancy agreed. 'My sentiments exactly!'

'Suit yourself then!' Frank went off in a sulk.

When Nancy went to look out the window, Alice followed her. At first she didn't say anything. Instead she just stood beside Nancy, stretching her neck to peer out the same window.

Being older and wiser, Nancy was well aware that Alice had something to disclose. Drawing her close in a hug, she asked quietly, 'When I've got a worry on my mind I find it's best to tell somebody, so what is it, child? Are you worried about your family, is that it?'

'No, they always manage to sort themselves out.' Alice assured her; though she had never really known what a proper, loving family was like, until Frank brought her home to this wonderful place.

Nancy persisted. 'Out with it,' she demanded. 'What's troubling you? Was it something your father said?'

Ashamed of the position her parents had put her in, Alice explained, 'You've been so kind to me . . . letting me stay last night, and making me that lovely silk under-skirt for my wedding dress.'

Nancy laughed. 'That dress has been hanging in my wardrobe since the day I got married. When I offered to make you an underskirt out of the lining, I knew I would have to take it in by a mile, so it was just as well you stayed over.'

She regarded Alice's slim figure against her own ample size. 'Back then, when I was just a young kipper, I was never as tidy-built as you are,' she exclaimed. 'Even after making you a long underskirt, there's still enough of that material over to make a barrage balloon!'

Alice laughed. 'That's not true, I'm sure, but I really appreciate you making me that lovely underskirt.'

'You're very welcome, so now why don't you tell me what's on your mind?' Nancy asked.

Alice told her, 'Just now, when Father rang, he had a favour to ask.'

'From me, or from you?'

'From you.'

'Well then, luv, I have a right to know what it is he's asking, don't you think?'

'Yes, but I don't like to say anything because you've already been so good to me.'

She went on, 'It's just that . . . he wondered if I could

stay here again tonight, because my sister Pauline's gone to stay with her friend in Bedford. I don't want to ask her not to go, because I know it's a special visit, so her friend can help her choose her bridesmaid shoes. It means though, that I'll be in the house without my parents.'

Nancy was worried. 'So your sister Pauline still hasn't got her shoes? Dearie me! She's left it a bit late, hasn't she?' Nancy thought she had never known such a disorganised wedding, and there were Alice's parents supposed to be high-flying business people. Either they didn't care enough about their youngest daughter's wedding, or they had much higher priorities to manage.

Alice explained about the shoes. 'Pauline and Mother have been arguing for days over who would choose them. In the end Pauline won. She always does, but there's not much time left, so that's why I can't ask her to stay in the house with me tonight, instead of visiting her friend.'

Nancy put Alice's concern to rest straight away. 'Look here, child! You are about to become my daughter-in-law, and I couldn't be more thrilled,' she announced proudly. 'My home is your home, and of course you'll stay here, and that's an end to it.'

Alice kissed her on the cheek. 'It's *me* that's thrilled,' she whispered, ''cause I'm about to have another mum . . . the best in the world!' Nancy flushed with delight.

Just then Joe arrived. 'Something smells good,' he said rubbing his hands together.

'Get your coat off and wash them mucky hands.' Nancy could smell the oil from the tractor engine. 'Your brother's upstairs, so make sure the pair of you leave the bathroom as you found it!'

While the brothers were away, Nancy and Alice put the finishing touches to the table.

Alice thought she had never seen such an amazing spread. She felt proud of herself for having helped.

Moreover, she had loved working in the kitchen with Nancy, because she taught her so much more than her mother had ever done.

The table was laden with a feast. There was a plump joint of best beef waiting to be sliced by Tom, and various dishes of steaming-hot vegetables. There were roast potatoes golden brown and dripping with meat juices; boiled potatoes dressed with butter and herbs; fresh green peas, carrots and light, fluffy cauliflower. The baby Yorkshire puddings were all soft and melting on the inside, while the outsides were brown and crispy.

A few minutes later everyone was round the table. Joe was about to start, when his mother caught his attention. 'Not yet, son,' she chided. 'Have you forgotten your manners?'

Joe was shocked. 'I forgot!' He apologised with a sheepish grin. 'Looks like I've been away too long, eh?'

Frank leapt at the opportunity to make a sly comment, 'Shame on you, Joe.' He gave him a knowing glance. 'What kind of company have you been keeping? Don't they say grace where you've been!'

Joe might have made some discreet retaliation, but unwittingly his father did it for him. 'Enough of that, Frank.' He gave his eldest son a stern look. 'I seem to recall a few weeks back, someone *else* forgot to wait for grace, didn't you, Frank?'

Reassuring Joe with an easy smile he admitted, 'It's not every family in the land gives thanks for what they've got, and that's all right; but we're farming stock, and throughout the generations it is something we care to do.'

He then checked to make sure everyone was ready, before folding his hands on the table.

It took only a moment for Tom to offer gratitude on all their behalfs. 'We thank thee Lord for this plentiful food and the roof over our heads, and for bringing Joe home to us. Amen.'

Afterwards, when they were all tucking in, Nancy asked Alice, 'So, what else did your father have to say, Alice luv?'

'Just that I was to stay here tonight if that was all right with you, and go home tomorrow. I'm to look in my wardrobe at the things Mother bought. You recall I told you, she went out to buy my shoes and veil? Oh and I'm to look at page fourteen of the leaflet on the table, because she hopes I like the bouquet she's chosen.'

'What!' Tom was astounded. 'I always thought it was the *bride*'s prerogative to choose her bouquet?' He stuffed a potato in his mouth and began chewing.

Nancy brought him up sharply. 'Tom!'

'What?'

'It's none of your business who chooses the bouquet, or anything else.'

'I never said it was.'

'Besides, how do you know it wasn't *Alice*'s idea for her mother to choose her bouquet?'

'It was not my idea,' Alice offered, 'but mother said if she was paying out a fortune on my wedding, she had every right to do some of the choosing.' She gave a sad little smile. 'To be honest though, I don't think that's why. I think it's because she never had a white wedding of her own.'

'Why was that?' Frank was learning more about his future wife and family, with every passing day.

Alice explained, 'She told me that she and Father decided not to spend money on fripperies, and that it would be far better to invest the money in their first restaurant.'

'I think they did right,' Frank declared. 'After all, look how they've used that money. Three restaurants up to now, and all because they started that first one with money that could have been wasted on paying for a big, fancy wedding.'

While Alice pondered sadly on his remarks, Nancy said she would have much preferred a white wedding, '. . . with all the trimmings, like me and Tom had.' She was quick to assure them, 'It was nothing posh mind, but I had the loveliest dress and we paid for the choir to sing in church. We hired the village hall for the best party ever, with a pianist and a flautist and we danced all night long.'

Sighing wistfully, she reminded Tom, 'It was the best day ever, wasn't it, Tom?'

Tom readily agreed, but added, 'To my mind, Alice's parents did right. They made a first-class business decision. That's why they now own three of the best eating places in the area.

'My own story is not so straightforward. Y'see, my father once owned all the land adjacent to this farm-cottage, only he fell on hard times and had to sell a good part of it. Fortunately, he arranged to rent back some acres and the cottage . . .'

'That's enough now, Tom!' Nancy often had to check him when he was being too forthright.

Joe had a pertinent question for Frank. 'So, if it was you, and you had a choice, you'd really go without a white wedding, and invest the money in a business, would you?'

'Too right I would!' Frank was adamant.

'In that case, I reckon it's just as well that it's the *bride's* family who are paying for yours and Alice's wedding.'

Frank nodded unashamedly. 'That's right. If it was coming out of *my* pocket, there'd be no fancy clothes, no big church do with a hundred people wanting to be fed and feted. Oh no! We'd be in and out of the registry office; a meal back at the house, then a few days looking about for a new and exciting enterprise.'

Glancing over at Alice, he smiled encouragingly. 'You

agree with me don't you, eh? You and me, setting out on our first big adventure together?'

Alice gave him her best smile. 'Sounds exciting,' she said brightly, as though she actually agreed. But she did *not* agree. And as she looked up she caught Joe's eyes. It was as if he could see right into her soul. She flushed slightly and looked away.

Unaware of the change in atmosphere, Frank went on glibly, 'But it's *not* my money, so now that my future in-laws have amassed their fortune they can splash it about all they like; if they want to give me and Alice the best wedding that money can buy that's up to them!'

Across the table from Alice, Joe saw how Frank's insensitive babble had dampened Alice's bright and sunny nature. He wished there was something he could do to bring back her smile. But he couldn't. That was Frank's role in her life now.

With Frank's embarrassing and thoughtless remarks out of the way, Nancy turned her mind elsewhere. 'By the way, Joe?'

Joe looked up. 'Yes?'

'With Alice staying here again tonight, you'll need to sleep on the sofa. Is that all right?'

'Absolutely!' He was just glad she wasn't going home yet. 'The sofa will be just fine.'

'Good! That's settled then.'

∼

Marred only by Frank's damning words about white weddings, the next hour proved to be the most pleasant Joe had spent in a long time. The meal was wholesome and delicious, and with the conversation focusing on local events in the farming calendar, he began to feel as though he had never been away.

Nancy had something to show them. 'Now then, look at this, everyone!' Grinning from ear to ear, she held up the leaflet. 'I got this from the post office in Blackhill,' she informed them. 'It's the information for the Spring barn-dance in the village hall.'

'Give over, woman!' Tom reminded her. 'We've no time for dancing. You know as well as I do . . . Spring is a busy time on the farm, what with lambing an' all. Besides, in case it's slipped your mind, we've a wedding to go to!'

Nancy shook the leaflet in his face. 'Ah, but the dance isn't for another three weeks, and anyway it's been carefully planned to work with the farming calendar,' she added triumphantly. 'We all know how much you hate these events, and how you make every excuse not to go dancing. Well, *we're* all going, aren't we, folks?' She waved the leaflet in the air.

'I would love to go,' Alice said, excitedly.

'Oh, well if Alice is going, then so am I.' Frank did not want other men anywhere near her. Alice was a prize he meant to hang on to.

Joe, too, was all for it, though for different reasons. 'Well, I'm raring to go!' he told Nancy. 'I haven't been to a village dance in a long time, and now I'm really looking forward to it.'

'Aha!' Nancy was jubilant. 'So there ye have it, Tom Arnold,' she told him. 'We're all going and so are you. It's either that, or you cook your own meals for the next six months.'

'Have sense, woman!' Tom groaned. 'I've a gammy leg, in case you've forgotten!'

'I have not forgotten,' she answered. 'But gammy leg or no gammy leg, you'd best get yourself to that village hall with the rest of us, and no argument. You can sit it out and sulk if yer afraid to join in, 'cause it'll make no difference to me.'

She gave him a shrivelling glance. 'Besides, you've never once danced with me in public anyway, and only once in private, and that was on our wedding night when you were blind drunk and couldn't care less who saw you.'

'That's not a nice thing to say.'

'Mebbe not, but I don't reckon it's nice if you're ashamed of dancing with your own wife in public.'

'Don't be daft, 'course I'm not ashamed.'

'Yes you are. I know it, you know it, and everybody in this village knows it.'

Tom actually had a flush of conscience. 'All right then, Nancy Arnold. If it's dancing yer want, it's dancing you'll get, but it'll be your doing if this old leg gives up the ghost.'

Alice clapped her hands and gave him a kiss. 'You'll enjoy it,' she promised.

Nancy's face was wreathed in a broad, happy smile. 'That's settled then, husband.' And flushing with pleasure, she laid the leaflet on the table.

When Joe picked it up, she told him with a twinkle in her eye, 'I expect the girls will be swarming all over you. In fact it wouldn't surprise me if you didn't find yourself a really nice girlfriend. That Rosalind Thompson always had an eye for you, and she's still not wed. Oh, she's had a few men-friends but nothing's ever come of it.'

Frank chipped in, 'That's because she only ever wants what she can get from them, then when their pockets are empty, she dumps them and moves on to the next victim. No wonder they call her the shark; given half a chance, she'll eat you for breakfast and spit out the pips!'

Joe laughed. 'She won't be interested in *me* then,' he quipped, 'I've got nothing worth the taking.'

'*You* said it, not me,' Frank said spitefully. 'Anyway, like I said, Rosalind Thompson doesn't want a serious relationship.'

Tom spoke without thinking, 'As I recall, didn't *you* have a bit of a fling with her at one time?'

Frank laughed it off. 'Not really. She might have wanted to get her claws into me, but I'm nobody's fool. I soon told her where to get off.' He smiled at Alice and was relieved when she smiled back.

He was furious with his father for mentioning the embarrassing fling he had had with that Thompson bitch.

Truth be told, it was Rosalind who unceremoniously dumped him, and not the other way round. He was heart-broken, until he found Alice Jacobs.

Frank had always been careful to make Alice believe she was the only one.

He had no intention of letting her find out that she was his consolation prize.

~

The conversation changed direction and continued over dinner, with Tom and Nancy having the occasional teasing dig at each other, and Alice thoroughly enoying their company.

Frank assailed them all with talk of his ambitions to have his very own farm, '. . . with a hundred acres of prime, crop-growing land; another fifty acres of pasture, and a stable filled with top quality horses straight from Ireland. I'll build us a fine house and hire enough experienced men to run the place, while the two of us travel the world,' he told Alice.

Joe was impressed at the scale of his brother's ambi-tions; though he was naturally dubious. 'So, how d'you intend funding this amazingly extravagant enterprise?'

Frank resented his question. 'Why, from Alice's *parents* of course.'

Alice was shocked. Like the others, she had no inkling

that he was making such plans. 'You mustn't rely on my parents, Frank,' she cautioned him gently.

'Why not?' Unlike the others, Frank was surprised and irritated by her remark.

'You don't know what they're like where money's concerned, or you would never have included them in your plans.'

She revealed a snippet of information. 'The only person they ever helped was my sister Pauline. She was always naturally good at hairdressing, and she learned her trade well. When her employer was ready to sell up, he offered it to Pauline, and she asked Mother to buy it for her. You see, it was always Mother's dream to own a hairdressing salon for the well-off. So she went along with Pauline's business plan, and it was a huge success. There are five salons now, right across the county. Father is tied up with his own business, so it's Pauline who oversees them. She works long and hard because she revels in it. But the deeds to each and every shop are all in Mother's name.'

Worried, she glanced at the others. 'I'm really sorry,' she apologised, 'but it's best if Frank knows the way things are.'

'So the hairdresser's shops are all in your mother's name, but what does that matter to us?' Frank persisted, 'I'm talking about a loan, a safe, secure loan for something I know inside out. I'm a mature man, tried and tested, and as far as I know, neither of your parents know the first thing about farming the land, or raising animals, or anything else that makes a farmer's day. Now then, Alice my love, am I right, or am I not?'

Frank did not appreciate having his plans cruelly dashed, especially in front of everyone.

'Yes, you're right, of course you are,' Alice answered kindly. 'But *you* had your father to share the load, and I'm sure he taught you everything you know. The way my parents will see it, is they had no one to lead or teach them; they had to learn the ropes the hard way, on their own with little or no guidance. They'll tell you how they had to make sacrifices in order to get their first business off the ground, and that they did it themselves without asking help from anyone.'

She gave a wry little smile. 'When we were growing up, we heard it all, time and again. She lightly mimicked her mother. '"We did it all on our own, and you girls will have to do the same when the time comes!" They'll expect you and me to do the same, Frank. To make our own way in life, the way they did.'

Frank still did not accept her explanation. 'You've got it all wrong,' he insisted. 'They must approve of me or they wouldn't have sanctioned our marriage; or be spending an absolute fortune on our wedding. Besides that, you're their flesh and blood . . . their baby daughter. It goes without saying, they'll want to see you living in the style to which you're accustomed.'

Alice agreed. 'I won't deny they're spending a fortune on our wedding, but that's only because it will be a show-case for their friends, and you're right, Frank . . . they *will* want to see us living in a fine big house with land. But they'll expect *us* to work hard and provide it.'

Frank was open-mouthed with disbelief. 'I'll believe that when I hear it from *them*!'

Throughout this exchange, Tom and Nancy had remained quiet, listening but not wanting to interfere. But now Tom spoke his thoughts. 'If you don't mind me saying, Frank, I can understand what Alice is trying to tell you. And I have to say, I fully agree with her parents' view-point. A man has to make his own way in this world. That way he remains his own man, not indebted to anyone. It's the only way he can be proud of what he's achieved.'

Frank strongly disagreed. 'You don't understand,' he

argued, 'If I'm given a kick-start, then I'd be on my way and never ask again.'

Alice intervened. 'Trust me, Frank. I know my parents. They're just not those kind of people.' She went on with quiet sincerity, 'There's just you and me, Frank. It's up to us, and no one else.'

'Well said!' Nancy exclaimed. With every passing minute she was learning more about this quiet girl who Frank had chosen to spend his life with.

'You're wrong, all of you!' Frank rounded on Alice. 'When I mentioned my plans to your father, he seemed really interested. You'll see! When we're wed and I'm a part of the family, they'll be falling over themselves to set us up with a business of our own.'

Seeing how agitated he was, Alice reluctantly conceded, 'Perhaps it's *me* that's got it all wrong.' Though she knew it was not.

Having remained silent throughout, Joe now added his contribution. 'There's something you appear to have forgotten,' he reminded Frank. 'If you're so intent on building your empire, and so sure you'll get the help you need, then you won't be here for Dad. Have you thought of that?'

Frank assured him, ''Course I've thought of that. Unlike you, I would *never* let Dad down.

'What I plan to do won't happen overnight, Dad, not even with Alice's parents helping me out. I'll still be here with you for a good while yet. Meantime, Joe can learn the ropes inside out, and of course we'll need to let go of Jimmy, because he's a bloody liability! There are plenty of sensible, hard-working blokes who would jump at his job.'

He congratulated himself, 'So like I said, it will all work out in the end.'

Tom thought differently, but he wanted this particular conversation ended. 'Course it will, son,' he said jovially, 'course it will.' There was a hint of sarcasm in his voice.

Later, when the time was right, he would have a heart to heart with Frank. Somewhere along the line, his eldest son had become too full of his own importance, and that would never do!

Nancy felt the same but kept her own counsel. She was disappointed to hear Frank talk that way in front of everyone. Such delicate issues should remain between a man and his partner, and no one else. At least not until it might be finalised and others needed to know.

Determined that the evening should be a success, she kept the conversation going on a lighter note, and soon everyone was in much better humour.

The apple pie was served and enjoyed, and the meal finished with a glass of homemade cider, and then it was time for Frank and Joe to check the animals and make sure the lambing-pens were secure. In the meantime, Alice and Nancy cleared the table, while Tom went to snooze on the sofa.

'God help us, will you look at that?' Nancy brought Alice's attention to the round, pink belly bursting out of Tom's shirt. In fond tones, she told Alice, 'Fat belly or no fat belly, I wouldn't change him for the world!'

They were taken by surprise when suddenly the middle button of Tom's shirt flicked off and went skidding across the room and out of sight. 'It was the apple pie that did it,' Nancy screeched, and the two of them laughed until they ached. 'It'll take me a month o' Sundays to find that button,' Nancy tittered, dabbing her tears with the end of her pinnie.

~

When a short time later Frank and Joe returned and the wine was brought out, Tom awoke, complaining, 'There's a draught in 'ere.'

71

'That's cause you've lost a button and there's a bare patch on your belly,' Nancy pointed out dryly; though she was aching to laugh out loud, and so was Alice. 'It came at us a hundred miles an hour,' she declared with a straight face, 'you're lucky it didn't knock somebody's eye out!'

Tom was having none of it. 'If you'd sewed the damned thing on properly in the first place, it would never have worked itself loose!'

Nancy refused to take the blame. 'It's that big belly of yours!' she retaliated. 'You look like you're eight months pregnant! Too much booze and apple pie, that's what's done it.'

Ignoring her, Tom filled everyone's wine glass. 'Here's to us!'

Without further ado, they all toasted the forthcoming wedding. After that they sat and chatted, with another glass or three to warm the cockles. Tom was unusually merry, and Nancy was well on her way to being three sheets to the wind.

Apart from Frank's embarrassing declaration, the evening had been a great success; though things had been learned and the true nature of certain people revealed.

Frank believed he was right and that Alice was wrong. Tom had seen a side to his eldest son that he did not particularly like, and Nancy had deliberately put it all out of her mind, because like Alice, she was already thinking ahead to the two most exciting events on her personal calendar. The wedding, and to a lesser degree, the barn-dance.

After washing up the dishes and feeling all the merrier with the wine, Nancy even did a little Irish jig to show Alice her favourite dance. 'The nuns taught us at school.' She put her arms stiff by her side. 'You should never jiggle your arms about, because then all your energy goes into your arm movements, instead of down to your feet.' And

to prove her point she went
feet a tapping, and arms stretc
as two pokers.

Everyone clapped to Nancy'
a happy smile on their face.

'Give over, woman!' Tom la
the tooth to be prancing abou
you'll likely not be able to wal

'You're just jealous because y

'I could if I tried,' he argue
is, if the rest of my shirt butto
might happen!'

Nancy laughed. 'We'd all ha

Reverting to his original
'Whether you like it or not,
youngsters anymore. We're a bit
far too old to be happy.'

'Away with you, Tom Arnold!'
too old to be happy. You're onl
your way to the knacker's yard.

To prove it, she hoisted her
the same spot, she let her two
furious tapping of the Irish jig.
taught me this one.'

Seeing Alice tapping her feet a
grabbed hold of Alice who soc
furious rhythm; though both
collapsed with exhaustion in no t
for now,' Nancy clasped her che
Tom,' she told her husband, 'I r
the tapping after all.'

In the meantime, having he
share of cider, Frank was feeling
off to bed.' He gave Alice a slop
drunkenly up the stairs.

Later, when the time was right, he would have a heart to heart with Frank. Somewhere along the line, his eldest son had become too full of his own importance, and that would never do!

Nancy felt the same but kept her own counsel. She was disappointed to hear Frank talk that way in front of everyone. Such delicate issues should remain between a man and his partner, and no one else. At least not until it might be finalised and others needed to know.

Determined that the evening should be a success, she kept the conversation going on a lighter note, and soon everyone was in much better humour.

The apple pie was served and enjoyed, and the meal finished with a glass of homemade cider, and then it was time for Frank and Joe to check the animals and make sure the lambing-pens were secure. In the meantime, Alice and Nancy cleared the table, while Tom went to snooze on the sofa.

'God help us, will you look at that?' Nancy brought Alice's attention to the round, pink belly bursting out of Tom's shirt. In fond tones, she told Alice, 'Fat belly or no fat belly, I wouldn't change him for the world!'

They were taken by surprise when suddenly the middle button of Tom's shirt flicked off and went skidding across the room and out of sight. 'It was the apple pie that did it,' Nancy screeched, and the two of them laughed until they ached. 'It'll take me a month o' Sundays to find that button,' Nancy tittered, dabbing her tears with the end of her pinnie.

～

When a short time later Frank and Joe returned and the wine was brought out, Tom awoke, complaining, 'There's a draught in 'ere.'

'That's cause you've lo
patch on your belly,' Nanc
was aching to laugh out lc
at us a hundred miles an hc
face, 'you're lucky it didn'

Tom was having none of
thing on properly in the f
worked itself loose!'

Nancy refused to take th
yours!' she retaliated. 'You
pregnant! Too much booz
done it.'

Ignoring her, Tom filled
to us!'

Without further ado, the
wedding. After that they s
glass or three to warm the
merry, and Nancy was wel
sheets to the wind.

Apart from Frank's en
evening had been a great su
learned and the true natur

Frank believed he was ri
Tom had seen a side to hi
particularly like, and Nancy
of her mind, because like A
ahead to the two most exc
calendar. The wedding, and
dance.

After washing up the dish
with the wine, Nancy even
Alice her favourite dance. 'T
She put her arms stiff by her
your arms about, because th
your arm movements, instea

A few minutes later Tom followed, then Alice, and then Nancy. 'Are you sure you'll be all right on the sofa, son?' Giving Joe the folded blanket and a pillow, she offered her cheek for a goodnight kiss. 'It was good of you to give up your room for Alice.'

'Don't you worry about me, Mum,' he smiled cheekily. 'You've tired me out with watching all that dancing and tapping. Give it a few minutes and I'll be out like a light. Go on . . . you get off to bed. You must be worn out with all that jigging about.'

Growing serious, Nancy lingered a moment before asking quietly, 'Frank didn't spoil your homecoming with the arguing, did he?'

Joe was quick to put her mind at rest. 'Course not. Frank is Frank.' He forced a smile. 'Nothing changes in that respect.'

Nancy lingered nervously. 'Sometimes I wonder about Frank,' she confided in a whisper, '. . . he should never have spoken out like that, embarrassing Alice in front of everyone.'

Joe promised her, 'I'm sure he didn't mean to upset anyone, and I don't think Alice was embarrassed; in fact I think she quietly gave him food for thought. So, don't you worry. It'll all be forgotten in the morning.'

Nancy gave a sigh of relief. 'It's so good to have you home, son.' She then ambled her way across the room and on up the stairs to a well deserved good night's rest.

Joe smiled when he heard her cussing herself as she went, 'Whoops there, Nancy; keep your balance! Hey! I reckon you've had a drop too much wine.' She gave a hearty chuckle. 'I reckon we *all* have. Dearie me! I expect we'll suffer for it in the morning.'

'You're right, Mum!' Muttering to himself, Joe pulled the blanket over his head. 'I expect we will.'

Later, when the time was right, he would have a heart to heart with Frank. Somewhere along the line, his eldest son had become too full of his own importance, and that would never do!

Nancy felt the same but kept her own counsel. She was disappointed to hear Frank talk that way in front of everyone. Such delicate issues should remain between a man and his partner, and no one else. At least not until it might be finalised and others needed to know.

Determined that the evening should be a success, she kept the conversation going on a lighter note, and soon everyone was in much better humour.

The apple pie was served and enjoyed, and the meal finished with a glass of homemade cider, and then it was time for Frank and Joe to check the animals and make sure the lambing-pens were secure. In the meantime, Alice and Nancy cleared the table, while Tom went to snooze on the sofa.

'God help us, will you look at that?' Nancy brought Alice's attention to the round, pink belly bursting out of Tom's shirt. In fond tones, she told Alice, 'Fat belly or no fat belly, I wouldn't change him for the world!'

They were taken by surprise when suddenly the middle button of Tom's shirt flicked off and went skidding across the room and out of sight. 'It was the apple pie that did it,' Nancy screeched, and the two of them laughed until they ached. 'It'll take me a month o' Sundays to find that button,' Nancy tittered, dabbing her tears with the end of her pinnie.

~

When a short time later Frank and Joe returned and the wine was brought out, Tom awoke, complaining, 'There's a draught in 'ere.'

'That's cause you've lost a button and there's a bare patch on your belly,' Nancy pointed out dryly; though she was aching to laugh out loud, and so was Alice. 'It came at us a hundred miles an hour,' she declared with a straight face, 'you're lucky it didn't knock somebody's eye out!'

Tom was having none of it. 'If you'd sewed the damned thing on properly in the first place, it would never have worked itself loose!'

Nancy refused to take the blame. 'It's that big belly of yours!' she retaliated. 'You look like you're eight months pregnant! Too much booze and apple pie, that's what's done it.'

Ignoring her, Tom filled everyone's wine glass. 'Here's to us!'

Without further ado, they all toasted the forthcoming wedding. After that they sat and chatted, with another glass or three to warm the cockles. Tom was unusually merry, and Nancy was well on her way to being three sheets to the wind.

Apart from Frank's embarrassing declaration, the evening had been a great success; though things had been learned and the true nature of certain people revealed.

Frank believed he was right and that Alice was wrong. Tom had seen a side to his eldest son that he did not particularly like, and Nancy had deliberately put it all out of her mind, because like Alice, she was already thinking ahead to the two most exciting events on her personal calendar. The wedding, and to a lesser degree, the barn-dance.

After washing up the dishes and feeling all the merrier with the wine, Nancy even did a little Irish jig to show Alice her favourite dance. 'The nuns taught us at school.' She put her arms stiff by her side. 'You should never jiggle your arms about, because then all your energy goes into your arm movements, instead of down to your feet.' And

After Nancy had gone, he lay awake, thinking about Alice.

He felt it his duty to be best man at his brother's wedding. Once he'd made up his mind, he vowed that whatever else happened, he would keep his distance from Alice.

He promised himself to think only of her as his future sister-in-law, rather than the girl he had fallen head over heels in love with.

This evening though, when he saw how she had dealt with Frank's boasting, in a firm but tactful manner, and afterwards her childish joy as she danced with his mother, he knew then, that he would always think of Alice as the girl who stole his heart.

He could see his life stretching before him, when Alice would always be there; his brother's wife, and in time the mother of Frank's children.

He made himself a heartfelt vow. 'However hard it might be, I'll stand beside him as best man. I'll stay to see them married. Then I'll be swiftly away to make something of my life.'

If he was to keep his sanity, what other choice did he have?

CHAPTER THREE

LYING THERE ON the sofa, knowing Alice was just a few steps away, Joe found it difficult to sleep.

He had promised himself he would leave straight after the wedding, but then what? Wherever he went, Alice would be on his mind, and try as he might, he could not envisage a life without her.

Of course there had been flings with other women. He was a red-blooded man after all. He was lonely and they were there, but he'd never wanted to get serious with any of them.

It was always Alice. It always would be, and the strange thing was, although they had only met twice he felt as though he had known her forever.

He did not know that even now, while he was thinking of Alice, she was thinking of him.

~

Upstairs, seated on the edge of her bed, Alice wondered about Joe, and his brother Frank; tonight she had realised how very different they were.

She had witnessed a side to Frank that she had never seen before.

She had been shocked and ashamed to hear how he

expected a share of her parents' money like it was his God-given right. Moreover, he had stubbornly refused to listen to reason. Instead, he came across as being self-important and unable, or unwilling, to recognise his own faults.

For the first time, she began to wonder if he had ever really seen her as being his partner for life, someone to build a future with. Could they trust and support each other like married couples do?

What *real* part would she play in Frank's empire-building, she wondered. Did he expect her to be seen and not heard, while she raised his children like the timid little wife, watching from a distance while he shut her out in the same way her mother had done; as though her opinions didn't matter?

Feeling ashamed and guilty for thinking that way, she decided she must give him the benefit of the doubt.

His attitude tonight had been unfortunate, but it could well have been the drink talking, she thought hopefully. No doubt in the light of day, he would be mortified to know what he had said.

After deliberating, Alice came to the conclusion that, for better or worse, Frank was her man, and soon she would be his wife. When and if they were ever able to own their own farm, it went without saying that she would surely be involved in any decision making.

So, with that in mind, she decided that the sensible thing to do was to put Frank's unfortunate outburst well and truly behind them.

After all, it had been a wonderful evening; Joe was home, and with all the excitement and the wine, things were said which otherwise, may never have seen the light of day.

Moreover, because she had put him straight with regard to her parents' dubious generosity, the subject would probably never arise again. As far as she was concerned, that was an end to it.

Her thoughts turned to Frank's brother, Joe.

Alice saw how Joe had remained silent, carefully listening to Frank, and studying the situation before speaking his mind.

Alice had been grateful for Joe's intervention. She appreciated Joe's quiet, confident approach, which in her opinion had helped to calm a difficult situation this evening.

She liked Joe. Yes! She liked him a lot.

Consumed with all manner of thoughts and unable to sleep, she got up from the bed quietly so as not to wake Frank. She was agitated, and for some inexplicable reason, she suddenly felt deeply sad.

Carefully now, she tiptoed across the landing and into the bathroom; pausing only when she heard what sounded like rhythmic rolls of thunder coming from Nancy and Tom's room. 'That'll be Tom sending home the sheep,' she thought with a little grin.

Once inside the bathroom, she cleaned her teeth and had an all-over wash, before going back to the bedroom where she put on her nightgown and brushed her hair.

Afterwards, she lay on top of the bed; half-dreaming half-thinking, but with not an ounce of tiredness in her body. Instead, she felt unusually restless.

She had to get out. She needed to breathe the cool night air. 'Maybe I'll go to the barn and check to see if the falcon is all right,' she said softly to herself. Yes! She decided that would be a good thing to do.

Barefoot and in a hurry, she threw her pink robe around herself, tied the belt tight, turned up the collar and went like a whisper down the stairs and silently out the door.

Relieved to have got away from the house without waking anyone, she set about negotiating the darkened path to the barn; while underfoot the way was uncomfortable without shoes, yet she seemed not to notice.

It seemed to take forever, but at last she found herself standing at the barn door. Once there, she carefully lifted the bar, and pushed open the heavy door.

It was dark inside. 'Now where did I see Frank put the lamp?' she muttered to herself. One evening when they came back late from the field together, she had watched as he put the tilly lamp safely away, and she remembered it was up high.

It was too dark to see. Going up on tiptoe, she ran her hand along the upper wall, and there nearest the window, she found a shelf. Very carefully, for fear she might dislodge something heavy, she gingerly walked her fingers along the shelf, until her hand alighted on a metal object.

She thought she could feel the iron handle and the glass dome. 'That's it!' Clutching it in her two hands, she brought the object down, giving a sigh of relief when she realised it actually was an old tilly lamp.

Reaching up again, she found the box of matches, and with the door open she was glad to see how the moon had risen and was shining a low, ghostly light, to help her see what she was doing.

Carefully now, she raised the glass dome from the top of the lamp and placed it tenderly down. Striking a match along the rough side of the matchbox, she put the flame to the wick.

Almost at once, the wick spluttered into life and lit the barn with a soft, yellow glow.

Giving a sigh of relief, Alice now carried the lamp high as she made her way to the far end of the stables.

Once there, she climbed on to the bales of hay, so she could see the falcon more clearly. 'Hello, you!' Thrilled when the bird turned to peer at her through bright, beady eyes, she saw how the mellow light from the lamp appeared to give its feathers a bronze, velvety sheen. 'Oh, but you really are a magnificent creature!' In awe, she climbed higher, until she was almost on a level with the cage.

Leaning on the wooden rail, she stared up at him, amazed by the rich, vibrant colours in his wings, and the strong, clean shape of his head, so perfectly angled, and dark as night.

She studied him for what seemed an age, her mind and memory drinking in that raw, wild beauty.

Alice had never been that close to a falcon before.

It was an experience she would never forget.

~

In the farmhouse, Joe lay on the sofa, half awake, contemplating the future. He did his best to shut Alice from his mind, but she clung to him, as though she was touching every nerve and sense in his body. She was like an addiction; the more you had of her, the more you wanted. 'You're a damned fool, Joe!' he hissed. 'That kind of thinking can only bring unhappiness!'

For a moment he was alert, sitting up and listening. A short time ago, he thought he heard a noise, but then he put it down to the old creaking floorboards. 'Best try and get some sleep,' he assured himself. 'What with Jimmy being an outcast, I dare say Frank will need all the help he can get tomorrow.'

Lying down, he drew the blanket up. Then he sat up, got out of bed, and begun pacing the floor again. Twice more he prepared to sleep, and each time, sleep eluded him.

He made his way to the kitchen, softly so as not to wake anyone. Once there he filled the kettle and put it on to boil. 'A hot drink,' he decided, 'that should help me settle.'

He made the tea and sat at the table, but still he was unable to settle. All manner of disturbing thoughts raced through his mind, of prison, and the way of life that had driven him almost to the brink of insanity. Prison was a place of destitution, a place where there was no joy, and everyone was out for themselves.

Some men, like him, may have been innocent of the crime laid against them, but there were others . . . evil beasts who fed on violence and intimidation. Men who had committed murder and probably worse.

Things went on behind those walls; bad things that Joe would never again want to witness.

His thoughts shifted to Frank and how he would have set himself against these men. Joe knew Frank would have given as good as he got in there. Because deep down, he was made out of the same mould.

In fact, Joe truly believed that if he had not come along when he did, Frank may well have beaten Jimmy to death.

Sickened by the idea, he made himself think of those two good people who had raised them. Frank did not take after either of their parents, he thought. Nor did he take after their grandparents, because they too, were good folks of old farming stock: honest and sincere, and totally dedicated to their way of life.

His mind turned again to Frank, and the lovely Alice, who was soon to share Frank's life, in as intimate a way as a man and woman could be. 'How did Frank manage to snag a girl like Alice?' he wondered aloud. Then he remembered Frank could be very persuasive when he set his mind to a purpose.

He had grown up in Frank's shadow, and he knew the score. He knew things he had never told anyone; like the time on his third birthday, Frank tied him to a post in the bull's field, and then pretended to run off and leave him, until the bull began to show an interest and Joe became frightened and started crying.

Frank released him, but not without threatening him, 'If you say anything to Mum or Dad, I'll take the horse whip to you!'

Shutting out the bad memories, Joe took a sip of tea. After the hard work in the field today, he felt bone-tired, yet his mind was still too active for sleep.

Slouched over the table, he soon decided he must get some rest, or he would be fit for nothing in the morning. Rinsing his cup, he placed it on the drainer.

As he turned from the sink, he imagined he saw a light somewhere out there in the dark.

His first thought was a poacher, or one of the gypsies parked in the long grass two miles down the lane. 'Dammit! They'll be after the lambs!' He wondered if he should call the family, but then decided against it. 'I can handle this,' he muttered, 'No point in waking the others.'

Hurrying to the sitting room, he quickly pulled on his trousers and boots. Grabbing his coat he threw it on over his crumpled shirt. 'The buggers!' he kept saying. 'Thieving buggers!'

Before rushing out the front door, he reached under the sideboard and drew out his father's shotgun. Checking it through, he then tucked it under his arm.

Careful not to alarm the others who were still fast asleep, he softly switched on the porch-light then closed the door before walking along the path. Wary and alert, he was now ready for unwelcome intruders.

A few minutes later, having located the source of light, he was amazed to see that it was Alice in the barn. He was even more amazed when he saw how she had her hand halfway in the cage, her fingers tenderly stroking the falcon's wings. The bird made no move to back off.

Instead, he had his head turned towards her, as though studying her.

In all the years he had been growing up on this wonderful farm, Joe had seen many amazing things, but he had never seen a wild bird so close and easy with a human.

Mesmerised, he remained out of sight, watching and listening; reluctant to let Alice know he was there.

'I'm glad Joe saved you,' Alice spoke to the bird softly. 'It would have been so cruel to let you die out there.'

Having stood the lamp on a safe, upturned metal crate, she sat on the hay bale, her fingers delicately stroking the falcon's head, while unperturbed, the bird preened his feathers and occasionally trained his glowing eyes on her.

Oblivious to Joe's presence, Alice addressed the falcon as though he understood. 'We're all looking forward to the village dance,' she explained. 'Nancy's right, when Joe turns out all dressed up in a suit and tie, smiling that deep, quiet smile, the girls won't be able to take their eyes off him.'

She mulled over the evening in her mind. She could see herself and Nancy, leaping and dancing, and laughing so much they could not go on.

She laughed now. 'You should have seen us.' Excitedly sharing her joy, she described the evening. 'Me and Nancy were doing Irish dancing, oh but it was such fun!' As an afterthought she added sadly, 'in fact, it was the best fun I've ever had.'

Unaware that Joe was watching her every move, she stretched out her legs and set her feet a tapping. Happy of heart, she giggled at the thought of her mother's disapproving face. 'I can't even *imagine* what Mother would have said if she'd seen us?'

In a way, she wished her mother *had* seen them. That way she would know how the other half lived, and how you could enjoy life and be happy with what you had, rather than be miserable wanting the world.

She recalled Tom's remarks about her mother choosing her bouquet. Nancy was so different from her own mother. Alice often felt like she'd been a sorry mistake. Her mother always gave Pauline a free rein on everything, they discussed business, clothes and were generally as thick as thieves.

Alice had never felt close to her parents.

Her father was a stern man, who rarely resorted to cuddles or small talk. Unlike his wife, he did not treat Pauline any different from his youngest daughter. He treated them the same; always encouraging obedience as they grew up, and advising them when they were adults. Whenever he had close discussions with his wife, it was always about business and money.

Alice was fond of her father.

Her mother though, had caused her much heartache, in that she treated Pauline as her equal, while her youngest daughter was of little consequence.

Alice opened her heart to the falcon. 'It was Mother who said I should ask Nancy if I could stay here for a couple of nights.' She had thought that was a strange thing to do, especially with the wedding so near. Yet she was glad Nancy had said yes. 'I expect Mother wants me out of the way, while she and Pauline arrange my wedding day.' That thought gave her little consolation, but if she had complained and been difficult about it, the consequences would no doubt have been uncomfortable.

'Tom was right,' she declared bitterly. 'She should not be choosing my bouquet. It was a selfish thing to do.'

A thought occurred to her. 'Mother likes to control my life, but I've always thought how strange it was, that she never tried to dissuade me from seeing Frank. When I told her I had a boyfriend, she was really pleased. Then, when Frank asked me to marry him, I was sure Mother would hit the roof, but she never did. Not once did she argue about it, or try to put me off. Not even when she discovered he was a farmer's son, and not a wealthy property owner, or a businessman.'

She gave a low, cynical laugh. 'She wouldn't care who I was marrying, as long as I was out of her way. I'm glad Frank asked me to marry him! He's a good man. Oh, but if it had been Pauline and not me, who was marrying anyone less than an old money-bags, she'd have thrown a fit.

'It just goes to show that she wants rid of me, even if it means handing me over to someone she believes is beneath her,' Alice thought uncomfortably.

Alice had never really thought about it before, but it was strange how her mother let her choose her own husband to be, while she set about making all the decisions with regard to the wedding.

Her mother had completely taken over the wedding day arangements. She even insisted that Alice changed the dress, because she said it did nothing for her at all, while everyone else thought it was beautiful. Then the bouquet was chosen without her even asking if Alice liked it. And she carried on when Alice wanted *two* bridesmaids, Pauline and Alice's old school friend Mandy Baker.

She mimicked her mother's sharp, shrill voice. '"You're a selfish girl, Alice Jacobs! The wedding is already costing us a fortune! Think yourself fortunate that you've got your sister Pauline as bridesmaid. Now let that be an end to it!"'

Alice had to explain to Mandy, how she could not be bridesmaid after all. 'It must be *my* fault,' she chided herself now. 'Somewhere along the way, I've allowed it to happen. It's always been the same; Mother speaks and I listen. Mother chooses and I agree. Mother disapproves, and the idea is eventually dropped; unless of course, it's Pauline with the idea.'

She grew angry. 'It's time I stood up to her, like Pauline does!'

She gave a wry little smile. 'I've always known I was the unwelcome child. The accident that should never have happened.'

Regret tinged her voice. 'I've always tried too hard to please her, to make her love me, like she loves Pauline.' Her voice broke. 'I wish I could handle Mother like Pauline does, but then, I don't enjoy arguing. Pauline seems to thrive on it, which is not surprising, seeing as Pauline is Mother in the making.'

Silent for a time, she drew pleasure from watching this wild creature; encaged much like she had been all her life. 'Are you frustrated . . . locked up in that cage?' she whispered. 'I expect you want to spread your wings and fly away.' Her love of animals embraced all creatures, which was why she found working at the vets to be especially rewarding.

Curious, the bird cocked its head from side to side, as though taking in her every word.

'You're the lucky one,' Alice told him. 'When Joe lets you out of here, you can soar up to the Heavens, free as the air that carries you.' She continued to stroke his neck and face tenderly.

'We're a lonely pair you and me, aren't we, eh?' she remarked. 'You and me in the dead of night, all alone in this dark old barn.' She gave a laugh. 'I hope you realise I should not be out here, cavorting with a strange male,' she tutted. 'I'll have you know, I'm getting married on Saturday.'

There followed a long silence, and Alice contemplated the future. When she spoke again, it was to voice a sneaking doubt. 'I hope I'm doing the right thing,' she confessed in a whisper. 'I thought I loved Frank, but now I'm not so sure. I'm not even sure if I really know him at all.'

She leaned back into the hay. 'What am I saying? Of *course* I love him. I wouldn't be with him now if I didn't love him!'

The enormity of what she had said was shocking to her. 'No! Frank means the world to me. I can't wait for Saturday to come.'

She remained there, slumped into the hay, eyes closed and head bowed, and her heart sore. Was she fooling herself? Was she marrying Frank just so she had someone to love her? Or was she doing it to get back at her mother for rejecting her? No! She would *never* do that. She did love Frank! She really *did* love him!

The sound of her quiet sobs echoed across the barn.

Just a few strides away, Joe was torn by emotions. He had heard everything. He felt her pain. He needed to hold and comfort her. He wondered if he should make his presence known, or leave quietly.

Hesitant, he took a step forward, making as much noise as possible, deliberately allowing Alice time in which to compose herself.

Startled, Alice looked up, anxious to see who had discovered her there. Fearful that they may have overheard, she quickly sat up, waiting to see who it was out there, in the half-light.

On realising it was Joe who had found her, she was immensely thankful, feeling instinctively that any snippet he may have overheard would go no further; though of course she hoped he had heard nothing at all.

'I'm sorry, Alice,' Joe explained with a lop-sided grin, 'I didn't realise it was you! I thought I might find a pack of thieves, looking to steal goods or livestock. I happened to catch a glimpse of light from the tilly lamp, so I thought I'd best come down and investigate.'

Carefully, he laid the gun on the ground and sat beside her. 'So, what are you doing out here, in the early hours of the morning? Come to check on our little friend, have you?'

Alice merely nodded; while discreetly wiping away the tears.

Joe felt his heart melt. 'Did I frighten you?'

'No.' Fearful he would know she'd been crying, Alice kept her gaze averted.

'Is there something wrong, Alice?'

'No.'

'Do you want me to go away, leave you alone?'

Panic-stricken and in need of a friend, she grabbed hold of his coat. 'No! I would like you to stay. Please, Joe? Stay with me, just a while longer?'

Joe sat beside her. 'Why don't you tell me what's wrong?' he enquired gently.

'There's nothing wrong.' She gave him her brightest smile. 'Why would you ask that?'

Joe paused a moment, unsure of himself, and yet not wanting to deceive her. 'I have a confession to make,' he said in a low, sorry voice.

Instinctively wary, Alice asked him, 'What do you mean a confession? What *kind* of confession?' Something about Joe's expression worried her.

Joe chose his words carefully. 'Just now as I came in, I thought I heard you crying.'

'Oh?' Smiling, she put on a brave face. 'So you thought I was crying, did you?'

Joe looked her in the eye. 'You *were* crying.' He gave a reassuring smile. 'I think I might know when a girl is crying, but don't worry. I promise, your secret is safe with me.'

'I'm sorry, Joe. You're right, I *was* crying, but it was nothing, really. Just pre-wedding nerves. I expect every bride gets them.'

Joe was careful not to reveal how he knew of her doubts concerning Frank. Instead he reached out, and placing his hand beneath her chin, he lifted her face to look at him. 'Frank upset you tonight, didn't he?'

Alice drew away, 'Yes . . . I suppose.'

'He didn't mean to,' Joe assured her. 'Sometimes he lets his tongue run away with him; speak first, think later, that's Frank I'm afraid.' He laughed. 'You were more than a match for him though,' he said proudly. 'You let him know you were not a woman to be messed with.'

Thinking of her mother, Alice laughed at that. 'Did I really come across as a woman not to be messed with?'

'Oh yes!' Joe was adamant. 'You even made *me* nervous!' he said jokingly.

Alice laughed at that, and then she was smiling, shaking her head in disbelief. 'Good Lord! I'd best be careful, or I might turn into Mother!'

Joe was curious. 'Would that be so bad?'

Alice laughed, 'If you knew my mother, you wouldn't even ask that,' she promised with a hearty chuckle. 'Trust me, it would be the end of life as we know it!'

Joe laughed out loud, 'I can't wait to meet her.'

'She'll be there on Saturday,' Alice promised light-heartedly. 'She'll be the one with the biggest hat and the sergeant-major voice. The slimmer version beside her, will be my older sister Pauline.'

Joe was intrigued. How could such a dainty, lovely creature like Alice have a mother of that description? 'So, how does Frank get on with your family?'

Alice shrugged. 'He's only really met them twice. The first time, so my father could inspect him, and then again when he was invited to have tea. Of course, he's seen them when he's been collecting me, but Father works long hours in his study and Mother is never that sociable. A wave of her hand and she's away.'

'I see.' Joe couldn't help but wonder how Frank would fit into such a formal family as this.

Alice went on, 'I think Frank was quite impressed with Mother. She made sure he had everything he wanted; an extra slice of cake, or another pot of tea, and even a glass of wine to end the evening. Father talked a lot about business, and Frank seemed comfortable with that. In fact, he came away quite pleased with himself.'

'I'm not surprised,' Joe remarked. 'As you witnessed for yourself this evening, Frank is ambitious. It's in his nature to aspire to greater things.'

Joe could easily imagine how Frank would have made more of himself than he really was. Tonight for example, he appeared to think he'd got Alice's family wound round his little finger.

'My father has always been ambitious like that, and my mother is the same,' Alice revealed. 'Do you think it's a bad thing to be ambitious, Joe?'

'No, I don't think that.' Though knowing Frank, Joe had his doubts. 'Shall I tell you what I really think?'

'Yes! I'd like to know.'

Joe worded his thoughts carefully. 'Frank is headstrong. Sometimes he needs someone to hold him back. At first, he'll find it virtually impossible to keep you in the manner you've been used to, but there is no doubt he'll work his fingers to the bone. You will never want for anything, and in time, who knows, he may well give your father a run for his money.' He had to smile. 'If not, it won't be for the want of trying.'

Without being vindictive, he felt he had to be honest. 'The thing is, when Frank sets his mind to something, he wants it right away. Unfortunately, it doesn't always happen like that.'

Joe went on in a serious voice. 'He needs guidance,

someone to draw the reins in now and then.' He went on reluctantly, 'You might just be the one, Alice.'

Alice was flattered. 'Do you really think so?'

'Yes, I do.' Against all his instincts, Joe reassured her. 'I really do think you could handle Frank, where no one else can. Tonight for example. You didn't yell or argue. You just told him quietly that it was never going to happen, that there was no point in him expecting your parents' money. You stood up to him, and I'm proud of you. That took some guts, Alice Jacobs!'

'Thank you, Joe.'

When she smiled up at him, Joe's heart bounced in his chest, and for a moment he couldn't speak. Instead, he gazed into those wonderful, dark-blue eyes and his heart turned over. 'You really are an amazing little thing,' he murmured, 'Frank is a very lucky man.'

Beneath his intense gaze, Alice felt oddly uncomfortable, but not in a bad way. It was a feeling she had never before experienced, a feeling of someone looking right into your soul, to know you better than you knew yourself, to read your emotions like they were an open book.

She felt worried and excited, all at the same time.

Suddenly she knew. 'You heard me, didn't you?' she whispered harshly. 'Just now, you heard what I was saying. You heard it all. Didn't you, Joe?'

Joe nodded his head. 'Yes, I heard.' He felt ashamed. 'I'm sorry.'

Alice clambered up. 'I've got to go!' She began to move away, the tears rolling down her face. 'Please, Joe, don't tell Frank. I didn't mean it, none of it! I didn't know what I was saying. It's not that I don't love him, because I do. Only what with Mother taking over, and then Frank behaving like that tonight, I don't know how I feel anymore . . . I just don't . . .'

'Ssh! Don't cry, Alice.' Impulsively, Joe drew her into his arms.

Alice nestled into him; the faint, dry smell of his work-jacket offering an odd kind of comfort. She felt as though she belonged here, in Joe's strong embrace.

In that instant they were in each other's arms. It was like a dam had burst and then they were kissing, long passionate kisses that surprised and thrilled.

Shocked at her own response, Alice tentatively pulled away. 'No! We shouldn't . . . this is bad, Joe.' Her head was saying one thing but her heart was saying another.

'I understand.' Joe released her. 'Don't blame yourself, Alice,' he whispered. 'It was my fault, not yours.'

Stunned by what had just happened, Alice stumbled backwards.

Behind her, Joe sat down in the hay, head bowed; his feelings in chaos, when he thought of the enormity of what might have been. He felt deeply ashamed, but he still wanted her so much he could hardly breathe.

Deeply shaken, he went over the dizzy madness of the past few minutes. 'I'm sorry.' He didn't look up; didn't want to see her walking away. Suddenly, his every sense was heightened, and he knew she was there, standing right before him.

He raised his head to look up, and there she was; hands motionless by her sides, and her blue eyes gazing down on him, alive with emotion.

In that unforgettable moment, Joe saw his own powerful feelings mirrored in her eyes. Without a word, she held out her arms and Joe folded her to him. 'I love you,' he whispered, 'I always have.'

When he carried her deeper into the darkness where no one could see, Alice went willingly; wanting him every bit as much as he wanted her.

In the darkest corner, he gently laid her down. Alice

knew it was meant to be. She had never been more content.

It was a shocking truth, but it was the truth and right now here in Joe's arms, shrouded by the darkness . . . she had no regrets.

Their lovemaking was both fierce and tender; fierce in its hunger, and tender in the taking.

For Joe, it was something he had always known would happen. For Alice, it was her very first time, and she believed with all her heart that it was right to be with Joe.

Afterwards, Joe asked in a whisper, 'Are you afraid? Do you regret what we've done?'

Alice shook her head, her eyes alight with the joy of being in Joe's arms. 'No' she whispered, 'I'm only sorry it had to be now.' In his embrace, it was as though time did not exist.

Later, she may regret this night, but not in this moment, safe and bathed by his need of her.

She had given herself freely, without reservation; without a thought for the consequences.

Without fear of what tomorrow might bring.

~

Jimmy the farmhand had been making his way back from a night in the pub, when he decided to take a shortcut through the farm.

Harbouring a grudge after Frank had viciously whipped and humiliated him, he had lost himself in drink and was now well and truly inebriated.

As always when fuelled by booze, he broke into song; caterwauling and laughing as he tripped and stumbled towards his modest little cottage.

In his condition, it was not easy to negotiate his way home, especially in the dark, which is why he failed to see the spade propped against the wall. After stumbling over it, he lay on the ground, laughing and cursing. 'What damned idiot leaves a spade across the path?'

When both himself and the spade was upright again, he wagged a finger at the spade. 'Aha!' Replacing it against the wall, he laughed. 'Didn't get me that time, did yer, eh?'

Haphazardly continuing on his way, he rounded the wall and came up towards the barn. 'What's that then, eh?' His attention caught by the flickering light, he went as carefully as he could. 'Why would anybody be in the barn, at this time o' morning!' Stooping low, he went on at a careful pace. 'Ssh!' Feeling more afraid than drunk, he managed to keep himself upright as he approached the barn door.

Once there, he steadied himself against the wall as he peeped inside. On seeing that the place appeared empty, he shook his head in disbelief. 'Some daft idiot's left the lamp on.' He started forward, 'best turn that bugger off.' He shook his head. 'Set the damned barn alight that could!'

A wicked thought stopped him in his tracks. 'Hey! If that lamp was to tip over, the whole place would be cinders in no time.' He gave a devious smile. 'Mebbe the farm-house with it an' all!'

The drink may have fuddled his thinking, but his intention was clear. 'Take a chain to whip me, would he? Give me the marching orders and take away my living, eh? Bastard!' The more he thought on Frank's treatment of him, the angrier he grew.

As he inched forward, he was made to stop and listen. Alarmed on hearing low voices and the sound of someone emerging, he crouched down and hid in the shadows. 'Jeez! So, there *is* somebody inside after all, eh? Hmm! Thieves, grabbing what they can lay their hands on, is it?'

He shrugged. 'What do I care, eh? Let the buggers 'ave the lot! What's it to me, eh? Nothing!'

Inching back, he crept deeper into the shadows, to a place where he could see them, but they could not see him.

First, the light was extinguished, and then the two figures came out, close together, the man with his arm about the girl, who appeared to turn and look up at him.

Intrigued, Jimmy came closer; frustrated when he was unable to recognise them. 'They don't appear to be thieves,' he reasoned. 'So, who the divil are they?' He sniggered. 'That bad bugger Frank and his woman I expect, escaped from the others, to have it away in the barn?' It irritated him that he couldn't see them clearly enough.

Deciding to take a risk he slipped closer, but as he set one foot forward, the couple moved furtively away, towards the house. Excited and curious, he slithered along through the shrubbery towards them, still hidden, still undetected.

He watched as they picked their way through the darkness. And now they were in the porch.

For one split second, the soft glow from the porch light partly bathed their features and Jimmy almost fell over with the shock of it. 'Bloody Hell!' Rooted to the ground, he had recognised Alice; and there was something familiar about the man, but it was not Frank, he was sure of it.

He waited, his whole body tingling with excitement as the man paused for Alice to go into the house before softly closing the door behind her.

When the man turned round to light a cigarette, Jimmy's suspicions were well and truly confirmed. 'Lord above!' He shivered with excitement. 'Frank's brother!' His heart was beating so fast he feared he might pass out.

~

When he believed it was safe to go inside, and unaware that he was being watched, Joe finished his cigarette, before dropping the tip on the floor and grinding it into the earth. He took a moment to think, and wonder if tonight had been just one fleeting, magical experience, or the start of a whole new beginning. He hoped so. With all his heart, he hoped so; though it concerned him that on the way back to the house, Alice had been very quiet.

Was she already regretting it, he thought sadly. Or like himself, was she concerned about Frank and the family, and how they would take the news.

He could not be certain that things would turn out as he prayed they would. In all fairness, he had left the decision for Alice to make. She knew that whatever decision she came to, he would abide by it. After tonight, and the long, intimate talk they had while still in each other's arms, he never doubted her love, not for one minute. Alice loved him, he knew that with absolute certainty.

Right now, with the aura of Alice still on him, he was the happiest man alive. It was never his intention to hurt anyone, especially family, and yes, the cloud of guilt lay heavy on him; but that was the price he was willing to pay, if it meant he and Alice could be together.

From his hiding place, Jimmy kept his eyes firmly on Joe, watching as he gingerly opened the door and went silently inside.

Sniggering to himself, then unable to contain himself, laughing out loud manically he loped off into the darkness. 'Well now, fancy that, eh?' Breathless, he turned against the tree to empty himself of the booze put away that night. 'Joe and his brother's woman, well I never. Whoever would 'ave thought it?'

He roared with delight. 'Not Frank, that's for sure. Oh, but won't it wipe the smile off that smug face of his when he finds out, eh?'

Tonight he had accidentally discovered what was potential dynamite to the Arnold family, and to Frank in particular.

'Now then, Jimmy boy,' he chided himself. 'Don't get too carried away just yet. This is no time to go barging in like a mad bull. You need to think this through,'

So many questions rampaged through his simple mind. 'How do you deal with this pleasurable information?' He flicked his tongue over his lips as though savouring a tasty meal. What to do? Do you go straight to Frank Arnold, and watch the look on his face when you tell him what's been going on, right under his nose?

'No, wait . . . wait a minute!' He reminded himself how he still bore the marks of that wicked chain on his back. He must be very careful not to sign his own death warrant, because there was not the slightest doubt in his mind that the man in question was capable of killing.

'I could blackmail Joe.' He swiftly discarded that option. It was fairly obvious that Joe had returned to the fold without a respectable penny to his name. Besides, he reminded himself that it was Joe who saved his skin from being lacerated, and more.

'Or I could wait until Frank and Joe have gone out across the fields, then slip a note under the door, addressed to Tom Arnold. That old bugger would raise hell and damnation, there's no doubt about it.'

Jimmy reminded himself that he had no grouse against any of the Arnold family, other than Frank. At different times, both Tom and Nancy had been good to him. In fact, if Tom had not pleaded with the landowner to let him rent the cottage, he wouldn't even have a roof over his head.

So, he concluded that he would not deliberately hurt the old couple; though if they got caught up in the fray, that would be a different story, and not altogether his fault.

Their oldest son though, was a very different kettle of fish. 'I have to teach that son of theirs a lesson!' he decided. 'And it might not be a bad thing if they were to learn what he was really like. There's a badness about that Frank! He's got a murderous heart if ever I saw one!' Moreover, Frank Arnold cared for no one, not man, woman nor child.

His hatred of Frank was like a canker inside him. But how to punish him without hurting the others too much? How to make him suffer, without getting himself killed?

The discovery he had stumbled on this night was like a bomb waiting to go off.

'Be careful, Jimmy boy,' he cautioned. 'Take your time. Think it through, and be sure to get it right.'

Oh yes! He would need to think long and hard about this one.

Maybe, if things went his way, he might never use this exciting information. He didn't really want to, because in hurting Frank with it, he would also hurt Joe and Alice. Joe had always been good to him, and so had the rest of the family, so in telling what he had seen, he would hurt them too. On the other hand, it would be good to see Frank get his comeuppance.

He sloped off. 'We'll see,' he muttered. 'We'll just have to see, won't we?'

PART TWO

~

Suspicions

CHAPTER FOUR

Nancy was all of a dither. 'Just think, in a few more days you'll be a real part of this family, all legal and everything.' Smothering Alice in a bear-hug, she brushed away the tears. 'You'd best go,' she said, 'before you have me babbling like a two year old!'

'That's right!' Frank had started early that morning, but now he was back at the farmhouse, all washed and changed, and ready to take Alice home. 'We don't want your mother sending out a search party for you, do we, eh?'

Leading Alice by the arm, he walked her to the black Ford saloon; his one and only extravagance and his pride and joy. 'Mind you wipe your feet,' he joked as he watched her climb in, 'after all, I don't know where you've been, do I?'

Laughing, he did not see Alice's worried expression as she sank into her seat. If only he knew, she thought nervously.

After lying awake for most of the night, thinking of Joe and what they had done, Alice was sick with worry. She hated herself for having allowed it to happen, yet even now she wanted Joe so much, it was like a physical ache that would not go away. Those few hours with Joe had never been sordid. Instead, they had been amazing. Joe had awakened a part of her that had lain dormant.

Alice knew without a shadow of doubt, that for all her life she would remember what happened, and her heart would always belong to Joe.

But she also knew, with deep sadness, that a future with Joe was impossible.

She still felt a degree of love for his brother. She had promised to be Frank's wife, and now she did not have the heart to walk away; especially when he hadn't really done anything to hurt her. Instead, he had always been faithful to her, consoling her when she was hurt, taking care of her, and loving her.

At the end of a long, sleepless night, she had come to what she believed to be the right decision. The plain fact remained; she had promised to be Frank's wife, long before Joe came back on the scene.

Joe, on the other hand, was a man who represented something she was not used to. He was a man with the freedom to go wherever he wanted; a man with a sense of adventure; a man who would never want to stay in one place for too long.

There was no denying she harboured deep feelings for him, Wonderful, powerful feelings that swept her to dizzy heights. And yet they frightened her. She was drawn to him like she had never been drawn to any other man, including Frank.

Joe was the fantasy, a figment of her girlish dreams; the knight in shining armour. Joe was her way of proving that she was a woman through and through, lonely and needy, and there he was; without any condition or demands. And now the fairytale was over. Daylight brought reason, and reality beckoned.

Soon no doubt, Joe would be on his way again, tasting adventure in far flung places. He would soon forget about her.

Frank on the other hand, was reality; safe and reliable.

There was no joy in her decision. Instead, she had begun to wonder if she even knew what love was meant to be.

With Frank she felt comfortable. She knew him, and she was content that their future was planned, even though there had never been the same feeling she felt for Joe.

Her emotions were all over the place. One minute she was thrilled because in Joe she believed she had found a soulmate, and the next minute she was riddled with doubt and shame.

Frank was uncomplicated, and she really did love him; though she asked herself, if she loved Frank, why did she give herself to Joe?

She blamed it on the madness of the moment. Or maybe she needed that intimate kind of love. When Frank tried to persuade her to make love, she had told him she wanted to wait until they were man and wife.

The importance of saving her virginity until the wedding night had been drummed into her so often by her Victorian-minded mother. Succumbing to Joe may have been her way of showing her mother that she was not to be ordered about, or treated as though she did not have a mind of her own.

Alice had felt closer to Joe, in spirit and heart, than she had ever felt with anyone.

Was that real love, she asked herself, or was it pure excitement, the thrill of danger. Something she had never been allowed to experience. And yet, when she and Joe had made love, she felt so alive, so different, as though she could fly without wings.

She thought about it now, the touch of his mouth on hers; that clear, shining emotion in his deep, dark eyes when he looked at her . . . in a way that Frank never had.

For as long as she lived, Alice knew she would never

forget that special, wonderful way he made her feel; almost as though they belonged together for all time.

But it was over now and, rightly or wrongly, she turned her mind to the wedding day.

Startled by Frank's voice calling out, she quickly put Joe to the back of her mind.

'Tell Joe I'll be back quick as I can, I'm just off to visit Alice's folks,' Frank informed his mother. 'Meantime, he'll know what to do. Oh, and tell him to keep a lookout for that no-good Jimmy Slater!' He shouted a curse as he climbed into the car. 'If he steps foot on my land again, I'll have him. Once and for all!'

Alice was curious. 'What's Jimmy done wrong?' She had always liked Jimmy. He was simple but kind, a decent sort, though occasionally a bit worse for wear with booze.

'Don't you worry your pretty head,' Frank said. 'Leave Jimmy to me, eh?' Patting her on the knee, he started the car and shifting into gear, drove off in a skid. 'Must get this gearbox checked out,' he grumbled under his breath. 'Damned thing's snatching again!'

Inside the house, Tom had heard what Frank shouted to Nancy, and he was none too pleased. 'I'd like to know what he means by that.'

'What? About Jimmy you mean?' Nancy pursed her lips. 'I'm sure I don't know what he meant.' She turned her mind to making them a pot of tea.

'No!' Tom was persistent. 'I didn't mean what he called Jimmy. I meant what he said about Jimmy being kept off *his* land!'

Nancy was preoccupied, thinking of the washing and the baking, and the wedding that loomed ever nearer. 'Well, I expect he had a bit of a run-in with Jimmy,' she said. 'You know what he's like when he's had a few.'

Groaning with frustration, Tom stood before her. 'Will

you stop faffing about, and listen to what I'm saying. Frank said to keep Jimmy off *his land*!'

Having got Nancy's full attention, he went on in a quiet voice. 'The main fields are long gone, but that tiny parcel of land is all you and I have to show for a lifetime of work. We sold everything we could to find the money to buy that bit o' land. We sat through winter with hardly any coal in the fire, and there were times when we couldn't even afford to walk up to the pub for a drink and a chat with our neighbours. So, *now* d'you see what I'm telling yer? Our Frank appears to think the little field belongs to him! He needs to remember how it was back then. After my father, and his grandfather sold the main holding to our landlord, we did well to get back what little we could. In the main, we're just tenants now, with just a few acres to call our own. It's mine and yours and Frank needs to remember that!'

Nancy smiled knowingly. 'Did you really think I'd forgotten how we struggled to get it back, Tom?' she said quietly.

'Well then!' Tom snapped angrily. 'Frank needs to stop and think, before he lays claim to what doesn't belong to him!'

'Hey now!' Nancy warned him. 'Don't go getting yourself all riled up. It'll bring on your indigestion.'

'Bugger the indigestion!' Tom retaliated. 'I do not take kindly to him thinking he has a right to what's mine an' yours.'

'Ssh now, Tom. I can understand why you're angry, but getting all wound up like this won't put it right, will it now?'

Being fully aware how Tom had long resented the fact that he could no longer work the land, Nancy's heart went out to him. 'Think on this, Tom love,' she urged. 'You and me won't be here forever, will we? In time, that small, precious piece of land will go to Joe and Frank anyway.'

'I know that.' Tom had been made to accept that he was past the heavy work, but his spirit was still fighting fit, as he now demonstrated, 'I also know that you an' me have grown older, and I may have a gammy leg and a weak back . . . I do know all that. But we're nowhere near dead an' gone yet! I for one intend to dance at our son's wedding and hold his newborn in my arms, so don't you count us out yet woman, 'cause I'm not ready to go!'

And to Nancy's delight, he even gave a one-legged jig to prove it.

'You daft old bugger.' Plonking a firm kiss on his cheek, Nancy had a twinkle in her eye. 'All right, I get the message; there's life in the old dog yet, eh?'

The twinkle developed into a smile. 'So? How about you and me go upstairs and try to rekindle our youth, eh?' She gave him a wink for the fun of it.

'Ooh, hey, woman!' Wide-eyed and stumbling, Tom took a few steps back. 'Steady on! I don't know as I'm ready for all *that*!'

'All right Tom love, don't start panicking. Just let me know when you're good and ready. It's been a while since you and me had a bit of a tumble. I'll be looking forward to that, an' no mistake.'

Turning away, she could hardly keep a straight face. 'So now that's settled, are you ready for your tea?'

Grateful for small mercies, and thankful to be changing the subject, Tom had the last word. 'That son of ours is getting far too big for his boots!' he declared. 'What with expecting Alice's family to fork out a fortune so's he can build an empire, and now claiming what's yours and mine. I reckon it's time I put him right on a thing or two.'

His younger son, Joe, was very much in his mind. 'Besides, apart from that, we have another son, who's finally decided to come home where he belongs.'

Nancy agreed with a nod of the head. 'Our Frank doesn't mean anything by it,' she promised. 'It's just that sometimes he gets carried away with himself. He always has. Even as a boy he had a temper and a strong will.'

As a mother, Nancy had been quick to recognise the anger that filled her first child, though over the years she had seen him mellow. Until now she truly believed he was over his earlier difficulties. 'You're right though, Tom,' she conceded now. 'For my part I'm just thankful that Joe's got the wanderlust bug out of his system, and he's back in the family fold. So, like you say Tom, we have *both* our sons to consider, and like it or not, Frank needs to remember that.'

~

At that very moment, Joe was examining the fence, where the playful lambs had trampled it down to ground level. 'Little devils. If we're not careful we'll have them munching at the crops and that would never do.'

He was in buoyant mood, thinking of Alice, and daring to believe they might actually have a life together. He wasn't taking it for granted though, especially when Alice had said hardly a word as they walked back to the house last night.

All he could do was wait for her decision, which would need to be soon, with the wedding so near. What if Alice saw last night as being a huge mistake? What if she still wanted to be Frank's wife?

If that's the way it was to be, then he must accept it and make plans to leave as soon as possible.

In the meantime, he had to be patient and focus his energy on the work in hand, which was to find the lamb that had pushed its way through the fence and strayed from the fold.

~

Not too far away, meandering along the lane towards the main road, Frank was puzzled as to why Alice had lapsed into silence. 'You're unusually quiet,' he remarked now, 'are you all right?'

Alice was quick to reassure him. 'Of course I am. Why shouldn't I be?' She was still thinking about Joe.

Frank had another question. 'Alice?'

'Yes?'

'You're not having regrets, are you?'

'About what?' Her guilt was tenfold.

'About the wedding, what else?'

'No, of course I'm not having regrets about the wedding.' In truth she was having regrets about everything: the wedding, Joe; her own shameful behaviour last night in the barn. This morning all she could think about was Joe, when her mind should be on her wedding day.

Suddenly, Frank was cursing. 'What the devil's going on now!' He slammed the brakes on. 'I should have taken it to the garage when it first started playing up.'

Scrambling out of the car, he stripped his shirt off, raised the bonnet and peered inside. 'Looks like the battery's come adrift!' he shouted. 'Look in the boot, there's an oil rag in there. Fetch it, will you?'

Alice did as she was asked, and Frank got to work. 'It'll only take a minute,' he promised, and it did.

'Look at the state of you!' Alice drew Frank's attention to the oil and muck all over his arms. 'You can't get back in the car like that.'

'I don't intend to,' he said, 'I'll have a quick swill in the brook, then we'll be on our way.'

Rather than be left on her own, Alice went with him; running away shrieking with laughter when he came towards her, his arms open wide as though to grab her.

Lighter of foot, she kept him at a distance. 'Get off!' For one fleeting moment her worries about Joe disappeared beneath her girlish laughter. 'Can you imagine Mother's face if I walked in with my dress all smothered in oil?'

With that in mind, Frank backed off. 'We don't want to upset the family now, do we?' It wouldn't do to blot his copy book when he had their money on his mind.

So, while Alice sat on the boulder with her bare feet dipped into the cool water, he washed his arms.

That done, he took her by the hand and together they walked across the field and up the hill back to the car. 'You looked like a little nymph down there,' Frank teased. 'You're a wild thing at heart, but you're *my* wild thing, and woe betide any man who tries to take you from me.'

Without warning, he grabbed her by the waist and swung her round to him. 'Let's make love right here, right now,' he demanded, his gaze coveting her face, and his arms wound so tight about her waist, she could hardly catch her breath.

'Let me go, Frank.' Her quiet, firm voice belied the fear inside her.

'Why should I let you go, tell me that?' He was so close, she could feel his warm breath bathing her face. 'Anyone would think I was a stranger and here we are, just a few days from being man and wife.' He shook her playfully, 'Go on then, tell me, why should I let you go?'

'You know why,' she answered meaningfully.

'Oh, yes, of course!' He laughed, a harsh, raking laugh that made her cringe. 'So now we're back on that are we?' he snarled. 'Oh yes, I forgot, silly me! We can't make love, because your mother wants you to save your virginity until you're respectfully married, is that it?'

Alice gave no answer. She thought of Joe, and the way they had made love last night. It was so right. So beautiful. In all her dreams, she could never have imagined it to be like that.

'Alice?' Something about her quietness had stirred a fear in him.

Alice looked up, but said nothing.

Strangely subdued, Frank suddenly asked, 'Do you love me, Alice?'

'Yes,' she replied.

Frank met her gaze. 'You don't sound so sure.'

'I *am* sure.' But was she? After Joe, how could she be so sure?

'I do love you, Frank.' She needed to convince him, and herself as well, 'I don't want us making love . . . not yet. Not until we're married.' She paused, looking at him in such a way that made him feel unsettled, unsure and afraid. 'Please, Frank, it's only a few more days.' With Joe still heavy on her mind, she needed time.

Her sincere words softened his mood. 'All right then, my beauty. I'm sure it will be all the better for the waiting.' He gave a confident little wink. 'I'm just grateful that I'm marrying a virgin, and not some tart who's been spreading herself about.'

When she made no comment, he laughed out loud. 'Oh, I see! You've got no answer to that, so does it mean you're turning me away, while all the time you've got a man hidden away somewhere . . .' he smacked her rear end, '. . . giving him what should be mine, is that it?'

'That's a terrible thing to say, Frank Arnold!' Going with his mood, Alice forced a laugh. 'The truth is . . . I've got a man for every day of the week.'

Enjoying the banter, he wagged a finger in her face. 'You little tease,' he said, giving her a shake. 'And here am I, thinking you were the quiet, shy little thing, and all the time you're a secret Jezebel!'

Suddenly he had tight hold of her hand and was running her up the hill. 'All right then, I suppose I'll have to be patient,' he conceded. 'But I'm warning you . . . it had better be worth the wait.'

From the far side of the field, Joe heard their laughter and came to see. He instantly recognised them, chasing up the hill, with Frank now calling back to Alice, 'Come on, slowcoach! We'll never get you home at this rate.'

He saw Frank help Alice inside the car, then he saw it begin to move slowly away, and now Alice turned her face towards him. Convinced that she had seen him, he remained there, returning her gaze, and watching until they were gone from sight.

For a long time he remained in that same spot. 'She's gone,' he whispered, 'she's gone.'

Striding across to where the lamb was grazing, he collected it into his arms, and placed it safely inside the fence, then secured it tightly behind him. 'Looks like I've got my answer,' he said under his breath. 'She seemed happy enough, and that's all I want for her.'

Now, he had to make up his mind. Did he stay to be his brother's best man? Or did he go back right now, pack a bag and disappear?

~

When he returned to the farmhouse some time later, he was still undecided as to what he should do.

It was Nancy who innocently made the decision for him. 'I've ironed your shirt for Saturday,' she told him excitedly as he came into the kitchen, 'and your shoes are all polished and ready.'

She then folded her arms about him. 'When I stand in

that church and see my two sons side by side together . . .' A tear brightened her eye, '. . . I shall be the proudest mother in the world!'

Joe saw how she was, and he knew he must stay.

After all, no one would ever know their secret, not his parents, and not Frank. Thankfully, there were only two people who knew of their lovemaking, and that was himself, and Alice.

That much at least, he was thankful for.

~

Alice had seen Joe, and she knew he had seen her. She suspected he now realised that she was going ahead with the wedding. It would not be an easy thing to do, because Joe had awakened a part of her soul that would be forever his.

Yet Frank was the man she must marry, because if she chose Joe, it would split his family apart, and her own family would banish her from their lives. That in itself would not break her heart, but she had seen how happy Nancy and Tom were on seeing Joe home again. If she deserted one of their sons to be with the other, they would be devastated.

There were so many reasons why she could not be with Joe. In time Joe would see that, and forgive her. Right now, she was convinced that following her head instead of her heart was the right thing to do, for all concerned.

'Here we are.' Frank steered the car up the gravel drive to the house. 'I like this house.' Sick with envy, he observed the long casement windows and the grand entrance with its deep porch and heavy wood-panelled door. 'One day we'll have one just like it. We'll find a plot with land some-where deep in the countryside, and we'll design the house together.' He drew the car to a halt. 'That would be my dream come true. What say you, Alice?'

'I wouldn't care about the house being as grand as this

112

one,' she said honestly. 'As long as ours is a happy home, filled with laughter and children, I'm sure I would be content.'

'Oh, so you've decided to show your face at last, have you?' Having seen them arrive, Alice's mother rushed out in a flurry to greet them.

With her thick, greying hair wound into a bunch at the nape of her neck and her tall, straight figure clothed in what was obviously a very expensive brown tweed two-piece, she made an authoritative figure.

When she complained about the heels on her shoes being ruined as as she crunched her way angrily through the gravel, Alice knew she was in for a lecture.

'Have you no sense of responsibility? You were supposed to be home hours ago. Honestly, Alice! I was beginning to wonder if you'd changed your mind about getting married, what with the final fitting of the dress still waiting to be done, and we have to inform the hairdresser on how we want your hair dressed, and then there are a thousand other things you need to help with!'

Totally ignoring Frank, she took hold of Alice by the arm. 'For goodness' sake, child, have you no sense of urgency? Don't you realise how time is racing away? What did I tell you? I said to be home first thing today, so what kept you, that's what I'd like to know?'

'I'm sorry, Mrs Jacobs, it was my fault entirely,' Frank intervened. 'I've been having trouble with the car lately, and on the way here it broke down. We had to stop while I fixed it, which took a bit of time I'm afraid.'

'Yes, well, you should have seen to it earlier, but never mind, she's here now, and like I say there are so many things to deal with, poor Pauline and I are quite worn out.'

'It was you who wanted me to stay over for another night,' Alice reminded her. 'Oh, and how's everything with Uncle Larry?'

'Like I told you, he's very upset, but never mind that for now. With this wedding to organise, I think I have quite enough to deal with without worrying about someone else's marriage problems.'

Taking control of Alice, she led her inside. 'The dressmaker is already here, waiting to do the final fitting,' she announced grandly. 'It's total chaos! I've got the florist in the sitting room waiting for me to go through everything with her, and Pauline has gone into Bedford town to change her shoes. Apparently they pinch her toes.'

'Why didn't she put them on and walk about in the shop?' Alice asked. 'She would have known then, and it would have saved her going back.'

Angered by Alice's innocent remark, Maureen Jacobs tutted, 'You know very well, Pauline will not try shoes on in the shop, especially if there are other customers about.'

Not wanting Frank to hear of her daughter's personal problems, she lowered her voice to a whisper, 'Have you forgotten your sister has this unfortunate business with her feet?' She wafted her face with the back of her hand. 'Foot sweat can be extremely unpleasant. The poor girl is a martyr to it!'

She ranted on, while keeping a firm grip on Alice's arm as she marched her through the hallway.

Bemused but not wanting to alienate his soon to be mother-in-law who he believed would help to set him on a path to riches, Frank followed a few steps behind. 'Is there anything I can do, to help with the wedding arrangements?'

Her answer was painfully direct. 'I'm sorry, Frank, but this is no place for you at the moment,' she retorted with a frosty smile. 'Have you eaten?'

Thinking he was about to be asked into the hallowed living room, Frank offered his best smile. 'Well thank you, yes I had a little breakfast, but I'm a working man, and working men are always hungry.'

'Ah! Well in that case, you may as well go through to the kitchen. I'm sure Cook will find you something. After that, you might want to hurry home. We've got lots to sort out and I'm sure you have too. Beside, you won't want to be underfoot.'

Disappointed that she wanted rid of him, Frank replied cockily, 'I'm already sorted.'

'Are you really?' Pausing in flight she turned to regard him yet again. 'As I recall, Frank my dear, the last time we spoke you were still waiting for your brother to come home. Up to that point you had no best man. So are you saying the matter has been resolved?'

'That's exactly what I'm saying, yes.' Like most people, he had no liking for this arrogant woman, but he needed to keep her sweet for his own purpose. 'Everything is fine,' he assured her. 'My brother Joe is home, and more than delighted to stand beside me as my best man.' He winked at Alice. 'All we need now, is the bride.'

'You've been fitted with your suit I hope?'

'Yup. Fits a treat it does.'

'And you've got the ring safe, have you?'

'Safe as houses.'

'And you have a note of when the cars arrive, do you?'

'My mother has it all written down in big black letters. Don't you worry. Everything is fine and dandy. To tell you the truth, I've never been so organised.'

'And are you clear about who goes into which car?'

'Of course.'

'Well!' She forced a smile for his impudence. 'I really am impressed. It seems like you've left nothing to chance.'

Frank agreed. 'Like I said, all we need now is the bride.' He glanced about; there were doors on every side. 'Er . . . which one leads to the kitchen?' The last time he was here, they were ensconced in the dining room for most of the evening; except for half an hour when they were offered drinks in the drawing room.

'Through there.' Pointing to a narrow door beside the stairway, Maureen Jacobs found Frank a bit too brash for her liking; but the fact that he was ready and willing to take on the responsibility of her youngest daughter, certainly warranted a polite, even friendly manner. After all, she didn't want a daughter of hers being left on the shelf.

Nodding his thanks, Frank went gingerly through the narrow door. 'Hello . . .' Seeing no one in sight he shouted again, 'Hello . . . anybody here?'

'Oh, Mr Arnold!' Emerging from the pantry, the Jacobs' cook, a little grey-haired woman, was all smiles. 'I thought I heard you out there, talking to Mrs Jacobs.' She clapped her hands together. 'Oh, but it's so exciting!' she exclaimed. 'I can't wait to see Alice in her wedding dress.'

She was instantly mortified. 'Oh, but *you* can't see her in it, because it's bad luck, don't you know?'

Frank gave a genuine smile. 'Everybody and his cousin has told me the very same,' he groaned. 'But . . .' lowering his voice, he gestured towards the door, '. . . the High and Mighty have marched Alice away, so I don't supppose there's a chance in hell of me seeing her until the wedding, is there?'

Lucy chuckled. 'Fraid not. So now, you've been sent for something to eat before you make your way home, have you?'

'That's about it, yes.'

'What d'you fancy then?'

'What have you got?' Frank rubbed his hands together in anticipation. The smell of fresh-baked bread filled his nostrils, and his stomach growled hungrily.

'Do you want savoury or sweet?' the little woman asked.

'Savoury.'

'Well, I've got ham on the bone with some fresh-baked bread. Or I've got baby meat pies and chutney, oh, and I've got a couple of chicken legs left over from last night.' She looked like a little bird as she bent forward to ask in a whisper, 'What's it to be then?'

Frank's mouth was watering. 'It all sounds tempting.'

'So?'

'So, I'll have the chicken legs! But don't bother with all the niceties,' he told her, 'I'll take them with me and munch on the way if that's all right with you?'

'Are you sure?' Proud of her kitchen and cooking, Lucy was horrified. 'Won't you at least have a nice cup of tea before you leave?'

Sometimes it got very lonely in the kitchen; and though she had heard through the village grapevine that Frank Arnold was a law unto himself, she hardly ever paid mind to idle gossips. Besides, the company of a man like Frank was better than no company at all.

Frank refused the tea. 'I need to get back,' he explained, 'I've left my brother ploughing the bottom field, and it's been some long time since he was let loose on a tractor and plough.'

Lucy shrugged her narrow shoulders. 'Makes no difference to me whether you have tea or not,' she declared, 'but as the kettle is already on the boil, you might as well have a cup of tea while you wait.' She gave him a merry smile, 'All right?'

'Have I got a choice?'

'Not really.'

'Tea it is then.'

Pleased with her powers of persuasion, Lucy ordered him to sit down while she made it.

When Frank was seated, she made a pot of tea, and brought it to the table, along with cup and saucer, and a plate of biscuits and cake. 'There y'are,' she announced.

'See how fast you can shift that little lot, while I get your chicken legs ready.'

'You sound like my mother!' he laughed. 'She bosses me about an' all.'

'Hmm!' The little woman wagged a finger. 'Quite right too. It's a mother's job to keep her offspring in their place! I know, because I've got a couple of my own.' Having imparted that snippet of information, she disappeared into the pantry.

While Frank tucked into the biscuits, she began muttering and moving about, before eventually reappearing with a brown paper bag. 'There y'are,' she said merrily. 'Now go on . . . be off with you and get yourself ready for the big day. Oh, and I'll be there . . . somewhere in the background, waiting to throw my little bag of confetti.'

As he went towards the door, she came up behind him. 'Mr Arnold?'

When he turned, she spoke to him in a whisper, 'I do wish you all the best, I really do.'

Puzzled by her attitude, Frank thanked her, but when she spoke again, it was to issue a covert warning. 'Me and your mother are one of a kind,' she said, 'we're straightforward women and if we have anything to say, we'll say it to the person intended and not behind their back. What I mean is, what you see is what you get with some people. But not everybody's like that. Other people might put on a front, when behind your back they can be very spiteful.'

'I'm sure they can.' Frank thought it might be time she retired and put her feet up.

Lucy went on in a hoarse whisper, 'All I'm saying is, with Alice you have a beautiful little soul; a girl with a heart of gold. She'll be a loyal wife to the end; even if some others turn out to be a disappointment . . . if you know what I mean? Never expect more than you will ever receive.'

'Right! Well, thanks for the advice. I'll certainly keep it in mind.'

He didn't know what else to say, except, 'I do know what a gem I have in Alice, and there is nothing I wouldn't do for her. I assure you, she will be safe enough with me if that's what you're worried about?'

The little woman smiled. 'Go on then, young man . . . get yourself off home. I'll see you at the church on Saturday. Oh, and tell your mother I'll be looking to catch up with her. It's a long time since we had a good natter.'

She quickly closed the door on him, talking to herself as she went across the kitchen, 'They may be my employers and he may be marrying their daughter, but they have no liking whatsoever for that young man.'

She shook her head and sighed. 'I've heard them talk about him, and I know what they're saying. They don't care tuppence for Frank Arnold, and while Mr Jacobs may have some regard for his youngest daughter, his wife sees Alice as a burden she can't get rid of quick enough!'

She stomped about, reaching into cupboards and getting out her pots and pans. 'It's Pauline this and Pauline that, and just because she's turned out to be a good businesswoman like her parents, it does not make her a better person than her younger sister. In fact, Alice is twice the lovely person she will ever be!'

Making herself a fresh cup of tea she crossed to the table and sat down. 'Disgraceful.' She nibbled on her ginger-snap. 'That's what it is, downright disgraceful!'

~

Standing outside the kitchen door, Frank paused a moment, turning Lucy's advice over in his mind. 'She's losing her marbles, silly old bugger!' One thing did intrigue him though. 'What did she mean "behind your back they can be very spiteful"? That was an odd thing to say.'

Dismissing her babbling, he followed the sounds of Alice speaking and her mother's loud voice. Before he had gone even a half-dozen steps, he heard Maureen Jacobs screeching madly at some poor person: 'I distinctly ordered WHITE roses! If you're not able to provide them, then I'll find someone who will!'

Alice intervened. 'It's all right, Mother,' she insisted, 'I prefer red roses anyway. They're my favourite, you know that.'

'Please, Alice, do not interfere. I will have what was ordered, and that is that!'

Frank retraced his steps. 'Lucy's right,' he muttered, 'This is no place for me just now.'

Heading for his own car, Frank recognised the black saloon now approaching the house. He also recognised the man who climbed out of it.

Ronald Jacobs appeared every inch the businessman; strongly built and grey at the temples, he held himself with the kind of well-bred authority that made you look up to him.

Excited, Frank decided to linger a moment or two, hoping to somehow creep into the older man's good books. 'Hello sir, and how are you today?' Flashing his best smile, he changed direction and made his way towards the other car.

'Ah, Frank!' The older man swung his briefcase out of the car. 'So, you've delivered my daughter safely, have you?'

'I have, yes, and now I'm on my way back. There's lots of work to do before the big day, as I'm sure you under-stand.'

The big man gave a reserved kind of smile. 'It's always good for a man to work.'

Frank saw his chance and he took it, 'Of course we don't own all the land,' he explained. 'My father rents all but a small parcel of it from the landowner who bought it some years ago from my late grandfather. My father has worked the land for many years.'

Ronald Jacobs applauded such initiative. 'Good man! What with the War now well and truly behind us, the country is in dire need of building up. We could do with a few more of your father's sort, yes indeed! Sort this country out in no time at all, it would.'

'Yes, sir, you're right!' Impatient, Frank still had an eye to his big chance, never mind the country's needs. He had more pressing needs of his own. 'One day I mean to have my own acreage,' he confided proudly. 'Rich, prime land that stretches away as far as the eye can see, and for your lovely daughter, I'll build her a house fit for a Queen!'

He lowered his voice, 'Mind you, it might take years, being that I'm just an ordinary working farmer.'

'Well done all the same!' The older man appeared delighted. 'Very commendable attitude, Frank!' Shaking Frank by the hand he wished him well. 'I'm pleased we've gone into certain matters that had concerned me. I see your vision and I like the way you plan forward. Yes indeed. It certainly seems as though my daughter Alice has managed to get herself a man with purpose. A man after my own heart.'

He felt the need to add, 'I'm very gratified that you have ambitions to build my daughter a house that would be fit for a Queen, but that kind of achievement does not happen overnight, so in the meantime, I'm sure you will both be more than happy with the cottage we've had reno-vated for you to occupy for the time being.'

'Oh, and we are grateful, sir. It's a lovely little place,

right there beside the spinney and overlooking the whole of Bedfordshire.' Frank reiterated his own ambition. 'But I still have vision, sir. I also have a plan, which one day maybe you and I can discuss?'

'Mmm.' The big man looked towards the house, 'I really must go now. Like you said, there's work to do. Give my regards to your parents.'

'I will, thank you.'

Pleased with himself, Frank had a grin on his face as wide as the Mersey tunnel. 'He's taking the bait!'

Once inside the car, he whooped for joy. 'It's only a matter of time before I've got the old bugger eating out of my hand!' Nothing would stop him now, he thought. 'The world is my oyster. With Alice as my wife, anything is possible!'

~

Behind him, Ronald Jacobs remained in the porch, his wary gaze watching Frank's car as it cleared the drive and headed on to the road. 'Hmm!' He shook his head. 'He must think I was born yesterday. Cunning and brazen as you like, asking me to finance his venture into buying land. Not in a million years will I!'

Thrusting his key into the door lock, he entered the house. Damned young upstart! he thought. If you want something badly enough, you'll work all that much harder to achieve it. There are no handouts, not in this life.

He was still muttering to himself as Maureen came bursting out of the living room.

He gave her a peck on the cheek, and peered behind her to the closed living room door. 'Is Alice in there?'

'Yes. Don't go in. She's in her wedding dress, and oh, Ronald, she really does look lovely.'

'I'm sure she does, and I look forward to seeing her

on the day, but I'm not so sure about that young upstart she's about to marry.'

'Oh, and why's that?'

Leaning forward he asked her, 'Are you sure we're doing the right thing in allowing her to marry this man?'

'What are you getting at? I thought we'd already discussed it in length. We both agreed that she was old enough to be married, and that she could do with the discipline. We've tried to train her into socialising and our way of life, but she is not the slightest bit interested. She won't even be drawn into helping Pauline run her salon.'

'Ah, well, if you don't mind me saying, I blame Pauline for that. The one time Alice turned up at the salon, eager to learn the ropes, Pauline threw her in at the deep end and then complained vehemently, when everything was less than perfect.'

Addressing her more cautiously, he took his life in his hands. 'Pauline is much like you, my dear . . . strong-minded and sometimes a bit of a Sergeant-Major, while Alice is rather sensitive. You and Pauline might get better co-operation if you didn't always treat her like a child straight out of school. She is an intelligent, hard-working young woman, and in my opinion for, what it's worth, she deserves to be treated as such.'

'My! my!' Maureen was genuinely surprised. 'Defending Alice all of a sudden is it? Some time back, you were sulking because she left your offices to work at the vets, taking care of the animals there.'

'Well, I've had time to reflect, and I've come to the conclusion that she already knows more about animals than she cares to learn about filing cabinets. At least the veterinary profession is well-respected, if poorly paid.'

She continued to taunt him. 'She's out of control, that's the trouble.'

'All right! All right! we should be thankful. She appears to have found some sort of purpose, and who knows, her unpredictable behaviour may soon be a thing of the past.'

'I hope so.' Maureen Jacobs was out of patience with her wayward daughter. 'I'll be the first one to celebrate if she ever attains a responsible attitude to our family values. Look how she behaved last Thursday when we had important guests for dinner; instead of wearing the sensible dress I chose for her, she came down in a bright pink top and swirly skirt. I was ashamed, to say the least.'

'Really?' He smiled at that. 'I thought she looked quite lovely. Brightened up the place she did.'

Ronald felt the heat of Maureen's disapproval, and quickly added, 'I do agree with you, though. Being a wife and consequently a mother, must certainly give her some semblance of discipline. I'm just sorry we weren't able to find someone more suited to the family than this Frank Arnold fellow.'

'You know very well, Ronald, we have endlessly tried to match her up with the more eligible young men, but she preferred the company of this Arnold person. In the end we had little choice but to accept him, or have a spinster on our hands.'

'But will she be happy with him, my dear? That's what worries me.'

'Yes, because like I said, he was her choice. I think she'll be happy. I also believe we're doing the right thing. Before too long, people will start to think she's gone wild, and uncontrollable. I mean, all this running off on her own; paddling in the brook in bare feet and preferring to be with the creatures rather than civilized people. It simply will not do, Ronald! You know as well as I do, we have a reputation to uphold.'

He nodded. 'You're right. The responsibility of

marriage and children should definitely quieten her down though. And as I say, she does appear to have a deep affection for this young man . . .' he paused, '. . . although I can't say I agree with her choice.'

Maureen Jacobs was intrigued. 'I had an idea you were not taking to him very well,' she said, '. . . why is that?'

The big man leaned forward in confidence. 'Unless I'm very much mistaken, he just tried to coax me into backing him on a grand idea he's got in mind. Oh not in so many words, but he's a clever young devil all the same. He claimed it was for Alice.'

He gave a rueful look. 'Now then, my dear, what d'you think to that?'

'I think he's got a damned good cheek, that's what I think!'

'I quite agree. Like I say, he did not so much as come out with it altogether, but he went about it in such a way, I knew straight off what he was getting at. I must admit though, I do have a sneaking admiration for him; he used clever tactics, which might well have worked on someone less alert than myself.'

His manner grew serious. 'He's got the wrong idea, if he imagines for one minute that marrying Alice gives him access to the family fortune. It will never happen. In fact, I've already set things in motion to that effect.'

'In what way?' Maureen was intrigued.

'All in good time, my dear.' He tapped the side of his nose to imply secrecy. 'No one gets the better of Ronald Jacobs,' he concluded, 'especially not a cocky young farmer with ideas above his station!' As he spoke his voice rose in anger.

'Ronald, ssh!' She glanced towards the living room. 'We have visitors. The florist is in there, and the dressmaker is in the throes of changing the hem on Alice's gown.'

'I see. Well, in that case I don't suppose dinner will be

on time. That's a pity, because I have to say I'm ready for a good meal.'

'Oh, dear!' She gave a long sigh. 'I really could have done without all this business. There are so many people in and out, and I haven't had a minute to myself. All the same, it will all be over before we know it, and I for one will not be sorry.'

He smiled at that. 'I thought all mothers were supposed to enjoy their daughter's wedding day?'

'I don't know about that. All I know is, after Saturday, Alice will be someone else's responsibility, and I for one will not be sorry.'

'You know I adore you, my dear,' Ronald said, giving her a bird-peck on the cheek. 'Sometimes though, I do believe you think of our children as a real liability.'

'Don't be ridiculous!' He had touched a raw nerve, especially with regards to their youngest daughter. 'Look, I'll tell Lucy to get on with the meal as usual, and I'll get rid of these people as soon as I can.'

'Right, well, I'll be in the office if you need me.'

With that he strode away and closed his office door behind him; greatly relieved to be shutting out the world.

'It's all right for some!' she called after him. But he was already out of hearing distance, and glad of it.

~

'Joe?'

Alice's voice whispered across the field to where Joe was seated on the bank, deep in thought. Torn two ways about his promise to be Frank's best man, he was sorely tempted to walk away and keep going. Now, the sight of Alice coming towards him was deeply unsettling.

'What are you doing here?' Getting up he stood before her, his eyes momentarily drawn towards the cottage. 'If anyone sees you out here with me at this godforsaken time there would be awkward questions to be answered.'

She moved forward, a vision of loveliness, with a childish air of innocence. 'I couldn't rest,' she admitted, 'I keep thinking of . . .' she hesitated before lowering her voice, 'of that night together, you and me.'

When Joe made to speak, she raised her hand. 'No, please let me speak. I need to tell you something Joe.' She quickened her words, afraid that if she didn't say what was troubling her, then it would burden her for the rest of her days. 'That night . . . you and me, it was wonderful, Joe. I will always cherish the memory, but that's all. It was wrong. I'm promised to your brother, and he doesn't deserve to be deceived in such a way. I do love you, Joe. I think I always will, but I love Frank too. Soon we'll be married, and I mean to keep my vows.'

Joe had listened in silence, but now he spoke. 'I understand.'

'Do you, Joe?' There were tears in her eyes as she saw the pain in his face.

'Yes, I do, and now you need to go. Get ready to make your vows and put all this behind you.'

When she stepped forward he retreated a little. 'Go, Alice,' he urged. 'Quickly, before you're missed. Soon everyone will be awake and wondering where you are.'

There was a moment when he thought he would take her in his arms and hold her to him, but then she was gone, and he was alone again.

'I will never stop loving you,' he murmured, watching her slight frame retreat into the distance. 'Goodbye my darling Alice.' His voice disappeared on the breeze, and with bowed head and heavy heart, he made his way back to the cottage.

CHAPTER FIVE

'JOE! ARE YOU ready yet?' Nancy's voice carried up to the bedroom, where Joe was finishing dressing for the big day.

'Yes, I'll be right down!' Since seeing Alice in the early hours he had not slept a wink. Stepping into his black polished shoes, he tied the laces into a strong bow. Taking his tie from the bed, he slung it round his neck and tried several times to knot it correctly without much success.

After the fourth attempt, he gave up. 'Damned, stupid thing!' He glanced at himself in the long mirror. 'The trouble is, Joe Arnold, this is not your day.' It was Frank's day, and Alice's, and he had to accept that, albeit reluctantly.

He tried knotting the tie one more time, but again without success. 'You're not used to wearing ties,' he told himself. 'neither are you comfortable with being turned out all smart and dandy.' He was more like Alice, going with his instinct, and wearing what he felt comfortable with.

Drawing a deep sigh, he lowered his voice to a whisper, 'One thing's for sure, Joe Arnold, you won't be comfortable witnessing the union of the woman you love to a brother you can never respect.'

For a long, heavy moment he fell silent, thinking about Alice. These past few days had been a real trial, with his thoughts constantly returning to that all too brief but magical time in the barn. With her, he had shared a love he'd only ever dreamed of and now, in the blink of an eye, she was gone forever.

He respected her choice, because there was little alternative. Where the future was concerned, he could not envisage any other way than to put as much distance between himself and Alice as possible, once the marriage was absolute.

At the same time though, he would keep in touch with his parents. Unlike before, they would always know his whereabouts.

He blamed himself for what happened between him and Alice, that night in the barn. He should have followed his instincts and stayed away, at least until the wedding was over. Not for the first time, he wondered how he might feel when the moment in church was imminent.

His greatest fear was that when he handed over the wedding ring he might unwittingly reveal his feelings, in an unprotected glance, or the whisper of a smile.

He smiled now at the thought of her. And what about you, Alice? When you give your vows before the altar, how will you feel? Will you believe them from the bottom of your heart? Or in that moment when you become man and wife, will you regret having done it? Will you be happy?

In spite of everything, he wished her happiness with all his heart.

'Joe!' Nancy sounded frantic, 'What the devil are you doing up there? The car's here already!'

'All right, I'm on my way!' Joe took one last look in the mirror. 'At least you look the part,' he told himself. 'Just remember why you're here. Your brother asked you to fulfil a duty, and like it or not, that's exactly what you must do.'

Joe came running down the stairs two at a time. 'At

last!' Nancy grabbed hold of him. 'Look at the state of your tie. Come here, let's get you ready and on your way.' With a flick of her wrist and a flourish to finish, she stood back to admire her handiwork. 'There! You look a real gent. Now get off with yer!'

Looking smart and civilised, Frank was already in the car. 'What the hell are you playing at, Joe? If we're not careful we'll have the bride there before us!'

He had been in a sour mood ever since waking, and now, some hours later, his mood had not mellowed. 'I'm a bag of nerves as it is,' he complained all the way to church. 'I wish we'd gone straight off and got wed in a registry office, but Alice and her mother would not hear of it!'

'I should think not.' Joe thought he was a real misery.

Frank was beyond pacifying. 'Bloody women! The idea of a big white wedding was not my idea. If we'd just gone to a registry office, we could have saved a heap of money and there wouldn't be all this bloody panic!'

Joe reasoned with him, 'You shouldn't deny Alice the right to choose what kind of wedding she wants, and besides, how could *you* save money, when it's Alice's parents who are paying for it all?'

'Well, for your information, the wedding was not Alice's choice. It was her mother's . . . showing off to her friends and clients, that's what it's all about. As for the money, Alice is their daughter so she has a natural claim to their wealth.'

He gave a sly little grin. 'As a matter of fact, the minute Alice is my wife, I'll have as much a claim to it as she does.' He groaned. 'Jeez! I hate all this wedding stuff! All the fuss and palaver, I'll be glad when it's over.'

Joe said nothing. For very different reasons, he also wanted the day over and done with.

While Joe and Frank were driven to the church, the Jacobs household was also in panic.

Alice had been shut in her room for almost an hour. 'What on earth is she doing up there?' Maureen Jacobs demanded of her daughter, Pauline. 'We're all ready and waiting and here she is, locked in her room and refusing to open her door to anyone.'

'Huh!' Pauline snorted, 'I'm not surprised. She's always the same, you should know that by now.'

Wearing a straight gown of cream silk, with a sparkly tiara on her head and clasping a ribboned posy of red rosebuds, Pauline looked every inch the bridesmaid; as her doting mother constantly reminded her. 'You look absolutely stunning, my dear!' she announced on first seeing her dressed. 'In fact, you look good enough to put the bride to shame.' The idea of which put a smile on Pauline's face. That had been her intention: to belittle Alice's special day.

Behind the smile was a rising envy. Unable to find a man who was prepared to put up with her dictatorial manner, she was now being made to witness her younger sister getting married, and as far as Pauline was concerned, nothing could be more humiliating.

The prospect of playing second fiddle to Alice did not please her; although she consoled herself with the knowledge that Frank Arnold was nothing special. He was just a farmer, with no land of his own and no future. Besides which, according to the local gossip, he was a man of unpredictable temper, ready to fly off the handle at the slightest provocation. If that was true, then he was exactly the man to tame her wayward sister.

'It's time to go, everyone!' Looking distinguished and dapper in his smart grey suit, Ronald Jacobs arrived to usher them out to the relevant cars. 'Tell the driver of the first car to wait. I'll go and bring Alice down.'

'She won't come down.' Maureen informed him angrily. 'She won't even speak to anyone.'

'Nonsense! The poor girl is probably overawed. It is her wedding day after all, so she's allowed to be a little nervous. I expect all she needed was a moment or two on her own.'

'Go on then!' Maureen was out of patience. 'See if you can succeed where we failed!'

'You get in the car.' He shooed them out. 'I'll go and reason with her. Alice will not respond to bullying, as well you know.' It was a cleverly disguised accusation, which Maureen begrudgingly took note of.

'Off you go then!' He urged them away, before climbing the stairway with a sense of purpose.

'Alice?' Ronald tapped gently on the door. 'Mother and Pauline have already gone to the car. It's time to leave.'

When Alice called back to say she wasn't ready, he tapped on the door again, this time though he was less patient and spoke to her in a much sterner voice, 'You'd better get your skates on, my dear. I'm afraid we have to leave right now. The cars are waiting, and I am not moving from this spot until you open that door!'

'Give me a minute, Father, please!'

'I'm sorry, Alice, but this is no time to be dithering. I should imagine Frank and Joe are already at the church, and it's high time we were on our way. So come on now, Alice. Open this door.'

When she remained silent, he changed tack. 'It's not like you to be so inconsiderate, and besides, I've waited all morning to see my beautiful Alice in her wedding gown. Please, dear . . . come on out . . . for me, eh?'

Inside the bedroom, Alice remained seated at the dressing table. Her head was bowed as she relived her night with Joe. Until this morning, she had managed to convince herself she was doing the right thing, but now the doubts were beginning to creep in.

'Alice!' The sound of her father growing angry made her panic. 'Alice, I need you to come out of there, this very minute!' He coaxed her in softer voice, 'Grandad and Grandma Beck have been sitting in their car for a good ten minutes or so. You know Grandad has had a poorly spell of late, so it really isn't fair to leave them waiting like that.' He knocked on the door a little harder. 'Alice . . . please!'

Slowly the door inched open, and when she emerged, he was visibly shocked, 'Oh, my dear . . . you look amazing.'

Taking Alice's hands in his, he walked her towards him, his eyes alight with pride. 'Is this really little Alice Jacobs?' he asked brokenly, 'my little girl, all grown up and looking like a princess?'

Seeing her like this had been a real jolt for him. She had always been the tomboy; climbing trees and running wild, with nothing and no one able to tame her, and now he could hardly believe what he was seeing. 'You're so lovely my dear.' His eyes welled with tears. 'My little Alice . . . amazing. Absolutely amazing!'

The high-necked ivory gown had been her mother's choice. Fitted at the waist and billowed to the hem, it was somewhat heavy for Alice's slight figure, but even so she carried it with a certain unique quality that only she could. The flowing, figured veil that might easily have swamped her, instead exaggerated her fine features and shining dark-blue eyes.

Her long hair, which naturally hung loose and wild, was bound with pink flower-clips and wound into a spray of curls at the top of her head with a wide band of veil threading it all together.

It was not her mother's choice of dress that brought about the beauty in Alice. Instead, the beauty was in her warm nature and in the quality of spirit that shone from her.

Maureen too, was forced to admit, 'You really do make a lovely bride, my dear.' Splendid and regal, she led the way.

'I'm ready now, Father.' Calmed by his presence and made confident by his heartfelt remarks, Alice felt able to face the day.

'I'm proud of you, my dear,' he whispered as he walked her to the car. 'Every man in that church will envy me, having you for a daughter.'

At this moment in time, he imagined he could forgive her anything.

He had no way of knowing that the true test of his forgiveness was already in the making.

~

The imposing old church in the nearby town of Leighton Buzzard was filled to capacity with friends and neighbours. There were strangers too, made curious by the rumour that the daughter of Ronald Jacobs was marrying a farmer's son.

The ceremony went without a hitch; though when the congregation was asked 'If anyone here knows of any reason why these two should not be joined together in marriage' Joe kept his silence and bowed his head.

And so they were married. To the haunting sound of the organ, Frank and Alice walked up to sign the register, as man and wife, every step they took like a knife in Joe's heart.

Everyone smiled as the couple made their way down the aisle, and outside they were congratulated and showered with confetti, Maureen and Pauline noticeably more restrained than the rest of the congregation.

The sun shone and everyone appeared happy. Outside, the guests began to form little groups while they waited for the cars to arrive and carry them the few miles to the Grand Hotel, and a lavish reception.

During the initial rush, Joe had kept his distance. Now though, in the moment before Frank and Alice got into the car, he went to shake his brother by the hand. 'Am I allowed to kiss the bride?' he asked.

'So long as it's just a peck. I can't have my wife being man-handled by all and sundry,' Frank joked.

Just then, Frank turned round and went off to speak to the driver.

Joe took the opportunity to kiss Alice gently, his insides nervously churning as he told her in a whisper, 'You look lovely, Alice.'

With the memory of their liaison strong in her mind, and now the touch of his mouth on her cheek, Alice blushed to her roots. 'Thank you, Joe . . . I . . . I didn't mean to hurt you,' she stammered.

'You've done nothing to hurt me, Alice.' His answer was a warm and forgiving smile. 'All I want is for you to be happy . . .'

Started as Frank slapped him on the back. Joe swung round. 'Everything all right is it?'

'Of course. Can you think of any reason why it shouldn't be?' Frank chuckled.

Joe ignored the question and said, 'I'll see you both at the hotel.'

'Come on then, wife!' Without further ado, Frank took Alice by the arm. 'We'd best get to the reception, and receive our guests.'

Alice went with him, and as she climbed into the car, she turned to look at Joe. For a fleeting moment, he thought he saw the look of regret in her eyes. 'I hope you haven't made a mistake, Alice, my love,' he whispered. 'For all our sakes.'

~

The reception was lavish. The guests were pampered and the food was presented in a fashion fit for a king.

The toast was taken, then Joe gave a short speech, and everyone gave a resounding ovation.

The evening that followed was unforgettable.

When the band struck up for the first waltz, Frank swung Alice on to the floor, holding her close while he swung her round to the music. Everyone clapped before swarming on to the dance floor, until there was no room to move.

The band played on until the small hours and everyone danced or excitedly chatted about the wonderful day, and the lucky couple. As the night wore on, the dancing got faster, and the guests got merrier.

Glad to leave her kitchen responsibilities behind, little Lucy danced until her bones ached. She felt excited and privileged to be here. Moreover, this was the very first time in her uneventful life that she had enjoyed fine food, cooked by someone else, then prepared and served on fine china and silver-platters, polished so high you could see your face in it.

The height of the evening was when the fat, red-faced butcher gave her a full-blown kiss on the mouth, then promptly collapsed in a heap at her feet; he was so drunk it took three men to carry him off.

After a few dances, Frank made his way to the bar, while Alice wandered over to her friend Mandy, who was still smarting from not being asked to be bridesmaid. It wasn't long, though, before the two of them were deep in conversation, and all was forgiven. 'I must admit, I was disappointed not to be your bridesmaid.'

'I'm sorry,' Alice apologised, 'I always meant you to be, but you know what Mother is like, when she gets a bee in her bonnet. Once she'd decided that Pauline was going to be the only bridesmaid, there was no reasoning with her.'

'It's all right, Alice, don't you worry.' Mandy was a big girl, with a less than shapely figure. She had never been in the front row for a pretty face, and Mandy Baker knew full well why Maureen Jacobs did not want her for a bridesmaid. In her warped mind, she probably thought Mandy would lower the tone of her daughter's wedding.

'I really don't mind,' she assured Alice; although in truth she had been bitterly disappointed. 'I do know what your mother is like once she makes a decision, and I know I wasn't pretty enough or slim enough for her, but you and me won't ever fall out over it, because all I care about is that we're still friends.'

'What!' Alice threw her arms round Mandy's neck. 'What are you saying? Of course we're still friends. You will always be my friend, as long as we live.' The very idea of Mandy not being in her life was unthinkable to Alice.

She and Mandy had known each other since before going to school; right from the day Mandy and her family moved into Brighill village, and Mandy's father took up the vacancy of blacksmith.

From that very first meeting some fifteen years ago, when Maureen Jacobs took Alice on her pony to have its hooves trimmed, Mandy and Alice had been inseparable.

Maureen Jacobs, however, was horrified at the friendship, but she needed a blacksmith for her horse, and there was only one in the village. And so she reluctantly suffered the clumsy, chubby little Baker girl, for no one's sake but her own; and that of her precious horses.

So now, with Alice having mended their friendship, the two girls chatted and laughed, and talked of plans for the future; until Mandy became flattered and flushed, when a young man approached her and asked her to dance.

Throughout the evening, Joe had kept a watchful eye on Alice. The moment Mandy was whisked away to dance, he first reassured himself that Frank was still propping up the bar, before snatching what he knew would be his last chance.

He quickly made his way across the floor. 'Would the lady care to dance?' His smile enveloped her, 'Unless you're afraid I'm got two left feet and no sense of style?'

Alice laughed at that. 'It sounds like a description of me, not you.'

'Oh no! I can't have that. I've seen you dance,' he told her, 'all the way across the land and through the brook like a wayward nymph; no shoes, and not a care in the world. Am I right?' He led her on to the dance floor.

'Maybe, but that's not dancing.'

'It is in my eyes.' He drew her into his arms. 'Did I tell you how lovely you look?'

'Mmm.' With his strong arms about her, and the easy way he took her into the slow, rhythmic steps of a waltz, she felt herself relaxing too easily into his embrace. 'Joe . . . ?' She drew back a little, her worried gaze trained on his face.

'You don't need to say it,' he whispered. 'I know, because I feel it too.' Afraid he might say too much, he wisely suggested, 'I'd best take you back . . .' Suddenly he was wrenched away as Frank forced his way between them. 'Well, well! Aren't we nice and cozy?'

Joe resented the manner in which Frank took control of Alice. Frank's fist was so tight round the lower part of Alice's arm, the blood ebbed from his knuckles. 'Don't do this, Frank,' Joe said in a harsh whisper. 'We were dancing, that's all . . . just dancing. Afterwards I was coming to tell you, I'm leaving tonight. It's time I struck out on my own . . . make a future for myself. Much like you and Alice intend doing.'

Frank laughed out loud. 'So! You shout your mouth off when you think *I'm* planning to desert Dad, but here you are about to take off like a scared rabbit into the night!'

He gave a sly little snigger. 'Look what happened the last time you went off on your own. You and I both know it didn't turn out the way you would have liked, did it, eh?'

Taking note of the warning expression on Joe's face, Frank decided to stop right there. It wouldn't be clever to rile Joe, he reminded himself. Not unless he wanted Joe to reveal secrets best left undisturbed.

The best thing was to shut his mouth and let Joe go; the quicker and further Joe went, the better he would like it. 'Bugger off then!' he snapped. 'We don't need you anyway!'

From across the room, Tom had witnessed the heated exchange between his two sons, and knowing how it might escalate, he hurried over. 'It's late,' he told Frank, 'and you've had too much to drink.'

'So?' When Frank swung round, Joe managed to prise his brother's grip from Alice's arm. Before Frank could confront him, Tom had Frank by the shoulders. 'Come on, Frank, time to go home.'

Frank shrugged him off. 'I'm not ready to go home yet,' he seemed suddenly sober; though still slightly unsteady on his feet. 'Me and Alice have to dance the new day in yet. It's a tradition, Father. Or have you forgotten?'

Without another word and with surprising tenderness, he laughingly took Alice into his embrace. 'Me and my wife are duty bound to dance the new day in, and that's what we're gonna do!'

He turned his attention on Joe. 'Y'see, Joe, this is my wife, and she only dances with her husband, isn't that right, sweetheart?' He kissed Alice on the neck. 'Me and and nobody else.'

As he swirled her about on the dance floor, Tom voiced

his disgust. 'I don't know what the devil's got into him, but he never could hold his booze.'

Tom was relieved that the little fracas had not attracted too much attention, but during Frank's rant, he had been painfully aware of the sinister undercurrent between Frank and Joe.

Remembering the manner in which Joe had taken to Alice when they had first met, and after what happened here tonight, it only served to confirm Tom's belief that the feelings Joe had for her remained as strong as ever.

It worried him so much so that he told Joe, 'Don't be too long before you make your way back, son. Your brother seems to be in one of his moods.'

Joe was concerned, for both his father, and for Alice. 'In that case, it might be best if I stayed to keep an eye on him.'

'No.' Tom was adamant. 'I'm suitably familiar with his tantrums. If you step in, it might only make matters worse. No, you go on, son. Go home. I'll handle him, don't you worry.' He gave a little chuckle. 'He might think he can get one over on me, but he hasn't managed it yet, and he never will.'

Joe understood. 'You might be right,' he conceded. 'Me being here does seem to rile him up, so I'll get off, but if there's any trouble send for me, and I'll be back here in no time at all!'

Tom shook his head. 'There'll be no trouble, not now.' He patted Joe on the shoulder. 'The way things are with him, you're best away from here.'

As Joe turned away, Tom stopped him with a firm hand on the shoulder. 'Apart from all this, it's good to have you home, son.'

Despite his growing suspicions about Joe's dangerous feelings for his brother's wife, he truly meant what he said.

It really was good to have his second-born home again.

~

Having taken heed of his father's words, Joe made to leave.

When he got to the doorway, he glanced back to see Alice looking over Frank's shoulder at him. She even gave the whisper of a smile.

Ashamed, Joe dropped his gaze and left.

Behind him, Frank talked and laughed, and whispered sweet nothings in Alice's ear.

When the music stopped she looked up to where Joe had been. The door was swinging shut. He was gone.

Along with her happiness.

~

'Come on, wifey!' It was now in the early hours. 'Goodnight everybody!' he waved to one and all. 'Me and Alice are off to our brand new love-nest.' He gave a meaningful wink. 'All on our own, with no one to bother us.' To Alice's embarrassment, his meaning did not go unnoticed.

Believing his dreams had all come true at once, Frank was convinced that the cottage given to them by Ronald Jacobs, was just the start of things to come.

Alice reminded him, 'I need to say goodnight to my parents, and besides, I haven't seen Grandad and Grandma for a while . . . they must be outside. They would not be best pleased if I went away without saying cheerio.'

A short while after she went in search of them, Frank decided to follow her. 'Grandparents . . . worth a bob or two, best keep in with 'em.'

Ronald Jacobs had been delighted when his parents

agreed to come to the wedding. Due to a bitter confrontation between Maureen and his mother Tricia, his parents had refused all invitations to their son's home.

Joshua Jacobs himself had little liking for his daughter-in-law; and as ever, his loyalties were to his wife.

Having returned from a brisk walk around the grounds with his wife, Joshua was pleased to see Alice making her way towards them. Smiling broadly, he stretched out his arms to receive her. 'So, here you are, my dear. I was afraid you might go away without coming to say goodnight.'

A man of considerable stature, he made a formidable sight, with his iron-grey hair and steel-blue eyes.

Having started the family business many years ago, he now trusted his son Ronald to run it; though he retained some shares in the business, together with keeping a wary eye on all transactions. He was proud to see his son taking the business from strength to strength.

Alice buried herself in his hug, and then it was the turn of her grandmother, who cradled her long and hard.

Considered to be a woman of elegance, with her sleek, silver hair, and quiet, caring nature, it was well known Tricia Jacobs did not suffer fools gladly. Intelligent and trustworthy, she had stepped back from her husband's business enterprises, and instead immersed herself in numerous deserving charities. Since then she had earned an admirable reputation for her tireless efforts at rehousing the homeless.

Maureen could never understand why Tricia ploughed so much energy into helping homeless people and their very different views were a matter of great contention between the two women.

Maureen took the view that, 'Anyone can secure themselves a home, if they're prepared to work hard enough!'

The comment had caused such bitterness that neither woman was prepared to apologise. Tricia had no fondness for Maureen, and though she hated to admit it, she believed her eldest granddaughter Pauline was made in the same cold mould as her mother.

Amazingly, Alice was a completely different creature. Because of her caring nature and simple beliefs, she had earned a permanent place in Tricia's heart.

Delighted now that her favourite granddaughter had sought them out, she cast her eyes over Alice's beautiful gown. 'You look lovely, as always,' she croaked. Her voice suddenly choked with emotion.

'What are you thinking Grandma? I look lovely *but*?' she wanted to know.

Tricia laughed out loud. 'You know me too well, Alice Jacobs!'

Alice persisted. 'Ah! I was right then. So there *is* a but?'

'Yes, there is, and I mean to keep it to myself.'

'I won't let you, Grandma. I'll follow you everywhere, and keep nagging, until you tell me what it is you don't like.' When pushed hard enough, Alice had a real stubborn streak in her.

Tricia took a moment, but she knew Alice well enough to realise she would keep her word. 'All right, bossy boots!' Tricia lowered her voice to a shameful whisper. 'If I'm honest I think I would rather have seen you in a simpler gown. Something nearer Pauline's, less fluffy and ornate.'

When her husband glared at her, she realised the gravity of her thoughtless comment. 'Oh, Alice, I'm terrible!' She gasped with embarrassment. 'I should never have said anything.'

Mortified, she grabbed Alice by the hands. 'I'm just a silly old woman who should know better! Here it is, your wedding day, and I'm complaining about your dress.' She made a sorry face. 'I expect you'll hate me forever now, won't you?'

Alice laughed. 'Course I won't, Grandma!' she assured

her with a fond smile, 'I would never hate you, and anyway . . .' Alice leaned forward and whispered, 'I agree with everything you say. Y'see, Mother chose my dress and I had no say in it. Mandy thought the same as you, so without Mother knowing, we fiddled with it here and there, trying to flatten the skirt, making it less like a blown-up balloon.' She giggled. 'We did our best, but after what you just said, I think we failed.'

Tricia was greatly relieved. 'Oh, Alice, I've always cherished the fact that you and me could always talk straight with each other, but today was not the day to poke my nose in. In any case, to be honest, the dress does not matter one jot, because you would still look lovely covered in a brown paper bag. It's *you* Alice! *You* that shines out. Not what you wear.'

'Quite right!' Grandfather Joshua totally agreed. 'You're like a breath of fresh air,' he said. 'You're a natural and lovely person without airs and graces, and you don't give a stuff for money or possessions. I for one find that to be most endearing, especially in this material world we live in.'

Just then, Frank stumbled up to them. 'Alice is not like me,' he hiccuped. 'I want the world, and I'm prepared to work for it.' He steadied himself. 'I learn quick, I do. I'm . . . ambitious.'

Afraid that Frank might be making a nuisance of himself, Tom hurried over to apologise. 'Sorry about this, Joshua . . . Tricia.' Taking control of Frank, he promised, 'He's had a few too many, but I expect he'll suffer for it in the morning.'

Joshua assured him, 'It's his wedding night. Most bridegrooms are put to bed legless on occasions like this. Don't worry, Tom, we've all seen it before.'

'Well, *I* certainly have!' Tricia revealed with a sideways glance at her husband. 'On *our* wedding night, you were out of it, well before the last waltz. I've never really forgiven you for that!'

Frank laughed out loud. 'Oh! So he m . . . barrassed ye, did 'e? Like I'm . . . m . . . barrassing my poor ol' dad!'

Grandfather Joshua wisely changed the subject. 'Tom, do you need a hand with him?'

Tom graciously brushed his offer aside. 'No, but thanks all the same. You enjoy what's left of the evening. I'll make sure Frank and Alice get home safely.'

Alice kissed her grandparents. 'Is your room booked and everything?' she asked worriedly.

Tricia assured her it was. 'Grandad thought it would be more sensible to stay here than suffer the three hour drive home to Blackburn, and I agree.'

'So, what time are you leaving tomorrow?'

'Not before midday,' Grandad interrupted. 'That way, we get a lie-in. I know you're newly wed, but I hope we might be able to see you before we leave.'

Grandma Tricia reminded him, 'We only visited the cottage once before, and now we're not really sure how to get there.' Having worked with Ronald to secure the cottage they felt proud.

Tom put their minds at rest. 'It's a devil of a road . . . just a little lane really. The thing is, they all look the same at the best of times, and the signs are non-existent. Look, I'll come and fetch you,' he promised. 'You can follow me there. Midday is it?'

'Thank you, Tom, yes . . . midday. We'll be waiting for you.'

~

While Tricia said her goodbyes to Alice, Joshua went in search of his son, Ronald, all the while an overwhelming sense of disappointment tormenting him.

'Father!' On hearing Ronald calling, Joshua spun round. 'Ah, Ronald! Just the man I need.'

'Why? What's wrong, where's Mother?'

'Your mother's saying goodbye to Alice and Tom's helping take Frank back to the car . . . he's drunk.'

Moving nearer, Ronald confided in a quiet voice, 'Between you and me, Father, I'm still not sure we've done the right thing in letting Alice marry a man like that.'

Joshua was concerned. 'Really? And why is that?'

'Well for one thing, just look at the state of him . . . drunk as a Lord, without a thought for his new wife.'

'If that's all you've got against him, it's as well you weren't there to see *me* on my wedding night.'

Ronald admitted, 'It isn't just that,' he said. 'It's the rumours I've been hearing this past few days . . . about Frank Arnold having beaten some fellow to a pulp. He's also been seen brawling in the village. Apparently he can't be reasoned with.'

'Did you know this before you agreed to the marriage?'

Ronald felt the need to defend himself. 'I had heard that he was quick-tempered when he thought he was in the right, but I didn't pay much heed. I mean . . . any man can be awkward if he believes he's in the right . . . you and me included.'

The older man agreed. He recalled a heated board meeting not so long ago, when he found himself in a bitter confrontation with a newly appointed colleague. The young upstart had the gall to ridicule a well-devised plan, which Joshua and a colleague had painstakingly put together. At one stage, Joshua thought he could happily have smacked the other man to the floor.

'What other rumours have you heard, and is there any truth in them?' Joshua asked.

Ronald relayed what he knew, 'There's nothing else,

but the trouble is, how do you track down a rumour? How can you get to the source of it? I've asked discreet questions, and come up with nothing substantial. I thought about tackling Frank with what I'd heard, but I have no proof.'

Joshua gave it some thought. 'You were probably right not to say anything,' he told his son. 'Sometimes rumours are spread by envious people, or someone who has a grudge, or even just for the sheer pleasure of causing pain.'

Ronald had another reason why he did not vigorously pursue the rumours. 'Alice has never been happier,' he said, 'I don't think she would take it kindly if I was to wrongly accuse her husband of fighting and brawling in the streets.

'I know Alice thinks the world of him, but to tell the truth I've never really been in favour of her marrying Frank Arnold. But Alice is old and wise enough to make her own choices. She chose Frank Arnold. We either accept that, or we lose her, and I'm afraid that's the way of it.'

The older man considered for a moment, before telling his son, 'They do say there's no smoke without fire, so it might be wise to just keep an eye on things. Make sure Alice is well taken care of, and that she's content. Oh, and it wouldn't hurt to keep your ear to the ground with regards to her husband.'

He added, 'I think it might be best if you did not say anything about this to your mother.'

Joshua then touched on another matter. 'Oh, and I need a word . . .'

Ronald groaned. 'Oh, look Father, if it's that warehouse down by the river, I'm already dealing with it. I've got two quotes already, and I'm expecting to have the final one . . .'

'No, no!' Joshua put up his hand. 'It has nothing to

do with that. You had a query about that land. You asked my advice and I gave it, so now it's up to you.'

Visibly relieved, Ronald wanted to know, 'If it wasn't that, what's so urgent we need to discuss it right now?'

'Your mother . . . and your wife, that's what!'

'Oh, not that again!'

'Look, son, I really am sorry about this ridiculous rift between Maureen, and your mother. I thought maybe between the two of us, we could knock some sense into their heads, what do you think?'

Ronald tutted. 'Damned ridiculous if you ask me!'

'Nobody's asking you . . . *either* of you!' Tricia had come up behind them and heard enough to know what they were discussing. 'If it's about me and Maureen, I think you should leave that to us!'

Ronald pleaded with her. 'Look, Mother . . . I know Maureen can be uncompromising,' he admitted, '. . . but I wish the two of you would put your differences aside, if only for Alice's sake.'

Having spent the past ten minutes or so searching for her father, Alice hurried across the room towards them. 'I've been looking everywhere for you,' she told Ronald. 'I've already said goodnight to Mother, and I have to go now.'

She apologised. 'Frank's had a bit too much to drink and now he's snoring his head off in the back of Tom's car. Tom's already taken Nancy home, and now he's taking me and Frank, and I mustn't keep him waiting.'

She had overheard their conversation and it saddened her. 'Don't worry about Mother and Grandma,' she gently chided her father. 'You know they'll make up soon enough anyway.' Alice looked at her grandmother. 'One minute you hate each other, and the next you're off shopping for new hats.'

Tricia laughed. 'You're right,' she told Alice. 'We should

be ashamed. Look, all of you, I'm willing to try and put our differences aside. But only if Maureen is prepared to meet me halfway.'

'I'll try and make her see sense!' Ronald promised before bidding them goodnight. 'See you tomorrow.'

As he went away, he muttered under his breath, 'Women! Huh! They cause more trouble than an army of men put together!'

Alice gave them each a goodnight kiss. 'I'd best go.' Raising the hem of her gown she took off at a run. 'Tom will be wondering where I've gone.' Almost out of earshot, she called out, 'See you all tomorrow.'

'Goodnight!' they shouted in unison, with Ronald promising, 'I'll make sure someone gets a vehicle to you, so it's there in the morning if you need it!' He then wished his parents goodnight, and headed back to the bar.

Left alone, Joshua and Tricia returned to the question of Alice's mother. 'You know very well I've tried several times to make the peace with Maureen, but she won't hear of it. Like I said, I'm willing to bury the hatchet, but I refuse to go cap-in-hand to such a hard-hearted creature. I ask you! What would *she* know about being thrown out of her home because her husband's lost his job and they can't pay the rent.'

Tricia stopped when she saw the frustrated look on his face, 'Oh, I'm sorry, Josh. I know I get passionate about my commitments, but it irritates me that Maureen can be so hard-hearted.'

She let him into her confidence. 'I know she's our daughter-in-law, and I know I shouldn't say this, but to be honest Joshua, I can't stand the woman!'

Joshua was not surprised. 'You will try and make the peace though, won't you?'

'Yes, but like I said, she has to meet me halfway.'

'Well, in that case let's hope our son has inherited the same powers of persuasion as his father.'

That made her smile. 'Come on husband,' she linked her arm with his, 'I'm ready for my bed. We're not teenagers any more, just two old codgers, not used to staying up this late.'

Off they went, arm in arm; happy as the day they first met, some fifty-odd years ago. Still friends. Still watching out for each other.

CHAPTER SIX

AFTER THE TWO of them had struggled getting Frank up the narrow stairway and into bed, Alice offered Tom a hot drink before he made his way home.

Tom thanked her but declined. 'As you know, I had to take Nancy home after she got one of her headaches. She's bound to be wondering where I am.' He gave her a hug. 'You're a fine young woman,' he told her softly. 'I'm proud to see you and Frank get wed, and it's a real pleasure to have you in the family.'

Deeply moved, Alice planted a fleeting kiss on his ruddy red cheek. 'Love you, Tom,' she said; and from the look on his face, it seemed he already knew that.

Alice followed him to the front door, where he stood a moment gazing about at the cottage, all newly renovated and furnished with the finest that money could buy. There was a sturdy floral chesterfield under the pretty bay window, a small red sofa with matching cushions by the fireside, and a walnut sideboard with curves and niches, and here and there, a couple of smaller pieces of furniture in the same beautiful wood. 'By!' Taking off his flat cap, Tom scratched his head in wonderment. 'This place puts our present to shame!'

He seemed genuinely upset. 'Your family give you all this, and from me and Nancy you get a bedspread!'

'Don't say it like that!' Alice chided, 'Your present was one of my very favourites. All those beautiful patches of bright-coloured material, and that exquisite silk border. It's a lovely present, Tom.'

Alice could only imagine how long it had taken her mother-in-law to match up each piece. 'It must have taken Nancy weeks and months to sew it all together,' she said. 'It really is the most beautiful thing, and the fact that it was all sewn and finished with love, only makes it all that more special.'

Tom agreed. 'I must say, my Nancy is a real perfectionist. Lord only knows how many late nights she sat up patiently stitching away, and more often than not undoing a great chunk of it, when it didn't satisfy her eagle-eye.'

'And it shows,' Alice replied. 'It will always be precious to me and to Frank. Even when we're old and grey, it will still be keeping us warm in our bed.'

Tom laughed at that. 'Old and grey, eh?' He gave a great sigh. 'You'd never know it, but me and Nancy were young as you once upon a time.'

Suddenly, all the long years weighed heavy on him. 'Well, I'd best be off.' He turned to leave, 'Mind you, I'm not altogether happy leaving you like this; what with Frank out like a light.'

He made a face. 'I know it's his wedding night and all that, but it's *your* wedding night too! He should have had more sense than to drink himself three sheets to the wind.'

Alice assured him she would be fine. 'Thank you for everything, Tom,' she said.

Tom nodded. 'Night then, my dear.'

'Night, Tom. Oh, and can you please tell Nancy I'll be round in the morning, to see how she is.'

Tom promised he would tell Nancy, though as he got into the car and drove off, he couldn't help but chuckle to himself. 'So you'll be over in the morning, will yer?'

He had really enjoyed the day; the wedding, and the gathering afterwards. It did his old heart good to know that his son had taken a wonderful girl for his wife. 'Alice will do my Frank proud.' He had no doubts whatsoever about that.

He chattered to himself as he drove along the darkened lanes, 'She's a fine girl with a lovely nature, and she's loyal into the bargain.' He could not be more pleased. 'In time she'll provide me and Nancy with grandchildren . . . hopefully mebbe even a boy or two, so as to keep the Arnold line going strong.'

The idea brought him huge contentment; there was only one thing missing to make their lives complete. He wished Joe would find himself a nice girl to wed. He'd love to see him settle with children running round his feet instead of keeping wandering off like a lost soul.

Content that Tom was at last on his way, Alice drew the downstairs curtains and climbed the stairs, cautiously, so as not to wake Frank. She was thrilled with the cottage, though her mind was drawn to Joe.

In the bedroom, she found Frank exactly where she and Tom had left him; half-dressed and sprawled across the bed, with the eiderdown loosely thrown over him. 'Sleeping like a baby,' she whispered, drawing the eiderdown up to his chin.

For a long moment, she gazed down on him, at the rugged face and the thin-lipped open mouth, now emitting gentle, rhythmic snores. 'I wonder if we'll be happy together?' she murmured. 'I hope so, Frank, I really hope so. I'll do all I can to make this marriage work, and I will never again deceive you.'

Even though she hated herself for the time she had spent with Joe, she still had not been able to rid herself of the powerful and shocking emotions that carried her into his arms that night. Though shameful and forbidden, it was an amazing and wonderful happening, and because of it, she knew her life would never be the same again.

Determined to put the memory behind her, she told Frank in a whisper, 'I *will* be a good wife, you'll see, and I will never again do anything to damage our future together.'

After sealing her promise with a kiss, she stood up straight, unfastened the wedding dress and let it slide to the carpet. She then tiptoed to the chest of drawers. On opening it, she reached into the big drawer at the bottom, and pulled out her nightgown and slippers.

She then slipped on her nightgown and slid her feet into the soft, fluffy slippers; a present from her friend Mandy.

On her way to the bathroom, she gently closed the door behind her, before having a thorough wash at the sink.

Taking extra care to wipe the layer of lipstick and rouge from her face, she was astonished to see that the hitherto white hankie was smothered bright-red. 'Hmm! Looks like Mandy went a bit mad with the make-up box! Somehow I didn't notice before.'

Dropping the hankie into the bin, she thought about her dear friend, Mandy. 'I wonder what *she'd* say, if she knew about me and Joe and what we did?'

Not for the first time, shame engulfed her. Hurrying to finish, she returned to the bedroom where she climbed into bed beside her new husband.

Leaning on one elbow, she reached out with the tip of her finger, tenderly tracing his lips, and brushing back a lock of hair from his forehead. 'I did a wicked thing, Frank,' she whispered. 'You didn't deserve that, and I'm sorry.'

The feel of her slim, warm body against his must have filtered through Frank's senses, because he began to fidget and mumble, and when he unexpectedly threw his arm over her, Alice instinctively cringed, feeling somehow threatened.

After a few minutes he settled again, and she gently lifted his arm from about her. Turning her back on him, she closed her eyes and tried to sleep. But sleep did not come easy.

Restless and worried, she turned this way and that, her mind alive with Joe, and the wrong she had done to Frank. Even then, in her heart of hearts, she knew without a shadow of doubt that it was Joe she wanted. But Joe would soon be gone and Frank was now her husband. That was the brutal truth.

'I'll keep my promise though,' she whispered to Frank, 'I'll do my best to be the wife you want.'

That's what she told Frank, and it's what she kept telling herself, but in her deepest heart, she could see only Joe.

Joe, the wanderer; the brother of her husband.

Joe, her first lover.

Joe. The man who had stolen her heart and soul, when she wasn't looking.

Was it the same for Joe? she wondered.

Right now, at this very moment while he was strong in her mind, was he thinking of her? Or had he put all memory of her out of his mind and his life forever. The idea of such a thing was too painful to imagine.

'Hey, wifey!' Frank's thick, slurred voice cut into her thoughts. 'What's wrong with you?' Grabbing her by the shoulder, he flipped her round to face him.

'Look at you, eh?' His smile became a leer. 'Alice Jacobs, now Alice Arnold. My brand new wife.'

The moonlight seeped in through the window, masking the leer on his face. Right now, he had only one thing on his mind.

He did not see her regrets. He saw only the shadow of

her face and the full, virgin mouth, waiting to be kissed. And he saw the woman . . . *his* woman. Like the young fillies on the farm, Alice was now ready to be broken in, and he could hardly wait.

Leaning up on one elbow, he looked at her through bloodshot eyes. 'I think I had a bit too much to drink . . .' he laughed. 'One minute I was falling to the floor, and the next minute I'm lying in my own bed with this lovely young virgin lying beside me.'

When she made no reply, he gave her a shake. 'Hey! What's wrong? Cat got your tongue? You woke me up, did you know that? You woke me up with your muttering and chattering, and shifting about.'

He licked his lips. 'Couldn't wait, is that it?' he asked meaningfully, 'want me that bad, do you?' His laugh sent shivers down her spine. 'Waited too long already, have you?'

Clambering on to his knees, he clumsily straddled her. Reaching down with both hands, he grasped the neck of her nightgown and ripped it from seam to seam, laying bare her small breasts, and her pink, youthful skin.

'My, my!' He stroked her breasts with the flat of his hand, groaning as his need of her surged through him. 'Mine at last, eh? You kept me away for too long, but not anymore, because now you're mine.'

Stroking her face, he whispered lovingly in her ear, 'My shy little Alice. Mine, for the taking.'

Teasing the tip of his wet tongue over her nipples, he told her, 'I just need to gaze at you, lying there so young and fresh.'

Alice thought the look he gave her was tainted with evil. 'I know you've never been with a man in that way,' he murmured. 'I'm no angel though. I've had women by the plenty, and I know a thing or two.'

The smile abruptly disappeared. 'I want you so bad. It's

such a shame though, because right now you're still intact and innocent, but once you're broken, it can never be the same again.'

Sliding his arms beneath her slim body, he arched her towards him. 'I can't wait anymore,' he whispered huskily. 'Can't wait . . .'

Alice began to panic. For a long time, she had waited for this moment; to be made his wife in every sense of the word. Now though, she was nervous. Afraid that he would read her mind, and see Joe there.

'Not yet . . . please, Frank . . .' When she instinctively tried to get up, he pushed her down, pinning her to the bed with manic strength. 'Don't worry,' he whispered harshly in her ear, 'I'll be gentle. I won't hurt you.'

He laughed in her face, a soft, disturbing laugh. 'You should be grateful,' he boasted. 'It's just as well that I'm the first bloke to have you! Anybody else might go at you like a mad thing, and tear you apart. But not me . . .' He smiled, 'I'll break you in easy. So you be a good girl. Lie back, and it'll be over before you know it.'

Without love or emotion in her heart, she lay there, waiting for her husband to claim his marital rights, and hoping that even now, she might be able to give him back some of the love and loyalty she had promised him.

And so he took her, not in the gentle manner he had described, and not with any thought for her.

Instead, he was wantonly cruel, and with every vicious thrust, her fear of him heightened to repugnance. Closing her eyes, she prayed her ordeal would soon be over.

When at last he finally rolled away, grunting and exhausted, she hid her face in the pillow, silently crying.

Lying beside her, naked and uncovered, Frank was sweating hard. 'Phew! That was good.' Rolling on to his belly, he wrapped his two hands around her face and kissed her hard on the mouth. 'I know I said I'd be gentle,' he whined like a spoilt child, 'but I got carried away. There's no need for you to worry though,' he insisted in a firm voice, 'the worst is over now.'

Alice wondered who this stranger was; this uncaring, selfish creature she had never seen before.

Realising she had made the biggest mistake of her life, she wished with all her heart that she had gone with Joe, wherever in the world he chose to be.

But it was too late. She was tied in marriage to this man, and like it or not she must live with it. There was no place for fantasies in her life. Not now. Not ever.

Inching closer, he was in her face, his eyes boring down on her, and the stale odour of booze filled her nostrils. 'I'm told a woman's first time is painful, but you did enjoy it, didn't you, wifey?'

It was more a demand than a question. 'I *said* you did enjoy it, didn't you?' Reaching over her head, he switched the bedside light on to see her all the better. 'Well?'

Nodding her answer, Alice drew the remnants of her nightgown together, visibly shocked when he grabbed her by the wrist, telling her softly, 'I asked you a question.'

'Yes, Frank!' She visibly cringed from his touch. '. . . I did.'

'What kind of an answer is that?' His features hardened. 'Say it, Alice . . . you did enjoy it!'

'Yes, I did enjoy it like you said.'

'Good girl!' He rolled on to his back, quiet now, as though turning it all over in his mind.

Pleased with his manly performance, he hoisted his arms behind his head. 'What are you doing?'

His avaricious gaze followed her every move, as she collected her dressing gown from the back of the chair. 'I need to visit the bathroom,' she muttered. 'I won't be long.'

Drawing the robe tight about her, she fastened the belt and went quickly away.

'Take your time,' he said, 'we've got all night, and all day as well . . . if I choose to.' He spied the celebratory bottle of champagne her parents had placed on the dressing table. 'Bring me the bottle. When you come back, we'll drink a glass or two to celebrate our union.'

'Can't we leave it until the morning,' she asked. 'I mean . . . haven't you had enough already?'

His face hardened. 'What, you think I'm drunk?'

'Well, no, but . . .'

'Just get the bottle . . . please my love?'

While Alice went to get the bottle of champagne, he noticed the torn nightgown on the carpet, 'Sorry about the nightie.' Taking the bottle from her grasp, he promised, 'I'll get you a new nightie . . . all pink and pretty, with buttons down the front . . . easier to get at you, eh?' He gave a knowing wink.

In the bathroom, Alice let the tears flow. She thought of the painful and degrading way he had taken her just now; while with Joe, their lovemaking had been fulfilling and magical. He was incredibly caring, and while she was in his arms, she never wanted it to end.

The tears coursed down her face. I don't know who Frank is anymore, she thought. I don't think I love him. Maybe I never did. She was certain of one thing; she never wanted him to touch her again.

Suddenly there was a loud pop, and she knew he had opened the champagne. 'As if he needs any more alcohol,' she whispered worriedly. But, as she was already beginning to learn; right or wrong, Frank Arnold took whatever he wanted, whatever the consequences.

Turning on the tap, she cupped her hands and splashed her face with water. She then ran the water into the sink and taking flannel and soap, she bathed herself from head to toe; feverishly rubbing at her skin until it was sore and bruised. Even then, she still felt used and dirty.

~

For different reasons, Frank was also going over the experience of the past half-hour; not because he believed he'd been thoughtless and aggressive with Alice, but because he felt uneasy about the truth of it. 'Alice!' Taking another long swig from the bottle, he called again, this time more vehemently, 'ALICE WHERE ARE YOU? GET IN HERE!'

When he got no answer, he grew angry and impatient, 'Alice!' He scrambled out of bed in such a rush that he got caught up in the eiderdown. 'Bloody thing. Damn and bugger it!'

Snatching up the eiderdown that his mother had painstakingly sewn together, he tore it to pieces, square by square, until it lay at his feet in a tangled mess.

He now turned his attention to the bed sheet, and the persistent nagging thoughts in his fevered mind continued to grow.

He noticed how the corners of the sheet were tucked neatly underneath the mattress, but what really intrigued him was how spotlessly clean and white the sheet was, with only a crease here and there to show where Alice had lain.

Something struck him as odd, and yet it wasn't alto-gether clear in his mind. Maybe it was because she had been too quiet and forgiving, he thought, while he had perhaps been a little over-excited and rough. Maybe he should have been more careful; especially with her being a virgin.

He continued to stare at the bed. Something was not right, he thought. Something curious, and the more he thought about it, the more he was convinced.

It wasn't long before curiosity became suspicion.

When a moment later he burst into the bathroom it was to find Alice frantically covering herself with the robe.

'Frank!' Startled, she asked, 'Can you give me another minute. I need to clean my teeth.' It was the first excuse that came to mind.

'Oh, I see . . . clean your teeth is it?' Muggy-headed from the effects of too much booze, he remained by the door, his eyes raking her body; almost as though he was raping her all over again.

Nervously Alice asked again, 'Please, Frank . . . I'll only be a minute, then I'll be back to you . . .' Again the guilt. Always the guilt; and now the anger, '. . . if that's what you want?'

Still, he made no move towards her. Instead, he asked in the quietest voice, 'What I *want* . . . is the truth.'

Alice was shaken. 'What do you mean? What truth?'

Hard-faced, he asked point blank, 'Have you been with another man, before me?'

Momentarily stunned into silence, Alice was slow to reply. 'I . . . what do you mean, Frank?' She gave a nervous little laugh, 'That's a strange thing to ask . . . especially on our wedding night.'

If Frank was uncertain before, her nervous response only heightened his suspicion. 'Don't treat me like some bloody fool!' he snapped. 'I asked a question, and I want an answer. Oh, and it had better be the truth, or so help me, if I find out you're lying to me . . .'

In an instant, he had her by the shoulders, his face leanng into hers. 'D'you think I've never broken a virgin before? Well I have! More times than I care to remember. So I know how it is. D'you hear me, bitch . . . I know how it is with you women!'

Forcing her head up so he could look square into her eyes, he smiled, a quietly invasive smile that unnerved her, even more than his ranting. 'So! Was there a man before me? Don't you lie to me, Alice, because I'll know!'

Alice was in no doubt. He suspected! Somehow, he suspected, and now he meant to get at the truth. 'I've no idea what you mean, Frank,' she brazened in a small voice. 'What am I supposed to tell you?'

'Who was it?'

She tried to brave it out. 'There was no one, Frank . . . just you.'

For a moment the air was thick, and when he spoke again, there was real menace in his voice. *'I'll ask you again . . . I wasn't the first, was I?'*

When she opened her mouth to speak, he spread his hand across her face. 'No more lies! I want the truth . . . NOW!'

Alice dropped her gaze to the floor, her heart beating wildly. 'Don't do this, Frank,' she asked. *'Please . . . don't do this . . .'* Clutching her robe, she wrapped it tighter about her. 'I'm getting cold, Frank. Let me get dressed, and then maybe we can talk about this.'

Smiling, he shook his head. 'Talk your way out of it, you mean?'

'No, Frank! You've got it all wrong.' His suspicions were uncannily true, but how could she admit that she'd slept with his brother? That it was Joe who had taken her virginity?

And even more damning was the fact that she had willingly gone to him that night; even though she knew the truth would bring trouble and heartache in its wake.

'Listen to me, Frank. There is no one else!' Again, the lies, and the shame. Never before had she lied in such a way, but at that moment, faced with Frank's dark mood, she could see no other choice. 'There is only you, Frank.'

'Liar!' Snatching her by the scruff of her hair, he shook her like a rag doll. 'You've had someone else, I know it.

I can smell him!' His face crumpled with hatred. 'Was it good with him, eh? Was it better with him than with me?'

'Get off me, Frank!' Desperate to escape his grip, Alice suddenly realised that until now, she had never seen Frank drunk. Now though, with the stench of booze still on him, and his loud, aggressive manner, she wondered if it was the drink at the root of his suspicions.

After all, he had always been possessive of her, and besides, how would he know he was not the first man she had slept with. Since that night with Joe, she had been so careful.

Intermittently swigging from the bottle, he continued to rant, 'You led me to believe that you were saving yourself for me! When all the time, some bastard was taking what was mine!'

Continuing to shake her, he cruelly mimicked her voice, 'I'm saving myself until we're married, Frank.'

Raising his fist he punched her hard across the face, yanking her upright when she slumped against him. 'You thought I wouldn't find out, didn't you, eh? Well, you should have known that Frank Arnold has been about a bit, and he's not one to be taken in. Oh, but you . . . You took Frank Arnold for a fool, when nobody else ever could!'

He laughed, a deep-down laugh that sent a shiver through her. 'Think o' that, eh? You! Just a slip of a thing . . . you actually managed to get one over on me! So! Thanks to you, I would be a laughing stock if this ever got out!'

He began shaking her. 'No man or woman has ever been able to make a fool outta me . . . until now! Oh, and there was me, idiot that I am . . . thinking you were something special. Thinking you were different from all the others.'

Increasingly agitated, he threw her aside. 'Bitch!' He

began pacing the floor. 'What in God's name did I ever see in you? I could have wed any number of women, worthless tarts who had nothing but the shirts on their back; they'd spread theirselves across the back seat of my car and we'd have a bit of fun. They lived in places you wouldn't house a dog. But I'll tell you this for nothing! They weren't cheats and they weren't liars. What you see is what you get with them.'

He ranted in a low trembling voice, as though talking to himself. 'Blind! That's what I am . . . blind and stupid! To think I could have chosen any one of them, but no, I chose you . . . the shrinking violet. The pure one . . . or so I thought!'

He took a long, hate-filled look at her. 'Looking so innocent and all the time, you were rotten to the core. I've always managed to steer clear o' your sort. The trouble is, you had a family with money. In my book, that makes a real difference.'

Screaming, he pointed a finger at her. '*You!* You took me for a damned fool! And even now when I've all but caught you bang to rights, you won't admit it . . . why won't you admit it, eh? Afraid I might cut him up a bit, well you'd be right about that, because if I ever get my hands on him, he won't *walk* away, that's for sure! They'll have to carry him away!'

Alice tried another tack. 'Listen to me, Frank! I married you, not him . . . *you*! We're man and wife. I belong to you now. Isn't that enough?'

'Ah! So now you admit it! You *did* have another man when I wasn't looking. Tell me . . . was it before, or after me? Did you and this bastard have it away while you were promised to me?'

Seizing her by the neck, he pulled her violently towards him, his voice a mere whisper, 'Were you saying yes to him at the same time you were saying no to me?'

'It wasn't like that!' Admitting defeat she looked him square in the face. 'All right! I did wrong, I admit it. But it will never happen again, you have my word!'

'I knew it!' Bundling her down the stairs and into the kitchen, he threw open all the drawers until he found a large pair of scissors. 'And all this time you kept on denying it.' He was like a madman. 'I know what you're up to. You want people to believe I'm losing my mind!'

'No, Frank!' In fear for her life, she pleaded with him, 'I just want for us to talk it through sensibly . . . please Frank . . . think what you're doing. It doesn't have to be like this.'

With a twist of his arm, he had her at his feet. 'There's only one way to treat a trollop like you.'

When he brandished the scissors in her face, there was no doubt in Alice's mind, that he would maim, or even kill her.

But Frank Arnold was too clever, or too cowardly to kill her now. Yes, he wanted her dead, along with the man who had taken what was his. The pair of them would answer for it. But not just yet; not until he'd had his pound of flesh.

'So, are you ready to tell me now who was it?'

Gripping her neck in a powerful hold, he kept her head down. 'Well?'

With the long blades of the scissors cold against her skin, Alice remained very still.

'One more chance!' He squeezed her neck. 'All you have to do is tell me who he is.'

Defiant, Alice shifted her gaze away from him. 'I can't.'

'What was that?' he goaded her. 'I didn't quite hear what you said?'

He relaxed his grip on her neck. 'His name? That's all I need to hear. Nothing else. No "Sorry, Frank", or "It was all a mistake". I don't need that! I just need his name.'

There followed a deathly silence. 'Don't test me, Alice. You haven't known me long enough to realise what I'm capable of.'

Alice remained silent.

'So you won't tell, eh?' The ensuing silence was almost deafening, before he spoke again, 'Seems to me you need a lesson, on how to loosen your tongue.'

With an iron fist, he kept her pinned down, while with the other hand he used the scissors to slice remnants from her robe, and when there was little of it left, he began to chop wildly at her hair, all the while softly sniggering, like someone demented.

Terrified, Alice could see the long strands of hair falling to the floor. She could feel the stabs of scissor blades in her scalp and all the while her mind was filled with his laughter. All she could think was that he must finally have lost his mind.

Truly believing that when he was done chopping her hair, he would take her life, she knew now that even if she was to give Joe's name, Frank would not let her go. He would kill her and then he'd go after Joe. And so she remained silent, save for the quiet sobs that she could no longer hold back.

Frank's rage knew no bounds. Haphazardly hacking at her hair, he seemed oblivious to the spurts of blood that meandered slowly down her face; and the raw patches of skin on her scalp, where only the wispy stumps of her long, thick hair remained.

Exhausted and triumphant, he stood over her. 'Now then, bitch! Are you ready to give me the bastard's name? Or do I have to finish you off?'

Sick with pain, Alice looked up at him, but said nothing.

For one fleeting moment, he was affected on seeing her distress, and for some strange reason he even entertained a sneaking, twisted admiration for her loyalty.

But he was too far gone to stop now. Someone had to be punished. Someone had to pay the price for making a fool out of him!

He had an idea. 'Maybe I should leave you here nice and secure, while I visit your precious family, eh? They've got a nerve to think they're a cut above me, but they're not. How can they be, after breeding rubbish like you?'

He started talking to himself; loudly outlining his plan, as though perfecting it in his mind. 'Somebody should rid the earth of people like that! I could do that! I could make sure they don't wake up in the morning. I know where they live. I had a real good look round when I was there.'

Grabbing her face with both hands he made her look up at him. 'Make no mistake! I can be in and out of that place, without anyone ever knowing I was even there.'

Deeply shocked, Alice clung to him, pleading for their lives. 'No Frank! Think what you're saying! You can't do this . . . they'll catch you and lock you away in a dark place. You wouldn't like that would you, Frank? Please, Frank!' But she could see he was past reason. Jealousy and madness had taken over.

Suddenly he flung her across the room, where she landed badly against the wall; and while she was still reeling from the impact, he rushed at her again, shaking and slapping her. When she slithered to the floor, he dropped to his knees and took her into his embrace. 'Aw, look at what you made me do.' He began rocking her backwards and forwards, tenderly wiping the blood from her face. 'Why won't you give me his name?' The hardness crept in. 'Is it because you love him more than you love me, is that it, eh?'

He made her a promise. 'I won't hurt you anymore,' he whispered, 'if you tell me who it was that you slept with . . . who took what was mine, eh? You have to tell me!'

Gripped with pain, Alice was determined as ever. She turned away.

'All right, have it your way.' He threw her aside, saying with a hint of approval. 'You might be a dirty trollop, but you're a stubborn bugger if ever I saw one!'

His manner changed. He was insanely calm. 'So now, you're making me do something wicked. Something I will not enjoy.'

He turned from her, his attitude surprisingly matter-of-fact. 'Now you be a good girl while I find some rope, because I'm not done with you yet.'

When he left her there, Alice thought this was her chance, but when she tried to stand up, her legs buckled beneath her. Every bone in her body hurt. Time and again she made the effort to escape, and each time she crumpled to the floor. 'God help us,' she muttered. 'Please God, help us!'

On his swift return, Frank saw that she had moved and he was greatly amused. 'There you are. Y'see . . . you're just too stubborn for your own good.' He began tying her hands behind her back, and then he tied her legs together. 'Stubborn,' he kept saying. 'Too stubborn for your own good.'

Alice looked up at him, wanting to speak, yet not wanting to tell.

'Ah!' He wiped a trickle of blood from her mouth. 'So, now you want to tell me something, do you?'

Alice spoke in a whisper, 'Don't hurt them . . . please.' He would, she thought, he would murder her entire family without a second thought, because he was insane . . . completely and utterly insane.

He groaned, 'Oh, dear, and I thought you were about to give me a name.' He tied the knot twice over and prepared to put the gag on her.

'Now then, I don't want you calling out, or any such

silly thing like that, not that anyone would hear you, way out here. Listen, I'll lock the door behind me, so you won't be disturbed.'

Leaning forward he whispered in her ear, 'What I have to do won't take long. I'll be back before you know it.'

Alice was desperate. If she continued trying to protect Joe, her family would be murdered, of that she had no doubt. If on the other hand she told him about Joe, he would finish her off and then hunt Joe down.

Just now, he had given her a choice, and time was running out. Any minute now, he would stuff the gag in her mouth and there would be no second chance.

Her mind was in chaos but she had to make herself stay calm, think.

Joe was young and able, she reasoned, and if it came to an outright fight, Joe may well be a match for his brother.

Her parents were old, and could not defend themselves against Frank's manic strength. After all, he was their son-in-law, and when he knocked on the door, they would naturally assume that he had come for help of sorts. They would have no reason to believe he was there to harm them.

What to do? What to do?

When Frank stooped to thrust the gag into her mouth, she panicked. 'Joe!' His name filled the room, and then she was sobbing. 'Just one time . . . one time, that's all.'

She saw his mouth fall open; she saw the horror in his eyes, and she looked away, her voice almost inaudible as she pleaded for Joe's life. 'It wasn't his fault . . . it was me! I went to him of my own free will. *I'm* the bad one. Listen to me, Frank! You were right. It's *me* you need to punish.'

He wasn't listening. Instead he was rocking back and forth, as though in a daze, his face wreathed in disbelief.

He stared at her for a second or two, then he stared at the floor, and now the rocking got faster and faster as he whispered over and over, 'You and *Joe*!'

Suddenly he rammed the wet cloth into her mouth. When she put up a fight, struggling and biting, and screaming for help, he hit her hard across the side of the head, while driving the rag between her teeth and into her mouth with such force, she found it difficult to breathe.

Slowly shaking her head, she raised her tear-filled eyes to his, silently pleading for him to cut her loose; for someone, anyone to help her.

'Oh, dearie me . . .' He took pleasure from tormenting her. 'Turning on the tears now is it?' His answer was a vicious slap to the face. 'Don't try the tears on me, because it won't work!'

As she fell away he issued a warning, by putting a finger to his lips, 'Ssh.' It was a clear instruction of how unwise it would be to try and plead with him in that way.

As he went out the door, he spoke to her as though everything was quite normal, 'I'll do what I have to do, and then I'll be back. I'm glad you told me the truth, it makes everything so much easier. You really are a bad girl though, and as you must know, bad girls should be punished.'

He smoothed back his hair and wiped his forehead, as though brushing off any visible signs of what he had done to her. 'First things first though. People have to be taught a lesson. After that, you and I need to talk.' He smiled at her, as though nursing a secret.

Keeping his gaze fixed on her for a moment; he watched her desperately struggling, and he gave a bright, happy smile. 'Bad, Bad girl!'

He then closed the door behind him, calling as he went, 'Don't you worry now. I won't be long.'

Then she was all alone in the eerie silence.

~

Straining to see around her, Alice looked for a possible means of escape; though when she tried to move, the ropes cut into her flesh.

Frank was off his head. Somehow she had to find a way to stop him. If she couldn't find a way to raise the alarm, Joe would die, and so would she.

She heard the slam of a door, the car engine starting. And then the crunch of ground under wheels as the car moved off.

In the ensuing silence, all that could be heard was the rhythmic ticking of the grandfather clock; and the muffled sound of her sobbing.

As the morning light began to fill the skies, Frank drove like a man hellbent on killing himself; careering back and forth across the lane, he seemed oblivious to the deep ditches on either side.

'I'll bury the two of you together, that's what I'll do!' He sneered wickedly at the thought. 'You and the trollop, side by side in a deep, black hole.'

His laughter echoed across the fields.

'You're a dead man, Joe!' He thumped the steering wheel. 'A dead man!'

~

Rising with the daylight, as he had done all his farming life, Tom made his way down to the kitchen, only to find Joe already there. 'Hello, son. I didn't know you were up and about.'

Joe smiled. 'I don't know if up and about is the right description,' he groaned. 'More like dragging my feet.'

Tom chuckled at that. 'Feeling the worse for wear, are you?'

'You could say that, yes. I think I stayed up past my bedtime last night . . . what with you and me finishing off that bottle of whisky and talking till the early hours, I feel like something the cat dragged in.'

'It'll pass, once you're out in the fresh air, don't worry.' Tom had truly enjoyed being with Joe, and although he had not managed to get much out of him with regard to where he'd been this past year, he consoled himself with the fact that the two of them were at least enjoying each other's company; something they had not done in a long time.

'Oh, but wasn't it good?' he said warmly. 'Your mother tucked up in bed and you and me down here putting the world to rights?'

Joe readily agreed, 'It was good, yes.'

With Joe having already brewed the tea, Tom just needed to pour himself one out, then add the milk and three spoons of sugar. 'By! I need this!'

Joe was deep in thought. 'I missed you when I was away,' he said now, taking Tom by surprise. 'Last night with the two of us talking together and laughing at nothing, I realised how much I'd missed being here.'

'We'll do it again tonight if you're of a mind,' Tom said, waddling to the table. 'Want one?' He raised his mug of tea.

'Got one, thanks.'

Collecting his own mug of tea from the table, Joe took a long gulp of it. 'As for doing it again, I think I'll give it a miss.' He groaned, 'I've got a head that feels like two!'

'It was a damned good wedding, don't you think, Joe?'

Joe nodded. 'It was, yes.' Though it cut him to the heart, he thought Alice looked lovely in the church. 'I hope they'll be happy.'

'D'you mean that, Joe?' Tom reminded himself of how Joe had long been attracted to his brother's wife.

Joe was alarmed. 'What d'you mean?' he asked sharply. 'Of course I want them to be happy. Why shouldn't I?'

Tom apologised, 'I were only thinking how you haven't yet managed to find a girl to share your life with. If you were just the smallest bit envious of Frank, I would understand it.'

Deliberately ignoring the last comment, Joe told him, 'You don't need to worry about me, Father. The right girl will come along when she's meant to. Until then, I'm young and content enough to wait.'

Relieved, Tom took a long, deep breath, held it a second or two, then blew it out with the statement, 'I'm very pleased to hear that, son.' He had another question. 'So? What are your plans now? You didn't say much about that last night.'

Joe had thought long and hard on that one. 'What would you like them to be?'

Tom looked him in the eye. 'Me and your mother want you to stay right here, with us; for as short or as long a time as suits you.'

He leaned forward. 'Listen to me, son, I don't ask where you've been or how you fared, but I do know that since you've been back, there are times when I've glanced at you, and you've been miles away . . . kind of haunted.'

Joe smiled a wistful, sad smile that touched old Tom's heart. 'I'm not haunted,' he promised, 'though I will admit I had my bad times while I was away.'

He wanted so much to confide in his father, about the ugliness of prison life, and the loneliness that had taken over him. More than that, he desperately needed someone to understand about his feelings for Alice, the one girl he could not forget. 'Some day when I'm ready, I might tell you all about it,' he told Tom 'But for now, I just need to do what makes me comfortable.'

'I see.' Tom leaned back in his chair, 'And being here with me and the family, has that made you feel comfortable?'

'Yes, Dad, it has,' Joe told him fervently. 'It's been really good, being here with you and Mum.' He made no mention of Frank, because Frank was the enemy; and always had been.

Tom confided his own feelings, 'Like I say, for what it's worth, son, there is nothing me and your mother would like better than for you to stay here.' He added thoughtfully, 'Not just because Frank is planning on acquiring his own farm; though if I'm honest that is a consideration. No! It's just, well, we want you here at home with us, where you belong. I can tell you have a lot on your mind, and I'm sure there'll come a time when you'll share your troubles with us, but for now, don't you think it makes sense for you to stay, and be kind to your-self for a time?'

He persuaded in a fatherly way, 'That way, son, you'll have no one to answer to, and there'll be plenty of time to decide what it is you want to do with the rest of your life.'

Joe had a question of his own. 'Do you really think Frank will strike out on his own if he gets the finances to do it?'

Tom had no doubt. 'Frank is my son and I love him, but I know what he's like . . . what he's *always* been like. Truth is, if he gets an idea into his head, there's no stop-ping him! If Frank Arnold is hellbent on doing some-thing, he'll see it through to the end.'

He paused, before going on in a quieter voice, 'I'm afraid your brother is a law unto himself. If he means to become the gentry landowner, he'll walk over anyone who gets in his way, and he won't give me nor his mother a second thought.'

He lapsed into deep thought, before confiding in a whisper, 'Between you and me, there was a time when me and your mother got really worried about him. He was such a difficult boy, so unpredictable . . . we never knew what he'd be getting up to next.'

Looking straight at Joe, he asked, 'I don't suppose you recall the time he tied that boy round the tree . . . nigh cut the poor little bugger in half with the rope he did!'

Surprised to see how his father had seemed to age just by talking about Frank, Joe wanted to put his mind at rest. 'We were just kids, Dad. We were playing cowboys and indians, that's all.' He was quick to assure him, 'Looking back, I agree it was a silly thing to do, but I don't think Frank meant any harm.'

Tom shook his head vehemently. 'It was a cruel and spiteful thing to do,' he said sharply. Then in softer tone, 'He doesn't get it from me or your mother, that's for sure!'

Joe had seen how his father was going back over the years and it worried him, because if he was dwelling on that particular episode, what else was he thinking about? Did he suspect that Frank had murdered their little dog? And what about all the other things Joe knew and had never told . . . did he know about them too?

Joe quickly changed the subject. 'So, you want me to stay, do you?'

Tom's face brightened. 'O' course we do! Me and your mother were talking about it in bed last night . . .' He added with a mischievous twinkle in his eye, 'There's nothing much else to do when you get to our age.'

'Right, well, d'you want to know a secret?'

'Only if it's a good one.'

'Well, first of all, I should tell you, I had already decided to leave straight after the wedding.' When he saw his father's expression fall, he went quickly on, 'Now though . . . after Frank told us of his plans to move on, I've decided to stay. I want to work here, with you and Mum. Like you say . . . I need to take some time to decide what I want long term.'

Added to that, he needed to stay close in order to keep a wary eye on Alice. 'So, Dad, I don't reckon I'll be going off on a new adventure for some time to come.'

Tom's eyes filled with tears. 'Oh, son, that's the best news you could have ever given us. Wait till I tell your mother. Oh, she'll be that pleased!'

A few minutes later, Nancy came into the kitchen, yawning, and in a cranky mood. 'I thought when you got to a certain age, you were allowed to have a lie-in; especially on a Sunday!'

'Ah, but you're a farmer's wife, so you need to be up with the lark,' Tom declared, a secret little smile written across his ruddy-red face.

Nancy noticed it and was instantly suspicious. 'All right, husband! What have you been up to?'

'Nothing!' He gave a sideways wink at Joe.

'So why have you got a face like the cat that got the cream?'

Tom held out his half-empty mug. 'If you'll be so good as to top that up, I might tell you why.'

'Hmm!' She took his mug and filled it up, then brought it back but held on to it. 'Go on then . . . explain!'

'Give us me tea.'

'Not till you've told me!'

'You're a wicked woman, Nancy Arnold!'

'I'm still waiting!' She kept the mug out of his reach.

Tom knew he wouldn't get his tea until he told her. 'You might be pleased to know that our son, Joe, has just told me he won't be leaving, and that he's staying here with us. Now then, woman, what d'you think to that?'

Nancy's response was to drop the mug in front of Tom. 'That's wonderful news!' Grabbing Joe in a bear-hug she squeezed him till he hurt. 'You don't know how happy that makes me, son,' she told him tearfully, 'I got it into my head that once you'd done your duty as best man, you'd be away and then we might never see you again!'

Joe opened his heart to her. 'I'll be honest with you, Mum, all the time I was away, I was never happy, not really. Oh, I saw different places and I tried this and that, but this place, and all of you, were never far from my thoughts. So! I'm back now, and for the time being at least, this is where I want to be.'

When they were all sat round the table sipping their tea, Tom and Joe began planning the work schedule for the day.

'It'll be no use relying on Frank today,' Nancy chipped in with a knowing wink. 'He'll not see daylight for a few hours yet I'll be bound.'

Tom pretended to be shocked. 'Whatever are you implying, woman, at your age an' all?'

'Aw, shut up you!' She flicked the dishcloth at him. 'We've had our day. Now it's the young 'uns turn.'

Joe tried to hide the pain in his face and he was reminded again that Alice was now firmly Frank's woman, though he had to smile at the banter between his parents.

These two were not wealthy; they didn't even own the roof over their head and yet, just having each other, they had everything, Joe thought. They were uniquely happy, and totally content with the life they had made together.

Joe could not help but wonder if he would ever have a marriage like theirs: honest and open, with laughter in their hearts and children round the table.

For one precious moment, he allowed himself to think of Alice, and his heart was sore.

'Right then, Dad.' Pushing thoughts of Alice from his mind, he got out of his chair and glanced up at the wall clock. 'It's quarter to six . . . time I got started.'

Nancy scrambled out of her chair. 'Don't you go off without the sandwich and flask. It'll only take me a minute.

I already sliced the meat, and the kettle will be singing in no time at all.'

Joe thanked her, before addressing his father. 'Where would you like me to start this morning, Dad?'

'Well, I'm not sure. Whatever you think is the most urgent, I suppose,' Tom replied thoughtfully. 'The trouble is, I'm not altogether up with everything. Frank never thinks to keep me informed. I reckon he thinks he's in charge and I don't matter . . . the cheeky devil!'

He rubbed his fingers across his stubbly chin; a familiar trait whenever he was thinking hard. 'Are there any jobs half done?' he asked, 'I could never be doing with jobs half done!'

'Well, there's that fencing at the top of the rise,' Joe said. 'By the looks of it, Frank's already made a start on it, and I do believe it's the next job on his list. The thing is, I noticed the sheep have already moved on to graze the banks up there. With only half the fencing done, they could well work their way down and on to the crops, and besides, if anybody walking the rise should lose their footing, it's one hell of a dangerous drop from the top, down to the craggy bottom, with nothing solid to stop their fall in between.'

Tom agreed. 'You're right,' he said. 'The fencing along that ridge should be Frank's first priority! It has to be finished, but it's a hard job on your own. Look, you get the stuff up there and I'll see if I can't get Jimmy Slater to come up and give you a hand.'

Joe reminded him, 'Frank won't like that. Him and Jimmy had a bit of a disagreement.'

Tom gave a weary sigh. 'D'you know what it was all about?'

Joe deliberately played it down. 'Something and nothing.'

'I see, and Jimmy came off worse. No matter. There'll

be time enough for me to get to the bottom of it, but for now, disagreement or not, that fencing needs doing. Moreover, I reckon I should make something very clear to you, son.'

'Oh?' Joe was eager to be gone. 'And what's that?'

'Just that, *I* have the last word on any decision with regards to this farm.' Asserting his authority, he went on, 'Frank might like to think he's in charge, but he isn't; not when it comes right down to it.'

He spoke with deliberation. '*I'm* the one whose name is on the rent book, and *I'm* the one who pays the rent.'

There was one other thing he thought Joe should know. 'If your brother is so determined to strike out on his own, I'll be hoping to rely on you heavily, Joe. If there comes a time when you want to go your own way, then that's entirely up to you. In the meantime though, if Frank does walk away, any decisions with regard to this place, will be for me and you to make.'

'And what about *me?*' Nancy's voice sailed across the kitchen. 'I suppose I'm just a woman, so I don't get a say, is that it?'

Winking at Joe, Tom swung round. 'Do you *want* a say?' he asked her.

'Don't be silly! Don't you think I've got enough to do, without running the farm as well!'

The two men burst into laughter, while Nancy flounced off, secretly smiling. She was pleased to the heart with everything she'd heard.

A moment later, she returned with a bag for Joe. 'Here! Don't forget your flask and sandwiches,' she told him. 'And make sure you take a coat. It might look warm what with the sun shining, but it can change at the drop of a hat, as you well know.'

Collecting his coat from the back of the chair, Joe picked up his bag. Thanking Nancy, he gave her a peck on the cheek and when they thought he'd gone out the door, he came quickly back. 'I forgot! I haven't fed the falcon. I'd best do it now . . .'

'No need!' Nancy waved her hand. 'I'll do it . . . or Tom will. You get off now, son. Like your father said, we'll try and get a hold of Jimmy to come and give you a hand.'

She made her way over to the dresser. 'I've an idea Frank wrote his number by the telephone.'

While she rummaged, Tom asked Joe, 'Did Frank leave the tools up there with the fencing?'

Joe searched his memory. 'I'm pretty sure the rolls of fencing are still up there, but I noticed the tools are lying in the back of the wagon.'

Tom groaned. 'How many times have I told Frank not to leave tools out in the open! Tools cost money! Leave 'em out and they get rusty, which means in time the tools aren't fit to do the job they were got for.'

He went to the drawer and got out a set of keys. 'Here!' Throwing them to Joe, he advised, '. . . the wagon keys.'

When Joe said he would prefer to walk, Tom insisted, 'You don't want to be carrying tools all the way up there. Besides, it'll be handy to throw the old fencing on, and you might want to bring back any new fencing that's left over.'

Having found Jimmy's telephone number, Nancy handed it to Tom. 'You can get hold of him, while I see to the bird.'

Tom swiftly handed the paper back. 'It was you that wanted a damned telephone in the house!' he argued. 'You know very well, I don't like the blessed thing. Everybody shouting at each other 'cause they can't hear properly.'

When he slammed the paper down, Nancy ignored his tantrum and turned to Joe. 'Do like your dad says and take the wagon,' she advised. 'If it turns wet or cold, you'll be able to sit in there with your tea and sandwiches.'

'Not a problem.' Joe took his leave, calling back as he went, 'Oh, about the falcon! You'll find his tin of food on the floor beneath the cage. And mind you're careful with him, Mum. He's a bit nervous, and his wing is still not strong enough. I don't want him escaping . . . at least not for another day or so.'

'Go on with you!' Nancy called back, 'I've lost count of the times you've come home with injured creatures. I think we've had enough practice looking after them, don't you?'

Joe went on his way smiling. 'See you later!'

Once outside, he climbed into the wagon, turned the key and shifted into forward gear; there was a crunch and a whine, and then he was off. 'I don't know about the tools getting rusty,' he chuckled, '. . . but this old wagon seems to be getting a bit tired an' all.'

Bumping over ridges and skirting potholes, he wended his way up to the highest point, constantly shifting gear and hanging on to the steering wheel, as the road got rougher. 'It's as well the sheep have an appetite for the scrub up here,' he muttered, while being shaken top to toe, 'because it's fit for nothing else!'

Busy concentrating on the way ahead, Joe had no idea he was being followed.

Keeping his car well back, Frank stayed close enough to keep an eye on Joe. 'Looks like he's headed for the rise.' He was satisfied with that. 'The further away from peeping eyes, the better.'

At the foot of the bank, he drew into the spinney. Hiding the vehicle in the shrubbery, he then collected the shotgun from the back and, securing it tight under his arm, he proceeded up the bank; ducking and diving so as not to be seen.

On foot he moved with speed and cunning: like the hunter after its prey.

'That's it, Joe!' Excited and nervous, he kept after him. 'On your way to do the fencing is it? You took my woman, and now you're taking my work!'

Like a man possessed, he snaked his way up to the heights, his hatred like a clenched fist inside him. 'You're a dead man, Joe!' he kept muttering. 'A dead man!'

~

Back in the farmhouse kitchen, unaware of the tragic events already unfolding, Tom enjoyed another mug of tea.

After several times trying to contact Jimmy, Nancy dropped the big, black receiver into its cradle. 'Stupid thing!'

'What? Can't you get him then?'

'No!' She stood, hands on hips, wondering what to do next. 'I can't get through!' she grumbled. 'There's some silly devil at the other end crackling a paper bag or at least that's what it sounded like!' Frustrated, she marched into the kitchen.

Tom smiled. 'I told you them things weren't worth the space they take up, didn't I, eh?'

'Tom Arnold! If you don't want strangling, you'd best keep your tongue between your teeth!'

For a moment there was silence, then, 'Nancy?'

'What now?'

'I wouldn't mind another piece of toast before I see to the falcon.'

It was a moment or two before Nancy returned with a plate of toast. 'You eat that,' she instructed, 'I'll go and feed Joe's bird. You can't be climbing up to the cage, not with that gammy leg. You'll likely slip and do yourself a damage. *Then* where would we be, eh?'

He sighed. 'Now that I'm getting old, you think I'm useless, don't you?'

Nancy smiled. 'I've *always* thought you were useless,' she teased, 'but I love you anyway.' And to confirm it, she gave him a kiss on the mouth. 'Eat your toast,' she said,

He had other thoughts on his mind. 'What about Jimmy?' he asked. 'Joe can't manage that fencing on his own. It's a job for two men.'

'When you've had your toast, you can have another go at getting hold of Jimmy. I've tried and got nowhere, and anyway, I've the bird to see to.'

Prepared for any weather, she donned her hat and coat.

Before she left, she informed Tom, 'Go on then! Get on to that telephone, before Jimmy leaves the house, because then you'll not be able to get him at all, and like you said, our Joe can't do the fencing on his own now, can he?'

With Nancy gone, Tom got out of his chair and ambled across to the telephone, where he gingerly picked up the receiver. He then noted the number on the piece of paper that Nancy had left there. Slowly and carefully, he dialled the number and held the receiver against his ear. 'Hello, who's there?'

He waited a moment, before asking again, this time with impatience, 'Who's there?' He held the receiver away from him, then he pressed it back to his ear and when there was no sound, he replaced the receiver into its cradle. He tried again. He picked up the receiver, dialled the number and listened. 'Ah! It's ringing!' His face lit up.

He waited, and waited, and it went on ringing, and then his patience ran out. 'Bloody rubbish thing!' The receiver bounced as he slammed it back into its cradle. 'I'd best get Nancy.'

He was just opening the front door to go and find Nancy, when he heard her yelling for him, 'Tom! Come quickly!' Her screams echoed across the yard.

Rushing as fast as his dodgy legs would carry him, he burst into the barn. 'What in God's name . . . *Nancy*! Whatever's happened?'

Nancy was in a heap on the hay bale, rocking back and forth, and sobbing like he had never seen her sob before. 'Look, Tom!' She could hardly speak. 'Look at what they've done!'

When he got to her, she held out her hands and lying there, badly mutilated and dying in agony, was Joe's falcon. 'Look, Tom!' Nancy sobbed. 'Who could have done such a terrible thing!'

Deeply upset, Nancy pleaded with him. 'Help it, Tom, it's in such pain. We have to do something. Help it, Tom . . . please, help it!'

With tears rolling down her face, she handed him the bird, its eyes wide open, and its body shivering with pain. 'I'm sorry, Tom, love . . . but we can't let it suffer.'

'All right, Nancy, I understand. Ssh now.' Tom had never seen her so distraught.

Choked with emotion, he took the bird, and for a split second he felt its body twitch in his hands; he saw the way its wing had been viciously torn out, and his old heart broke with the sadness of it all. 'Go inside, love,' he murmured to Nancy, 'I'll be along in a minute.'

Quietly sobbing, Nancy left, touching him reassuringly on the arm as she went. 'Oh, Tom, who could have done such a cruel thing!'

Once outside, she thought of Tom, and the awful thing he had to do. She couldn't go back in, and she couldn't leave him. So she sat on the wall, and waited.

Inside the barn, Tom swiftly and gently put the bird out of its misery. 'Such a beautiful thing.' As he lifted it to wrap it in the hessian sack, he tenderly stroked its warm, broken body, his grief giving way to anger. 'If I ever find out who did this . . . !' He choked on the words. 'Wicked buggers! Cruel, sadistic buggers!'

Looking about until he found a spade, he then took the bird outside. Deep in thought, he didn't see Nancy there, so he started digging beside the beech tree, and when the hole was deep enough, he tenderly placed the bird inside. 'There!'

Carefully now, he covered it over with soil. 'You've got a tree all to yourself . . . you can fly away, or you can just watch the world go by.'

When Nancy's hand touched him lovingly on the shoulder, he turned to see her homely face so sad, and those pretty eyes red-raw from crying, and he loved her more than ever.

'Oh, Nancy, love!' Grabbing her to him, he held her for a moment, and when he spoke it was with puzzlement. 'Why would anyone want to harm Joe's bird?' he asked. 'If you ask me, it was no accident, but a deliberate, wicked act of cruelty.'

'How d'you mean, Tom?' In truth, Nancy had harboured the very same thought. 'You talk as if it wasn't someone who happened on the bird and did it in a moment of spite. You make it sound as though someone might have purposely set out to do this.'

Tom relayed his thoughts carefully. 'Think about it, Nancy. The cage was still hanging exactly the same since Joe put it there. I couldn't see any signs that some animal might have climbed up and forced its way into the cage. Oh, I admit, it's possible for a rat to have got to it; there are plenty of rats on a farm, that's for certain. But if had been a rat, there'd be nothing left of the bird.'

He pictured the bird in his mind. 'It was no four-legged creature that attacked that poor bird,' he deduced, 'it didn't have any damage; except for the wing that was torn out and thrown aside.'

He went over what he'd seen. 'The only sign of inter-ference that I could tell, was the door of the cage being left wide open . . . as though someone had deliberately reached into the cage and taken the bird out.'

As they walked back to the house, they were lost in thought, each remembering a time when Frank was their only child. When Joe came along, Frank was deeply resentful. There was a time as the boys got older, when at every opportunity, Frank would accidentally hurt Joe in some cunning way, and wherever possible he'd set out to destroy everything his younger brother had.

Nancy and Tom each had these memories.

They each had their suspicions.

But voicing them outright was another thing altogether.

~

Alice was exhausted. She had struggled so hard to get loose, but was strapped up so tight it was almost impos-sible to move. Moreover, the deep scissor-wounds on her scalp were causing such pain that even moving her head was painful.

Whenever she tried to shout, all that came out was a useless, muffled noise.

Desperate, she tried shuffling again, inching her bottom along the floor. It was painstakingly slow, and the move-ment of dragging herself along seemed to tighten the ropes about her wrists and ankles. 'You have to get help!' she told herself over and over '. . . You have to stop him!'

She had seen the malice in Frank's eyes, and she knew now what he was capable of. There was no doubt in her mind that he would kill Joe without an inch of compas-sion. After that, he would be back to taunt her with the news, before killing her too.

Blaming herself for telling him what happened between

her and Joe, she was determined to somehow get out of the cottage, and raise the alarm.

She gritted her teeth and continue to inch her way towards the door.

After what seemed an age, she realised that at last, she was actually making progress; albeit agonisingly slow. Keep going, Alice! she thought, to herself. Keep going! The thought of Joe in danger spurred her on.

Time and again, she had to stop and take a breath. But to give in now, would be suicide, she knew that.

When at last she was within reach, she shuffled the last few inches to the front door, where she fell against it; so weak, and in such pain, she wondered if she would die there.

For the moment she was unable even to raise her head. So she stayed like that, trussed-up and muffled; with every last ounce of strength used up.

When she felt her senses slipping away, the voice in her head would whisper, 'You can't give up, Alice.' With Joe heavy in her mind, she found a new determination.

She brought her gaze to rest on the small bolt in the bottom panel of the door. Being an old cottage with low, ancient doors, the two bolts were set one in the top panel and the other low down.

By fidgeting and rolling, she managed to position her mouth near to the bolt, which was undone, with the long handle jutting out. She then thrust her mouth forward, hooked the gag over the bolt-handle, and pulled. When finally the cloth was out, she drew in great gushes of air, filling her lungs and yelling out, for someone to help her.

Having heard Frank lock the door as he left, and knowing that she was too isolated for anyone to hear, Alice looked in vain for a sharp object that she could back up against and cut the ropes around her wrists, but every movement was laboured by the fact that she was still not free.

Twisting from side to side, she tried to reach the bolt, to see if she could cut the ropes that way, but it was impossible. Desperate that at any minute he might burst in through the door, she cast her gaze about the room, searching for a means of escape. But there was no easy way out. She couldn't think straight. What to do? What to do?

The only other feasible chance she had was through the window. It was near enough for her to get to, and low enough for her to hitch herself up to the wide, flat window ledge that jutted out at the base.

Having inched herself on to the ledge, she soon realised it was not as easy an escape as she thought. The only glass pane that might open was the small one across the top, impossible for her to open, and even more impossible for her to fit through.

Remaining on the window ledge, she took a moment to think.

Examining the window, she noticed how there were six small panes; each one of them encased in its own little lead-frame. They were then linked together in a larger frame; which was attached to the stonework on either side.

Alice saw how the stonework was uneven in places, which meant every now and then, little gaps appeared all round the frame, where over the years, the lead had shrunk away.

This was her only chance to get out before he came back for her! She couldn't sit about and hope her grandparents got to her first.

With every ounce of strength left in her, she launched her weight again and again at the window, hoping it might give; though each thrust of her weight took its toll on her. And the weaker she grew the more she realised that no one was coming to help.

Any minute now, Frank would come in through that door. He would torment her, and then he would finish her off.

CHAPTER SEVEN

S TILL SEARCHING FOR work, and deeply bitter about the way Frank Arnold had treated him, Jimmy emerged from the spinney.

Seeing a nicely rounded piece of fallen branch, he stooped to collect it. 'That'll keep the home fires burning a while longer,' he chuckled.

Taking a moment to string the sizeable collection into a bundle, he then set off back to his cottage. 'This little lot will keep the fire going of an evening,' he muttered as he went. 'Thanks to that swine, Frank Arnold, I need to watch the little bit of money I've saved.'

At every place he'd been to ask for work they'd turned him away, with the empty promise that if anything came up, they'd be sure to contact him.

Jimmy didn't believe them for one minute. He knew Frank Arnold had been telling everyone not to take him on, because he was trouble.

'If it weren't for that devil, I'd be earning a wage instead o' counting pennies, and foraging the spinney for bits o' firewood!'

He had been toying with an idea. 'I reckon I should have a word with old Tom. He knows I'm a good worker. All these years, he's never had cause to complain. Huh!

I bet if he knew how Frank had beaten me wicked like that, he'd have something to say and no mistake.'

Just then he came out on to clear ground. 'By!' Throwing down the sizeable bundle of firewood, he settled gently on to it, legs open wide, arms folded across his knees. 'If the Lord ever created anything more beautiful than this, I've yet to see it!'

From this one particular point, he could see right across to the far-off lake, and in between the land positively danced before his eyes, curving up then down, with all manner of different shades linking arms one into the other; green grasses; mustard coloured crops, and trees of every shape and magnitude.

Sometimes, when the sun shone and the shadows played on the land, everything shifted and moved, as though united in some kind of magical dance.

For a time he just sat there, looking and listening.

On such a day as this, the world was so still, if you listened hard enough, you could hear your own heart beat, Jimmy thought.

After a time, his thoughts returned to Frank Arnold. 'Mebbe I *should* have a word with Tom,' he mumbled. 'Trouble is, when it comes right down to it, blood's thicker than water, and rightly so. Mind you, I'll never understand how such nice folk as Nancy and Tom Arnold ever created a monster like that!'

As he stood up to resume his journey home, he paused, his eyes drawn to the far bank which led up to the rise. 'What the devil's that?'

Placing the palm of his hand across his forehead to shut out the daylight, he peered down. There's somebody there: what's he playing at? Jimmy wondered.

He focused hard, drawing back when he thought he recognised the figure. 'Is it? I'm sure . . .'

Screwing up his eyes he looked again. 'If I'm not mistaken, that's Frank Arnold . . . what's he doing? Looks like he's holding a shotgun.'

Jimmy watched for a time, trying to work out what Frank was up to. 'He's either hunting a rabbit or two, or he's ready for the funny farm, otherwise why is he lurching along like that . . . keeping low, hiding in the shrubberies? What's he up to now, the mad bugger!'

Shaking his head, he collected his bundle and ambled along. 'Now then, long way or short way home?' he asked himself. 'Short way means I'll be back sooner so's I can change into summat smarter; that's if I'm still of a mind to go and have a word with the butcher . . . see if he might have a vacancy in the shop, seeing as Cathy Lucas is due to have her baby any day now?'

The thought of serving in a butcher's shop did nothing to excite him. 'It'll be better than nothing though,' he reasoned. 'At least it'll give me a wage coming in, until such a time as I find work on the land.'

He decided on the shortest route. 'A job in a shop is better than no job at all,' he said. 'So then, Jimmy! It's a wash and change then straight down to the village. Who knows, you just might be lucky this time.'

By changing direction, he had to climb the hill, before he went down again. As he did so the land fell away and the high banks expanded into a plateau. From there he caught sight of Joe fixing the fencing.

'Joe!' he called out. 'Hey, Joe!' But the wind carried his voice to the elements; and when he began waving, he realised that Joe was too far away and too intent on his work, to see him. Jimmy had always liked Joe. He was a different kettle o' fish to his brother, that's for sure!

With Frank popping into his mind, he glanced back. There was no sign of him, and then suddenly, there he was . . . low down, making his way along the edge of the spinney. Jimmy gave a cynical laugh. 'Them poor rabbits don't stand a chance, not with Frank Arnold after their furry tails!'

Sniggering, he went on his way; spurred on by the hope that today, he might find work.

~

The clock chimed. 'Good Lord! The day'll be gone before we can turn round,' Tom was rummaging in the long-cupboard by the stairs. 'Nancy?' When there was no reply, he called again, this time louder, 'Nancy, love!'

Nancy came hurrying in from the kitchen. 'There's no need to shout. What's the matter?'

'Have you seen my shotgun?'

'No.' Still reeling from the shock of finding the bird like that, she had no enthusiasm for this conversation. 'What would I want with a shotgun?'

'Do you know if Joe took it with him?'

'I didn't see, but I wouldn't think he'd need a shotgun to put up fencing, would you?'

Tom closed the cupboard. 'No, you're right but what about Frank? I don't think he would take it without asking me, though he can be a sneaky devil when he wants.'

He was nervous all the same. 'I meant to lock it up in the cabinet,' he said. 'Only, what with everything, I can't remember if I did, and now I can't even find the keys to the cabinet!'

'I shouldn't worry,' Nancy told him. 'I expect Frank locked it away, and in all the excitement he must have put the key into his pocket.'

'Yes, I expect he did. He knows I'm strict about that shotgun being locked away when it's not needed. But like I say, I can't even find the key to the cabinet.'

Nancy was concerned. 'Why d'you want the shotgun?'

Tom was reluctant to say, so he merely skated over the truth with a white lie. 'I'm off to check the yard for signs of rats and such,' he said. 'The last thing we need is a pack o' rats running round the place.' The kind of rat he was thinking of did not have four legs and a tail.

Nancy wiped her hands on her pinnie. 'I'll go and look in Frank's trousers. They're still here, and the key might be in his pocket.'

As she turned, all hell was let loose. 'Tom! Nancy! For God's sake open the door!' The door was being kicked so hard it almost burst off its hinges.

Tom swung the door open, ready to give their visitor a piece of his mind. 'Jimmy! What the devil . . .' His eyes were drawn to the sorry bundle in Jimmy's arms. 'Good Lord above . . . is that . . .' He thought he recognised Alice, but the face and head were so bloodied and broken, he wasn't sure.

Jimmy was frantic, his words tumbling one over the other as he tried to explain, 'It's Alice! She's hurt real bad! I thought she were dead . . . she were just lying there . . . oh, she's not dead is she Tom? Only I thought she were dead . . . I had to bring her here . . . I didn't know what else to do . . .'

'Quick, Jimmy! You'd best get her inside.' While Tom took charge, Nancy was rooted to the spot. White as a sheet with her hands clasped over her mouth, she was unable to take in what she was seeing.

'Lie her on the couch, Jimmy . . . quickly now.' He led Jimmy through. 'Oh, dearie me, what's happened to her? Where did you find her? Where was she? Jimmy! What happened?' The questions poured out in a nervous torrent.

Watching as Jimmy gently laid Alice on to the big old couch, Tom felt sick to his stomach. 'Stay with her, Jimmy,' he instructed. 'I'll phone the ambulance.'

Seeing how Nancy was running her hands through her hair, her stark gaze fixed on Alice's ravaged scalp, he spoke sharply, 'Nancy! You know what to do, love! Get some warm water and towels.'

Nancy snapped out of her trance and went away in a hurry.

Losing his fear of the telephone, Tom dialled the emergency number and asked for an ambulance. 'Straightaway, yes! Yes . . . Alice Arnold . . . she's been attacked. She's in a real bad way . . . quickly, please. As soon as you can!'

After giving his address, he turned to Jimmy, who by now was trembling so much he could hardly speak. 'I found her lying there. I didn't know what it was at first,' he stuttered, 'I had to pass the cottage . . . it was the quickest way. I saw the window . . . all smashed to pieces it were, an . . . well, I didn't know . . . I didn't see nobody there.'

Seeing how badly affected Jimmy was, Tom quietened him. 'So, you found Alice at the cottage?'

'Yes, at the cottage. She was on the ground outside . . . she weren't moving. I thought she was a goner, Tom. I really thought she was . . .'

Openly sobbing, and greatly relieved that he had got her to safety, Jimmy started gabbling. 'The window was all broken . . . there were pieces of glass lying outside. Alice was all mixed up in it.' He took a deep breath. 'Oh, Tom, I don't understand . . . why was she all tied up like that? Will she die, Tom . . . will she?' And then he went all to pieces again.

'Hey!' With Nancy now tending to Alice, Tom held Jimmy still. 'Ssh now, Jimmy, you need to tell me. Where's Frank? *Did you see Frank?*'

Still in shock and sweating profusely, Jimmy wiped the flat of his big hands across his face, while he made an effort to concentrate. 'Frank?'

'*Think*, Jimmy! Did you see Frank?'

'Yes . . . I did.' The memory of Frank creeping along by the spinney loomed large in his mind. 'He wasn't at the cottage.'

'Where was he then?'

Jimmy shook his head.

'Concentrate, Jimmy. When you saw Frank, where was he? Was he safe? Had he been attacked? Jimmy! Where did you see Frank?'

Jimmy knew. 'He was near the spinney; he was heading for the rise.'

He paused, a terrible memory coursing through his troubled mind, of that night when he saw Joe and Alice in the barn. One thought led to another. 'Oh, Tom! Was it Frank who hurt her? Did he find out what they did in the barn? Oh, Tom! I never told that I'd seen Alice with him . . . I never told no one!'

He grew angry. 'He's not a good man like you and Joe. Frank hurt me too. If Joe hadn't stopped him, he would have killed me for sure!'

'Jimmy!' Thankful that Nancy was too busy with Alice to have heard what Jimmy had said, Tom grabbed him by the shoulders and drew him away, his voice little more than a whisper as he asked Jimmy, 'What did you mean just now, when you said you'd seen Alice in the barn. *Who* was she with? What exactly did you see, Jimmy?'

Thinking he would get the blame, Jimmy clammed up. 'I never saw nothing!' And beyond that he would not be drawn.

Realising this was not the time, Tom decided not to push him any further; though he was anxious about what Jimmy had let slip. Who was Alice in the barn with? It couldn't be Frank, or Jimmy would not be so nervous. Joe's name sprang to mind, but he could not let himself believe he and Alice could do such a thing.

He tried to reason it through. Joe had saved the falcon, and Alice was fascinated with the bird, so that must have been what Jimmy saw; Joe and Alice, in the barn, and it was as innocent as Alice taking an interest in how the falcon was doing.

Or was he just trying to cover up the truth, he asked himself. Was it really something unthinkable? Enough to send Frank over the edge?

Realising he may have let slip too much, Jimmy was pleading. 'I never saw nothing!' He was frantic. 'Nothing at all!'

Tom decided now wasn't the time to press the matter. All he knew was that he desperately needed to find his two sons. 'Jimmy, listen to me! You said you saw Frank at the spinney, and you think he was heading up to the rise. Have I got that right?'

'Yes . . . he was hunting rabbits . . . making his way up to Joe.'

'He was hunting rabbits, you say?'

'Yes!'

Tom's heart sank. 'Think hard, Jimmy!' Placing his hands on either side of Jimmy's shoulders, Tom turned his head so that he was looking straight at him. In a harsh whisper, he asked, 'Did Frank have a shotgun with him? I need to know! *Could you see if he had a shotgun?*'

Jimmy nodded, 'O'course! He was hunting for rabbits, that's why.'

In the middle of tending to Alice's battered body, Nancy turned to look at Tom, and she saw her own dark thoughts echoed in Tom's face.

They were both thinking the same: of how Frank had a destructive streak in him. They were each recalling all those years ago, when Frank had hurt that little boy.

And now Alice had been trussed up with ropes in exactly the same way.

There was no doubt in their mind that Frank had done this to her.

Tom was fearful that Frank had learned of what Jimmy saw, and that he was out there now, armed with a shotgun, and headed straight for Joe.

Intent on helping Alice, Nancy cut away the remnants of the bathrobe; at the same time trying to maintain Alice's modesty by means of a sheet.

Behind her, Tom was quietly addressing Jimmy. 'Listen to me, Jimmy, I don't want you telling Nancy what you told me, about what you saw in the barn . . . you and me, we can talk about that later. Okay? Nancy must not be worried about all that. Do you know what I'm saying, Jimmy? *Nancy must not be told!*'

Jimmy promised, 'I won't tell, 'cause I don't know nothing!'

Tom nodded. 'Good! Now then, Jimmy, I have to go and find Frank. I want you to stay here with Alice and Nancy. Will you do that for me?'

'All right, Tom. I'll do that.'

'Right!' Tom gave him strict instructions. 'After I've gone, you're to lock all the doors and don't open them, not to anyone at all unless you see the ambulance outside. Do you understand what I'm saying?'

'Yes.' Jimmy lowered his voice to a whisper, 'Will you tell me something, Tom?'

'Go on. I'm listening.'

'Did Frank hurt Alice, like he hurt me?'

Tom's silence was answer enough.

Shocked and afraid, Jimmy leaned against the chair, then he sat down, and stared at the floor, thinking back to when he saw Joe and Alice coming out of the barn. He was glad he hadn't told anyone about that, because if he had, then he'd be the one they blamed.

'Jimmy!' Tom shook him. 'Don't let me down! I'm counting on you to look after the women.'

'I will!'

'All right, but listen, Jimmy! Keep all the doors locked until the ambulance comes. Oh, and try to get in touch with Alice's parents. Can you do that for me?'

Jimmy assured him, 'Don't worry.' But it soon went out of his mind.

'And now I need you to do something else for me.' Tom did not want Nancy to know what he was planning.

Jimmy was eager to help. 'All right, what d'you want me to do?'

Tom answered in a whisper, so as not to alert Nancy, 'Get Carter out of the stable,' he said. 'Saddle him up, and I'll be out directly.'

Jimmy was horrified. 'But, Tom, you haven't ridden him since . . .' he glanced down at Tom's gammy leg, '. . . since . . .'

Tom gave Jimmy a gentle push towards the door. 'Go on. Quick as you can!' He then glanced at Nancy, bent over Alice and doing whatever she could to help her.

Nancy looked up to see him watching her. 'I'm so worried, Tom,' she told him sadly. 'She's in a terrible state. Was it . . . *him*, Tom? Did *he* do this to her?'

Tom went to wrap his arms about her. 'We'll soon know,' he said. 'I'll see to it, don't you worry, love. You take care of Alice. I'll be as quick as I can.'

Fearing the worst, Nancy kissed her beloved husband. 'Be careful.' Nodding, Tom prompted Nancy, 'Jimmy will ring the Jacobs soon as he can. You see to Alice. She's the important one.'

As he turned to leave, Nancy glanced through the half-open doorway. When she saw Jimmy lead the horse out of the stable, she was frantic. Knowing she could not leave Alice, she called out to him, 'No, Tom! You were lucky not to have lost your life the last time he threw you! You said he was crazed! You swore never to ride him again . . .

that you'd only keep him because he was an old friend. I won't let you ride him . . . I won't!'

Determined, Tom yelled back, 'This is an emergency, Nancy! Frank has one vehicle and Joe has the other. If I go on foot, I'll never make it up to the rise, not with this gammy leg, and you know as well as I do there's more at stake here than me riding an old horse.'

Nancy knew that what he said was the truth, but it did nothing to ease her fears for his safety.

Tom understood and ran back to reassure her. 'Look, Nancy love. What happened that day maybe it wasn't Carter's fault. Something could have frightened him. I don't believe Carter has an ounce of nastiness in him. He carried me backwards and forwards over these fields for nigh on twenty years. He would never have reared and kicked out like that, if he hadn't been startled by something like an adder in the grass, I don't know what it was.' He knew it was Carter's fault and that he had proved to be unpredictable but he didn't want to worry her.

He turned away. 'All I do know is that I have to get to the boys as fast as I can!'

Nancy knew he was right. 'Go on then, Tom. Stay safe.'

'I will!'

While Nancy watched over Alice, Jimmy had to give Tom a leg-up, though once he was in the saddle and had hold of the reins, Tom was at home again. 'Old habits die hard, eh, Jimmy?'

Jimmy watched him ride away. 'Don't forget to lock all the doors!' Tom called as he headed towards the spinney.

With Tom gone, Jimmy ran frantically round checking all the doors and windows, while Nancy persevered with Alice, keeping her as comfortable as was possible, and tenderly talking to her, while trying to hide her deep shock at the extent of her brutal injuries.

When Nancy had cut the last of the ropes, she could

see where they had worked through, laying open the skin beneath. 'Oh, Alice love, whatever made him do this to you?'

Visions of that little boy haunted Nancy's mind. This was the same pattern of cruelty; though what he had done to Alice was much more vicious.

Frank had trussed the boy up so tight the ropes had split his skin in two places; while Alice had been subjected to an avalanche of terrible and barbaric treatment. Her lovely hair was butchered and torn. From what Nancy could see, Alice's tormentor had shown her no mercy. Quickly now, with the wounds accessible, Nancy went to the kitchen and brought back a bowl of warm water and a flannel.

She tested the water before dipping the flannel in. 'Jimmy, see if you can find the salt, will you? Oh, and a spoon.'

A moment later, Jimmy returned with the packet of salt; the tiniest measure of which Nancy stirred into the water.

With the greatest of care, she applied the warm solution to the gaping wounds on Alice's body.

It broke her heart to see how Alice's lovely hair seemed to have been hacked to the roots in places, 'Just like the falcon.' Hot, blinding tears flowed down her face. 'Alice's beautiful hair . . . torn away.'

She saw how Jimmy was nervously pacing the floor. 'Jimmy?'

'Yes, Nancy?'

Nancy discreetly wiped away her tears. 'I think it might be a good idea if you were to watch for the ambulance from the window.'

'All right, yes.'

A few moments later and much to Nancy's relief, the unmistakable sound of bells shattered the air. 'They're here!' Jimmy's excited voice rang through the house.

Having treated Alice's injuries as best she knew how, Nancy went quickly upstairs, returning a few minutes later with a clean sheet and a blanket, both of which she lovingly swathed about Alice; the sheet first, which would not stick to the wounds, and then the blanket for warmth. 'Got to keep you warm, child,' she murmured. 'You don't need pneumonia, on top of everything else.'

Suddenly, Alice stirred and Nancy grew excited. 'Alice! Alice, love?' But Alice appeared to have slumped unconscious again. 'They've come to help you, dear.' Nancy persevered. 'You're going to the Infirmary. You'll be well taken care of now.'

The burly ambulance men made their way into the sitting room. After swiftly assessing the situation, and taking a short statement from Nancy, they were in no doubt about the seriousness of Alice's condition. The stretcher was brought, and Alice was tenderly secured on to it.

Once Alice was on the stretcher, she opened her eyes, to look straight at Nancy. 'Ssh, child!' Nancy could see how Alice was desperately trying to tell her something. 'It's all right. You must save your strength for now. We'll talk later . . .' But Alice would not be calmed, and when she tried to reach out, Nancy took hold of her hand. Leaning down she felt her voice breaking. 'Don't try talking, sweetheart,' she pleaded softly, 'you're on your way to hospital. Everything will be all right now,' she assured her. 'Me and Tom will follow on.'

When she tried to draw away, Alice held on to her. 'What is it that can't wait for you to tell me?' She leaned closer. 'All right, I'm listening now. So, what are you trying to say?'

Alice had the words in her head, but she couldn't seem to get them out. '*My* . . . fault.'

Nancy shook her head. 'No, no! You could never have done anything to warrant this!'

When Nancy leaned closer, Alice whispered in her ear, 'Me . . . and . . . Joe.' Tears ran down her cheeks. 'Help . . . Joe.' Her mind was in chaos. She was back there, launching herself at the window again and again, and when it buckled beneath the onslaught, she felt herself falling, and then nothing but Nancy's soothing voice in her ear.

Alice wanted to tell her everything, but now she didn't even have the strength to speak. All she knew was that Frank had hurt her, and that Joe was in danger, and she wanted to tell them it was her fault. She needed them to save Joe.

'I'm sorry! We must get her to the Infirmary!' Already moving with her towards the door, the ambulance man was anxious. 'We have to go now.' He added as he went, 'You do understand, the police will need a full statement.'

Nancy nodded, but she could tell them very little, for she knew nothing of the events leading up to this nightmare.

As they carried Alice out, Nancy assured her, 'We'll find Joe. Me and Tom will be following on to the Infirmary. Meantime, I've got a few calls to make, and I need to be sure Tom is safe. You're in good hands. We'll be with you, quick as we can.'

Jimmy stood beside her as she watched them leave. 'Will she die, Nancy?' Jimmy was so afraid.

Nancy told him she would be well taken care of. 'I should have gone with her.' She ran forward, waving her hands, but the driver didn't see her. 'What was I thinking, I should be with her.'

'They'll look after Alice,' Jimmy assured her. 'Besides, Tom needs you to wait, and you have calls to make.'

He suddenly remembered. 'Oh, Tom asked me to call Alice's parents! I forgot. I'm sorry Nancy. I forgot.'

Like Nancy, Jimmy was fearful that once Tom caught up with his sons, anything could happen. All else had slipped his mind.

Felling guilty and ashamed, Nancy was torn between going after Alice, or waiting to see if her husband and sons would return safely. 'I can only wait,' she decided. 'But I must call Alice's parents. I'm so afraid,' Nancy muttered aloud. 'I have to wait for Tom.'

She promised herself that Alice was in good hands now, while out there, Tom was searching for his sons, one of whom had a shotgun. It did not bear thinking about.

She reassured herself that she was doing the right thing waiting for Tom. Her every instinct told her, this terrible situation was not yet over.

'I tell you what, Jimmy,' she said. 'Why don't you go and make us both a nice cuppa tea, eh? It'll calm our nerves. While you're doing that, I'll ring Alice's parents but not go into too many details. I'll just tell them she's hurt bad and on her way to hospital. I'm hopeful they'll go straight there.'

Three times Nancy tried the Jacobs' number, and each time there was no reply. 'Where the devil is she? Out with that daughter of hers, I'll be bound!' She replaced the receiver, then picked it up and tried again. 'Jimmy!' she called out. 'Jimmy, I need you to go over to the Jacobs'. If you don't find them at home, leave this note.' She scribbled a message and handed it to him.

Jimmy groaned. 'Tom said I was to stay here and look after you.'

'Never mind about that. Do as I ask, there's a good man,' Nancy cajoled. 'Once you've done that, you can go after Tom, while I keep trying to reach the Jacobs on the phone.'

Still grumbling, Jimmy set off at a run, leaving Nancy frantically dialling their number. 'I should have gone with her,' she muttered to herself, 'I should have gone with her.'

Realising she needed another plan, Nancy's thoughts turned to Mandy. Flicking through the book beside the telephone, she opened the page, picked up the receiver and began to dial.

The telephone rang at the other end for what seemed like an age, before Mandy's mother answered. 'Oh, Jean, it's me Nancy. Listen Jean, I haven't got time to go into detail, but Alice has been taken to the Infirmary, and I wondered if there's any way you could get Mandy to sit with her until me and Tom get there. No, we don't know how it happened, but I have to tell you, she's in a bad way.'

She listened for a moment. 'Yes, it is very worrying. No, it's not anything broken as such, at least not that you can see, but she's taken a terrible beating . . . shocking! And I can't seem to get hold of the Jacobs. Look, I have to go, Jean. Tom will be here any minute and I need to be ready. Oh, thank you, yes, I'd appreciate that.'

After replacing the receiver, Nancy stood a moment, her head bowed in prayer. 'Please, Lord keep Alice safe, and bring my men home safe and well.' But she had a bad feeling, and try as she might, she could not relax.

'I'd best go and get myself ready. As soon as Tom's back, we'll be away,' Nancy muttered to herself as she made the sign of the cross. 'Keep them safe Lord. Keep them all safe.'

As she made her way upstairs, Nancy continued, 'First the falcon, then Alice, and now Tom's out there searching for the boys.' She had to ask the question, 'Why did Frank take the shotgun and when did he get a hold of it?' One thought led to another. There's no reason why Frank should be stalking Joe. What's happened between them? What's made him so mad?

Nancy had not fully understood what Alice meant, but having spent time in the barn while Joe was tending the falcon, Alice had obviously seen the bond between Joe and the bird. Maybe somehow, Alice had heard about the falcon being attacked, and she was concerned that it would upset Joe?

Not knowing what Alice was so desperate to tell her and with all manner of suspicions running through her mind, Nancy was clutching at straws.

The shocking things that were happening seemed to draw her back to Frank's turbulent childhood. Creatures that were brought home by Joe, damaged and in pain. How was it that he always managed to find them like that?

She reminded herself how Frank had been such a secretive, moody boy; envying every little thing his younger brother had in his life. Even though right from birth, the two boys had always been loved and treated the very same, Frank seemed to have always resented his brother.

And what about the matter of the falcon? It was Joe who found the injured falcon. He loved it, tended it, and if it had survived, Joe would have launched it to the skies, and freedom.

Reluctantly, Nancy was forced to ask herself. Was it Frank who had attacked and destroyed that poor bird? And what about Alice? What bad thing had happened to cause all this pain and suffering? Was Frank to blame?

Her motherly instinct recoiled at the idea that her own son could actually do the terrible things that had been done to Alice. And yet, the more she thought about it, the more she feared that Frank might be deeply involved.

There were too many coincidences, she reasoned. Too much of the past repeating itself. If her suspicions were right, what could have happened to raise such evil in her own son? And how was it possible that two brothers could turn out to be so different when the same blood flowed through their veins?

With these disturbing thoughts churning over in her mind, and her husband Tom out there determined to confront Frank, Nancy could not rest easy.

~

At that very moment, high on the ridge, Tom was about to witness a scene he never in his life thought to see.

Having dismounted the horse before the going got more difficult, Tom left Carter to simply meander about in search of fresh green grass.

It had been a while since Tom had climbed this far away from the house, and he took a moment to catch his breath.

'I'm feeling my age,' he muttered under his breath, 'I reckon I'm ready for the knacker's yard!'

Stretching to ease his back, he looked eagerly about; what he saw galvanised him with fear. A short distance away, partly hidden by the sparse shrubbery, Frank stood a short distance from his brother, his shotgun trained at Joe's heart.

'*Oh, dear God!*' Tom took off, sliding and stumbling as he went, but at that moment he felt as though he had the strength of ten men. 'FRANK! PUT THE GUN DOWN, SON. THINK WHAT YOU'RE DOING. THIS ISN'T THE WAY!'

'Go back! Don't you come any nearer!' Taken unawares, Frank eyed Tom warily, but kept the shotgun trained at his brother's heart.

Joe had also been startled by his father's appearance. 'Go back, Dad. Leave it to me and Frank.' He was ready for that split second when Frank might lose concentration, which would allow him to make a move on him. But it would not be easy. Frank had backed him into a dangerous situation. With the deep gully below him, and the shotgun aimed at his heart, there was no safe place to go.

Closing in, Tom kept calling out, desperate to calm Frank. 'It's all right, Frank!' he shouted, 'Whatever it is, we'll sort it out between us. Listen to me, Frank . . . put down the shotgun!'

Unable to keep his balance on the craggy ground, Tom tripped and fell in his haste, while constantly pleading with Frank as he came nearer. 'Have sense, man! Whatever it is, it can't be so bad you'd want to shoot your brother, and what about your poor wife, eh? What in God's name were you thinking to do that to her?'

Turning to Joe in disgust, Frank snarled, 'Did you hear that? My poor wife.' Keeping the shotgun levelled at Joe, he laughed, a soft, evil sound that only served to confirm Joe's suspicions, that his brother had finally lost his mind.

'D'you want to tell him, Joe? D'you want to tell him why I had to punish her . . . why I can't bear to look at her?' His smile deepening, he found a measure of comfort in telling Joe what he'd done. 'I promise, you wouldn't want her now, Joe. No man will ever want her again!'

Frank thought of how he'd left Alice bruised and battered, bathed in her own blood, and half-scalped. He didn't care. He had no compassion, no regrets, and it really hurt him to think she had somehow got the better of him.

'So! The bitch got away did she? I should have finished her off when I had the chance. I should have made sure she got everything she deserved!'

A darker mood settled over him. 'I can see I'll have to do it proper next time!'

Joe was shocked to the core. 'You crazy bastard! What have you done to her?' Out the corner of his eye he could see Tom hurrying his way towards them. 'Stay back, Dad!'

His immediate instinct was to leap at Frank and tear his head off, but he knew he would have to be careful, or both he and his father would pay the price. He had to bide his time, and hope Frank might drop his guard for that one, split second, and he would have him!

For now though, Alice was uppermost in his mind. 'What did you do to her, Frank!' His fists clenched by his sides, he demanded, 'What the hell is wrong with you? What did you do to Alice?'

Frank was silent for a moment, then he gave a kind of smirk. 'She's craftier than I thought,' he muttered, as though talking to himself. 'Witch! I was sure she'd be dead by the time I got back.'

At the sound of Tom's voice pleading with him to put down the gun; he swung round. 'You'd best not try anything . . . either of you.' He looked from one to the other. 'I won't hesitate to kill the pair of you if I have to!' He instructed Tom to come closer where he could keep an eye on him.

Tom had no choice but to do as he was told, so he moved closer to Joe, stopping only when Frank was satisfied that they were near enough for him to keep a wary eye on them, yet far enough apart so they couldn't rush him together.

Joe was desperate. 'Where's Alice, Dad? What did he do to her?'

Tom continued to reason with Frank. 'Listen to me, son,' he said quietly. 'You've done a bad thing, but thankfully you haven't killed anybody. If you put the gun down and come back to the farmhouse, I promise we'll do what we can to help you.'

When it seemed as though Frank was listening, Tom made the mistake of moving forward. But he quickly halted when Frank yelled at him. 'Stay where you are, or

Joe will go first . . . then you! And don't think I'm bluffing!'

'I don't think that, son. I know you're angry, but I don't understand what all this is about. Talk to me, Frank. Why are you doing this? You're only making matters worse. Look!' Stretching out his arm, he asked calmly, 'Give me the shotgun, son. Come home with me.'

Frank ignored his plea. 'Where's the bitch now?'

'She's in a shocking state, Frank.'

'I said . . . where is she?'

'Safe in hospital, I hope.'

The colour drained from Joe's face. 'Hospital?' He turned to Frank. 'You'd best shoot me now, Frank, because the first chance I get, I'll make you pay for this. I'll kill you, Frank, I swear, I'll kill you for this!'

Tom looked from one son to the other. 'This is not the way, Joe,' he warned quietly. 'Alice will be all right. She took a beating, but God willing, she'll be fine.'

The last thing he wanted was for Joe to learn the truth of how deeply Alice had suffered, and how when Jimmy brought her home in his arms, they had feared the worst.

With clenched fists, Joe glared at Frank, and spoke in a quiet, trembling voice. 'It's me you want to hurt, not Alice! It was me who did the wrong, but oh, I forget! Even as a kid, you preferred to hurt those who couldn't fight back. That's right isn't it, Frank. You were a bully then, and you're a bully now!'

'Shut it!' Frank aimed the gun at Joe's head.

'Leave it, Joe!' Tom saw the pure evil in Frank's eyes and for one terrible moment he really thought he would pull the trigger.

Joe took a chance. 'I've always known about the bad things you did, Frank. I know how cruel you can be, and how you always pick on them that can't fight back. I know how much you enjoy inflicting pain on others. Like that little boy you tied up and nearly choked to death; or the animals you maimed and killed over the years. You were even jealous of Mum and Dad's little dog. I always knew you'd killed it, Frank. Deep down I think they knew it too. You were a sadistic bully when we were kids, and nothing changes, does it, eh?'

'Don't goad him, Joe.' Tom looked up at Joe, and the younger man was devastated to see how his father had suddenly grown old. 'I'm sorry, Dad,' he told him.

Tom smiled, but it was a sad smile. 'I knew,' he said sadly, 'I always knew.'

Seeing his father defeated like that, Joe's rage welled up inside him. 'Come on then! What are you waiting for? If you want an apology for what me and Alice did, you'll wait forever! So, you beat her up, did you . . . put her in hospital, you cowardly bastard? Well, come on, big boy, man to man, you and me! I'll take you on right now! Let's see if you can beat *me* up like you beat her up. Let's see who's the better man, eh? Or are you too much of a coward to give me the punishment I deserve, eh?'

Frank merely smiled, in that sly, knowing way Joe knew so well. 'Oh, you'll get your punishment all right. First though I need you to tell Dad what you and Alice did to me. I need him to know that the trollop deserved everything she got, and that it won't be over until I've pulled this trigger!'

Joe changed tack. 'Alice is no trollop, Frank. She made a mistake in promising to marry you, but it was more your fault than hers. You saw the land and the opportunities that came with the package and you bamboozled her. The truth is, Alice was too young to know her own mind. She was unsure and didn't want to hurt your feelings. I took advantage of that, so in the end, we're *both* cowards! You and me, Frank, we're blood brothers, made out of the same mould. Alice made a mistake and I took advantage of it, so in a way that makes me almost as bad as you. But there is a difference. I was weak; I did a selfish thing, whereas you deliberately target the weak. You hurt them just for the pleasure of it. You're sick, Frank. You need help.'

Incensed by the truth in Joe's words, Frank screeched, 'TELL HIM WHAT YOU DID!'

Tom was both shocked and saddened. He knew Joe had feelings for his brother's wife, but he had hoped his suspicions were unfounded. Now though, he knew different. But he had to calm Frank. He had to make him lose concentration; he had to save the situation if he could and to his mind there was only one way.

In a quiet, shaking voice, he spoke to Frank, '*You* tell me, Frank! I need to hear it from *you*. What could be so terrible that you should want to hurt Alice like that? What makes you so intent on murdering your brother, *and me;* because make no mistake, if you pull that trigger on Joe, you'll have to kill me too.'

He took a moment to look at Frank, deep down into that dark, wickedness that he and Nancy had somehow bred, and he made a vow there and then. 'I mean every word I say, Frank. Kill Joe, and I swear before God, I'll send you back to hell!'

Because of the manner in which he spoke, with anger and shame, no one doubted his word.

Tom fervently believed that whatever the provocation, nothing in this world should make a man do the terrible things that Frank had done to Alice. 'You say you're here to punish Joe . . . *kill* him even. So, what is so mountainous and unforgiveable that you should do these terrible things. I want to hear it from *you*, Frank, so why won't you tell me?'

Frank snapped back, 'Because *he's* the one, him and that bitch! All right, you want to know the details, well I'll tell you . . .'

In a rage, he confirmed what Tom had already feared.

'That bastard took my woman before I did!'

Out of control, Frank waved the shotgun haphazardly before eventually training it back on Joe. His voice quivered as he went on, 'They stood at the altar like two innocents! They stood alongside me, as though nothing had happened. *Can you believe that?* They stood there: he gave the ring and she gave her vows. Like it didn't matter what they'd done before. Like *I* didn't matter!'

Consumed with rage, he warned Tom in a cold voice, 'They deserve to die! If you try and stop me, you'll pay the price. Don't forget, I've got nothing to lose.'

In a last ditch effort to calm him, Tom asked, 'How do you know they did these things? Who told you that? Think what you're saying, Frank. This is a bad thing; how can you be so sure of it?'

'Oh, I'm sure,' Frank snarled. 'The trollop told me herself!'

He turned on Joe. 'You thought you'd been clever, didn't you, eh? You thought I wouldn't find out about you and her . . . fornicating behind my back . . . laughing at me! Making a fool out of me!'

'It wasn't like that, Frank!'

Joe needed to convince his brother that he had not meant it to happen. 'I'd already planned to leave,' he revealed. 'I know what we did was wrong, and so does Alice, but it's *you* she married. It's *you* she wants. She told me that herself, Frank. You have to believe me . . .'

'Liars, the pair of you! I knew there was something . . . but she wouldn't admit it at first. But I knew, and in the end I got it out of her. She didn't want to tell me, but I *made* her!'

Keeping a wary eye on Tom, he took a step closer to Joe, his manner much calmer. 'I'm not sorry for what I did to her,' he growled. 'The bitch got what she deserved . . .' his finger curled round the trigger. 'It's your turn now, Joe.' When he looked Joe in the eye, there was madness in his smile, his voice a mere whisper. 'I hope you rot in hell!

'No!' As Tom lunged forward the ear-splitting crack of gunfire echoed across the valley; Tom saw Joe's chest burst open and he felt the blood splash on his face. Joe was falling before his eyes, ever downwards, arms out and a look of shock on his face as he seemed to float in slow motion to the gully floor, where he settled against the boulders, his face up towards the skies; his body broken.

'Dear God above!' Deeply shocked, Tom threw himself at Frank, punching and screaming. 'You've killed him, you mad bastard!' As the reality consumed him, he could hardly breathe. *'I should have smothered you at birth!'*

Throwing him aside, Frank held him in his gunsights. 'I could pull this trigger and it would all be over for you,' he said, 'but I've decided that would be too easy. Leaving you *alive* would be the best punishment of all. That way, you can spend the rest of your life remembering what your son and that bitch did to me. You'll blame yourself for not being able to save your precious Joe, and every minute for the rest of your life, you'll see him, lying down there, looking up at you. And the guilt will drive you crazy.'

Too dazed to think straight, Tom sobbed helplessly. 'What in God's name have you done?' Torn apart by what he had witnessed, he pleaded, 'Don't leave him, Frank . . . help me get him up . . . there might still be a chance . . .'

Tom never saw it coming. Without warning and with all his might, Frank swung the butt-end of the shotgun. When the older man slumped like a felled ox at his feet, Frank simply turned, spat on the ground, and walked away.

Nancy was frantic.

She was rushing about, collecting what she thought Alice might need: nightclothes, toiletries, a scarf for her head. Though she was mindful of the state Alice was in, and how it might be some time before she was strong again.

She couldn't shake the terrible image of Alice's damaged face from her mind, and though somewhere deep inside she knew it was Frank who had done it, she prayed like never before, that she might be wrong. How could she ever again want to look on her eldest son's face, if it turned out to be his doing after all?

She was sick with worry about Tom, and ran to the top of the landing. 'Jimmy!' She peered over the bannisters, 'Look again, will you?' she called down. 'Is there any sign of him yet?'

Jimmy gave the same answer, 'Not yet, no.' He rushed outside to scour the horizon again.

On his way back in, the telephone was ringing. 'Answer it, Jimmy!' Nancy called down. 'See who it is!'

Gingerly, he collected the receiver into his bulky fist. 'Hello, who is it please?'

Holding it away from his ear, he waited for the caller to speak. 'Oh, Mandy, yes all right, I'll go and fetch her.'

Nancy was already hurrying across the room to take up the conversation. 'Hello, Mandy, what's wrong, love?' She feared the worst.

When Nancy replaced the receiver it was to tell Jimmy that she had to go to the hospital immediately.

'Is it Alice?' Jimmy was frantic. 'What's happened?'

Ignoring Jimmy, Nancy made for the telephone. Quickly dialling the number, Nancy waited a moment. 'This is Nancy Arnold. I need a taxi now, please . . . yes, right away.' She gave her address, together with the destination, 'Bedford hospital, and it's very urgent!'

Within minutes, carrying her coat and a heavy bag, she was pacing up and down at the front gate. 'It's all right, Alice, love. I'm on my way.'

She was anxious about Tom but she knew she couldn't wait any longer.

She thought it alarming how in the space of a single day, her whole life and that of her family had been turned upside down.

In a surprisingly short time the taxi arrived. 'Don't forget what I said, Jimmy.' Nancy reminded him as she climbed into the back seat. 'Go and find Tom. See if everything's all right. Tell him Alice is asking for me. Tell him I waited as long as I could, and now he'll just have to follow on as best he can.'

'Don't you worry, Nancy,' Jimmy reassured her, 'I'll find him, and I'll be sure to tell him what you said, and I'll keep trying the Jacobs' number.'

Before locking the doors behind him, he stood and waved as the taxi carried her off, down the lane and out of sight. 'Find Tom,' he muttered over and over as he ran across the fields. 'Find Tom!'

With fear in his chest like a clenched fist, he ran down to the brook, where he then followed it for a distance, before heading up towards the rise.

At first he went at some speed, eager to find Tom, worried about Joe, and remembering what had happened to Alice.

As the way grew more difficult, he slowed down, calling as he went, 'Tom! Where are you?'

He stopped awhile to take a breather, then he set off at a brisker pace. When the frightened horse came careering wildly down the bank towards him, he almost lost his footing. 'Carter!' His heart skipped a beat. 'Where's Tom? Have you thrown 'im off, is that what you've done? Oh, you bad creature!'

He shouted out loud. 'Tom, where are you?' His voice echoed through the hills and died away. There was no response, no sound, other than the heightening breeze whipping through the valley.

He glanced back; Carter had skidded to a halt, and was now grazing quietly on the fields. 'Carter . . . here!' He gave a long, soft whistle, the like of which Tom used to call Carter in from the fields. 'Let's go and find Tom, eh?'

In answer, the horse violently threw his head back and began scraping the ground with his hoof. 'Woah, woah boy!' As Jimmy started towards it, the horse became increasingly nervous, loudly whinnying and ready to take flight.

'Easy, boy . . . easy.' Jimmy was convinced that something bad must have happened to scare him like that.

'I can see you've got no stomach for going back up there eh.' He spoke calmly. 'You stay here then,' he said. 'Don't go anywhere, Carter! Stay right here!' He had a feeling that one way or another, he might need that faithful old horse.

Continuing on his way, he had a bad feeling. Something's wrong, he thought to himself. Where's Tom? Did he find Frank? Something's gone wrong, I know it! And where's Joe?

Knowing Frank better than most, he knew he could not rule out anything.

When he got to the top of the rise, Jimmy looked this way and that, searching for Tom, hoping to catch sight of the brothers, but there was no one in sight.

Cupping his hands about his mouth, he shouted to the elements, 'Tom . . . where are you?'

Nothing.

Again, 'Tom! . . . Joe!'

Nothing.

As he quickened his steps, he realised that the

misshapen bundle on the ground before him was Tom.

For one agonising moment he recalled his horror at finding Alice and now, on seeing Tom, his first instinct was to turn and run; to let someone else deal with it, and he was ashamed at such a cowardly thought.

He now inched forward, sickened by what he found. Tom's face and head were caked in blood, and he wasn't moving.

'Don't let him be dead. Please don't let him be dead.' Unsure what to do, he continued to stare down at Tom, his eyes big as saucers, his mind in chaos.

He noted how Tom was lying, very still, face up, and to Jimmy's mind, he was already gone from this world. 'It was *him*, wasn't it, Tom?' He muttered to himself, 'Frank's the only one I know who's capable of such a thing. Oh, but what sort of cowardly man is he to do this to his own father?'

He fell to his knees. 'I'm sorry, Tom. He's your son I know, but he's an evil man. I've always said he were dangerous. I tried to tell you what he was like but you wouldn't listen. *Nobody ever listened!*'

Gathering Tom into his arms, he began to quietly sob. Suddenly Tom opened his eyes and whispered brokenly, 'Help me . . .'

'Tom!' Jimmy was laughing and crying all at the same time. 'God! You gave me such a fright.'

Aware of how fragile the older man was, Jimmy asked, 'What shall I do, Tom?' With extraordinary tenderness, he slid his two arms round Tom's plump body, shifting him into a more comfortable position. 'I thought you were dead, Tom . . . I really thought you were dead! You're too heavy for me to carry all the way down the valley, so shall we wait together and hope they send someone to look for us? Or shall I go back and raise the alarm? I don't want to leave you here, Tom, but even if we tried our damnedest, I don't reckon you'd ever make it down, not the way you are. Besides, if I moved you . . . put you upon Carter, I might do you a damage.'

Partly veiled by blood, the extensive wound on the side of Tom's head was shocking to see. 'You need help badly, Tom. So, will you be all right if I leave you here while I fetch help?'

Finding it hard to concentrate his mind, Tom was genuinely terrified that Frank might come back to finish the job. He tried to tell Jimmy this, but his throat felt strangled and he couldn't get the words out.

Fearing that Tom would actually consider making an attempt at the arduous journey back, Jimmy had to be brutally honest. 'You'll do yourself in if you try and make it down,' he told him. 'It's difficult enough for a healthy man, never mind someone who's badly injured. Don't even think of it, Tom,' he urged. 'You'll never make it!' Even as he spoke, Tom's breathing had grown increasingly laboured.

Like Jimmy, Tom realised he would never make it down the high banks. There was no strength in his body, and with every minute that passed, he felt as though he was drifting further away. And the thought of Joe lying down in the gully, was like a knife through his heart.

When he accepted Jimmy's argument with a small nod of the head, Jimmy gave a sigh of relief. 'You'll have to trust me, Tom,' he said. 'I won't let you down, you know that.'

He leaned closer. 'I'll be back in no time,' he confided, 'I'll fetch help . . . I will! Ripping off his jacket he placed it over Tom, 'Meantime, you need to keep warm.

'Carter's waiting at the bottom . . . he'll take me the rest of the way.'

He saw the whimsical little smile on Tom's lips, and he knew what he was thinking . . . that Jimmy had not sat astride a horse since he was catapulted off the previous summer. Having sailed through the air he ended up in a hawthorn hedge; bruising both his pride and his rear end.

Tom was desperate. He needed to let Jimmy know about Joe, but as the minutes ticked away, he felt himself sinking fast. Fearing his time had come, he was determined to hold on, aware that Joe depended on him.

Taking a minute to make Tom more comfortable, Jimmy showed his anger. 'Frank did this, didn't he? And what about Joe . . . where's Joe?'

In reply, all Tom could do was slowly move his hand on the ground. Pointing his finger towards the edge of the rise, he summoned every last ounce of strength. 'Joe.' He needed Jimmy to know that Joe had been shot, and was lying at the foot of the gully.

It wasn't the mumbled name that alerted Jimmy. It was the look in Tom's eyes, and the determined manner with which Tom was twitching his finger, as though pointing to something. 'What is it, Tom?'

'*Joe*.' Exhausted, Tom fell back, his sorry gaze trained on Jimmy, as though willing him to understand.

It took a moment for Jimmy to realise what Tom was trying to tell him. He clambered up. 'What, Tom? Is Joe down there in the gully?'

Relieved that Jimmy understood, Tom gave the whisper of a smile; then safe in the knowledge that Jimmy would find Joe, he closed his eyes and sank into the darkness.

Jimmy ran to the edge and looked down into the gully. 'Oh, my God! Joe!' He screamed out Joe's name, but Joe was long past hearing.

Running back, Jimmy was disturbed to see how the older man looked pale as death. 'Don't you die on me, old man!'

On touching Tom's hand he was shaken by how cold

it was. 'Must keep you warm,' he mumbled. 'Must keep you warm!'

Swaddling the coat tighter about Tom, Jimmy kept talking. 'I'm going now, Tom, but I'll be back . . . d'you hear me, Tom Arnold! I'll be back, for you and Joe . . . I promise!'

Tom made no response. In his deep subconscious, all he could see was Joe broken and battered, lying in that deep gully.

Somewhere inside he blamed himself, and the guilt was tenfold. Just as Frank had promised.

Skidding and tumbling down the high banks, Jimmy found Carter where he had left him. 'Come on, boy . . . we have to get help quick. Don't you let me down now!'

He approached the horse softly. 'Don't fight me, boy, I won't hurt you,' Jimmy lightly coaxed him. 'I don't relish the idea of climbing on to your back, but we have to get help. We need to trust each other; you have to go like the wind. Don't do it for me! Do it for Tom . . . and Joe,'

Jimmy continued talking real soft, until he was close enough to stroke Carter's face. 'Tom's always taken care of you, so now it's your turn to help him.'

With great caution he climbed on to Carter's back, and for one frightening moment Jimmy was certain the horse would bolt and throw him off.

Somehow though, the old horse appeared to sense that Tom was hurt and needed help, and when Jimmy gently put his heels into his soft fleshy sides, Carter went off at a trot, then he was cantering, and when they got to the straight he took off like the wind.

With Carter galloping at high speed towards the village, Jimmy urged him on. 'Come on, Carter! Keep going! We're nearly there, boy!'

As they neared the village, Jimmy's mind was in chaos.

From start to finish, this was the worst day of his sorry life.

From what he had seen, he had to believe there was no hope for Joe. But Tom was still alive, and that was enough to drive him on.

'Faster, Carter . . . C'mon!'

Tapping his feet against the horse's plump belly, he yelled into the wind, 'Faster, boy . . . Faster!'

And as always, the faithful old horse gave everything he'd got.

PART THREE

~

July 1952

Turned Away

CHAPTER EIGHT

A LICE WAS ANXIOUS.
She had waited for this day for so long, and now that it was here, she was afraid and alone, unsure of her future.

After eight long weeks in hospital she had been told she would be allowed home. And now she had to ask herself where home was.

Impatient, she had already packed the canvas bag that her father had brought the day before. The contents consisted of two nighties, a hand-held mirror, a draw-string bag of toiletries, a pair of slippers and a hair-brush.

The absence of her mother and sister throughout her time at the hospital had not really surprised Alice, but her father had visited as often as he could, as had her grand-parents. On one occasion, her father brought her an incredibly soft and expensive hairbrush. 'The shop assistant said it would gently massage your scalp,' he explained, kissing her awkwardly on the forehead.

Her father was clearly ashamed and embarrassed at how Frank had contacted the newspapers with his deceitful version of what happened, to try to save his own neck. Consequently, the story was reported in newspapers far and wide, together with a graphic and twisted description of the sordid reason behind his merciless attack on his family. Frank had slyly twisted the truth to try to gain public sympathy.

In spite of a wide-scale operation by police to track Frank down, they had not yet been successful in rooting him out.

'Ah, so here we are then, all packed and ready to go!' Big in heart, body and voice, Nurse O'Conner's claim to fame was that she had actually kissed the blarney stone and two days later found the man of her dreams. Sadly, a year later he ran off with the Avon lady.

'So, me darlin'!' Bustling about in that familiar manner Alice had come to know so well, she asked, 'Ye'll be going home, to that fine father of yours, will ye?' Lifting Alice into the chair, she wagged a finger. 'Didn't I tell you I would pack the bag? You couldn't wait, could ye, eh?'

Alice apologised. 'Sorry.'

'Ah, sure it's all right. Take no notice o' me. I'm in a bit of a cranky mood this morning.'

She made Alice comfortable in the chair. 'Sure, ye know what I'm like when I sleep too long. Only I took a wee dram last night . . . just celebrating like ye do. Y'see, I don't normally take the drink, only me brother was staying with me. He's an awful bad influence so he is!'

She giggled. 'Hey! Ye should have seen Sister's face when I turned up half an hour late. It was like the day of judgment I'm telling ye!'

Having told the tale, Nurse O'Conner promptly broke another rule by seating herself on the edge of the bed. 'Now then, me darlin', where's your little friend this morning? What's her name, Mandy, yes, that's it: stocky little creature with a big smile.'

'Mandy said she'll come and see me once I'm home,' Alice replied. 'Mind you, I'm not really sure whether my mother is happy about taking me in. Father says she's pleased to have me, but I don't know about that.' She gave a wry little smile, 'You do know, she hasn't been to see me, not even once?'

'Ah sure, I'm well aware of that!' Nurse O'Conner tutted. 'If ye don't mind me saying, I can't understand your mother. I know she has not set foot in this hospital, not to give a hug nor comfort of any kind. What kind of a mother is that, if ye don't mind me saying?

'I could never turn me back on a daughter of mine. I'd be worried out of me mind, so I would. I mean, just look at the sorry state ye were in when they brought ye here. Sure we didn't even know if you'd survive the night let alone two months.'

She assured Alice, 'If I was yer mammy, I'd have moved heaven and earth to be with ye, so I would!'

Alice had come to accept Nurse O'Conner's outspoken manner. It was part of her reliable, no-nonsense nature. She loved people and was passionate about everything, and to Alice that was a fine thing.

Nurse O'Conner suddenly stopped short. 'Will ye listen to me . . . calling your mammy as though I had a right!' She tutted loudly. 'I've got a big gob so I have. Sure one day somebody will try and shut me up and there'll be an almighty fight so there will!' She clenched her fist and punched the air.

Alice laughed out loud. 'They would never do that,' she said. 'You're too well loved by everybody, and I for one don't know what I would have done without you giving me a lecture when I felt sorry for myself, and threatening to abandon me when I threw a tantrum. You've been more than a nurse to me. You've been a good friend . . . someone I could talk to in confidence.'

Nurse O'Conner brushed aside her comments. 'Ah, sure that what I'm here for,' she declared with a broad smile, 'I have to keep you lot in line, so I do!'

Alice recalled how she had woken from a long, dark

sleep to see that rosy, round face smiling down on her.
'You were there for me, right from the beginning,' she
told her now. 'You were there when I closed my eyes and
then again when I woke up.'

Nurse O'Conner laughed out loud. 'Will ye stop now!
Ye make it sound like I *haunted* ye!'

Having monitored Alice throughout her ordeal, she had
come to know and like her. She witnessed the fear when
the nightmares took hold, and she felt her pain when she
cried out in the night; often calling for Joe, the man she
clearly loved.

She asked again, 'Yer father's coming to collect ye, isn't
that what ye said?'

Alice nodded. 'That's what he told me, yes.'

'Will your mammy be with him d'ye think?'

Alice shook her head. 'I don't think so. She's too embarrassed and angry.' She looked up. 'You do know what I
did, don't you?' she asked in a shamed whisper. 'Before
Frank and I were married, I slept with his brother Joe. So
now everyone knows I'm a trollop of the worst kind.'

The nurse shook her head. 'All they know is what they
read in the papers, which half the time is a lot of lies and
old rubbish . . .'

Alice interrupted, 'No! It's true!' She could not deny it.
'It's *all* true, every word of it.' The awful knowledge of
what she had done was like a weight on her soul, and yet
the one single thing that warmed her heart and kept her
going through the darkest hours was the memory of being
in Joe's arms.

Even now after all that had happened, she truly believed,
that was where she belonged.

When the tears pricked her eyes, she turned away. 'I
did a terrible thing,' she murmured as though to herself,
'. . . a shameful, unforgiveable thing, and I deserved what
Frank did to me.'

'Don't say that, child!' Nurse O'Conner was shocked. 'The things he did to you, were cruel beyond belief... *barbaric*, that's what it was! Oh, and look how he attacked his own father and brother.' Making the sign of the cross she added softly, 'It's a mercy no lives were lost; though it's a terrible state of affairs all the same.'

Alice had spent every waking moment thinking of Joe, praying with all her might that he was okay and that Frank had not done what she feared he would.

When she learned from her father that Joe had been seriously injured, and was lying in the intensive care unit at a specialist hospital, she was devastated but thankful that he was alive.

Spurred on by the news Alice had been determined to regain her strength as soon as possible. The idea of seeing Joe again had kept her spirits up and made her determined to recover.

Joe was the reason she was so thankful to be leaving now.

Nurse O'Conner was still chattering on, 'I don't mind telling you, when they find Frank Arnold, they should hang him by the neck, and be done with it.'

'Nurse O'Conner!' Sister Maitland's voice cut through the air. 'Have you forgotten where you are!' Hurrying up the ward was a small, wiry person with piercing green eyes and an air of authority. 'What are you doing, sitting on the bed like that? Explain yourself!'

'Oh! Sister Maitland!' Horrified, Nurse O'Conner leapt off the bed. 'I was ... er ... I was just ... er checking the bed.'

'Oh? So you were checking the bed, were you?' This was not the first time Sister Maitland had cause to discipline Nurse O'Conner, and from her experience it surely would not be the last. 'And might I ask, *why* you were checking the bed?'

Alice discreetly interrupted. 'It's my fault, Sister,' she apologised, 'I felt uncomfortable through the night and Nurse O'Conner wondered if there was a lump in the mattress or something.'

'Oh, I see!' Giving Nurse O'Conner a wary glance, she said, 'So, did you manage to find this lump?'

'No, Sister! Not yet I haven't, but I'll keep at it so I will.'

'Somehow, I don't think that would be advisable.' Sister Maitland was on to her. 'I think it might be safer to leave the matter there.' It was a veiled but definite warning all the same, prompting Nurse O'Conner to quickly shut her mouth and leap to attention.

Addressing Alice in a softer tone, Sister Maitland asked, 'So then, Alice, you're all ready to leave are you?'

'Yes, Sister.'

'And you'll be going home to your parents, will you?'

Alice nodded. 'Yes, Sister.'

'Will you be wanting transport arranged? You're still quite weak, and not back to full health, my dear. You must remember to treat yourself kindly and rest often. It will take time for you to feel anything like your old self.' She glanced at Alice's medical notes. 'Follow the guidelines, oh and don't forget to keep your hospital appointment. That's very important!'

'Yes, Sister. Thank you, I will.' In answer to the older woman's question she explained, 'I won't need transport though; my father is collecting me.'

'That's good! Well, the doctor is on his rounds as we speak. It'll be a while before he gets to you, so maybe if Nurse O'Conner is not too preoccupied with the lump in the mattress, she might get you a nice hot cup of tea while you wait.'

'Ah sure, I can do that, Sister. I'm away at the double so I am.'

'And while you're at it, Nurse O'Conner, please observe

the rules of this hospital; one of which is that you do not sit on the patient's bed! Rules are put in place for very good reasons, and I will thank you to remember that!'

'Yes, Sister, I'll remember that, so I will!'

Looking from one to the other, Sister Maitland again addressed Nurse O'Conner. 'By the way, there is one more thing you should consider . . .'

'Yes, Sister?'

'Contrary to what you nurses imagine, I am not as gullible as you might like to think.'

Knowing exactly what she meant, Nurse O'Conner chose to act the innocent. 'I'm sorry, Sister, but I don't think such a thing!'

'Enough of that! What I'm saying is this: I have eyes and ears and I rarely miss a trick.' Narrowing her eyes, she asked meaningfully, 'I hope you understand what I'm saying, Nurse O'Conner?'

'Yes, Sister, I'm sure I do.'

'Good!' Striding briskly away, she had the whisper of a smile on her face.

There was no doubt in her mind that Nurse O'Conner would think twice before breaching the rules again.

~

It was an hour later when Doctor Edwards arrived at Alice's bedside. A tall, lanky figure of a man, he had Sister Maitland at his side. 'Sorry for the delay,' he told Alice, who had been growing increasingly anxious. 'It's been a busy morning.'

Collecting Alice's notes from the foot of the bed, he stood, head bent, as he read them. 'Mmm,' he kept saying, 'mmm . . . yes. How are we feeling today, Alice?' When she was brought in he thought he had rarely encountered such shocking injuries.

Now though, after extensive treatment and tender care, Alice had come through her ordeal, not entirely unscathed or completely healed in body and mind, but she was at least stronger in spirit and looking more like the lovely girl she had evidently been before.

'I'm feeling much better in myself, doctor.' Alice had been seriously depressed by her appearance when she was first able to see into a mirror. Back then, her confidence had been at rock bottom, and even today her injuries were still painfully evident.

'I'm ready to go home,' she said bravely.

'And are you feeling able to face the outside world?'

Alice took a moment to think about that. Her physical scars were visible but fading fast, and her scalp was almost healed.

When she was first admitted, they had to shave her head in order to treat the deep wounds. Now her long tresses were gone, but her hair had grown into a strong, elfin-like cap, which, according to Nurse O'Conner suited her well.

'If I'm not ready now, I never will be,' Alice replied.

His question was the one she had asked herself time and again, ever since she was told she might soon be discharged. She had not found the answer then, and she did not have the answer now. All she knew was that she had to leave the security of this place and confront whatever waited for her on the outside. 'I really am feeling much stronger now,' she informed him confidently.

In truth though, after two months in the care of medical staff, and a kindly psychologist who had brought her through the worst of her nightmares, Alice was desperately afraid of what life held for her out there.

'Yes, I'm ready now!' She was adamant. 'It's time to step out into the big wide world.'

He nodded his approval. 'Sister Maitland tells me your father is on his way to take you home?'

'He is, yes.'

Alice read the discreet glance exchanged between him and Sister Maitland. 'I know my mother hasn't visited,' she assured them lamely, 'but she's a very busy lady. I'm sure she'll be with my father when he comes for me.'

'You may feel stronger now, Alice, but you must not push yourself in any way. No heavy work or getting into heated situations of any kind. You're bound to be vulnerable and shaky for a time. You've been here with us for two months, and you've had a strong support team about you. When you leave here it will take all your courage and strength to pick up your life again,' the doctor told her carefully.

'I do understand that, doctor, and I *will* take care,' she promised. 'I can't deny I'm feeling a bit shaky, and I'm a little concerned as to how I'll cope, but I will do it!'

She knew the only way to get on with her life was to face it head on. 'I'm so grateful to you all for everything,' she said.

The doctor smiled warmly. 'It's what we do, Alice.'

For more pertinent reasons, he felt the need to re-assure her. 'After a long stay in hospital, it's only natural to feel suddenly alone and abandoned, so I'm here to reassure you that if you're worried about anything, anything at all, there are people here who can help.'

He could not help but wonder if her return home would be as straightforward as she might expect.

Alice also had her doubts, but for very different reasons. 'I'm sure I'll manage.' She had no choice.

The doctor turned to the nurse. 'Draw the curtains please, and go about your other duties. Sister and I will tie everything up here, thank you.'

With a discreet little wink at Alice, the nurse closed the curtains and left the room.

It took a while for him to check the many wounds, sustained by the vicious assault on her body.

On the whole the doctor was delighted that they were healing well. Most of the scars were faded now, although some were more distinct than others.

A few minutes later, having checked her blood pressure, lungs and heart, he assured Alice, 'The wounds have healed well, and most of the scars are all but gone. As for the injuries to your scalp, I'm delighted to say that at long last, the hair is beginning to grow on those deeper-wounded areas. Given time, I'm confident that you really will get back your full head of hair.'

When the doctor then glanced up at Sister Maitland, and she gave a curt little nod, Alice started to panic. 'There's something else, isn't there?' She looked nervously from one to the other, 'What is it, doctor . . . what's wrong?'

The doctor addressed her in quieter tones. 'As you know, we did a series of tests when you first arrived here . . . all very usual, all necessary in order to carry out our work.'

He again exchanged a discreet glance with Sister Maitland, before going on in a gentle tone, 'Alice, you should know that during the more recent routine tests I have discovered something else.'

'What is it? What's wrong with me?'

'Well . . . having carried out the usual tests prior to you leaving us, I decided on an extra test, and . . .' he hesitated. Acutely aware of Alice's background and unsure as to how she would take it, he simply and quietly announced, 'It appears you're pregnant, Alice.'

Alice felt the blood drain from her face. Staring from him to the Sister, she realised what he was saying, and yet she could not take it in. Pregnant! No! It wasn't true. How could it be? Raising her head, she looked again at the doctor, then at Sister Maitland, and now she was crying, not loudly, not intently, but silently, the tears rolling down her face.

Sister Maitland was quickly beside her. 'Alice, it's all right,' she kept saying, 'It's all right!' She suspected that Alice was thinking how could she keep a child whose father had tortured her within an inch of her life and left her for dead?

Alice heard the Sister's voice, but it wasn't all right. It was unthinkable! 'Are you sure?' she heard herself whispering the question. 'How can you be so sure? You might be wrong, doctor. Please . . . tell me you're wrong.'

She heard his answer and it struck her to the heart. 'The tests don't lie, Alice. You're two months' pregnant . . . give or take a few days.'

Leaning forward he placed his hand over hers in a gesture of sympathy. 'There is something else you need to know,' he told her.

Alice had hardly taken in the news of her being pregnant, and now she was fearful of the news he was about to impart. In her dazed frame of mind, she truly believed it could not be worse than the news he had already given her.

Silently, she waited, until he began quietly, 'As far as we can tell, you appear to be carrying twins.'

All Alice could hear in her head, was the devastating news that she had *two* babies growing inside her. Two babies, and she had no idea whether Joe or Frank was the father.

It was too much to take in all at once, and so she closed her mind to anything else he had to say. Feeling as though she might pass out, she took deep breaths to steady herself.

The doctor gently explained how the pregnancy appeared to be moving along as well as expected, but that they would need to monitor her regularly, and she must take care of herself.

'I must leave you now,' he apologised. 'Sister Maitland

will bring you some leaflets and other necessities to take away with you.'

As he stepped away, Alice called him back. 'Please, doctor, don't tell anyone else about this,' she pleaded. 'Especially not my family.' She thought of Tom and was grateful that he too, was recovering well.

'If that's what you want, then I shall respect your wishes,' he answered. 'Although I hope you might be sensible enough to confide in them.'

Alice looked away.

~

The doctor called Sister Maitland aside. 'She's taken the news badly,' he whispered. 'Moreover, she's asked me not to divulge the news to anyone, but of course I never would.'

Sister Maitland understood. 'I think if I was in her shoes, I might feel exactly the same.' She glanced back at Alice, who was listlessly staring out the window.

'Poor thing,' Sister Maitland murmured. 'No one should ever have to go through what she's been through. Yes we all know she made a mistake, but she's paying dearly for it. She's been defiled in all the papers; tortured and left for dead by her husband, who's still on the run from the police. As for the brother . . . Joe isn't it? From what we know, he could still die. If he does, then there's no doubt she'll be pilloried for that as well.'

Shaking her head forlornly, Sister Maitland lowered her voice even further. 'On top of all that, she now finds herself two months' pregnant!'

'She's proven herself to be a strong young woman,' the doctor reminded her. 'There are many women out there who would love to be told they're pregnant . . . even carrying twins. Alice will cope.' He was sure of it. 'From where I stand, that young woman is a true survivor.'

Sister Maitland was not so certain. She looked at Alice, noting the wide, frightened eyes and the frantic manner in which she was twisting her hands together, and all she saw was a lost soul.

It was all too much to deal with; especially for one so young. The last thing Alice needed was to lay herself open to more punishment; from the press, the public, and possibly more so, from the women in her own family.

Sister Maitland had been trained not to get emotionally involved, and that was how it should be. A true survivor, the doctor had said.

'Very well, doctor.' Sister Maitland sealed her approval with tight lips and a curt nod of the head. 'You're right of course. Alice has already proven herself to be a survivor, and I'm hopeful that she will learn to cope with the news she's been given.'

Secretly, the doctor was also a little worried. 'Maybe you could have a word with her?' he asked discreetly. 'Try and put her mind at rest?'

Sister Maitland explained, 'First, I have an urgent call to make. But after that, I have every intention of popping back to have another chat with her.'

'Good!' Satisfied, the doctor turned on his heel and went smartly away.

With Alice strong in her mind, Sister Maitland went away in the opposite direction to tend to her duties.

The moment the two of them were out of sight, Alice picked up her bag and crept carefully through the ward. Her body was still very weak but she had to get out of the hospital. Afraid now to go to her parents' house, she needed to get away before her father arrived! How could she tell him that she was carrying twins . . . that she didn't even know who the father was? And if they were to find out, her mother and sister would taunt her mercilessly.

Her mind was playing tricks on her. Who was the father?

One night she was with Joe, and another she was with Frank. As far as she knew, she could have been made pregnant by either brother.

After all that had happened, it was a devastating situation to be in.

She couldn't stop thinking about the babies, already growing inside her. It was a lonely, cruel world they would be coming into. When they were old enough to ask questions, what would she tell them?

Should she confess how she had slept with two brothers; one her new husband, the other his brother, and all in the space of a few days? The shame was hers, not theirs, yet one day they would learn the truth and pay the price.

Unless she got right away from this part of the world, they would always suffer hostility from those around them. They would be derided and scorned; pointed out in the street as though they were lepers. There would be no peace for them anywhere. Children at school would taunt them mercilessly.

No! However much she tried to protect the children, she would not be able to, because everyone would be asking the same questions that she was asking herself now. Who did they belong to? Who was their father?

Parents would tell their children that Alice Jacobs was a tramp, and the slander could penetrate the minds of her own children. Because of that, they could end up hating her, and rightly so.

Could she bring the children into a world of pain like that? What was she going to do?

Somehow, when she had got her thoughts together and before the pregnancy went on much longer, she must find a place where she could hide away, somewhere she could think clearly.

But where would she go? She had nothing but the handful of belongings in that canvas bag, and because of the heartache she had caused them, she would rather die than ask her family or the Arnolds for anything.

Of course she could always turn to her friend, Mandy. Even then, it would be a selfish thing to throw herself on the mercy of her one and only true friend.

During the many times Mandy had been to see her, not once had she mentioned the reports in the newspapers, or questioned Alice about the truth of it all. Instead she had sat and comforted her, and wisely talked of mundane things, always reminding Alice that she was there for her, if needed.

But deep down, Alice felt unable to turn to even her closest friend.

Should she get rid of the pregnancy as soon as possible? Oh, but what a wicked sin that would be. Dear God, who could she confide in? Who could she trust? Who would help her decide what to do?

She thought of Joe and suddenly felt a burning desire to find him, to be close to him but, blinking back tears she knew bitterly that she couldn't. Not now.

Hurrying away from the building, she was deeply conscious that many people were looking at her as she stumbled across the car park, blinded by tears and oblivious to the fact that she was weaving dangerously in and out of oncoming vehicles.

Ronald Jacobs was turning into the car park when he almost mowed her down as she ran across his path. 'For God's sake . . . *Alice*!' Safely bringing the Jaguar to a halt, he leapt out and went after her.

After a few minutes of frantically searching, he found her huddled on a bench, rocking herself back and forth. 'Alice! Whatever's wrong? What are you doing out here?'

When he sat down beside her, she fell, exhausted, into his arms. 'I'm sorry, father, I just had to get out.'

'What's wrong, child?' He held her tight. 'Has someone

said something to upset you?' He knew from recent experience how cruel people could be; even those who should know better.

Alice looked up at him, her face swollen from crying. 'I can't go with you, Father,' she said. 'Please . . . leave me alone. Just go!'

'I shall do no such thing!' He was amazed. 'I don't understand. Does the doctor know you're out here like this? Weren't you supposed to undergo a final examination before being discharged?' When she gave no answer, he gently shook her.

Alice discreetly brushed away her tears, 'It's all right. The doctor saw me.'

'And?' Sometimes he felt out of his depth.

'He said everything was fine.'

'In that case, why are you so upset?'

'I don't know. I suppose I'm just so relieved to be out of there.' She could not tell him the real reason.

Having seen the state she was in when he found her, Ronald said adamantly, 'As for leaving you here, you know I would never do that, Alice. I want you home with me, and besides . . . where would you go? You need plenty of rest and good food, and a place where you can feel safe, where someone will make sure you're taking care of yourself.' He drew his arms around her carefully. 'You're coming home with me, and that's an end to it.'

Mentally and physically drained, Alice did not have the strength to argue. Maybe for now the best thing might well be to go home with her father. If she could bear the company of her mother and sister for as long as it took to arrange more satisfactory lodgings, then she would take up her father's offer and be grateful.

With two months already gone, time was of the essence. Alice knew she would need to make a decision, sooner rather than later, on the matter of her pregnancy. Her heart told her she could never have the pregnancy terminated. Her head said she must.

For now, her mind was all over the place.

The night before she had finally dropped into a fitful slumber where Frank filled her dreams with horror. This morning, she had woken in a sweat, fearful that she was about to leave her safe haven. She was filled with dread at the thought of returning home, where no doubt her sister and mother would make her life difficult.

And now, the daunting news that she was pregnant with twins was like a bombshell. All she could think of was to keep running and it would all go away. But it didn't and it never would; not unless she made some painful and harsh decisions.

The day had started off badly, and now, feeling unbelievably weary, she was on her way home with a dark feeling of dread in the pit of her stomach.

One thing she remained strong about however, was that *no one* must know she was pregnant. Not her father, and not her mother, and especially not her sister Pauline.

She reminded herself that it would not be too long before she began to show. Once that happened, the outside world would know. And the vicious gossip would start all over again.

Accepting that she had little choice, she reluctantly conceded. 'All right, Father,' she smiled up at him; a tired little smile that touched his heart. 'Let's go home, eh?'

'Good girl! Firstly, I need to let them know you're leaving.'

Collecting her canvas bag he walked her to the car, his arm taking her weight as she leaned heavily on him.

Knowing Alice better than most people, he was concerned that she had not told him everything.

Later, when she was rested and the two of them were alone in the house, he fully intended to discover the truth of it.

While helping her into the car, Ronald was shocked at how feather-light she was. 'You need fattening up, my girl!' he chided. 'You need some good, healthy meals.'

He left her there, safe and warm, to return and explain how he was taking her home. Fortunately Nurse O'Conner was easily found and he returned in a few minutes.

On the way back to the house, he continued to make a fuss of her, and in spite of her fears, Alice was grateful for his genuine concern.

It occurred to her how her father would be sickened if he knew the absolute truth about Joe, and that night, and the news that she was two months' pregnant.

'What happened, Alice?' He was pressing the question yet again. 'Why were you running from the hospital? Did someone recognise you . . . did they taunt you with what they'd read in the newspapers?'

Strangers had taunted *him*, and the rest of the family. That was why his wife and daughter Pauline were so loath to visit Alice.

Last night he had warned them both. Alice was coming home, whether they liked it or not!

'No one taunted me, Father,' Alice answered. 'I just felt as though I couldn't breathe in the hospital. I had to get out, that's all, but I'll be all right once I'm home, you'll see. I'll be able to think straight, without doctors and nurses constantly fussing round me.'

'I hope so, Alice.' For some odd reason, he did not altogether believe her excuse.

She asked after Tom. 'I'm glad you let me know about Tom,' she said. 'Did you tell him I was sorry about what happened to him?'

'Of course I did. I told him we were *all* sorry.'

'How is he?'

'He's well enough,' her father told her. 'Thankfully, his wounds are now completely recovered.' He thought it best not to mention the fact that Tom had barely spoken a word since the attack and Nancy was sick with worry.

Desperate for information, she asked, 'What about Joe? How is he?'

'The last time I heard, he was in the intensive care unit.'

'Oh.' For a moment Alice lapsed into silence, as did Ronald.

Eventually, Alice spoke. 'Father?'

'Yes, child?'

'Do you blame Joe, for what happened?'

'If it's all right with you, sweetheart, I would rather not discuss it.' His hope was that she might leave all those dreadful memories behind and start afresh. She was still recovering from her injuries, both mental and physical. Yet she was young and her self esteem would return. In time, God willing, she might well carve out a life for herself.

It would take time though, and much courage; and shocking though it may be, she was still married to Frank Arnold.

The lawyer had warned, 'Closing the marriage will not be straightforward. It seems the wheels of justice turn slowly.' Which in layman's terms meant it would cost a great deal of money. But Ronald Jacobs was a man of means, and if he could rid his daughter of that crazed monster, then it would be worth every penny.

Alice persisted. 'So you *do* blame Joe, don't you?' His long silence told her as much.

'I did not say that!'

'It wasn't all his fault,' she was emphatic. 'I'm just as much to blame.'

'Water under the bridge, Alice. Best to let it be, don't you think?'

She persisted, 'Where did they take Joe?'

'I don't know.' Although Ronald knew of Joe's whereabouts, he had no intention of telling her. '*No one* knows!

Except the family of course, and they're not likely to tell *us*, are they? They seem to be keeping themselves to themselves.'

Something in his tone made her suspicious. 'You would tell me if you knew, wouldn't you Father?'

'Of course . . . if I believed it was in your own interest.' He was not usually so evasive, but on this occasion he thought it for the best.

'You *do* know! Please tell me, Father. Where is he? I must see him! I need to know that he's all right.'

'Enough, Alice. The subject is over!'

'Please, Father, it's important I see him.'

Growing increasingly uncomfortable by her persistent questions, Ronald brought the conversation to an end. 'Because of the press and such, the family have kept his whereabouts a closely guarded secret. If they had wanted you to know, they would have told you, so now let it be! No more questions. All anyone knows is that Joe's injuries warranted him being moved for specialist treatment.'

'What . . . in London, you mean?'

'Alice, what did I just say? I will not have you tormenting yourself. I'm unable to tell you where Joe is, so it's no good you asking me.'

'But London is where these specialist places are, isn't that right?'

'I have no idea! Look here, Alice, isn't it enough for you to know that Joe is being well taken care of? What you should realise is you need taking care of! I didn't want to bring this up, but you have to remember that cowardly swine who nearly killed you is still at large.'

'I know that, Father, but I'm more worried about Joe!'

Frustrated, Ronald swung the car into the kerbside and brought it to a halt. Wrenching on the handbrake, he addressed her sternly. 'And *I* am more worried about you! Listen to me, Alice! I'm sure Joe is safe enough. He has his own family to worry about him. It's you I'm concerned about. I'm quite sure wherever he is, Joe is being well taken care of. Now, as far as I'm concerned, that's an end to it!'

Alice knew when her father meant what he said.

She would need to use other means in order to locate Joe's whereabouts.

A moment later they were back on the road and an uncomfortable silence filled the car until Alice broke it.

'Why did Mother and Pauline never come to see me?'

For a long moment Ronald gave no answer. Then he reached out to take hold of her hand in a comforting manner. 'They were wrong not to come and see you,' he conceded angrily. 'The thing is, Alice, these past months, it has been very difficult for them . . .'

'For *all* of us!' Alice was not sympathetic.

Returning his attention to the road, he went on. 'People have not been too kind to our family. Apparently, your mother and sister have been made to endure much abuse from strangers.'

Alice wondered if they'd exaggerated in order to gain her father's sympathy. 'And of course they blame me, is that it? The thing is, father . . . if they didn't think enough of me to visit, how come Mother is allowing me into her home?'

'It's *your* home too, Alice. And mine!'

Alice strongly believed there had been trouble about her returning to the family fold. 'I won't live in a war-zone, father,' she remarked worriedly. 'I would rather find myself a place to stay . . .' Not the cottage, she thought, it was filled with bad memories.

Ronald interrupted, 'Out of the question, child! And besides, there's no need for that. Your mother and I had a long talk only yesterday, and she's absolutely fine about having you home.'

He gave a smug little smile. 'I have news by the way.'
'What?'

'My news is about your sister, Pauline.'

'Oh, Mother's bought her another salon has she?' Alice was not prepared for what she was about to hear.

'No need,' he confided. 'Pauline has gone one better than that.' He gave a little laugh. 'Would you believe, she's got herself married? She never told us . . . just went off and did it in a hurry.'

Alice was amazed. 'She always said she would rather die than have some man spending her money and lording it over her.'

'Ah, but this man is different. He's a wealthy man in his own right. They met at a business convention and when they got chatting, she learned he was the proud owner of some of the finest hairdressers' in the business. After that, she seemed intent on keeping hold of him.'

Alice listened, but said little. Suddenly, the strain of the day was taking its toll on her.

Ronald explained, 'His name is Tony Jackson. He has a fancy place in the suburbs of London, As far as I can tell, they seem made for each other.

'At least she's getting a life together.' Alice felt despondent.

'One day, you'll get your life together again. And you will, Alice. It might not seem like it now, but mark my words, there *will* come a day when all this heartache and pain is well and truly behind you.'

Alice was sorely tempted to confide in him about the pregnancy; but she decided this was not the time. Besides, if she went for the option of ending the pregnancy, it would be for the best if he never knew the truth.

Strangely enough, she felt guilty at the idea of denying him what he obviously desired . . . to be a grandfather.

On the other hand, he might well be right; that the day

would come when she would finally get her life together. If and when that day came, there might even be a chance for her to provide him with grandchildren.

For the briefest moment she allowed herself to believe that her future and Joe's lay together.

But then she reminded herself of how it was pointless hoping for anything; especially when their lives were in tatters.

You may wish all you like, she thought sadly, but in the end, Fate will be the one to decide the outcome.

'Tired are you, sweetheart?'

'A little.' In truth she felt as though she could sleep forever.

Ronald was concerned at how quiet she was, and how in these past few minutes she had slid down into her seat, her eyes closed and her face deathly pale.

'Let's get you home, eh?' he said gently. 'A hot drink, and maybe a little to eat, then it's straight off to bed for you my girl!' Not for the first time he wondered if they had discharged her from hospital before she was truly well enough. 'Perhaps they should have kept you in for another week or so,' he remarked. 'At least until you were much stronger.'

Alice was no longer listening. Her mind and heart was with Joe. Would she ever see him again, she wondered. And if she did, would he want to know her after all the pain and heartache she had caused?

'Alice?'

'Yes, Father?'

'Are you all right?'

'Yes, Father.'

'A few more minutes and we'll be home.'

He hesitated, before revealing the news. 'I forgot to mention, your sister and her new husband may well be there. It seems Pauline can't wait to introduce you to him.

Is that all right with you, Alice? If not, we can sidetrack them for now . . . I can easily smuggle you in the back way and straight up to your room. I'll tell them you were too tired and that you'll meet up later. Shall I do that?'

'No, it's all right, Father.' Alice could imagine how smug and satisfied Pauline would be, and it was not something she looked forward to. On the other hand, she remembered what her father had told her, about Pauline and Mother having been snubbed and humiliated because of her.

Alice felt as though she owed the family, and meeting Pauline's husband might well prove to be the opportunity to build bridges. Besides, it was only polite to meet this Tony Jackson. After all, he was Pauline's husband, and part of the family.

She hoped he might succeed where everyone else had failed.

'No need for the cloak and dagger stuff,' she smiled at him, 'No, I think I'd like to meet the man that has made Pauline go soft!'

Ronald had to chuckle. He understood her remark; in fact he actually agreed with her.

These past difficult weeks he had witnessed both harsh words and bitchiness from Pauline and his wife.

But his greatest nightmare was the fact that Frank Arnold was still loose out there somewhere. He had proven himself to be seriously unhinged, without a shred of compassion or mercy. There was no denying he had reason to want revenge, but he had crossed the line, and having failed to exact the ultimate revenge on Alice, was he hellbent on finishing the job, at whatever cost?

It was a frightening prospect, and one that had haunted Ronald's every waking moment.

Thankfully Alice had pulled through; but her deep affection for Joe Arnold was a constant and worrying issue. It had already come close to taking three lives.

By the grace of God, Alice and Tom Arnold had survived.

Joe's extensive injuries on the other hand were still very much life-threatening.

He glanced at Alice now, his heart turning at the frailty of her. She had always been such a naturally joyful girl, with a passion for everything simple, everything in nature.

With his youngest daughter, what you saw, was what you got.

Today though, she was different; more like a river, running fast and clear on the surface, but underneath, in the shadows, there lived all manner of turbulence.

She was frighteningly vulnerable, and he knew from the way she spoke of Joe, that she needed protecting against herself.

To that end, he had already decided that he would have to keep Alice and Joe apart by whatever means possible.

~

'Well, here we are, home again, my love.'

Thankful to have her back, Ronald swung the Jaguar into the drive of the big old house. He then got out, and rounded the car to help her out. 'Take it easy,' he said, when she stumbled. He caught her to him. 'You mustn't forget you've been in hospital for the best part of two months. It'll take a time to get your strength back.'

'I'm fine, Father . . . stop fussing!' Alice was deeply nervous about coming back to the family fold. 'I don't want Mother thinking I can't take care of myself.'

'You're not fine!' Ronald knew she was deliberately putting on a brave face. Her long silences on the way here were a real source of concern to him. 'I really needed to speak with the doctor. No matter! I'll make an appointment to see him in the week.'

Alice began to panic. 'Why would you want to see him?'

she asked. 'I already told you . . . he was obviously satisfied with my state of health, or he would never have let me leave. Besides, you saw him yesterday and he told you exactly the same, didn't he?'

'Well, yes, but . . .'

'Well there you are. So, don't go wasting the doctor's time.' Alice knew only too well how persuasive her father could be. The last thing she needed was for him to bombard the doctor with questions.

Once inside the porch, Ronald called out, 'Maureen!'

When there was no answer, he reached into his jacket pocket for his house key. He was about to put it into the lock when suddenly the front door was flung open and there stood Pauline.

'Ah! So, the prodigal daughter, returns?' She stepped back, into the shadows. 'Come in, why don't you?'

Alice and her father went through to the drawing room, and there, standing to attention beside the fireplace, was her mother, looking regal and sour-faced as ever. 'Well, Alice, here you are, back home again. When you got married to that Arnold fellow I really thought you had left this house for good. Apparently I was wrong, wasn't I?'

'Maureen!' Ronald cut in. His stern face was a clear warning. 'Your daughter has just been discharged from hospital. Have you nothing more encouraging to say to her?'

Maureen Jacobs was a proven expert at hiding her true feelings, so now she put on a smile, and spoke with a softer voice. 'Why of course, Ronald dear. I was only thinking of Alice, and how she would prefer that none of this business had ever happened. I didn't mean anything harsh.'

She stepped forward stiffly to plant a fleeting kiss on Alice's forehead. 'I'm well aware of our responsibilities, Alice. So you really mustn't fret. I know you must feel very guilty about what happened, but I'm sure the whole shocking business was not altogether your fault.'

Her implication was well disguised, but Alice was not fooled.

And now it was her sister Pauline's turn to pile on the sweetness. 'Alice, this is Tony . . . my husband.' She drew him forward.

Tony Jackson was a man who looked to be in his mid-thirties, with fine dark hair scraped back, and the air of a businessman about his stocky person. 'We're almost a whole month married,' she smirked, 'and deliriously happy.'

She turned to him. 'Isn't that so, darling?'

Sliding an arm around her shoulders, he was obviously embarrassed. 'If you say so, my dear. As you know, I would have preferred a big wedding for you, but you swept me off my feet, and now you're the best thing that ever happened to me.'

Pauline's smile stiffened. 'Really Tony, you are such a tease.'

Ronald quickly interrupted. 'Look, Maureen, poor Alice is worn out. She needs to rest. Here, take this . . .' Handing his wife the canvas bag, he explained, 'I wonder if I could leave Alice in your capable hands, my dear? Tony and I have this important issue to thrash out.'

Maureen was none too pleased. 'Can't it wait? I had planned on getting my hair done. It's all arranged. They won't take kindly to me breaking an appointment.'

'What? Not even when your daughter is straight out of hospital? I'm sure they wouldn't mind at all.'

'How long will you be?'

'A few minutes . . . ten at the most. It's just a matter of tying up a few loose ends, but time is of the essence, and it needs to be done sooner, rather than later.'

Having heard her mother's whining protests and excuses, Alice was deeply uncomfortable. 'It's all right,' she interrupted. 'I don't need looking after. I'm well enough to be discharged from hospital, so I'm well enough to take care of myself.'

She looked from one to the other. 'The last thing I want is to interfere with your routine. Please just go about your business as always. I really am capable of looking after myself.' In fact, she was beginning to wish that she was back at the hospital.

Ronald proudly smiled. 'Independent as ever, eh? Well, I'm sorry, child, but you're going to be looked after, whether you like it or not.'

Addressing his wife, he told her, 'I shall leave you to it, my dear. Make sure Alice doesn't do anything too strenuous. She's still very weak. When I get back, we can maybe discuss taking on a nurse part-time . . . kill two birds with one stone so to speak. The nurse can keep an eye on Alice, which will leave you free to do whatever it is that you do.'

He gave a sigh. 'I don't know why I didn't think of it before . . .' In truth, he had foolishly believed his wife would want to take care of her youngest child. 'Oh, and Pauline, I wouldn't be at all surprised if your sister was ready for a hot drink of sorts?'

Pauline was visibly shocked at being given an order, and when Alice began protesting, he gently shushed her. 'Father knows best,' he chided, 'We need to get you strong again.'

Placing a hand on Tony's shoulder, he suggested, 'Let's head away to the office for our little chat. Better make it short and to the point.'

Pauline bristled. 'Oh, and what little chat is this, might I ask?'

Tony discreetly reminded her, 'You remember our discussion yesterday?'

He gave her a meaningful look and Pauline said no more.

The minute the two men were out the door, Maureen dropped the canvas bag at Alice's feet. 'You might be able to wrap your father round your little finger, but I will not let you pull the wool over *my* eyes. I can tell you right now, you are not wanted in this house. Your sister and I have suffered intolerable insult and injury because of you! People of a certain kind, pointing at us in the streets . . . jeering; yelling obscenities, and all because you find it amusing to play one brother off against another!'

When her mother paused for breath, Pauline had her say. 'You should be ashamed! What kind of a trollop would promise herself to one man in marriage, and then crawl into bed with his brother? You're a disgrace . . . you've dragged the name of this family into the gutter, and I for one wouldn't care if I never clapped eyes on you ever again!'

'That makes two of us!' Closing the distance between herself and Alice, Maureen calmly raised her hand and slapped Alice across the face. Shocked, Alice reeled back in the chair.

'Oh, dear me!' Maureen lent forward, her face almost touching Alice's. 'Why don't you tell your father that I slapped you? Then I can tell him how you got hysterical . . . swearing at me and your sister Pauline. You lost control, and no wonder, after what you've been through . . . all that suffering and pain, it's a wonder you haven't gone completely out of your mind!'

The sight of Alice in tears and clutching her face spurred her on. 'You should know by now, Alice, you might be Daddy's little favourite, but I'm a better liar than you will ever be. So for your own sake, don't set yourself up against me, because you will lose out every time!'

Pauline emphasised her mother's warning. 'The best thing you can do is get as far away from here as you can. No one would miss you . . . except maybe Father, who is fast becoming a deluded old man where you're concerned! Oh, but then he never could see the faults in you, could he? Last born first loved! Always Daddy's darling. Alice this . . . Alice that! Never Pauline. And then you wonder why I detest you!'

As Alice scrambled to get out of the chair, her mother held her there. 'You're *nothing*, Alice! I was overjoyed that one of the Arnolds had taken a fancy to you . . . enough to want to marry you. I couldn't get you out of my house fast enough. But now here you are again, trying to creep your way back in. You've no idea how much happier we are without you.'

Shocked and dazed at the bitter onslaught from both women, and with her face stinging from the spiteful slap, Alice saw red. 'I don't want to be here!' she told them angrily. 'I never meant to come back, but Father insisted.'

Her mother placed her two hands one on each arm of Alice's chair. 'I want you out of here, and when you're gone, the door to my home will never again be open to you.'

Alice looked into her mother's eyes. She glanced up at her sister, and their hatred of her was like a palpable presence.

'I want you to go,' Maureen hissed. 'Before your father comes back. You have caused him a great deal of worry. *He* won't tell you . . . old fool that he is! But, because of you his most valuable customers have deserted him. Long-standing, lucrative contracts have been cancelled. He's lost money and status; his pride and reputation is in tatters.'

'Yes! And even then, after all the harm you've done . . . he *still* tries to protect you!' Pauline shouted. Grabbing Alice by the shoulders she began shaking her backwards and forwards, like a rag doll, until Alice felt her senses going. 'Leave me be!' she pleaded. 'Stop it!'

Finding it hard to catch her breath, Alice began to panic.

'Mother! Make her stop it!' she yelled. But her mother made no move to help. Instead she looked on, her face impassive.

Buckling under the ferocity of Pauline's jealous rage, Alice was desperate. 'Leave me alone . . . get off me!' But Pauline was like someone demented. 'Pauline! Get off me!' When Maureen made no attempt to intervene, Alice blurted out the only thing that might make Pauline stop. 'I'm pregnant!' That was the last thing she wanted them to know, and now it was out, and they were shocked to the core.

The silence was deafening. Pauline fell backwards, a look of disbelief on her face, and Maureen stared at Alice, as though she was seeing a stranger.

When Ronald's voice softly shattered the silence, Alice realised the dreadful enormity of what she had done.

'Alice . . . did I hear right?' The two men had entered the room, just as Alice called out.

Alice did not look up. Instead, she sat hunched and desolate in the chair.

'Alice! Answer me!' He came closer. 'Did I hear you say you were . . . *pregnant*?'

Quietly sobbing, Alice appealed to him, 'I'm sorry, Father. I only found out this morning. I wanted to tell you, but not like this. Never like this, no!'

For what seemed an age, Ronald stood silent, his sorry gaze resting on Alice. '*Whose is it?*'

Pauline laughed aloud. 'How would *she* know?'

'BE QUIET!' Ronald was devastated. 'Or leave the room!'

Sulking, Pauline crossed the room to be with her husband, while Ronald returned his attention to Alice. 'I want the truth, Alice. Who's the father of this child?'

Ashamed, Alice dropped her gaze.

'So, does that mean you *really* don't know?'

Alice gave no answer; but to her father, the silence was answer enough.

'I see.'

Suddenly Maureen was screeching, 'I want her out of here! She's no better than a tramp who jumps into bed with any man who'll have her, and now she's carrying a brat and she doesn't even know who the father is!'

While Maureen was yelling, Tony quietly took Pauline out of the room. 'This is not our business.'

Like everyone else, he knew the sordid story of Alice and the brothers, and in truth he had a certain compassion for her sorry situation. But he was only new to this family, and did not want to be seen as interfering.

~

Into all of this commotion, Joshua and Tricia arrived.

As they climbed out of the car, they were pounced on by Pauline, who gleefully greeted them. 'Hello again! Your darling little grandaughter is inside, but I wouldn't go in there if I were you!'

'Whatever do you mean? What's going on?' Tricia was anxious.

'All hell just broke loose in there . . .' Pauline started.

'Pauline!' Tony ushered her away. 'I'm sorry,' he apologised to the grandparents, 'but, well, there's been a bit of an upset.'

While Tricia hurried towards the house, with Pauline excited to accompany her, Joshua asked him, 'What kind of an "upset"?'

'It's *Alice*'s fault!' Pauline angrily informed Tricia. 'It's *always* Alice! She's caused so much trouble, and she doesn't even seem to care!'

'I can't believe that for one minute!' Tricia was aware of the animosity Pauline had for her sister.

Behind them Joshua was quizzing Tony, who explained there had been a row, while deliberately omitting the news of Alice's pregnancy.

Tricia however, was already finding out the truth.

As she approached the open front door, she could hear Maureen's raised voice. 'You just can't see it, can you? Your precious daughter knew exactly what she was doing! She got herself into this predicament, and I'm telling you now, if she stays under this roof, I'm leaving. It's her or me, Ronald!'

'Good heavens!' Tricia was shocked and angry. 'My granddaughter is just out of hospital, and her mother's screaming like a fish wife! Whatever are they thinking of?'

Quickly now, she hurried across the hallway, while Pauline gleefully slunk back to the men.

As Tricia approached the sitting room, she was almost knocked over when Alice came bursting out in floods of tears. She collided full on with her grandmother. 'Good lord, Alice!' Reaching out, Tricia took hold of her granddaughter and crushed her in a hug. 'What in God's name is going on here, child?'

Distraught, Alice confided, 'I can't stay here, Grandma. Mother doesn't want me, and I don't blame her. I'm a disgrace to everyone.'

When Ronald came rushing out, he was astonished to see his mother there. 'I'm sorry,' he muttered. 'There's been a bit of a row, but it's all right now.' He held out his arms to Alice. 'Come back in, Alice, please. It won't happen again, I promise.'

He felt suddenly old, and immensely tired. He was too long in the tooth for all this upheaval. Even though he loved her dearly the news that she was pregnant had shocked and saddened him.

Holding on to Alice, his mother took control. 'I have no idea what happened here,' she stated, '. . . and I don't need to know.' She gave him a look that only a mother could when chastising her child. 'Alice is coming to stay with her old grandma for a while, and I'm looking forward to having her. So, Ronald! Is that all right with you, son?'

Secretly relieved, Ronald nodded. 'If that's what Alice wants.'

'And will *Maureen* be in agreement with that?' Tricia made no mention of the fact that she had heard Maureen say he must choose between her and Alice. After her outburst, she had chosen to disappear and sulk in her room,

'Maureen will agree, yes. Absolutely!' Whether she agreed or not was of little consequence to him. He had witnessed the true feelings his wife felt for her youngest daughter, and it had cut him deeply.

When he now reached out for Alice, she went to him, her head buried in his chest as they held each other. 'I'm sorry, child.' His voice was heavy with emotion. 'I haven't protected you very well, have I?'

Alice looked up. 'It's not your fault,' she whispered. 'None of this was ever your fault.'

'Do you really want to go with your grandmother?'

Alice nodded.

'All right then. Maybe in the circumstances, it might be for the best.' He addressed his mother, 'What about Father? Will he be all right with this?'

Having ambled across the drive, Joshua had heard enough of the conversation to understand at least some of the situation. 'From what I understand, it seems Maureen lost her temper over some silly nonsense . . . *whatever that may be.*'

'All I can say is, judging by what I've seen and heard, your daughter coming home with me and your mother would probably be the best thing for everyone.' He looked Ronald in the eye. 'Would you agree with that, son?'

'I think so, yes. For the moment it will be best for Alice, and I know she'll be safe enough with you and mother.'

Placing his two hands on Alice's shoulders, he moved her back a step, so he could look into her face. 'You know I don't want you to go, don't you, Alice?'

Alice looked up, her heart breaking, not for herself, but for him. 'Yes, Father, I know that.'

'But can you see that it's for the best . . . at least for now?'

'Yes. Thank you, Father.'

Concerned that Alice appeared frail and ill, Josh intervened. 'We'd best not come in, son. Give our excuses to Maureen,' he said. 'It's more important for us to get Alice settled. After all, the poor girl has only just come out of hospital. We don't want her heading back that way again, do we now, eh?'

'No, of course not!'

Asking for a moment alone with Alice, Ronald watched his parents walk to the car. 'I truly am sorry, Alice.

Reaching down, he kissed her on the forehead. 'You've been through so much,' he whispered. 'And now even your homecoming is ruined. I failed you, child.' He had got over the initial shock of hearing her news. 'You're barely a woman, and here you are, after everything you've gone through . . . and now, you're left carrying a child.'

He had witnessed such strength and determination in this young woman, his daughter. He felt both proud and ashamed. 'You don't deserve all this pain.'

'I'll be all right, Father,' Alice assured him. 'Really I will.'

Collecting her canvas bag and keeping a tight hold of her, he walked Alice to the waiting car. 'Will you tell your grandparents about the pregnancy?' he asked.

Alice answered with conviction, 'No. At least not yet.'

A worrying thought occurred to her. 'You won't let Pauline or Mother tell anyone, will you?'

Ronald's face was set like stone as he answered quietly. 'You've no need to concern yourself with that. They know which side their bread is buttered! They won't say anything.'

Only now did it occur to him to ask, 'What will you do about your situation?'

'I'm not sure, Father. I need to think.' Alice knew exactly what he meant.

Ronald took a deep breath before offering her a way out. 'Don't be angry with me for saying this, Alice, but it isn't just the child you have to think about. It's yourself too. You must do what's right, for *both* your sakes.'

It was comforting to know that if she took the route she was loathe to take, then she would at least have her father's support. 'You mean, if I decided not to have . . .'

'Ssh!' He placed a finger on her lips. 'Don't explain to me,' he said gently. 'Whatever you decide, I'll be there for you, I promise. But only *you* can make that decision.

She thanked him. 'I understand.' She wondered what he would say if he knew she was carrying twins. That they were not talking about taking the life of *one* child, but two.

'Don't fret over it just yet,' his voice broke into her thoughts. 'There's time enough, and when the decision has to be made, it will be the right one, I'm sure, for the both of you.'

A few moments later he helped her into the car. Then he waved her off, deeply regretting the manner in which her homecoming had ended.

From behind the curtains, Maureen watched the car turn out of the drive.

'Good riddance!' she muttered.

PART FOUR

~

A week later

Harsh Decisions

CHAPTER NINE

IN THE WEEK that Alice had been with her grandparents, July had tripped into August without anyone barely noticing.

Alice had gained strength both in mind and body, and she was sitting on the swing in the garden, quietly contemplating her future, when a familiar face peered round the corner. 'So, here you are, Alice! I knocked on the door, rang the bell and shouted out, but nobody came, so I thought I'd best come and find you.'

'Mandy!' Alice was always delighted to see her friend. 'My grandparents are out, and I was so deep in thought, I didn't hear you.'

To Alice, the sight of that stocky little figure, with the round cheery face and mop of dark curly hair, was always a welcome sight.

'So, how are you feeling today?' Throwing herself beside Alice she set the swing in motion. 'You look good!' she declared with a grin. 'In fact, I reckon you've actually blossomed since I last saw you.'

Alice laughed. 'You only saw me three days ago.'

'Well, three days, three weeks, makes no difference. You're looking better every time I see you; stronger in yourself, if you know what I mean?'

Alice knew exactly what she meant. 'At long last I'm

beginning to come to terms with everything,' she admitted. 'My wounds are healed and I feel more at peace inside.' She tapped her chest, 'Thankfully, the nightmares have gone away, and I'm sleeping much better.'

As was her way, Mandy gave her an embracing hug. 'After all this time, you're beginning to seem more like the Alice I know.' She held Alice at arm's length. 'Look at you! Your hair is growing again; no sign of any scars that I can see. And your pretty eyes are shining more brightly than ever.' She was so pleased to see how Alice was recovering that she felt the need to wipe away a tear. 'Look what you've done now!' she accused Alice jokingly. 'You've got me blubbering!'

Alice laughed. 'That's not *my* fault,' she said. 'You blubber at anything! You always have.'

They now laughed at the truth of it until Mandy brought the conversation to a more serious level. 'You will never know how worried I've been,' she told Alice. 'Worried that you might be scarred forever. Worried that you might not make it.'

Alice intervened. 'I *do* know how worried you all were,' she assured her, 'and I love you all the more for it.'

For a while they sat in the bright August sunshine, chatting and laughing, and putting the world to rights. 'I've shut up the shop!' Mandy confessed. 'Old Patsy has gone off to her sister's for a few days and left me in charge, so now I can choose which hour I close for lunch.'

Alice knew all about Mandy's old tricks. 'Don't you mean which *two* hours you can shut for lunch?'

'Ah, yes, but if I take a longer lunch, I always stay on later in the afternoon,' she reasoned. 'Besides, that's when I sell the most flowers.'

Alice was intrigued. 'How come?'

'Because all the blokes have finished work, then they start to think of the girl they're taking out that night, and they spend money like there's no tomorrow: red roses; pretty wrapping paper, and even a big bow to finish.' She winked cheekily. 'Suits me, because then Patsy thinks I'm the best flower seller ever. One of these days she'll be duty bound to give me a raise.'

'You're a devil!' Alice loved her like a sister; at least more than she had ever loved her true flesh and blood sister.

'You know what, Alice?'

'What?'

'I reckon you've even put weight on.'

'You're imagining things.' Alice felt a surge of panic. But then, she was still only nine weeks' gone, and hardly showing.

Mandy persisted. 'I'm telling you! Honestly, I can see it in your face. You've got little rosy cheeks, where before you were all thin and pale. Oh, and look here . . .' taking hold of Alice's arm, she gently pinched the flesh. 'I couldn't have done that a few weeks back. You were like a stick insect!'

Alice gave an inward sigh of relief. 'It's Grandma's good food, and this lovely sunshine.' Her thoughts turned to Joe. 'Mandy?'

'What?'

'Do you *really* not know where Joe is?'

'I've already told you. No, I don't!'

She had heard the gossip though. 'I think his where-abouts are being kept secret, because of Frank. If he knew where Joe was, who's to say he wouldn't risk being captured, just as long as he was able to finish his brother off.'

Alice had thought of that too. 'I'm worried, but I can't even imagine how Tom and Nancy must feel.'

Mandy nodded in agreement. 'Wherever Joe is, Frank won't rest until he finds him.'

Alice detected something in Mandy's voice that made her suspicious. 'You know where Joe is, don't you?'

'No, Alice, I do not! And I haven't come across anyone else who knows either.'

'*Someone* must know.' Alice had grown increasingly desperate. 'He can't have just vanished from the face of the earth. It's like there's a conspiracy to keep me from seeing him.' Alice told Mandy how she had thought about going to see Tom and Nancy, and asking them as to Joe's whereabouts.

Mandy had her own thoughts about that. 'I'm sorry, Alice, and you might hate me for saying it, but they might not welcome you and besides, don't you think it would be best if you never saw Joe again?'

'Best for who?' Alice had heard it all before; from her father, and her grandparents, and even people who had no business telling her what to do.

'Well, best for *you*, of course!' Mandy feared for her friend. 'When you were in hospital, all you could talk about was Joe. Joe this and Joe that, and now that you're out, you're still talking about him.'

'That's because I love him, Mandy. Even when he went away for all that time, I thought about him a lot, and when he came back to be best man, I knew I'd made a big mistake in promising to marry Frank.'

'So, why did you go through with it?'

'I'm not really sure.' Time and again, while she was recovering in hospital, Alice had asked herself that same question. 'I suppose it was because I'd already promised myself to Frank.'

'But . . .' Mandy hated herself for asking the question, but she had to ask, '. . . you were with Joe before the wedding, so why didn't you tell Frank you couldn't marry him?'

Reliving it all in her mind, Alice took a moment to

answer, 'The truth is, I felt ashamed. I knew what I'd done was wrong. I felt that I'd committed a terrible crime, letting Frank down . . . and his family and everything. I imagined those fleeting moments with Joe could never be repeated. I was so sure he would go away, and I would never see him again.'

In her mind's eye she could see herself in Joe's arms, and it was magic like she had never known before, and would probably never know again.

'Being with Joe was so beautiful,' she murmured.

That was her strongest memory of her time with Joe; the sheer beauty of their love, of being together in that way. Then afterwards, when it was over, the fear and the guilt was crippling.

Listening to Alice, and seeing that look in her eyes, Mandy only now realised that Alice truly loved Joe in a way she could never love Frank.

As always, Mandy was straight with her. 'None of that really matters now,' she said. 'You need to remember, Alice, it's partly Joe's fault you almost died, and even now, his brother is still out there. Hopefully he's a million miles away from here, but the fact is, he wanted you dead on account of what Joe did!'

Mandy fell silent for a moment, thinking about how Alice and Joe had each paid a terrible price for what happened that night, and having heard the furtive whispers, she also knew how Joe's parents feared that Frank might return to finish what he started.

'Mandy?'

'Mmm?'

'If you *did* know where Joe was you would tell me, wouldn't you?'

'D'you want the truth?' Mandy took a deep breath.

'You know I do,' Alice said pleadingly.

'Then, no. I would *never* tell you.'

For what seemed an age, the chasm of silence between them deepened, until Alice spoke, her voice quivering, 'So, you would never tell me where he was, not even if I was desperate to see him?'

'No!'

'Not if I had something very special to tell him?'

'Nothing could be so special that you would risk your life. So, no,' Mandy was adamant.

'Not even if you knew that I might be carrying his child?'

Mandy reeled back, as though physically struck.

Abruptly bringing the swing to a halt, she turned about and stared at Alice, her face opening in disbelief. Then she looked away, her voice harsh as she asked Alice, 'Is that why you want to see Joe so much? So that you can tell him you're pregnant with his child?' There was the merest hint of disgust in her voice.

'No, Mandy. It's not just that. Don't look away, Mandy . . . please?' Alice fully realised how afraid Mandy was. Afraid for her; and now, afraid for the unborn child. 'Please, Mandy . . . look at me.'

When Mandy turned round, it was obvious that she was desperately shocked and concerned at what Alice had told her. 'You know what this means, Alice?' she said shakily. 'What if Frank ever finds out that you're carrying Joe's child? It doesn't bear thinking about!'

Alice knew she had to tell it all, in order for Mandy to understand. 'The thing is, I don't really know if Joe *is* the father.' She added quietly, '*Frank* might be the father for all I know.'

Mandy was taken aback. 'I didn't realise you actually slept with Frank on your wedding night. For some reason, I imagined the trouble started earlier on?'

Alice took her time in replying, because even now she could hardly bring herself to talk about it. 'No. It didn't happen like that.'

'So? Everything was all right, until you told him about Joe. Is that what you're saying, Alice? You slept with Frank, and *then* you told him about Joe?

Reluctantly, Alice nodded her answer.

'But why would you do that? Why tell him? Was it because you had a guilty conscience?'

'No.'

Alice recalled everything. 'Frank was in a drunken stupor and I was glad, because I thought he wouldn't bother me. I though I'd have time to think about what to do.'

It all came back, like a moving picture in her mind. 'I couldn't bear the thought of him touching me. I knew I had made a terrible mistake in marrying him, but it was too late.'

Her voice fell to a whisper as she relived that night. 'He woke up. He just . . . took me. It wasn't love. It was nothing like love?'

'How do you mean?' Mandy could see the torment in her eyes. 'He forced himself on you, is that what you're saying, Alice?'

Alice hesitated. 'Frank was like a crazy man. I couldn't stop him. He was like a wild animal. He was rough, and hurtful. He tore at my clothes and when I wanted him to stop, he got angry. Afterwards, he seemed to know somehow . . . about me, that I'd been with another man. He started asking questions . . . demanding to know who I'd been with. He forced me to tell him, about me and Joe. He was out of his mind, and oh, he hurt me so bad. He cut my hair, tied me up. He kept saying all these terrible things, about what he would do. He wouldn't stop hurting me. I thought it would never end.'

When the memory began to swamp her, she paused, her two hands clasped to her face.

Mandy pulled Alice towards her. 'It's all right,' she whispered. 'I understand. And it was wrong of me to question you like that.'

Realisation dawned on her. 'So either of the brothers could be the father?'

Alice broke away. 'How can I know?' she asked. 'I was a virgin before Joe. How can I ever be sure who the father is?'

Mandy understood. 'So what will you, do, Alice? Will you have this baby? Did the doctor advise you at all?'

'He told me I had to make up my mind quickly. I've already got my next appointment, and because of everything that's happened, I'm to see a hospital counsellor at the same time.'

'Good!' Mandy approved. 'I can understand that,' she told Alice. 'It's a difficult situation . . . and you will have to make a difficult decision.' A thought occurred to her. 'When is your appointment?'

'Friday.'

'That's tomorrow!'

'I'm to be there at 12:30 p.m.'

'Do you want me to come with you?'

Alice shook her head. 'Thank you, Mandy, I appreciate that, but Grandma said she wanted to take me.'

Mandy was pleased. 'Your Grandmother is a kind and wise person . . . she'll help you decide.'

'Mandy?'

'What?'

'The doctor told me something else.'

'It's nothing bad I hope . . . I mean, you are on the road to a full recovery, aren't you?'

'So they tell me.'

'So, what else did the doctor say then?'

'The thing is, I'm carrying *twins*.'

For the second time in the space of minutes, Mandy was visibly shocked. 'You're . . . *what*!'

Scrambling off the swing, she began pacing the ground. 'Look, Alice, nothing has changed, not really. You still have to think carefully, about the consequences. Not just for their sakes, but for yours too. Bloody hell, Alice! You were lucky to get away with your life, never mind all of this on top! If it was me, I wouldn't think twice! I would *know* what to do.'

'Would you?' Alice already suspected what Mandy was thinking.

Mandy stopped pacing and came to sit on the swing again. Looking Alice in the eyes, she told her quietly, 'I would end it.'

'Why?'

'Well, because!'

Mandy knew how difficult it would be for a girl like Alice, to do, what in Mandy's opinion, was a necessary evil.

So, she drew her thoughts together, and tried to present her many reasons in a valid way. 'It's the only thing to do, Alice.'

Though she partly understood Mandy's thinking, Alice needed cast-iron reasons. 'In what way?'

'Well, firstly, unless you can somehow find out who the real father is, you'll be denying the children their right to know the truth. I mean . . . what will you do when they get old enough to ask questions? What will you tell them . . . that you're not sure who their father is; that you slept with both brothers in the space of a few days, and that one of the brothers is their father, and the other is their uncle?

'Think about it, Alice!' she urged. 'You have to let them go, or it could mean a lifetime of unhappiness, hard questions with no answers, and a good deal of misery for all three of you. Besides, if you had the babies, it would mean you would never be free of Frank.'

Alice had thought of all that, over and over, until she could think no more. 'There might be a way of knowing who the father is,' she said now. 'There must be some test they can do that will confirm whether Joe or Frank is their rightful father.'

'No, Alice, it still won't do! Think about it. Say they could do a test. Say they discovered that *Frank* was the father, how do you think the children would feel, once they knew what he did to you and Joe, not to mention his own father? Oh, and don't delude yourself that they will never know the truth, because they *will* find out, you can count on it!'

In her desperation to convince Alice, Mandy believed she might have to be cruel to be kind, so she left no stone unturned as she went on, 'If you decide to tell them everything, it could backfire. They could turn on you.'

'Maybe they would, but then it would only be what I deserve.'

'There are other things to consider as well, Alice.'

Mandy pushed her argument. 'What if it was proven somehow that Joe was the father? What makes you think they would accept him, any more than they would accept Frank? Once they knew the whole truth, how do you think they might cope; two innocents, brought into a world of lies and deception.'

She went on relentlessly, hoping that Alice might realise the danger of going ahead with the pregnancy.

With everything Mandy said, Alice felt her heart and her hopes sink. 'You're painting the worst possible picture,' she said. 'We can't know *what* they might think, or how they would feel.'

'Maybe. But once they're in possession of the true facts, they would have no peace of mind. They would be forced to live with the knowledge of what happened, and who would they turn to? Think of it, Alice! You must know it would be cruel to put them in that situation.'

Alice was distraught. 'But, I would always be there for them. I would never let anyone hurt them. Never!'

'You would not be able to control it, Alice. People can be malicious, and children more than most.'

Alice tried to explain. 'The thing is, I can't seem to think straight. I'm not sure what's right or wrong any more.'

It was as though she was in the middle of a nightmare, and she couldn't wake from it. 'I want to do what's best for them, but I'm not God! I don't know what the answer is!'

She went on, 'I had thought that maybe we could move away . . . take on a new life, new names, all of that. It's possible . . . isn't it?'

'Oh Alice, listen to you!' Mandy said wearily.

'What do you mean?'

'I mean . . . your babies are not even born yet, and already you're planning an escape route.'

For the sake of Alice and her babies, Mandy remained resolute. 'All I want is for you to realise the enormity of what you're doing,' she pleaded. 'I don't want to see you hurt anymore, but if you go ahead and have the children, you must realise how hard your life will be.'

Mandy's voice softened. 'I know I shouldn't force my own views on you like this. You're my best friend, Alice, and I love you dearly. You asked me what I would do, and I've told you. If I've hurt you with my answer, I'm truly sorry.'

Alice was deeply shaken, but she appreciated Mandy's honesty. Alice knew she had her and her unborn babies' best interests at heart.

'I think I always knew what you would say,' she told Mandy now. 'In truth, I thought the very same, but I keep coming round to the idea that everything might work out all right, and that it isn't my place to end two innocent lives.'

Mandy understood her quandary. 'All right, I agree that it will be the hardest thing you may ever have to do in the whole of your life. All I'm saying is, don't think of what's happening right now. Think of the future. Think of the repercussions on everyone; especially the children. But, when all is said and done, Alice, whatever anyone says, *you* are the only one who can decide.'

'I know,' Alice replied. 'Tomorrow, I'll make my decision, and that will be an end to it.'

For a long time they sat on the swing, gently swinging back and forth, each in deep thought; each of them afraid of what tomorrow might bring.

~

It was early afternoon when Tricia drove up in her black Ford car. She parked it outside the front door as always, then she collected her shopping bags and carried them into the house. 'Alice!' she called out as she went straight through to the kitchen, where she dropped the bags on the chair.

'Alice, I'm home!' Crossing to the sink, she quickly filled the kettle with cold water from the tap, and switched it on to boil. 'Wherever is she?' She looked out the window and across the garden to the swing, and still there was no sign of Alice.

While the kettle came to the boil, she wandered back down the hallway, pausing only to pat her hair in the mirror as she went.

She peeped into the sitting room, and checked the sun house. When there was still no sign of Alice, she went upstairs and frantically searched every room, and now she was hurrying back down in a state of panic. 'Alice? Alice, where are you, dear!'

Flinging open the library door, she gave a sigh of relief,

on seeing Alice curled up in the window seat, fast asleep.

Treading quietly across the carpet so as not to wake her, she stood a moment, to regard Alice, so small and vulnerable, with the harrowing experience of late etched on her pretty young features. 'Oh, child . . . what's going to become of you eh? But I'm so glad you trusted me with the truth, about the babies.'

'I'll leave you to sleep, child.' Tricia whispered. 'It's what you need.' She was concerned to see how pale Alice was. 'You must stop fretting, sweetheart,' she continued, moving a stray lock of hair from Alice's temple, 'You need to concentrate on getting stronger.'

Taking off her coat, she slid it gently over Alice. 'I'll call you when tea's ready.' She then kissed her softly on the forehead, and quietly tiptoed away.

A short time later the two of them were seated at the kitchen table, enjoying a pot of tea, with fresh scones bought by Tricia that morning. 'I don't want you worrying about tomorrow, Alice,' her grandmother urged. 'Once the decision is made, you can then concentrate on looking to plan your future . . .' she chose her words carefully, '. . . one way or the other.'

They talked fleetingly of Alice's dilemma. 'You will always have a home here with me and your grandfather, if that's what you want.' But Alice was already forming a plan in her mind.

When her grandmother got up to clear the table, Alice helped, while Tricia chatted on. 'Your grandfather said I was wrong not to take on another housekeeper when Martha retired, but I'm really enjoying myself taking care of the home and everything. I admit I do have a woman in to do the ironing and hoover under the beds, because my back won't allow me to do that.'

She gave a resigned smile. 'Mind you, dear, it's not beyond the realms of possibility, that in the future I might be forced to take on another Martha. Like your grandfather insists on reminding me . . . I'm not getting any younger.'

While she chatted, Alice grew more determined.

She could not get Joe out of her mind. Somehow, she had to see him, to speak with him. She needed to know that he was truly on the road to recovery.

The only thing she knew was that Frank had injured Joe so badly it was touch and go whether he would survive, and even if he survived, the early diagnosis was that he may suffer a degree of permanent damage.

But he was alive! She knew that much, and in knowing it, her yearning to see him grew stronger with every new day.

'Alice! Are you all right?' Tricia was concerned.

'Yes, Grandma, I was just thinking, that's all.'

'Oh, I'm sorry, child. Here I am, wittering on like a silly old woman, while you have such a weight on your mind.' Tricia repeated her support. 'We'll see it through together, eh? You won't be on your own. I'll be there with you tomorrow.'

'Whether you agree with my decision or not?'

'I meant what I said before, child. No one is judging you. You're facing a very difficult time, and you can rest assured that your grandfather and I will support you; as will your father.'

Sliding an arm about Alice's shoulders, she told her, 'There are people who love you dearly. You must never forget that.'

It was late afternoon when Alice decided she could put it off no longer.

While her grandmother snoozed in the sitting room, she went up to her room and refreshed herself with a wash and change of clothes; choosing a pretty grey dress with the white trimming at the hem and neck. She had been grateful that her father collected her things from the cottage, because she never wanted to go there again.

Brushing her hair, she noted with relief how the minute patches of raw scalp were now barely visible through her new hair. She dabbed some powder on her cheeks, a touch of lipstick for colour, then she slipped her feet into her low-heeled sandals. 'I hope you're doing the right thing, Alice,' she whispered into the mirror, '. . . for everyone's sakes.'

Downstairs, she wrote a note for her grandmother:

Dear Grandma,

I felt I needed some fresh air, so I'm going for a walk. I won't be too long,

Alice.
XX

Softly letting herself out of the front door, she then closed it quietly behind her, before setting off down the lane.

Growing increasingly excited by the purpose of her errand, she quickened her pace. On reaching the stile from the lane to the field, she climbed over, jumped down on the other side, and went at a run down the long field.

Like a wild thing let loose, she ran until she thought her heart would burst, on and on, through the fields, then across the high lane that skirted the village, and now she was headed for the woods, her heart soaring as she realised that this was the first step towards seeing Joe.

Stumbling into the woods, she fell against a tree, breathless and exhilarated, her laughter echoing through the high branches, where the breeze carried it away to the skies.

She felt free, and it was amazing! *Life was amazing!!*

And all she could think of was Joe, and the two new lives inside her.

Suddenly her mood sobered, and she felt incredibly sad.

Leaning against the tree trunk, she slid to the ground, where she sat for what seemed an age, tears spilling down her face, and her heart heavy with the burden of what she must do.

After a time, she clambered up and went on. 'You have a way to go yet,' she chided herself. 'Think of Joe . . . keep thinking of Joe.'

She pushed through the thicket; slowly at first, then faster, and now she was blindly running, thrusting back the branches that crossed her path; falling and tripping in the dense undergrowth, until she burst out into the sunshine, where she took a deep, invigorating breath. 'Not much farther now, Alice,' she told herself.

After a mile or so up hill and down dale she could see the house nestling lower down in the valley. She knew that house so well, with its tall cylinder chimneys; rickety outbuildings, and the sprawl of land, enclosed in that familiar white fencing.

Cautiously now, she approached, down the bank and up again, towards her beloved brook, where she had spent many a wonderful hour in its cool, welcoming waters.

She kicked off her shoes. Holding one shoe in each hand, she stepped into the shallow water and paddled up and down, gently kicking her feet as she luxuriated in the cool water's soothing touch. When she was refreshed, she sat on a boulder and wiped her skin dry with the tail end of her skirt.

Eager to be away now that she was so close, she slipped her sandals back on and set off, up the field and on towards Tom and Nancy's house. It was only then that she began to realise the enormity of what she was doing.

With the stark realisation came the niggling doubts. 'Be careful, Alice,' she warned herself. 'Remember, they could have told you where Joe was before . . . if they had wanted you to know.'

As she drew near she recognised Nancy in the garden; as always she was dressed in the familiar pretty floral dress made by her own hands, and that plain blue pinnie she always wore when going about her housework.

On the ground beside her was a wicker basket spilling over with clean, white bed sheets, which she plucked out one by one, to hang on the line. They blew in the breeze, like the great sails of a mighty ship.

Warmed by the sight of that dear woman, and yet feeling suddenly anxious, Alice sat down on the grass to watch Nancy at her work.

This was the first time in many a long week that she had been in striking distance of Tom and Nancy's cottage, and the sight of it now was tugging at her heart, creating a medley of emotions within her.

When suddenly Nancy looked in her direction, Alice lay flat on the ground, hoping she had not been seen. Nancy drew out another sheet and Alice was within a heartbeat of turning around and going back.

She chided herself, 'No, Alice! You came here with a purpose, and you have to see it through. It'll be all right . . . it really will.' And yet, she could not be sure of that.

She paused when she heard the engine of a car start up.

Keeping low to the ground, she looked down towards the cottage and at once recognised the long, black saloon car, which she knew belonged to the landowner.

As the car went down the track and away, Alice noticed Tom leaning on the doorway. When the car was out of sight, he went back inside.

Having now hung out all the sheets, Nancy ambled up

the path to the cottage, with the wicker basket under her arm.

Taking nervous steps towards the cottage, Alice paused to collect a posy of wild flowers from the hedgerow, now alive with drifts of pretty pink daisies and handsome colts-foot, remembering Nancy always liked these.

Clutching them to her, Alice went tentatively across the garden to the front door, which as ever, was open and welcoming.

With her heart beating ten to the dozen, she went forward.

She hesitated for a moment. Was she doing the right thing in coming here? How would they greet her?

She tapped on the door.

When there came no reply, she tapped again a little louder, until Nancy emerged from the kitchen at the end of the passage. 'Hold yer horses . . . I'm on my way!'

Wiping her wet hands on her pinnie, she came forward, a ready smile on her face. When she saw who it was, her ready smile quickly faded. 'Good Lord! Alice! What are you doing here?' There was no welcome, no acknowledgement of past friendship.

'I need to talk with you, Nancy.' Alice nervously clutched the flowers. 'Please, Nancy . . . a minute, that's all?'

Nancy gave no answer, but constantly glanced behind her. Alice held out the flowers. 'Please, Nancy. I just need a minute or two, that's all I ask.'

'Then you ask too much!' Growing increasingly nervous, Nancy seemed not to notice the flowers. 'Look, Alice . . . I can't ask you in. I've nothing to say to you. Go away. I don't want no trouble.'

She cast her gaze over Alice. 'You ought to be at home with your grandparents.' She spoke sternly, 'Please, Alice! For all our sakes, go away. Before he sees you.'

'I can't go away, Nancy.' Alice had not forgotten the

reason that drove her here. 'I'm not here to cause trouble,' she promised. 'I'm here because I'm worried about Joe. No one will tell me where he is, and I can't rest. I know he's in a hospital somewhere, and it's all my fault, but I love him, Nancy, I really do.'

In a sudden move that startled Alice, Nancy grabbed hold of her. Without a word, she ran her away from the house and down towards the barn, where she quickly shoved her inside. 'Look at the state of you!' she gestured to Alice's torn feet and general state of chaos. 'Good grief, girl, are you trying to put yourself back in hospital, or what?'

Taking the flowers from Alice's hands, she laid them on a hay bale, and began brushing the leaves and debris from Alice's skirt.

Plucking the bracken from Alice's hair, she continued to warn her, 'You should not be here! You should not even be out on your own. You must know how bad things have been for us. Tom is in a bit of a state. Look, just take yourself off home.'

'It's too bloody late for all that!'

Tom was making his way towards them. 'Have you no shame? Is there no decency in you?'

When he took a step forward, fists clenched and his face set hard, Nancy feared his intention. Skilfully, she stepped between them. 'Leave it, Tom! We don't want you doing something you might regret!'

Her voice was stern, her manner formidable. 'Go back to the house. I'll deal with this.'

In all the years they had been married, Nancy had never known her husband raise an angry voice to her, but he raised it now, and it shocked her. 'I WANT HER OUT OF HERE!'

In a controlled voice he told Nancy, 'If you're so fond of the little hussy, then you're welcome to pack your bags and go with her!'

Taking hold of Alice by the shoulders, he held her in front of him, his face not an inch from hers; his deep sadness written in his eyes.

In a low, broken voice, he demanded, 'Have you any idea, what you've done to this family. Oh, I'm not saying Joe was innocent in all of this, and Frank neither.' His fingers dug hard into her shoulders. 'What you did might seem like a game to you, so what d'you care if your shameful behaviour has ruined all our lives. This was a peaceful, happy home, and now me and my wife can't even speak civil to each other. We've lost it all, d'you see?'

He leaned closer, his voice almost inaudible, as though he was talking to himself. 'Everything's gone wrong! One minute we're all under the same roof, a family together at last. Then suddenly it's all snatched away. I've got one son fighting for his life in hospital . . . and even if he gets through it, he may never walk again!'

Viciously thrusting her away, he went on angrily, 'As for his brother, he could be anywhere! Probably on the other side of the world for all I know . . . running scared, knowing that when they catch up with him, he could face a lifetime in prison. *And all because of you!*'

He paused, and when he now spoke it was in a deliberate manner, as he drove home every devastating word. 'No wonder Joe hates you,' he growled. 'He can see how wrong he was, and now he's broken and crippled, and he never in his life wants to see you again. That's what he said. And he meant every word!'

'Tom . . . please . . .' Nancy had never seen her husband like this, and it frightened her.

'So! Get away from here! Leave us be!' Alice was shocked when he grabbed her by the arms. 'Don't try pleading with me, because I know what you are. You're a hussy, that's what you are. A bad apple, rotten right through.'

Dropping his voice to a harsh whisper he told her, 'I don't want to hear how sorry you are, because sorry means nothing to me. D'you hear what I'm saying, Alice Jacobs?' He deliberately used her maiden name. 'Being sorry will never be enough!'

Tightening his hold, he roughly marched her towards the barn door, startled when Nancy called out, 'No, Tom! Please don't hurt her.'

Frantic, Nancy ran between them. 'For God's sake, Tom . . . Alice is carrying our grandchild!'

'Don't give me that!' Visibly shocked, Tom took a step back. 'She's lying. She would say anything to get her claws into this family again!'

Alice couldn't help but fleetingly wonder how Nancy had discovered the truth, but whispers spread fast and eventually the truth will out and she was glad, because now she knew exactly what she must do.

Since being told about the babies, she had been troubled and confused about whether she should keep them, or end the pregnancy. Now though, her mind was suddenly clear. The decision was made, and because of it, her heart was easier.

'I didn't know,' she told them quietly. 'They only told me the day I was leaving hospital.'

For a moment the silence was deafening.

Looking from one to the other, Tom smiled, a slow, hesitant smile that never reached his eyes. 'You're a liar!' He addressed Alice shakily, 'I don't believe one word of what you say, and even if you were telling the truth, I wouldn't care one way or the other, because it would not belong to this family, and neither do you. You never have, and you never will!'

Looking her in the eye, he leaned forward. 'You were the worst thing that ever happened to us. You split my family. You hurt my two sons, and left them broken. You've driven me and mine out of our home and off the land that I've worked since I was a boy.'

The emotion flooded his face, as he went on. 'Inch by inch, mile by mile, we gave blood, sweat and tears to the very land we're standing on now. Me, and my father before me.'

When Alice opened her mouth to ask how she could have done such a thing, he placed his finger so tightly against her lips, she felt them go numb. 'You were not the only visitor here today,' he revealed. 'There was another visitor besides you. And *neither* of you brought good news to this house.'

As he went on, his face began to crumple, and now the bitter tears flowed down the narrow crevices in his sad old face. 'Your sort would never understand.'

'I *do* understand!' she protested. 'I've seen for myself how much you love this land, and I know it would break your heart if you were to lose it.'

He smiled, a sad smile that touched her deeply. 'No,' he whispered. 'You can't understand; *nobody* can. Y'see, the land is like a person. When it becomes neglected, it starts to die, and when it dies, the man who spent his life caring for it, well, he also dies a little . . .' Making a fist, he thumped his chest. 'In here!'

His sadness was overwhelming, as he addressed Alice in a broken voice, 'With my boys gone, there's no one to work the land. I'm too old and useless, and Jimmy can't carry it on his own. I can't afford to pay for outside labour, and now the landlord wants us out, so's he can replace me with some fancy townie. Someone with new-fangled ideas. Someone who can rip out the hedges to make bigger fields, in order to produce bigger crops. Someone who would modernise and force the land to produce more than it can yield. But I only own a small part of it, and that will never be enough to sustain us. The landlord is a good man, but he has the last word and wants us out, and because of what you did, he's got his chance. And I for one will never forgive you for it.'

Alice was distraught. 'He can't just kick you out! You must have rights. He can't do this!'

'Shows how little you know.'

Casting her a disdainful glance he told her again, 'The landlord claims I'm not able to sustain my position and he's right. So, you'll be pleased to know that I'm finished. We're *all* finished, you've seen to that!' With his anger rising again he took her by the shoulders and shook her hard. 'Don't you ever tell me you understand, because you never will!'

Alice pleaded with him. She told him that she never meant for any of this to happen, but while she pleaded, Tom stopped listening.

With Nancy looking on, her face raw with grief, he turned his gaze to the door, looking across the magnificent sweep of land that he had proudly tended for all these years.

His heart and soul were alive with memories, of when he was a young man striding the fields with his father; each of them fired with the love of this beautiful place.

'I was never so fortunate,' he murmured, keeping his gaze to the land. 'Unlike you and yours, I never had much land of my own. Never had the means, y'see.'

He gave a quiet little smile. 'Show me a farmer who's rich, and I'll show you a speculator; a man who never sets foot on the land itself; a man who looks at the fields from a distance. In his cold, calculating mind, he sees a crop of money.'

His smile grew wistful. 'The farmer on the other hand, who lovingly cradles that same land through drought and blizzard . . . he sees only the beauty in the golden swathes of a crop of wheat, or the endless drift of well-kept pasture, where every cow is known by name. And in springtime, the newborn lambs prance and play to their hearts' delight. They have a full and satisfied life, like the farmer who cares for them.'

When he now raised his gaze to her, Alice realised how all the fight was gone from him. 'Beauty, and continuity,' he said. '*That's* what the farmer sees, and that's why he pours his very soul into keeping the land content, because when the land is content, then so is he.'

For a moment he was silent, living his memories, thanking the Lord for the life he had lived, but regretting this day, when it would all come to an end. 'I spent my life toiling other folks' land,' he finished. 'When we came here, the land was all used up and drained. We breathed life into it . . . me and my father, and my sons after me. Since then, I've watched the seasons come and go, and I've been more content than any man has a right to be.'

He scowled. 'But no more, thanks to you, I've lost the sons who worked alongside me, and the land that gave me everything. There are no crops to plan for. No money to be earned, and no one to help.'

As he went on, Nancy could be heard quietly sobbing in the background, and when Alice started over to her, Tom drew her back. 'Leave her be!' he warned. 'Thanks to you, we've been given our marching orders. Our lives as we knew it, are over. That's what you did to us, Alice Jacobs. We never had a slut in the family before, and you're not wanted here, not now. Not ever!'

His anger knew no bounds as he forced her out the door; even when she fell to her knees, he could find no forgiveness in his heart.

When Nancy ran forward to help, he snatched hold of her and held her back, his thoughts in chaos as he strode angrily to the cottage; that same delightful home where he had always found shelter and security. Not now though. Because now he was being forced to leave it behind. His family and his world were falling apart.

Broken in spirit, Alice watched them go; that dear homely woman, and this haunted man who was almost unrecognisable as the proud and gentle soul who had welcomed her into the family. Her heart ached because of all she had done to them.

Alice took a moment to catch her breath against the back wall of the barn. Her mind was in chaos.

She felt emotionally battered and hopelessly lost, and all she could remember were Tom's bitter accusations of how she had destroyed the only things he had ever loved; his family, and his home.

And now he had no work, no help, and soon, no home.

He had blamed her for all these things, and even in her wildest nightmares, she had not realised how deep the tragedy had gone. It wasn't just her and Joe, or even Frank.

It was all her fault.

All her fault! Dear God what had she done? How could she ever put it right?

When she got up to leave a short time later, she could hear them inside the cottage, loudly arguing; something she had never witnessed between these two kindly people before.

'How do you know she's with child?' Tom demanded to know. 'She could be lying, and you're soft enough to believe her!'

'It's true, I'm telling you!' Alice could hear Nancy saying that she'd bumped into Mandy's mother at the shops. 'Apparently, Mandy accidentally let it slip and made her mother promise not to tell anyone, but you know what her mother's like. She's a nice enough soul, but she can't help having a loose tongue.'

'No matter!' Tom retaliated. 'It's none of our business. Do you hear me, woman? I don't want to hear any more about Alice Jacobs or the bastard she's carrying!'

'You can't blame Alice for everything,' Nancy yelled back at him. 'It takes two to make a baby, or are you saying she got *herself* pregnant?'

'I don't give a bugger who made her pregnant! For all we know, it could be the butcher's bastard, or any other young man she may have taken a fancy to.'

'Don't talk nonsense, Tom. Calm yourself.'

Alice could see Nancy was concerned for Tom's health. 'You'll give yourself a heart attack if you don't stop all this shouting and yelling . . . getting all worked up. Carry on like this, and before you know it, you could be lying in the Luton and Dunstable alongside your son. Sit down, man! I'll make us a cuppa, then we can talk sensibly about what to do.'

'There's nothing to be done!' Tom flopped into the chair. 'We've lost everything, Nancy, and that's the awful truth of it. A month from now we'll be out on the street, and at our age that's not a pleasant prospect. What in God's name are we going to do, eh? Where do we go from here?'

Disturbed by everything she had learned, Alice began her journey home.

She felt overwhelmingly heavy of heart and her entire body was suddenly too much of a weight to carry her.

Deeply disturbed by what Tom had told her, she also felt a feeling of exhilaration wash over her.

'Luton and Dunstable hospital . . . that's what Nancy said.'

She quickened her step, and now she started running, as though desperate to find Joe, and explain. She needed to tell him how much she loved him, and that she would look after him . . . she would find a way to help Tom and Nancy . . .

Suddenly a sharp pain in her side caught her unawares with such a force that she was made to sit down and rest.

When a moment later the pain grew worse, she began to suspect there might be something wrong. 'Please . . . oh, please! Don't hurt my babies,' she whispered. 'Not now . . . please, not now!'

Scrambling up, she tried to go forward, but the pains were crippling; and when the cramp buckled her insides, she could hardly breathe.

Anxious, she took another short rest before setting off again. The pains had eased, but she now felt herself falling, until almost without realising, Alice felt her senses slip away.

When the blessed darkness came over her, it was like a quietness of soul. There was no trauma, no anxiety.

Crumpling to the ground, Alice lay there, and all around her, the silence thickened.

CHAPTER TEN

TIRED AND HUNGRY after the long drive back from London, Joshua was glad to be home.

The business meeting had dragged on, and he was now kicking himself that he could have done a better deal.

I could have squeezed a higher figure out of him, he thought as he drove into the lane. Damned broker! I was not ready to sell that land until I'd acquired planning on it.

Easing his car along the side of the house, he smiled. Mind you, he thought, I did make a handsome profit without even lifting a finger. I suppose when it comes right down to it, I actually made a killing.

Though he loved to grumble, Joshua was quietly satisfied with the result of his hard bargaining.

Switching off the engine, he noticed the unfamiliar car parked outside the front door.

'Joshua!' When Tricia came hurrying out of the house, he threw open the door and ran to meet her.

'Tricia! What's wrong? Whose car is that?'

'It's the doctor,' she told him as they hurried along. 'Alice had a fall, but don't worry, she seems to be all right, thank God! Oh, but I've been so worried, I rang the office and they said you'd already left. There was no way of contacting you.'

'Had a fall you say?'

'That's right. It seems she went to see Tom and Nancy. According to Nancy, Tom was really upset and asked her to leave. Nancy was concerned, what with Alice being pregnant, so she went after her, and found her slumped in the field. The doctor said she was lucky not to have had a miscarriage.'

'Dear God! And you're sure she's all right now?'

As he opened the door to let her through, Tricia explained, 'At first the doctor considered sending her to hospital, but he was satisfied that the babies were safe, and Alice was only slightly bruised.'

As he ran up the stairs, Joshua voiced his concern. 'Maybe he should send her to hospital for a proper check-up anyway. Just to be on the safe side?'

'Are you saying I haven't given her a proper check up?' The doctor, a small-framed, squat figure was on the landing, preparing to leave.

'I didn't mean any such thing.' Smiling, Joshua shook him by the hand. 'I merely want the best for my grand-daughter.'

'Very commendable, but I can promise you Alice has been thoroughly checked, and if I had the slightest doubt that she was in any danger, I would have despatched her to the hospital in double quick time.

'Mind you! She's very lucky that she didn't come to any real harm when she blacked out. We must be thankful for Nancy Arnold and her caring nature; if she had not gone out looking for Alice, who knows how long she might have lain there?'

Tricia and Joshua were thinking the very same. 'From now on, I will want to know where Alice is at any given moment!' Tricia declared. 'I blame myself. I should have been watching her more closely.'

The doctor smiled at that. 'Why is it, when any accident happens to those we love, we always blame ourselves? The truth is, we can't wrap them in cotton wool. We all need the freedom to make our own mistakes. That's how we learn, and that's how it should be.'

On that prophetic note, he excused himself and departed. 'I've left a prescription beside the bed,' he informed them. 'Just a little something to help her sleep . . . make sure she gets the rest she needs.'

'If we're worried, we'll call you!' Joshua declared.

'Yes, you do that,' the doctor answered. 'Though Alice will be fine I'm sure. I'll pop back day after tomorrow. Meantime, you need to make certain she doesn't overdo it.'

Alice was sitting in bed, able to hear their conversation. She felt incredibly tired; every bone in her body hurt, but her mind was clearer now that it had been for a long time, 'Thank you, Nancy,' she whispered. 'The doctor's right. If it hadn't been for you, who knows what would have happened?.'

Somewhere in her deepest heart she believed that Joe was the father, because it surely must be true that babies were conceived out of love, not out of fear and pain.

Placing the palm of her hand on her stomach, she could feel the warmth of those two innocents inside her. She even imagined that she could hear their little hearts beating.

Just then the tap on the door shattered her thoughts. 'All right to come in, dear?' Joshua poked his head round the door. 'I've been hearing all about your escapades, and I need to make sure you're all right.'

Alice smiled back at him. 'Come on in, Grandfather,' she said, opening her arms to greet him. 'We've been waiting for you.' She glanced at Tricia, who was right behind him. 'Grandma's been up and down the stairs, looking for you.'

Hugging them one after the other, Alice told them fondly, 'I don't deserve you two. You've always gone out of your way to help me, and here I am . . . causing you anxiety. It's not fair.'

Joshua would have none of it. 'You're our grand-daughter, and we love you,' he said firmly. 'When you love someone you break all the rules to help them.'

That made Alice think. 'I've got something to tell you,' she confessed.

'Oh, and what might that be?'

Joshua drew up a chair, while Tricia sat on the edge of the bed, their whole attention focused on Alice, who was nervously fidgeting with the corner of the sheet.

'Don't keep us on tenterhooks,' Joshua groaned. 'You've no need to be nervous with us, my dear. We're old and ugly enough to cope with anything.'

'You speak for yourself!' Tricia winked at Alice in a bid to ease her nerves. '*You* might be ugly,' she told him, 'but I'll thank you not to paint me with the same brush.'

Alice laughed out loud, relaxing a little. 'Grandfather isn't ugly either,' she told them truthfully.

She had no way of knowing how they might react to her news.

Coaxing her, Joshua reached out and placed his hand over hers. 'Whatever it is you need to tell us, you'd better spit it out,' he urged her. He added with an encouraging smile, 'Besides, there's a brandy waiting for me down-stairs.'

Alice took a moment to think about what she had to say. It would change her life as she knew it, and to all intents and purposes, it was bound to change theirs too.

In fact, because they were the only ones she could turn to at the moment, it could even possibly turn their lives upside down.

In the end she knew there was only one way to say it,

and that was out loud, and quickly. She prayed they would not be too shocked. 'I've decided to have the babies!' There! It was said.

With wet eyes and the whisper of a smile on her kindly face, Tricia leaned forward, her two hands holding Alice's. 'Do you think I didn't already know that?' she said. 'I knew it the minute the doctor said you were fortunate not to have lost the babies. I saw your face, and I knew you would never be content until you held the little ones in your arms. Am I right?'

All this time, Alice had struggled making a decision. She had tortured herself with guilt and doubt, and now that it was truly settled in her mind, she was greatly relieved, so much so that she could not hold back the immense relief that soared through her, and brought forth tears of joy.

'You're right, Grandma,' she whispered. 'The doctor said they could have died, but I know now my babies wanted to live. *They* made the decision. Not me.'

Like his wife, Joshua was excited at the thought of newborn babies in the house . . . his great grandchildren; though he was not altogether convinced whether it was the right thing for Alice to be raising two children without a husband, and with all the stigma and future uncertainty a situation of that nature would inevitably create.

He prayed she had made the right decision. She was still very young, and so much had happened in these past weeks. But like Alice said, the decision was made and knowing her, he also knew that once her mind was made up, there would be no turning back. Alice had always known her own mind, and he was proud of her for that.

'You can count on us, my dear,' he promised sincerely. 'We'll be with you all the way.' Crooking his fingers under her chin, he raised her tear-stained face to look at him.

'You, me and your grandmother . . . we'll get through this together. All three of us, yes?'

'Yes, Grandfather.' Alice flung her arms round him. 'Oh, yes, please!'

And so, rightly or wrongly, they now had to see it through.

And the more he thought of it, the more Joshua let himself believe that the presence of these two little beings, in this house, alive and well, might just bring them a degree of hope and joy to help them forget the bad things.

With a clearer mind, Alice had one more thing to ask of her grandparents. 'I will never be able to thank you for what you've done for me . . . taking me in, and caring about me the way you did. And even now, when I've decided to have the babies, you're happy for me. I didn't tell you this, but you need to know; Tom turned me away. He was angry and upset. He blames me for what happened to his sons. He threw me out . . . told me never to contact any of them again.'

Tricia was horrified. 'I always believed Tom Arnold to be a real gentleman. How can he put all the blame on you, when there are others involved. He should remember the part his own sons played in all of this! Frank Arnold nearly killed you!'

Alice defended Tom and Nancy both. 'I don't blame him,' she confessed. 'Tom and Nancy are kind and lovely people. The thing is . . .' Looking up to her grandfather, she hesitated before going on nervously, 'Because of what happened, because of what I did . . . they've had so much heartache. And now they've lost everything.'

Joshua knew his granddaughter well, and he sensed her concern. 'What are you trying to say, Alice? What exactly do you mean they've lost everything?' He had heard rumours, but thought them to be just that. 'Is there something you think I should know?'

Alice faltered. She knew it might even further alienate Tom and Nancy if she was to reveal their sorry situation. They would be ashamed.

'Alice!' Joshua persisted, 'There's something on your mind, isn't there? If you don't tell me, I can't help.'

'No! It's nothing,' Alice quickly backed off. 'I'm just saying, they've been really worried, that's all.'

Tricia could understand that, and said so. 'We've *all* been worried, Alice. And we're not through it yet . . . none of us.'

Because of her grandmother's remark, Alice felt the need to clarify her own situation. 'After I've had the babies, you do know my mother won't tolerate me going back home?' she told them. 'I know my father wants to do what's best for me, but Mother made it clear that she didn't want me there. So I'm thinking, she won't want the babies either, will she?'

Tricia knew what she was getting at, and quickly put her mind at rest. 'I should hope not!'

Joshua butted in, 'Alice, listen to me, dear. If we thought you were contemplating taking the babies away from here once they were born, your grandmother and I would be most disappointed.' He turned to his wife, 'Isn't that so, Tricia?'

Tricia smiled. 'My sentiments exactly.' She laughed. 'I almost feel as if they're my babies too,' she teased.

Alice was amazed at the depth of their love. Overfilled with emotion she threw herself into their arms; more safe and content than she had felt in a very long time.

There were other issues though, which continued to play on her mind.

Her heart ached for Tom and Nancy, but it would be too selfish and cruel to burden her grandfather with the truth; particularly as her grandparents had done more than enough for her in her hour of need. Besides, Tom and Nancy were proud people and would not thank her for interfering.

She kept the matter of Tom and Nancy strong in her mind all the same. If there was any way in which she might possibly help them, she would be only too glad to do so.

But it was Joe that she could not stop thinking about, and now she knew where he was she had to see him, whatever it took.

~

The following Friday afternoon, Mandy went with Alice to the hospital for a check-up.

'I never want babies!' Mandy was adamant. 'All that bawling and sicky stuff, and dirty, stinky nappies. Ugh!' She made a face that had Alice laughing.

'I'm sure it's not *all* like that,' Alice protested. 'They're also all soft and pink, and when they smile it's like a little ray of sunshine.'

'Oh, yes? And you're an expert now, are you?'

'No, but I saw a woman in the corner shop the other day and she had this beautiful little baby girl . . .' She had often day-dreamed about what sex her babies might be. 'I would like a little girl,' she confessed. 'But if there's a boy as well, I'll love him just the same.'

'What if it's *two* boys?' Mandy argued. 'Think about that! Not only would they be a real handful but there'd be no long hair to plait and comb, no pink ribbons, and no pretty little dresses to wear. What's more, they'd be hankering after football and boy-things and all that boring stuff!'

Alice laughed. 'I could always pretend they were girls,' she teased. 'No one would ever know.'

'Yes they would!'

'How would they?'

Mandy gave her a curious glance. 'Well, because they're different, aren't they?'

'Are they?' Adopting an air of innocence, Alice had to stop herself from laughing out loud.

'Well, yes! 'Course they're different!'

'In what way?'

'Aw, come on, Alice! You know very well . . . they've got these *things*, haven't they?'

'What's that supposed to mean?' By now Alice was having great difficulty in keeping a straight face.

'Well, their little, you know, dangly bits . . .'

When Alice burst out laughing, Mandy was embarrassed. 'You little horror!' Playfully slapping Alice across the shoulder, she revealed, 'You knew perfectly well what I was getting at, and you just wanted to aggravate me. Some friend you are!' And just to prove her point, she gave her another slap.

She gave her yet another slap as they chased each other up the street, the sound of their laughter echoing from the rootftops as they fled into the hospital grounds.

Sobered by their surroundings and the reason for Alice being there, they approached the desk, where Alice duly gave her name to the receptionist.

The receptionist was a pleasant bony woman, with a peculiar, sing-song voice, 'Take a seat in the waiting area,' she sang. 'The doctor will see you in a moment.'

In fact, it was fifteen minutes before the doctor arrived, after which he ushered Alice inside. 'Wait here,' he told Mandy.

Inside the examination room, Alice was already getting undressed. 'Well, everything appears to be just fine,' the doctor gestured for Alice to sit down and get dressed. 'Your blood pressure is very slightly up. That's to be expected, though we'll keep an eye on it. Other than that, you're carrying well, and hopefully you'll go full term without any problems.'

Sitting on the edge of the desk, he asked her, 'Are you absolutely certain you want to take the pregnancy to full term?'

'If you mean do I want to keep my babies, the answer is yes. Like I said, I've thought about it long and hard, and after I collapsed in the field, I got to thinking, what if the babies had died? What if I never had a chance to get to know them, to hold them or love them?'

Alice was certain. 'I do want my pregnancy to go full term.'

The doctor nodded. 'I'm very relieved to hear it,' he confessed. 'Otherwise it might have been a very difficult thing to deal with.'

'Oh?' Alice was intrigued, 'How's that?'

He explained, 'Terminating a pregnancy is something that should never be taken lightly. There are many issues to consider. Firstly, there's the matter of how far along you are. Then there's the actual procedure of termination, and to be honest, they don't always go to plan. Then there's the emotional and psychological problems, which can take years to erase, if ever.'

He studied her for a moment. 'Then of course there are times when we see problems, and find it necessary to refuse the procedure.'

'You don't see problems with me, do you doctor?'

'Of course, your circumstances are slightly different from the normal, what with the injuries you sustained and the danger of inflicting more surgery on you at a time when you are vulnerable. You needed time to consider all the options. However, terminating a pregnancy in the later stages is always a serious issue, and often dangerous, which is why we needed you to make a decision sooner rather than later.'

He stood up. 'However, that particular dilemma is now thankfully resolved. But, I do have other issues for you to deal with.'

'What kind of issues, doctor?'

'Well, first and foremost, you need to put some fat on your bones. You're far too thin, and you look tired. I'll speak with the nutritionist, and also the physiotherapist. Between the two of them they should be able to get you strong in body and mind, ready for the birth.'

He began scribbling on to his prescription pad. 'Meanwhile, remember to take one of these a day. You can collect them at the pharmacy by the front entrance. Oh, and you must book your next appointment at the desk. We will need to see you on a regular basis.'

On that note, he wished her well, and reminded her to be careful with the medication. Then he saw her out the door.

~

Mandy was waiting to meet her, eager to hear what the doctor had said.

The two of them chatted all the way to the bus stop.

'Everything's fine. He doesn't see any problems, but he says I need fattening up.' Alice smiled. 'With the twins growing inside me, I'm sure I'll be fat as an elephant soon enough!'

'No! He's right!' Mandy was adamant. 'Compared to me, you're like a stick insect.' She made a face. 'Mind you, compared to me, *everyone's* a stick insect.'

'Don't be hard on yourself,' Alice chided. 'Besides, I am not a stick insect.'

'Yes, you are! There's nothing of you, nobody would ever guess you were pregnant!'

In an impulse, Alice flung her arms round her friend. 'You're right!' she laughed excitedly. '*I'm pregnant!* Oh, Mandy, I'm so glad I've decided to go ahead with the pregnancy. I don't think I could have lived with myself if I'd chosen to terminate.'

'I knew you wouldn't do it,' Mandy confessed. 'All the time you were agonising over it, I knew all along it would never happen.' She knew how such a thing would have haunted Alice forever and a day.

For a time they walked along in silence; arm in arm, each deep in thought. When they got on the bus, Alice voiced her feelings about Joe, and how desperately she needed to see him.

'Why can't you leave it be?' Mandy asked worriedly. 'Especially after what Tom said.'

'I can't leave it be,' Alice confided, 'I won't rest until I've seen Joe and talked with him.'

'Oh, and how will you do that, when you don't even know where he is?'

'I think I do.'

'How can you? As far as I know, they haven't told anyone.'

Alice explained, 'After Tom sent me away, I overheard Nancy telling him to calm down. Then she mentioned Joe, and said something about Luton and Dunstable. That's what Nancy said.'

'But you won't go, will you? I thought Tom said that Joe didn't want to see you anymore?'

Alice had been thinking about that. 'To tell you the truth, Mandy, I'm not sure I believe Tom,' she admitted. 'He might be saying that just to keep me away.'

Mandy disagreed. 'Will you be cross if I speak my mind?'

'No. I really *want* you to speak your mind.'

'All right then, I will.' She had to say it, even if Alice might feel hurt. 'Listen, Alice. You can't get away from the fact that in doing what you did, you and Joe set off a series of catastrophes. I mean, think about it. *You* ended up in hospital for weeks on end, and almost died. Tom was hurt, and *Joe* is still hospitalised. According to what Tom told you, we don't even know if Joe will ever be the same again.'

'You're right, and I blame myself. I should never have gone into the barn that night. It was wrong, and I *knew* it was wrong, but I still let it happen!'

Her voice broke with emotion. 'Sometimes, when I can't sleep, I think about that night. I remember how wonderful it was, not dirty or sordid, but kind of magical. I will never forget how it felt with Joe's arms around me. I love him, Mandy. I can't help what I feel.'

She had thought long and hard and she knew what she must do. 'I wouldn't blame Joe if he regretted it though, and even if it's true that he never wants to see me again, I would never blame him for that either. The trouble is . . .'

Mandy completed the sentence for her. 'You just can't believe Joe would never want to see you again, that's it, isn't it?'

Alice nodded. 'I need him to say it to my face,' she said. 'I need to see it in his eyes. More than that, I have to satisfy myself that he's on the road to recovery.'

When Alice talked of Joe, she was so alive her eyes shone and her face lit up from the inside. There was something about her that was different, and amazing.

'You really do love him, don't you?' Mandy asked now.

'With all my heart,' Alice replied softly. 'From the very first moment I saw him . . . just after Frank and I started going out together. He took me to see Tom and Nancy, and Joe was there. He smiled at me, and something happened. It was like he could see my thoughts . . . like he was in my head. I was drawn to him then, and soon after he'd gone away, I found myself thinking about him.'

'So, if you felt like that, why didn't you end it with Frank?'

Alice shrugged. 'I don't know. I suppose I thought it was nothing . . . that I was just excited to meet Frank's brother or something. I really don't know!'

She smiled at the memory. 'That first meeting, Joe seemed a bit mysterious. He hardly spoke. He just smiled, the kind of smile that creeps right into your insides.'

She took a deep breath. 'Then he suddenly went away. One minute he was there and the next he was gone. After that, I kept thinking about him, wanting to see him.'

She felt a bit like a schoolgirl with her first crush. 'When I think about it now, I must have fallen in love with him right from that first meeting, only I didn't know it. Not until he came home to be Frank's best man. That was when I knew.'

The smile slipped away and in its place was a sense of desolation. 'I swear to you, Mandy, if I could turn back the clock, I would have thought twice about going through with the wedding. It was the wrong thing to do. I see that now. Tom was right; it was all my fault. I went to the barn. I watched Joe handling the bird and my heart was aching to be with him. I should have walked away, but I didn't, and for that one moment of weakness, a lot of good people have been hurt.'

Sliding an arm round her shoulders, Mandy told her not to blame herself. 'It takes two,' she said comfortingly. 'Just remember that.'

Deep down, Alice knew she was right. 'I would still change things if I could.'

'Well, you can't!' Mandy told her sharply. 'What's done is done, and besides . . .'

She gently patted Alice's belly. 'You need to concentrate on these two little monsters. Before you know it, you'll have 'em dangling one from each little titty. And don't forget what goes in the top, must come out the bottom. There'll be so many nappies to wash and change, you won't know which way up you are!'

Alice laughed at that, but soon the mood was sober again, and her intention resolute.

One way or another, she had to find out the answers for herself. Had Tom told her the truth? Did Joe actually say that he never wanted to see her again?

And what could she do, to stop Tom and Nancy losing everything they had worked so hard for?

~

Neither Mandy nor Alice had noticed the dark saloon that followed them all the way from the hospital, and was still tailing them now.

They didn't see how, even after they had climbed aboard the bus, the car stayed close.

It kept a discreet pace all the way to the bottom of Aspley Hill, where Mandy got off. 'I'll see you in the week,' Mandy called as she stepped down off the bus. 'Look after yourself!'

'You too!' Alice waved from the window, and soon Mandy was gone, leaving Alice feeling lonely, and a little sad.

In all this time, Frank had never been far away. He watched them now from his car window. He watched Mandy until she was out of sight. He then eased the car forward, still pursuing the bus, still wary that someone might recognise him; though he had taken every precaution.

Having carefully tipped the brown trilby low on his forehead, he could easily see out, while ensuring that his face was well hidden from prying eyes.

When Alice got off the bus, he followed, keeping enough distance between them not to alert her.

When she turned to go up the drive, he drew the car over and proceeded on foot, making sure to keep close to the hedge.

As Alice entered the porch, he remained behind the gate, watching her; thinking how if it had been part of his plan, he could have have abducted her with ease. For now though, it served his purpose to closely monitor her movements.

'You got free of me last time,' he growled. 'But now that I know where you are, there'll be time enough to finish the job!'

He felt only loathing for the woman he had taken for a wife. He had never really loved her. She was merely a means to an end. He had hoped she might afford him wealth and status the like of which he had never known before. He knew now it had all been a pipe dream, because the family wealth would never have been his.

More than that, she had shamed and hurt him. All that time she had kept him waiting for her virginity until they were married, and then before the event, she willingly gave herself to his brother.

The wish to see her dead remained strong in him.

Added to which, the discovery that Joe was still alive was like a thorn in his side.

Once he knew Joe's whereabouts, he would wait for his moment, and when it came, his plan was to kill two birds with one stone.

The idea made him smile.

He watched now as Alice put her key in the lock, but then she swung her head round nervously as if sensing his presence before pushing open the door. He dodged back into the hedge; secure in the knowledge that she had not seen him there.

After Alice had gone inside, he went back up the lane to his car. Once there, he quickly climbed inside, started the engine and moved off.

A short time later he drove past his parents' cottage without even a thought for them.

He drove on for another mile or so, before turning into a narrow cart track, then he continued on for another mile.

When he reached the fork in the road where it opened out in three directions, he turned the car about and parked it under the far-reaching branches of an old beech tree.

Satisfied that should he have need to make a quick exit, he would have a fast and clear way out, he now stopped the engine, switched off the ignition, and got out of the car.

Locking the car, he dropped the keys into his jacket pocket, and continued on foot, along the familiar and well-used track.

After a while, he found a broad tree stump nestled into the hedge. Pleased with himself, he settled down to wait for his prey.

Digging into his jacket pocket he took out a packet of cigarettes. He slipped one out and, putting it between his lips, he dug into his pocket for a second time, located a match and struck it on the sole of his shoe. He cradled the flame against the breeze, and lit the tip of his cigarette.

After enjoying a long, slow drag of the cigarette, he blew out the smoke in a perfect ring. 'You haven't lost it, Frank old son!' he chuckled, his gaze now trained on the stile and the field beyond. He glanced at his watch. 'He shouldn't be too much longer,' he murmured. 'A man of habit . . . always has been!'

The minutes passed, then an hour, and now Frank was weary and irritated. 'Where the devil are you, Jimmy?' he muttered. 'I know this is the way you always come, with your poaching bag over your shoulder, fit to burst, you thieving git!'

He sniggered. 'You always were a better thief than a farmhand!'

~

Not too far away, crouched down at the deep end of the brook, having skilfully snatched them from the slow-moving waters, Jimmy was busy hooking up the last of his catch. Violently flipping and twitching, the fish were already gasping their last.

By the time he had them all neatly strung, he was confident of his meals for the next few days, and the thought of them lying on his plate, all fat and juicy, made him salivate.

He'd cook them up with a nice dab of butter and serve them with a few well-chosen root potatoes and veg which would be discreetly removed from Farmer John's allotment. Oh, and a jar of cider to wash it all down. 'By! You'll be living like a king on this little lot,' he chuckled to himself.

He went on his way, content with the world; except for the absence of regular work and the fact that the few pounds he'd managed to earn here and there was not enough.

Whistling merrily, he knotted the end of the twine to secure his fine catch. That done, he tied the whole ensemble around his waist in a knot. 'Time I was off home,' he muttered. 'Don't want all the dogs and cats in the area getting a sniff of you lovely things!'

He laughed. 'Dopey fish! You never learn, do you eh? I put the bread on the hook and I drop the hook into the water, and being the greedy, daft buggers you are, you take the hook like you were born to it.'

He smacked his lips. 'Before you know it, you'll be dancing and sizzling in the pan, ready to fill old Jimmy's belly.'

Still chuckling at the thought of his meal, Jimmy quickly covered the distance between himself and Frank.

Jiggled about by his jaunty stride, the fish swung and danced around his hips; the strong unpleasant odour rubbing off on his duffle coat, but did he care? Not Jimmy. No way.

His mood was such that he even began singing. It was an old pub song, a bit randy and bawdy in nature, but one of Jimmy's favourites.

It was also the signal that told Frank he was on his way.

Jimmy's merry song came to an abrupt halt as he climbed over the stile, and he was grabbed from behind by the scruff of the neck. 'Well now, Jimmy, you sound far too happy for my liking!'

Frank had him fast by the throat. 'I'm glad you're in good voice though, because I want you to sing for me while you're at it. D'you think you can do that, Jimmy? Can you sing for your old friend, Frank?' With immense strength, he yanked him over the stile. 'Well?'

Jimmy's eyes were big and scared. This was the moment he had dreaded. His every instinct had warned him that Frank was never far away, and that when he did show his face, he was bound to seek him out. And he was right. He couldn't stop trembling.

'Don't hurt me, Frank!' His throat was squeezed so tight between the other man's fingers, the words came out in a gargle. 'What d'you want?'

'I want answers, Jimmy.' Frank thrust his face close to Jimmy's. 'Information, and lots of it! That's what I want . . . for now.'

'I don't know nuthin'!' Jimmy's Adam's apple bobbed up and down with fearful speed.

'Is that so?' Frank shook him hard. 'Well, I tell you what we'll do, shall I?'

Jimmy nodded.

'I'll release my hold on you, and then I'll tell you what I need to know.'

He smiled, a slow, evil smile that made Jimmy's skin crawl. 'Then, you can answer my questions, and if the answers suit me, well then, Jimmy, I might just let you go on your way. So! Is that a deal?'

Jimmy nodded again.

'Good! I knew you'd see the sense of it.' Just to make sure he had his full attention, he squeezed his fingers tighter round Jimmy's neck.

When Jimmy made a strangled sound, he grabbed him by the shoulders. 'One other thing,' he warned. 'If you talk to anyone . . . *anyone at all,* about me being here, I'll have to hunt you down and shut you up . . . for good.' He smiled into Jimmy's face. 'Now then, Jimmy. Do we still have a deal?'

'Yes, Frank.'

Keeping Jimmy close, he asked, 'Why was Alice at the hospital today?'

'I'm not sure.'

For a long moment, Frank stared at him. 'Tell me what you know.'

Only too aware of what Frank was capable of, Jimmy opened up. 'I honestly don't know. It might have been something and nothing.' He dared not reveal what he'd overheard, about Alice being pregnant.

Frank grabbed him by the neck. 'Are you telling me the truth, or is there something you're covering up? You'd better answer me, Jimmy!'

'Like I said . . . I don't know why Alice was at the hospital, Frank. I expect it was a check-up or summat. I mean . . . she was hurt bad, wasn't she? Maybe she has to have regular appointments, I don't know!'

Seemingly satisfied on that point, Frank had another question. 'She didn't see me, but I followed her today. I was right behind and she never knew. I followed her to the hospital, and then I followed her back to her grand-parents' house.'

Jimmy recalled what he knew. 'There was a lot of

trouble. When they let Alice out of the hospital, your dad said he didn't want her there . . . not after what she did. It seems her mother didn't want her neither. Rumour has it, that she went to stay at her grandparents' house. At least, that's what I heard.'

'So nobody wanted her, eh?' His delight was obvious. 'Well now, I can't say I'm surprised. I mean, she's got what she deserves, hasn't she? She's nothing but a filthy little tart! What woman would sleep with the brother of her husband to be . . . Who would do such a shameful thing, Jimmy?'

Jimmy said nothing. He didn't want to rile Frank any more than he was already.

'Is she seeing anybody?' Frank spat out the words. 'Is she cheating again?'

Panicking, Jimmy shook his head. 'I shouldn't think so! I don't imagine that for a minute. Honest, Frank, I only know what I know . . . that you hurt her bad and she was a long time in hospital, then she went to live with her grandparents. I don't know nuthin' else. Honest to God, I don't!'

Knowing what a coward he was, Frank believed him. 'I'm surprised you even know that much,' he chuckled. 'People know what a gossip you are, don't they, eh? Nobody tells you anything as a rule. They feel they can't trust you to keep it to yourself. Isn't that so, Jimmy?'

'Yes, that's right, Frank, nobody tells me nuthin'.'

'Ah, but you still manage to find out in your own devious little way, don't you, eh?'

Jimmy felt proud. 'Yes . . . sometimes.'

'There you go then! That's why I came to you, and nobody else, Jimmy. I knew I could count on you to let me know what's been going on since I've been away.' He paused, his eyes boring into Jimmy's. 'So, what else has been going on then, eh?'

'I don't really know nuthin' else, Frank.'

'Don't you lie to me now, Jimmy, because I wouldn't like that. Y'see, it would make me really angry.'

'Please, Frank! I'm not lying. I don't know any more.'

'All right then, but now I have another question.'

He paused, before going on in a low, deliberate voice. 'This time, I want you to think very hard before you answer, because this one is more important to me than you know.'

'I'll try, Frank. I really will!'

For a long moment Frank waited.

He watched Jimmy squirm and he bided his time, and when he thought Jimmy was about to break, he said harshly, *I need you to tell me where Joe is.*'

Jimmy had been afraid he might ask that.

'Well!' Frank was impatient.

'I'm sorry, Frank. I don't know that one. *Nobody* knows, because Tom and Nancy have kept it all to themselves. Y'see, they didn't want Joe to be bothered. They wanted him to be quiet, so he could mend without anyone being a nuisance. And they didn't want Alice going near him neither.'

He saw no harm in explaining. 'She kept asking after him d'you see? She asked anyone who might know, but nobody did, because Tom and Nancy never told. When Joe was moved away from Bedford hospital, they asked the hospital never to say where he was; especially to the newspapers, and especially when they kept hanging about, waiting for you to turn up, Frank.'

He nervously finished, 'I expect they're still watching for you, Frank.'

'Ssh!' Frank put his finger to Jimmy's lips. 'I don't want to know that. What I want to know is where Joe was moved to, and why.'

He gave Jimmy a suspicious look. 'Are you sure you don't know where he is?'

Jimmy nodded.

'If you're hiding something?'

'I'm not!'

'Mmm. All right then. Now you listen carefully. Being on the run does not mean you're altogether unaware of what's happening in the outside world. Like everyone else, I read the papers.'

He lapsed into deep thought, before revealing his ideas. 'It's a shame I didn't manage to finish Joe off, but there'll be other chances. I'm a patient man as you well know.'

He smiled. 'You and me, Jimmy we've had our differences but we can put them behind us now, can't we, eh? We need each other, you and me, don't you think?'

Jimmy made no response, and Frank was too deep in thought to notice.

He gabbled on, 'I knew they'd taken him to Bedford hospital. And I thought there was little hope that he might survive. Unhappily for me, he proved them wrong, but he was hurt bad; at least I got that right anyway!'

He persisted in his questioning. 'You say my parents didn't want Alice going near him? Is that right?'

'They really turned against her, Frank. Especially Tom.'

Frank smiled at that. 'I can't say I'm surprised. Dad was always a stickler for doing the right thing. Every bad thing that ever happened to our family was caused by what she did!'

He had a rare stab of conscience. 'I'm sorry I hurt my dad. But it was his own fault. He should never have got in the way.'

He frowned. 'As for Mum, well, she's always been too damned soft . . . seeing the good in everybody. I wouldn't be at all surprised if she hadn't tried to stop Dad from getting rid of the little bitch!'

His voice fell to a whisper, and for a moment he seemed totally oblivious to Jimmy's presence: 'Mum needs to realise that we've all had our lives ruined by her dear little Alice! Oh, but she'll learn! One of these days, somebody will need to teach her a lesson she won't forget!'

There was such a rage in him that when Jimmy took a step back, Frank was on him. 'Where d'you think you're going?'

'I thought . . . I just thought . . .' What he actually thought was that Frank had gone completely mad; that he was talking about hurting Nancy . . . his own mother; and that really spooked him.

Shaking him hard, Frank put the question again. 'I'll ask you one more time. Where's Joe?'

'I don't know, Frank! Truly, I don't know. It's a secret.'

'You'd better not be lying, Jimmy!'

'I'm not lying. I wouldn't lie to you, Frank, you know that.'

Frank did know it, and he said so, but he remembered what Jimmy had told him earlier. 'You said they didn't let on where Joe was, because they didn't want Alice going to see him?'

'Yes, that's right, Frank.'

'So, that means he must have thought she *wanted* to see him?'

'Oh, she did. She still does. Mandy's mother is a real gossip. She chatters about what Alice said to Mandy, and the word is that Alice is desperate to see Joe.' The second the words were out, Jimmy could have bitten off his tongue, but it was too late to take it back, and now Frank was seething.

'Is that so?' He was silent for a while, his mind alive with such hatred he could taste it. 'And has she seen him?'

Thinking Frank's question was a trick, Jimmy shook his head vehemently. 'If I knew that, I might know where he is, but I don't.'

'And I don't really know what to do with you, Jimmy.'

'What do you mean, Frank?'

'Well, I mean, you haven't told me an awful lot, have you? You've told me about the bitch being turned away from the cottage, and that she has a longing to see Joe.' He glared at him. 'Are you sure there's nothing else I should know?'

'I told you she'd gone to her grandparents.' Jimmy could see his life ending there and then, and he began to panic. 'You can torture me if you like, Frank, and I won't be able to tell you anymore, because I don't *know* anymore. I keep myself to myself. I don't like being round people. They stare at me. They think I'm stupid!'

Growing anxious, he started gabbling, 'I've told you how your dad means to keep Alice away from Joe, and I've told you she intends to find out where he is. Anyway, that's what Mandy's mum says, and I believe her.'

'Bugger off, Jimmy!'

'What?'

'I said . . . bugger off!'

Jimmy was visibly relieved. 'So you're not gonna hurt me then?'

'Oh! Now you've got me worried, Jimmy.'

'Why?'

Frank was cruel to the bitter end. 'Well, there must be a reason as to why you think I should hurt you.'

Taking hold of Jimmy's collar he drew him forward. 'Am I right to be suspicious, Jimmy? *Is* there a reason why I should hurt you? You know what? I'm beginning to wonder if you're hiding something from me. Are you, Jimmy? Are you hiding something?'

'No!'

'Right, then you'd best do as I said, and bugger off . . . before I decide to take you to pieces.'

Jimmy did not want telling twice.

He knew from personal experience how dangerously unstable Frank was.

Taking to his heels, he clambered over the stile and ran like the wind down the lane, with Frank laughing and calling out, 'RUN JIMMY BOY! I might take a mind to come after you. Remember what I said . . . one word about me and what we've been talking about, and I'll have you!'

Jimmy knew it, which is why when the string broke from round his waist and his well-earned meals fell to the ground, he didn't even stop to collect them.

Frank saw it, and laughed out loud. 'You're a prize dimwit, Jimmy,' he chuckled as he went on his way. 'Thick as a plank and twice as gormless!' But he secretly thanked Jimmy for the information he'd given him.

'So, now all I have to do is get to Joe. First though, I need to find out where he is.'

It was a dangerous risk he was prepared to take, what with the police hot on his tail. But it would be worth it, just to finish the job he started.

As he went back to the car, his mind was spinning. 'So! we've got a badly injured patient who's been moved from Bedford hospital to somewhere else. So, why did they move him, eh?

'It seems he's got injuries they can't deal with. Yes! That must be it. Mmm! Chances are they had to move him because he needed special treatment, or delicate surgery, and they weren't equipped to deal with it at Bedford.'

Frustratingly, Jimmy had not been able to tell him which hospital Joe was in, so now he had two real choices; neither of which were safe, or desirable, but either one would stand a good chance of allowing him to find Joe.

He could wait till nightfall and go cap in hand to see his parents, and wheedle the truth out of them.

Or he could risk being seen in public to have another word with Jimmy, who seemed able to find out anything if he set his mind to it.

By the time he got to his car and started his way back

to his hideout, he was satisfied that his second choice was the better one.

What was even more satisfactory, was the fact that he need not wait until morning. He would execute his plan later tonight, then if it worked out the way he wanted it to, he could be at Joe's bedside sooner rather than later.

He congratulated himself, 'The best plans are always the simplest.'

Putting his foot down on the accelerator, he arrived at the canal in no time.

Driving into the shadows, he eased the car alongside the bins before making his way up the towpath to the old barge which was moored nearby.

Scrambling aboard, he tapped on the small panelled door that led down to the cabins. 'Hello there!'

Back came the slurred voice, 'What d'yer want? Get away from 'ere, yer little bastards!'

Frank pushed open the door. 'It's me, Jack . . . it's Fred.'

'Don't know any bloody Fred.' Screwing up his eyes to see through the dim light, he warned. 'Clear orf, or I'll set the dog on yer!'

There was a lot of rustling and banging around, and when a shadowy figure appeared at the other end of the living quarters, Frank warily began his way forward.

'It's not kids!' he said. 'It's me . . . it's Fred. Don't you remember? We met in the pub and you offered me a place for the night? I went out because I had something urgent to attend to, and now I'm back!'

'What's that you say?' The older man peered at him. 'Are you the bloke from the pub?' There was a flickering of light and a whoosh of flame as the candle was lit. 'Bugger me, Fred! You 'ad me worried there. I thought it were them bloody kids back again . . . aggravating little ratbags, they want doing away with! If they so much as show their faces again, they'll 'ave my boot up their arse, an' no mistake!'

Needing to be sure he still had a hiding place to come back to, Frank told him, 'I've only popped back to collect something and put my head down for a couple of hours. That bit of business I were telling you about just now, well, y'see, it's not done yet. I have to go out later, just for an hour or so, then I'll be back.'

'Bloody hell, Fred!' The other man was none too pleased. 'You're in and out, then it's the kids throwing things at the barge, and now when you've woke me up, you're off out again.' He groaned. 'Happen it might be best if you find . . .'

Suspecting he was about to be shown the door, Frank quickly closed the short distance between them. 'You're a good mate, Jack,' he purred. 'I don't know what I'd have done if you hadn't taken me in. I appreciate it, Jack, and you won't go short, not if I can help it.'

He slapped the skinny man on his bare shoulder. 'Listen to me, Jack. To show my appreciation, what if I was to collect a bottle of the hardstuff on my way back, eh? How would you like that?'

'Ha, ha! That's me man!' Jack liked it a lot. 'Yer crafty old beggar, Fred! You know how to please a fella, I'll say that for yer.'

He leaned forward, fouling the air with his body odour and boozey breath. 'Hey! Yer couldn't make it *two* bottles, could yer?'

He gave a toothless grin. 'It'll help me forget the mindless little bastards who keep tormenting me!'

Because this hiding place was ideal, Frank was relieved. 'Two bottles it is then!' It was either that, or shove the filthy bag o' bones over the side. 'First though, I need to put my head down,' he reminded him. 'I've had a long enough day already.'

'That's all right wi' me, Fred. So long as yer don't forget what you promised, eh?'

The skinny man returned to his bunk, while Frank remained by the door, huddled in the chair and sleeping lightly.

In the dark recesses of his mind, he was busy hatching the details of his plan. 'I'm on to you, Joe,' he whispered. 'I think I've worked out where you might be.'

Feeling satisfied, he drew his coat about him and settled back. 'We'll soon find out if I'm right!'

'What's that yer say?' Jack heard him mumbling.

In reply, Frank made a series of loud, snoring sounds. 'I see . . .' Jack chuckled. 'Talking in yer sleep is it?' He turned over. 'Yer chattering don't bother me, matey. So long as yer bring the bottles back, yer can chatter and snore to yer 'eart's content!'

He gave a low chuckle. 'Mind you! Once I've got me mitts on them bottles, I'll up anchor and away. As for you, matey, well, you can go to buggery for all I care!'

To him, Frank was just a stranger in a boozer who'd bought him a drink. 'I gave you a bed for the night, and that's all yer getting! Yer ain't sliding yer feet under *my* table for months on end, no siree! Bottles or no bottles!'

Slithering further into the bed, he smiled at the prospect of the booze he was about to enjoy.

What he could not have known was that Frank had heard, and with every cutting word, the bargee had well and truly sealed his fate.

CHAPTER ELEVEN

IT WAS MIDNIGHT by the time Frank arrived at the Luton and Dunstable hospital. With dogged determination, and keeping his ear to the ground, he had found out where Joe was.

As always, the place was lit up inside and out. There were ambulances arriving and departing; people rushing to and fro; some carrying stretchered casualties; and others waiting anxiously as their loved ones were rushed into the emergency ward.

On the far side of the front entrance two women in nurse's uniform stood chatting and smoking, and stamping their feet on the ground as the late night cold air enveloped them.

'Bide your time, Frank,' he murmured, being careful to keep a low profile. 'You don't want to be charging in there like a bull at a gate. You need to be calm and quiet . . . wait for the right time, and the job will be a good one.'

He smiled at the thought of dealing Joe a hammer blow, without physically lifting a finger.

He constantly took a mental note of the exterior layout as he went.

During his time on the run, Frank had learned the many wiles and tricks of a convict. He now reminded himself that it was wise to clock every possible exit, and anything else that might aid a quick and easy escape should it be needed.

He took a while to familiarise himself with the building itself. There were four different entrances to the hospital; the main one, the one for emergencies only, a side entrance for staff and porters and possibly deliveries, and a more discreet one, which he assumed to be the boiler house and storage place, and which might possibly hold an inner access to the hospital corridors.

'If I can get in, then I can get out!'

He began to relax. In the event of anyone raising the alarm, such information would serve him well. As would the fact that he had parked his car in a most strategically favourable position; with its nose pointed to the exit, and no possibility of anyone parking between him and a clean escape.

Fastening his jacket, he sleeked back his hair, which he had deliberately grown much longer than normal. He then put on the discreet, rimless spectacles he'd purchased some time ago. That done, he headed for the main entrance; his shifty eyes constantly darting about, looking for anything that might pose a threat.

Feeling confident, he sauntered through the main doors.

On seeing the little shop at the corner, he approached it cautiously. For a moment he lingered, pretending to browse, while discreetly surveying the whole area.

'Want some flowers, dear?'

A little woman had emerged from inside to fill the flower-buckets. 'Two bunches for six shillings,' she informed him. ''Course if you only want *one* bunch, that'll be four shillings and five pence.'

Frank opted for one bunch, and quickly counted out the money.

'Which colour, dear?' She held up two bunches of roses. 'Pink or yellow?'

'Either will do.'

'Oh!' She seemed surprised. 'I'm sorry. I assumed you might be taking them in for your wife and new baby.' She smiled. 'How silly of me. I got the idea you might be a nervous new daddy.'

A moment later she had wrapped the yellow roses and collected his money. 'I'm sorry I jumped to conclusions,' she apologised. 'I hope whoever you're visiting will like the flowers. They're fresh in this morn—'

Before she'd finished talking, he was gone. 'Miserable devil!' she grumbled. 'Anyone can make a mistake!' Then she reminded herself and felt guilty. 'Don't be too harsh, Eva,' she chided herself. 'The poor man is probably worried about his sick relative.'

Looking very much like the concerned visitor, Frank held the flowers before him as he went to the reception desk. 'Excuse me . . .'

When the young nurse glanced up, he noticed she was quite a looker and he thought if this was a different occasion, he might well be tempted to ask her out. But he was on a very delicate and dangerous errand, so he kept focussed. 'I understand my cousin was brought here, but I don't know which ward he's in. I wonder, could you please point me in the right direction?' He gave his most encouraging smile.

Instantly at ease with him, she smiled back. 'I'll do my best,' she offered. 'What's your cousin's name?'

'It's Joe . . . Joe Arnold . . . transferred from Bedford Hospital.'

While she consulted her ledgers, he continued in a friendly easy manner, 'We're very close me and him . . . we virtually grew up together, but we kind of lost touch. I've been abroad this past year: on business . . . travelling with my company. As soon as my uncle managed to get hold of me, I cancelled everything and got back as quick as I could.'

She nodded. 'I see . . .' After returning her attention to the ledger, she glanced up. 'Joe Arnold . . . he's the young man who was attacked.'

'That's right! And I've travelled a long way to give him my support.'

She nodded agreeably. 'I'm sure he'll appreciate that,' she said. 'He doesn't have too many visitors.'

She thought of Joe Arnold, who was not much older than she was. From what she'd been told, he may never again stand on his own two feet. It was a daunting and terrible thing, especially for one so young.

'He'll be pleased to see you,' she told Frank. 'So far as I know, his parents have been the main visitors. Oh, and there's Bob of course. He takes a few minutes every now and then to chat with your cousin . . . lets him know what's going on in the outside world so to speak.'

She smiled. 'Mind you, I expect he enjoys a little break from the monotony.'

Being careful not to sound too interested, Frank enquired, 'Who's Bob?'

'Oh, I'm sorry!' She explained, 'The police have posted him outside your cousin's room. I expect they think he might still be in danger.'

'That's good,' Frank declared. 'It shows the police are taking this seriously.'

'Yes, but I'm afraid you'll need to tell him who you are and he'll question you,' she said. 'Bob's all right though. He's not too authoritative. In fact, he's a bit of a pussy cat really.'

Frank assured her, 'That's all right. I don't mind answering questions.'

In the light of what he'd learned, Frank was already

looking to take a moment and realign his plans. 'Like I say, I'm here to support Joe,' he said casually. 'A bit of inconvenience is neither here nor there.'

She added, 'Oh, but you'll need to wait a few minutes, because Nurse Barry is in there at the moment. She's doing her regular check-ups, but she won't be long now.'

Gesturing to the seating area opposite, she told him, 'You could wait there if you like. There's a tea stall at the back.'

She had another suggestion, 'If you want, you could go up to the next floor. There's a proper café up there. Well, when I say proper, I mean they sell biscuits and sand-wiches, and there are a few tables and chairs. It's where the nurses go to eat their lunch.'

Frank was relieved to have been thrown a lifeline. 'Good idea. In fact I am a bit peckish. Yes! Thank you. So, how long will the nurse be, d'you think?'

The young nurse shrugged. 'Ten, maybe fifteen minutes. Nurse Barry shouldn't be much longer than that.'

'Might I ask where the loos are?' He feigned embar-rassment. 'I was in a rush to get here. Sorry!'

'Down the corridor, on the right.'

Fifteen minutes later, she had completed her filing, when Nurse Barry came rushing up to return the medical tray. 'Got to go, Sally,' she said breathlessly. 'I didn't realise what the time was, and I promised mother I'd pick her up the minute my shift was ended. She's staying with me for a few days. She's not been well, y'see?'

'There was a visitor for . . .' The young nurse started to tell her about Frank, but the older woman cut her off. 'Sorry, can't chat. I've really got to go . . . but look, I know you finish today, and I just want to say the best of luck travelling. Be careful, and stay well. I hope you enjoyed your short stint at the desk. You did a good job.'

Reaching over the desk, she gave the young girl a quick hug then she was off, calling as she went, 'Mother will be in such a cranky mood if I'm late again! When you get back to university, work hard and you'll get where you want to go.'

She was still calling as she went headlong out of the doors and across the car park.

For a time, Frank kept his eyes peeled. He saw the nurse come hurrying to the desk. He saw her quickly leave and soon after that, he watched as the shift changed hands.

'If you're gonna do it, you'd best do it now!' he told himself.

Impatient to get inside with Joe, he seized the moment.

Staying in the shadows, he returned to the hospital foyer, where he sat himself in the area that the young nurse had earlier pointed out.

The busy hospital staff went about their duties with a zest, while visitors seemed to rush about as though they hadn't got a minute to live.

As for the cleaner, she seemed half asleep. Dressed in a green wraparound apron and pushing a galvanised mop bucket before her, she went about this routine act like a zombie, rhythmically swishing her wet mop across the floor, then viciously screwing it into the drainer until it was bone dry, before slapping it into the disinfected water for the umpteenth time, and starting the whole pattern over again.

Frank was mesmerised. He found he couldn't take his eyes off her as she walked up and down, softly humming to herself as she flopped the mop in and out. After a while, he was amazed and angry to find himself almost nodding off. He blamed it on the bargee who'd kept him up late with his loud snoring.

On seeing the policeman walking towards the desk, he

was excited, and a little nervous. This was what he'd been waiting for.

'You should never have brought me that tea.' The big man had a deep, gruff voice, and a baby face. 'Now, I need to visit the gents.'

'And enjoy a crafty ciggie at the same time, no doubt.' The young nurse was obviously familiar with him.

'So, d'you think you could keep an eye on the ward for me?'

The nurse assured him. 'When you've got to go, you've got to go,' she grinned. 'Yes, of course I'll watch the door. I've done it often enough, haven't I?'

He laughed. 'You needn't think you're sharing my wages though,' he joked, 'I've got a wife and kids at home.'

'So you keep telling me.' She gave him a cheeky grin, 'And I thought we had a future. Shame on you.'

He went away chuckling.

The moment she turned to collect something from the back desk, Frank made his move. He slid his way along the corridor and slipped softly into the now unguarded private ward where Joe was.

At first he was taken aback to see how Joe was trussed top to toe in a kind of traction mechanism. Flat on his back, with his chin in a collar cast, he was totally helpless.

Quickly over the first shock, Frank was delighted that Joe was in no position to shout or hit out. In fact it suited his purpose to see him restrained like that.

He was about to make his way across the room, when he heard footsteps. Quickly dodging behind the door, he held his breath. Like a cornered rat, he meant to escape at any cost.

He heard the footsteps stop outside the door, then he saw the handle move and he pressed himself flat against the wall, ready to make a run for it.

The door opened slightly, then a nurse took a step into the room, peered over at Joe, then backed away and closed the door behind her, leaving the intruder greatly relieved.

Taking a deep breath, he waited a second or two, before moving cautiously towards the bed where Joe was lying.

Acutely aware that he could well be trapped at any moment, Frank leaned over him, his voice low and excited. 'Well, well, well! Look at you . . . all strung up like a chicken ready for the oven.'

Joe had been sleeping, though not deeply, for he was too uncomfortable and restless. When he now heard Frank's voice, he opened his eyes to rid himself of the nightmare. But when he realised he wasn't dreaming and that it really was Frank, his face collapsed in shock.

The urge to fight was strong in him. He even made frantic moves to lift his arms, but they were like lead weights against his damaged body.

When he now opened his mouth to speak, Frank clamped his fist across it. When Joe began to struggle, it did not take much to squeeze Joe's mouth tightly shut. 'Be still!' he hissed. 'And listen!'

Against his bullish strength, Joe was helpless.

Frank leaned closer. 'I did have a mind to finish you off. But now I can see that would be a blessing for you. Besides, I can't think of any single reason to show you mercy.' He quickly observed the manner in which Joe was strapped down, and it made him smile. 'It pleases me to see you this way, Joe,' he whispered. 'I never expected it to be like this.'

When Joe closed his eyes in disgust, he went on, 'Not very pleased to see me are you? Want to get up and make mincemeat out of me, do you? Want to fight me . . .' He shook his head. 'Looks to me like your fighting days are over, Joe. You're a poor excuse for a man, and as far as I'm concerned, it's no more than you deserve!'

He gave a low, menacing snigger. 'You can't move. You can't do anything for yourself, can you, eh? Face it, Joe! You're helpless. So, what's it like? How do you feel when the nurse has to bring you a bedpan? Does she have to wash you, Joe? Are you treated like some old man?'

He was relentless. 'I'm afraid that's how it will be from now on, Joe. A broken old man, trapped in a young man's body.'

Joe continued to stare up at him, his eyes burning with hatred, knowing that every word Frank uttered was bitterly true.

For a long, delicious moment, Frank enjoyed watching Joe suffer, then suddenly his manner changed. 'I haven't got much time,' he growled. 'I need you to know that Alice is tracking you down. Before too long she'll be sure to find you . . . just like I did.'

When he saw how that information lit Joe's eyes with hope, he could have suffocated him there and then. But then Joe would be out of pain, and he didn't want that. He wanted him to suffer, until such a time as his situation was so unbearable, he would beg to die.

Never-ending suffering. That's what he wanted for Joe; not a swift, easy end.

He left Joe with one thought. 'Alice is mine! She's still my wife. If you give her just one inch of encouragement . . . if you so much as even let her touch you, I'll know about it. And I swear, I'll finish what I started. She got away last time. She won't get away again!'

He added, 'Don't even think about telling anybody about me being here, or what's been said, because if you do, I might just go ahead and do the deed anyway. In fact, you can be sure of it.'

He smiled into Joe's tragic eyes. '*You, more than anybody should know I mean exactly what I say.*'

He knew by the look on Joe's face, that he was reminded

of when they were boys. The animals that had suffered at Frank's hands, and the children who had been sent home in terror. Joe had told, but nobody listened, and the children were too afraid to speak out.

'And another thing, Joe,' he purred. 'When I finish Alice off, I'll be sure to enjoy taking my time about it. I mean it, Joe! If I have to do it, then it's your fault and not mine. So remember, if I find out you've been encouraging her, I'll make her suffer like you would never believe.'

He saw the tears of rage fill Joe's eyes but he cared nothing for his brother's pain. 'I've got to go now, Joe. But I'll be watching. I have my spies. I'll know if you go against what I've said. Make no mistake, I *will* carry out my threat, Joe. You know I will!'

His last words to his brother were delivered in a matter-of-fact way. 'I'm so glad I found you, Joe. You can't know how much of a pleasure it's been.'

His voice dropped to a whisper. 'With just a flick of the wrist, I could kill you here and now. But it would be far more satisfying to keep you alive. Like the living dead, eh, Joe?'

He chuckled. 'That's what you are, Joe . . . the living dead!'

Before removing his hand from Joe's mouth, he issued a final reminder. 'Think on what I said, Joe. If you so much as smile at her, Alice is gone . . . forever!'

'You cowardly bastard!' Joe had never wanted to hurt anyone so badly as he did now.

'Tut, tut, Joe . . . such language!'

Then, as quickly as he had arrived, he left.

Behind him, Joe was left thinking of Alice. So, she was out of hospital. Thank God for that.

But why hadn't his father told him?

Why did he have to hear it from that no good brother of his.

He focused on Frank's threats.

There was no doubt in Joe's mind that if he dared to make plans with Alice, Frank would do what he promised. After all, he had already tried to kill her once.

The worst thing of all was that he felt so helpless and trapped.

Maybe Frank was right. Maybe he would be better off dead than to be left alive like this.

More than once since being struck down, he himself had entertained that very same idea.

Yet, with the doctor's encouragement, he had never lost hope.

If it took years, and all his strength and courage, he had to walk again, to work, and live, and be with Alice.

But what of Alice? What would he do if and when she came to see him?

How could he turn her away, when all this time he had yearned for her, longed to see her face; to know she still loved him.

Every minute of every day he had kept alive the hope that Alice would come to him, and everything would be all right. It was the only thing that kept him going.

Every so often they took him out of the contraption, subjecting him to agonising exercises that seemed to tear his limbs apart. So many times he came close to giving up, but he didn't.

He endured the excruciating agony because of Alice, and his dream that they had a future together.

Alice was his hope, his reason to go on fighting.

What must he do now, in the face of Frank's warning? Rather than see Alice hurt in any way, he would cut off his own arm.

There must be a way to keep her safe.

In his mind he went through the options.

He could somehow involve the police . . . tell them that

Frank had been right here, making threats to kill Alice.

Another option would be to tell his father, and let him do what was necessary.

Or maybe he could ignore Frank's threat, and welcome Alice with open arms. And to hell with it!

He then went through the reasons why none of the options were suitable.

Even if the police caught Frank and threw him in jail, he would still find a way to get to Alice. Using any means at his disposal; enticement, bullying, or dirty dealing, he would use someone else to do the deed . . . an ex-prisoner maybe.

Frank was dangerous and unstable, enough to make things happen. He might even extend the threat to the entire family; after all, he had shown no compassion when his own father tried to reason with him. Instead he turned on him, leaving both him and Joe for dead.

A man like that would not even flinch at taking Alice's life.

Joe realised that if he passed the burden on to his father, that would be a cowardly and wicked thing to do, and it would paint him with the same brush as Frank. More than that, the end result might well be catastrophic, and Joe could not risk it.

Lastly, if he was to ignore Frank's threat, Alice would pay the ultimate price.

Joe knew his brother better than most, and he knew the true depth to his wickedness. He was convinced that come what may, Frank would find a way to carry out his threat.

~

Once outside the hospital, Frank slunk away, careful not to be seen or heard as he made his getaway.

'One down, one more to go.' He was satisfied that he had Joe on two counts. Firstly he was not about to inform on him, and secondly, he was so besotted with Alice, he would die rather than put her life in jeopardy.

Heading for the canal, he dodged the main walkway.

Keeping close to the towpath, his mind darkening with revenge every step he took.

After what seemed an age, he neared the barge, where he glanced up and down to make sure he was not seen, then staying low, he ran forward and silently climbed aboard.

'Who's that?' From the galley, Jack saw the shadow as it flitted in the twilight. 'Fred? Is that you?'

'Yes!' Frank made his way down. 'I've come to collect my stuff.'

'Well, I'm about to move on, so you'd best get what it is you came for, and be on your way.'

Having sensed trouble, Jack was hoping to be rid of him. He told Frank, 'If you'd have been another few minutes later, I'd have been well away.'

'Really?' Frank smiled. 'Where you off to then?'

'Oh, just meeting up with some old friends of mine. I haven't seen them in a while. The word came through the grapevine that they'll be at a certain place at a certain time, and that they'd be pleased to see me.'

'What place would that be then?' Frank suspected he was lying.

'It don't matter what place, does it, Fred eh?' Jack snapped. 'Like I say, if you hadn't turned up just now, I'd have been long gone.'

'Well, I'd best be quick then, hadn't I?'

'That's right, son. Be quick and out of it, then I can get on my way.'

The quicker the better, Jack thought, because there was something about this fella that put a deep-down fear into him.

Frank made his way through to the cabin at the front. 'I'll be gone before you know it!' he called back. 'I'll be sorry to leave you though. I've enjoyed my time here.'

'Yes! So 'ave I!' Turning the fried egg in the pan, Jack rolled his eyes. 'It'll suit me if yer bugger orf and never come back,' he muttered. 'Bloody weirdo!'

'Sorry, Jack, what did you say?' As he made his way into the galley, Frank heard his every word.

Startled by his sudden nearness, Jack swung round, but he was too late as Frank grabbed him by the neck. 'So I'm a weirdo, am I?' He stared down into Jack's terrified eyes. 'Tut, tut, and I thought we were friends.'

'We are!' Gurgling and choking, Jack pleaded, 'Stay if yer like. I won't . . . mind.'

'Bye, Jack. Oh, and don't you worry. I'll say hello to your friends for you.'

Reaching out, he snatched the heavy cast-iron saucepan from the stove and brought it down with an almighty thump against Jack's skull.

Swearing and cursing, he threw Jack's lifeless body aside, and cleaned up the blood.

Splattered from floor to ceiling and running down Frank's jacket, it had a certain smell about it; dry and musky, and to Frank's warped mind, the colours were amazing. Where it had spattered over the stove, it was bright pink, yet on his clothing and across the floor it was all shades of red. 'Pretty!' When he smiled, Frank had the look of a devil on him.

Quickly now, he plucked Jack from the floor and took him outside. After making sure there was no one watching, he propped him up on the wooden bench and carefully arranged him so that he looked much like a man at leisure. He found Jack's fishing rod, and fixed it under his armpit. The line dangled into the water.

Returning to the galley, he located a big hessian bag,

into which he placed the heavy saucepan, together with numerous other heavy objects. That done, he collected the length of rope from underneath the cabin steps.

He tightly closed the neck of the bag and tied one end of the rope around it.

He now carried the bundle outside, where he proceeded to tie the other end of the rope around Jack's lifeless body making sure the rope was of the right length to secure Jack to the bottom of the murky canal.

That done, he sat Jack upright on the wooden bench. 'You like the water, don't you, Jack?' He stared into the other man's lifeless eyes, which were open wide with shock. 'We had a good time though, didn't we, eh? You and me . . . a pint or two and a laugh. It's such a shame you have to leave so soon.'

Placing the flat of his hand on Jack's narrow back, he gently patted him, as though in comradeship. 'You mustn't worry. I'll look after the boat for you.'

With a hard thrust of his hand he simply pushed him over, afterwards looking excited and mesmerised as Jack's body broke the surface of the water.

Almost as though in slow motion before disappearing from sight, the murky waters opened up and swallowed him; then he was gone. 'Sorry, Jack.' In his madness, Frank sounded truly repentant. 'But you did bring it on yourself!'

A few minutes later the engine was started and the barge moved out, leaving behind the familiar sound of disturbed water slapping against the sides of the canal walls.

Frank's voice uplifted in song, which echoed through the air.

Behind him, a lone bird called his mate.

He had seen.

But he could never tell.

CHAPTER TWELVE

T HE FOLLOWING DAY Alice and Mandy arrived at Luton and Dunstable hospital. 'You go in,' Mandy was nervous. 'I'll hang about here.' She sat herself in the area where Frank had sat the day before. 'It's okay. I can read while I wait.'

She promptly picked up a newspaper from the table, 'Go on then!' She gave Alice a gentle push. 'You've been going crazy to see him, and now's your chance. Go on, Alice. You can tell me all about it afterwards!'

Alice was a bag of nerves. Torn two ways, she wasn't sure whether she had done the right thing in finding Joe.

She didn't know how he might feel when he saw her, and she whispered all that to Mandy now. 'There must be a reason why Tom didn't want me to find out where he was,' she said. 'Suppose Joe told him not to tell me.'

'Just go in there and witness the smile on his face when he sees you walk through that door,' Mandy said confidently.

Alice wasn't convinced. 'How do I know he still feels anything for me,' she asked. 'To tell you the truth, I wouldn't blame him if he never wanted to see me again. I was weak. It was me who went to Joe that night, and now it's Joe who's come off worse.' She was fast losing confidence. 'Oh, Mandy, I'm so . . .'

'Hey!' Mandy sat Alice down. 'Look! I've heard nothing from you these past weeks, except Joe this and Joe that. You've been a pain in the backside, and now that we're here, you're looking for any excuse not to go and see him.'

Suddenly rising out of her seat, she yanked Alice up. 'Right then! So you're not going in. You've changed your mind and now you don't want to see him. Fair enough!'

Linking her arm with Alice's, she smartly strode towards the door, taking a surprised Alice with her. 'Fine by me!' she declared. 'We'll go home then, if that's what you want!'

Alice was horrified. 'No!' She looked about, anxious that people should not think they were arguing.

When Mandy smiled, Alice knew she had deliberately pretended to be angry. 'Oh, Mandy, I desperately want to see him, but I'm worried. I don't know how he'll react. I don't even know if he wants me here.'

'Rubbish! Why would he not?'

'Because if it wasn't for me, he wouldn't be here. He'd be out in the field, working . . . it's where he belongs. Not shut up inside like this.' She knew how much Joe loved the outdoors. He was a part of nature; only truly alive when he could feel the soft earth beneath his feet.

'I know him,' she told Mandy now. 'And I'm sure that to be shut away in here must be like torture to him.'

Sensing Alice's predicament, Mandy was gentle with her. 'Go to him, Alice. Joe will be so pleased you're here. You see if he's not.' And as extra encouragement, she gave her another, gentler little push.

She watched while Alice explained to the chubby nurse at the desk. And when the nurse accompanied her along the corridor, Mandy smiled. 'Go to it, girl,' she murmured. 'Go see your precious Joe!'

Alice was surprised to find that Joe was under police protection; it only served to remind her that Frank was still out there. For the police to keep a guard outside his ward, they must believe that Frank had every intention of coming after his brother.

The idea made her shiver inside.

Alice was now put through the security procedure, and when Bob was satisfied she was allowed through. Tom was not happy with her being near Joe, but Joe had asked for her, time and again.

Softly opening the door to the ward, the nurse told Alice in a whisper, 'Don't be too alarmed by all the strapping, and if you need me, just call out. Oh, and try not to expect too much of him, will you?'

She then left her there, and returned to the desk.

Alice was shocked and upset to see all the strapping and mechanics that were holding Joe's damaged body together. He was very still. There was no sign of movement and his head was turned away. It seemed unreal.

This was Joe, she reminded herself. This was the man who had held her on that unforgettable night; the night when she came alive. The night when she knew what real love was. This was her lover. This was her soulmate.

Every sense in her body cried out for the injustice of it all.

Taking a step forward, she wiped away a tear. She was unable to forgive herself for the weakness that drove her into his arms. When the temptation came over her, she could have walked away, but she didn't. Even when she gave herself to him, there was still time to back off and run away. But she lacked the strength and the moment was too precious.

Because of her weakness that night, she had done this to Joe. She had brought him to this.

It was her fault, and no one would ever convince her otherwise.

Joe appeared not to have heard her enter.

For most of the night he had lain awake, tormented; he was filled with such a rage he could hardly bear it.

After hours of wrestling for a solution, he had not found the answer. And he was desolate.

'Joe?' Quickly wiping the tears from her face, Alice took a step forward. 'Joe, it's me . . . Alice.'

Thinking he must be dreaming, Joe slowly turned to look at her, and the joy he felt was alive in his face. 'Alice!' He took a deep, long breath, and let it out with her name, as though he had been holding it forever, 'Oh . . . my Alice . . .'

When she came forward, he longed to reach out and hold her, but his arms were restrained by his sides. All he could do was to watch as she came near, to see her face, so sad and lonely; such a friendly, pretty little face that took his heart and turned it inside out.

Now she was holding him delicately, and it was like his world had been dark and now it was bathed in sunshine. 'Alice,' he kept saying her name, 'Alice . . .'

Suddenly her face was Frank's face and he could hear the warning in his head. *I'll have to kill her . . . you know I will!'* And he knew what he must do. However painful it might be, he had to protect Alice.

Now, as she reached over to kiss him, he hardened his heart, and before his courage was altogether gone, he turned away from her, his voice low and hard, 'No, Alice! Leave me!'

'Joe! What's wrong?' Alice was taken by surprise at his sudden change of manner. 'Did I hurt you?'

Joe could not bring himself to look at her. 'You have to go,' he told her gruffly, 'You can't be here.'

'Why not?' Alice had seen the look of love in his face when she came through the door, and suddenly he was almost hostile. 'Why can't I be here, Joe . . . tell me?'

Joe gave no answer.

'Look at me, Joe . . . please. Do you really want me to leave?'

'Yes.'

'You blame me, don't you, Joe?' Her heart was dead inside her. 'You blame me, and you're right. I ruined your life. I'm so sorry, Joe. Please, Joe . . . can't you forgive me?'

For a while she pleaded with him, then realising she could be aggravating his recovery, she told him softly, 'I'm truly sorry, Joe. I hoped it would be different, but you've asked me to leave and I will.'

She paused on her way out.

She did not look back. Instead she told him, 'Before I go, I need you to know that I would give anything for this not to have happened to you. I love you so much, Joe. I always will.'

When he remained silent, she walked to the door, where she looked back just once, hoping he would call her to him.

When he kept his face turned from her, she knew it was over. 'Goodbye Joe,' she whispered. 'I'll pray for you to be well soon. Try to get well. For your parents' sake, and your own . . . please try, Joe.'

With her heart in pieces she said, 'Somewhere out there you have a life waiting. It might not be with me, but you *will* enjoy life again, I know you will. You must.'

A moment later, she was running headlong down the corridor, the tears flowing down her face. 'I'm sorry, Joe . . . I'm so sorry . . .'

Listening to her running footseps as she fled down the corridor, Joe lay there, numb of heart, dead in his soul. When he realised the enormity of what he had done, he called her name, 'Alice . . . Alice!' He wanted her back. He wanted Frank dead. He wanted to get up from this bed and run after her, to explain why he had to send her away.

He needed her to know that Frank would not hurt her as long as the two of them were apart. And if that's what it took to keep her safe, then so be it, because the alternative would be even more catastrophic.

Joe consoled himself with that awful knowledge, but after seeing Alice and aching to hold her, it was a small consolation.

The unbearable thing was, he could not do anything to stop Frank from hurting her. There was no way he could help her, because he wasn't a man anymore. He was a mouse! A frightened, useless little nothing; unable to protect the one person he had ever loved. Frank had wanted to punish them both, and he had done it in the most evil way of all.

Because of Frank, Joe was dying inside.

Alice was devastated, and that was the price they had paid.

But his darling Alice was safe, and that was what mattered.

~

Waiting to greet her with a ready smile, Mandy was amazed when Alice fell into her arms. 'He sent me away,' she sobbed. 'Joe sent me away.'

For a tense moment, Mandy just held her, then easing her away, she urged, 'Come on, Alice . . . let's take you home.'

She had half expected something like this to happen. Yet to see Alice so broken like that was hurtful.

In a small way, Mandy did not blame Joe. Nor did she blame Alice. It was one of those cruel tricks that Fate often plays on you. 'Maybe he'll come round,' she said as they walked away. 'Give Joe a day or two, and he'll realise how much he needs you.'

Alice shook her head. 'No, Mandy. He never wants to see me again.' She clung to her friend. 'And who could ever blame him? Oh but, Mandy, you should see what it's like. His body is strapped down, and he can't move his limbs. I'll never forgive myself for what I've done. And now he hates me, and I love him so much.'

Looking up at Mandy through red-raw eyes, Alice quietly vowed, 'I owe it to him to do as he says. I have to stay away . . . give him the time and space he needs to recover but I really don't know if I can be here and not want to see him. I have to leave, Mandy, I have to get far away from these parts.'

'But why would you do that?' Mandy could not imagine a life without Alice in it. 'This is where you live. It's where you grew up. This area is all you know.'

'I have to leave.' After her unhappy encounter with Joe, Alice was determined. 'If Joe recovers from his terrible injuries, and I pray he does, just think how he would feel if he should see me on the street, or walking across the fields? Don't you see, Mandy . . . I'll always be there to remind him of what happened to him, and to his parents.'

She walked along for a moment in complete silence, then in the softest murmur, she voiced an idea that was playing over in her mind.

'I can't help Joe directly, but I think there is at least one thing I can do to help make amends. Even if I have to go cap in hand, on my knees!'

Other than that, she would say no more.

~

While Alice and Mandy walked away, deep in conversation, Tom Arnold walked up from the car park, his step slow and ungainly as he negotiated the gravel walkway.

His head was down, as though in deep thought, and the smile that used to live on his kindly old face was gone.

Instead, the lines of his face were etched with worry and pain, and as he approached the hospital doors, he seemed to have aged, even beyond his mature years.

The nurse recognised him straight off. 'Hello, Mr Arnold,' she greeted him with a cheery smile, 'My! My! Your son's a popular young man today, isn't he?'

Tom was immediately alert. 'Sorry? What did you say?'

'Well, only that you're the second visitor for Joe in less than an hour.'

'You're saying our Joe had a visitor?'

'That's right. A young woman, very proper and polite she was, and pretty. Not striking or handsome, but . . . just kind of pretty.'

She was still chatting as he hurried away.

'Alice Jacobs!' He was fired with anger. 'It couldn't have been anybody else! That bloody woman, how did she find him? Why can't she stay well away from where she's not wanted!'

'Back again, eh?' Policeman Bob had taken a liking to Tom. He thanked his lucky stars that his own boy was not in such a bad way as this old fella's son. 'You're the second visitor today.'

He was surprised when Tom gave no acknowledgement, but merely nodded, as he hurried away. Usually he paused a minute to pass the time of day.

On hearing the footsteps, Joe had his eyes trained on the door, hoping that Alice had come back; then praying she had not.

'Dad!' Exhausted by the simple task of turning his head, he leaned back into the pillow. After the painful confrontation with Alice, he had neither the strength nor the heart for anything.

Tom came straight to the bed, his frown unfurling into a warm smile as he reached out to take hold of Joe's hand. 'How are you, son?'

Every time he came into this room, he felt the urge to lift Joe out of that bed and take him home. It took all of his control not to show his deep frustration.

'I'm the same as ever,' Joe smiled. 'Don't worry about me, Dad. I'll beat this, you wait and see. I'll be up and about in no time, then you and Mum will be wishing I was out from under your feet.'

Tom took hold of his hand and squeezed it. 'Never!' He tried to swallow the lump that filled his throat. 'The day you come home will be the best day of our lives,' he promised fervently.

After the landlord's visit, his promise was all the more poignant because at this moment in time, he didn't even know where home might be.

Seeing how tired his father was, Joe's heart went out to him. He knew how hard it must be for him, coming here, seeing him like this, and knowing that Frank was responsible. It was a dilemma no man should ever have to deal with.

'They got me upright today,' he revealed with a disarming grin. 'They swung the whole contraption on its head and it was almost as though I could just get out and walk away; only I couldn't, and my head felt like a ton weight on my shoulders. Mind you, it was good just to be upright, instead of lying flat on my back, staring at the ceiling.'

Tom was amazed. 'That's wonderful, son!' His spirits were lifted, 'Does it mean they're thinking of taking you out of all this . . .' he glanced at the restraining mechanism, '. . . all this rigmarole?'

Joe shook his head. 'I asked the same question,' he answered. 'But apparently, it's all to do with circulation, and a little respite from lying flat on my back for too long at a time.'

In his mind he relived the moment when they raised him forward. 'It was kind of weird,' he confessed. 'My legs felt like blobs of jelly, and my whole body seemed to sink down.'

He relived the moment in his mind. 'I had this huge urge to push my legs forward, but they wouldn't go.'

The fear inside him showed itself in his voice as he asked his father, 'You don't think it means I'm done, do you, Dad? I mean . . . if I didn't feel any strength in my legs, does it mean I can never walk again?'

Tom gave him hope. 'I'm no doctor,' he told Joe. 'But I'm sure they know what they're doing. They've got you this far. I don't reckon they're about to give up now.'

He went on encouragingly, 'As for not feeling any movement in your legs, you have to remember you've been flat on your back for a long time now. The muscles will have lost their strength. That's probably why they're doing this . . . to get them going again.'

He could see how desperate Joe was. 'If they thought there was no chance of you ever walking again, they wouldn't be putting you through all that, would they now, eh?'

Tom went on encouragingly, 'Think about it, son. You were shot; both your arms and legs were broken in multiple places, and your lower spine was fractured. I know it may not seem it to you, but I see an improvement every time I come in.'

He pointed out, 'There was a time when you were wrapped up like a mummy, unable to move your arms and legs, and you couldn't even turn your head. These doctors have done a fantastic job! I never thought they'd ever put you back together again, but thanks to their skilful work, you're coming on really well.'

Joe smiled at that. 'So, what you're saying is, I'm Humpty Dumpty am I?'

Tom was gladdened to hear him teasing. 'If yer like,' he replied with a grin. 'All I'm saying is, you were smashed up bad. These marvellous people have been able to knit your bones together and, as far as I understand it, they're hoping there will be no permanent damage.'

Tom was determined to lift Joe's spirits. 'You mustn't expect too much too quickly, son. Y'see, they can't just get you out of bed, and ask you to walk along the floor so's they can see how far you go. There's testing and trying, and being wary not to go too far too soon. Common sense tells us that much.'

'I know that, Dad,' Joe groaned. 'And I know I have to be patient, but there is so much I want to do. So many things I need to tend to outside of this place.'

There was one particular area that concerned him. 'I need to get back to work . . . help keep the farm going. The land needs maintaining. After the late crop it needs feeding and spraying, and there needs to be a working plan for next year. I should be out there Dad, helping you to keep on top of it all.'

'Listen to me, son. I don't want you worrying about things like that. You just concentrate on getting well. We're doing just fine,' Tom assured him. 'All we want is for you to get better. Right now, that's the only thing that matters to me and your mother.'

'Well, that's all very fine, Dad, but if the landlord sees the land being neglected what with me and Frank not there, how long will it be before he comes down on you like a ton of bricks? That's what worries me.'

Tom hated lying, but he didn't have the heart to tell Joe the bitter truth. 'Like I said . . . everything is in hand. The landlord has no need to worry, and neither do you.'

While Joe digested that information, Tom changed the

subject. 'This business of raising the bed and standing you upright. I reckon it's a way of getting you to the next stage . . . like actually coaxing you out of this contraption.'

He added worriedly, 'Look, Joe! You mustn't think the worst. You need to concentrate on getting better. Whatever it takes, and however long you have to stay here, keep telling yourself, that every day that passes is a day nearer to you coming home. All right? Can you do that for me, son?'

Joe smiled, that handsome, lopsided smile that was uniquely Joe. 'Everything you said is exactly the same as what the doctor said when I asked him.'

'There you are then!'

'I *will* think about what you said, Dad. And I have every intention that one day I might walk out of here on my own two feet.'

He was silent for a moment, thinking of Alice, and how much she meant to him.

Along with his parents, she was his strength. 'I have to get out of here, Dad, and to that end, I'll take everything they throw at me . . .'

The doctors had been encouraging too. Having explained how he still had a long way to go, they were confident he would come through it. Even though it was a slow and delicate process,

Yet however much they tried to reassure him, and however determined he remained, Joe was still fearful that he would never walk again.

'Being swung upright like that . . .' Joe could still recall every excruciating minute of it. 'I don't mind telling you, Dad . . . it was the hardest thing I've ever done. It was only a matter of minutes, but to tell you the truth, I was completely exhausted afterwards.'

In truth, he was feeling a little like that now. He was always thrilled to see his father, but the effort of just conversing really took it out of him. When his mother came to see him, she hardly spoke. She held his hand and seemed too upset to say anything, but Joe knew how deeply she felt, and he understood.

Like Nancy, Tom was immensely proud. 'You're a real fighter, Joe,' he told him stoutly. 'You do what you have to do, and one day, you'll be standing on your own two feet again. I know it, son. I just know it!'

Leaning over he took hold of Joe's two hands, and clenched them in his fists. 'Me and your mother . . . we're both so proud of you, son,' he said brokenly. 'We really thought we'd lost you.'

Joe felt uneasy. His father seemed unusually emotional today, and at times kind of preoccupied. 'What's wrong, Dad? Is there a problem? Is everything all right at home?'

Tom was instantly on his guard. 'Apart from wanting you home, there's nothing wrong. Why do you ask?'

Joe was persistent. 'Is it Frank? Has he been to the farm?' He feared for their safety. 'I know they haven't caught him yet, otherwise why would they stand a police guard outside?'

He had to be careful not to let slip that Frank had actually been here, issuing threats and demands.

Seeing how agitated Joe was getting, Tom cursed himself for allowing his mind to wander back to what the landlord had said. 'Hey! Now you listen to me, Joe! We've neither seen nor heard from Frank in all this time.'

Joe knew there was something on his father's mind. 'Something's niggling at you. What is it, Dad? If it's money you need, you'll find my savings book under the bed. Take it, Dad! You have my permission, you know that.'

'Stop getting yourself in a state, Joe!' Tom was frightened for him. 'There is nothing niggling at me, and even if there was, which there isn't, it wouldn't be money. Your mother and I have been very careful with our pennies over the years. As for Frank, you can get that out of your head right now. Frank is long gone, and may God forgive me, but I wouldn't really care if I never saw him again as long as I live!'

Frank had shown no mercy to anyone, least of all to his family. If it had been up to Frank, both Joe and himself, and Alice would be dead right now.

Although there was a time when Tom laid the blame at other people's door, he had begun to admit that Frank was little short of a murderer, and that was a terrible thing to learn about your own son.

'So, there's nothing else playing on your mind, is there?' Joe still wasn't altogether content.

'Nope! Except for wanting you to stay determined to get out of here. Oh, and I've got the blessed gout come back again. Soonever the summer months are behind us, it starts with a vengeance.'

Though he sympathised with his father's ongoing condition, Joe had heard his father complaining for as far back as he could remember. 'Are you taking your tablets?'

'Yup!' Tom replied doggedly. 'Your mother makes sure of it.'

'How is Mum?'

'Healthy as an ox.'

'Dad?'

'Yes, son?' He hoped Joe might be about to tell him why Alice had been there but he was disappointed.

'Are you on top of the farm work?

'Of course!'

'Okay, so who's helping you then? Don't try misleading me, and don't try telling me you're coping on your own, because I know that would be an outright lie. I want the truth, Dad. Who have you got working on the farm?'

'Hey! I'll thank you not to write me off just yet, young man!' Tom was frantically searching for time in which to find an answer. 'I'm still able to do the easier jobs. I can still sit on a tractor and contrary to your thinking my boy, I do know my way round a field. Oh, and I'm a dab hand when it comes to painting the barn.'

'You still haven't answered me. Who's doing the farm work? Who's keeping the pasture good, and spraying the crops? Who manhandles the hay bales, and fills the field troughs with water for the animals? I need to know, Dad. So, don't lie to me.'

Tom gave a loud sigh. 'Like I say, everything is under control. You've no need to concern yourself. All you need to do is think about getting out of here, all fit and well.'

'You still haven't answered me, Dad!' Joe was growing more suspicious by the minute. 'Who have you got working the land? Who's minding the animals?'

'Right! Well, there's Jimmy. He's worth his weight in gold. Then there's Lenny the blacksmith's son. He's a hard-working, willing young man, looking to earn a wage.' He puffed out his chest in a show of bravado. 'Then there's me and your mother. Between the two of us, we mop up the little jobs. And now I've answered enough questions, my boy.'

Having skilfully evaded the question without actually telling the truth, Alice remained strong on Tom's mind. 'I reckon it's time you answered a question for me.'

Joe was intrigued. 'What kind of question?'

Tom came straight out with it. 'What did Alice want?'

Joe was taken aback. 'How did you know she was here?'

'Never mind that, son. I just want to know what she was doing here?'

'She was worried about me.'

'Huh! And so she should be! What else did she want?'

When Joe gave no answer, he asked, 'Did she come here to cause trouble?'

'No.'

'So, what did she *really* want?'

Joe raised the image of Alice in his mind, and his heart grew quiet. 'Alice was here to apologise for her part in what happened, and I told her it was more my fault than hers. I did wrong. I knew she was marrying Frank, and I should have sent her away. Instead, I wanted her with me. I've always loved her, dad. I think you knew that.'

Tom had no wish to discuss the sordid details. 'Best leave it be,' he suggested harshly. 'It's water under the bridge.'

His main intention now was to keep Alice as far away from Joe as possible.

'I hope if she shows her face here again, you'll have the courage to send her on her way.' He didn't want to say this, but he felt he had to. 'You say you made a mistake in not sending her away before, but you have the chance to put that right. If Alice shows her face here again, I want you to get rid of her. Before she can get her claws into you again.'

He had a thought. 'In fact, maybe I should have a word with the nurse at the desk . . .'

'That's not your decision, Father,' Joe told him sternly. 'It's for me to decide, and if you interfere, I may never forgive you.'

He held his breath before revealing softly, 'She said she loves me, and you could not understand how wonderful that felt. I have to tell you, Dad, I still love her. So very much.'

Before Tom could say anything, Joe quickly added, 'You might be pleased to know I did not tell her how I felt about her. Instead, just as you suggested, I sent her away.'

Tom was delighted. 'You did right!' he said. 'I'm so glad you've seen sense at last.'

He had already decided not to tell Joe that Alice was

pregnant. And now he knew he had done the right thing.

Joe was wearied by the exertion of two visitors in such a short space of time. He had also found his father's visit to be deeply unsettling. 'I'm sorry, Dad, but I can't talk any longer.' He felt drained, and oddly disturbed.

Understanding that Joe was in need of his rest, Tom bade him goodbye. 'I'll see you tomorrow,' he promised. 'Look, son, I know it must have been hard for you to send her away, but you really did do the right thing. Later on, when you're fit and well, you'll see that, and you'll know it had to be done.'

With that he left.

After learning that Joe had actually sent Alice away, he went down the corridor feeling much better. 'You won't regret turning her away, son,' he murmured under his breath. 'She's out of your life now. And I for one am thankful!'

Somewhere at the back of his mind he remembered the look in Joe's eyes when he confessed to still loving Alice. 'You'll get over her, son.' For a fleeting moment, he felt Joe's pain. 'I know it must have been hard for you to turn her away, but she's the one who turned this family inside out, and well she knows it.' Even now, he could not forget that in giving herself to Joe, Alice had initiated the break up of his family.

His face hardened. 'Before she came into our lives, we were a close family.'

When he got to the desk and saw the nurse there, he made his way over. 'Excuse me, Nurse . . .'

'Yes, Mr Arnold . . .' Tom was recognised by all the staff. '. . . what can I do for you?'

Tom could suddenly hear Joe's voice in his ear, 'If you interfere, I may never forgive you . . .'

'Sorry, Nurse, er . . . just now, Joe told me you had him taking the weight of his own body today, and I just wanted to ask . . . what particular benefit did that have on Joe's condition?'

The nurse was only too pleased to inform him. 'It showed us that his bones were mending well, and that his muscles needed extra work before they could take the strains of considerable weight. On the strength of what we found, we're now able to increase his daily exercises.'

She suggested, 'To be honest, you need to discuss it with the doctor. Shall I tell him you'd like to see him?'

'Yes, thank you, that would be good. I'm sure his mother would want to come along, so when do you think the doctor will be available to see us?'

She consulted her ledger. 'Tomorrow he finishes his round about midday. Shall we say twelve thirty?'

'Yes, that's fine. We can see Joe straight after that.'

He thanked her again, before going on his way. 'God willing, he'll come on in leaps and bounds, and we can pick up our lives again.'

His heart sank. 'As for Frank, I don't know what will happen. All I do know is, he's shown a side to his nature that frightens me. When they find him, I've no doubt he'll be put away for a very long time.'

He shook his head in despair. 'I blame her!' he muttered. 'If my boys had never met Alice, none of this would ever have happened, and now because of her, my family as I knew it, is in pieces.'

As he walked on, he casually wiped away a tear, brought on by one son's wickedness, and another son's fight to be strong again. 'Help them Lord,' he whispered. 'Please help them both.'

After all, they were his sons, and he couldn't help but love them.

~

Lying helpless in his bed, Joe was desolate. 'You don't understand,' he whispered. 'You don't know how desperately I need her. You don't even know why I sent her away. It was Frank. He threatened to kill her, and he would do it without a moment's hesitation. That's why I sent her away, to protect her. Only she didn't know that, and I couldn't tell her.'

Life without her in it was empty and cold. And in that desolate moment, Joe didn't care if he lived or died.

'I love you, Alice.' He gazed out of the window at the brooding skies beyond. 'One day, God willing, I mean to hold you in my arms and tell you just what you mean to me and when that day comes, we'll never be apart again.'

It was a dream, that's all it was.

But Joe was a man of vision.

He believed that if he wished hard enough, his dreams really would come true.

PART FIVE

~

January 1953

New Hope

CHAPTER THIRTEEN

EDWARD BAXTER HAD stopped off at the local pub for a well-earned pint. 'You look shattered sir, if you don't mind me saying.' The bartender was used to the local landowner popping in on his way from London. 'Had a hard day have you?' While he chatted, he began pulling the big man's favourite pint.

'You could say that.' Edward Baxter was a man of considerable means; he was also a shrewd businessman who knew how to move in where there was rich picking to be had. 'Sometimes I wonder why I keep at it,' he confided. 'If I retired tomorrow, I could live the life of Reilly.'

He sighed. 'Wine, women and song . . . and every day in the sunshine. What d'you think?'

'I think if it were me, I'd be off like me pants were on fire!' The cocky young barman could never contemplate having that kind of choice.

'Ah, but y'see it's never that easy.' Edward Baxter knew the pitfalls. 'The more a man owns, the bigger his responsibilities, until they seem like a chain holding him back. In the end, you work because you forget how to stop. Then you forget how to enjoy life, and that's the sad thing.'

He climbed on to the bar-stool. 'It's not all glory,' he admitted. 'The city isn't what it used to be either. Once upon a time, it was straightforward. You saw a bargain and you got in there first. You were the man with the money, and the know-how to pick and choose, but it's very different nowadays. There are too many quick-witted fly-boys half my age who take risks I would never dare take, and you know what? However green behind the ears they are, they always seem to come up smelling of roses!'

The barman knew all about the young up and coming breed of risk-takers. 'It's the same in any walk of life,' he said philosophically. 'Take me for instance! It wasn't that long ago when I ran my own pub. I didn't own it, mind. But I worked my fingers to the bone and took it from a back-street pop-in kind of pub, to one of the best meeting place in North Shields.'

'Don't tell me!' The older man saw what was coming, 'The owner sold it from under your nose, and some fly-by-night snatched it for a song, when you weren't looking?'

'Exactly right! I never even knew it was up for sale, until the sign went up outside. I didn't even have a chance to arrange a loan or anything, before this brash little Jack the Lad sauntered in and started measuring up for the changes he intended making.'

'And then what?'

'Then I was looking for a job, and here I am. As for the pub I worked and sweated to build up, it's now one o' them new-fangled, fancy drinking places; more like a whore-house if you ask me. The word is, it's making more money than three pubs put together!'

He gave a wry little smile. 'Still! I've got regular work, and for now that's all I can hope for.' He gave a little tut, 'I don't expect you understand what I'm saying . . . you being a man of means an' all.'

'Oh, but I *do* understand!' Edward Baxter had known a few hairy moments in his life. 'Don't imagine I haven't had my bad patches,' he said. 'Oh yes! I haven't always been wealthy, and I'll tell you now, it was never money handed down, oh no! Yes, I made mistakes and I paid for them. But in the end, it was focus and determination that got me where I am today.

'Nothing is for nothing, and that's the way of it, my boy!' With that he took a huge gulp of his drink and set off on a coughing spasm.

The barman got him a glass of water. 'You'd best enjoy life while you've got the chance,' he merrily joked. 'Sounds to me you could be headed for the knacker's yard!'

'Huh! Cheeky young bugger!'

Quickly recovering, the older man placed a handsome tip on the bar. 'Stick to serving beer and not advice,' he joked back. 'And keep your eyes peeled! Your next opportunity could be out there, passing you by even as we speak. Go grab it, young man, and don't let the dust settle.'

Having enjoyed his pint, he went on his way.

He had a lot on his mind; foremost being the imminent eviction of Tom Arnold and his family.

Turning Tom off the land is not an easy thing to do, he murmured to himself as he drove away. But I had no choice. The decision is made. The papers are issued, and that's an end to it. If you want to stay ahead of the losers, you make decisions with your head not your heart, he mused. That's how Edward Baxter got to where he is today.

He took a deep breath. 'Tom Arnold had enough notice and chose to do nothing. So now the mechanics are in place, and rightly so!'

~

He had been home for over an hour and was beavering away in his office when the front door bell rang out its melody through the house. 'Who the devil's that?' Irritated, he raised his voice, 'Martha!' When there came no response from his housekeeper, he called again, this time in full volume. 'Martha get the door, will you!'

There came the sound of pattering feet running down the wood-blocked floor, then the closing of the front door. Then Martha tapped on his office door. 'You have a visitor, Mr Baxter, sir.'

Throwing down his pencil, he grunted, 'Who is it?'

The little woman looked flummoxed. 'Er . . . it's a gentleman . . . sir?'

'Martha! *What is the gentleman's name?*'

She bit her lip and looked decidedly nervous. 'I'll go and ask.'

'Martha!' He took in a deep breath that appeared to expand his chest to twice its size.

'Yes, Mr Baxter . . . sir?'

'A gentleman you say?'

'Yes . . . sir.'

'All right, Martha,' he said more patiently, realising he might have frightened poor little Martha.

Martha had arrived here some twenty years ago. A pretty young woman left on her own, it was only meant to be a short appointment, but somehow she'd stayed, time passed and here she still was.

His late wife had taken her on, and over the years Martha had been a jewel, worth every penny of her keep.

Suddenly Edward felt sad at the passing of the years, and the cruel manner in which it ravaged you when you weren't aware of it.

He thought of himself, and there were so many regrets. One day you were a young man, and then before you knew it, you looked in the mirror and there was this old person looking back at you, complete with wrinkles and silver hair.

Mentally shaking off his mood, he got out of the chair and made his way across the office towards her. 'You go about your business, Martha,' he said kindly. 'I'll see to this visitor.'

She gave a nervous little bow. 'Yes, Mr Baxter . . . sir.'

She hurried away, her shoes creating a rhythm on the floorboards. Edward thought a moment, then he was striding down the hallway with all the flourish and authority he could summon.

Waiting in the hallway, Joshua heard him coming, and he too, stood firm and authoritative, ready to meet this lion of a businessman head on.

It took Edward Baxter a moment to recognise him.

In the depth of a certain winter, he and Joshua Jacobs had shared the same compartment on a train to London.

They had struck up a casual conversation, though it had never evolved beyond that, because once in London, they had gone their separate ways and their paths had never again crossed – until now.

'Good grief!' He came forward with his hand extended in greeting. 'Joshua Jacobs! We meet again, only this time in more comfortable surroundings than a train compartment on our way to the London offices, eh?'

'When needs must.' Joshua recalled the incident well. 'If we hadn't had one of the worst snowfalls in many a year, we would never have left the cars at home, and we may never have met at all.'

Edward had enjoyed his company on that particular occasion, and he hoped the same would apply now. 'So! To what do I owe this pleasure?'

Having recently learned that Joshua was the grandfather of Alice, the young woman who was tortured and left to die by her husband, Edward was slightly embarrassed, and somewhat dubious as to how he should receive him.

'Forgive me for calling on you like this, without prior notice,' Joshua apologised. 'Only, I need to talk with you about a certain business matter, if you wouldn't mind?'

Intrigued, Edward gestured towards the drawing room. 'Of course! Come through.'

With Edward leading the way, Joshua followed, his gaze resting on the dark-oak panelled walls and the high, arched ceilings. This was a fine house he thought.

Having settled Joshua in the drawing room, Edward excused himself and went away to the kitchen, in search of Martha.

He found her day dreaming, as she rested on her elbow and watched the dog run round and round in the garden, trying to catch his tail. 'Martha!'

Startled, she swung round. 'Yes, sir?'

'I've settled our visitor in the drawing room. We would very much like some refreshment . . . say a pot of tea. Oh! And some of your little ginger cakes?'

Without waiting for an answer, Edward hurried back to his guest. 'Tea and cake will be with us shortly,' he informed Joshua who was standing by the French doors, admiring the view. 'Please, sit down and tell me what business brings you here?' Edward said warmly.

For a moment, Joshua appeared not to have heard. Instead, he turned and smiled at Edward Baxter. 'This is a magnificent place you have here.'

Edward explained, 'My father designed and built it. As a young man he worked the land this house stands on, and he tilled the fields as far as the eye could see. It was his dream to one day own the land, and build his own home.'

Proudly smiling, he walked across the room and stood beside Joshua. 'He worked like a dog from morning to night. When his farm work was done, he would go down to the village and earn money by mending leaky roofs . . . unblocking drains, and anything else that needed doing. He would squirrel every penny away, until one day . . . many years later . . . he was able to buy many acres of the land and build this house.' His voice caught slightly and Joshua could tell that Edward clearly still missed his father and talking of him was too emotional.

'I'm so sorry,' Joshua apologised. 'I didn't mean to jog painful memories.' He had always thought Edward Baxter was a man of some stern authority, yet here he saw someone who was damaged and still lost in the past.

'No, no!' Edward assured him. 'It was nothing you said.'

Just then, Martha arrived with the tray, which she placed on the low table between the deep leather chairs.

'Thank you, Martha.' Edward nodded and dismissed her with a smile.

Suddenly, Edward decided, 'I think we deserve something a bit stronger than tea, don't you?'

'Of course, yes . . . thank you!' Joshua was also partial to a drop of the good stuff.

'Whisky?'

'Please.'

So the whisky was poured and the first dram went down very well. 'So, what brings you here?'

'I need to see you about a matter that concerns me . . .'

Edward took another, longer swig. 'I see! And what "matter" would that be?'

'A delicate matter, but I'm hoping we might reach agreement on it,' Joshua answered.

'Delicate, eh.' Casting his gaze to the floor, Edward absent-mindedly swirled the glass between the palms of his hands, while he cast his mind back to a certain regrettable time many years ago. 'You know, there was a time when all of this might have been lost forever . . .' he made a wide arc with his arms, '. . . the house, the land. Everything my father worked so hard to build . . . all put at risk, because of me!' He appeared to lose himself in memories.

Joshua was embarrassed. Edward had clearly taken a

little too much whisky with his tea. 'Are you sure you want to discuss something so personal?' he asked, somewhat bemused.

Edward went on, 'Y'see, as a young man, I had a weakness for gambling. I was brash and over confident. I thought there was no one in the whole wide world who could bring me down. I simply couldn't lose. It was win, win, win, all the way. Until the tide turned, and I found myself up to my neck in debt. I was broke . . . with no place to turn. My credit was nil, and my reputation was in tatters.'

He paused. 'In the end I had to go cap in hand to my father. To hide the shame that could be brought down on us, he took out another loan on the house and cleared all my considerable debts. Some weeks later he suffered a severe heart attack. Within a month he was dead.'

He paused, took another swig of the whisky, and explained quietly, 'I knew I had to take care of my mother so, I rolled up my sleeves, gave up my bad ways, and took on Father's many responsibilities. I worked day and night until I had secured this place and won back my mother's respect.'

Taking a gulp of the whisky, he found solace in opening his heart and mind to someone who might understand. 'In all my life, before or since, I have never worked so hard. It made me realise how much of his life and leisure my father had given up for his dream, this land, this beautiful house.'

Joshua felt for him. 'I'm truly sorry,' he told him. 'But at least in the end you helped to save this place. I'm sure your father would have been proud of you.'

Edward gave a wry little smile. 'I don't know about that. Father was a man of principle. Forgiveness was not one of his traits, and even if I had died trying to make amends, I don't believe he would have ever have forgiven me.'

When Edward lapsed into deep thought, Joshua tentatively raised the reason for his calling. 'Much as I have enjoyed passing the time of day with you, there was another, rather pressing issue I need to discuss with you. Though if you would rather I came back tomorrow, then of course I will.'

Suddenly, Edward was all attention. 'No, dear me, no! I do apologise. So, what is this pressing matter you need to discuss? And what has it to do with me, might I ask?'

Unsure of how Edward might react, Joshua cleared his throat and explained. 'I'm hoping to persuade you to halt the eviction of Tom Arnold from the cottage.'

While Edward Baxter digested this shocking announcement, the rhythmic ticking of the grandfather clock pierced the silence that now filled the room.

Edward was fully aware of the circumstances which linked the Arnold family with the Jacobs. All the same, Joshua's outright request had totally stunned him. 'I'm sorry,' he replied stiffly. 'I can't do that.' His father had left him a duty, and he was no longer a man to shift his duties.

'But why not?' Joshua held his ground. 'Surely you are a man in charge of your own affairs?'

'That's by the by, and besides, you're too late,' Edward returned coldly. 'Tom Arnold has had more than enough warnings, and still the land is neglected. I already have another tenant . . . a very competent man with three strapping sons and a love for the land. He has admirable credentials, and years of farming experience behind him. In fact, he would not be looking for work had his previous employer not sold all the land for development.'

He reaffirmed his stand. 'You must have seen how badly neglected the land is, and there is no way forward, not with Tom Arnold on his own, and with just one man. You're a businessman! You must know I can not afford to see the land go to rack and ruin like that. I'm sorry. The answer has to be no!'

Now impatient for his visitor to leave, he stood up. 'I'm sorry you had a wasted journey. Like I say, everything is set in motion. Tom Arnold is required to be out before the end of the month, otherwise I shall have to take further, more drastic action.'

He gestured to the door. 'And now, I shall say good day to you, sir. It's a pity we part on a sour note.'

Joshua was not done yet. 'I have a proposition,' he said quietly.

'Not interested.'

'Let me buy the cottage? I'm prepared to pay over the odds for it.'

'The cottage is not for sale!'

'Then would you consider leasing it to me . . . as long a lease as you wish?'

'Never! If you don't mind, I consider our business to be concluded. Neither the land or the cottage is up for sale . . . lease or freehold it makes no difference.'

'Then please, find it in your heart to leave Tom and Nancy in the place they know as home. They've been there so many years, their heart and soul is written in every brick.'

'Sentimental nonsense!'

Realising the other man would not budge, Joshua was deeply saddened to be going back to Alice, with a resounding no to her request. 'I see there is no persuading you.'

At the front door he turned, with one last desperate, parting shot. 'Do you think your father would be proud of you? Do you really imagine, if he were still here, that he would have thrown Tom out of his home? I don't think so, and neither do you.'

'How dare you bring my father into this!' Rushing

forward, Edward flung the door open wide. 'Get out of my house.'

Seeing how he had touched a raw spot, Joshua dared to remind him, 'Tom Arnold has slaved on that land all his life . . . from boy to man. His blood is in the soil. His heart is embedded in every nook and cranny.'

He paused to let that sink in, before going on. 'He feels an affinity towards the land, just as your father did. All right, Tom has had a bad time of it, and he's lost the two sons who helped him keep things going, but Joe will be back, God willing! He, too, has the same passion for your father's land. I beg you to think what you're doing, Edward! Think how your father must have felt when he almost lost everything. And remember, that's exactly how Tom Arnold is feeling now.'

Enraged, Edward physically thrust him out the door, with the grim warning, 'Don't ever come back here.'

Joshua felt himself crumple and made his way to the car. 'I tried, Alice,' he whispered wearily to himself. 'Sorry, sweetheart.'

Turning the car around, he got a glimpse of Edward Baxter standing at the door, then suddenly he was waving, and calling out, and when Joshua stopped the car he was right there, peering in at the window. 'I'll say this about you, Jacobs. You're a persistent bugger!' He had the smallest whisper of a smile on his face.

Joshua apologised. 'Maybe I was unforgiveably rude. But when I see a wrongdoing, I feel duty bound to right it. This time it isn't my call. It's yours.'

'Are you prepared to put your money where your mouth is?' Edward leaned closer.

'In what way?'

'I could contract a couple of experienced farm hands to work with Tom and Jimmy for the next year to eighteen months, until Joe is able to help his father. They'll need wages and lodgings, and it will be *you* that foots the bill. What d'you say?'

Joshua could hardly believe his ears. Before the other man should change his mind, he leapt out of the car to shake him by the hand. 'Done! And many thanks. You won't regret it. You know it's the right thing to do.'

Before they parted, Joshua asked, 'What made you change your mind?'

Edward took a moment to reflect and his eyes began to smart. 'You were right. My father would never have approved of turning Tom out of his home, any more than he was proud of me, when I almost cost him everything he had worked for.' His voice dropped to a whisper. 'I know my weakness cost him his life, and I will have to live with that.'

Joshua saw his pain and he was humbled. 'No, Edward,' he spoke softly. 'Your father would probably have had that heart attack anyway. All those long years of working day and night when you were a boy; it was bound to take its toll. Don't punish yourself for something that was beyond your control.'

Edward looked up, his eyes bright with tears. 'Thank you,' he murmured. 'You can't know what those few words of kindness mean to me.'

'I mean it. Life is hard enough without taking on more blame than you have a right to.'

Edward smiled, and when the tears threatened to spill, he quickly turned on his heel and strode away. 'Let Tom know the eviction notice is cancelled,' he called over his shoulder. 'I'll be in touch!'

As he drove away, Joshua felt triumphant. He had helped both Tom and Edward Baxter.

'You think a man is rock solid and ice cold ruthless,' he murmured to himself, 'but underneath, we all have our ghosts to deal with.'

His thoughts fled back to the first year he and Tricia were married. Almost four months later the son she was carrying, was sadly lost to them.

It was a heart-breaking time.

Over the years they talked about it often between themselves, but never once had they discussed it with anyone else, not even family.

Such a deeply sad experience was best shared only by those who suffered it.

~

A few days later, Tom received a letter from Edward Baxter's legal representative.

Dear Mr Arnold,

I have had instructions from Edward Baxter, of Baxter Hall, owner of the cottage you inhabit and the land surrounding it.

I am to inform you that you will not be evicted from your home. However, you will be required to accept the following men to work under your personal and expert guidance for an unspecified period of time, in order to keep good the said land and buildings owned by the above Edward Baxter, and previously maintained by yourself and your sons.

Here enclosed is a form of acceptance to these conditions. If you are in agreement, please sign and return the form and we will be in touch with regard to the workmen, who will report to you for instructions concerning what work is required of them.

According to my instructions, once you are able to undertake the necessary work unaided, the men employed by Edward Baxter, will of course no longer be required.

Mr Edward Baxter will be calling on you at some time

in the near future, in order to clarify matters, and answer
any queries you may have.
　　Yours sincerely,

　　J.C. Clarence

As always, straight after breakfast, Tom had collected the letter from the postbox that was situated at the bottom of the garden path.

Nancy was busy packing her delicate china, and feeling totally lost as she tried to envisage a life away from this delightful home where they had been so happy for all these years.

'I really don't know how we'll ever cope . . .' she told Tom as he wandered in. 'I've never lived in lodgings before. The very idea of it makes me feel ill . . .'

Distraught, she flopped into the armchair and began to cry. 'I'm sorry, Tom . . .' she started. 'I can't even think about it . . .'

'Now, now, Nancy . . . don't upset yourself love . . .' He had torn open the letter and was on his way to console her, when suddenly he screeched out, 'OH MY GOD! NANCY!' He was laughing and crying all at the same time. 'We're not being thrown out after all!'

Now it was his turn to be tearful, but this time they were tears of joy. 'We can stay here! Oh, Nancy, did you hear what I said! we can stay!'

Flinging his arms round her, he read the letter to her, and afterwards the two of them danced across the kitchen floor. They laughed and hugged, and when the initial excitement was spent, Nancy wiped the tears from her eyes.

'I can't believe it,' she said brokenly. 'Read it to me again, Tom love! Just to be sure we're not dreaming!'

And so he read it, and for a long moment they were

silent, holding each other and thinking how the good Lord had smiled down on them. And Nancy had a thought. 'Tom?'

'Yes, my love?' He still could not stop smiling.

'If I told you I suspect Alice had something to do with this, would you be angry?'

At first he stared at her in astonishment. 'Alice.' There was hostility in his voice. 'Why the devil would you think *she* had something to do with it?'

'Alice *Arnold!* Whether we like it or not, Alice is still our daughter-in-law.'

Tom chose to ignore her very proper reminder. 'As far as I'm concerned,' he declared angrily, 'that young woman has devastated our family, and you should remember that! As for you thinking she may have had something to do with us staying on here, I can not imagine!'

'I can't be certain, but when you were out walking the other day, she came to see me,' Nancy confessed.

Tom's features stiffened. 'She was here? And you never thought to tell me!'

'I didn't tell you because I knew you would react like you're reacting now . . . with a sour face and a sharp tongue, and anyway she was here for just a few minutes.'

Now Tom was on his feet, staring down on her with a distinctly disapproving expression. 'I hope you didn't let her in!'

'I did, yes, and she opened her heart to me. Look, Tom . . . I know our family has been devastated but it's wrong to blame Alice altogether. After all, Joe could easily have turned her away, but he didn't.'

'No! Because she had him in her claws, that's why!'

'No, Tom. And I know you've always had your suspicions that Joe was attracted to Alice on the first day Frank brought her home.'

Tom was shocked. 'Whatever makes you say that?'

'Because I know you better than you think, and because I saw how Joe looked at her, like he'd known her all his life. I knew that was why he went away, and so did you.'

Tom could not deny it, but he was adamant. 'I don't want her in this house ever again! And as for her having something to do with us staying here, that is just ridiculous.'

'Maybe not so ridiculous, Tom,' Nancy explained. 'She came here because she was distraught about Joe, and all the things that have happened. She said she was sorry about her part in it, and that in a way she didn't blame Frank, because she and Joe had been wrong to do what they did. She was here to seek our forgiveness, Tom.'

'Well, she won't get it . . . not from me anyway. Never from me!'

'Think what you're saying, Tom,' Nancy urged. 'Think what it must have taken for her to forgive Frank. And I'll tell you now, whatever provocation he may have had, Frank was wicked to do what he did to Joe and to Alice. Yes, she did wrong, and so did Joe. But to my mind, Frank did much worse. And what about what he did to you? His own father!'

This was the first time she had disclosed her true feelings, and now she wanted Tom to realise how strongly she felt at what their son had done to this young woman.

'Don't you try and tell me he was justified, because to my mind what he did was unforgiveable. He hurt her bad, Tom, and tell me this, how would you have felt if that had been your own daughter? Frank deliberately tied her down and tortured her. He ripped out her hair and put her through hell! And I tell you now Tom . . . though I want him safe, I do not forgive him what he did. I don't know if I ever can!'

Tom had never seen his beloved wife so wound up before, and it shook him to his roots. 'Oh, I can see it all now! I can see she's got to you . . . just like she got to our two boys.'

'No, Tom! You won't let yourself look at the wider picture, will you? Alice is just a girl, Tom, a frightened, haunted girl. She looks ill, Frank, and she has nightmares, and she said if there was any way she could help us stay here in our home, she would move Heaven and earth . . .'

'Hmm! Anybody can say anything if they're looking to be forgiven! It means nothing. D'you hear me, Nancy! What Alice says means absolutely *nothing*! Not to me!'

Besides being angry at her for letting Alice in, his pride was dented. 'The reason we're staying here is because I know more about this land than any other man will learn in a lifetime, apart from the man who shaped it! They need me, Nancy. That's why we're being allowed to stay, and for no other reason that that!'

Nancy stood up. 'There's something else.'

'Oh, so now what?' His patience was at an end.

'Alice had seriously considered having an abortion.'

'Why does that not surprise me?'

'She decided against it though.'

'Well, at least she has the decency not to end a life before it's begun. No doubt she'll give the child to some stranger after it's born.'

'Does that worry you, Tom?'

'No! Why should it? As far as I'm concerned, it'll be a little bastard . . . best given away to somebody else.'

Nancy was shocked. 'May the Lord forgive you, Tom Arnold.'

'There is nothing to forgive. I suppose the next thing you'll be saying is that she's carrying our grandchild, and we should be looking forward to it?'

'Yes! Something like that.' Nancy smiled. 'Only it won't just be our grandchild. Alice is carrying our *grandchildren*.

She's having twins, Tom, and they're our flesh and blood. So, don't you think it's time for a little forgiveness?'

Reeling from the shock, Tom would not give an inch. 'To hell with her and to hell with them! I don't want her offspring! I want our sons back! I want us to be the family we were before she came along. You need to remember, Nancy . . . they won't just be *our* flesh and blood . . . they'll be hers too. And I for one want nothing whatsoever to do with them!'

In a state of rage and utter confusion, he stormed off.

When Nancy called after him, he quickened his steps, and sought refuge in the barn.

Huddled on a hay bale in the corner, Tom's gaze was drawn to the bird cage swinging in the rush of air that whistled through the cracks in the wall.

Images rushed through his mind; of his son Frank and the wickedness that was undoubtedly rooted in him. How did it happen, that a son of his should harbour such evil?

He watched a while longer, his painful thoughts creating an avalanche of images, as the cage swung backwards and forwards, creaking a tune against the silence.

In his mind he saw Joe, trussed up in that hospital bed, damaged and broken, maybe for the rest of his young life.

He also remembered Alice, made almost unrecognisable by what Frank had done to her.

And the wild bird, kept safe in that bird cage, while being tenderly nursed back to its amazing beauty in Joe's loving care.

The enormity of Frank's badness was a terrifying thing. So much pain, so much hatred.

Try as he might, Tom could not take his eyes off the bird cage, swinging backwards and forwards, backwards and forwards; the rhythmic creaking seeming like the cries of a creature in agony.

'What in God's name possessed you, Frank?' he murmured softly. 'How could you hurt a helpless little bird like that?'

He heard Nancy's voice in his head. 'She's just a girl, Tom . . . a frightened, haunted girl.'

Wasn't it odd, he mused, how he could feel so warm and comfortable in this draughty old barn, especially when these very walls had witnessed such badness.

And especially as this very barn was the place where it all began.

CHAPTER FOURTEEN

ALICE STOOD WITH the back door open, watching as the snow fell in droves, just as it had done all day long.

Now, in the late evening, everything was covered in white. Along the back footpath some little creature had picked its way up to the back door and back down again, creating a perfectly formed ladder right down to the end of the footpath, where it disappeared into the undergrowth.

Tricia came rushing in from the front hallway. 'Good grief, child!' She hurried to Alice's side. 'Whatever are you doing, standing there in your nightgown? Come away, before you catch your death of cold!'

In no time, she had the door closed and was leading Alice back to the kitchen table. 'Look at you!' Pointing to Alice's swollen stomach, she tutted. 'Only weeks to go before you give birth and there you are standing at the open door on a freezing cold January evening, trying to get pneumonia!'

Placing Alice carefully but firmly into the chair, she said, 'Sit there and do as you're told, young lady!' She then lost no time in making hot cocoa and frying up some crispy bacon, which she then put between two slices of bread and put in front of Alice. 'You've eaten like a little bird all day long!' she chided. 'So tuck into that; I do not want to see a single crumb left on your plate.'

Alice was used to receiving lectures on what to eat and drink, and how not to sleep on your tummy, in case she squashed the babies.

But she didn't mind. In fact it was comforting to have someone fuss over her.

In all these months she had not once heard from her sister or her mother, though her father had visited many times, always worried, always eager to know how things were going.

Alice was anxious. 'I don't like the idea of being cut open,' she told Tricia now. 'I'd rather give birth the natural way.'

'I know you would, child.' Tricia brought two mugs of hot cocoa, and slid one over to Alice.

'The thing is, you know what the doctor told us. You're small-built and you're carrying two babies. It could be difficult for you to give birth naturally. They've already explained, they're prepared to wait and see, and maybe when the time gets nearer, you might just prove them wrong.'

Alice worked it out. 'Only three weeks and a day to go until the date they gave me.'

Tricia reminded her, 'Ah, yes, but they couldn't say exactly which date the babies might arrive. What they said was, it could be a few days either way.'

'Well I don't mind, Grandma. I just want to hold them in my arms.'

Whenever she thought of these precious babies, Alice got all emotional. 'Wouldn't it be wonderful if I knew which sex they were?'

'Utter nonsense! I've never heard the like, and anyway, why would any mother want to know whether they were having a boy or a girl . . . it would spoil the surprise.'

Alice laughed. 'I think having twins was enough of a surprise for me!'

'Have you still not settled on names?' Tricia was excited about her new great grandchildren.

Alice put her out of her misery. 'I'll tell you what. For the second names, I'll keep Father and Grandfather's, together with two of my own choices for first names. That's the boys. Then I'll do the same with the girls . . . your name and mine for second names. And two others for first names.'

'Not your mother and sister's then?' Tricia was not surprised.

'Nope.'

Tricia understood. She was well aware that neither Maureen nor Pauline had been anywhere near this house, or even bothered to ask after Alice's well-being.

'Right then.' Tricia was anxious that Alice should eat well. 'You'd best eat that sandwich before it goes cold. Unless of course you think it's too disgusting to eat. Is that it? You don't like my cooking?'

'No, it's not that at all,' Alice promised. 'It's just that I'm not really hungry.' The truth was, her grandmother was not used to cooking for herself these days. She had a wonderful little woman from the village who took care of all that; leaving her free to go off on her much-loved charity work.

Tricia tried another tack. 'You may not be hungry, but what about your babies?'

'I think they'll be happy if I just drink my cocoa.'

'Every last drop?'

'Of course.'

Tricia smiled at her. 'Very well then, but you really must try and eat more.'

'I will.'

'Promise?'

'Yes, I promise.'

'Right then. I'll be off to my bed. And you had better be close behind me, or I'll have to come down and fetch you.'

Alice returned her peck on the cheek. 'Goodnight Grandma.'

'Goodnight, child.'

Tricia made a confession. 'I know you've not been sleeping lately,' she revealed. 'I've lain awake in bed, listening to you, walking up and down before creeping down the stairs, then creeping back up again. It's how I knew you were down here for so long. That's why I came looking for you . . . only to find you gazing out the back door with nothing on but your nightgown.'

Her voice dropped to a kindly tone. 'I know I'm an old nag, but I do worry for you, Alice. You need to take care of yourself,' she said softly. 'I know you've been through a terrible time, and I know you worry about Joe, but you have two little babies to think of now, and oh, you do look so tired all the time.'

Throwing her arms round Alice, she held her close for a moment. 'I really do hurt for you, child,' she said. 'Your grandfather and I love you so much. You do know that, don't you?'

Alice assured her that she did know that, and that she loved them back. 'I honestly don't know how I would have coped if it hadn't been for you and Grandfather.'

Tricia smiled at that. 'Oh, you would have coped,' she promised. 'You might be a little thing, but you have a big heart and a streak of stubborness, high as a mountain.'

She gave her another peck on the cheek, then she was gone, and Alice was all alone in the cavernous kitchen.

For a long time, Alice sat there, her mind alive with thoughts of these past months. 'Darling Joe; I wish we could be together,' she whispered. 'But I know we can't.'

She walked across to the window and looked out. The snow was still falling, now knee-deep in places. 'I miss you so much, Joe. I think about you all the time, and oh, I do so much want these babies to be yours.'

Stroking her hand across her stomach, she suddenly thought about Frank, and the fear inside her was palpable.

Raising her eyes upwards to the vast, brooding skies, she spoke in the smallest of whispers. 'Don't let them be *his*!' she pleaded. 'Please, Lord . . . I couldn't bear the thought of Frank's children growing inside me, but I can't snuff out their lives.'

It was partly that fear that kept her awake at night. And the questions; always the questions. Where was he? Was he hiding low, planning his next move? Was he watching her, even now?

Instinctively, she backed away from the window.

But one pressing question remained.

Had she done the right thing in not ending the pregnancy? And the answer came back loud and clear. It was right and proper, to give these innocents little ones the chance of life. After all, what happened that night was not their fault.

It was her's and Joe's, and it was only right that she and Joe should be the ones punished.

Upstairs in her bed, Tricia lay awake, waiting for Alice to come upstairs.

Twice, Joshua had opened one eye to watch her stirring, and each time he had asked worriedly, 'What's wrong with you? Why can't you sleep?'

'I'm just a bit restless,' she told him. 'Now stop fussing, and get back to sleep. You're keeping *me* awake now!'

All the same, she was anxious. Alice was deeply troubled, she knew that, but hopefully once the babies were born and she was able to hold them in her arms then life might seem more worth the living.

There was something else too.

Just now, when she was speaking with Alice, she noticed the pink flush on her face. It reminded her of the time when she herself was expecting.

Just prior to Alice's father being born, she too had that same pink flush and felt uncomfortably warm and bothered. So much so that she could hardly bear to be inside the house.

Was Alice feeling like that? Was it why she had been standing at the back door in her nightgown? Because she was hot and uncomfortable?

Tricia chided herself. 'I'm imagining things,' she muttered, 'Alice still has over three weeks to go yet.'

'What did you say?' Joshua rolled over.

'Nothing!' Tricia shoved him back to his own side. 'You get back to sleep!'

After a few minutes she heard Alice come up the stairs and then she heard her close the bedroom door. 'Silly old fool that I am!' she smiled. 'Worrying about something and nothing, when there's still plenty of time yet.'

With that thought in her mind and Alice now safely in her bedroom, Tricia soon dropped off to sleep.

Very soon, the house was quiet.

Alice however, was wide awake. She had climbed into bed and wanted to sleep, but she couldn't. So after a while she got out of bed and threw open a window.

Now she was seated cross-legged on the window seat, watching the snow continue to fall, very quickly covering everything sparkly white.

As always when she was alone and quiet, her thoughts went to Joe. 'The woman in the post office told Grandfather that you were beginning to take a few tentative steps on your own two feet. Oh, that's so wonderful, Joe!' she said to herself.

She closed her eyes for a moment and she could see

his face, that familiar wonderful face with those hand-some eyes and the mop of hair that seemed to have a mind of its own.

She wondered if he was looking up at the same sky right now, watching the snow tumbling down. 'I know you don't love me Joe, and after what's happened, I can't blame you for not wanting me.'

Kissing her finger tips she blew it to the breeze. 'I'm sending my love to you anyway.'

She missed Joe so much. Since that day when he told her to leave, she had never gone back; though every minute of every day she had longed to see him again.

She had accepted his decision, because she had no real choice. Even so, nothing could stop her from loving him.

There was no other man she would ever need, not like she needed Joe.

With a heavy heart, she climbed back into bed, and within minutes had drifted into a shallow, restless sleep.

~

In the early hours of the morning, Tricia was woken by the sound of what seemed like a heavy thump. 'Alice!' Scrambling out of bed, she ran to Alice's room. As she flung open the door, Alice fell into her arms. 'I don't know what's wrong,' she sobbed. 'I think the babies are coming . . .' When suddenly she grasped her lower abdomen and yelled out in pain, Tricia knew there was no time to waste. 'It's all right,' she led Alice back to the bed. 'Try to keep calm, Alice. We'll get you to hospital. Don't worry, child . . .'

Just then Joshua burst into the room. 'What is it?' He took one look at Alice bent double and groaning and his heart sank. 'Oh, dear God, the babies are coming . . .' Like all men he was lost as to what he should do next. 'I'll phone the ambulance, shall I?'

As he hurried out of the room, Tricia called after him, 'Hurry, Josh. Tell them it's urgent! Make sure they know she's three weeks early!'

'Oh, dear! Oh dearie me!' Joshua almost fell headlong down the stairs in his hurry to get to the phone.

From upstairs he could be heard issuing instructions as to how the ambulance should get there, and then he was running back in a panic. 'They say they might need to wait until the snow has cleared. They're not sure they can get along the lanes, but they'll do their best, and keep in touch.'

He had an idea that might just save the day. 'The Land Rover!' He went running back down the stairs. 'It's not the most comfortable thing in the world, but that old Rover can get through anything!'

Before anyone could stop him, he was away, determined by one means or another to get Alice to hospital.

In the meantime, Tricia got Alice as comfortable as she could, rubbing her back and keeping her calm. All the while Alice clung to her, intermittently crying out as the pains grew stronger, and the time between got short and shorter.

Tricia was no expert, but she knew enough to realise that the babies were on their way; they were not waiting for anyone.

Going to the window, she saw Joshua opening the garage doors. Quickly now, she flung open the window and yelled down to him. 'Joshua!' When he seemed not to have heard, she yelled again, this time louder. 'Joshua . . . Joshua, look up!'

This time Joshua turned and saw her. 'There's no time! You have to get Nancy!' Tricia recalled how Nancy delivered a baby once when the girl in the butcher's shop went into labour without warning. 'Hurry, Joshua! Tell Nancy she's needed . . . fast as you can!'

Joshua jumped into the car as quickly as he could,

the big wheels leaving wide, flattened tracks of snow as he sped off. 'Don't let them die!' he prayed, as his hands gripped the steering wheel tightly. 'You look after my girl, and them little babies. Or I'll never forgive you!'

~

Tom heard the roar of the engine as the Land Rover skidded and fought its way up to the cottage door. 'What the devil . . . !' Grabbing his trousers he threw them on and ran down the stairs. 'Damned lunatic . . . what's he think he's playing at . . .' When there came a hammering and banging enough to knock the door off its hinges, Tom put his back to it and yelled out, 'You'd best get away from that door if you know what's good for yer! I've got a shotgun and I know how to use it!'

When Nancy came running into the hallway, Tom shouted out, 'Get away from here, Nancy. It's them bloody gypsies! I've seen 'em parked up in that bottom field. I knew they were trouble the minute I clapped eyes on 'em!'

When there came another hard banging on the door, he shouted, 'I've told you . . . clear orf! Unless you want a blast o' shotgun pellet up yer arse!'

'Tom! It's me!' Joshua tried to get himself heard above all the shouting and commotion. 'Tom! It's me . . . Joshua!'

Nancy heard. 'Get outta the way, you silly old fool!' With one mighty swipe she pushed him away from the door.

The minute she had the door open, Joshua was in. 'Alice needs you!' he said breathlessly. 'Tricia says the babies are on their way and there's no time to lose . . . please, Nancy. You've got to come. The ambulance can't get through, and it's too risky to put her in the Land Rover.'

'My wife is not going anywhere!' Tom was adamant. 'Whether Alice is having her babies or not is none of our concern. So you can go right back where you came from, and tell her that!'

'You don't speak for me, Tom Arnold!' Nancy said quietly but boldly. 'Did you not hear what Joshua said? Your daughter-in-law is about to have our grandchildren, and the ambulance can't get through. You can stay here if you like, but as for me, I'm ready to do anything I can to help.'

Still dressed in her nightgown, she ran back to get her shoes and long coat. As it was knee deep in snow along the path, Joshua carried her out to the Land Rover. 'There's a blanket in the back,' he said breathlessly as he sat her in the seat. 'It's an old picnic thing, but I dare say it'll keep you warm if you need it . . .' Reaching inside the back, he got it out and spread it over her knees.

As they drove away, Nancy looked back to see Tom, still standing at the door; a small, solitary figure that made her heart ache. 'He's a good man,' she told Joshua. 'It's just that he's finding it hard to deal with everything that's happened.'

'I know.' Joshua had also suffered a few bad moments these past months. 'Like you said, Tom is a good man. Just give him time. He'll come round, you see if he doesn't.'

Nancy kept her gaze on Tom for as long as she could. 'I'm sorry, Tom,' she whispered. 'There's already been too much pain and unhappiness. Maybe it's time we started looking forward.'

When they got to the big house, Alice was wrapped up and beng loaded into the ambulance. 'We managed to get through in the end,' the driver said, '. . . but it might help if you were to go in front of us on the way back. We followed your earlier tracks but the road's still a bit dodgy out there.'

Joshua was only too pleased to do whatever he could, zig-zagging and and creating a wider, flatter trail, to give Alice a smoother ride.

On arriving at the hospital, Alice was quickly whisked away.

While she was gone, Joshua, Tricia and Nancy walked up and down. They chatted and talked of Joe, and Alice, and even Frank, while they waited for news of Alice and the babies.

~

Three hours later, when they were huddled in the chairs, half asleep, they received news that Alice had given birth to two healthy babies. 'Two perfectly beautiful boys,' the nurse assured them, and told them that Alice was doing fine.

On realising that everything was well, all three of them shed a tear. 'Think of it! Two grandsons!' Nancy was laughing and crying all at the same time.

'Dearie me!' Joshua felt proud of his own part in it all. 'I was thinking of selling it, but I think I'll keep that Land Rover now.' He was that excited he didn't really know what to say.

Tricia was very quiet.

'Are you all right?' Joshua asked her.

With tears in her eyes, she told him. 'We're so lucky, you and me. We have a wonderful son in Ronald, and a lovely granddaughter, and now . . . two new grandsons. What have we ever done to deserve it?'

Her heartfelt comment made them all stop and think.

PART SIX

~

January/February 1953

A Price to Pay

CHAPTER FIFTEEN

B Y A MIXTURE of luck, accident and devious means, Frank Arnold had avoided capture for many months.

Having kept himself to himself, he took on the lonely life of the modest man he had so callously murdered, and travelled freely up and down the many miles of waterways; showing himself only when needing to earn money in the fields, or to purchase fuel and necessities.

Occasionally he would venture out on a dark night to look for the kind of woman who did not mind spending the night with a stranger.

Wily and cunning, he was also a bitter, driven man. A man who had lost all sense of reality. And the only thing on his mind was revenge on those who had ruined the life he knew before.

'Alice! That bitch!' Murmuring her name, he stood at the back of the barge, skilfully shifting the tiller this way and that, gliding along the water as though he was born to it. Having worked with engines all his farming life, and tracked straight lines up and down a field, the barge was not too great a mystery.

His one aim in life was to mete out a just punishment on those who had belittled and deceived him. It was the one thing that kept him going.

He had a plan, and he was biding his time.

He also had a thirst.

That was why he now made his way down to his favourite watering hole.

As he came round the curve, a cavalcade of ducks and swans flew up into the air, quacking and calling and making a flurry in the sky. 'Gerrout of it, you buggers!' Frank had no love for birds; they made a mess of his boat, and soiled his washing-line.

His foul mood lifted when he saw the old pub before him, tucked back on the towpath, and looking warm and inviting. The Glen in the vale of Stoke Hammond was a haven. This old place was visited by every boatman up and down the canal.

Anticipating that pint glass overflowing with amber nectar, he licked his lips as he came round, gently and easy, taking the barge further up the towpath, so as not to be too easily noticed. Drawing into the side, he threw off his line and moored the barge with ease. Like someone born to it.

Once the barge was secure, he then put on his duffle coat and pulled the woolly hat down over his forehead. As ever, he maintained a low profile, and kept his wits about him.

'Right, sir! What's it to be then?' The barman had seen him arrive. He also knew him to be a man of few words.

Frank sidled up to the bar. 'A pint of your best.' As always he avoided eye contact.

'Bit nippy out there, eh?'

'You could say that, yes.'

'Travelled far have you?'

'Far enough.' He kept a civil tongue, but in his head he was thinking. 'Get a damned move on! I'm not here for idle chit chat.'

'There you go, matey.' The barman slid the pint over to him, and Frank slid the coins back. Then without another word he walked away to seat himself in the far corner, by the window.

From here he could see the barge, and anyone who dared go near it.

As he tipped the glass to his lips, he heard the murmur of men talking. Seated at a wooden trestle outside the window, they were discussing the time of day and the recent freak storms in Britain that had taken the lives of over four hundred people.

The conversation moved on to which horse might win in a certain race on Saturday; while the women present among them talked of the forthcoming coronation of Elizabeth the second.

Ignoring them, and pleased to be out of sight, Frank again took a long slow gulp of beer, savouring the flavour as it hit the back of his throat.

As the voices wafted up to him, Frank suddenly realised they were talking about him.

'It's time they caught that wicked bugger!' one woman declared angrily. 'What he did to his wife was unbelievable. He must be mad as a hatter!'

'Yes, but what I want to know is where the devil is he?' That was her companion. 'It's like he's vanished off the face of the earth.'

'You're right! And it now begins to looks like the police are scaling down the search, more's the pity.'

A man's voice intervened. 'According to the papers, they did arrest somebody, but it turned out to be some poor devil who happened to be in the wrong place at the wrong time.'

The first woman interrupted excitedly, 'Apparently, the police are keeping an eye on the maternity unit at Bedford.'

'Why?' That was the first man.

'Well, because according to the papers, she gave birth

to twins, and for some reason, that's where they still are . . . in Bedford maternity unit. Think about it, Lenny. If he tried to kill his brother and his wife, what's to say he won't harm the babies?'

A new voice chipped in, 'What about the brother . . . the one he crippled?'

There was a small silence, before someone else said, 'They don't say too much about him, do they? It's like they're more interested in the woman and her babies; probably because they think it's her he'll go after.'

One man had a strong opinion on Alice. 'I'll tell you what . . . she was wrong to sleep with his brother. Any man would go out of his mind if that happened.'

'She may have been wrong, but that Frank Arnold was worse! He tried to kill three people; all family. As far as I'm concerned, he should be locked up and left to rot!'

When the men began discussing the next Australia versus England cricket match at the Oval, Frank gulped down his drink, and made a hasty exit.

His shortest route was straight out the front door and past the group he had heard talking.

Frank caught the eye of the woman. For the longest few seconds when their eyes met each other's, the woman felt a cold shiver go through her; while he found delight in imagining his hands locked around her neck, choking the last drop of life out of her.

In the space of a heartbeat, he held her with his hard stare, before quickly turning and hurrying away.

Climbing on to the barge, he went straight to the calendar, which was hanging behind the cabin door.

He carefully studied the fine red line that ran from the date of his wedding, to a date which was two days away.

'Damn and bugger it!'

Tearing the calendar off the wall he tore it to shreds. 'How could I get it so wrong?' He began pacing the floor.

It doesn't matter! he thought. Because now he knew, and he would need to rearrange his plans.

In turmoil, his mind raced ahead as he frantically started the engine and drew in the mooring line.

Within minutes he was going down the water full speed, talking to himself and making plans that would put him back in charge. 'I'll show her!' he kept saying, 'I'll show the lot of 'em.'

Behind him, the little group were getting ready to leave. 'Did you see that bloke?' the woman said.

'What bloke?' That was her companion.

'That fella in a long coat and woolly hat? He left a few minutes ago.'

One of the men chuckled. 'I saw him,' he said. 'I've seen him here before . . . a bit of a loner I reckon.'

'Damned weirdo!' she answered quietly. 'He kept staring at me . . . real strange like.'

Laughing out loud, the other woman gave her a playful shove. 'Give over, Sal!' she said. 'It's more like you were staring at *him*!'

The fat man added to the merriment. 'We all know you're on the lookout for the next big romance.'

As they walked away, the woman kept glancing over her shoulder, watching, as the barge disappeared under the little bridge. 'There's something really scary about that bloke,' she muttered.

Merry from the drink, the fat man laughed. 'He's probably thinking the very same about *you*!'

They all laughed at that, though once they were in the car, she recalled the look in his eyes as he stared at her. Try as she might, she could not get the image out of her mind.

CHAPTER SIXTEEN

'I HATE PUTTING YOU to all this trouble, Father.' Alice felt guilty. 'Every day for two weeks you've picked me up and brought me to the hospital. Grandfather said he would take turns, or I could even get on the bus . . . or get a taxi. I don't like taking you away from your work. I know how busy you are.'

Ronald shushed her. 'I only lose an hour in the morning,' he explained, 'I don't intend losing sleep over that! Besides, work will be here long after I'm dead and gone.'

He added, 'Bringing you to hospital is my pleasure, and I get to see my grandsons. Anyway, I only bring you in. Grandfather collects you.'

He gave a contented grin. 'So! You don't need to order a taxi, not when you've got your own little taxi service. Besides, your grandfather and I would not have it any other way. Oh, and don't forget these two little people are very special. Us two men mean to stay close to them . . . if that's all right with you?'

'Well, of course!' Alice was shocked. 'Why would you ask such a thing when you know perfectly well, I'd be deeply hurt if you *didn't* want to be close to them!'

Ronald smiled at her. 'Well, there you go then. So stop nagging at me and Grandfather. Doing our bit to help makes us feel useful anyway!'

'Dad?'

'Yes?'

'Can I ask you something?'

'Ask away.'

'You will tell me the truth, won't you?'

'Of course.'

Alice paused, unsure as to whether he would even want to discuss it.

'Well, come on then!' He negotiated the entrance to the hospital, drove into the space and brought the car to a halt.

Switching off the engine, he asked again, 'So, what's on your mind, Alice? I'm anxious to get in and see my grandsons.'

When again she paused, he looked at her, and from her worried expression, he knew what she was thinking. 'It's your mother, isn't it?'

Alice nodded.

'I'm sorry love. Your mother is very stubborn. I've tried to persuade her but she's not having any of it!' He gave her a consolatory kiss on the cheek. 'Don't worry yourself over it, sweetheart,' he urged. 'It's her loss, not yours.'

Alice was saddened, but not surprised. 'And Pauline?'

He shook his head. 'The same!'

Seeing how he, too, was upset, Alice tugged at his sleeve. 'Come on then! Stop hanging about when there are two wonderful little boys waiting to see their grandad!'

As they walked into the hospital arm in arm, Frank watched from his hiding place at the back of the car park.

'How very cosy!' he sneered. 'Pity though! You two had better make the best of it while it lasts!'

Every day for a whole week he had watched the very same scene. Alice's father bringing her in the morning, then her grandfather taking her away at night.

Having previously found a way inside without confrontation, he had managed to gain knowledge of the layout, and he had taken the trouble to make sure there had been no changes in and out of that place.

On each of his little exploratory trips he had skilfully dodged the police presence, and even found his way to the maternity unit.

And now after careful planning, he was almost ready to strike.

Chuckling to himself, he wended his way out of the car park, then down to the bus stop, where he boarded the bus.

Some time later, he got off at the canal bridge. Glancing furtively about, he then walked down the towpath and climbed on to his barge.

Once inside the cabin, he went straightaway to the far corner, where he turned the carpet back and drew out a fold of paper, which he then took to the galley, laying it out carefully on the drainer.

Flattening the creased paper with the palm of his hand, he took a minute to familiarise himself with it; making certain he had missed nothing out. After being painstakingly careful and devious, he did not intend to fail now.

Sketched on to the paper was a map of the hospital. Now, using the tip of his finger, he traced every corridor, every exit and entry, and when he touched the outline of the maternity unit, where he knew Alice's babies to be, he smiled, a deep and devious smile that betrayed his intent.

After a while, he took a pen from his pocket and began writing in untidy scrawl, alongside the map:

ALICE

MORNING
Arrives with father at eight-thirty. (He stays 15–20 minutes.) He leaves. She stays on.

<u>EVENING</u>
Grandfather collects her at eight-thirty. (He stays 30 minutes.) They both leave.

<u>HOSPITAL STAFF</u>
<u>Baby care unit</u>

<u>MORNING</u>
First nurse arrives at seven. Leaves at nine. (Give or take fifteen minutes.)

Second nurse arrives at ten. Relieves first nurse. Stays two hours – leaves midday – (give or take 10 minutes.)

<u>AFTERNOON</u> Too many people. (Morning; 9a.m.-10a.m.) is best. No nurse. Brats quiet. Alice goes for a little walk for fresh air.

The barge swayed back and forth as he danced around the cabin. 'Ha! Thought they were rid of me did they?' He had waited so long. 'Tomorrow, *I'll* be the one doing the visiting! I'll teach them a lesson they'll never forget!'

Pent up and excited, he could hardly wait. 'In and out . . . quick as a wink. They won't even know what's hit 'em!'

The next thing to do was to take the barge nearer to the hospital in order to make a quick getaway. 'Now then . . . where's the best place to be?' he asked himself. 'Out of sight of prying eyes, yet with a clear run out of the area.'

A smile whispered across his face. 'Ah, yes! The very spot!

'See where kindness gets you, eh, Jack?' he giggled. 'It

gets you a final resting place in the deepest part of the canal. Poor Jack. Never to be seen again.'

In no time at all the engine was quietly ticking over, and the barge moved forward, silently slinking through the water.

Softly whistling, he steered the tiller left and right, before taking up a middle course, away from the towpath, where strolling lovers might grow curious.

~

The following morning, unaware that her sons were in danger, Alice walked with her father to the car. 'I can't believe how well they're doing,' Ronald remarked. 'After Father's mad dash through the snow, and the race to get you here, I never thought the babies would thrive like they have.'

He put an arm round her as they walked on together. 'Alan Joshua . . . and Michael Ronald.' He gave a proud nod of the head. 'Fine names for fine boys.' Though he asked, 'I thought you didn't want names that could be shortened?'

Alice had changed her mind. 'Maybe they won't be shortened, and if they are, well I won't really mind Ron and Al, they're manly names don't you think?'

He agreed. 'Yes, I think so, and I'm sure the boys wouldn't mind at all.'

After seeing her father off, Alice returned to the unit, where the nurse was busy weighing the babies one by one. 'My! But they're doing just fine!' Nurse McDonnell was a little Scottish person with a heart of gold, and a smile as wide as the Mersey tunnel. 'If they keep gaining weight like this, they'll be walking themselves out of here before you know it.'

When she now glanced up at Alice and saw her wipe

away the tears, she placed the second baby in the cot and slid an arm around Alice's shoulders. 'Aw, hen . . . you shouldn't be crying! You should be shouting from the rooftops. My babies are strong and well!'

Alice laughed through her tears. 'Ssh! You'll wake them all up!'

'Ah, but your two are the only ones in this unit now,' the nurse told her. 'The other wee ones are back in the main unit. They're coming on in leaps and bounds and, as you know, tomorrow they're also due to go into the main unit.'

Alice hugged her back. 'I can't thank you all enough,' she said. 'With them being early like that, it really frightened me.'

'Aw, they weren't all that early. Besides, they're chunky little fellows. That's why they were fighting to come out . . . because there wasn't enough room for them in that little frame of yours.'

Like everyone else, the nurse had followed the story in the papers. Having met Alice though, she saw a gentle soul, and someone who had suffered terribly for her mistakes.

'You must be so thrilled,' she told Alice now. 'These babies are a credit to you. Another few days and I wouldn't be surprised if the doctor didn't tell you to take them home . . .' she laughed out loud, '. . . before they start climbing out of the cots and making for the door!'

Just then the door in question opened and in bustled Nurse Baker, a tall thin person, the exact opposite to her jolly comrade. 'Have they been bathed?'

'Yes.'

'Fed?'

'All done.'

'So, it's just a change and weigh?'

The Scottish nurse winked at Alice. 'That's it, yes. Oh,

and it's just the twins. The others are already back in the main unit.'

'Well, thank you, looks like you've already done most of my work.'

'Aw, not at all! Since the other two have gone, it's left me with spare time, which I expect will be used up the minute Matron finds out.'

'Well, it suits me today, because I've been told to report to Matron the minute I've finished here. And don't ask me what it's about, because I don't know.'

Nurse McDonnell had a wicked sense of humour, which had got her into trouble on more than one occasion. With another wink at Alice, she quipped, 'I expect Matron's found out you keep disappearing into the cupboard with Doctor Jackson.'

With a straight face and pretending she had not heard, the other nurse told her sharply, 'You might as well go now. I'll take over from here. Thank you.' And before she could change her mind, Nurse McDonnell scurried away.

Leaning over the cots, the nurse looked from one baby to the other, remarking thoughtfully, 'Just look how they've come on! Such handsome little fellows, one blue-eyed, the other brown-eyed and from my experience, that's not altogether usual.'

She smiled at Alice. 'Mind you, I've only ever seen two sets of twins, one set of boys, totally identical in every way, and another with one of each sex, so I suppose it's a bit silly of me to compare, isn't it?'

'I suppose so, yes.' Alice had not liked this nurse the first time she met her, and she didn't like her now. 'While you're seeing to the babies would you mind if I took a little walk to the front door and back?'

The nurse appeared relieved. 'Not at all! I expect you've been here since early on. It'll do you good to get a bit of fresh air and a cup of tea . . . though the tea from the machine isn't the best in the world.'

She glanced at the babies, kicking their legs and twisting their little fingers against the cot side. 'They're no trouble,' she told Alice. 'Once they're all weighed and changed and smelling nice, I'll leave you to it.'

Alice went to her sons and stroked their heads, talking baby talk and thinking what a fortunate woman she was to have two such beautiful, healthy sons. 'Nurse?'

'Yes?'

'I'd rather stay and help, if that's all right?'

'Oh, no, dear! That's quite unnecessary,' she answered condescendingly. 'It's best if I just get on. The sooner I'm done, the sooner you'll be able to give them another cuddle or two, eh?'

Alice leaned over the cot to kiss her babies and softly tell them that she would be back very soon. Then reluctantly, she left, with the intention of being no longer than half an hour.

That was more than enough time for a cup of tea, and a breath of fresh air, and besides, she would much rather have stayed with her babies if that surly nurse had allowed her.

Alice wasn't in the mood for tea.

Instead she went out the front entrance, where she leaned against the wall, breathing in the cool, clean air. Biding her time until she could go back in and be with her babies. 'Miserable thing!' she muttered, 'I wouldn't get in the way. All I want is to be near my babies.'

She gave a little secret smile. 'I wonder if she really does keep disappearing into the cupboard with that doctor?' Somehow she could never imagine that woman being warm-blooded enough to want a man anyway.

It wasn't long before her thoughts brought her to Joe. And as always, the longing started. Nancy told her the other day that he was walking on his own two feet with much more confidence now, and Alice thought that was wonderful.

She had never stopped missing him, or loving him.

But somehow or another she had to reconcile herself to the fact that he did not want her. So, it looked like it was just her and the babies, and the family who loved them.

She thanked the good Lord for that much at least.

Alice was deep in thought when suddenly everyone seemed to be running about in a panic.

When she heard someone shouting, 'HE'S GOT THE BABIES!' she ran back inside to grab the policeman who was running down the corridor towards the baby unit. 'What's happened? What's going on . . . what's this about the babies . . .' Even as she was screaming the questions at him, she knew. Her every instinct told her that it was Frank. He had somehow got past the police and taken her babies. 'Oh, no . . . please . . . don't let him harm them . . .'

She was running now as fast as she could towards the unit. When she saw the policeman throw open the door, the nurse she had left in charge of her sons was sobbing in a corner. Nurse McDonnell was comforting her.

When she turned to speak with the policeman, she saw Alice. Running forward she took hold of her. 'I'm sorry, Alice! I'm so sorry . . .'

Behind her the other nurse was gabbling her story to the policeman. 'He looked respectable,' she said choking back tears. 'He told me he was looking for Alice, and that she told him to wait in the unit, that she'd be back in a minute. He asked me if he could look at the twins and I showed them to him, but then he threw me to the ground. I couldn't stop him. He took the babies . . .'

She was hysterical. 'It wasn't my fault! I didn't know . . . he just knocked me down. Like a crazy thing he was . . .'

The policeman turned to Alice. 'Mrs Arnold, do you know who this man was?'

'It's Frank. It must be Frank. He's crazy! He'll hurt them, I know he will. Please! You have to get my babies back!' she cried helplessly.

Within minutes more police had arrived. Alice was taken aside and a policewoman tried to calm her. 'Come away,' she said. 'You come with me. Leave them to do their job . . . they'll find him. You come with me.'

Alice tried to run outside, and when the policewoman grabbed her back, she fell into her arms, sobbing like her heart would break. 'Please . . . get my babies back . . . he wants to hurt them, and they're so tiny.'

'We will. He can't have gone far, and they're after him now. You let me take you home now. Your family will need to know what's happened. All right?'

Alice didn't want to leave. 'I need to stay. I need to be here when they bring them back.'

Eventually, it was Nurse McDonnell who persuaded her. 'We had your father's number, and I've telephoned him,' she told Alice. 'He's aware of what's happened, and he says he's on his way to fetch you right now.'

By the time Ronald arrived, Alice was in pieces. 'Come on, sweetheart.' He thanked the policewoman. 'I've got her now,' he said. 'Her grandmother's waiting for her at home.'

When the policewoman explained that they were fearful that Frank Arnold might go after Alice too, Ronald agreed that the policewoman should accompany them.

Settling Alice in the back of the car with the policewoman beside her, Ronald got into the driving seat and quickly left, relieved to be getting Alice away from the heightening chaos.

~

Back at the Police Station, the woman from the pub was adamant that the man who had stared at her was the same man who they were looking for. 'I saw him,' she said. 'It played on my mind. In the end, I rummaged in the drawer and got some old newspapers out that I keep for lighting the fire. It's him! It's Frank Arnold, I tell you! He got on this barge and went away, but it was definitely him . . . look!'

Taking the newspaper cutting out of her pocket, she showed it to the policeman 'That's the man I saw . . . Frank Arnold . . . I tell you it was him!'

She now had his interest, 'Are you absolutely certain this was the man you saw getting on to that barge?'

'It was, I tell you! He got on the barge and he went away. Painted dark brown it was, with blue all round the windows. It was him I tell you!'

She was still talking, when the police clerk ran off to fetch a senior officer.

~

Having grabbed both babies and shoved them into one cot, Frank had run like the wind, dodging and diving, keeping low as he scurried down the back ways and alleys. Breathless but jubilant, he clambered aboard the barge. 'I've done it!' he laughed and sniggered. Placing the cot on the bed, he stared at the tiny infants squashed up to each other, and seeming no worse for their ordeal.

'Little bastards!' There was no pity in his heart; no love or compassion for these helpless infants. Only revenge and hatred, and a black heart filled with murder. 'She'll suffer now, won't she eh? Oh, but I won't do you in . . . oh, no. I'll just let you lie there and starve to death, and if you start bawling, I'll just have to stuff your mouths up, won't I, eh?'

Going to the window, he glanced out. 'They'll never find me,' he gloated. 'How will they know where I am, eh? They won't! They'll be looking here and there, and all the time I'm down here, in this dark little corner, far enough away so they can't even see me.'

He stood for a full minute, just looking down at the infants. 'Who do you belong to, eh? Me, or Joe?!'

Going to the cupboard, he flung open the door and searched for the bottle he had put there earlier. When his hand alighted on it, he drew it out. 'Ah. A drop of this will do me for now.'

Popping the cork out, he tipped the bottle to his lips, gurgling and spluttering as the fiery liquid spilled from his mouth.

He sat down beside the cot, looking and smiling. 'She wants you, but she can't have you, because now I've got you. She can never have you . . . because all she deserves are years of pain and regret. When you die, it'll be her fault, not mine.'

He took another slug from the bottle, laughing and singing and poking the babies until they cried.

In the midst of song, he thought he heard a noise outside. 'What the devil's that?' He got up and peered out the window and then he saw them . . . dark blue uniforms creeping up the towpath looking for him. Looking for the bastards.

Snatching the cot, he climbed outside. 'That's him! That's Arnold!' A chorus of angry voices shattered the night air.

From the back of the growing crowd, Jimmy brought Joe gently forward. 'Take it easy, Joe,' he urged. 'I wish now I'd never let you persuade me to bring you. I should never have told you.' There were times when he opened his mouth before he engaged his brain, and this was such a time.

When Joe heard what was happening, he had to be here. He had to confront his brother . . . make him see sense.

His gaze went to Alice. She looked wretched. Contained in the arms of a burly policeman, she constantly fought to surge forward, her face soaked with tears as she called out to Frank, 'Don't hurt my babies. Please don't hurt them.'

Out of his head with booze, Frank climbed to the back of the cabin. 'Come another step nearer and I'll throw them in the water!' He took another step back. 'I mean it!'

The order went out, 'Back off!'

Then one of the officers inched forward, his hand up to calm the situation. 'Just give me the babies,' he said quietly. 'Listen. You're frightening them. You don't want to be hurting them, Frank. Just come down and we'll talk.'

'Keep back!' Shaking his fist he warned, 'If you come one step closer, I'll drown 'em, I will!'

With Jimmy's help, Joe now wended his way through the police. He called up to his brother, 'Don't do this, Frank.' His voice was calm, while inside he was in turmoil, wishing he had the strength to launch himself at this man who was his own flesh and blood. 'You've done some very evil things in your life Frank, but you must not harm those babies. Come down, Frank. Come down. Those innocents have done you no harm.'

Suddenly Alice was at his side, and as he looked down on her, he could feel her pain. 'Go back,' he murmured, but she would not.

The official's voice called out to Frank, 'Be sensible, man! So far you've not murdered anybody. Let's keep it that way, shall we?'

He dared to take a small step forward, and as he did so, Frank took a step back. He was dangerously balanced on the edge of the barge. 'THE BITCH HAS TO SEE THEM GO DOWN . . .' He gave a low wicked laugh. 'I want to see her face when they disappear under the water.'

Now he was waving his fist and shaking the cot, working himself up into a rage. When he began laughing he went backwards and lost his footing. The cot went up in the air. One small bundle rolled back to the floorboards, the other went with him, backwards and down, into the murky depths.

Everything happened at once. When a frantic cry went up, Joe kept Alice back. One policeman ran to collect the child from the cabin floor, while two others threw off their jackets and shoes and dived into the murky depths.

In Joe's arms, Alice prayed like never before, as they could only stand helplessly while the policemen came up several times for air. The water was deep and dark, and it was difficult to see.

When they finally surfaced, one of them had the cot in his fist.

As he handed the cot up to the helping hand, he shook his head, a look of sadness in his eyes.

Some time later, the divers moved in.

It took a while, but eventually, they found two bodies. One was Frank Arnold. The other was the baby.

Once they knew the whole story, people said it was poetic justice.

Acting on information and other suspicions, the police later discovered another body in the murky dark waters further away; that of Jack, the bargee.

Some said that with the drowning of Frank, Jack had taken his revenge, but that the tiny innocent had been caught up in the evil that was Frank Arnold.

CHAPTER SEVENTEEN

O N A GLORIOUS June day, in the church at Husborne Crawley, Joe stood tall and proud as the music started. He wanted to look round but he made himself wait, because this was a moment he wanted to keep in his heart forever.

When finally he did look round, he saw her walking up the aisle towards him, and no man could have been prouder. Alice was about to become his wife.

At long last, after many trials and much heartbreak, they were together, and it was a bittersweet moment.

But there was one, very precious matter to tend to, before they made their marriage vows.

Smiling, Alice walked up to him, and together they went with the priest to the font at the side of the altar, where they christened the boy with the brown eyes, 'Michael Ronald Arnold'.

After the christening, his grandfather Ronald took the boy, while Joe and Alice made their vows. Mandy was there, all dressed up and looking pretty in her bridesmaid dress. Pauline and Maureen had dressed to the nines for the day, but throughout they kept their distance. No one expected anything different.

Afterwards, Alice and Joe went into the small churchyard on the hill, where they stood beside the tiny resting place cradled amongst the rhododendrons.

Alice laid her bouquet and, kneeling there, she prayed that the good Lord would hold her lost baby in His arms and keep him safe.

Then, with feelings of joy and sadness, she walked down to the arch, with her husband at her side, and their son Michael, safe in his embrace. 'I love you, Alice Arnold,' Joe whispered. 'I love you too,' she said, and they held each other for a precious moment.

~

Later, back at Tom and Nancy's cottage, Tom came up to Alice. 'I've been a silly old beggar!' he said.' I didn't believe it was you who kept me in our beloved little home. You even chose to bring the celebrations back here. I owe you everything. And I gave you nothing.'

Alice hugged him. 'You gave me more than enough,' she said. 'You gave me the man I love, and now we have a son, and people who love us. We have a house of our own, thanks to Edward Baxter, who bought another cottage especially for us. So, Tom, what else could anyone else want?'

Another voice intervened. 'Nothing at all!' Nancy said, and then she told everyone to go out to the barn and start up the dancing. 'And for them that don't want to dance, the food's waiting,' she said. 'So, go on! Get to it!'

Merry music echoed through the air, until the early hours of the morning.

Outside, away from the noise and the crowd, Joe and Alice strolled awhile. Joe smiled down on Alice. 'I've loved you forever,' he murmured.

'Somehow I always knew you and I belonged together,' she confided softly.

There was a long moment of silence, when they looked back on all that had happened. 'It's been a bitter journey at times,' Joe said. 'There were moments when I thought this day would never happen.'

He took her in his arms with a kind of fierceness. 'I will always look after you,' he promised. 'I won't ever let anyone hurt you or the baby, ever again!'

'I know,' she said.

This was not the end.

It was just the beginning.

Josephine Cox

INSIDE:

- Exclusive extract from **Midnight**, out February 2011!!

- Sign up for news and competitions at www.josephinecox.com

- Register for **Chatterbox**: The Josephine Cox Newsletter

- Don't miss Josephine's other books

Midnight

Harmful Things

Part One
Bedfordshire
2008

Chapter One

"JACK, WAKE UP!"

Disturbed from her sleep, Molly slid across the bed to him, "I'm here, Jack. You're safe." Wrapping her arms about him, she kept him close.

Lost in the darkness, Jack heard her faraway call.

Beneath his body the earth was soft and pliable. It gave him a feeling of warmth. He was not alone though. Something else was here. Something shocking.

He heard Molly calling, and he knew instinctively she was his only way back. "I've got you," her voice soothed him. "I won't let anything hurt you!"

With each crippling nightmare, Molly was there for him. She had learned to be patient; to watch and wait.

"I have you safe, Jack," she promised now. "I won't let you go."

For as long as he could remember, Jack had fought his demons. Always in the darkness, alone with feelings of guilt. And the knowledge that someone was watching. They never came after him though. They watched and waited, but they never once came after him.

Everything remained the same. Hazy, shifting shadows, dancing in the moonlight. And all round him, the shapes, and the eyes … oh, the eyes! So cold. And blue as the deepest sea.

He could hardly breathe. He had to go back. He needed to get away from here.

He could hear her calling still. He knew she would save him. But for how long? So many times he'd escaped, only to be drawn back, time and again. To this place. This lonely place.

The darkness and the images had long haunted him; almost to the edge of madness.

"Jack! Look at me, Jack!"

Molly's gentle voice quietened his heart.

Desperate to leave, he was compelled to stay. He could never leave. Not until he understood.

Why had the visions plagued him all these years? Why would they not let him be? He needed to forget, to feel safe.

"Ssh now." Folding the corner of the bed sheet, Molly wiped away the beads of sweat that poured down his face. "Jack ... listen to me. It's just a dream," she murmured, "I'm here, sweetheart. I won't let you go."

Leaning into him, her voice whispered through the shadows. Softly she coaxed him, "Open your eyes, Jack. Come away now."

Most times she could waken him, but this time he resisted. And it made her afraid.

Closing her fingers about his flailing fist, she drew him closer, her voice firmer, more persuasive, her fears very real, "Jack! You need to open your eyes and look at me."

Suddenly, without warning, the fight went from him. His clenched fists fell heavily by his side and Molly felt his whole body tremble and shiver.

Calmer now, he turned to look on her, his eyes scarred and heavy with what he had seen, back there, in that place. "Midnight," he whispered brokenly, "...always midnight."

The remnants of a shadowy memory lingered like a cloak over his mind. "Where is it, Molly?" he whispered. "What does it mean?" He gave an involuntary shiver, "Why won't it let me be?"

For what seemed an age, Molly searched for an answer, "It isn't real," she promised. "It was just a dream. A bad dream, and now it's over."

When he slowly shook his head, she placed the palms of her hands about his face, "Let it go, Jack. Don't think about it now." Like many times before, she saw how deeply it affected him.

Softly, she kissed him, once on each side of his face, much like a mother might kiss her child. "It's gone now," she told him, "… maybe it won't ever come back."

"Maybe," he leaned into her embrace, "…maybe not." He knew it would be back.

Drawing on her strength, he needed to believe that maybe one day the nightmare really would go away. Molly believed it. So why couldn't he?

He smiled, a sad, quiet smile, because he knew the truth. Molly meant well, but she didn't know what it was like. How could she?

All his life the nightmare had haunted him, and not only when he slept. Sometimes in the daylight hours, something bad carried him back there. Something urgent. Something deep in his psyche.

As a boy he might be playing in the street with his pals, when the darkness would suddenly come over him and he would creep away to hide in some quiet corner.

The other boys began to tease him. They laughed and said it was no good having Jack Raynolds on your side at football, because halfway through the match he would suddenly run away to pee in a dark corner.

He was sad when they stopped asking him to play in their team. Sad and ashamed.

He never told them the truth. He never told anyone.

If he had, they might have thought he was off his rocker and should be locked away, like that woman on Tamworth Street who drowned her newborn twins before killing herself. He heard the cruel talk, about how she should rot in Hell.

The thought of it filled him with a different horror. So he told them nothing and he was lonelier than ever.

He wanted to tell, but he daren't. In all his life, he had never betrayed the awful secret he carried with him. He began to believe he must have done a bad thing. If not, then why was he afraid to close his eyes and sleep?

And what about the drawings he'd made at school? Bad, frightening things that created weird shapes onto the paper, almost as though something or someone else was making the pictures and not him.

The teachers were angry. They took the drawings away. They said he should pay attention and listen to what was asked of him, instead of allowing his imagination to run riot.

They never understood.

It wasn't their fault. How could they see what he could see? Trapped in that lonely hellhole, so real and terrifying. Was it his warped imagination? Or was there really a place like that somewhere?

What a shocking thought … that it might actually exist outside of his nightmares.

Surely that could never be?

Or could it?

As the years passed, the fragmented images remained, as did the feelings of helplessness. He had so many questions and no answers.

What really haunted him was the reason behind it all. Had some terrible happening triggered the images in his mind? Or was it merely a deep-down terror of the darkness?

Jack wondered if he would ever know the truth, and more importantly, would he really want to?

All he had ever wanted was for it all to go away. Instead, the nightmares were growing stronger, more persistent.

Molly was right! He should be seeking help, asking questions, fighting back. Instead of being the victim.

But what if he didn't like the answers? What if it wasn't a nightmare, but something more physical. Some dreadful, creeping thing that threatened his very existence. He wanted to know. But he was afraid.

website
Have you logged on yet?

www.josephinecox.com

- Chat
- Blogs
- Book updates
- Competitions
- Events
- Extracts
- Photos
- and more

You'll find features, giveaways
and competitions, have the chance
to chat to other fans, and you
can read Jo's very own blog!

Don't miss out –
become a member today!

chatterbox

The Josephine Cox Newsletter

If you would like to know more about Josephine Cox, and receive twice-yearly updates, just send a postcard to the address below and automatically register to receive Chatterbox, Josephine's free newsletter. The newsletter is packed with exciting competitions plus news and views from other fans.

CHATTERBOX
Freepost PAM 6429, HarperCollins Publishers
77-85 Fulham Palace Road, Hammersmith, London, W6 8JB

GO GREEN!

You can now read Chatterbox online! If you want to find out more about Josephine, and save the environment at the same time, simply log on to www.josephinecox.co.uk to read the latest issue in full.

THE LONER

Home is where the heart is – but it's also where the pain lies…

Young Davie Adams is all alone. Devastated, he flees his hometown of Blackburn to escape the memories of the worst night of his life. With little more than the shirt on his back he sets off on a lonely, friendless road, determined to find his father.

Two people are stricken by his departure – Judy, his childhood friend who is desperate to reveal a secret she has kept close to her heart for so long, and Joseph, his grandfather, who is racked with guilt about that fateful night.

Exhausted and afraid, Davie finds friendship and a place to stay but when fate deals him another disastrous blow, he must decide whether to keep running or return to face his demons…

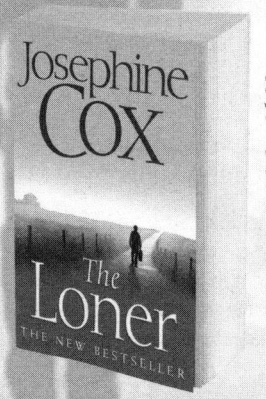

978-0-00-730205-5 • £6.99

Save 10%

when you buy direct from HarperCollins – call 08707 871724.

Free postage and packing in the UK only.

SONGBIRD

Madeleine Delaney, holds a dark and dangerous secret, one that she has carried with her for over twenty years…

Madeleine is the star of the show at the Pink Lady Cabaret Bar. Her angelic voice and striking looks capture the hearts of many. But she only has eyes for club owner, Steve Drayton, a devastatingly handsome but terrifying man.

Then one night, she witnesses a horrific crime and her life is irrevocably changed forever. The kindness and friendship of one girl, Ellen, rescues Madeleine. But in order to survive, they must flee London, leaving those they dearly love behind, and danger is following them wherever they go…

978-0-00-722115-8 • £6.99

Save 10%

when you buy direct from HarperCollins – call 08707 871724.

Free postage and packing in the UK only.

BORN BAD

Harry always knew he would go back one day…

Eighteen years ago he made a decision that drove him from the place he knew and loved. In those early years he carved out a life for himself, and somehow, he had found a semblance of peace.

Every waking moment during those long aching years he was haunted by what happened when he was a boy. He had never forgotten that warm, carefree girl with the laughing eyes.

For Judy Saunders, the pain of her past has left her deeply scarred. Cut off from her family and stuck in a stormy marriage to a man she doesn't love, the distant memories of her first love are her only source of comfort.

Now for the first time in all those years, Harry is heading back and he needs to know the outcome of what happened all those years ago.

And most importantly, he needs to find forgiveness.

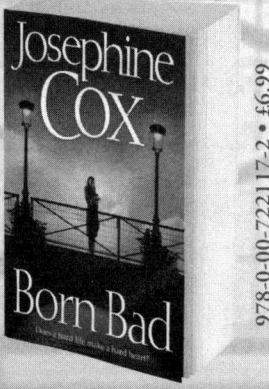

JOSEPHINE COX

Born Bad

978-0-00-722117-2 • £6.99

THE BEACHCOMBER

In the summer of 1952 two people arrive in
the pretty seaside hamlet of West Bay,
Dorset to start a new life.

Kathy Wilson dreams of turning the derelict Barden House into
a home free of the pain she suffered back in London. As the
summer stretches before her, she watches her cherished dream
take glorious shape – though she grows curious about the lonely
wanderer who strolls the beach below her window day and night.

His name is Tom Arnold. He also seeks refuge in West Bay,
needing a place to hide when the life he knew was brutally
destroyed by tragedy. Drawn to this aloof loner, Kathy feels a
bond forming that will radically change them both.

But the shadows and secrets that haunt Tom and Kathy will
not easily be dismissed. And as two wounded people try to find
the courage to open their hearts to love, the past threatens
their fragile new beginning…

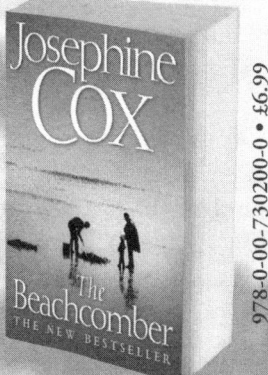

978-0-00-730200-0 • £6.99

Save 10%

LOVERS AND LIARS

In the sleepy Lancashire village of Salmesbury, childhood sweethearts Emily and John are secretly planning a life together when they are cruelly forced apart.

Already abandoned by her father, and unhappy at home, Emily is heartbroken when John leaves the village. Her life takes a devastating turn for the worse when she gives birth to a child. She dare not reveal the identity of the child's father or there will be a terrible price to pay.

Many miles away, John is trying to forget Emily and forge a new life. Having carried her in his heart for years, a chance encounter leads him to believe she has forgotten him.

Emily has never been able to banish thoughts of John. But when it looks as though history is about to repeat itself, Emily must put the past – and John – behind her and safeguard her daughter. But can she forget him?

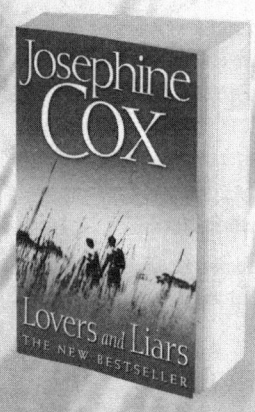

978-0-00-730201-7 • £6.99

Save 10%

when you buy direct from HarperCollins – call 08707 871724.

Free postage and packing in the UK only.

LIVE THE DREAM

Luke Hammond: handsome, rich, charismatic, cursed by private tragedy. Amy Atkinson: humble and kind with a good – but wounded – heart. When they meet by chance in a café run by Amy's best friend Daisy, a spark of love takes hold of their hearts.

But neither are sure that they can dare to love again. And what of Luke's public life, hidden from Amy? The owner of a large factory, he is a pillar of the community, married – though in name only. But Luke is also a sensitive and emotional man, whose greatest joy is retreating to his woodland cabin, nestled deep in the Ribble Valley, where he creates powerful paintings. Amy is torn between her head and her heart, but her sense of honour is paramount – and when she discovers his true identity, she is thrown into even greater turmoil.

Then disaster strikes the factory – and with it Daisy. Suddenly, the future looks troubled indeed…

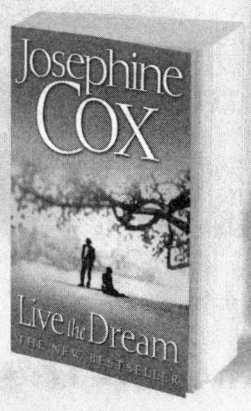

978-0-00-730202-4 • £6.99

Save 10%

when you buy direct from HarperCollins – call 08707 871724.

Free postage and packing in the UK only.

THE JOURNEY

Three strangers are thrown together by chance. It's an encounter which is destined to change all of their lives for ever.

When Ben Morris comes to the aid of Lucy Baker and her daughter Mary, he is intrigued by the story behind their frequent visits to the local graveyard. Later, invited into their home, an old Edwardian place suffused with secrets of the past, Ben hears Lucy's remarkable tale – one she must tell before it's too late.

The story of Barney Davidson, his family and the part Lucy played in his extraordinary life, is one of a deep, abiding love and an incredible sacrifice, spellbinding in its tragedy and passion. And it still exerts a powerful influence in the present day …

The Journey is Josephine Cox at her mesmerising best. Spanning decades, generations and continents, it will stay with you for ever.

978-0-00-730203-1 • £6.99

Save 10%

DIVORCED AND DEADLY

Footloose, fancy free and ready to get back in the game

Newly divorced Ben is back home with mum which is just where she wants him. But best mate Dickie has other ideas, and soon they are sharing a flat, up to all sorts and plotting Ben's future romantic adventures.

But being single isn't all it's cracked up to be.

Ben staggers from one disaster to another – all under the beady gaze of his ex, who may not want him but doesn't want anyone else to have him either! And then there's Ben's co-worker Poppy, who seems very interested in his escapades too – could she have plans of her own…

Laugh-out-loud funny and based on true stories that you just couldn't make up, *Divorced and Deadly* is the perfect feel-good read.

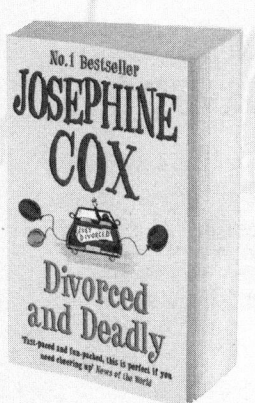

Save 10%

when you buy direct from HarperCollins – call 08707 871724.

Free postage and packing in the UK only.

'An especially searing account of state oppression and
Communist terror… Everything is held together by
Mukherjee's wonderfully inventive prose style'
Prospect

'A thing of wonder ... Does what a great novel should do... One of the most wonderful novels I've read for ages and ages'
Deborah Moggach

'Mukherjee confronts us with the deranged performances of both master and slave... *A State of Freedom*'s artfully handled piecing together of story fragments is held in tension by a counterforce of textual disintegration'
Spectator

'Harsh and vibrant... Mukherjee's deep knowledge of India and the West, allied to his never-failing curiosity about the ties that both bind us and separate us, makes him an outstanding chronicler of Bengali life, seen from within and without... In an age when so many fiction writers flimflam around in a cloud of unknowing, Mukherjee has an eagle's eye for the truth'
Rose Tremain, *New Statesman*

'It's a brave and frequently devastating novel whose themes of displacement and dehumanisation are all too timely'
Paul Murray, *Observer*

NEEL MUKHERJEE

Neel Mukherjee is the author of two novels, *A Life Apart* (2010), which won the Writers' Guild of Great Britain Award for best novel, and *The Lives of Others* (2014), which was shortlisted for the Man Booker Prize, the Costa Best Novel Award, and won the Encore Prize for best second novel. He lives in London.

ALSO BY NEEL MUKHERJEE

A Life Apart
The Lives of Others

NEEL MUKHERJEE

A State of Freedom

VINTAGE

1 3 5 7 9 10 8 6 4 2

Vintage
20 Vauxhall Bridge Road,
London SW1V 2SA

Vintage is part of the Penguin Random House group of companies
whose addresses can be found at global.penguinrandomhouse.com

Copyright © Neel Mukherjee 2017

Neel Mukherjee has asserted his right to be identified as the
author of this Work in accordance with the Copyright, Designs
and Patents Act 1988

First published in Vintage in 2018
First published in hardback by Chatto & Windus in 2017

Parts of this novel were previously published in *Granta* 130 and the
Harvard Review 50

penguin.co.uk/vintage

A CIP catalogue record for this book is available from the British Library

ISBN 9781784701734

Printed and bound by Clays Ltd, St Ives Plc

Penguin Random House is committed to a sustainable future
for our business, our readers and our planet. This book is made
from Forest Stewardship Council® certified paper.

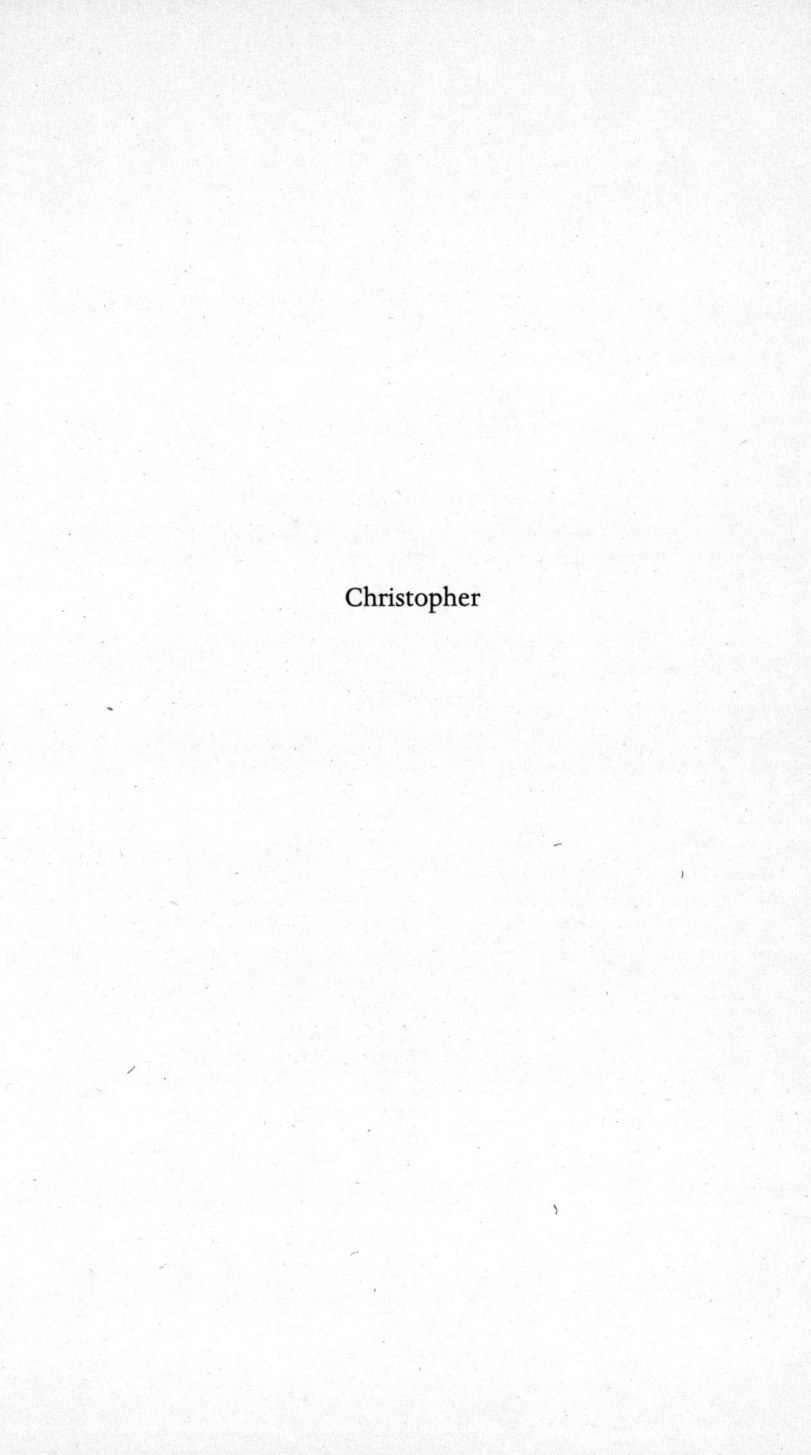

Christopher

After all, we make ourselves according to the ideas we have of our possibilities.

V. S. Naipaul, *A Bend in the River*

'Migrants? We are not migrants! We are ghosts, that's what we are, ghosts.'

Syrian refugee at the border of Austria,
August 2015

I

While trying to check the bill before settling – an old habit, inculcated by his father, of giving any bill the once-over to see that he had not been overcharged – he realised that he had lost the ability to perform the simple function of adding up the individual items and the tax that together made up the grand total. Standing at the reception desk, he tried again and again. Then he took out his wallet and tried to count the rupee and US dollar notes nestled inside; he failed. Something as fundamental to intelligence as counting was eluding him. In the peripheries of his vision he could see a small crowd gathering to look at him; discreetly, nonchalantly, they thought. The news had spread. It was then that he broke down and wept for his son.

He had hesitated about taking the boy to Fatehpur Sikri right after their lunchtime tour of the Taj Mahal; two major Mughal monuments in one afternoon could be considered excessive. But, he reasoned, it was less than an hour's drive and to fit the two sites into one day was the generally accepted practice. They could be back at their hotel in Agra by early evening and after an early night with the television and room service they could leave for Delhi, refreshed, the following morning. The reasoning prevailed.

When he mentioned part of this plan to the driver of his hired car, the young man, all longish hair and golden chain around his neck and golden wristlet and chunky watch, took it as a veiled order to go about the business in record time. He revelled in the opportunity to drive along the dusty, cratered slip road to Fatehpur Sikri at organ-jostling speed, punctuated by abrupt jerking into rest when impeded, and launching as suddenly into motion again. They passed a string of dingy roadside eateries, tea-shops, cigarette-and-snacks shacks. The bigger ones boasted signboards and names. There were the predictable 'Akbar', 'Shahjahan', 'Shahenshah', a 'Jodha Bai', even a 'Tansen', which was '100% VAGETARIAN'. There had been a speed-warning sign earlier: 'Batter late than never.' Not for the first time he wondered, in a country given over to a dizzying plenitude of signs, how unsettled their orthography was. A Coca-Cola hoarding adorned the top of one small shop, the brand name and shout line written in Hindi script.

'Coca-Cola,' the boy said, able to read that trademark universal wave even though he couldn't read the language.

'We can have one after we've done our tour,' he said, his mind occupied by trying to work out if another order to the driver to slow down to prevent the boy from being car-sick would be taken as wilfully contradictory; he worried about these things.

The boy seemed subdued; he didn't move from the bare identification of the familiar brand to wanting it. Ordinarily, he would have been compulsively spelling out and trying to read the names written in English on shopfronts and billboards. While he was grateful for his son's uncharacteristic placidity, he wondered if he hadn't imposed too much on a six-year-old, dragging him from one historical monument to another. He now read a kind of polite forbearance in the boy's quietness, a way of letting him know that this kind of tourism was wholly outside his sphere of interest but he was going to tolerate his father indulging in it. After a few questions at the Taj Mahal, which began as enthusiastic, then quickly burned out into perfunctory – 'Baba, what is a mau-so-le-um?', 'Is Moom-taz under this building?', 'Was she walking and moving and talking when Shajjy-han built this over her?' – they had stopped altogether. Was it wonder that had silenced him or boredom? He had tried to keep the child interested by spinning stories that he thought would catch the boy's imagination: 'Do you see how white the building is? Do you know that the emperor who had it built, Shahjahan, had banquets on the terrace on full-moon nights where everything was white? The moonlight, the clothes the courtiers and the guests wore, the flowers, the food – everything was white, to go with the white of the marble and the white light of the full moon.' The boy had nodded, seemingly absorbing the information, but had betrayed no further curiosity.

Now he wondered if his son had not found all this business of tombs and immortal grief and erecting memorials to the dead macabre, unsettling. His son was American, so he was not growing up, as his father had, with the gift of ghost stories, first heard sitting on the laps of servants and aunts in his childhood home in Calcutta, then, when he was a little older, read in children's books. As a result, he did not understand quite what went on inside the child's head when novelties, such as the notion of an order of things created by the imagination residing *under* the visible world and as vivid as the real one, were introduced to him. He made a mental note to stick to historical facts only when they reached Fatehpur Sikri.

Or could it have been the terrible accident they had narrowly avoided witnessing yesterday at the moment of their arrival at the hotel? A huge multi-storeyed building was going up across the road, directly opposite, and a construction worker had apparently fallen to his death even while their car was getting into the slip lane for the hotel entrance. As they waited in the queue of vehicles, people had come running from all directions to congregate at one particular spot, about twenty metres from where they sat in their cars. Something about the urgency of the swarming, and the indescribable sound that emanated from that swiftly engorging clot of people, a tense noise between buzzing and truculent murmuring, instantly transmitted the message that a disaster had occurred. Otherwise how else would the child have known to ask, 'Baba, people running, look. What's happening there?' And how else could the driver have answered, mercifully in Hindi, 'A man's just fallen from the top of that building·under construction. A mazdoor. Instant death, bechara.'

He had refused to translate. He had tried to pull his son back from craning his neck, but as the queue of cars moved, and their vehicle moved forward, through a chance aperture in the hive of people around the death, he saw, for the briefest of flashes, a patch of dusty earth stained the colour of old scab from the blood it had thirstily drunk. Then the slit closed, the car started advancing inch by inch and the vision ended. He saw his son turning his head to continue to stare at the spot. But had the boy really seen the earth welt like that, or had he just imagined it? There was no way he could ask him to corroborate. Worries came stampeding in: had the child seen it? Was he going to be affected by it? How could he establish if he had, without planting the idea in the boy's head? All of last night his mind had been a pincushion to these sharp questions until he had fallen asleep.

They returned now, summoned by the boy's unnatural quietness. By the time they got out at Agra Gate, having shaved all of ten minutes from the journey, the boy was looking decidedly peaky, and he felt that his own lunch had risen in rebellion, to somewhere just behind his sternum. The driver grinned: there was just the right touch of the adversarial in the gleam of self-satisfaction.

More than twenty years of life in the academic communities of the East Coast of the USA had defanged him of the easy Indian ability to bark at people considered as servants, so he swallowed his irritation, even the intention to ask the driver to take it more gently on the journey back, in case he couldn't control the tone and it was interpreted as a peremptory order. Instead, he said in Hindi, 'We won't be more than an hour.'

The driver said, 'OK, sir,' nodding vigorously. 'I will be here.'

He checked the car to see if he had taken everything – a bottle of water, his wallet and passport, the guidebook, his small backpack, his phone, his son's little knapsack – then shut the car door and held out his hand. The boy's meek silence bothered him. Where was the usual firework display of chatter and fidgety energy, the constant soundtrack of his aliveness?

He knelt down to be on a level with the boy and asked tenderly, 'Are you tired? Do you want to go back to the hotel? We don't have to see this.'

The boy shook his head.

'Do you want a Parle's Orange Kream?' he asked, widening and rolling his eyes to simulate the representation of temptation in the advertisements.

The boy shook his head again.

Behind him, on a grass verge, a hoopoe was flitting across. He said, 'Look!' and turned the boy round.

The boy looked dutifully but didn't ask what it was.

'It's a hoopoe. You won't see this bird in New York.' He supplied the answer gratuitously.

The boy asked, 'Is this a moss-o-moll-lom?'

'No, sweetheart,' his father laughed, 'it's not a mausoleum. It's a palace. You know what a palace is, don't you? A very good and powerful king lived here. His name was Akbar. I told you about him last night, remember?'

'That was Shajjy-han, who built a big big marble stone on his wife and she died and he was very sad and cried all the time.'

Every time he spoke, the American accent made his father's insides go all squishy.

'No, this is different. Akbar was his grandfather. Come, we'll look at it. It's a different colour, see? All red and brown and orange, not the white that we saw earlier.'

They passed some ruined cloisters, then a triple-arched inner gateway, solidly restored and, slightly further from it, a big domed building that was awaiting restoration work. Touts, who had noticed a man and a small boy get out of the car, descended on them.

'Guide, sir, guide? Good English, sir. Full history, you won't find in book.' Not from one voice but from an entire choir.

Beggars with various forms of crippledness materialised. From the simplest pleading, with a hand repeatedly brought up to the lips to signify hunger, to hideous displays of amputated and bandaged limbs, even an inert, entirely limbless, alive torso laid out flat on a board with wheels – this extreme end of the spectrum of human agony filled him with horror, shame, pity, embarrassment, repulsion but, above all, a desire to protect his son from seeing them. How did all these other people drifting around him appear to be so sheathed in indifference and blindness? Or was the same churning going on inside them? Truth was, he felt, he was no longer a proper Indian; making a life in the plush West had made him skinless like a good, sheltered first-world liberal. He was now a tourist in his own country; no longer 'his own country', he corrected himself fastidiously. He suppressed the impulse to cover the boy's eyes with his hands and said impatiently, 'Sweetie, can we move a bit faster, please.' It came out as a command, the interrogative missing.

Men came up with accordions of postcards, maps, guidebooks, magazines, photos, toys, current bestsellers in pirated editions, snacks, rattles, drinks, confectionery, tinsel, dolls, plastic replicas of historical buildings, books, whistles and flutes … He kept shaking his head stoically, a tight half-smile on his lips, and ushered his boy along.

The child, distracted one moment by a tray of carved soapstone figures, then another instant by a flashing, crudely copied replica of an inflatable Superman toy, kept stalling to stare.

'Baba, Baba, look!'

'Yes, I know. Let's keep moving.' He was so relieved – and grateful – that the cheap toys had diverted the child's attention away from the suppuration and misery that he almost broke step to buy one of those baubles.

That small manifestation of interest was enough. The loose, dispersed assembly of touts and peddlers now tightened into a purposeful circle.

'Babu, my child is hungry, hasn't eaten for four days.' The shrivelled girl with matted hair in the woman's arms looked like the living dead; she had no energy or will to swipe at the flies clustering on a sore at the corner of her mouth.

'Here, look, babu, babu-sa'ab, look . . .' A button was pressed and a toy came to mechanical life, emitting tinny games-arcade sounds of shooting guns as it teetered forward.

A man came up uncomfortably close and, with the dexterity of a seasoned cardsharp, fanned open a deck of sepia prints of famous Indian historical buildings and temples. A picture of a naked woman appeared and disappeared so quickly that it could well have been the prestidigitator's illusion. He was shocked; didn't the man see that he had a small child with him? Or did he not care?

The surrounding gardens, well tended by Indian standards, shone in the white-gold light of the January afternoon, yet, looked at closely, all that riot of cannas and marigolds and manicured grass lawns could not really disguise their irredeemable municipal souls. There was the typical shoddiness – straggly borders; lines that could not keep straight; a certain patchiness to the planting, revealing the scalp of soil through the thinning hair of vegetation; the inevitable truculence of nature against the methodising human hand ... and underpinning all this amateurish attempt at imposing order and beauty he could feel, no, almost *see*, what a battle it was to keep the earth, wet and dark now, from reverting to red dust in the obliterating heat of the Northern Plains in the summer. He bought tickets and entered the great courtyard of the Diwan-i-Am. The world transformed – in the burnished gold of the winter afternoon sun, the umber-red sandstone used for the whole complex at Fatehpur Sikri seemed like carved fire, something the sun had magicked out of the red soil in their combined image and likeness.

He looked at his son, expecting to see a reflection of his own wonder on the child's face, but all he could discern in that mostly unreadable expression was ... was what? Boredom? Across another courtyard, all blazing copper in the light, lay the palace buildings. He backtracked to consult the map etched on to a stone block towards the entrance, but with no reference point to indicate 'You are here' he felt confused.

While retrieving the camera and the guidebook from his backpack, he said to his son, 'Stay still for a moment, don't run off. We'll go to all those beautiful little palaces, do you see?' By the time he had slung the camera around his neck and opened the guidebook to the correct page, he could tell that the boy was itching to run across the courtyard. He tried to keep an eye on him while skim-reading the relevant page. Yes, he had found it – this must be the Mahal-i-Khas, the private palaces of Akbar. His head bobbed back and forth, like a foraging bird's, from page to surrounding environment. When he had established beyond any doubt that the two-and-a-half-storeyed building on the left, which had a touch of incompleteness to it, was Akbar's private apartments, he caught hold of his son's hand and made to enter the building.

But he had been spotted leafing through the travel-guide, his hesitation and momentary lostness read shrewdly. A man materialised behind him and began to speak as if he was in the middle of a talk he had been giving: 'The recesses in the ground floor that you will see were meant for his books and papers and documents ...'

He wheeled around. The sun caught his eyes and dazzled him. All he could make out was a dark, almost black, sharply pointed face, a human face on its way to becoming a fox's; or was it the other way round?

'If you go up to his sleeping chamber, the khwabgah, on the top floor,' the man continued, 'you will see fine stone latticework screens along the corridor leading to the women's quarters, the harem. These jaalis protected the women from the public gaze as they went back and forth from the khwabgah.'

The man spoke with practised fluency. If he was trying to advertise his skills as a guide to get hired, then there was nothing in his manner or his speech that betrayed this purposive bent. If anything, he seemed almost oblivious of his presence and his child's.

The sun had blinded him so he turned his head away, both to face his son, whom he was afraid to let out of his field of vision for any duration, and to signal to the man that he was not going to be needing his services. The buildings that lay in the slanted shade were an earthen matt pink. Elsewhere, the red sandstone that caught the sun burned a coppery-gold. When he turned around to see if he had shaken off the tout, there was no one to be seen.

In the rooms on the ground floor of the emperor's private quarters he was held by the flaky painted decorations depicting flowers and foliage; these faded ghosts still managed to carry a fraction of their original life-spirit. They had been touched up, restored, but with a brutal mugger's hand. From the vantage point of the courtyard, the interior had looked poky and pitch-dark and he had wondered about the smallness of the chambers and, correspondingly, the physical stature of those sixteenth-century people: did they have to huddle and stoop inside? Was it light enough to see things in there during the daytime? Why were there no doors and windows? What did they do for privacy? And then, the crowning question: did he know just too little about the architectural and domestic history of the Mughals?

Now that they were inside, the idea that the rooms were cramped somewhat diminished but the feeling that they were, or could be, dark remained. Was it something to do with his vision, or from having just come in from the brightness outside? He blinked several times. The interior seemed to shrink, expand and then shrink again, as if he were in the almost imperceptibly pulsating belly of a giant beast. In the pavilion at the top, where Akbar used to sleep, faded frescoes, nibbled away by time with a slow but tenacious voracity, covered the walls. But the fragments seemed to be under some kind of wash; a protective varnish, perhaps, but it had the effect of occluding them under a milky mist. A winged creature, holding an infant in front of a cave in a rockface, looked down at him from above a doorway. It looked as if it had been assembled from large flakes of once-coloured dandruff. His heart boiled against the cage of his chest.

'Baba, look, an angel!' the child said.

He closed his eyes, gripped his son's hand, turned his face away, then back again and opened his eyes. The angel continued to stare at him. There was intent in those eyes, and even the very first touch of a smile in those delicately upturned corners, as if Persian artists had brought forth a Chinese angel. He shut his eyes again; the face of the fox-guide, accompanied by shifting confetti-links of floaters, flickered across his retina.

Outside, the courtyard, large enough to be the central square in a city where the crowd congregates for the beginning of a revolution, held scattered groups of colourfully clothed visitors. The spiky phalanx of red cannas blazed in their plots. A square stone platform, bordered by jaalis, rose from the centre of a square rectangular pool, filled with stagnant water, virulent green with algae. Four raised narrow walkways, bisecting each side of the square, led to the platform. The musical rigour that the Mughals had brought to the quadrangular form struck him again; he riffled through his guidebook to read something illuminating about this pool, Anup Talao.

'Baba, can we go to the middle? There are lanes,' the boy said.

'I don't think we are allowed to,' he said, then tried to distract him by summarising the few lines on the feature: 'Look, it says here that musicians used to sit in the centre there, on that platform, and perform concerts for the emperor and his court.' After a few beats of silence, he added, 'Wasn't that interesting?', hearing his own need to keep the boy engaged fraying with exhaustion.

'Why aren't we allowed to?'

'Well,' he thought for a second or two, 'if people were allowed in, we would see a lot of tourists here walking in and out, posing on the platform, taking pictures ... but there's none of that, do you see?'

It was better outside – the relative darkness inside had, oddly, unnerved him. But the pressure of tourism was relentless, bullying. Surely they hadn't come all this way to stand in the sun and look at pretty buildings from a distance, when they could be inside them, poring over the details, going into every room of every palace, absorbing what the guidebook had to say about each and then re-looking, armed with new knowledge?

In the strange and beautiful five-storeyed panch mahal, each ascending floor diminishing in size until there was only a small kiosk surmounted by a dome on top – eighty-four, fifty-six, twenty, twelve and four columns on each level, respectively, his guide told him – arches between columns took the place of walls and he had been glad of the light and the breeze that came in unimpeded.

Outside once again, he noticed the squares marked on the courtyard, with a raised stone seat at the centre of the regular cross formed by the squares, and pointed them out to his son. 'Do you see the squares in the four directions, making the four arms of a big plus-sign?' he asked, tapping a few with his feet and indicating the rest with his pointing hand, 'Here, and here, and this ... do you see?'

The boy nodded.

'Show me the plus-sign then,' he asked.

The child danced around, stamping on each square, repeating his father's 'Here ... and here, and this one ...'

'Good,' he said. 'Do you know what they are for?'

'This square has X on it, and this one,' the boy said, jumping on each of them.

'Yes, so they do. Do you know what these squares are doing here?'

The boy shook his head and looked at him expectantly.

'This is a board game, like Ludo or chess. It's called pachisi. Instead of having a small board at the centre, which is surrounded by a circle of a few players, they had a big one marked out permanently in this courtyard.'

His son stared silently, as if digesting the information.

'But do you know why it's so big? I mean, so much bigger than a Ludo or a chess board?' He was hoping the child was not going to ask what Ludo was: why should the ubiquitous board game of the endless afternoons and evenings of his Calcutta childhood mean anything to an American boy? That worn question of his son's disconnection with his father's culture reared its head again, but weakly. He pushed it down, easily enough, and offered the answer to the question he had asked, by reading an excerpt from a nineteenth-century book quoted in his travel-guide: 'The game of *pachisi* was played by Akbar in a truly regal manner, the Court itself, divided into red and white squares, being the board, and an enormous stone raised on four feet, representing the central point. It was here that Akbar and his courtiers played this game; sixteen young slaves from the harem, wearing the players' colours, represented the pieces, and moved to the squares according to the throw of dice. It is said that the Emperor took such a fancy to playing the game on this grand scale that he had a court for *pachisi* constructed in all his palaces ...'

Again, that expression of wide-eyed nothingness on the boy's face. He explained the quotation slowly, in simple words, pointing to the squares and the stone seat, to spark some interest in the boy. The child's face lit up for an instant. He hopped from one square to another, then another, finally sat, cross-legged, on one of them and chirped, 'Am I a piece in this game?'

'You could be,' he laughed.

'What will happen when you throw the die? Will my head be chopped off? In one clean stroke?'

Before he could answer, a voice behind him intervened sharply, 'Get that child out of that square!'

He wheeled around. It was the man with the face of a fox. His eyes glittered. The moustache looked animal too.

'Don't you know it's bad luck to have children sit in these squares? Do you know what happened here? Don't you know the stories?'

He was sufficiently annoyed by the man's hectoring tone to protest: 'Show me a sign that says children are not allowed on this board. It's part of the courtyard, anyone can walk on it. And who are you, anyway?'

'Look around you – do you see any children?'

Almost involuntarily, he turned around: to his right, the extraordinary symmetry of the detached building of the Diwan-i-Khas; behind him, the jewel-box of the Turkish Sultana's house; and in the huge courtyard on which these structures stood, not a single child to be spotted. All those colourfully dressed tourists he had seen earlier seemed to have vanished. There were one or two to be seen standing in the shapely arches of buildings or colonnaded walkways, but there was no one in the courtyard and certainly no children. Incredulous, he turned a full circle to be sure he had let his gaze take in everything. No, no children. The man too was gone. There was a sudden, brief vacuum in his chest; then the sensation left.

'D-did you see the ... the man who was just here? Where did he go?' he asked his son.

The boy shook his head.

'But ... but you saw him speaking to me, didn't you?' He was nearly shouting.

'Speaking? What?' the boy asked.

Of course, the child wouldn't have understood a word; the man had been speaking in Hindi.

'B-but ... but ...' he began, then that futility was inside him again, making him feel weightless.

He extended his hand to his son and caught the warm little palm and fingers in his grip and wanted to hold on to them to moor himself and at the same to scrunch them, so fierce was the wave of love and terror that suddenly threatened to unbalance him. He took the boy and ran into the Turkish Sultana's house but was blind to the ways craftsmen had made every available surface blossom into teeming life with dense carvings of gardens, trees, leaves, flowers, geometric patterns, birds, animals, abstract designs. At another time he would have been rooted to the spot, marvelling, but now his senses were disengaged and distant and all he saw was the frozen work of artisans and their tools. In one of the lower panels, the heads of the birds of paradise sitting on trees had been destroyed. An animal, crouching below, had been defaced too, making it look much like the lower half of a human child, decapitated in the act of squatting; it brought to mind ritual sacrifice. A small thrill of repulsion went through him. The mutilated carvings had the nature of fantastical creatures from Bosch's sick imagination; left untouched, they would have been simply beautiful. Then the dimness started to play havoc with his perception. Shapes and colours got unmoored and recoalesced in different configurations. It was like discovering a camel smoking a pipe, formed in clouds in the sky, shift and morph into a crawling baby held in the cradling trunk of an elephant, except there was no movement here, no external change of shape to warrant one thing becoming another.

He forced himself to read a few lines from the relevant section of his guidebook but they remained locked too; signs without meanings. He asked his son, 'Do you like what you see? Can you tell me what these are?' He couldn't make the words come out animated.

The boy shook his head.

'All right, let's go look at something else.' No amount of beauty could counter the permanent twilight of the interiors.

The baize-table lawns and the begonia shrubs radiated light like a merciless weapon. A ripple passed through the blazing froth of bushes, as if the vegetation was shuddering at his presence. Almost dragging his son along, he ran towards a small, perfectly formed building, standing in the flag of shade that it flung on the pied stones of the courtyard. Mariam's House, the guidebook said. It was the colour of something that had been sluiced indelibly in blood in its distant past. Under the stone awning three-quarters of the way up, the ventilation slots – surely they were too small to be windows? – looked like blinded eyes, yet the house gave the effect of looking watchful. It struck him then, suddenly, a feeling that the walls and stones and cupolas and courtyards were all, as one organism, watching him and his son.

And something was: another angel, this time above a doorway. Barely discernible through the slow, colourless disappearing act that time and the well-intentioned but wrong kind of preservative varnish had together enforced on it, it still managed, through some inexplicable resurrection, to fix him with its eye. It was like looking into the face of ancient light transmitted back from the beginnings of time.

He took hold of his son's hand to return to the car, moving as fast as having a six-year-old physically attached to him would allow. The larger half of the site remained unvisited; he had had enough. The very air of the place seemed unsettled, as if it had slipped into some avenue where ordinary time and ordinary circumstance did not press against it. Then, with rising anxiety, he knew what was going to happen next, and it did. From the dark inside of a square building, the fox-man came out and stood under the domed canopy of a platform at one corner of the building. He could see the man so clearly, so close, that it was as if all the distance between them across the courtyard had been telescoped into nothing. Then the man retreated into the dark again. He had known the exact sequence of events beforehand, even known the bending of distance that would occur, known that the platform on which the man had stood was called the Astrologer's Seat even though he had not visited that section of the palace quadrangle. He felt himself pursued by the place as they ran out, retracing the route through which they had made their way into and through the palace complex.

While waiting for the car, he dared to look up: the sky was an immense canvas of orange and red, not from the setting sun, it seemed to him, but from the red sandstone that burned, without decaying, under it. Everything was ablaze.

On the road back, a huge, slow procession of shouting men, hundreds and hundreds of them, coming from the direction in which they were travelling, stalled all traffic. The car windows were rolled up instantly; the protestors were within touching distance. The vast, crawling snake seemed to be an election rally, although he could not tell – the posters were all in Urdu, a language he couldn't read, and he couldn't make out a single word amidst the shouting of slogans. They could have been in an utterly foreign country. The boy had his nose pressed to the window; he had never seen anything like this.

'We just have to wait until it passes, right?' he asked the driver. A pointless question. The driver shrugged.

Time in this country flowed in a different way from the rest of the world. It was the flow that had carried him a long time ago, when he was a boy, growing up in Calcutta, but now he could no longer step into it: he had become a tourist in his own country.

The rally seemed endless. Occasionally, it stopped alto̧. After forty minutes of sitting inside the car, the driver said, 'The, moving.'

A brave taxi up ahead had decided to cut through a narrow lane on the left – a dust-and-straggling-dead-grass path, really – with the hope of rejoining the main road at a point further up where it would already have been traversed by the rally. Like mechanical sheep, cars started leaving the main route and entering this side-lane. Their driver was quick – he manoeuvred the car sideways with manic energy and was into the path before the rush to get in there created total gridlock. But he was still behind a few vehicles and the juddering stop-start stop-start stop-start movement down an unmetalled alley was the modern equivalent of running the gauntlet. Soon they came to a complete halt. The procession, well behind them, still seemed to be in full spate, but at least they were now not in the flow of something volatile and unpredictable.

He must have dozed off. The next thing he knew was a shadow blooming inside the car at the same time as he heard a timid pattering on the window next to the boy. A bear, standing on its hind legs, was looking in, its muzzle almost pressed to the glass. There was an irregular patch of mist that changed shape in rhythm to the animal's breathing. Its pelt was a dark slate-grey shag-cushion of dust and tiny insects and bits of straw and grass. Up close, the hairs looked coarse and thick, somewhat like the quills of a hedgehog. Behind him, a man extended his arm forward and tapped on the glass with his black fingernails. The child pushed back on the heels of his palms and moved backwards, trying to burrow into his father's lap, but couldn't turn his fascinated head away. The man outside looked eerily familiar – he had the sharp, pointy face of a rodent's and a moustache that seemed alive. Surely he must be dreaming? They were still in the country lane, and the terracotta late-afternoon light had turned to ashy dusk, but that ... that man

w ... He felt that the spinning of the earth carried
the slot of a roulette machine and delivered him
that were endlessly repeatable, each ever so slightly
he other, all more or less the same.

by the unblinking gaze of father and son, the bear-
wallah tapped on the glass again, and made a shallow bowl of his
palm to beg. Those glittering, scaly eyes indicated a sickness that
would finish him soon. Inside, he was too frozen even to shake
his head in disapproval. At a signal from his keeper, the bear lifted
its paw and replicated the human's begging gesture. The chain,
attached to the animal and run through the space between two of
its fingers, obliged clinkingly. He saw the head of a huge iron nail
driven through the paw – or was it a callus? The claws at the end
were open brackets of dirty gunmetal. The paw could easily smash
the window, reach in and tear out the child's entrails. He tried to
ask the driver to shoo the man away but no sound emerged from
his throat. He tried again.

'Driver, ask them to move on,' he said in a kind of low rasp. He
couldn't bring up his arm to mime 'Go away' to the beggar.

The driver lowered his window and barked, 'Ei, buzz off.'

The man paid no heed; the begging from both creatures continued. Presumably at another signal from the man, the bear
nodded, then grinned. Where it met the teeth, the gum was a
bright pink but further up the colour of cooked liver with a violet tinge. There were sticky threads of saliva gleaming whitely
against all that dirty ivory and raw flesh. Then the animal started
shaking, as if it was having a malarial fit. The boy screamed,
once, twice.

He shouted, 'Driver, why isn't he going? Ask him again, now.
Ask!'

The driver complied, his command issuing more forcefully
this time. The traffic unclotted. As the car moved to life, the pinning gaze of those scaly eyes receding backwards seemed to have

become a solid, unfrayable rope. Then motion and the gathering dark severed it.

The boy coughed all night and kept him awake. Occasionally, he cried out in his sleep loudly enough for him to turn on his bedside lamp, get out of his bed and go to his son's to see what was wrong, to soothe his nightmares away.

Towards the end of the night, the child woke up with what he could only call a howl and continued to cry with an abandonment that brought back to mind the inexplicable and seemingly endless runs of crying during infancy. He couldn't establish now if the boy was still lodged in his world of dreams during this fit or whether something in the real world, colic or feeling ill or an onset of some sickness, was making him scream like this. Questions had yielded nothing.

Should he ring for room service and ask for a doctor? Surely a hotel of this class would have access to one? The boy's forehead and neck were not hot.

'What is it? Tell me, what is it?' he asked over and over again, reaching the edge of anger on the other side of his helplessness.

Then, a tiny chink in this wall of repetition: 'I feel afraid,' the boy managed to articulate.

He bobbed afloat on a swell of relief. 'Afraid?' he asked. 'Afraid of what? There's nothing to be afraid of, I'm here with you. Here, I'll sleep in your bed, my arms around you. Everything will be all right.'

But the child wouldn't stop. He caught something in his son's gaze, a brief focusing of his eyes on something behind his shoulder, as if he had seen something behind his father, something that made him wail louder, before the focus dissolved.

He turned his head to look. There could be nothing outside the wall of windows – they were on the sixteenth floor of the hotel. The dark glass reflected back at him a dramatically lit-and-shadowed scene of his staring face, twisted around on the stalk of his neck; his son lying on the bed with his mouth open in a rictus of horror and pain; the white bed linen twisted and roped and peaked in the great turbulence that was being enacted upon it; the whole tableau shading off into the darkness that framed it. As his vision moved away from that sharp chiaroscuro foreground of the reflection, he could see, in the refracted light from the hotel grounds, the skeleton of the skyscraper on the other side of the road. On the very top few floors, he could make out the scaffolding – was it still the bamboo-and-coir-rope of his childhood or had they moved on to something more reliable and advanced nowadays? – and the billowing pieces of sackcloth or plastic or whatever it was that the workers had set up there. He wondered, not for the first time, what purpose those sheets served. A safety net, perhaps? They had certainly not prevented one of them from meeting a terrible end yesterday.

By the early hours, not far off from dawn, his son exhausted himself to sleep. He drifted off too, one arm around the boy. The light woke him; he had forgotten to draw the curtains in the night. Next to him, the child was dead.

II

When I think of her – not often, admittedly, before I decided to write this – the first image is always from an evening in July. The night before, it had rained like I had always imagined it must have done during prehistoric eras, the Pleistocene or the Triassic, say. It brought back my boyhood, lying awake, listening to the sound of relentless sheets of water coming down, imagining a low, red, early-era sky, and strange vegetation and fearful creatures and dangerous landscapes pelted by a downpour that must have been untempered, closer to a natural cataclysm than just simple, heavy rainfall. It even brought back the memory of Bible classes in school, of how all the fountains of the great deep woke up and the windows of heaven opened and it rained upon the face of the earth for forty days and forty nights.

There were dark rain-clouds covering most of the sky next morning but at least the rain had let up for a while. My parents' living room, on the first floor of a block of flats in Bombay, had an unimpeded view of the sea, which was no more than a few metres away, across the Band Stand in Bandra where, in British times, the band used to gather and play every afternoon. Now between the window and the sea was a road, forked at our end by a narrow, tri-angular sliver of green, at the vertex of which stood a pair of solid-looking, heavy metal statues, all chunky cuboids and rectangular masses and straight lines, some city council's idea of cubist primi-tivism. The pedestal on which the figures stood bore the legend *Time is / Too late for those who wait / Too swift for those who fear / Too long for those who grieve / Too short for those who rejoice / But for those who love / Time is eternity.*

As if in response, Band Stand, and the mile-long seafront prome-nade, dotted with concrete benches and sea-poison trees at regular intervals, had become the focal point for romancing couples in the afternoons and evenings.

The Arabian Sea, a placid pond for most of the year, became ruffled and turbulent in its bathetic, minor-mode way during the monsoon, and this morning it looked wild by its standards, with white breakers crashing, one after another, on to the black, rocky shore, which was now totally submerged, the sea having swollen and reached the brim of the sea wall. The horizon was an inky bank of clouds. Far away, I could make out the painted red hull of a fishing boat. It looked like a child's paper contraption that would soon unravel on the wild slate-grey surface which it rode, tossed almost rhythmically like a seesaw.

I had a meeting in Colaba at 10 a.m., which meant that I had to leave early in order to avoid the notorious morning traffic. These were the days before the Bandra-Worli Sea Link, so it could – and sometimes did – take two hours to travel a distance of twenty kilometres. In another couple of years the Sea Link would open, shocking everyone that something which had nominally been under construction for decades, with nothing except a few fist-like stubs rising from the surface of the sea across the Reclamation (as it was called) to show for it, could be finished so quickly. Who knew what kind of pressure the World Bank, which funded the majority of the project, had brought to bear on the stalled rusty machinery of corrupt politicians and bureaucrats and construction companies to get it moving again?

Last night's rain would mean flooded roads and waterlogging, so the prospect of a long, stop-start journey into town seemed almost inevitable. I left home just after eight. Amit, my father's driver, usually reported for duty slightly later in the day but he had been asked to come early that morning. By the time the car reached Mahim, the skies opened again. Despite the windscreen wipers semaphoring furiously back and forth, I could barely see anything in front and nothing very much at all through the streaking wall of water which was the passenger window. The whole world seemed to be deliquescing. After twenty minutes or so, the strafing abated somewhat although the rainfall continued; a seen-through-streams-of-liquid kind of visibility was restored; the world became that of an Impressionist painting. At the obligatory traffic standstill at Haji Ali, I saw that the long walkway on the sea leading to the offshore mosque was nearly obliterated to the sight by the spray, so that the mosque, wreathed in low mist, looked as if it were floating in the air, untethered from its umbilical cord connecting it to land. Normally the walkway, a gauntlet of seriously maimed, crippled and diseased people begging, would be a seething corridor of people, either making their way into or out of the mosque. I was too mesmerised by the fairytale dream-vision castle it had transformed into to pay much attention to the long-range view of plagued humanity seeking succour. Then the traffic lights changed, the boys selling pirated copies of bestsellers, self-help books and glossy magazines, out even in this weather, dispersed and the car left the scene of accidental enchantment.

It was that evening, around six o'clock, while Baba and I were debating whether to bring forward our routine pre-dinner drinking – a couple of whisky-and-sodas for each of us – by half an hour to six-thirty, that the doorbell rang.

'Who could it be?' Ma asked, almost to herself. 'It's too early for Renu ...' Renu was the cook.

I got up, went to the door and opened it. Renu was standing on the other side of the threshold. Or not exactly standing; she had one hand stretched out, holding on to the doorjamb to support herself, as she swayed on the balls of her feet. On her desiccated face her bloodshot eyes were swimming. Her hair, normally oiled and combed tightly on to her scalp and tied into a loose bun at the neck, was dry and frizzy, escaping in disobedient wisps all over.

'Are you all right?' I asked her, then turned my head to say to my mother, who was already halfway to the front door, 'It's cooking-aunty.' I could never bring myself to call Renu by her name and add a suffix such as 'di', older sister, or 'mashi', aunty, either of which would have been the expected or normal thing to do.

'I had no sleep last night,' Renu began. 'The police came in vans and asked us to get out of our rooms. The sea was rising because of the rain, they asked us to get out, they thought our jhopri was going to be swallowed under water.'

She could barely stand straight on her feet.

'Not a wink of sleep,' she said. 'They chased us out at ten, then asked us to go back in around midnight, then they came at two again and drove us out. I've had to work all day after a night of no sleep ... I can't keep my eyes open. So I was thinking, I know it's too early, but if I start now and cook something quickly, I ... I could ...'

Something about her unbending sense of duty pierced me. I said, 'Nothing doing. You go home right now, there's no need to cook tonight. You go get some sleep.'

Ma added her voice to this – 'Yes, Renu, don't worry about cooking this evening, you go back home.'

Renu hesitated. Even in this state of extreme exhaustion, she felt some compulsion to resist something so easily given – it wasn't right, it wasn't the normal order of things for families to intercept a servant's unarticulated request and accede to it. And yet I could see on her face relief, so much stronger than professionalism.

Before she could make another weak attempt – not because she was insincere but because she did not have the necessary energy – I forestalled her and repeated, 'Shush, not another word. We'll see you tomorrow morning. You need to sleep. Go.'

She was not a person much given to smiling, or expressing any kind of pleasant emotion, but the imprint of gratitude beneath that wrung-out face was unmistakable, a silver-gelatin film beginning to take on the lineaments of the photographic negative in its chemical bath.

I asked, 'Where did all of you go when you left your homes?'

'We sat on the road, here, right here,' she said, pointing in a vague westerly direction.

'You mean in Band Stand? Just outside our house?'

'Yes, there.'

'But it was pouring . . .'

She inclined her head sideways, a way of saying yes that stoically dealt with her plight.

I said, 'Listen, if it happens again, you come straight here and ring the bell. I'll tell the guards downstairs that you may come in the middle of the night and they're to let you in. You come and sleep here in the living room if you get thrown out of your home again.'

Ma said, 'Or the kitchen. You can sleep in the kitchen.'

I was tempted to turn slightly sideways to give Ma a look, but I controlled myself. It was an old, old battle between us and it had just let me know, gently, that it was still there, deferred and waiting, waiting to be roused from its sleep.

Instead, I carried on looking at cooking-aunty and said emphatically, 'There's much more space in the living room. Come and sleep here if you need to.' A bit too emphatically.

She gave a dismissive wave of her hand, a gesture that doubled as a goodbye, as she turned to take the stairs down – 'Achha, achha, we'll see, but there's no need, they say that it's not going to rain so much tonight.' That was the closest she was going to get to a smile.

I wanted to ask her so much more: the layout of her living quarters in the slum, how many people had been dragged out of bed and made to stand out in the driving rain all night as a way of preventing death by flooding, how close the slum was to the sea . . . but she was gone.

It was the year before this incident that I first met cooking-aunty, on my regular January visit to Bombay.

It became obvious soon enough that she did not like me. She was my parents' new cook and she'd been with them only a few months. A Bengali cook, they had wanted; stressing especially the cook's origins, when the previous one, a Maharashtrian woman from the fishing community, the Koli, proved to be too limited – and, no doubt, too foreign – for their sophisticated Bengali palates. My father was nearing sixty, my mother nearly fifty-eight; too late for them to experiment with regional Indian cuisines, especially in view of the fact that they were Bengalis, a people not known to think that anything other than their own culture – be it culinary, literary, linguistic, artistic or anything else – was worth engaging with.

On one of the fortnightly phone calls to my mother, she explained to me how difficult it was to get a good cook in Bombay but, after a month of looking, she thought she had found someone who met the requirements. 'She works for six homes but she's just lost one of them,' Ma said. 'She'll be looking to fill that gap. I hope I get lucky enough to bag her.'

'Six homes?' I asked. 'That's a lot. How does she fit them all in? She must work at least twelve hours a day, if not fourteen.'

The next time I rang my mother, Renu was working for them. This, as far as I can remember, was in July or August, so it would be five or six months before I was to meet her.

My design job in London was flexible. I worked for a progressive, thinking-outside-the-box class of trendy outfit, the kind of place that was being talked of as the future of both working and the workplace, in publications such as *Wallflower**, *i-D*, *Wired*, so it was possible for me to bunch together all my statutory leave in January and take off for the entire month to India.

Over the months preceding my visit, I had asked Ma a couple of times about their new cook and she had sounded cautiously pleased. I had never known Ma to be effusive about domestic staff, so I took it as a reasonably good sign when she had said – and I'm conflating several snatches of conversation here – 'She's all right. She's lived most of her working life outside Bengal, so she's either forgotten or doesn't know traditional Bengali cooking. I have to tell her what to do. I caught her putting onions and garlic in a light fish stew. And she puts hing in everything, can you believe it? I don't know where she picked up this kind of cooking. In non-Bengali households, clearly.'

And so it went; carping was a way of praise with my mother.

I need to say a little about my interest in food because it touches, if only glancingly, upon our story. I cooked for myself in London and entertained friends and work-people at home, of course, but my engagement with food ran deeper than the functional. I loved eating, I thought about cooking and recipes and different culinary cultures a lot of the time, and one of my current assignments, perhaps because this enthusiasm of mine was widely known, was to write and design a full-length book devoted entirely to regional Indian breakfasts, state by state. A young editor, at an imprint specialising in beautifully produced cookbooks, had spotted a blog on breakfasts across the world and mentioned it casually at a dinner with friends of friends. Someone in that serendipitous chain thought that I was some kind of authority on Indian food, and a project had been born – a lavish and substantial book, sitting on the intersection between food- and travel-writing. It was not an original or underexplored territory but we were enthusiastic and all agreed that what it lacked in novelty, it could make up for in content, visual feel and production values.

There was work that one did in a kind of professional, mandatory, bread-and-butter kind of way, and there was work that caught the tindery and flammable bits of one's passion and began a long, slow, steady combustion; this book was the latter. The research and sourcing of recipes were the easy bits. I was continually asking my mother to give me recipes from classical Bengali cuisine, particularly those that had been handed down generations within families, each family tweaking a given dish in ways that made a new, different thing of it. For example, my mother, in the days when she used to cook, or at least instruct the several persons, over time, who were employed to cook, had only two ways of making kalai dal (called 'biuli' in our family; most of the rest of India call it 'urid dal'): one in which the boiled lentils were spiced with fennel seeds and julienned ginger; the other where the lentils were toasted first, then boiled, and spiced with whole red chillies and hing spluttered in very hot oil. Both methods had been learned from her mother. But in my paternal grandparents' home, my mother once said to me, they cooked the same lentils in a completely different style: lots of finely chopped garlic, whole dried red chillies and that quintessentially Bengali spice, panchphoron – a mixture of equal amounts of fennel, cumin, fenugreek, nigella and mustard seeds – were sizzled briefly in smoking-hot mustard oil, then added to the toasted and boiled lentils. 'Some old Oriya cook's influence, no doubt,' Ma had dismissively added.

Now I thought I could pick up a couple of things from my parents' new cook's repertoire. It would add a certain spark to my annual visit.

Around noon on the day after I arrived in Bombay, I was sitting by the window in Baba and Ma's long, uncluttered living room, looking out to an imperturbable sea under a clear, sunny sky. It was low tide and the expanse of madly serrated and pitted black rock that was the beach here had emerged, glistening, the extremity of some enormous mythical undersea creature. The outcrop was dotted with men going about their morning ablutions: there were a couple bathing in the rock pools; quite a few of them washing their clothes, first stretching their sheets and towels and vests on the rocky surface and running a bar of soap along them vigorously, as if grating a carrot, then threshing the soaped clothes on the rough rocks to get the dirt out, and finally rinsing them ... creamy rings of suds had formed around some of these men. Slightly further out, towards the sea end of the rocks, there were three or four men, each standing at a spot they considered to be sufficiently apart from the rest, pissing into the sea. Two boys appeared along the promenade-wall, their arms hugging plastic bags full of flowers, presumably the clear-out from a temple or a shrine, and, hopscotching along the rocks right to the edge of the sea, flung everything they were carrying into the water. I could see the orange marigolds and dried leaves and other assorted vegetation and rubbish disperse in a wide garland, which lost its shape as the circumference became bigger and bigger.

Ma was doing her usual thing of ministering to me fussily: 'Do you want more tea?', 'Why aren't you eating the fruits? The papaya is very nice', 'Tell me when you want the upma heated up.' All she wanted to do was to serve me. On the first day, it felt comforting, as if I had regressed to childhood. By the third week, I would be thinking of the solitude of my mornings in London with such intense longing that I often barked at her to leave me alone. Sometimes her face would crumple and she would go quiet. At other times, she would strike back: '*Alone, alone,*' she would mutter, 'this is what you've learned from living abroad, you've lost all understanding of family and affection and how to live in society and be less self-centred.'

On the dining table, under a sizeable fine-mesh cover, sat small bowls of chunks of papaya, red jewels of pomegranate arils, halved guavas; and a large bowl, covered with a saucer, of upma, coarse-grained semolina cooked with mustard seeds and curry leaves and onions. It had fried cashews thrown in sometimes, or peanuts, or a small handful of peas. It was a South Indian breakfast dish and my mother knew it was one of my favourites, so she had asked the cook to prepare some this morning. By the time I had got up, the cook had left.

The upma was delicious. I had no idea why, but it was one of those things that I never cooked for myself in London, although it was a very simple and quick affair. In a divided life that was lived in two countries, separately and in rigorous succession, maybe I had saved a few things to belong to each of them solely, without flowing between the two.

'This is lovely,' I said. 'I could eat this for breakfast every day.'

'You can hardly call it breakfast at this time of the day. Here, have some more,' Ma said, getting up to serve me.

The young woman who cleaned and did the washing up was going about her business as Ma and I chatted.

'Is she new?' I asked, indicating the cleaning woman, confident that she wouldn't understand Bengali.

'No, she's been with us for nearly a year,' Ma said, then addressed the woman in Hindi, 'Milly, this is my son. He lives abroad. He has come here for a month.'

My mother's Hindi was more than competent; unusual in a Bengali woman but, then, she had spent nearly twenty years in Bombay because my father's work had brought them here in the mid-1980s. It was assumed that after my father's retirement they would move back to Calcutta (Kolkata, now) but, to be fair to them, they had found Bombay – that was the name of the city then, and the name I still use – not an unsympathetic place, growing more and more over time to like its energy and urban, unprovincial personality.

The introduction was more an advertisement of my mother's pride in her son than a courtesy extended to a maidservant, and Milly probably read it correctly: she refused to look at me, smile or nod or do whatever it was she did in these situations and instead turned her face away, as if in a calculatedly opposite response, and carried on with the dusting.

'How friendly,' I said in English.

'Achha, enough,' Ma hastily added, indicating with a gesture for me to stop being so openly critical of Milly's attitude.

'But she won't understand what I'm saying,' I persisted out of sheer cussedness.

'Uff, stop now, will you?' There was real annoyance in my mother's voice. I was surprised, but I assumed that she was going to explain later, so I shut up. I dutifully lifted my feet while Milly swept the floor with the broom, then again when, on all fours, she swabbed it with a wet cloth dipped in water and wrung out, working it in wide arcs. The room filled with the odour of citronella oil.

When Milly went to the kitchen, my mother said in a breathless run of sotto voce, 'She's from Jharkhand, she's a Christian convert, she says she understands Bengali and English', then ran off to the kitchen to supervise Milly.

Jharkhand. It was one of India's newest states, carved out of the southern and eastern part of Bihar only three or four years ago, after decades of agitation and activism by tribal peoples and backward castes – they had that dreaded Indian distinction, the branding iron of an acronym: OBC, Other Backward Castes – for a separate state where their interests and welfare would not be counted as nothing. It was also one of India's most troubled states, with a strong Maoist presence and, consequently, brutal state-sponsored repression. It was the repository of vast mineral resources, and the state was not going to let a bunch of ragtag militants and expendable tribal peoples whining about their ancient land rights get in the way of those riches.

Perhaps Milly belonged to one of those tribes that had been displaced by mining companies grabbing their land? Perhaps her life did not hold much for her there: from Jharkhand to Bombay was a long distance for her to have come to work as a domestic help. (My mother's generation still called them servants. My politically correct tag had not a jot of correlation to their status: their position in the Indian social hierarchy or economy had never changed.)

I went to the kitchen to deposit my empty bowl and spoon for Milly to wash up and discovered her sitting cross-legged on the floor, in the corner between the fridge and the cupboard, almost hiding, a plate heaped with food on her lap, eating her lunch. In the couple of awkward seconds that I was there, wishing I had not walked in on her eating, all kinds of childhood strictures about not watching servants eat flooded back, along with a new kind of discomfort.

Milly did not look up. I fled.

After Milly had gone, Ma filled me in on her background over the course of the day as I pottered around aimlessly, doing nothing at all and enjoying the lazing. I even paid a kind of passive attention to Ma's intermittent chatter – chit-chat about her friends and neighbours, gossip about celebrities and Bombay film stars culled from glossy magazines. It turned out that even Ma had noticed that Milly did not talk to, or even look at, men, so my mother had assumed that the girl had an unpleasant history with them and had left it at that. What she had done instead was to engage the young woman in conversation during the hours that she came to work and, in the process, had pieced together a sort of surface narrative of her life.

It went something like this: Milly was married to a man from Jharkhand who worked as kitchen staff in a low-end restaurant in Bandra. They had a daughter, who was around three or four years old, and a son, who was just under one. Milly was pregnant when she began working for my parents, so Ma decided to give her a heavy meal every day. The good practice had continued, I was cheered to note, even though Milly, I assumed, had stopped breastfeeding.

'But where does she leave the children when she goes to work?' I asked.

'With her husband, of course,' Ma answered. 'He does the evening shift in the restaurant.'

'Does she come from far?'

'No, no, she lives just around the corner, in the slum along the sea wall on that side,' she said, indicating with her hand the direction towards Taj Land's End, the luxury hotel which sat on the tip of this centre-west finger of Bombay jutting out into the sea and forming the top part of the curve of land nestling Mahim Bay.

'Is there a slum there?' I asked; I had no idea. 'But where? I thought there was only the sea on the other side of the wall.'

'Have a look when you're out there for your morning walk,' she said.

Around seven in the evening, Renu arrived to cook dinner. She was short and dark and could have been any age between forty and fifty-five. The way she wore her sari Bengali-style, with the aanchol thrown over on the front but her head uncovered, made her look even more shapeless than she was. My mother introduced us. Without looking at me, Renu nodded at Ma, almost imperceptibly, and asked her, 'What shall I cook?' This, I gathered, was the order of things – she would arrive and, while still standing just over the threshold, ask my mother what she wanted for dinner, then she would go into the kitchen and set about her business.

Ma, indicating me, said, 'While he's here, he's going to be in charge of these things. I'm on holiday now. Mind you, he's a very good cook. And he loves eating.' She tried to sound amusing, as if encouraging Renu to step up her game for the visiting son, but in a bantering, tongue-in-cheek kind of way.

Renu, looking impassive and unimpressed, gave no sign that she had even registered this and instead asked Ma again, 'Tell me, quick quick, what you want cooked. I have to go at seven-thirty, they turn the tap off after half an hour, I can't stand here all day.' She made a gesture, even gave a ghost of a forced smile, that lent her impatient words the cast of a joke, too; the implied insubordination in her words would otherwise have been intolerable.

Ma repeated, 'He'll tell you.'

Renu continued to look resolutely at my mother.

Her voice was like a child's tin recorder made by an amateur, with every stop hitting the wrong frequency. It reminded me of nails scraping down a blackboard, or the pitch of a screech of metal on metal that seemingly existed merely to shred the uninsulated edge of nerve-endings. This voice was the most immediately conspicuous thing about her and unignorable.

I said, using the most formal and respectful version of 'you', 'Let's go into the kitchen and see what there is ...'

These things are difficult to give cast-iron evidence in support of, but I could sense that she hadn't taken to me. It was as if she had developed an invisible force field around her. She seemed to be surly – even impertinent – by nature, but my unease seemed disproportionate to the brusqueness of her manner. What was it that was really bothering me?

'Show me what's in the fridge,' I said, 'and we can decide after that. Achchha, this morning's upma was delicious, I've never had such good upma. You can make that again. What do you think are your best dishes? We can have one of those tonight.'

I jabbered on; even recalling it now is a touch neuralgic. Instead of answering the question, she emptied the contents of the vegetable crisper on to the floor and on the worktop, running through them one by one, 'Here. Green bananas. Spinach. Green papaya. Cauliflower. Cabbage. Brinjal. Carrots. Spring onions ...'

The language she spoke in, although identifiably Bengali, had flecks of hybridity marking it – she had earlier used the Hindi expression for 'quick quick', now she said 'palak' for 'spinach'.

'What about green-banana koftas?' I suggested.

'No,' she said peremptorily. 'If you want to eat koftas, you tell me the day before – it's a lot of work and it takes time.'

A deep-seated, almost hard-wired, cultural training injected outrage into my system at the fact of a servant answering back. But no sooner had it manifested than the overriding educated-liberal reaction to the retrogressive nature of that first response pushed it down. I had managed to put my finger on what was bothering me. The knowledge was shaming. The whole cognition process had taken a fraction of a second.

'Yes, yes, of course koftas take a long time,' I wittered, 'that's true, very true. OK, then, what about brinjal bharta? And green papaya with prawns? Are there prawns in the freezer? Let's see what fish there is in the freezer.'

My mother, who must have been listening from the living room, called out, 'Yes, your father bought lots of fish last weekend from the fish market. The freezer is full.'

This was one of the Bengali rituals my parents had held on to: the man, too busy or elevated to be involved in the domestic drudgery of daily or even weekly grocery-shopping, made an exception for buying fish because fish held a special place in Bengali cuisine and only a man could discern the freshest and the best specimens. Baba went to the big indoor fish market in Khar every Saturday morning to stock up on weekly supplies.

Renu now took out shallow Tupperware boxes from the freezer, prised open the lids and rattled off the names of the fish each held, 'Rui. Pomfret' – she pronounced this as 'pom-plate' – 'Rawas. Bombil ...'

Bombil. I stopped her there. It would be only a mild exaggeration to say that this fish, also known as Bombay duck, was one of my main reasons for visiting the city at least once every year. Laid out on the fisherwomen's concrete, the collected fish looked like congealing grey snot with a pinkish tinge, just one step up from liquid in the solidification ladder. Shallow-fried after a light dredging in semolina, or stuffed with a hot coriander-and-chilli green chutney and then fried, it was, in the words of my friend Ankita, 'life-changing'. You realised that there seemed to be a purpose in the near-incapability of the flesh in holding its form – that very amorphous nature transformed into the signature buttery meltedness after cooking.

I asked her to fry some bombil. 'That should be enough, no?' I asked, trying to be democratic. 'Green papaya, aubergine, bombil fry.'

Renu gave a nod and began her preparations. She went about them as if powered by some restless wind. Half a dozen things were started simultaneously: the container of frozen Bombay duck was left in the sink, under running water, to thaw; pots and pans were taken out; the vegetables that were not needed for the evening meal were returned to the fridge; a chopping board and knife appeared . . . she seemed to have ten hands.

Without looking at me, she asked, 'Rice or chapatis? And would you like a dal?'

I noticed that she too was using the most respectful form of 'you' in the conjugations of her verbs to talk to me; also, that her Bengali was slightly awry – if I had to translate her question literally, it would be, 'Will you take some dal?'

'Chapatis,' I answered. 'Dal . . . yes . . .' I hesitated.

'Jaldi jaldi, I'll be in trouble if they turn the tap off before I get to it,' she said again. This time the ameliorating gesture or smile was missing.

I curtly said, 'Whichever dal you think goes best with chapatis' and left the kitchen, making sure to draw shut the sliding door that divided it from the living room.

Keeping my voice down, I said, 'Well, a personality like good mustard oil – it goes straight up your nose', trying to make a joke of it.

My mother indicated to me in signs and whispers that we should speak about this only after Renu had left.

'But what is all this going-to-the-tap-on-time business?' I asked, my voice still low.

'She has to get her water from the municipal tap,' Ma said. 'The corporation water supply is limited to fixed hours, so she has to be there, at the tap, during those times, otherwise she'll be without water for an entire day.'

'But what water?' I was still baffled.

'Water for daily use – bathing, washing, cleaning . . .'

'Doesn't she have water where she lives?'

'She lives in the slum over there' – again, that pointing towards the west – 'there's no running water in the slum.'

'You mean the same slum where Milly lives?'

Ma nodded. Then she added, 'Renu can't abide her.'

'Who, Milly?'

'Yes. I'll fill you in later.'

Half an hour later, Renu came out of the kitchen, made for the front door with the words, 'I'll be back soon' and left.

Ma said to me, 'In a couple of minutes you'll see her, if you stand at the window.'

Yes, there she was, I could discern, standing in a small queue, with two large buckets and what looked like an industrial-sized plastic container. The promenade was full of people – strollers, wooing lovers, children – and the road crawling with buses, motorbikes, auto-rickshaws. The snack-vendors had come out in force, drawing good business from the evening crowd. All life, and all of life's motions and sounds and energies, seemed to be concentrated there. In the island of green, where the tap was situated, there were three old men on the red stone bench, three or four stray dogs, half a dozen children running around. The big trees around it blocked the orange sodium-vapour light and kept most of the area in the shadows. In the balmy sea breeze the trees stirred, making the dappled mass of orange light and black shade sway and move.

Baba returned from work and I went to the kitchen to fix us drinks. The kitchen looked like a chaotic, thick still-life that was not quite still. The pressure cooker, presumably with lentils inside, was on the hob emitting dying staccato whistles, the fire underneath it turned off. On a stainless-steel plate, the bombil were lying dusted in salt and turmeric. On another plate, the giant, flaky pat of a flame-charred aubergine rested. The worktop between the cooker and the sink was entirely covered with onion skins, vegetable peelings, wilted coriander stalks, garlic husks, sprinklings of flour, a careless scattering of green chillies, a disfigured finger of ginger. In a big steel mixing-bowl sat a lump of kneaded dough. In another small container there was rice soaking under a couple of inches of water. I could barely find space on a surface to rest our glasses and pour whisky and cubes of ice into each.

'The kitchen is a mess,' I said, handing Baba his drink.

'Don't worry, she'll clean it all up before she leaves,' Ma said.

'Tell me now about why she can't stand Milly.'

Ma began, 'Renu is a difficult person, as you saw. She's very lippy—'

Baba interrupted us. 'I can't believe the two of you are sitting gossiping about servants,' he said with mild distaste.

Ma turned to me and said, almost in a whisper, 'Later'; she always conceded to my father.

I was in no mood to start an argument with Baba; we had clashed before on the subject of masters and servants several times and it would be ploughing the same arid furrow now. While swallowing the words I could have used to challenge him, a memory from my boyhood came back with sudden, sharp-edged clarity.

It was the year before we left Calcutta for Bombay and it must have been either during the school summer break or on a Thursday or Sunday, since I was at home during the day. It was the height of summer, June or July, around one in the afternoon, when the sun was at its most killing. The temperature must have been touching forty degrees, if not slightly above that, because the tar on the roads had gone all soft and yielding. Baba sent out our live-in maid, a girl called Nisha, who couldn't have been more than eleven or twelve years old, to get some batteries from the general store in the main market, which was about a fifteen-minute brisk walk from our home. In just over half an hour Nisha returned but with the wrong batteries. Baba shouted at her and sent her out again immediately. Nisha, crestfallen, made the trip a second time. This time it took her slightly longer than half an hour.

'Wrong batteries, again,' Baba roared and flung the packet at the wall. Nisha cowered. Her face looked shrivelled. My mother appeared but she looked timid too.

'Do you have nothing in your head?' Baba raged at the girl. 'I told you to ask for the small red ones, not the big ones. Small, SMALL, do you get it?'

My heart was rattling in my ribcage.

Ma said, 'Why don't you write it down for her? She can show the chit to the shopkeeper.'

'But the shopkeeper can't read,' Baba said. He turned to Nisha and barked, 'Go now. Ask for the small red batteries. Small ones. Go, go!'

I could see her chin quivering but she fled. How could she, or any of her kind, have answered back? She was making the trip a third time in this temperature, which felt like it could turn a human into vapour within minutes, and she hadn't had the chance to sit down to rest a bit and cool off and have a drink before she was dispatched again. I ran to the front veranda to see her tiny figure; it was running instead of walking, getting smaller and smaller as it reached the end of our long residential back street and turned the corner. There wasn't a single human around in this heat, not even a stray dog or cat or the ubiquitous crows. The houses stood dreaming, utterly still, heavy with shadows on one side, flayed by burning light on the other. I was baffled by why she was running; wouldn't walking be cooler, safer?

When she returned, it was with the wrong batteries again. Baba took one look at them, gave out a sound between a snarl and a groan, scrunched up his face and bared his teeth, an expression halfway between feral and despairing. He tried to utter some words but they didn't emerge. Ma, who looked stricken, interposed herself physically between Baba and Nisha.

Nisha's mouth twisted and opened; she could no longer check her tears. There was no restraint to it – she sobbed and hiccuped as she cried. Her knees bent and I couldn't tell if she wanted to sit down and cry because it would be easier, or if she wanted to fall to my mother's or my father's feet and beg to be excused from being sent out again. I could hear my own blood pumping away furiously. Perhaps I had even begun to tremble. All I could think of was how the girl had had to run around without any food or water, for it must have been a long while since her breakfast and it was well past lunchtime. She was ripe for a heatstroke.

Then I noticed her feet. There were tiny black stone-chips, of the sort that were used to create the surface of roads, sticking to her soles in small clusters, and singly, here and there, an archipelago in an atlas. It all fell into place: she had taken off her slippers because they kept getting stuck to the road, made slightly gooey in this heat, impeding her journey to and back from the shop; but the road was too hot for her bare feet, so she had been obliged to run in order not to get blistered. The tar, beginning to melt, had had an adhesive effect on the area of contact between the skin of her soles and the stone-chips, some of which had come loose and got stuck to her feet.

A switch tripped: with all the cold fury that I could summon to my voice, I turned to my father and said, 'Aren't you ashamed to send this little girl out in this heat so many times? She has been running from pillar to post without so much as a sip of water ... And you, a big, able, pampered man, standing here, giving orders to a slip of a thing ...'

I rolled my fist into a tight ball and brought it up, as if to punch him. My mother screamed.

That was a turning point, and both my parents and I knew it. Something in the very air between us had been cleaved and it was going to make its presence felt every time the subject of domestic servants came up.

Later I found out that my parents had been baffled, more than anything else, by the side I had chosen to take: I had, inexplicably to them, crossed over to the wrong side of the 'us versus them' equation. Years later, in a similar situation, my father had taunted me, 'Turned out to be quite a Gandhi type, haven't you? All that expensive education I'm paying for is teaching you all kinds of fancy posturing.' It had made my blood boil then; it still had the power to bring it to a low simmer if I dwelt on it for any length.

Baba's comment on gossiping about servants animated that memory, but now was not the time to make the three of us acknowledge its presence, not one day into my month-long visit here, so I tinkled the ice against my glass as Baba went to change into his home clothes and Ma and I sat making inconsequential chit-chat. I was a world away from them, yet I could choose – and I did choose, for most of the time – to let this temporary suspension of my London life feel cosy and cocooning, as if I had escaped back to the age of irresponsibility.

Cooking-aunty returned and went straight into the kitchen. In an hour's time, she put the food, in covered bowls and serving dishes, on to the dining table, set out plates and cutlery, said, improbably, 'Bye' in English to no one in particular while standing at the front door, then was gone.

'She never says "Bye". What's got into her?' Baba said; Baba, who normally never paid attention to domestic staff, or engaged in any way with them apart from paying their salaries.

'Maybe she's thrilled to have a shaheb in the house and to cook for him,' Ma joked.

I went to the kitchen to pour us another drink. It was spotless.

The conversation meandered in a pleasant, aimless way, touching on mildly interesting things that were neither urgent nor terribly serious. It was all very agreeable, although I think both my mother and I were mindful of steering away from the topic of 'the minutiae of servants' lives', as my father would put it, certainly in his presence. But my curiosity had been piqued and I wanted to ask her to tell me a little bit more about Renu; she seemed so determinedly truculent, something so out of character for a cook that I wanted to will into being events and causes more profound than the simple explanation of personality.

Beyond my mother cryptically saying 'Jealousy' to my question of 'Why can't Renu stand Milly?', we didn't get much further on the topic. The food was simple and textbook-perfect. The grammatical error in spicing, as it were, that my mother found so offensive in cooking-aunty's food, and that she thought she was prone to, was nowhere to be tasted: the green papaya and prawns had been spiced with cumin and bay leaves, with garam masala and ghee added right at the end; the aubergines were a mushy tomatoey medley, with caramelised onions and ginger and sparkling with raw fresh coriander and green chillies. It was as if Renu was countering, successfully, an accusation that had been silently – and not so silently – levelled at her and under whose yoke she laboured in my parents' home.

'Everything is exactly as it should be,' I said to my mother. 'Why did you say she has no clue about the rules of traditional spicing?'

Ma grimaced and said, 'Yes, she hasn't messed this up, but you wait and watch. It all depends on her moods.' Then she repeated, 'It's because you are here.'

An idea was slowly taking on edges and shape in my head. I wanted to sound it out with my mother. She knew about my current project, the regional Indian cookbook. In a way, she had seeded this project in me: years ago, she had sent me one of a series that Penguin published – *The Calcutta Cookbook*. It was atrociously printed and organised, the index was a hot mess; clearly the people behind the book had no idea how to go about producing a cook-book. But that series – an Assam cookbook, a Goa cookbook, a Parsi cookbook, and so on – was an inspired idea, if woefully executed and commissioned, with some gems lurking here and there. *The Calcutta Cookbook*, for example, had any number of brilliant recipes, among them things I had always heard talked about, but had never eaten, such as a beetroot-and-egg dish, khagina, and a toasted moong dal with mango ginger. Amazingly, it featured the street food-stall favourite of the '80s, chow mein. Indians have always known that there is nothing called Indian food, only different, sometimes wildly and thrillingly different, regional cuisines. This is a fact that has been flattened out in the West. Wouldn't it be worthwhile, if only for the makers of my book, to produce something that amounted to a manageable guided tour around these regional cuisines?

So, prompted by that thought, I asked Ma, 'Do you think she'll be able to give us recipes from ... from her part of Bengal?' I had no idea where this was.

My mother snorted with open contempt. 'What do you want Medinipur recipes for? What special things do they have, anyway? Why not go for a selection of general Bengali food? I can give you those recipes.'

I knew her ego had been slightly dented – why should her son ask this upstart cook for authentic Bengali recipes when she herself could give me any number of them, and better ones? – but she was entirely justified in her point. It was enough to give readers an idea of the differences between the different Indian states without having to get into the micro-details of intra-state district divisions. It was a cookbook after all, maybe even a coffee-table item, not a history-and-sociology book.

Over the next few days I mulled over the idea, called various friends who were well placed to help me with the book or had friends in the states that I would be visiting for research. I lazed around at home, read, wasted time online, depleted my father's fine and seemingly inexhaustible collection of single malts and, above all, ate some food that Ankita would surely have called 'life-changing' or, literally translated from the Bengali, 'life-turning'.

Milly came in around noon and on one occasion, when my mother was out somewhere, I gave her lunch, arranging all the dishes on a plate and telling her what each was. They were all leftovers from the night before, or even two nights previously, and Renu had done a fine job. In my rusty Hindi, I struggled to find the correct words for spices or vegetables whose names I had only ever known in Bengali and English and had to ask Milly once or twice if I was right or wrong. It was painful to watch her seized up with shyness or inhibition or whatever it was, so I quickly exited the kitchen, resolving never again to talk her through the dishes in future.

One day, as Milly was eating her lunch in the kitchen, the doorbell rang. I opened the door; it was Renu, with a plastic bag of vegetables and greens. She had already done her morning schedule and wasn't due to come in again until the evening. Before I could say 'Come in', she launched into an explanation of her untimely appearance.

'Tonight's vegetables,' she said. 'No green bananas, coriander, curry leaves, chillies, pumpkin in the pheeej ... so I thought I would get some because I was going that way' – indicating the vegetable market – 'and it would save you having to go out.'

She had taken off her slippers outside the threshold.

'I'll put them away, don't worry,' she said and ran into the kitchen. I heard the sound of the fridge door being opened, vegetable trays being brought out and pushed back in, the scrunching of plastic bags, but not a single word between Renu and Milly. Then Renu came out and left the flat in one swift movement like a puff of wind. She didn't look back at me sitting in the living room, didn't say 'Bye' or 'I'll be back in the evening', just pulled the door shut from the outside and left.

She came back at half-past six to cook dinner. I had got into the swing of things by now, so I was ready with the menu – cabbage thoran, a Tamil pumpkin dish with tamarind and mustard paste, chicken chettinad – and with the recipes for two of the dishes she had never cooked before, the pumpkin and the chicken. Surliness I had come to expect from her, but not the degree of borderline rudeness that was on show that evening. She didn't look at me once, spoke minimally (and when she did, it was with extreme curtness) and snapped at me, twice, when I paused in the reading out of the recipes because I could see that she was doing three different things at the same time – taking out the vegetables from the fridge, putting the cut-up chicken in the sink to wash, taking out the cooking pans and wok from a cupboard – and would perhaps have preferred me to read them to her when she had a minute to pay attention.

'Arrey, read, read, I don't have all the time in the world,' she said.

'I was waiting for you to listen. So many instructions at once, you may forget what goes in when—'

She cut me short with a very Bengali expression of contempt – 'Arrey, dhur' – then repeated, 'Read, read. I'll remember.'

I was taken aback. With any other person I would have asked for the reason behind the edgy tone, or taken mild offence, but the difference in our social and class standing prevented me from doing either. How on earth did echt-Indian people, who had no notion of taking lip from people they considered their inferiors, react to her? Or did she let herself go only at my parents' home because my mother didn't indulge in the hallowed Indian practice of shouting at servants, certainly not in my presence? I read out the two recipes, one after the other, decided against asking, 'Will you remember?' or adding, 'Do ask me again if you need reminding', and went to the living room.

I caught my mother's eyes, raised my eyebrows and said in English, under my voice, 'Bad temper today. Best avoided.'

Ma, also switching to English, asked, 'What happened?' She had clearly not heard the brief exchange; besides, there wasn't much to hear – it was mostly in the realm of tone and attitude and facial expression. 'Shall I say something to her?'

'No,' I said firmly. 'Absolutely not. She's just in one of her moods this evening.'

'We're getting a bit tired of her moods. Sometimes she can be completely out of order.'

The conversation could potentially lead to a minefield, the 'correct' way for servants to behave, so I hastily and energetically tried to steer both of us away from the subject. It worked or, rather, Ma thought better of it, and I was relieved that we had avoided unpleasantness. Or so I thought; because sitting down later that evening to eat the food Renu had cooked brought everything back with renewed vigour.

Every single dish she had cooked was wrong. She had committed the cardinal sin, in my mother's books: adding hing to the thoran. The pumpkin tasted of nothing, despite containing two of the most powerful ingredients in Indian cuisine, tamarind and fresh mustard paste. At first I couldn't put my finger on what the chicken was lacking – it wasn't bad; it just wasn't the dish it was supposed to be – then I realised that she had left out the aromatics, cardamom, cloves and cinnamon, that were supposed to be fried in hot oil right at the beginning. It was clear to me that she had not been able to retain – as who would? – the long list of ingredients for not one but two dishes, and the subsequent processes for each, slightly involved and complicated in the case of the chettinad chicken, that I had read out only once.

My father was indifferent, but my mother was incensed and jubilant at the same time: here was evidence for her point about Renu being a hit-and-miss cook who didn't really have a proper understanding of the fundamental grammar and syntax of cooking. I felt nervous that we were again going to embark on the business of servant-bashing; such excruciatingly uncomfortable territory. Ma complained at length and my discomfort grew, to the extent that I found myself feeling slightly protective of cooking-aunty and defending her.

'Hing is not an entirely unintuitive addition to thoran, don't you think?' I pleaded. 'If there are already mustard seeds, curry leaves and coconut, hing seems to be naturally a part of that.'

Ma remained unconvinced. Baba, to his credit, added, 'The chicken is actually lovely. I don't know what it's supposed to be like in its perfect incarnation but this is great.'

I wanted to lean over and give him a hug, which was a complete no-no in my family and would probably be seen as a frivolous Western affectation.

Ma made a face but didn't counter this. Instead, she said, 'This is what we have to put up with, these moods. At first I thought: you put up with the kicks of the cow that gives you milk; but recently things seem to have worsened.'

Something clicked inside my head. 'She saw Milly here today, when she came in to drop off the vegetables,' I said.

'Aha. That must have set her off,' Ma said.

'But I don't understand why,' I said, genuinely baffled. 'You say it's jealousy, but jealousy about what?' While feeling nervous about edging close to this fraught subject, I was inwardly preparing myself to stare my father out on this one; I was too curious to let it pass.

'I can't quite tell the reason,' Ma said. 'Maybe something happened we don't know about – they both live in the same slum, after all. Or it could be that Milly has a husband, two children ... I can see how that would eat into Renu.'

'Doesn't she have children?' I asked.

'I think she has a daughter but doesn't have much to do with her.'

'What do you mean you "think"? You either know or you don't.'

'I dimly remember her saying something to me a while ago. I don't remember her exact words but I got the impression that she was married off early, she had a daughter, the husband perhaps used to beat her, which is why she left. I don't remember if she abandoned the daughter too when she left.'

'This was in Medinipur?' I was fascinated.

'Yes. I don't know which village.'

'Do you think I could ask her?'

Ma looked panicked. 'No, no, no need to do that. No need to upset her further.'

Baba said, 'Here we go again' and got up from the table.

'Please, don't go asking things to her,' Ma said again. 'No need to raise her to our heads, she'll take even more liberties with her behaviour and think we're giving her some kind of licence. Best not to become informal with servants, one must always maintain a distance with them.'

Rocks ahoy, I thought, and willed myself not to react; she did not mean it to be a bait.

The next morning Renu was back and I decided not to engage her in conversation. Usually I would compliment her on the previous night's cooking – she never responded, but I felt that she was secretly pleased to be praised – but today I withheld any such comment. Instead, I went out to have my first look at the slum.

I crossed the road and walked down the three steps to the paved area that marked one end of the promenade. Where the paving ended, the black rocks and sea began. There was a narrow path along one end, clinging to the last of the tyre shops and tea-sellers and snack stores, on what I only now noticed was a raised wall against which the sea lapped. The path curved around behind what I saw from my parents' living-room window as shops, trees, a tiny playing field, all bordered by this wall, which obstructed the view of the path running along it. I was on it now. It was so narrow that if two people could walk abreast on it, the one nearer the sea would be in constant danger of falling in. The water was barely inches below the lip of the wall. The path was muddy, with footprint-shaped puddles here and there. Was it submerged during high tide? I had a view of the slum spread out in front of me, on my left. It looked like the back of a huge black beast in camouflage, huddling low, perhaps dormant, lying pressed against the sea at two ends, its surface feathered with plastic on the roofs, mostly black, with an occasional flash of blue. When the breeze lifted, it seemed the beast's feathers were being ruffled. I pressed myself flat against what I assumed were back walls of houses to allow people behind me to pass. I followed them, with some misgiving, self-conscious about how I clearly stood out as an outsider. To my great relief, people noticed me but not in any egregious way; they didn't stare, or make comments, or even look curious or interested.

I realised that this outer path ringed around the sea-side perimeter of the slum and that even narrower alleys led off it into the interior. I took one of them. There were rooms packed on either side. I felt that if I stretched out both my arms, wingspan-style, the tips of my fingers could just about touch their exterior. Room after room after room, then another alley, easily missed because of its narrowness and the density of the living quarters. In fact you had to look hard to distinguish any passage at all threading through the houses, since it was often a practice rather than a physical thing; people made their way through the narrowest of spaces along the front, sides, backs of houses; a path was whatever people decided to tread. There were people walking, sitting, standing, doing nothing in particular, moving in and out of rooms. The interiors were so dark that I could barely make out anything, maybe a corner of a pallet, or just an expanse of floor, a section of a plastic chair. A woman was fanning a burning oven outside her front door in an effort to get the wood to catch. A small group of children ran around aimlessly; maybe they were playing a game. There was a motorbike parked outside one of the houses. How did they ever get it in here? People were now looking at me. My discomfort escalated and it was not only because of the stares. Edicts from a middle-class upbringing on looking into other people's lives through their open doors and windows combined with a liberal sensitivity, acquired later in life, about treating the poor as anthropological fieldwork or a tourist attraction, to produce a mixture of dread, guilt and self-loathing. I turned tail.

The question that most occupied me afterwards was whether each of those rooms was the entire house and home of one family.

Of course, I didn't tell cooking-aunty that I had seen the slum where she lived. I felt mildly depressed for the rest of the morning and when she came out of the kitchen to ask what we were planning to have for dinner, I gave a straight answer – chicken stir-fried with basil and nam pla, dry green beans with pork mince, garlic, nam pla and chillies – instead of the 'Why, I thought you needed to be told, just once, and just before you started!', which I could have delivered with a big grin to normalise the situation, at least to myself. I asked her if she was familiar with nam pla – she called it 'nampa' – and she gave a surprising answer: 'Yes, I cook with it in that house all the time. They eat a lot of this kind of food.'

'What house?' I asked.

'Oh, one of the houses I cook for over there.' She lifted her hand above her head and pointed behind her in a vague gesture that also managed to be typically dismissive.

That evening, I took her through the process, brief and very simple, of cooking the two dishes. Half an hour later, she slid the kitchen door open, peered out and said, 'I can't find the nampa.'

'Have you looked carefully?' Ma asked. 'It's in that cupboard to the right of where the glasses are kept. You know it.'

'Yes, I put it there myself. It arrived two days ago, I remember. You showed it to me.'

'Do you remember what it looks like?'

'Oi to, a small bottle, black cap.'

'Are you sure it's not there? Let me have a look.'

Ma got up and went to the kitchen. She came out after a few minutes. 'I can't find it. I looked everywhere it could be.'

'It can't have gone running away,' I said. 'Let me have a look.'

In the kitchen, I opened every drawer, every cupboard, looked in the overcrowded fridge, taking out every prehistoric jar of mustard, olives, kasundi, oyster sauce, marmalade, pickle from the door. It seemed that the Law of the Fridge was universal across cultures and continents: things went there to die slowly and be forgotten. But no; no nam pla in the fridge, although an unopened bottle wouldn't have been put there in the first place. I asked the usual questions – who put away the shopping that day, was there a sort of unspoken rule about which things went where (of course there was) – and got predictable answers. I looked inside the cupboards below the worktop, the spaces where flour and potatoes and onions were stored, and in the space for the blender, spice-grinder and rolling pin, even in the cupboard for plastic bags and the drawers for Tupperware. Nothing.

All four of us were now caught up in the search. Even Baba gave suggestions – have you looked here, or there, or what about that spot ... For half an hour we were entirely consumed by finding a bottle of fish sauce; absurd and bathetic.

We gave up. I was left alone in the kitchen with cooking-aunty. I could see that everything for cooking the dishes had been prepared – the chicken diced, the garlic and chillies finely chopped, the beans cut into short lengths, the pork mince defrosted. I was contemplating whether to take an auto, go to the shop next to

Mehbooob Studios and get a new bottle, when Renu said, 'That person took it, I know.'

'Who?' I had no idea what she was talking about.

'Oi je, the one who comes to clean.' The words were accompanied by that indicating-dismissing gesture of her hands that I was beginning to get familiar with.

It took a few beats to sink in. 'Milly? But why on earth would she do that?' I was genuinely nonplussed.

'I'm telling you,' she insisted.

'But why?'

'Because she's like that.'

'Like what?' I was annoyed. I wasn't going to let this go.

'I'm telling you,' she repeated.

'And I'm asking you what use she would have with it? Do you know if she's going to use it to cook? Why take something like that?'

'No, not to cook. She took it just like that. She'll look at it, show it to people. She's like that, I'm telling you.'

I said, 'I don't think so', trying not to let my anger inflect my words, tone or expression in any way. 'This does not sound convincing to me.'

'I'm telling you—' she began again, but I cut her short.

'Use soya sauce instead,' I said curtly and left the kitchen.

In the living room my mother asked if we had found it. I said no, put a firm lid on what was bothering me and proceeded with the usual chit-chat and drinking. I didn't want to talk about it in front of my father at all, so I waited until we had finished eating and he had gone to bed, then asked Ma to come to my room.

'Listen,' I said, 'Renu thinks Milly stole the nam pla. I was a bit flabbergasted. I don't believe her at all but I can't work out what's going on.'

Ma was baffled too. 'She said that to you? Did you ask her why she thought so? I mean, what an odd thing to steal.'

'Or: what an odd thing to accuse someone of stealing.'

'Yes, yes, that's what I meant.'

'What's going on, do you think?' I asked.

'I have no idea. Unless she dislikes Milly so much that she's trying to sow seeds of suspicion ...'

'So it could be possible that Renu hid the nam pla in order to blame Milly?'

Ma was nodding her head slowly as she fit the pieces together. 'My god, how low of her. She was accused of stealing in an earlier job, so she is using that now against someone else ... It's all beginning to make sense.'

'What do you mean: stealing in an earlier job? What job? Stealing what? Why didn't you tell me before?'

'Again, this is something I heard, I don't remember from whom. Or I pieced it together. Or maybe when Renu told me that she used to cook for the ONGC homes near Reclamation – you've seen those ugly buildings many, many times, I'm sure – and that they fired her, I made up the bit about false charges of stealing.'

'What false charges of stealing? Did you just pluck it out of the air?' My confusion was increasing rapidly.

'I think she was accused of stealing and was thrown out of one of those homes where she used to cook. But she's very trustworthy. I have left money and jewellery unlocked in the house several times while she has been here on her own. She has even had the keys to the flat, when we were out of the city. I would trust her with everything. I'm certain that those charges of stealing were trumped-up ... You know how it is here: anything goes missing, the first person the blame falls on is the servant, who may well be innocent.'

Oh yes, I knew all about that. I remember watching, when I was a child in Calcutta, one such servant, accused of stealing money and jewellery from the family for whom he worked, being beaten in public as a way of extracting a confession. I had run to join the watching throng. It wasn't only the men of the accusing family who had a go at him; neighbours, residents of the street, distant friends, even strangers joined in. News that a thief had been caught and was being beaten brought a huge crowd to watch the entertainment; the punishments got more extreme, more cruel. At one point I remember someone lifting him by his ankles and swinging him around in a circle, his head so close, during each revolution, to a pile of jagged, broken bricks that it repeatedly hit that mound, tearing open his forehead and the back of his head. He shrieked every time the collision happened, and I saw blood on his face.

I could no longer recall what I felt as a child witnessing this: thrill? Sympathy? Pity? Outrage? The man was howling, 'Babu, I didn't steal anything, I swear on my children's lives, I haven't touched a thing, please let me go, I beg you, please.' What I did remember very clearly was my mother turning up and saying to the family in question that she had come to protest against their barbaric behaviour. And I remembered the reaction: the woman leading the accusation and chivvying on the beating and the cheerleading had rounded on Ma, jeered at her and said, 'If you had had your own stuff stolen, would you have come here to preach? Keep your high-mindedness to yourself.' Then she had turned round and tried to do some rabble-rousing against my mother. Ma had caught hold of my hand and dragged me away. I could still hear the vulgar Bengali equivalents of the taunts 'Goody-two-shoes', 'Holier-than-thou', which were thrown at our retreating backs.

I briefly toyed with the idea of first finding out in which flats in the ONGC buildings cooking-aunty had worked, then enquiring about the episode at each of them, but gave up on the idea as a foolish one.

The following evening, halfway through her cooking, Renu poked her head out of the kitchen and announced, 'The nampa bottle is back.'

My mother looked at the floor; I got up to go to the kitchen, largely to avoid meeting Ma's eyes.

Renu pounced the moment I entered: 'See, I told you, she's brought it back, I told you, she took it, did her thing with it and now she's returned it. I told you.'

That high-pitched voice, grating my nerves raw; I felt the pop of an ache beginning behind my right eye. I didn't know what to say. The bottle stood on the counter. It was unopened.

I forced myself to ask, 'Where did you find it?'

'In the cupboard, where it was supposed to be. She brought it back this morning, when she came to clean, and slipped it in there. I know how she works.'

I had had no reason to open that particular cupboard all day, so I couldn't disprove her. Besides, my embarrassment was so acute that I made some kind of non-committal sound and left the kitchen.

The food at dinner that evening was perfect.

In my remaining couple of weeks in Bombay, I increasingly engaged Renu in conversation; in the mornings, especially, because often my parents would be out, but also in the interstices of giving her instructions in the evenings.

'Find a job for me in your country,' she would say, only half-joking.

I would say, 'There are no private cooks where I live. Only restaurants have cooks.'

'How do you eat, if you don't have someone to cook?'

'We make our own food.'

'Huh, how is that possible?'

'We learn how to cook. Everyone there knows how to cook at least a few things. Then there are shops where you can buy ready-made meals. You bring them home and heat them up.'

That silenced her. Then she came back with a shy question: 'They are as good as aunt's' – referring to herself, of course – 'cooking?'

I didn't answer this point. Instead I said, 'Besides, where will you live?'

'Why, don't you have room in your place?'

The thought of explaining immigration, labour, living, houses, wages, class occurred to me for an instant; I felt defeated almost immediately.

She got in through that tiny gap: 'I can sleep in the kitchen.'

Before I could find a white lie in lieu of an explanation, something emollient, I burst out with 'That's not possible.' Ashamed, I retreated to the living room, worrying that I had hurt her feelings.

Another time: 'Will you take a dal tonight?'

I said, 'No, no need, there's a lot of food already, I don't want to upset my stomach.'

'I am your aunt, this aunt's food will never cause an upset stomach.'

Over those weeks, she told me she came from Medinipur, from a family of rice farmers. They owned the land they cultivated, so they were not poor, or certainly not the kind of poor one associated with the term 'Indian farmer'.

'You go visit my village one day?' she asked.

I made polite noises. She told me about her brothers and widowed mother, how the land had been divided among the three children after their father died. Her brothers cultivated it now.

'Did you not get your share of the land?' I asked.

'Yes, I did, but I sold it to my brothers. How could I cultivate it myself?'

'You didn't marry?'

Her face shut down. 'Oh, a long time ago.' The dismissive gesture again, without any of its usual complements. 'I've kept a bit of land to build my house after I stop working and leave Bombay.'

'Great. You know when? And you'll go back to your village? Why not stay in the city?'

'Naaaah, this is not our country. I'll go back when I have saved enough money to build a house. My own house.'

So she had savings. I didn't know why it surprised – and gladdened – me. I had no idea what her outgoings were, but if she worked in six homes, earning anything between four to six thousand rupees a month at each, her income wasn't insubstantial. Was that why she lived in a slum, so that she was saved from the lion's share of her earnings being devoured in Bombay rent, one of the steepest in the world? I found myself strangely invested in this aspect of her life, willing her to work longer, in more homes, to live frugally, so that she could save more, to the extent that I caught myself clenching my fists and my jaws, imagining a speeding up of her efforts and a commensurate escalation of the figure in her bank account. And I thought about what it must be for her to experience the kind of working life that she had, every day the same, yet each slightly different, all her actions repetitive, yet sometimes with a minuscule possibility of uniqueness.

'You go there and see my old house and the land where I want to build my new home,' she said in a tone of warm, easy familiarity, even intimacy.

Often, when she came in the morning to cook breakfast and lunch, I would ask her to cook lunch for exactly two, Ma and Baba, since the fridge was groaning with leftovers. I loved leftovers and I could happily eat them for lunch every day, but Baba wanted to take something freshly cooked every morning to work, something simple such as rice, a vegetable dish and some fish. Ma, too, I think, liked something different from what she had the previous night, although she was slightly nervous about confessing this to me. Renu, naturally enough, often cooked enough to serve between four to six people, since that was easier to do than cook for one. The outcome was such a surfeit of cooked food at home that we all struggled. But Ma explained, 'Eat what you want, no need to feel the pressure to finish everything. We can always give it to Milly.

She is always happy with the season of plenty that happens when you visit, I can tell. And she can also take the excess food for her children.'

One such morning, around eleven, when it was time for Renu to leave after her stint, she came out to the living room and said to me (Ma was out), 'The fridge is full of food. Why aren't you eating anything? You must eat up the stuff in there, otherwise it'll spoil, then I'll be scolded by your mother.' Her tone was playfully chiding; taking some liberties and sailing riskily quite close to a few unbreachable boundaries of class; it was a measure of how easy she felt with me, and how fond she had become. We still addressed each other using the most respectful form of 'you'.

'Why don't you take some of it with you? Honestly. There's so much ... I can put it in tiffin boxes for you,' I said.

'Naaah, I don't need it, I eat only one meal a day, rice and boiled vegetables. I have no use for all that.'

Here was my opening to ask about her living arrangements. But before I could open my mouth, she had achieved a complete tonal shift: 'I know everything, you give it to that person.' (It took me a while to work out who she was referring to, since third-person pronouns are not gendered in Bengali.) 'I caught the person in the kitchen the other day,' she said, 'eating the food that I cook. I cook it with my sweat and with love – and you give it to her? I felt my whole body sizzle when I saw her. How dare she?'

She had suddenly become like a storm confined in a room. Her ugly voice had ratcheted up in pitch and volume. 'She knows her moves – the way she worked her way into your mother's life ... Why is your mother so fond of her? That woman must have done some witchy thing, some kind of spell. She's exactly that kind. She leaves her children at home and goes out every day, what kind of woman does that? Her husband works, why does she need to?'

'Enough,' I cried. Perhaps I hadn't said it loudly, or urgently, enough – she showed no sign of abating but her tone changed from angry to pleading.

'You come back home from foreign. Your parents' lives are empty without you. I know, I see them every day. Before you arrive, they only talk about you. "Renu, my son is coming, he likes to eat this, he likes to eat that, you have to cook well every day," your mother says. Your father goes and gets all this fish – they don't eat so many kinds themselves when you're not here. I know what it is to have the jewel of your eye live in foreign. My brother's son, he lives in a far-away country. You come back, it's not good for you to be away from your parents. They're getting old. You're a young man, we'll find a good girl for you, you marry and have children, your parents will live the rest of their days in happiness. I say that to my Dulal as well, but who listens to me?'

By the time she reached the end, that slightly forced tone of jauntiness had come back. It was her insurance, should she have found herself accused of stepping out of line in her conversations with people above her station. Whether, this time, the return of the tone was the result of her awareness that she had allowed herself to take liberties, I couldn't tell.

I returned to India a year later.

The book had changed personality during work on it in London in the interim: it was no longer centred on breakfasts; its full title, *Real Indian Food: Recipes from Homes Across India*, gave an accurate idea of its nature and contents. The idea still was that the recipes should be reproducible outside India without making the cook or the browsing reader nervous about recherché ingredients and labour-intensive processes, and, for a completely different kind of reader and cook, without making anything appear watered-down, inauthentic, giving cause for the bitter *ressentiment* crowd to wield that age-old stick used to beat Indians who resided abroad – 'tailoring things for Western tastes and sensibilities'.

The time for my annual visit to my parents came round. I had already decided that I would travel to four or five different cities and towns, meeting up and staying with people, getting recipes from them and, most importantly, eating their food. My editor joked that I was following in the footsteps of Matthew Fort's *Eating Up Italy*; I had to be mindful of making our book different.

It was inevitable that Calcutta should be the first city on the itinerary. I stayed at my uncles' home in Shyambazar. It was a huge three-storey house: each of my two uncles had an entire floor to himself and his family, while the ground floor was rented out. The cook, whom I've always known as Thakur, the generic Bengali term for a cook, because everybody called him that, was still in charge of the food, as he was before my father left for Bombay with my mother and me. I didn't visit my uncles in Calcutta often; in fact, I had been back only about five or six times since I left for England. This gave rise to a lot of affectionate passive-aggressive banter ('Now that you live in London, you don't deign to visit your poor relatives', etc.), which I used to find enervating but had learned, over time, to negotiate light-heartedly. What made it all worth it was Thakur's cooking, despite the food torture that goes in the name of hospitality in Bengali homes. (My mother resented the fact that Thakur didn't accompany us to Bombay as our family cook, choosing to stay on with her brothers instead. In a way, she was forever looking to find a Thakur whom she could install permanently in her life. Everyone would always fall short of his standards; Renu had lost even before she had joined.)

Thakur surpassed himself again; I felt he did exactly this every time I visited. The food wasn't dressy; far from it. Things just seemed to come together alchemically in his hands, the final thing far greater than the sum of its parts. Rice-flour pancakes, delicate as muslin handkerchiefs, served with coriander chutney for breakfast;

a simple lunchtime dish of potatoes, prawns and spring onions; a teatime snack of very quickly deep-fried flattened rice, served with fried green peas and chillies on the side – it was difficult not to talk about these things using suspicious words such as 'magic'. If I were to get the recipes from him and pass them on to Renu in Bombay, would she have been able to get them right? No doubt she could have replicated them, perhaps even exactly, but that surplus Bengalis called 'hand', would be missing – by the very fact that she wasn't Thakur meant that his food cooked by her wouldn't have his 'hand's' touch.

I spoke to Ma every evening on the phone and one evening, while I was giving her news of her brothers and sisters-in-law and nephews and nieces, besides of course a detailed account of what we were being served at breakfast, lunch, tea and dinner – 'four meals a day' was a Bengali idiom – I heard someone talking in the background and Ma responding, 'Achha, enough, you go to the kitchen now.'

'What's going on?' I asked.

'Ufff, Renu. She's saying that you must go visit her home in Medinipur. I mean, *really*.'

Why not? I thought. 'All right. Why don't you ask her to call her brother and let him know? We can work out a date.' It was instinctive, not thought through, but suddenly seemed like an interesting idea.

Ma was first incredulous, then aghast. 'Are you out of your mind? What will you do there?'

'Why? I'm here on holiday, sort of, and it'll give me a glimpse of small-town India. It'll be interesting, no?'

'But there's nothing to see in Medinipur!'

I failed to convince Ma that my visit was going to be a different kind of tourism, not about pretty or famous sights.

'But it's not going to be comfortable,' she wailed. 'Where are you going to stay?'

'Why, in cooking-aunty's home?'

I knew what was bothering her – the traversal of class boundaries, the queasiness that derived from the dissolution of certain impermeable, separating membranes that the intimacy of the son of a master going to stay in the home of a servant entailed. It brought out the rebellious teenager in me; I pushed back.

Two days later, the driver who worked for my uncles, Jishnu-da, was taking me to Garhbheta, where we were going to be met by Shankar, one of Renu's nephews, at a locally well-known sweet shop, Mouchak, and he would direct Jishnu-da to the village, Putihari.

After the hell of driving through Haora district and the squalid small towns of Medinipur, things felt less dirty, less squashed in and claustrophobic, the more we got away from human settlements. The road began to cut through large stretches of countryside with nothing, for considerable intervals, to mar it. We had to get out at a point about five or six kilometres from the village; Shankar said the narrow road was not fit for cars; he had organised people to carry my luggage. I only had a small backpack; I didn't need any help at all, but Shankar was adamant. I knew I had to put up with this intense servility that passed as hospitable behaviour; the guest was a god in Bengali culture. I still hadn't got over the moment when the car stopped to pick up Shankar and he fell at my feet to do pranam.

Jishnu-da was going to return the following day to take me back to Calcutta. The car, conspicuous in a place like this, had brought out people, mostly men and children, who stood gawping with undisguised curiosity. Some of the bolder children came forward and gathered close to the car, looking up at me unblinkingly. An old man at the door of a one-storey brick house about twenty feet from where we were parked called out to Shankar and said something that I couldn't catch. Shankar said, 'Na, na, pishi's people, he has come from Calcutta. He lives in London.'

'Dulal's friend?' the man asked.

'Arrey, na, na. I said, he's from London.'

'That's very far away. Ask him if he has come by ship or plane.'

I was desperately trying not to look at Shankar's face. The boy – he couldn't have been more than twelve – whom he had asked to carry my bag was sent ahead of us with my backpack. I fixed what I thought was a blandly pleasant and interested look on my face and followed Shankar. I could hear the boys behind us getting a bit manic. One of them broke into completely unintelligible chatter in a non-language, which I later understood was his attempt, maybe, to imitate English. Two of them started to sing a current Hindi film song that featured a phrase of English – 'Will you be my chammak-challo?' – but they sang the first four words as an aurally approximate gobbledygook. They kept saying 'hello' repeatedly and breaking into giggles. The word began to saw through my right temple, which had started throbbing.

Shankar must have read something in this because he turned to the boys and shooed them away. It took some tenacity; the boys retreated a bit, but carried on with their antics from a distance until they got bored of it and dispersed.

Putihari came as a pleasant green surprise: trees, bushes, creepers everywhere, neat courtyards with mud and thatched huts, ponds, banana flowers on trees, huge, spiky lumps of jackfruit low on the trunk, date palms, tall coconut and betel-nut trees, bamboo groves, and fields surrounding the village on all sides, dotted occasionally with a built structure, sometimes even brick houses, a lot of which looked either abandoned or half-finished. The winter sun was delicious. I saw bori drying in the sun, and some reddish-brown grain or seed set out on kulos in a courtyard flanked by flowering red hibiscus. The fields which had crops on them were the colour of golden sand in the sun. Other parcels of land looked waiting for something to be sown on them, or were dotted at regular intervals with what looked like tough hay-like stubble. Shankar kept up his patter, calling me 'sir', which I asked him not to do several times. Shankar had hardly any English but he insisted on dredging up a word here, a word there, and throwing them at me randomly: 'Flower', he would sing out, pointing to a tagar bush, 'Duck' when we passed a green pond, 'Hen' at a particularly showy rooster preening in the sun. He had clearly been to school, where he had had some rudimentary English lessons. I was still not making eye-contact with him.

Wherever we passed a home on the way, people came out to stare. Shankar pointed to a low L-shaped house of exposed brick and tin roof about twenty metres away and said, 'We're nearly there.' It stood on the edge of a vast rice field traversed by raised earth aals. The house had grown up piecemeal, concrete rooms added as and when resources had permitted. The earth courtyard was impeccably clean, with a border of flowers at one end, at the bottom of a low wall, and two trees on either side of the residential quarter, one a sour plum and another one I couldn't identify. The veranda in front had wooden pillars on which the roof-awning rested. A green parakeet in a cage hanging from a cross-beam eyed us sideways. There was a blue-painted tin gate, rust smudging it generously, where one of the arms of the L ended and the low wall began. Beyond it lay two squat, rectangular structures, unconnected to each other, it seemed, one with a tin roof and ventilation crosses towards the top of the wall, the other a thatched one. They seemed also to be separated from the main building by an empty stretch; what lay in it I couldn't see because my view was obstructed.

A whole reception committee was awaiting us; exactly what I had feared. Leading the charge was a dark man with greying hair and moustache, somewhere in his mid-fifties, I guessed. He was wiry but had a paunch. Another man was standing a few steps behind him; his younger brother, it was obvious. I assumed they were both Renu's brothers, although I couldn't discern any resemblances to her. Five children, three boys and two girls, of varying ages from six to twelve, I guessed, were standing in the courtyard, staring at us unblinkingly. A woman at the doorway quickly covered her head with her aanchol. Two men in their thirties or forties stood by a tree in the courtyard, one on either side of an empty plastic chair. The boy who had been sent ahead with our luggage, clearly the domestic help, came out of the house, looked at us and ran off.

The dark, wiry man came forward with his hands folded in pranam, head slightly bowed. 'Come, come,' he said (using the highest form of 'you', although I was nearly a quarter of a century younger), 'how kind of you to bring the dust of your feet into the hut of the poor ...', then, turning to the children, his tone changing, he barked, 'Ei, you lot, don't you see who is visiting, touch his feet immediately, he has come from London.' I retreated, lightning-quick, as if I had seen a snake approaching, almost shouting, 'No, no, no, absolutely no need, really, no, I forbid you, no, NO.' The children halted, looking at my face, then at the face of the man, in ping-pong manner.

The older man was Raja, his brother, Ratan; Renu was the middle sibling. The woman I saw when we came in was Ratan's wife, Mamoni. Raja's wife, Lakshmi, was inside, busy with chores in the kitchen. I was introduced to the women as 'my wife' or 'my sister-in-law'. I learned their names later when I heard their husbands call out to them.

We were taken to a dark room to be introduced to Raja and Ratan's mother, a frail woman who looked very old and clearly couldn't hear very much. Raja-da shouted, 'Ma, he's come from London.' His Bengali was accented, I had noted earlier, but not in the way Renu's was, which was slightly closer to pidgin, with the odd Hindi word here and there.

'No, I've come from Calcutta,' I said over my unease, adding a strained laugh to neutralise what could be construed as a corrective sting.

The woman could neither hear nor understand what was going on; her watery eyes were focused elsewhere. Even on this cool afternoon, I was sweating. As we were leaving the room, I heard her croak, 'Dulal, eli naki?', *Dulal, is that you?*

I had not paid much heed to Renu talking about Dulal being the apple of her eye, but his name had repeatedly come up in the last hour. I was so dreading the imminent discussion of sleeping arrangements, and the state of the toilet that we were about to be shown, that the question about Dulal got pushed to the background.

Raja-da said, 'You take some tea? Would you like to wash your hands and face first? Let me show you where the bathroom is.'

I followed him through the L. There were only three rooms, two of which were each occupied by a brother and his family; in fact, the room in which the old woman lay dying was shared by Raja, his wife and the two oldest children, a boy and a girl. The third room, in the corner where the two arms joined at right angles, was the size of a box, used for some purpose I couldn't identify – storage? A room in transition, about to be used as another bedroom? This was when I noticed that the floors were not concrete but compacted mud. Did I imagine the slight smell of cow-dung at that very moment of realisation? I didn't understand how rooms could be so bare and so cramped simultaneously: there were few possessions; the whitewash was peeling; a calendar from a shop in Garhbheta, Sri Bishwakarma Hard-Ware Co. & Sons, was hanging from a nail at an angle; a lizard had stationed itself on the top of the wall where it met the tin roof; a long, brown graph of a termite colony made its way close to where two walls joined. There was nowhere for me to stay, but there wasn't any conceivable way I could apologise for putting them to so much trouble – and, I would imagine, embarrassment and shame, too – without drawing attention to my understanding of their stretched lives. Better to go through the remaining hours feeling like an insensitive ogre of privilege, trampling through their hardbitten lives. Not for the first time I wished I had listened to my mother; I had failed to imagine how other people live. But why did Renu insist on me visiting if she knew, as she must have done, that this visit would fairly bristle with all kinds of awkwardnesses and contretemps?

Behind the short arm of the L, at the back of the house, lay a large vegetable patch and a pond. The larger part of the pond was obscured by the low brick box with cross-shaped windows that I had seen from the front courtyard; this was the bathroom. It had an unpainted tin door riddled with rust, which ended a good eight to ten inches above the floor. Inside were a latrine set in the floor, three buckets and a tin drum filled to the brim with water, and a large red plastic mug hooked to the rim of one of the buckets. There were no taps. A thin coir rope, attached to two nails on opposite walls, hung in a slack convex along the breadth of the bathroom. On it were slung two thin gamchhas.

Raja-da said, 'We bathe in the pond. We filled buckets for you in case you are not up for jumping in. Can you swim?'

Then he stopped and looked at me and gave a laugh, part invitation, part dare: 'Want to try it?'

I hesitated.

He said, 'It may be too cold for you ... it's the month of poüsh, after all. Anyway, the buckets and drums have all been filled up for you.'

We went back to the front room; I was going to sleep there, he said. 'The bed's big enough for you? You'll fit in, yes? If not, you can sleep on the floor – we have enough shataranchi, duvet, blankets, sheets. We'll make it really comfortable for you, don't worry about it.'

'No, no ... not worried at all,' I hastened to say.

'Think of it as your own home, do you understand? Your uncle's home, mamar-bari. You call Renu "cooking-aunty", so this is your mamar-bari, right?' He laughed at his own witticism; he was as uncomfortable as I was, perhaps even more.

The boy, Chanchal, brought in tea, and trailing him came Mamoni and Lakshmi, bearing huge bowls of puffed rice – they looked like white hills – and an enormous plate of fresh batter-fried aubergines.

Lakshmi said, 'Eat them quickly, otherwise they'll get cold, they've been taken out of the hot oil just now. There's more coming.'

I thought of doing the typical Bengali coy demurral act, faced with so much food, but dismissed it almost as soon as I had thought it; greed was too powerful.

'Eat up, eat up,' Raja-da urged. 'You don't get this kind of food in London, I bet.'

He was right. The aubergine fritters were perfection of their kind. The crispness of the kalonji-flecked batter giving way to the near-oozy softness of the aubergines, the puffed rice adding its own different crunch to the mouthful, the sharp heat from the powerful green-purple, squat local chillies ...

'Enjoying it?' Ratan-da asked. 'I can tell that you are.'

Yes, he could: I had closed my eyes while munching.

Ratan-da's children were lined up against the wall, watching us as they would a gripping circus act: mouths slightly open, eyes huge and round as owls'. The youngest of the lot, an intrepid girl of six, came forward and handed me something: a picture post-card. I turned it over, saw the German stamp before realising that I might be seen to be reading the words of the sender, so I turned it back again: a picture of an old, beautiful bridge over a river with a castle in the background, with the words 'Heidelberg Old Bridge and Castle' on the bottom left edge.

'Tell him, who sent this?' Raja-da coaxed her gently.

The girl had reached the end of her courage; she ran back to join her two brothers.

'Who sent it?' I asked.

'My elder son. Dulal. He studies in Germany, in Heidelberg.'

I stopped chewing and looked up. Was he joking?

'He's been there for three years now. This muri-beguni that you're eating is his favourite. He eats it every afternoon when he is visiting.'

'What does he study?' I brought myself to say. My voice was hoarse.

'Orrey baba, now you've got me!' he laughed. 'I don't understand that stuff, it all goes over my head. We are foolish, unlettered farmer-types' – he used a common Bengali expression, mukhyu-shukhyu chasha bhusha manush – 'how can we tell you what he studies?'

'But what is his subject?'

'Phee-jeek, he studies phee-jeek, that's all I can say,' he said.

I took this to mean Physics.

'My younger son may be able to tell you better,' he said, then hollered, 'Khokon, ei Khokon, come here for a minute.' In the time that it took for the boy to arrive, Raja-da said, 'He, too, goes to school, the same school that Dulal went to, Ramkrishna Mission in Narendrapur.'

It was a highly reputed school in Calcutta, with a long track record of academic success, and apparently difficult to get admission to. Before I could phrase any questions – and I knew I would have to do so carefully – Khokon came into the room.

'Tell him what Dada studies. You know I don't understand such things,' his father said.

'Physics,' the boy said. 'Particle physics. He's doing a PhD. He'll be called a Doctor at the end of his degree, but it's not a medical doctor.'

He stood taller as he was saying this. I even imagined his chest was puffing out. Education had leached away some of the accent that his father and uncle had. Maybe he, too, would go abroad to study, or become a real doctor, a medical one.

In the event, I didn't have to ask anything; the story came out over dinner. They could barely stop talking about him; all except the women. Dulal's mother, while serving me food, mentioned him for the first and last time: 'He is my son, he lives so far away, my mother's heart is restless and anxious. I can't sleep at night. I worry about him all the time – is he eating properly? Is anyone looking after him? What'll happen if he falls ill? So many worries in my head. It's all very well that he's studying, that he's going to make a name for himself, but all I want is for him to come back.'

We sat out on the veranda to eat. A long sheet had been laid out on the floor, against the wall, so that we wouldn't have to sit on the cold floor. I wondered if they ate in the bare, poky inside in the winter and whether they were making a sort of celebratory ceremony of dinner tonight – eating off banana leaves instead of ordinary plates, for example – because they were at pains not to let their handicaps impinge upon my comfort. The children and I were fed first. They wouldn't listen to my repeated requests that all the adults should eat together; this, in reality, meant only three men, since the women would have eaten only after all the men were done; it was an unshakeable rule. Again, I read this to be hospitality doubling as a diversionary tactic, turning my attention away from the more ordinary food the family would be eating, fewer dishes perhaps, after the guest had been given the best that they could barely afford. The food wouldn't go down my throat.

My mother would have called the menu vulgar but it pierced me: breaking all rules, they had cooked fish ('From our pond') and egg because they couldn't perhaps stretch to meat. The fish wasn't special and the cooking was workaday, uninspiring. I deduced that Lakshmi and Mamoni were functional cooks. Shame and pity made my eyes prick; I stuffed my mouth with more food; everything was more delicious than I could have imagined.

Raja-da said, 'We brothers went to our village pathshala, we didn't have much education. I was determined to send my boys to school. I want them to have a different life, a better life. This life of a farmer, cultivating rice, growing a few vegetables ... it's a difficult one. We struggle. Our days are not easy. I don't want this for my boys.'

'Your daughter goes to school too?'

'No, we can't ... can't afford it, after sending the two boys. Dulal's education was taken care of by Renu. She loves him more than anything else. More than her own daughter. When Dulal was born, we were dreaming about how we wanted him to grow up and have name, fame and wealth, and Renu said, I am going to take care of his studies, I will work and earn money and put him through school. That's why she went to Bombay. Someone told her that in Bombay they paid cooks lots of money, thousands of rupees. So she said, Dada, I'll go to Bombay and earn money and save and send money home for Dulal's school.'

My hands were shaking. I couldn't keep them steady enough to pick the bones of the fish, to mingle the flesh with the gravy and the rice, form my fingers into a spoon to bring the mixture up to my mouth.

Raja-da continued, 'She earns a lot of money now. She works at a lot of places, four or five or six. Your home, too. Saving has become a habit for her. She has very few needs, she lives very simply, spends very little. She saves everything. And she sends money to Dulal in German country. He got a full scholarship but the plane ticket, the clothes – it was a lot of money.'

He paused, thoughtful now, as if the very memory of that amount was sobering. He brushed it aside and said, 'All that money, Renu provided.'

I had to say something. If I didn't say something, I couldn't trust myself to speak again in the company of my hosts.

'He must have been an exceptional student to go to Heidelberg on a full scholarship,' I said.

'Yes, he is very bright,' Raja-da said. His face was aglow in the dim yellow light of the sooty hurricane lamps. 'He got a scholarship from Ramkrishna Mission to go to IIT in Kharagpur. Then he came first in IIT, got a gold medal. His teachers at IIT said to him, You must go to foreign land to study. All his fees were paid for in IIT, we only had to pay for his food and clothes and hostel and transport. Renu took care of everything.'

A star student at the elite IIT. Something in this broken country worked. I had reached a place of what I could only call wonder. The parakeet, which I thought was dozing, began to shuffle about on its perch. Ratan-da's son got up to feed it whole chillies. The bird made a noise that sounded like a cross between crooning and tsking.

'Didn't she get married? Where are her daughter and husband?' I asked.

From Raja-da's slight stammer when he began to answer my question, and the way his wife and sister-in-law exchanged a glance, then looked down, I got the impression that I had stepped into awkward territory.

'Yes, she got married, but ... but she left with her daughter,' Raja-da said. 'The man ... turned out to be ... n-not good, he drank, gambled, so she left. We brought up the girl, Champa. She was five years younger than Dulal. We married her off last year, she's moved to Muchipara with her husband. Renu always wanted to go to Bombay and find work, I told you. She thought only of Dulal, how she could make the words of the astrologer, who came to see the boy when he was born, how she could make his words come true. The astrologer said, "This boy is going to grow up to make a big name for himself one day." The words scored a deep line in Renu's mind.'

I noticed how the moment the conversation came back to Dulal, the ease and flow returned. I had so many questions about Renu but I could hardly ask any of them now.

At night, under my slightly oily-smelling lumpy duvet, I worried that sore over and over: how much had it cost them, and not just in terms of money, to host me? Was someone going without a duvet, or even a bed, because of me? Who slept in this room? Where were they sleeping tonight? And then more shaming thoughts. The rice had been the cheap, thick-grained, reddish rice of the area. The food had been the paradoxical combination of oily and watery. Were the sheets and pillowcases clean? There was no running water, so they had been washed in the pond, in which they bathed, washed their dishes and did god knows what else. How was I going to use that bathroom? They had no electricity – how unbearable did it get under a tin roof in the summer? The sweets after dinner – there had been three different kinds – had been of bad quality, rancid and stale, from a low-grade sweet shop. Why didn't they serve the sandesh, made from the new season's date molasses, that I had brought as a gift from Girish Ghosh? I felt ashamed but couldn't stop myself from thinking the small, mean thoughts; the mind really was the unruliest and basest of human attributes.

I returned to Calcutta, spent one more day there, went to Bangalore and Kochi to visit friends as part of the research for the book, then returned to Bombay. I had given my mother an indication, in our phone conversations, of what I had learned about Renu in Medinipur, but I hadn't asked Ma any of the questions that were bothering me. Now they came gushing out.

'What I can't understand is this: wouldn't that ne'er-do-well husband have claimed Renu's portion of the land after she did a runner? Or the money that she sent home for Dulal's education? He must have kicked up a fuss,' I asked.

'Difficult to know,' Ma said. 'Maybe the brothers closed ranks against him. Remember, they needed Renu's money, so it was in their interests to fend him off. I wouldn't be surprised if they helped her run away.'

Yes, of course; that hadn't occurred to me.

'That could be the reason why Renu sold off her portion of the land to her brothers. So that her husband couldn't claim it,' Ma said.

'But what about the daughter?'

'If he was a useless drunk, maybe it was a relief to him not to be saddled with the responsibility of looking after a child and providing for her.'

'No, I'm talking about something different. How did Champa take it, being brought up by her uncles, her mother away, sending money for her cousin's education? It must have been obvious to her that her mother preferred Dulal to her.'

'You are forgetting something – she's a girl, she's got no expectations.'

It was true; I couldn't say anything to this. I tried another angle: 'But she is Renu's daughter, while Dulal is her nephew. Isn't blood supposed to be thicker than water and all that?'

Ma made a face, as if to say all things took second place to a talented boy in a family, especially if they were poor. She said, 'Who knows what they worked out between them?'

'And you don't think I could ask Renu to her face?'

Ma whinnied like a panicked horse. 'No, no, I absolutely forbid you,' she said. 'You will go away in a couple of days, it's I who will be left to deal with her every day. I don't want to field any consequences of you and she becoming friendly.'

'But what consequences? What do you mean by friendly? I'm only going to ask her a few questions about her life. She may respond positively to someone taking an interest in her. God knows, the people who have domestic help don't exactly treat them as their equals.'

'Ufff, this "equals" business again. You live abroad, you don't understand the culture here, you shouldn't come trampling in with your fancy notions. There will be difficulty for us to clean up afterwards.'

'You still haven't managed to explain the nature of the difficulty,' I said heatedly.

She replied with equal irritation, 'I have said several times before. It'll only set you off on your word-chopping and equality high horse. We'll be going round in circles.'

With that, she left the room. I was too riled to see her point of view.

When Renu arrived that evening to cook, I thought I discerned a curiosity on her face that made it almost mobile. I also knew she wouldn't say anything in front of my parents; she understood that I had a different, more informal and, yes, friendlier dynamic with her, which was a world apart from how she related to my parents or, indeed, to all the people in whose homes she worked.

A fine tension had descended between my mother and me. I went into the kitchen, drew the sliding door shut and said, 'It was wonderful. They fed me till I was bursting. And such good food. I ate fish from your pond, aubergines and chillies and cauliflower from your vegetable garden. It was all so so delicious. I met your family, your brothers, your sisters-in-law, your nephews and nieces ...' I knew I was babbling but I couldn't seem to stop myself.

Renu continued to acknowledge impassively what I was saying with a curt nod or an 'Achha', but without once looking at my face – she was busy taking stuff out of the fridge. I had the impression that she was either embarrassed by the gush or didn't know what it was and, therefore, what to do with it. Or was I talking so much as a way of preventing her from saying anything that I would have found embarrassing?

'All right, tell me, what are you going to take for dinner?' she asked.

I said, 'I heard about Dulal.'

She looked up sharply.

'Why didn't you tell me about him all this time?' I asked.

She didn't reply – she had gone back to arranging the vegetable drawer in the fridge.

I didn't know what to say after this or, more accurately, what to say to her. Anything would have come out as platitudinous or sentimental or false, but perhaps those things only to my ears and not to hers?

What came out after this internal debate was no less stilted, although I meant every word: 'He studies in one of the best places in the world. I know you're all very proud of him. You should be: he has achieved extraordinary things. I was very happy to hear about him. And very proud, too. And ... and ... you made him.'

She dismissed it with that gesture of hers, that performance of half-joking impatience: 'Arrey, leave all that, tell me, jaldi jaldi, what will you take for dinner?'

I ignored her, reading her words and gesture correctly for once, I thought. 'Do you know what he'll do after he finishes his studying? Will he come back?' I could imagine a successful future for Dulal as a professor in IIT, or at the Tata Institute of Fundamental Research, or even the Bhabha Atomic Research Centre, but being the person I was, I thought he would be better off working at CERN or any number of European or American universities.

'Who knows what he'll do? We've never been able to tell what goes through his head. He says he's going to come back in two years.' Pause. 'Two more years of sending money,' she said, then quickly tried to dispel the burden of the last few words by her usual dismissive tics.

'I said to him: stay as long as it takes to finish what you're doing, you don't need to think of money ... But who listens to me?' The shift in tonal gear this time was to mock-carping, a time-honoured Bengali way of expressing deep affection.

Then, another shift with: 'He says he's going to come back and build me a house. We shall see.' She said it shyly, almost coyly, with a touch of self-deprecation, as if it was his fault for choosing her, of all people, to be a beneficiary of his generosity. But there was a grain of disbelief in there, too: would she be so lucky to have that come to pass, in reality?

'I'm going back home day after tomorrow,' I said.

She turned her face away but not before I saw a dimming on it.

There was a long silence before she said, 'You'll come again when?'

'After a year. Maybe before that. I don't know. Shall I give you your money now?' I left money for her, Milly and the driver after every stay at Ma and Baba's.

She nodded; she had, refreshingly, never been coy about money. I took out two five-hundred-rupee notes and stretched out my hand. She indicated the big tin of puffed rice on top of the fridge and said, 'Leave it under that, I'll take it on my way out.'

She came in the next day, my last evening in Bombay, cooked in total silence except to say to me, while I was giving her my usual instructions, 'You come back home. Nothing doing, all this living far away.'

On her way out, she turned at the threshold to face me, said, 'Travel safe. Dugga dugga' and shut the front door behind her.

I call my mother on a blowy, wet November afternoon. We talk about nothing in particular for a while. I tell her about things from my life in London that she will find interesting. I ask her what they had for dinner, something I always do when I call her at this hour, just as they're about to go to bed. Soup, she says; chicken soup.

'You've taught Renu how to make chicken soup?' I ask. 'That's quite an achievement.'

'Renu doesn't work here any more.'

'What?'

'I had to let her go.'

I can't speak; Ma, it seems, isn't inclined to, either.

'But why? When?' I ask.

'Last month, just before Pujo.'

Contrary to her character, she isn't volunteering any information.

'But why?' I repeat.

'She was behaving very badly with me.'

Silence. I have to wring everything out of her.

'What do you mean, behaving badly?'

'Shouting at me. I've been putting up with it for a good while now. Even the minimal dealing that I have with her, telling her what to cook and, sometimes, how to cook something ... she managed to be hostile and unpleasant even about that.'

'God! This is unbelievable.'

'One Sunday she came in to cook lunch and had some kind of a meltdown, shouting that I had messed up her whole day. Bringing things out of the fridge and setting them down with a clatter, banging the fridge door ... it was quite something. I was speechless.'

'But why?' I'm a damaged vinyl, the pin stuck on a scratch on the surface.

'Who knows? Maybe because I asked her to come a little later than usual? I was really taken aback. And you know what her voice is like ... Your Baba came out of the room and ... and just asked her to leave, said: All right, if this doesn't suit you, leave – leave right now.'

My chest is hammering.

'And?'

'She left. She looked shocked, as if she had been slapped. She hadn't expected what was coming.'

'Then?'

'Then what?'

'What happened after that?'

'Nothing. I rang a few days later to ask her to come collect her outstanding salary, she didn't pick up her phone. I sent a message through Milly . . . apparently she slammed her door shut on Milly's face.'

I can tell Ma is uncomfortable talking about this. How is she reading my silences, I wonder? I can spare her. I shouldn't put her through this. I change the subject with 'Anyway, what's happened has happened, no use thinking about it now' and talk about other things.

But it is she who asks, 'How's the book coming along?'

I can't answer but I must say something, talk. The November late afternoon has darkened and I need to turn the lights on.

III

III

No one knows where it has come from. Some children discover it against the big burunsh tree on the corner of the track that turns behind Sattu's house and leads eventually to the paved road going down to the valley.

– Look, a puppy, someone says.

– No, that's not a dog, it's too big, look at its face, someone else says.

– Look at its paws, another one.

– It's shivering, he says. No, it's too young to walk, it hasn't learned how to walk yet.

They throw stones at it, sticks and pieces of twig, to see what it will do or if it can run off. It shivers and looks at them, then frantically away, left and right and forward, as if searching for an exit. Its confusion tickles the boys – they laugh and jeer and throw more stones at it. It wobbles, runs a few inches, then stops, runs another few inches, stops again and shivers. The boys laugh and laugh.

They pick it up – will it bite? will it scratch? – and take it to Puran's father because he will know what the creature is. It trembles and whines and nearly leaks out of the large, shallow bowl of Puran's enclosed arms.

On the way they see Lakshman returning to the village down the path from Deodham, carrying a load of kindling on his back. The boys have a name, the whole village has a name, for Lakshman and his brother, Ramlal – shyal jyonlya, the fox twins. There is a rumour in the village that their mother, now dead – she died shortly after childbirth – was a witch, or had some kind of unhealthy relations with animals, which is how the brothers had come to resemble pointy-faced foxes.

– What do you have there? Lakshman asks Puran.

– An animal. We don't know what it is.

– Let me look, let me look.

– It's a puppy, he says.

– But it has very big claws, a boy says.

Lakshman notices that they are unlike any puppy's claws that he has ever seen. The nails are huge and curved, like miniature swords, but its face could be a puppy's. Or even a calf's, yet it is smaller than a newborn calf. Then it strikes him – could it be a bear cub? He is so surprised that he thinks it out loud.

The boys are thunderstruck. Bhaloo? they keep saying.

– Where did you find it? In the forest? Lakshman asks. – Here, give it to me, he says, setting down the stack of kindling.

The trembling, blinking creature is slightly larger and weightier than a fat dog. The pelt is dark grey and short, hugging the skin close. The snout is white in a line up to the bottom of the forehead. The animal will simply not stop squealing, despite the calming sounds that Lakshman makes.

A dog with a tail like a pennant comes barking and circles Lakshman, its head held up, its barking turning more and more manic. He knows this dog – her name is Jhumru and she belongs to the people who have built the new guesthouse on their plot, separated from their own home by a section of terraced land. They spend the larger part of the year in Morabadi, where they have another house. He orders the dog to stop barking, but the smell of the bear cub is stronger than a human shout. He takes a stick and threatens her but she retreats only half a dozen paces, barking continuously. Then she follows Lakshman, a few steps behind him.

The boys speed off to herald the approach of something different from the ordinary run of their lives. Minutes later, Lakshman reaches the old baanj that passes as the centre of the village; there are about a dozen people congregated there and more keep coming, once the cub is set down. Two other dogs join Jhumru and the chorus of barking becomes maddening. He has to shoo them away several times, but they position themselves outside the circle of people and continue to bark. Opinions, questions, comments fly about.

– Haan, haan, bhaloo hain. I know it, I saw one like this a few years ago.

– Where did it come from? It's too far up in the hills for these animals.

– Where is its mother? It's too small … do you think she lost it?

One of the children breaks off a little stick from Lakshman's bundle of twigs and prods the cub repeatedly. This gives the other boys an idea and they too make for Lakshman's stack, but he barks and waves them away. The cub mewls for a bit, tries to shift about, then gives up on both.

– Do you think its mother is looking for it? Will she come in the night to get it?

– It sounds like the mewing of a cat. It's a cat, pretending to be a bear, ha ha ha ha …

– How did it survive the night? How come a panther didn't get it?

– We saw it near Suraj's home, just outside it, one of the boys pipes up, hoping this is going to help others answer the big question.

– A bear is a good omen, no? It's a gift from Golu.

– It must be hungry. Give it something to eat.

No one can spare anything for the animal. Someone at last manages to get hold of a dry chapatti, tear it up into little bits and throw it in front of the cub. It doesn't react. This is a trigger for one of the boys to start poking it anew with a stick, while indicating the pieces of bread with the reiterated words – Eat up, eat up. The cub remains where it is, trembling, uninterested in the food being offered.

The woman who had asked about its mother now says – It's too young to eat bread, it doesn't have teeth, it only drinks its mother's milk.

– Mash up the roti with water then, someone suggests.

Once again, this gives the children something to do. A glass of water is found, the fragments of the roti brought together on the ground, and the water poured on it. The boy wielding the stick uses it to prod the bits of bread to mix with the water and turn it into pulp. But the earth has already soaked up the water, so his efforts yield only a muddier version of pieces of chapatti. The prodding of the cub and the mantra of 'Eat up' begin again.

– You are a fool, someone scolds the boy – the mashing needs to be done in a bowl. How can you do it on the earth? You have now wasted a perfectly good roti.

A woman frees herself from the swelling loose ring of spectators, slaps the boy and drags him out of the circle to lead him home. Ramlochan's son collects the soiled remnants of the bread pieces and runs off to mash them in the proper way. More observations are made.

– The bear could be a bad omen. A lost young one, with no sign of its mother … this is not good.

The dogs try to nose their way past the human legs into the clearing in the middle. A kick is delivered to the most persistent one; it runs away, yelping.

– What if the cub brings bad luck on our village?

– How can it bring bad luck? Lakshman asks.

Ramlochan's son comes back and sets down a dented plate in front of the cub. In it is a dark-grey pulp. The cub moves its head away. The boy keeps turning its head to the food, sometimes forcing down its mouth on to the muddy sludge on the plate. The cub lets its snout be held against the plate – it has no option – but it won't eat.

– Let it go, it'll eat when it wants, Lakshman says.

Then there is a breakthrough. Ramlochan says – Some qalandar could have left it behind.

– Qalandar? There are no qalandars in these parts.

– Maybe the animal poachers working for them passed through our village and left a stolen cub behind by mistake.

No one can respond with anything to this possibility, but the mention of qalandars sparks off a chain of ideas in Lakshman's head.

– I could sell him to a qalandar. Where do I find one?

– They don't live in our part of the country. You'll have to travel far to find one. Down in the plains, the towns there.

Someone says – But we have seen them pass through our village, with their dancing bears. I don't remember how long ago. These people are always on the road, that's how they earn money.

– What are you going to do with the bear until we find a qalandar to take him off your hands?

– Where are you going to keep him? What are you going to feed him?

Lakshman's bright plan to make money from the bear has put in the shade the middle stage between now and that future: how would he afford the animal's upkeep when he struggled to feed his wife, Geeta, and his three small children, Sudha, Munni and Ajay, and now his brother's wife and two children, too, since Ramlal had gone to the plains to seek work on building sites. It was Suraj from the village who had planted that idea in the brothers' heads; not that any planting was needed, since a handful of men had already left to find jobs elsewhere, either in nearby towns and villages in the hills or much further down in the big cities of the plains – work as housekeeper, or security guard, driver, cook, and if any of those didn't pan out, there was always a job in construction. So Suraj had said – a job in construction.

– They are always building in the cities. Roads, houses, shops, building work was constant, one after another, it never ran out, never stopped. There was always work to be had, even in the monsoons. Buildings coming up everywhere, in every available space or land, nothing empty for long, the thirst for buildings was unending. So many people, you couldn't count them, they were beyond numbers, they all had to live somewhere.

– Year-round work? Ramlal and Lakshman had asked in wonder.

– All round the year, year after year. So much money to be made that your begging cloth will tear from its weight.

In one month Ramlal was gone.

That was two years ago. In that time, he hadn't returned to visit his wife, Radha, and his children, Jeevan and Meena. He had sent money – two hundred and fifty rupees once, five hundred another time and four hundred another, all three times through someone Suraj knew in a neighbouring village on the other side. Just over a thousand rupees in two years – he might not have bothered to move to the cities if that baby's-piss trickle was all that he had to show for it in two years. And how was Lakshman supposed to feed three additional mouths on five hundred rupees a year?

There are times, especially at nights, when Lakshman's youngest, two-year-old Ajay, and Ramlal's youngest, Meena, born two months before Ajay, start up every couple of hours, unable to sleep with hunger, or pain, or whatever bothers them, and the thin, angry wailing, like the rain during the monsoon that does not let up for days and days, becomes a fist that pummels and pummels Lakshman until he, too, is screaming, his lungs and throat white-hot with the will to stop that fist of noise coming down upon him and flattening him to husk. He screams curses and abuse at Ramlal for saddling him with the yoke of two families and wishes a painful death on him.

His children are indifferent at first – no one knows what a bear is. His oldest, Sudha, asks Lakshman if it's going to become a dog when it grows up. His two other children stare at it for a bit, then get bored – the creature doesn't seem to be doing anything. Ramlal's oldest, Jeevan, a boy of four, desultorily throws whatever he can pick up from the ground – bits of straw, leaves, snippets of twigs – at the squealing cub; most of them don't make it anywhere near.

Lakshman's wife, Geeta, asks in despair – Where will you keep it? There's not enough space for us inside.

As if in response, the cub pisses – a brief dribble, over before anyone can exclaim – and from its arse lets out an equally brief squirt, which lands on the floor and runs. The children laugh in scandalised horror.

Geeta says – Put it in a box and keep it outside. We can get a rope tomorrow to tether it. Without a box, a panther will get it, maybe even a dog.

An empty fruit crate is found. The cub is put inside and three heavy logs placed on it to keep the animal confined. It does not have the necessary strength to push against them from the inside and escape, but Lakshman worries that the logs won't pose much of a challenge to a big dog or a panther intent on getting to it.

– If we raise it, I can go around the towns here, or even to the cities, and make it dance on the streets and get money. There is a lot to be made in the cities, there are many, many people, more than you can count. They will all pay to be entertained. There is no work here in the monsoons and winters.

Geeta is sceptical – How will Radha and I look after the children and the home? How will we feed them?

– I will send you money, and Ramlal will, too. He stops, hearing the wrong note that he's struck, and tries again – I will send you money, I will come back in the summer, it's too hot in the cities then. And at other times as well.

All night he has his ears pricked to catch the sawing, rasping sounds that give away the presence of a panther on the prowl.

In the morning the cub is still in its tiny wooden cage, which reeks of excrement.

A month after this, Salim Qalandar arrives; the local veins of news have worked successfully and fast. It's almost as if he's sniffed out, like an animal on the hunt, the presence of a bear cub in one of the precarious huts perched on the outer rim of a village in the hills.

– Yes, it's a bear cub all right.

Salim's eyes are round with wonder and something else. He has a confident and seasoned way of handling the animal – the way he holds it, lifts it up by the skin of its neck, carries it, stretches it out, all speak of experience and ease. There is a white ruff under the cub's neck. Lakshman thinks it looks as if the animal is wearing a garland.

– It's a boy bear, Salim says – just a few months old. Any other time, we would have paid you good money for him.

He cannot stop touching and stroking and playing with the cub, but with a kind of absence of intent or concentration.

– Why not now? Lakshman asks. He is prepared to let go of his idea of using the bear as a stream of income if he can get ready money for it now. The animal seems to be a godsend, not a bad omen.

– Impossible to do it now, Salim says.

– Why? Lakshman persists.

– They've banned bear-dancing. If they catch you travelling with a bear now, making it dance, like we used to do, our livelihoods were dependent on this, all our community did this, but now if they catch you, they take the bear away and put you in jail for seven years.

Lakshman had not thought of this possibility, so the novelty of it makes it easy for him to treat it as something trivial.

– You give them something, some tea-snack money, and they'll leave you alone, no?

– Yes, we did that for a while, but they have become stricter and stricter. Who knows, someone powerful may be sitting at the top, asking the police and people to catch poor folk like us.

Salim falls silent, ponders a while, then says – They caught my brother, Afzal. He's breathing jail air now. They asked him to hand over his bear and even offered him a job in return.

– What job?

– Some useless shop or the other. Putting spices in little plastic packets and selling them. They offered the same to another man from our village. He went bust in three months – how many people can you sell spices to in a small, poor village to make a living? Who has money there to buy spices in little packets? In three months he made less than half the money he drew in from a good week's bear-dancing. From crowds who gathered to watch his bear dance, who threw money and clapped their hands. But the bear was now gone ... Afzal knew what happened to this man. He said – no, I'll run away with Bilkis (that's his bear), I'll run away with her to a town far away, they'll never find me, he had laughed.

– What happened then?

– Find him they did. They took away Bilkis. Allah alone knows where she is now. They sent Afzal to jail.

A long silence descends.

– He's still there, Salim adds at last.

Lakshman can't find anything to say. He still cannot quite bring himself to believe that someone can go to jail for making bears dance in public. It had been done for ages; he has known about it ever since he was little. Besides, what he cannot understand is why it should be prohibited now. It wasn't robbing, or killing, or stealing. Where was the harm in it? Before he can put the question to Salim, the qalandar has swerved him along a far easier track.

– But if you want to keep him – Salim says – I can do what needs to be done. He will then dance for you for ever.

This is what Lakshman wants to hear, this is what he has been hoping for from the beginning.

– You'll do it? Lakshman's eyes shine. What needs to be done?

– A rope needs to go through his nose. Then some of his teeth must be broken. You have to do them when they're very young, when it is easy to handle them and keep them down. You'll also need a special stick, the one that we qalandars have. But you'll have to pay me to do all this.

– How much? To Lakshman, the actions are of far less moment than their price.

– Five hundred rupees.

Lakshman looks stricken. Where is he going to get that amount of money? He feels oddly irritated: what does this qalandar think, that money falls from trees?

– Where will I get five hundred rupees? Are we emirs or sheikhs?

– How can I work without money? It's hard work I'll be doing, not anybody can do it. Very few people, only qalandars, understand it.

– But I cannot give you so much money, I don't have it.

Salim mutters something under his breath, then goes quiet. The cub seems to be gnawing on his wrist; Salim shakes him off. There is another long silence.

– All right, then – he says at last – you owe me money. I will return to collect it, don't ever forget that.

Relief makes Lakshman rashly generous. He says – All right, come back when you want, after the bear has grown a bit and I've made some money. I will pay you more than two hundred rupees now.

– Remember this, because I will be back. This bear-dancing is our work, Muslim people's work. You are not one of us, you will never prosper in it unless you repay your debt. Do not forget this.

A fire is lit with kindling and, after it catches properly, a log placed on it; Salim wants it to be a deep, slow-burning fire. When it reaches the desired temperature, which Salim seems to be able to gauge with his eye, he inserts one end of a long iron rod in it. He has already cut some thick oak branches into different lengths. There is a piece of rope, generously lubricated with mustard oil. Over the time it has taken to procure most of these things, the people who have given them have come over to see what is going on. They do not know what it takes to make a bear dance; it will be a unique experience. Salim chooses four men, one of them Lakshman, and explains to them what they need to do. Each of the four men wraps a length of cloth – a vest, a sweater, rags – around his hand.

As if impelled by some deep instinct, the cub has scuttled off into its box to hide. Salim reaches a hand in, pulls it out and places it on the open ground, then tethers it with a short length of rope to a sturdy stick planted deep and firmly in the ground.

– Now, he shouts.

The four men turn the cub on its back – it's squealing now, a thick, squeaky noise – and stretch out its four legs, holding down the paws with their wrapped hands so that its claws can't inflict any damage. It moves its head manically, but Salim soon puts a stop to that. He inserts the thickest of the sticks into the cub's open mouth while the two men pinning down the front paws hold down the ends jutting out, effectively fixing the head to the ground. Its mouth looks like an improbably pristine pink hole seeded with small white teeth. The sound that comes out of it now is some kind of a hoarse attempt at a whisper from the throat.

– Don't press down too hard on the stick, Salim shouts – just enough to keep its head from moving.

But it isn't moving any longer, unless the convulsion going through its exposed underside, rippling that white garland and issuing as a staccato hiss, can be counted as movement. The spectacle of a tiny cub and five big men is a mockery of scale and proportion: it's as if a cannon has been deployed to deal with a fly. With four quick but forceful taps using a shorter stick, Salim knocks out the cub's canine teeth. The hiss changes to an odd rasping. The pink streaks with thin ribbons of red. They spill out, mixed with saliva, from the open corners of the mouth. Salim winds a long piece of cloth around his right hand, then removes the iron rod from the fire. He holds it for a while, one end of it glowing red, briefly, before it turns an ashy black, closes his eyes and begins to mutter something, as if he's in a trance. The crowd that rings around this business has fallen into a total hush. The surrounding pines respond in unison to a passing breeze with their own swishing sound. Children form the innermost circle, the children from Lakshman and Ramlal's family, the toddlers on the hips of their mothers, a scattering of boys and girls from the village. Salim opens his eyes – they're unfocused, as if seeing through everything in front of them to something invisible beyond or under things. Even the pines hold their breath now. He lets out a demonic cry and with a short, thrusting movement, which seems bathetic coming after that sound, he drives the hot end of the rod through the area just above the dark grey tip of the cub's nose, pierces it in one go, brings it out, then drives it in again a few centimetres above that point, punching a hole through the bone.

The wail of a child punctures the hush with unexpected force. The cub cannot writhe or move – it is pinned into place at every point where movement can occur. Lakshman feels the tug from the sheer need to move express itself as tiny jerks in the joints of the leg that he's holding down; a cyclone manifesting itself as a breath of air. The red-pink open mouth, leaking liquid, would look as if a moment of utter, grinning glee has been frozen in time, had it not been for the unearthly squeal, dotted with a gurgling rasp, emerging from it. Then a smell alerts Lakshman – he notices that the cub is shitting, and dribbling a few drops of piss, not enough to wet the ground under him.

– Keep holding him down, but not too much force, remember, Salim orders.

He fetches the length of rope, now generously dripping mustard oil, and begins to insert it through the hole he has pierced above the cub's nose. The heat has cauterised the wound, so there's no blood, but there is the faintest whiff of burnt flesh. Lakshman looks into the bear's eyes, inches below his own face; they alternate between squinting, squeezing shut and opening wide. The pupils swim madly, left and right. A bead of sweat drops from Lakshman's forehead on to the animal's shoulder. Salim's deftness seems to have left him, as he has trouble threading the rope through the piercing. He fails once, twice, three times, shouts curses, then manages to do it at the fourth go. The sound that comes out of the cub – something Lakshman has never heard before – becomes weaker, as if the creature is running out of energy. Salim draws the end of the rope that has emerged from the hole and pulls it for a bit from the other side until both ends are more or less equal.

– The pain, Lakshman begins, but the words don't come out. He clears his throat and rephrases what he had in mind to ask Salim – He'll be all right, no? Soon?

Salim smiles. It is tinged with contempt, or certainly superiority.

– They are animals, their pain doesn't last. All these animals that live in the wild, in the forest, on the streets, you've never known them to need a doctor, have you? He laughs at his own witticism, a dry, hollow, foolish sound, and continues – They heal quickly, they're strong. It's we, humans, who are weak. He'll be all right in a few days. Don't let anyone go near him for a while. Keep him in that box and only you look after him, no one else.

Then Salim warns the men that he's about to remove the stick from the cub's mouth; the men should withdraw their hands off its paws simultaneously and move away.

A curious thing happens after it is released – it immediately retracts its legs from the stretched into a more natural angled configuration, but remains on its back, blinking, those eyes swivelling.

The crowd stirs into life.

– It'll run away now. Don't let it escape. Stand close.

– Don't go near it, it'll bite, stay away.

– Arrey, why isn't it getting up? Is it dead or what?

– No, how can it be dead, its legs are moving, see?

– When will it dance? Will it dance as soon as it gets up?

And get up the bear does, after what seems a long time, after some of the people are beginning to give it up as dead: it turns on one side first, then on the other, then lies on that side for a moment or two before standing. It falls immediately. A sound of amusement goes through the spectators in a weak ripple. It stands up again, the rope through its nose trailing on the ground like a giant noose. It wobbles and falls again.

– It's trying to dance, someone in the crowd says – but hasn't learned it properly yet.

– No, no, it's got to be trained to do that. The qalandar will teach it.

The squealing has now changed to an odd whimper. Its jaws remain open, like a panting dog's.

– Now you give it a name, Salim says to Lakshman. It's your bear for life.

– Raju, Lakshman says. His name is Raju.

Salim takes Lakshman through what he needs to do over the next few days – the fitting of the band that will sit above the nose, how to connect the mouth guard to the leash, the necessary information about feeding and where to keep him, and how to make the special stick that Lakshman could tie to the leash in order both to lead him and to prevent the bear from turning on Lakshman and attacking him, although this was extremely unlikely because Raju would now acknowledge Lakshman as his master and lord and do anything that he bid.

– Can't you give me that stick, that special stick you use? Lakshman asks.

– How can I get one here? I could find one in my village, Salim answers. Besides, you owe me money.

Before leaving, Salim reminds Lakshman – Don't forget, the bear is the lord of the underworld. The idolators and kafirs worship him because they say he has powers.

With that he is gone.

At night, Lakshman dreams of jaws, with pine trees growing inside, trying to grind him. From there the dream slides elsewhere but when he wakes up, to the sound of a wailing child, he cannot remember it. The taste in his mouth is metallic. Could he have been dreaming of his brother again? The weight of the grinding seems to be on his chest, on his entire body now, as if a huge invisible stone is bearing down upon him with the slow movement of a pestle. He pushes against air and goes out of the room into the open. He navigates in the pitch-dark by familiarity, then pisses against a tree, legs wide apart so that the stream doesn't touch his feet on its run back. The sound of the warm jet perforating a hole in the soil is disproportionately loud. By the time he finishes, his eyes are becoming dark-adapted. In the faint starlight, he can see Raju in the vegetable patch at the back, tethered to a baanj, as a darker lump of the night.

Lakshman stands there, waiting for his peering eyes to become more attuned to the dark. The lump shifts. He hears something between a snuffle and a snort. He has positioned himself in such a way that even if Raju advances, the shortness of the rope with which he is tied will ensure that there is significant distance between him and the animal, but Raju makes no movement towards him. Lakshman stands and waits, he does not know what for. He wishes he could see clearly what Raju is doing, how he is observing Lakshman. He stands there for a long time, at the end of which he is still unable to establish if Raju has been looking at him in the dark. Then he goes inside. The weight settles back on him again.

Lakshman comes in one day to discover Geeta cooking egg-and-potato curry for dinner. The children get one egg each, Lakshman only potatoes and gravy.

– Arrey, where's my egg? he asks.

Geeta is silent.

– You didn't hear me? Where's my egg?

The pared-down reply – Only for the children – comes in a manner that makes it obvious to Lakshman that she is hiding something.

He asks again. The same reply is returned but this time impatiently, with some heat. Lakshman feels an old, familiar roiling start up in him, but it must get rid of the surface confusion before it can get going fully.

– Why didn't you buy eggs for me?

Silence.

– You want me to force the answer out of you?

– Didi gave me eggs for the children.

It takes Lakshman a while to work out that she is referring to her employer, the woman whose husband's house, the big new one with the terraced garden, past the old bungalow by the hedges near the turning for the road up, Geeta goes to clean every day. City people, rich, holiday home in the hills.

– How come? Lakshman's confusion has been swept away.

– Her wish.

– She thinks I don't give enough to my children to eat? She thinks we're beggars?

Geeta, who has sensed from the beginning the approaching combustion of the very air around them, remains silent; any words would be fuel.

– Why are you so quiet? Did *you* go begging? Did you go and say – here he mimics her voice – Didi, Didi, the children are hungry, the children don't have enough to eat?

The children have become still as stones. Their plates are polished clean. Geeta steels herself against what's coming and sends up a quick, desperate, silent prayer.

Lakshman is trembling. His eyes have gone small. The mimicry continues – Didi, I'm begging, begging you for my children's food, they haven't eaten for three days, Didi, save us. The palm of his right hand, fingers curved inwards to imitate a beggar's gesture, suddenly stretches open as he leans forward, thought-fast, and slaps Geeta full on the face. She utters a short cry and topples over from her sitting position. No amount of experience in reading the signals – the small eyes, the silent crackle in the air, the subtle tremor in his hands and voice – has ever prepared her for the first blow. The girl, Sudha, starts whimpering. Lakshman turns to her, she cowers, he barks out – Shut your mouth or you'll be next.

Just as suddenly the rage leaves him; maybe it's Sudha's crying, or Geeta's prayer. He says to his wife – If I catch you bringing in food, or anything those people give you, I'll break your face. Understood?

Silence.

– Understood? he roars.

Geeta walks out.

Raju attempts to chew the wood of the fruit crate, which he has now outgrown. Children and adults no longer congregate outside Lakshman's back garden to throw stones and prod Raju into dancing. His novelty value has almost dissipated and the long, fruitless wait to be entertained has edged into boredom.

– When? the children ask.

– Soon, Lakshman answers. He does not know himself; the qalandar, Salim, who knew all the secrets, didn't tell him. Does he need to train the bear? How? By dancing in front of him and waiting for him to imitate? By getting hold of a damru and playing it to him? He does not know, and at times this fills him with panic. Is he saddled with a useless pet? Instead of bringing in money, will it be a steady and continuing drain on what little he earns? Another mouth to feed?

Just before the onset of the rainy season, he builds Raju a make-shift shed of wood and corrugated tin – stolen from the next village – with plastic placed on the roof under bricks and stones. His family huddles inside their two rooms, sometimes for days on end. The vegetable patch is washed away; in its place, there is an irregular rectangle of mud and puddles the colour of milky tea from which they have to salvage the junal, which they grill on coals and eat every day. The insects are so numerous in the mandua flour that Geeta is defeated by the business of sieving and picking them out. Mould spores everything that can be eaten, and objects and surfaces and damp clothes, too. The dense vegetation cladding the surrounding hills manages to look not green, but one with the grey of the skies.

Hearing a crash one night, Lakshman is aroused from his thin sleep. His first thought is that Raju has been attacked by a marauding panther. He goes with a torch and in the weak, faltering light cast by fading batteries he can make out Raju standing on his hind legs and the roof collapsed on to the mud. Rain falls on the tin and plastic, making a sound slightly different from the noise of the monsoon on the shed when it was standing.

In the morning Lakshman discovers that Raju has chewed the upright pieces of the thin, long wooden sticks that had held up the tin roof to his shed; the wood is in splintered little pieces not far from where the four pillars had stood before. Raju's wet pelt is covered generously in mud.

They leave him out in the rain for days until his battery of grunts and yowls drives a hot knife through Lakshman one night and he comes out with his thin guide stick, which he has fashioned as best as he could, following Salim's description and guidelines, and brings it down on Raju's flank and head and face and sides wherever he can, and on the tree trunk too, for he cannot see to aim in the dark. Raju cannot run or hide because he is chained to the tree with the rope that is only four feet long, so he lets out a run of cries that span the spectrum from roaring grunt to high-pitched shrieking without any punctuation, one modulating into another seamlessly. The noise wakes up everyone and the children begin to cry. Geeta runs out and shouts – Stop now! Stop! He'll keep making that hellish noise unless you stop. She takes the stick from his fevered hand and flings it into the dark.

In the grey, drenched light of the following morning, Lakshman comes out to find Raju cowering and whimpering at the sight of him. But Lakshman hasn't forgotten or forgiven yesterday, so Raju goes without food. The cub whimpers all day, digs up the earth around him while emitting that sound between grunting and snuffling that Lakshman is becoming familiar with, then continues with the whimpering. Lakshman comes out, bent on teaching him a few rules: the beginning of his training. He shouts out the 'Shhh' so forcefully that it ends in him spitting. Raju goes quiet. Encouraged, Lakshman raps out – Stop that din. Stop. Raju blinks, looks down, then away. Lakshman feels a stirring of joy inside him. It is stubbed out the moment he goes inside and hears Raju begin his whining again. He comes out and repeats the shushing and shouting. Raju obliges by falling silent for the duration of Lakshman's presence. Today, I have won, Lakshman thinks.

Geeta says – He'll keep up this racket unless you feed him. He's crying from hunger.

– No, don't feed him. He'll get food only when he stops the noise. He needs to learn this lesson now.

– He won't stop, I'm telling you.

The lid, that familiar, grinding weight, descends early now, when he is awake and alert, watching his children and his nephew and niece and his wife and sister-in-law. He cannot bring himself to focus on any one thing for long – it's as if his attention, something inside him, is bent on wandering and will not, cannot, be moored.

Geeta reads the slackness and goes out to throw some cucumber and ragi rotis to Raju. Loud slurping-snuffling noises, like an army of animals at a trough, over in seconds. Then silence that lasts and lasts. Everyone inside is holding his or her breath, including the two toddlers, Ajay and Meena. Lakshman refuses to look at Geeta's face. Later in the night, with the sound of the rain dotted occasionally by a whimper or a guttural croak, an image comes to Lakshman, an image that helps him hold off the weight falling on him again. It is the recent memory of witnessing Raju standing on his hind legs. He holds on to it as sleep takes him.

Their walks have been troubled from the very beginning. First, the gaggle of children following them, stubborn, mischievous and disobedient, refusing to disperse despite his repeated threats. Instead of disappearing, they let a slightly greater distance open up between them. Lakshman and Raju walk ahead. The children stop throwing stones and twigs and whatever missiles they can aim at the bear. Sometimes there are monkeys overhead, leaping from branch to branch, tree to tree, following them, but from a height. The most persistent problem is the dogs and their unstoppable barking. At times Lakshman has to turn back and threaten the dogs with the stick, or bend down to pick a stone and hurl it at the pack. Still they continue, if hesitatingly.

It is for Raju that Lakshman is anxious. Raju had seemed afraid of the dogs and halting in his progress, but after the first few excursions, the bear appears more or less indifferent to the volleys of barks and the presence of other animals. As they move deeper into the forest, the dogs fall off, one by one. The ground is thick with pine needles. There is no undergrowth, only the occasional pine cone, and fallen branches, covered with lichen and moss. Raju strains at the leash towards a cone or two; Lakshman obliges by leading him to them. That awkward, lolloping gait, as if Raju is moving forward clunkily while simultaneously swaying from side to side, interests Lakshman – is this because he is young and will learn to walk properly when he grows up, or do all adult bears move similarly?

And then it happens, by accident, and takes Lakshman by such surprise that he is left wondering what caused it. On a steep slope along a track, on the other side of which a small house is falling to ruins and its orchard and trees running wild, the sizeable patch of land surrounded by slack barbed wire and up for sale, Raju lets out a whimper, stands fully erect on his hind legs and does a brief trot before resuming his original position on all fours. Lakshman lets the rope go slack and finds himself speaking to Raju – How did that happen, huh? Do it again. Go on. Stand on your legs and dance.

Raju sniffs the ground.

– Come on, do it again.

Raju gives no sign that he has heard. In his impatience, Lakshman tugs at the rope going through the bear's nose. Raju squeals, jumps up and hops about. Lakshman lets out a whoop of joy and pulls unthinkingly at the rope again. This time Raju emits a yowl, while springing up and prancing again. Revelation floods Lakshman – so it's the rope. He feels the joy as a hollowing-out of his insides; such a lightness. He lets out another shout, pulls the rope again, this time to test the new knowledge, and when

Raju reacts, the cry of – Shabaash! comes out almost involuntarily from his mouth.

After he gives a demonstration back home, the children want to have a go at making the bear dance. Word spreads swifter than the rain falls. Soon there is a crowd and Lakshman half-teases (but only half) – I should be charging you for this. The rope is pulled numberless times; Raju can barely recover from one tug before another unseats him. Someone has brought Lakshman a damru so that he can shake it to produce the traditional percussion rattle that accompanies animal shows, a rhythm to which the animal dances. Lakshman tries his hand at it and pulls Raju's nose-rope. The animal stands up and executes a dragging-hopping movement on his two hind legs, squealing, his head held up, his mouth open. Lakshman attempts to synchronise the hitting of the bead against the hand-held drum's skin to Raju's movements, but each time the animal cannot sustain the dance after a few steps, maybe eight or nine, and goes back to all fours. Some of the children mimic dance moves when Lakshman starts on the damru. A few of them, the adamant and intrepid ones, get very close to Raju and poke him, or kick him, and run away to a safe distance to see if he will react and get up to dance again.

Lakshman's order – Dance! Dance! – sometimes modulates to pleading, in desperation, then switches back to angry shouts again. His face turns hot, he feels he has been humiliated in front of all these people who know him, even children. There is a white flash behind his eyes, that familiar friend, and for a few seconds he sits still. Then he drags Raju to his station, tethers him to the tree, makes sure that the knot is secure and brings down the thin stick on to Raju's back in one swishing movement that cuts the air. Raju flinches and squeals and tries to hide behind the tree but he is exposed on all sides. This attempt at self-protection liberates Lakshman – held now in the blindness of that white flash, he beats

Raju with unstoppable energy, with infinite and perpetual motion, the stick becoming the engine that drives his hand, the soul animating his body, bringing itself down like a malignant rainfall on the flanks, back, mouth, muzzle, face, legs, head of the animal, wherever it can land and strike, and Raju squeals and whimpers and growls and shrieks, a demented singer possessed by spirits, and then rewards Lakshman many times over by rearing up and hopping and prancing on his two hind legs, clutching the tree trunk with his forepaws as if it were a dancing partner and Raju were a singing and dancing actor out of a film and he, Lakshman, the director and music-director and dance-director all rolled into one. And Lakshman laughs and laughs and laughs until the stick drops from his hand and, with his sweaty palms, he is wiping his snot and tears and drool and trying to stop the sobs that come out of the stranger that he has become.

There is absolute silence from outside at night as Lakshman lies awake, his chest alive with a threshing, and heavy at the same time. No snuffling or rooting or gurgling sounds, not even the sound of loud breathing. In the morning he comes out to give Raju his food. The bear starts a kind of staccato mewling before Lakshman hoves into view and, at the sight of the man, cowers and tries to hide behind the tree trunk. Lakshman cannot bring himself to start the process of befriending – a terrible lassitude grips him. He flings the rotis towards Raju and goes inside. When sleep arrives, it comes smuggling a weapon – those dreams of fire, again.

It happened when Ramlal and Lakshman were little, both just old enough to have begun school. The Forest Department, which owned all the land that was not private – the land on the hillsides, the forests of baanj and chir, the valleys and ridges and banks – had invited applications from locals to tap the natural resources: collecting oil from pine-sap, honey from beehives, cultivating bamboo.

Their father had put in an application and, much later Lakshman found out, when he was an adult, also a little something in the right hands to expedite the process. And he had been successful. The news had spread immediately.

A day or two after this, Lakshman and Ramlal had woken up to the sound of commotion and an orange glow outside. The forest was on fire and their father was missing. Of that night, Lakshman remembered odd things: the breathing, whispering sound the fire made as it spread, so much more soothing than the punctuation of crackling and popping wood; the rhythmic, lulling creak of the high branches, then the whoosh and thump and pop of them giving in to the fire in a spray of sparks; the smell of pine and burnt wood; the sound of birds, confused, fleeing, so odd in the dead of the night ... Hypnotised by it all, still caught in the net of sleep, he didn't think about their father until he had picked up on the talk of the villagers gathered to witness the spectacle. Apparently, their father had rushed into the heart of the burning wood, trying to extinguish the fire, trying to save the area that had been allotted to him by the Forest Department, the portion set on fire by a jealous, malicious neighbour who had also bid for the same contract but had not been successful. But maybe all the explanation and piecing together had come later, when the boys had been told that their father's body could not be found because there was no body, only a length of black something, part ash, part charred matter that could have been a tree trunk. Had they seen that thing or had Lakshman imagined seeing it?

And, then, the new term attached to 'the fox twins' – bin mai babok – whereas previously they had been only chhor mulya, motherless. He remembered how a wealthy man, a raees admi's car had passed by some of them sitting on the low stone wall outside the school, and the car window had rolled down and the man's son, no older than he and Ramlal and the other boys hanging around aimlessly outside, had reached out his hand and given them tangerines, presumably at the urging of his father beside him. Not a single word had been exchanged. The car window had gone up soundlessly as soon as the boys had taken the fruits, and the vehicle had moved on as silently. While they had sat, peeling and eating the fruits, someone among them – he forgets who now – had pointed out the little segments of a tangerine that nestle among the larger, regular ones, and said that the little cloves, chhora, were for motherless boys: they had secretly been put into the fruit by their dead mother's soul for her children. The boy had given his anomalous segments to Lakshman and Ramlal.

The bear's pelt grows long as the days get crisper and shorter and nightfall arrives more quickly. Lakshman builds Raju another shed with wood and salvaged tin and even a scrap of tarpaulin, which he installs over the tin roof and secures with large rocks and bricks positioned so that they don't get dislodged in high wind or heavy snowfall. The tree to which Raju remains chained is inches away from the entrance to the shed. The eldest boy, Jeevan, his nephew, comes back from school and says that bears live in caves, that's what they were told by the teacher.

– See, I've built him a cave, Lakshman says to Jeevan, forcing himself to smile. He has always felt that he doesn't know how to talk to children, not even his own; not just what to say to them, but what tone to use, what manner, what kind of voice. The feeling has increased lately and it sometimes changes form to become that familiar lid again, a shutting-out of light and air.

– See, doesn't it look like a cave? Lakshman asks, baring his teeth.

The boy turns his face away.

Geeta grumbles that they will now have to find money to pay someone to come every day to clear the bear's shit from the shed.

– How was the shit better, lying outside, near the tree? Lakshman asks.

One day, before the weather turns really cold, Lakshman sees Jeevan feeding Raju by holding a roti high enough against the tree trunk so that the bear has to stand up to get it. This Raju does. Then Jeevan moves the second roti around the trunk, making Raju move on his hind legs to get it.

The following day, Lakshman takes Raju out to the woods, ties him to a tree and moves himself away a distance of eight or ten feet. Facing Raju, he goes down on all fours in an attempt to imitate the animal. From that position, balancing on one hand, he starts playing his damru with the other. At the first few beats, he gets up and does a little, hopping walk, then goes down on his palms and knees and stops playing the little drum. He keeps saying to Raju – You saw that? Now you do it. Go on, you do it, I'll show you again – and repeating the short suite of actions over and over. Raju blinks, yawns, scratches the trunk of the tree, circles it once, twice, sits down, sniffs the ground, looks towards Lakshman without betraying any signs of seeing him, lets out a series of different sounds, including a huff-puff one, but does not imitate him. Lakshman moves slightly closer and does his routine all over again. Raju watches him, impassive, blinking frequently, then walks back slightly as if to re-establish the original optimal distance between them. Lakshman grits his teeth; his mantra to Raju now comes out less gently coaxing, more impatient, more commanding. The second time Raju moves away – this time it seems that he wants to bring the tree between them – Lakshman takes it as a slap to his face.

– I'll teach you, sisterfucker, he spits out and lashes Raju with the stick. – You will learn, you will learn, he shouts, then, seeing Raju leap up and try to scurry away upright, in so far as forty-eight inches of rope could allow him to, even trying to hide behind the tree, Lakshman exclaims – See, sala, see! You can do it, you're just being difficult. What do you take me for? Soft in the head, haan? I'll teach you – and keeps hitting Raju. The bear whimpers and shrieks, tries to bite the stick, catch hold of it with his paws, but Lakshman is too quick – there's a fiend in him. The stick catches the bear's face twice, three times. Raju howls and tries to charge at him, upright, front paws held up, mouth a-snarl, a white thread of spit flying out from one corner, but is pulled back almost immediately by the limited length of the rope. Lakshman howls, too; with laughter.

After what he considers to be a period substantial enough for Raju to have forgotten the previous training session, Lakshman tries a different tack. He attaches a carrot to a long piece of thin coir rope and fills his pockets with several more carrots. He picks a different spot this time, far from the earlier location – a large tract of land, bounded by a low stone wall, with rusting spiked wire strung out here and there to mark it out as private, designated for some future use, probably a large house and gardens around and behind it. It has an orchard – the peach, apricot and apple trees all look dead, but they can be rejuvenated – and it is this phalanx of dormant trees that he has in mind for today.

He tethers Raju to a pear tree. To his great relief, Raju doesn't baulk at it. He ties the free end of the coir rope to his qalandar's stick, hiding the carrot end from Raju. The bear looks mournfully at the base of the tree. Lakshman plays the damru, slowly, hesitantly; an alertness comes upon the bear; he makes a brief whining noise. Lakshman moves back and aims the tied carrot to a point more or less four feet in front of Raju. The bear moves forward immediately, Lakshman pulls the carrot just out of his reach, Raju rears up on his hind legs. Wiggling the vegetable on the ground but still keeping it out of bounds, just so, stepping up the beat on the damru, Lakshman watches Raju strain at his leash, jig where he stands, walk around the tree to approach the carrot from another side, all the while erect; Lakshman is flooded with hope. He baits Raju a little bit longer, letting his own chatter fall in with the rhythm of the beats from the damru. At last he allows the bear his reward. Raju, ravenous, does not bother to sit down to eat it from the ground, but instead grabs hold of it and puts it in his mouth while still standing. Lakshman nearly leaps with joy. No sooner has he done that than a seed of doubt plants itself in his head: does this limited success mean that Raju is going to become habituated to dancing only when a carrot or something edible is dangled in front of him? That would make the actual street performances ridiculous. Who cannot make an animal dance by starving it a little first, then tempting it with food?

Lakshman repeats the first act but this time without the carrot. Raju works out soon enough that there's nothing in it for him, so he stands for a little while, ultimately settling down on all fours and returning to the vacant blinking and yawning. The hope leaches out of Lakshman. He waggles the rope a little bit more, even play-whips Raju with it half-heartedly, but faced with all the different combinations and exclusions – damru and carrot and chatter but no stick; or perhaps damru and chatter and carrot but the last only as something shown, not given; or maybe damru and chatter and stick but no carrot at all; or carrot right at the end of the day, not during training – Lakshman's mind reels. Deflated, he pauses the training. The same frustrated anger against the dumb, stupid beast begins to grip him again. He tames it in the only way he knows: he unties the coir rope and uses the stick to beat Raju into understanding what it is that he's trying to make him do. A monkey, which has been watching the entire proceedings from its perch on a tree, perhaps in the hope of stealing the carrot, lets out a chatter and runs away, leaping from the high branches of one tree to another.

Something behind the house catches Lakshman's eye, he doesn't know what, but it creates a moment's tense haze for him and lifts as swiftly. He walks back a few steps, scouring the ground with his eyes, trying to pin down what it is. It keeps eluding him, even though some sense tells him that it's staring him in the face. Stones of ber fruit, scrunched-up plastic, vegetable peelings, crumpled paper, grass, earth ... then he has it. Eggshells. Small white fragments of eggshells. There's a large piece with the curvature of either the top or the bottom end intact. He stands very still for a while, the next moment almost felled by the swell of pity that buffets him: pity for his children, who need the eggs, who perhaps look forward to the days when an egg might appear, and pity for Geeta, for persisting stealthily in defying him. The thought of her defiance disperses the sympathy as if it was so much dust held out on a palm to the wind.

Over the next few days he watches, silently and secretly. He goes out, bides his time somewhere out of sight until Geeta goes out to clean, then returns home to hunt for hidden eggs. He wants to know if Radha is in on the plan, but decides it will be unwise to confront her – it will be so much more effective if Geeta doesn't get wind of his strategy and is caught red-handed. For the same reason, he doesn't ask any of the children a straightforward question. She must be boiling the eggs and giving them to the children to take to school. But when does she do it?

He waits by the hedges next to the old bungalow, waiting for her to finish the day's job and come out. He does not reveal himself. He crouches behind a hedge as she passes by, counts to twenty, then peeps out. She is carrying a plastic bag. He lets her walk towards their house until he is certain that she is no more than a few paces from their front door. He sprints like a man possessed and enters his home before Geeta has had a chance to hide the plastic bag. She looks as if she has seen a ghost; her face goes slack and bloodless.

– Give me that bag, he pants.

She doesn't – cannot – move.

– Give me that bag, he thunders.

He snatches it out of her hands. Inside, there are four white eggs, one of them just broken from the force with which he has taken the bag. There are some stale chapattis in it, too, and a small plastic tub of leftover rice and another one of some sabzi, probably cabbage; crumbs from the rich people's table.

Geeta tries to run into the kitchen, in a foredoomed, pitiable attempt to get away; a mistake. He holds one of her wrists and, with his free hand, takes out an egg and smashes it against her face. He takes out the second egg, she turns her face away, he catches hold of her hair and twists her head to face his. He smashes the second egg on her nose with so much force that he can see a thin trickle of blood coming out of her nostrils, under the slimy drip of the transparent albumen and the opaque yellow splatter of the yolk. The tears and the twisted mouth add to the ugly mess that is her face.

Her wailing brings out Radha, who shouts – Stop it! Stop it now! Don't you have any shame?

Her relational seniority to Lakshman insulates her from being in any danger of receiving similar treatment, but this doesn't prevent him from threatening – If you don't stop screeching, it's going to be you next.

– How dare you? she retorts – Don't you have any shame?

Lakshman effortlessly modulates from rage to acid contempt. He says – What will you do? Complain to your absent husband? He fled the coop a long time ago, leaving me to deal with this zoo.

Radha has no answer. Geeta, too, has stopped her loud crying. His mention of Ramlal, however, has the effect of turning Lakshman's anger to ashes. A bitterness fills him, and a desolation. He has to force himself to complete what he has begun, but his heart is no longer in it. He says to Geeta – If this happens again ... He doesn't have the energy to finish it. He goes out to wash his hands of eggs and the disgusting smell.

By the time spring is giving way to summer, Raju has mastered a sustained dance to the playing of the damru. Lakshman had already worked out that all he has to do is pull on the rope through Raju's nose to make him leap up instantly and prance about as if red ants were biting his arse, but the trick has been to make him learn to hold that for five, ten, twelve minutes.

He waits for the big festival of Golu. There is bunting strung out here and there, and three different amplifiers, positioned in different parts of the village, blare out Hindi film songs throughout the day and evening. At night, the mountains seem to distort the sound in such a way that it's here one minute, gone the next, only to reappear from an unexpected direction, as if the sound had been torn into tiny paper fragments and scattered from the sky and dispersed helter-skelter by the breeze.

He feels lucky to have an unobstructed view of the high point of the worship – the sacrifice of fifty-three goats. He has waited outside the temple overnight to secure this prize position. The crowd is so vast that had he left it until morning, he would have been no nearer than the arches leading to the front courtyard of the temple. The saffron, yellow and orange of the low pillared structure and the sea of marigolds wherever he looks – marigolds in garlands and festoons and baskets and strewn about everywhere around the temple – meld into a blinding sun. All of life is here, with all its noise and colours and suffocation. Lakshman has a fractional view of the enclosure behind the temple in which the goats are penned. A whole field of black goats, a sea of goats, like the sea of people around him. He can smell them from here. The animals look docile, resigned, as if they have sensed what's coming. They have bright vermilion marks smeared on their foreheads, between their eyes, and marigold flowers around their necks or horns. Golu is almost hidden from his view, behind columns and the press of human bodies and heads in front of him. He can catch the occasional flash of the god's enormous white turban, or a segment of his white, squat body on the white horse, if there is a chink in the wall of people in his line of vision, or if he leans his head at a difficult angle, but there is no space to do even that.

A man leads the first goat, the biggest, fattest of the lot, reared for twenty-one days only on the fruit of the baanj and glossy jackfruit leaves, to the forked iron peg that has been permanently staked into the front courtyard, directly in front of the small, orange-framed door to the sanctum. What a blessing to be the first animal to be sacrificed, and what blessings will accrue to the young man who has been selected to bring the animals to the point where they will give up their life for Golu. Lakshman has long coveted this post, believing that such a service every year will make the god smile on him and remove all the giant boulders that sit in the middle of his life, obstructing its free flow. But, as in everything else, he has been unlucky. One chance at something, anything, just one chance – is that too much to ask? There is no getting away from Fate, but there is also no way of telling whether the story of his life is bound to continue in the same groove that it has run so far. What if there is a change? Is the god reading his thoughts?

The fattened goat, its head down, comes obligingly almost up to the peg, then seems to understand something and wants to turn back. Lakshman can tell this, because the man has to drag it for the last few feet. The drums are loud in the foreground, and the manically ringing bells, hundreds and hundreds of them, strung out on the red arches that mark the long approach to the front courtyard and on the red-painted wooden beams at the edge where the roof meets the columns, some rung by devotees and worshippers, other, lighter ones set off by the brisk breeze, mingle with the purohit's mantras, the shouts from the gathering, 'Jai, Golu Devta ki jai', the smoke from the incense, and Lakshman finds himself at once a part of this ocean and removed far from it, weightless, tiny, watching from above. When the feeling of suspension takes hold, there is a faint tingling in his fingers, accompanied by the sensation of every limb becoming thin and long like sticks and his head ballooning to a huge bubble while losing every weight it has, every mooring. He has to touch something, the shoulder or arm of the person nearest him, and clench and unclench his fists in order to remind himself of his tethered corporeality. Then he is back in the ocean again until the weightlessness tolls back and untethers him.

The man pushes the goat's neck in the space between the two tines of the peg. The animal has stopped thrashing. It doesn't even kick back with its hind legs. That perfect balance of absolute contraries again: in the thickness of the chanting, the drums, the bells, a stilled heart of hush. Waiting at the iron fork is the man from the Nath sect who will bring his sharpened khukri down on the goat's neck and sever it. The purohit is in a trance of chanting. The worshippers hold their breath – the blow has to decapitate in one stroke, otherwise thirteen years of bad luck will be sent down by Golu upon the village. The drums are now the aggregated percussion of the heart of every human gathered.

The khukri comes down in such a swift arc that there is no process, only the before and the after. The goat's head is not severed in one clean cut but hangs at the neck, making it look like a toy animal that a clumsy child has broken during play. The spurting jet of blood, the purohit's shout and the devotees' collective exclamation of horror are all one in Lakshman's senses. The man who had led the animal now brings the hind legs of the thrashing torso together, then the front legs, gathers it up as if it were an old mattress, hugs it to his own body and carries it out, his face and clothes sprinkled with blood. Lakshman sees his retreating back, as if he is fleeing a scene of crime, and the uncut head dangling from the crook of his arm like a dainty handbag picked up as an afterthought to the main spoils. A trail of shiny blood follows him.

The man with the khukri has turned to stone, his weapon down, its blade almost black with the fresh blood, and a small colony of dark spots directly under it on the green-and-white tiled area on which he stands. A group of people on Lakshman's right tries to move, jostling each other, and in the temporary space allowing some freedom of movement, he shifts, too, and catches a glimpse of Golu's marble-white face and full lips the colour of kaafal. The god's face, pleasant in its huge-eyed expressionlessness, is marked by something – Lakshman cannot tell what exactly – that makes him look offended. Then Lakshman is jostled too and he has to move with the segment of the crowd that he is in. The flash of vision is gone.

The restless people are stilled as the young man leads another black goat to its slaying spot. This time the animal is refractory, straining to turn back, trying to dig its hooves into the unyielding tiles. It lets out a single bleat, then stops, as if realising that no amount of crying will save it. The sound conveys something to the other goats in the waiting area and is echoed by creatures that have remained strangely silent. But here, too, the responsive bleats are half-hearted, resigned, and after a dozen wavering and low 'meeh-eh-eh-eeh', the restiveness is extinguished. What survives, at least for Lakshman, is the much sharper presence of their suf-focating odour.

The second goat is dispatched in one go, and the third, and the fourth ... A new smell begins to assert its metallic note, mild, almost evanescent compared with the cloud of goat-odour, but present nevertheless. Lakshman knows that this is the smell of blood. Years ago, when he was a boy, Ramlal had seen his twin's eyes water at the overpowering stench at this annual sacrifice for Golu Devta and had explained the different smells to him.

The lopped heads are quickly taken away and arranged in a cir-cle at the feet of the god's milk-white horse. They look deader than dead, separated from the bodies, with some of the bluish tongues sticking out slightly from a corner. A small wick is lit, between the horns, on each of the heads. Some of the wicks catch, others don't; those that do burn with a small blue flame for a short while, then go out. The runnel, especially built around the tiled forecourt, is filling up with blood, but there's more of it on the tiles and all around. The goat-usher skids more than once going about his work but manages to balance himself steady each time. The rising smell of blood brings back Ramlal to Lakshman's mind. He feels close to suffocation. The flesh of the sacrificed goats will be cooked and served to everyone in the village. He tries to catch a final glimpse of the god's face to check if his look of displeasure has been erased by all the blood that he has been offered. Some error of rhythm has occurred in the dance that had brought everything together, the flowers and blood and incense and bells and drums and chanting and people, people everywhere, their sounds and life. The slackness now unbinds all the component parts and sets them off in different directions.

Lakshman turns round and pushes his way out, his back turned to the temple, until he reaches the thinning end of the crowd. He picks up his pace as he walks past the stragglers and latecomers, past the school-building with its grey doors and windows and the playground on three small terraces, until he arrives at the knoll on the edge of the wood behind Bhagwan's house. Even at this elevated point, from which he can see the valleys fall away and roll into the distance under their cladding of forests, the lighter pine and darker oak coming together in a dense weave and, sometimes, a colony of human habitation that looks like a small cluster of doll's houses, even at this height Lakshman cannot shake off his shortness of breath, his feeling that there isn't enough air for him to breathe here. The mountains dazzle in the distance: he sees popping dark-and-coloured spots after staring at them for a while. He can't find what he always searches for, almost involuntarily, when he looks at them – the nearly shut, heavy-lidded eyes, the long mark for the nose and the faintly, inscrutably smiling lips of Shiva imprinted on the slope of Nanda Devi that Ramlal had taught him to discern when he was little.

On a golden afternoon when the boys were eight or nine years old, Ramlal had pointed out and named all the peaks – You see that blunt one, just along from the flat line, that's Mrithugni, and the one after that, with the two dips, the two curves, do you see? – here he had shaped the indentation with his hand, to make his brother understand better – that's Trishul, because if you see it from the other side, we're seeing it sideways, if we see it from the front, it looks like Shiva's trishul, do you see the three prongs of the trident?

And Lakshman, dumb with wonder, had nodded. Whether he had actually understood it at the time he no longer remembers.

Ramlal had continued – Then the one after it, on the right, here, follow my finger, that one is Nanda Devi. That is where Shiva lives.

Then a dramatic pause, after which – You can see him. Do you want to see him? I can show you how to spot him.

Still silent, Lakshman had barely been able to nod.

– Follow my finger very carefully now. First close your eyes and think of Shiva. Now open them and look hard at where I am pointing. See that front slope of Nanda Devi? You see it, with snow on top and on the front, with rock showing where there's no snow? You see it? Now look directly under that long, thin line of snow, just under that shadow. Do you see his two eyes? They are the curved lines under the shadow, one on each side of that black ridge that has no snow on it – that's the nose. Do you see the eyes and the nose? The eyes look a bit sleepy, no? That's because he has just woken up from his meditation. Why are you so quiet? Can't you see?

Of course, Lakshman could see – he could see the god's beautiful, lotus-like eyes, more closed than open, and the mouth, almost smiling ... there he was, the great god Shiva, his face imprinted on

Nanda Devi, his abode. And there he, Lakshman, was, gazing on it, a wonder revealed to a boy, and all the air, all the light and all the days were his to do what he wanted.

That evening Lakshman drinks four glasses of the bhaang-laced saffron-and-pistachio lassi they whizz up near the temple, an annual ritual at this time of the festivities for Golu. The hand with the bhaang is generous, in keeping with the mood around the occasion, and Lakshman finds himself, first, slowed down to the dragging, underwatery beat of his heart, then giggly in an escalatingly uncontrollable way. After a while the marketplace cants at an uncomfortable angle and he loses the ability to command any of his thoughts or the way a wildly rushing and random stream of them seem to make a playground of his mind. He is sure he saw Golu frown. That white, white skin, like wax made out of milk. So much blood. And that smell. The meat the day after at the communal lunch has always had the whiff of goat for him. His wife and children will love the mutton. A heavy shroud falls on him, and he is suddenly fighting for air and light, for breath. He heaves and retches and the grass beside him gets covered by a small, viscous patch of yellowish-green liquid, still smelling obstinately of pistachios and saffron under the sour overlay of sick. And yet even after there is nothing to bring up, not even the last drop of his bitter, green bile, he still finds himself under that recognisable lid. Now there is an immovable stone upon it, getting heavier by the minute. There is nothing to do, nothing that can be done about it.

When he wakes up, the helter-skelter film in his head has stopped but the weight hasn't shifted an inch. He observes himself, from a distance, watching the children play danda-gulli outside and feeling nothing. Geeta complains about the piles of bear-shit at the back of the house and how the man she is paying to clear it away has not showed up for the last three days and the stench is unbearable, this used to be a human house, not a zoo, and the children are distracted all hours by the bear, and the creature is going to eat them out of house and home, where is she going to find the money to keep feeding him, too, when there is barely enough for the children and the three adults, particularly now that Lakshman has stopped bothering with even the basic work that their scrap of land demands and she has to look after that on top of everything else, how is she going to do it, does he think she has ten hands, how are the vegetables going to grow …? Lakshman's right hand itches to slap her right across the mouth, but the feeling lasts for the tiniest moment before that dark crushing takes over again.

He goes out to the back. Raju recognises him now. He is standing up, trying to bite the tree trunk, but on seeing Lakshman resumes his normal quadruped position and tries to advance towards him, but the four-feet rope pulls him up short. Undeterred, he makes that odd guttural sound, punctuated by short squeaks here and there, that makes Lakshman think Raju is trying to say something to him in his own language. He moves closer and strokes the creature's back, tentatively, gingerly, ready to leap back if he shows any sign of attacking, but Raju continues to emit sounds that can only be of appreciation, even affection, and for the first time in god knows how long Lakshman feels that lightening he has felt once or twice, in the company of Raju, or while contemplating his future with the bear, far away from this village.

The following day when Geeta is out working in the Bengali house he puts a few things in a small sack – his ration card in its blue plastic sleeve; a few items of clothing (he doesn't have much: his shawl, a sweater and a snuff-coloured, skull-hugging woollen cap, a lungi, a pair of pyjamas, an old white vest, now the colour of dust); a small tin of puffed rice; a coil of rope; two half-empty boxes of matches, anything he can take away without it being missed. He picks random things – there aren't many to choose from – without any thought or reason. He ties the sack, flings it over one shoulder, picks up the damru and his qalandar's stick, goes out, unties Raju from the tree, takes the rope in the hand that holds the stick and whispers – Come, we're off. The bear makes slobbering noises and roots around in the earth with his snout, as if looking for something that he wants to bring with him on the journey. The sounds change to what Lakshman thinks of as yawning ones: mouth wide open, a long glimpse of pink, and those dots of mewling notes.

– Yes, you're happy. I know. Let's go.

He doesn't really have a plan except to stop at each small town at the end of a day's journeying and make Raju dance the following day, collect the money and move on, repeating this routine until he reaches the city where Ramlal is working on building giant homes and river-like roads and arcing bridges. Three to six months at the most, he tells himself; he will be home long before the trees have shed their leaves, certainly long before snowfall fells trees and closes the roads to traffic.

They take the steep paths through the hills, eventually descending to the only road that connects all the villages, but at a point several feet below his own, and several kilometres away. From this juncture, marked by a shop that sells everything, from candles and batteries to Maggi noodles, car lubricant and strings of small sachets of Sunsilk shampoo, they stick to the road. The periodic truck unsettles Raju – he jerks around at the end of his rope, moves his head wildly, whimpers and growls.

– Shush, shush, it's all right, it's only a car, you're going to be all right, no need to be scared.

A driver rushing past leans on his horn, doubtless at the sight of a bear. Raju goes berserk and pulls at the rope so hard that he drags Lakshman along with him over the verge into the trees and bushes. Lakshman shouts. Raju blinks in a baffled manner, then looks down and, after a few seconds, into the distance. The narrow two-lane road falls away steeply, in a scree of rocks and earth, to the shrinking green ribbon of the Rishabh river, rushing along the rock-and-boulder-strewn gorge far below. After Raju's reaction to the loud, horn-tooting lorries, Lakshman realises that it would be safer to walk on the other side of the road, the one that banks against the slope of tree-dense land.

They make their way down to the river for a drink and for Lakshman to splash his face with cold water. In the dappled shade of trees they come across a still stretch of water, an overspill from the river and now cut off from its parent by a narrow bank of sandy earth and grey-green rocks and a strip of paler pebbles. On the surface of that island of water float many brown leaves that have fallen from the trees. No sooner has Lakshman seen them than he thinks there is something not quite right about them, but he cannot tell what. As if someone has read his thoughts, the dry leaves move in unison, in a blink-swift movement, and the folded-up undersides of the drinking swarm of butterflies change to a flickering mosaic of oranges, yellows, browns and blacks, stippled by the dance of spots of lights and shade. Lakshman finds himself unable to move. Before the reaction to pull back Raju to stop him has managed to travel to his hand, Raju has taken three or four steps. The sound and the movement disturb the butterflies. Like handfuls of coloured paper thrown upwards by a playing child, they scatter, then flit away. Raju stands up, chatters and reaches out his paws to swat them. But they are far away from him and in any case they are moving and, finally, all gone. The skin of the water is now just a green, shadowy screen for the swaying points of light and shade.

At the first hamlet they reach, Talla Panchgarh, which is a loose straggle of low houses with asbestos or tin roofs, all distant from one another, Lakshman buys a big packet of sliced bread from a small roadside shop, some stale, soggy biscuits and a small paper packet of groundnuts to eat with his puffed rice later.

– Is that a bear? the shopkeeper asks.

– Yes. His name is Raju.

Then inspiration strikes – or a canny calculation.

– He can dance. Do you want to see him dance?

The shopkeeper shrugs.

Lakshman calls out Raju's name authoritatively a few times, strikes the ground with the stick, then detaches the chain from the thick collar around the neck at the same time as he frees the rope through the nose and the hole in the snout from the knot into which it has been tied to attach it to the muzzle guard. He tries to do all these actions as swiftly as he can while crooning in a very low voice. Before Raju knows it, the rope is in Lakshman's left hand and the damru begins to sound its beats, arrhythmically at first, then settling to the rhythm of whatever tune inside Lakshman's head is animating his right hand. His heart thuds almost painfully against his chest; this is the first performance he is giving outside his village. The knowledge transmits some kind of keenness to him. He tugs the rope hard. Raju, who has been looking confused, instantly stands up on his hind legs, squealing, then drops down almost immediately. The action produces a soaring, followed quickly by a deflation, of Lakshman's heart. Maybe he is losing his touch; he needs to practise and let Raju have his daily routine more.

Suddenly the rhythm of one hand synchronises with the movement of the other, and the beats of the damru and the tugs on the rope going through Raju's nose are as one. Lakshman watches – more feels than watches – this unity of rhythm spread and make Raju a part of its entity: the bear, too, now begins to keep moving on his back legs, shaking his head, as if marking beat or signalling a gentle yet sustained 'no'. The squealing has stopped. He looks like a giant dog, not much like a bear. The shopkeeper is smiling. Lakshman keeps up a patter – Shabaash! Dance, my Raju, dance. Little bear, little bear, dance. Yes, that's it, my little bear, that's it. Well done. Forward, now. Now a few steps back, that's it – that seems not much different from the private, one-sided conversations with Raju that he has begun to fall into when they are on the move.

The rhythm breaks; Raju falls on all fours; or maybe it is the other way round, Lakshman can't tell.

He opens the packet of bread and throws four slices to Raju. Before he can tie a knot in the plastic bag, the bread has been snaffled up and Raju has ambled right up to him, his snout trying to press into the packet. Halfway through leaping backwards and tautening the rope involuntarily, to bring about a safe distance between himself and Raju, Lakshman thinks, no, let me show him I'm not afraid of him, even if deep down I really am, and tries to slow down both actions so that they are more casual, more natural. Simultaneously, another bright idea occurs to him.

– Won't you give me something for making the bear dance for you? he asks the still-smiling shopkeeper.

The man is unwilling to part with any money, so Lakshman asks for food and water for the bear. These materialise, and not only for Raju: sweet biscuits; laddoos, sour, on the turn; some stale rotis; a lump of jaggery; some oranges, even, and a couple of squishy bananas. Raju, overexcited, breaks into a whole choir of noises. Lakshman puts away the jaggery and rotis, keeps an orange and a banana for himself, and gives everything else to Raju. In less than a minute, it's all gone. He sniffs the ground where his food has been, avidly, as if there's more of the stuff that is oddly eluding him, all the while making his grunting-snuffling noises. He comes up close to Lakshman, raises his clawed paws – Lakshman freezes with terror; those claws are like miniature swords – and brings them close to Lakshman's ears, touches his head and brings it down to the ruff around his neck. The grunt-snuffle changes to a panting mew, with a few guttural notes mingled in it somewhere, while Lakshman, with a dry tongue cleaved to the roof of his dry mouth, is unable to move. But after the first few moments with his head in Raju's chest, he realises that the bear intends no harm, and it is over in seconds.

Lakshman and Raju do not get to the first town until the beginning of the summer. If he can spend the next three months in this town by a lake in the valley, its houses and shops lined along the road and hugging closely the hill-slopes on both sides of the lake, he will have saved enough money to find a shelter for the monsoon months. So far he and Raju have slept under trees or behind houses in the lower slopes of the densely vegetated hills. The more they progress south, the more the hills open up, allowing for wider valleys, more space, until he feels one day that the tight fist in which the mountains have always held him is correspondingly loosened, sometimes even absent.

The lake is green and where its edges meet the road there is the usual rubbish of plastic bags, food wrappers, cigarette packets, empty cartons, plastic bottles, flowers, paper, unidentifiable debris, shit, wildly coloured algal blooms, stretches of green slime, slicks of some viscous chemical or other, colonies of sedge, foamy scum, all so dense as to form a solid, ragged border, immovable, unlike the water further in, which is ripply and wavy in its ordinary way.

They attract attention – a bear is not a usual sight – and are soon followed, first, by one or two street-children and then, a bit later, by a bigger group of children, seven or eight, even a couple of young men and street urchins. A refrain begins – Bear, bear, show us how you dance. After a while it has the effect of something blunt slicing through Lakshman's head, but he ignores the retinue. Raju follows him docilely, undistracted by the clamouring children. It's only when one or two of them pick up stones and start throwing them that Lakshman turns round and spits out – Do you have money to see him dance?

A slightly older boy, maybe thirteen or fourteen, it's difficult to tell, swaggers forward aggressively and asks – How much do you want?

Lakshman tries to argue reasonably – I don't have a rate. People gather around me and I make the bear dance. Then more people come, seeing that. I take whatever they give me at the end.

The boy says – So you're a beggar then.

The words wind him but he recovers quickly enough to snarl – Do you know, I can set the bear on you and he'll maul you to shreds in five minutes. Why do you think there is that band around his mouth?

The boy's swagger leaves him. The entire gaggle steps back, then halts. Lakshman turns back and continues in the direction he and Raju were walking. His back prickles in the way it does when one is being watched, but he senses that the boys are no longer following them. A stone lands behind him, almost getting his ankle, and a second one, hard on the heels of the first, strikes the ground, bounces up and hits one of Raju's back legs so that he gives a little startled jump. In one furious movement, Lakshman picks up two stones, wheels around and, screaming, hurls them at the fleeing backs of the boys.

– Motherfuckers! Sisterfuckers! he shouts. The stones he throws at them come nowhere near. Does he imagine their contemptuous laughs from this distance? He realises that he is snarling, a thread of sticky spit dangling from his chin. From their assuredly safe distance, one of the boys turns back to face Lakshman, goes down on all fours and does a mocking mimic of Raju's walk for a few seconds before he joins his running friends. The thread of spit falls to the ground.

It is at the third performance in this town that Lakshman notices the boy who had called him a beggar and then, in close succession, he thinks he recognises some of the younger ones' faces too. He has had slim pickings at the first two events – twenty-three rupees and thirty-four rupees, barely enough to feed him and Raju for three or four days – and although this crowd looks bigger, he is beginning to learn that this does not always translate into proportionate takings.

The act is lacklustre; Lakshman knows this. It's not only Raju who is in need of being trained into a routine, with different numbers, but also Lakshman, who is a novice, all at sea. These street performances, on the other hand, are developing by a sort of impromptu trial-and-error. He plays the damru and tugs at the rope going through Raju's nose; the bear gets up and scampers around as long as the rope is being pulled; Lakshman chants some repetitive words – See, see, the dancing bear, now he'll get up on his back legs, now he'll dance, see, see, dance, dance, dance – and that's the pitiable extent of it. Today he wants to try out something new: make Raju go round and round in a circle around him. He will have to work out a way of doing this without the rope encircling him; the easiest solution would be to remain standing and rotate as Raju describes a circle; but he wants to keep sitting because he feels tired. Not for the first time he wishes that he could sing a couple of songs – any old, or new, Hindi film songs would do – to perk up matters a bit, give the audience the illusion that this is a rehearsed performance, that Raju is dancing *to* his singing.

The desultoriness is broken when a child, no more than six or seven, pipes up – Can I ride the bear? I want to ride him.

A man, presumably her father, brings her out of the surrounding circle to the centre where Lakshman and Raju are.

– He won't bite or attack? he asks.

Lakshman quails before the question, but the calculation that results in the lie – No, no, he's a total baby, a paaltu bhaloo, wouldn't even know how to hurt a fly – easily overrides the fear. This business of letting small children ride Raju could bring in more money than simple bear-dancing.

The girl comes hesitantly towards Raju, one of her hands tightly clutching her father's. She stands about four feet away from the bear, watching him intently.

Suddenly, a shout from one of the spectators – It's not a bear, it's a dog in a bearskin.

Lakshman knows who said this without needing to look; yet he does look and his eyes alight instantly on that boy, as if some kind of mocking destiny had singled him out and presented him solely, to the exclusion of everyone else, to Lakshman's vision. The pinning focus dissolves; Lakshman can identify a couple of the other, younger boys from that earlier day by the lake.

There is the beginning of a collective titter, then another voice – The bear dances, and the fox pulls the rope to make him dance.

The tittering explodes. A collective chant goes up – Dog, fox, dog, fox, dog, fox …

The people are all gathered up into a derisive laughter. How did it all degenerate so quickly, the time between the strike of a match and the conflagration so short? Lakshman looks up around him. There are construction sites everywhere, flatland and hillsides gouged out, piles of brick, cement, sand, machinery, one or two heavy vehicles. Hotels? Why couldn't Ramlal work here, near his village? Why did he have to go so far, no one knew exactly where?

Most of the spectators have left, leaving only a desolate handful. Lakshman is rooted to where he is sitting by a bottomless exhaustion. Raju has sat down too; docile, deflated, it seems to Lakshman. There is a single one-rupee coin on the cloth spread out to collect what people give.

Before they leave the town the following morning, Lakshman goes to a grocery stall right at the end of a road lined with tea shacks and places selling fruits and vegetables, grains, rice, onions, garlic, gourds, potatoes. He looks through the produce, making sure the man in the stall has noticed Raju.

– Is … is he a bear? the man asks, his interest stoked.

– Haan. A baby one. Raju, he's called, Lakshman answers pleasantly. His heart is beating madly. He knows he's taking a big risk but they need to eat. He lets go of the rope in his hand and nudges Raju's back with his foot. Raju wiggles his bottom a bit but doesn't move. Lakshman nudges him again, this time more forcefully, while keeping up a patter to sustain the shopkeeper's initial curiosity.

– He's just a baby, very quiet, very friendly, like a paaltu dog. Aren't you, beta, aren't you a little doggy-woggy? Go, go to this new bhaiyya, go.

The plan, such as it is, is unfolding on the hoof. Lakshman bends down and, with his hands on either side of Raju's rear flank, urges him gently to make friends with the new bhaiyya.

Raju takes a few steps forward, seeing which the shopkeeper blanches and exclaims – You've let go of the chain? No! Don't let him loose, tie him again, tie him!

Lakshman disregards him – He won't do anything, ekdum bachha hain – as Raju begins to advance, the blinking, resigned confusion on his face intact.

The shopkeeper repeats his injunctions, his voice rising, the panic in it becoming uncontrollable now. Raju sniffs the ground, a sack of dirty potatoes, another sack of tired pink bruised onions, looks up and yawns. The shopkeeper gives out a strangulated shout, edges himself out from behind his scales, with the stack of polygonal black iron weights lying beside it, and runs out of one corner, almost tripping over a huge basket of shrivelled gourds at the threshold. He retreats into the narrow dirt alley adjacent to his stall. Raju, perturbed by the perplexing feeling of not being on a leash, and the proximity of food, snuffles and grunts and ambles towards the corn near the mouth of the alley down which the shopkeeper has fled. Fearing pursuit, he runs further inside, leaving Lakshman, incredulous at his good luck, to stuff anything he can lay his hands on into the sling-sack that he has improvised from the large sheet that he spreads out for people to throw money on, when he is making Raju perform. Dark potatoes; onions slipping out of their papery skins, mushy here and there; gourds; sweet-corn; mangoes; bananas; packets of white, sliced bread … until the thought of capturing Raju makes him pause and drop the sack, now impossibly heavy. But Raju hasn't worked out yet what the novelty of unshackled movement means; instead he is rooting around in a jute sack of half-rotting cold-storage carrots from last winter, snout in, gobbling them up with absolute abandonment. Lakshman can-not bring himself to disturb that unity of focus and concentration, so he carries on with his erratic pilfering. Then – while Raju is still lost to the world – Lakshman catches hold of the free end of the chain and gives it a tug, two pulls, three, before Raju registers and looks up. The sack is going to impede a fast getaway; fear is upon him now. He has a good idea of how easy it would be for the shop-keeper to raise a cry of *Thief! Thief!* and have a crowd of people instantly at his back. Slinging the sack over his left shoulder, he pulls Raju sharply and hurries to the mouth of the road and from there slips into the scatter of houses amidst the trees set back from the road, turns left and right and right and left randomly, in case anyone is following them, and at last reaches the final line of built structures beyond which lie only trees. He stops to catch his breath and ease the sack off his shoulder.

The town straggles into an isolated tea-shop or two, a tyre shop and the frame of a house being constructed, with iron rods stick-ing out of the foundation pillars like tall, thin reeds, and then gives out on to an empty road bordered by vegetation. A mile further on Lakshman comes across a small temple. Its outside walls are painted blue, there is a red pennant on the conical roof and gar-lands of drying marigolds festooned across the small grilled metal gate. Lakshman ties Raju to a tree, removes his own chappals and walks into the tiny courtyard in front of the gate. He expects to find an idol of Shiva inside but it's Hanuman instead, a mace in his left hand and a miniature mountain in his right, which is lifted up as if he is offering the mountain as a sweet to a particularly honoured guest. His face and body are painted blue too. Lakshman brings out the coconut, bows his head – more in concentration than devotion, for he has only one go at what he is about to do – then, with a force disproportionate to breaking the coconut in his hand, he brings it down on to the courtyard with something akin to fury, his teeth clenched. The coconut shatters and the fragments are dispersed wildly. There is a dark spray along the concrete where the liquid has exploded. Lakshman collects the coconut shards, reaches his hand through the metal grille and leaves the fruit on the floor of the sanctum. The prayer he says inwardly reminds the god that the offering is for the surprise gift of food, the blessing that had made his escape so easy, that he won't forget his part of the bargain and will remember the god with gratitude every time he looks after his servant.

The heat is beginning to bare its teeth, and by the time he and Raju have walked another mile, Lakshman, wet from head to toe, feels he is going to faint. Raju has the self-possession that only an animal can have.

They cleave to the shaded areas, following the movement of the sun, until that is no longer feasible. At its zenith, the sun has full, ruthless command over everything under it; nowhere to hide. There is nothing to be done except find some cover and while away the time until sunset, at which point they can begin walking again, but he cannot think that far ahead without drinking some water. An image flashes through his head: the water tank in Golu's temple back in his village, shaded partially by a neeli-gulmohar tree with its small grain-shaped leaves and, sometimes, the blue flowers strewn on its calm, green surface. After an hour of searching, when they reach what he thinks could be a stream, he discovers only a curving line of boulders and rocks, with a rare patch of yellow-green silt where the water has evaporated more recently.

Raju pulls him along, sniffing the rocky ground and, uncharacteristically, pulls at the chain around his neck, as if he wants to break free or lead Lakshman somewhere. Stumbling over stones, he follows Raju to a tiny puddle of water hiding in the dark opening under the point where two big boulders join their rotund stomachs. Before Lakshman can negotiate his footing on the stones and get down to it, Raju, flexing the chain to its tautest, manages to perch on one of the fat boulders, push his snout down into the opening, his body at a mad angle, and lap up the water. Lakshman can hear the loud slurping, followed shortly by the habitual grunting sounds. He pulls Raju away and peers into the crack. All the water is gone. He shuts his eyes tight – he can see popping colours – and opens them again: no, no water. Raju's enormous pink tongue is licking the mouth that houses it. He looks unperturbed, unreadable.

The world around Lakshman turns dark. Before he can think of a suitable punishment for the ungrateful animal, he detaches the nose-rope from the collar and gives it a furious tug. Raju squeals and leaps over the boulder. At that moment the punishment presents itself to Lakshman's conscious mind. He keeps pulling the rope without letting Raju descend on to more level ground, effectively keeping him hopping precariously from one rock to another, or sometimes jogging on one large boulder, the pain preventing him from finding an even surface on which he can at least balance while being kept dancing.

Lakshman lets out a crazed laugh – See, haramzada, what I can do to you? How does this feel, eh? How does it feel?

With each word, the pulling on the rope becomes harder, more manic. The sounds now emerging from Raju change to an infernal combination of shrieking and yowling, the switch between the two random. Lakshman feels fear and relaxes his hold on the rope.

Will Raju now leap at his throat? Will he charge and attack him with his nails? Lakshman drops the rope to pick up the stick to protect himself in that eventuality, forgetting that Raju is temporarily untied and can easily run away, particularly after what has just been inflicted on him.

But Raju doesn't escape. He sits on a rock, emitting that frightening shriek, which peters out gradually. Lakshman waits at a safe distance, stick held ready in his right hand. He swings between fear at a potential attack and anxiety at the possibility of Raju's escape. Raju, his shrieking now over, looks down at the ground, as if he is searching for something he has lost. He clambers down and presses his snout between the two round boulders to peer at the spot where the tiny puddle had been, but there is no comfort to be had from there any longer. The chain is now stretched out slackly on the stones. There is a reasonable length between its end and Raju's neck. With thudding heart, Lakshman catches hold of it but doesn't dare pull. He will reattach the nose-rope to the collar later, when he feels safe.

Two weeks pass. They perform at a crossroads – Lakshman is now desperate; they've eaten once in the last two days. Traffic is desultory: a truck every twenty minutes, a few cars. From the open windows of a couple of them empty packets of crisps and gutka are thrown out. Lakshman runs to the spots where these land, hoping to salvage something, praying that the people in the cars made a mistake, or were getting rid of unwanted food. Raju licks the shiny salty-oily innards of an empty packet of Kurkure. Not a single vehicle stops, no one gets out to watch a bear and his owner sitting at the roadside, the man shaking his damru, the bear trying out a few steps. After several hours of this, the heat becomes too unbearable for this half-hearted soliciting to continue. When it's dark, Lakshman makes his way with Raju to the railway tracks. The heat is hardly any lower at night, when the baked earth radiates it back in its weak revenge on the sun.

There was a far higher density of people and their settlements along the tracks. They wouldn't starve around here, or die of thirst. But he works out quickly that these thin strings of slums, and sometimes even small villages, will not provide them with sustenance for more than a day or a night. Besides, there are too few people to make more than one bear-dance worthwhile; or even one – they do not have anything to spare for roadside entertainment.

Lakshman and Raju live off bread and tea, dal and rice, bananas, the occasional samosa or fried snack, pakoras, sweets, biscuits, fritters. How little one can get used to, he thinks, not for the first time, coveting the food of others, all the while trying not to think of food. At a depleted reservoir under a railway bridge, he strips off and washes himself and his clothes. He spreads out the wet clothes on scrub bushes; they are dry in minutes. He sees Raju, tied to a tree whose trunk casts a shadow as thin as a piece of loose thread, digging up the ground in the four-feet radius allowed him and apparently eating the dry dust and earth. When Lakshman reaches him, he notices, but only after close inspection, that Raju has discovered a long line of black ants and has eaten all that have been within his reach. He has dug up the earth around him hoping to discover a network of nests. Lakshman untethers him and leads him along to where he can spy more ants. They seem to be more readily visible to the animal's eye than to the human's. The glare of the burning soil doesn't make things easier. In a moment of both optical blindness and indulgence, he lets Raju lead him in a zigzag, spiral, circular dance, chasing tiny, scattering black insects, all of which the bear appears to be mopping up with the pink extended cloth of his tongue and devouring with sureness and ease. The grunts and unnameable range of sounds coming out of him seem to Lakshman to belong to the same arsenal out of which his pain is expressed. Would Lakshman, if he had his eyes shut, ever be able to distinguish between the two kinds? The unexpected gift is exhausted all too soon. He thinks Raju looks mournful.

– Chaley, he asks, we have a long way to go. He wants to stroke the bear's head but holds back.

Scourged by the hot winds, they can barely proceed. The very air has become an invisible fire. Lakshman has salvaged empty, discarded bottles of Bisleri along the way. He fills up whenever he gets a chance, often from tea-stalls and roadside eateries. At least water is one thing he doesn't have to pay for. Besides, the novelty value of a bear prises open some people enough to offer food. But a substantial amount of their erratic and meagre supply of food comes from foraging. It occurs to Lakshman that Raju is much the best equipped to do this and it may be in his, Lakshman's, interests even to let the bear free and follow where the animal's nose and instincts lead him, but that, of course, he cannot do.

They find watermelons lying among their decaying leaves like dark green boulders in a field. Lakshman waits until it is pitch-dark, then gorges himself on four of them, breaking them open with the side of his hand. He gets the runs through the night and soils his trousers. He exhausts his supply of water cleaning himself, but there's no way he can wash his pyjamas until he comes to another pond or reservoir. Disgust fills him, and shame, until he feels he can taste them as the rebellious ball of phlegm at the back of his throat, impatient to come out. Like a helpless child, he surrenders to tears, tears of self-pity and anger. How did he get here, squatting yet again to let another brief, hot squirt come out of his sore sphincter, when he had a home, more to eat than he has now, his wife to look after him, children to carry on his line and take care of him in his old age?

The density of slums increases near the level-crossings and stations of bigger towns. It feels as if the greedy, unruly sprawl is restless in its desire to subsume the iron tracks within it. Pigs, dogs, snotty children with matted hair, rutted earth that will turn to large stretches of puddle-pocked fields, sewage, open drains, narrow lanes with rickety houses closely huddled along them like too many bad, crooked teeth in a mouth, signage everywhere, on walls, on make-shift boards, on the front of houses and shops, signage in Hindi, which he can read, but often in languages he doesn't know but can tell are Urdu and English. And garbage, garbage everywhere, inseparable from the humans and animals and buildings and shops, each seemingly flowing into the other, with no lines to mark the boundaries. In the narrow roads and lanes, the thickness of traffic – rickshaws, cars, motorbikes, buses, lorries, bicycles, scooters – stuns Lakshman. How is he ever going to penetrate to the centre of these towns and make Raju dance? He can barely cross the road. An odd thing happens. So far on their journey, Lakshman has fol-lowed Raju, now this reverses itself; Raju seems to want to hide behind Lakshman, making it awkward for him to hold on to the chain with his hand behind him at an angle to his shoulder. And . . . and . . . who knows, what if the animal, in a moment of wildness, attacks him from behind?

But the sheer numbers mean that they attract attention, which, Lakshman is beginning to understand, he can attempt to harness. Set inwards a little distance from the railway-edge of the town, Lakshman and Raju put on their show under a tree near the crossing of three roads, in the narrow margin between an open drain and the stream of traffic, the band where fruit-sellers and snack-merchants sit during the day. A sizeable crowd gathers around them, impeding the passage of traffic. Encouraged by the number of people, Lakshman tries to up his game – he sings snatches of Hindi film songs which are currently all the rage and which he has heard blaring out of loudspeakers everywhere along the way. He doesn't know the lyrics, only the refrain or the catchphrase, but that seems to be enough, coupled, crucially, with Raju's antic movements, to bring some entertainment to the gathering.

Halfway through the act, Lakshman feels an odd sense of detachment steal over him after he inadvertently notices Raju's eyes – blinking, unfocused, looking at nothing, or seeming to be looking at something beyond what is in front of and around him. It is as if he is not present. Lakshman begins to feel that he, too, is looking at himself in a different way, from a distance: a man playing a damru, mouthing repetitive words of command or cajoling, singing snatches of popular songs, with a funny black-and-grey animal circling him on its hind legs, sometimes shaking itself rhythmically, sometimes bringing up its front paws to its face as if in a namaste. In this state of flotation, Lakshman feels that he has done this before many times, this roadside performance, including this very one, in this very place, at this very hour, so much so that he can predict the next few seconds of the action. All his life is becoming the repetition of the same few actions, unfolding in slightly different destinations.

A corpse is borne past them on a pallet with its retinue of mourners. Ram naam satya hai, Ram naam satya hai. Lakshman, pulled out of his reverie, instantly notes that the dead body passed him on his left side; an ill omen. His heart goes out of the performance. He tries to wind it down but a child, accompanied by her father, wants to ride Raju. Lakshman, pushing down his anxiety, asks for an upfront payment before he assents. The man gives him ten rupees. Scarcely believing his luck, he lets go of the rope pulling Raju; the bear sits down immediately. Lakshman attaches the rope to the collar – in a sign of how much he has been trained, Raju goes on all fours, thinking that it is time to go. The girl is seated on him gingerly, the father's hands on her, steadying her, unwilling to let go, should anything untoward happen.

Lakshman's heart is a mad drum only he can hear. The trick will be to keep Raju in this position. Will he be able to understand the change in signals – *leash* and damru, not nose-rope and damru? The corpse-bearers. He should not be attempting this on a day a corpse has passed on his left. The girl's legs come down the sides of Raju by only a few inches. She holds them out; she is not relaxed and clearly having second thoughts. The father keeps up a comforting patter. Lakshman adds his voice to it, but more to keep Raju comfortable and steady. Instead of playing the damru, he lets Raju see that he is standing up and tugs gently at the collar band, hoping, praying, willing that Raju is going to start walking slowly, thinking that they are moving on from here.

And Raju does exactly that. He starts walking, the girl balanced on his back, the father at her side, reaching out to keep his hand on his daughter, and Lakshman following no more than three feet behind, chain in hand, crooning – Chal, mera beta, chal, chal, mera Raju, mera chhotu, chal, chal.

Halfway through Raju's navigation of the circle, the crowd erupts into applause.

The following day, at around the same time, Lakshman and Raju begin their act again. But this time Lakshman advertises before he begins – Come, come, come one, come all, come to see the bear that gives children rides on his back, a gentle bear, a paltu bhaloo, a bear who is a child himself; come, come, only ten rupees a ride, ten rupees only. He shakes his damru as he chants this in a sing-song. Raju shakes his head. People think he is doing this in harmony with the rhythm of the damru. Raju gives ten children rides on his back. Lakshman has to turn away a few more because he judges them to be too heavy for the bear. He makes just over a hundred and eighty rupees that evening.

He orders two plates of dinner at a shack – rice, roti, dal, sabzi, egg curry – and gives one to Raju, then buys fruits and laddoos for both of them. Raju shits – an enormous pile – near where the pigs are wallowing on a spreading hill of garbage, sewage and mud as they try to find a slightly secluded spot where they can settle for the night. Lakshman picks the back of a dawakhana, shut for the night; a narrow ledge that forms the top stair of a flight of three leading to a collapsible iron gate, heavily locked, at different points, with five padlocks. The place has the great advantage of a gulmohar tree a few yards away on the lane that leads to the main street. Lakshman ties Raju to this tree, checks and rechecks if the day's takings are in the inside pocket of his trousers, and settles down to wait for sleep to come.

He dreams of fire again, vast, swift-flowing streams of it spreading out with absolute abandon, absolute freedom, and wakes up sweaty and terrified. His first thought is of his money. He takes it out of his inside pocket and counts it – it's all there, slightly damp from its proximity to his underwear, which is wet with the sweat from his groin and thighs as he had lain dreaming. Before his heart has stopped rattling, he decides he has to stow away the money in a safer place: so many people have seen him make money, who knows what is going through their heads, if one or two of them are not petty thieves, pickpockets – after all, these places are full of people who are up to no good. Who can be trusted these days? Certainly not strangers in a strange town. He has heard of thieves who can slit pockets with such a sharp knife that the sleeping man who is being robbed does not feel the slightest disturbance to awake him. It is so skilfully done that he doesn't even become aware of the theft as soon as he wakes up. Only when he searches inside his trousers or shirt to use some of the earnings does he find that his hand has gone clean through a hole.

The brainwave startles even him. He takes the money, folds each ten-rupee note on its horizontal axis and moves towards Raju, who gets up from his sitting position immediately. Lakshman crouches and contemplates him for a while, wondering how he is going to do it. Raju yawns – Lakshman can see the flash of his teeth and gums and tongue, and even his throat in the diffuse moonlight, and a brief gust of his rotten breath hits him. That view of the inside of Raju's mouth makes him even more nervous. Moving quickly,

Lakshman loosens the collar-band around Raju's neck, chanting meaningless words in his usual cooing sing-sing tone all the while, and inserts the thin strip of folded money carefully under the band. He realises that he has forgotten the stick. His hands shake as he keeps one firm finger pressed against the notes, tightens the band and eases his finger away. There. The money is now safe. No one will ever dream of that as a hiding place, should they want to rob him. Besides, even if they guessed, who would dare approach a bear?

The early hint of rain is beginning to touch the sky and the air when Lakshman and Raju arrive in the outskirts of what seems like a small, contained town – Varadapur, the black letters against the yellow-painted stone sign says. It is too small for trains to stop here. The afternoon fills with the milk of mist, low-lying in the open fields before the human habitations begin. Lakshman can smell it mingled with the odour of cow-dung – it is not mist but smoke from the chulhas being lit for the evening cooking. The sky turns a dark purple at the hinge of dusk and darkness; Lakshman fears a tremendous downpour, but it only spits for a few minutes, just enough for the dry earth to release that subtly rotting smell, then stops. Lakshman reads it correctly: the end of summer is here. He is lucky that the imminent monsoon coincides with his arrival in Varadapur, where he can look for some kind of shelter for the next three or four months.

A walk down the only paved road running as the spine of the town reveals something unusual: a series of almost identical buildings on either side of the road, near the centre. They are each four storeys high, with the outside of the curved front verandas all painted a rectangle of yellow, which must once have been the colour of ripe mangoes but is now closer to muddy shit. But still, compared to the greyness of the exposed concrete elsewhere – the paint must have been erased by years of rain, sun and neglect – the tenacious yellow is startling. Surrounded by overgrown ferns and weeds and set back from the road in what looks like a thinning jungle of pines, the buildings are all in such a state of dilapidation that Lakshman cannot tell at first if they had once been occupied and are now abandoned, or if the construction work had been discontinued at a very late stage. Floors and railings of some of the balconies are missing; the short, flying-bridge-like stairways connecting one building to another on each storey are broken and dangling in mid-air; leaking pipes have left indelible lines of rust, all exactly in the same spots on the different buildings; broken and missing windows, some boarded up, some like hollowed-out eyes, give on to the darkness inside, others have rusted or missing grilles. The buildings have compounds abutting them and shared with the others; clearly a housing complex. The yards are cracked, rife with weeds, barely visible. It is a spectacle not of ruin but of the process of ruination. This is the kind of place where ghosts live.

Lakshman's first thought is that if these buildings are derelict, with no signs of inhabitation, he and Raju may be able to find a temporary home here, before moving on towards the plains after the end of the monsoons. In whatever state of disintegration, one of these could still offer a roof over their heads to protect them from the rain. But months on the road, one day here, the next day somewhere else, living like a bird or a wild animal, have sharpened a certain kind of instinct in him and he decides to wait until it's dark before exploring the buildings. In the interim, he walks around for a while, taking in the town, always on the lookout for ideal places where they might be able to perform, spots that are likely to attract the largest possible numbers, the location of the shops, the ragged streams of slums on the periphery ... The reconnaissance reveals a large school, set in its own grounds, now just a stretch of loose, level dust, and a BDO complex.

Lakshman discovers that he can get a square meal of dal, rice and sabzi every day at around one o'clock at the canteen of the

BDO for five rupees only. And he finds out the history of the ghost buildings. They were built to house the employees of a big national machine-tools company, which had to close down its operations in Varadapur after ten years. Most of the inhabitants had left, either because they got a transfer to another branch, or because they lost their jobs and could no longer live in accommodation that came with their work. The company had done nothing with the houses, letting them stand and rot instead. A few of the flats still have people living in them – who knows what their rights are? But a lot of them are empty, probably unsafe, given that time has eaten into them so thoroughly. Most are inseparable from the wild undergrowth surrounding them, even during the dry months, nests to insects, reptiles, animals. This much Lakshman pieces together while he and Raju have tea and samosas at a roadside stall. The usual group of stragglers and curious people with nothing to do, nowhere to go, hang around asking questions – Doesn't he bite? Does he attack with his claws? How old is he? Where did Lakshman find him? Is Lakshman a qalandar? Will Raju dance now? When will they put on their act? He dodges and parries and gives partial replies, calculates what sort of answers are going to serve him best. They talk aimlessly for a good while – about whether the monsoon is going to arrive on time, about the school, about the temples in Varadapur. This last subject breaks down a certain invisible barrier; the men understand now that Lakshman is not a real qalandar – that is, not a Muslim. He knows he may have to stay in this town for some time, so he makes an effort to be warm and friendly and get to know the familiar faces. He buys matches, a candle, and tries to push away the thought of what he might need to live in one place for longer than a day or two, for that thought is a trap, the enormous lid.

When it's totally dark, he walks back with Raju towards the ghost housing complex. He steps over the low stone wall that marks the margin of the road and stands amidst the dried ferns, behind a tree, calf-deep in undergrowth, and watches, letting his eyes become adapted to the darkness. After what feels to him a long time, he thinks he can make out a light at a window on the second or third floor in a building east of where he is standing, a good distance away. The one closest to him has been entirely devoured by the dark. He ties Raju to a tree and makes his way, slowly and carefully, to this one, afraid to strike a match to see where he's planting his feet. The rustle of his footsteps is too loud to his ears. He can hear Raju sniffing around in the earth. He wonders how close he is to the building when he receives a small shock – he can suddenly see weak firelight framing the edges of an imperfectly boarded-up window. Someone is in there: a place to avoid. He cannot see anything around him, he doesn't know in which direction he can, or should, move. He lights a match and in its brief lifespan can only make out cracked concrete and weeds at his feet and shadowy details of a corner of a wall, maybe even a door or a doorway, but all is shadow and flicker before darkness reasserts itself. It doesn't seem like such a good idea to have come here in the dark. The thought of criminals and miscreants using this as their den occurs to him and he wants to run away swiftly – it doesn't look as if it's going to rain tonight, another night under the open sky would be perfectly possible.

He doesn't understand what pulls him along, surmounting the fear, to explore. He lights his candle; impossible to move without it, now that he is almost within the housing complex. In that weak yellow glow, he navigates himself away from the house in which he had seen some light to a building diagonally behind it, across a cement compound shared by both. In this one there is an electric bulb on one of the top floors. There is a doorway to his right, lead-ing into pitch-darkness. He enters; the candlelight is as useful as a wet paper bag; still, it's the only thing he has. He trips over a raised bit – a stair – and falls. The candle escapes from his grip and rolls away, but fortunately continues to burn. Lakshman grabs hold of it and looks at where he has fallen: two stairs, leading to a landing, on either side of which are two identical doors, or rather one set of doors, shut, and another doorway with its doors missing. He enters and finds himself in a large empty room. The floor is littered with dried leaves, bits of broken brick, inches of dust, unidentifiable debris and rubbish, broken glass near the window, which is missing all the panes from the wooden frames, a strew of dried pellets that look like goat-droppings … Something scurries away across the floor. A rat? The walls are stained and cracked and, in places, oddly furry. There is a dark patch in one corner of the floor, near the window, where the room seems to slope, or it could be a shadow, an area where the candlelight doesn't reach. There is a doorway next to it, presumably leading further inside the flat to the other rooms.

Lakshman has exhausted his supply of fearlessness; he cannot bring himself to explore the whole place in the dark. He wants to check if there's anyone living, or hiding, here but doesn't know how to go about it: should he call out? Should he bring in Raju first and then go looking with him? The presence of a bear could protect him from all manner of things. Besides, he feels lonely without Raju. He turns and heads out, candle in hand, his neck and back prickling with fear, an atavistic fear of something getting him from behind. It's odd that dark open spaces, such as fields, copses, forests, roads, do not hold this terror for him, only dark interiors, rooms, the insides of houses.

He tries to retrace his steps but is certain that he is losing his way. In desperation, he lets out a loud whisper – Raju, Raju.

Nothing except a general rustling.

He calls out, now using his whole voice – Raju, Raju.

An answering sound reaches him, something between a chatter, a yawn and a squeaking. Lakshman's fear dissolves.

The spectacle that greets Lakshman at first light, after a sleepless night of fears and discomfort, gives him a shock. The interior is filthier and more dilapidated than candlelight had revealed. To Lakshman, who has some sketchy knowledge of buildings, renovation and decoration, everything in here has crossed that line beyond which it cannot be cleaned, restored or repaired but has to be destroyed and begun, from scratch, again. That dark area he saw yesterday is not a shadow but a huge tongue of slime that has survived, wet and gleaming, all through the blood-evaporating summer. There is a bloom of orange mould – or is it rust? – occupying one-third of the ceiling. The wall in which the doorway is set is spored by a rash of black spots. There are paw prints in the dust and splotches of paan- and gutka-spit on the floor and splattering the lower third of the walls. Through the doorway that leads inside he crosses a short passage that gives on to what used to be a kitchen and an empty room beside it; the wall between the two is broken. Doors lean off their hinges and the wood at the bottom is eaten away in wildly serrated curves. The sink in the kitchen looks dry – there is no running water, Lakshman checks – yet all the pipes are corroded by rust, some sections into a fine filigree work. How could everything be so dry and yet marked so much by the wet at the same time? The small window in the bathroom, missing all its glass, looks out on to the side of the adjacent building that is a mirror image – a vertical series of identical tiny bathroom windows with the rusty, disintegrating cages of the grilles protecting the small bedroom verandas two or three feet away from them, repeated on each level. The rust scars from the metal bars outside the bathroom windows and the veranda grilles score the side of the building in thick orange tracks. Lakshman takes in the bathroom. The rajma-shaped toilet on the floor, with a raised, ridged rectangle on each side to plant the feet on, is full of dried leaves and has turned the colour of dried blood from, presumably, white; a huge colony of cockroaches on the walls, some scurrying about, most of them still and waiting; again, that strange mixture of opposites, slime and mould on one hand, extreme aridity on the other. The bedroom, while of a piece with the rest of the flat, is comparatively less afflicted. In here Lakshman sees the first and only piece of furniture in the entire place – a broken chair, partially burnt, with a large lick of soot on the wall behind it. Apart from this, the flat contains only the gathering rubble of its own slow disintegration. It is this room that Lakshman decides to make his home for the rainy season, and the front room, Raju's, with the bars on the window serving as the tethering post. If anyone tries to enter, a bear just inside the entrance will serve as an effective deterrent, Lakshman hopes.

There is a tiny nub of panic in him: he has to make the bulk of his money for the next three months in the days – no one knows how many – before the rains begin. He goes out with Raju and finds a temple. A blue-faced Shiva, smiling subtly, is enshrined there, sitting on a cow, one leg raised and folded over, the other one hanging. Lakshman buys a garland and a watermelon from one of the men who have spread out their wares on jute sacking or baskets just outside the temple, on the verge of the road. There's much excitement among them – Look, look, a bear's arrived! Lakshman offers the flowers and fruit to the dozing priest, who wakes up, takes in Raju with a glance, then sits up and says – Stay away, stay away, this is a temple, can't you see? It's not for people of your kind.

Lakshman retorts – I'm not a qalandar. I come from Deodham, I'm a kayasth. If I were a Muslim, I wouldn't have bothered to come here. Which Muslim brings offerings to Shiva?

The priest looks suspicious but accepts the marigold garland and the watermelon, if reluctantly, then rings a little hand-bell, sprinkles some water on him and murmurs something hurriedly that sounds like a mantra. Lakshman sits, feet tucked under his bottom, and brings his head down on the first step of the three leading to the tiny vestibule where the priest is stationed, looking at him with unmasked distaste. Against the wishes and hopes of tens of millions of people in the country, Lakshman prays for a big delay in the onset of monsoon.

When he raises his head, the priest asks – A bear, huh? Let's see him dance.

Lakshman says – There aren't enough people here.

The priest says irritatedly – If you put in some effort to get people here, there would be. It's a temple, there are crowds here at certain times.

Lakshman understands why the priest is keen to have him put on a show in the temple precinct. He weighs it up and finally says – Thik hain, I'll do it, but not now, it's getting too hot, we won't be able to get many people. You tell me when the crowds come, which times of the day, and we'll be here.

The priest, too, does some kind of inner calculation before he agrees – Come on Friday, come early in the morning, six or seven. Friday is the big day of worship here.

Lakshman and Raju are at the temple early on Friday morning. The flower-sellers, fruit-sellers, vendors of relics and puja paraphernalia are all there. The purohit doesn't show any sign of recognising him. There are, however, around eight or ten people, mostly women, who have come to worship. They are all distracted by the presence of a bhaloo and a bhaloo-wallah. Lakshman sets up his station a few yards from the temple. He begins playing the damru and the sing-song chant inviting people to come and see the dancing bear. Lakshman keeps this up until enough people have gathered, maybe twenty or thirty. A couple of cars have stopped and their passengers have come out to see what's going on – who knows if they'll stay? These people have more money, Lakshman knows, than the townspeople. He begins to sing his incomplete film-songs while tugging on the rope that goes through Raju's nose. Raju jigs and cavorts and walks round in a circle. How dirty and dusty his pelt looks, Lakshman thinks, but look at his claws – they look like miniature swords made out of grey iron. The butterflies on that stream: how beautiful they were; and Raju enchanted, too.

On a whim, Lakshman says – If you give him something, he will take it, he knows how to accept things.

He knows he is tempting Fate but hopes that Shiva, so near him, will send him his blessing. Lakshman leads the upright Raju around in a circle. The bear's front paws are held near his throat, as if he is a supplicant in this court of spectators. Lakshman picks out a man from the inner circle and says – Give him something, go on, something small, a fruit or a vegetable, he'll take it. The man looks embarrassed; he doesn't move. But the man next to him says – Here, take – and fishes out a banana. Lakshman gently touches his stick to Raju's front paws. The animal extends one of them towards the fruit and, miraculously, as if Shiva really has seen what is going on in Lakshman's head, Raju makes a bowl of his paw – Lakshman can see the grey pads, like stones held in the bear's palm – and lets the man give him a banana, which he wolfs in an eye-blink, even as the people are clapping and expressing their amazement at his darling cleverness. Lakshman is, to begin with, stunned; he recovers himself quickly – it wouldn't do to let anyone guess what a fluke the trick was – and lets his heart swell with gratitude for Shiva.

At the end of the performance, Lakshman goes around collecting money – Show the joy you had from clever Raju. Give with open hearts and open hands. Give from your heart. Make little Raju happy.

As soon as the people disperse, the purohit approaches Lakshman and asks for his 'fee'.

– Fee? Lakshman falls from the sky.

– That prime space beside the temple, you think it comes free?

– But . . . but you didn't mention anything about money that day. Had I known, I would never have come here, I would have gone somewhere else.

– Gone where? Where else would you have got such a crowd in a town like this? The fee is hardly for my use, it's for him – the priest indicates the idol inside.

Lakshman doesn't have the opportunity to hide part of his takings and offer a fraction of the remainder to the priest, for everything unfolded right under his nose.

The priest says – Give it as an offering to the god. If you don't, he'll be angry. And you know how terrible his anger can be.

Lakshman capitulates, initially out of a vague sense of fear, but later, while nursing the sore from being stung by the priest, he thinks that perhaps the bribe was not such a bad thing, for it bound the priest into a certain tie of obligation. Besides, he really needs the god on his side for the rains to be delayed.

Back at the ghost building, he secretes most of the money he has managed to retain under Raju's collar, keeping on his person only what he thinks is necessary to buy food. That evening, indoors, Lakshman feeds Raju and, in a rare moment of intrepidity and affection, strokes his neck and back while keeping up a chatting and crooning. Raju answers with his own spectrum of sounds, more eloquent than usual. Lakshman has never been able to read them, to understand the emotions or wants behind them, but tonight he takes them to be Raju's pleasure at being stroked; the bear's expression of gratitude and friendliness for the human who looks after him. Raju's vocalisation of whatever he feels doesn't let up; instead, it gets louder. Lakshman is afraid that anyone living in these buildings – so far invisible and inaudible – will pass by, hear it and come over to investigate. He tries his usual twin approach, soothing followed by threatening, but tonight Raju won't be placated. What on earth has got into the cursed creature? It doesn't take long for Lakshman to find out – the diminishing of the noises and the appalling stench are almost simultaneous. He swings between despair and rage: who will clean up the mess? His living quarters are now defiled. And the only reason he hadn't kept Raju tied to a tree or post outside was because he was afraid of being discovered. Because Raju had always done his business outside, it had never occurred to Lakshman that such behaviour was not fixed or regular, governable by rules that applied to humans. What keeps him from punishing Raju is the fear that the resultant yowling might attract attention. He bites down on his fury.

The following day he has a choice: whether to set up near the temple again or find a new spot. He weighs up the pros and cons of each option and decides to go for the former. The priest wants a bigger cut of the day's income. Lakshman has no negotiating power.

He knows he is getting good at the performances, with his patter and singing and soliciting, but his heart is not in it today. The heat and the humidity are pressing against him like a wall on either side. He wants to smash the priest's head against the concrete stairs on which he had laid his own to worship that first time. The man's spilt brains would be a suitable offering to the god. Lakshman gives him half of what he has made and asks him to exchange his, Lakshman's, handfuls of loose change for paper currency. Away from the public, he hides the notes under Raju's collar. The sky has darkened.

He is beside himself with worry. At night, he wakes up every twenty minutes or so, waiting for the sound of rain, which doesn't happen. The mugginess is suffocating. He has covered Raju's shit with newspapers. He worries about Raju, now tied to the nearest tree outside, being discovered. Then he catches the distinct sound of a child crying somewhere in the building, or maybe in the adjacent one, and freezes. Rustling and creaks and taps, ordinary night sounds that would have gone unnoticed before, now become magnified to his ears as preludes to imminent discovery and disaster. When nothing materialises, he ventures out to check on Raju. A low chatter greets him, as if Raju understands the need to be quiet. The moment disappears as Lakshman looks up and notices lights at no fewer than four windows in the housing complex and one on a higher floor than his in the building he is in. Fear and incomprehension jostle for supremacy inside him. How could anyone live in his building? The staircase leading to the upper floors is broken and ends in a huge yawn of suspended jagged concrete halfway up the landing above his floor. Absent-mindedly, he strokes Raju's head, forgetting to be afraid of him. Raju raises his paws and tries to bring Lakshman's head down. Lakshman, now alert, gently tries to move away but Raju positions himself closer to him, brings his lowly chattering head to his master's chest and holds him in a brief hug before letting go.

All morning it drizzles weakly. Lakshman avoids the temple and walks in the direction of the school. He is surprised to discover that the loudspeaker broadcasting the latest film songs, which he has been hearing since waking up, is located within the school premises. Preparations for some kind of a festival or function are under way. There are more snack-sellers, balloon-wallahs, drinks-sellers, sherbet-wallahs than he had noticed the first time he walked past it. Raju is overexcited, as are the vendors and other people who see them arrive. A stage has been set up beside the school building. In the wings of the stage, entirely open to the view of people on the road, a girl, in garish costume and make-up, is trying out dance moves, oblivious to being watched. She looks very pleased with herself, then she breaks into a grin and a giggle, as if she is about to play a big prank on someone. She disappears into the building. A gaggle of girls comes out next, each one dressed to the nines. They, too, dance to the song that's blaring out of the sound system – 'Aankhen do' – until an adult, presumably a teacher, comes out and admonishes them. They scatter, helpless with giggles, and run inside. Lakshman discovers from the cold-drinks-seller that it's a three-day festival to celebrate the founding of the school.

Raju and Lakshman are a huge hit when they perform. The crowd is the largest they've ever had. Lakshman throws himself into the act, singing along to some of the songs that are playing on the public address system, much to the delight of the girls, their teachers and guardians. People buy Raju all kinds of things – chana garam, ber, cucumber, peanuts – to have the pleasure of watching him take them in his paws and eat them.

For three consecutive days, Raju and Lakshman repeat their gig. The takings are beyond any of Lakshman's previous imaginings. Raju's collar band swells; Lakshman thinks he will need to replace it soon with a wider, tougher one. He wonders if he has enough to send home – he will have to take it all out one evening and do a count – but how is he going to send it? Through whom? Someone once told him that a post-office could arrange these things.

On the third day, as they walk towards a roadside eatery on the way back to the housing complex, a day almost tremulous with the weight of the stillness and waiting that come before the skies open, someone calls out to him. He turns round. A man he doesn't immediately recognise is saying to him – Salaam, ji.

Then the wave of recognition crashes over him. Salim Qalandar.

Salim says – So. He's grown big, hasn't he? But he doesn't make a move to stroke or pet Raju, only looks at him intently.

Lakshman still hasn't managed to gather his thoughts.

Salim says – Yes, very big.

Pause.

– And I see you've put him to good use. He's making good money for you. Here he hums a line from one of the songs that Lakshman has sung in the most recent gig – My name is Lakhan, mera naam hain Lakhan – and lets out a great cackle. It sounds so sinister that Lakshman loses what few words he had scrambled together inside his head.

– You owe me money, Salim says. The transition from laughter to business is like the crack of a whip.

– I can't give you the entire amount, Lakshman at last finds himself able to speak.

– Why? For three days you were raking it in with both hands.

– It's not as much as you think. Most of it is loose change, in coins. You know well how it works.

– You can pay me some of it. You can be sure I'll come back for the remainder.

Lakshman does a quick calculation. It defeats him: he cannot be certain of the amount he has stored under Raju's collar. Then another thought strikes him, more terrifying: does Salim know about his hiding place?

Just to be rid of Salim as soon as possible Lakshman says – You can have everything I've earned today. Here you go. I'm keeping back ten rupees for chai-paani, here, see.

– I know these tricks, you forget that I was a qalandar. A real one. This is not *everything* you've taken today.

– On my mother— Lakshman begins.

– Cut it out. Who'd believe a fox like you? All right, I'll take this now, but don't forget … He leaves the rest unsaid.

When he is gone, Lakshman feels that the whole encounter was a dream. He has only the disappearance of the day's income to show that it was real. As he walks past the low stone wall, he cannot tell if it is the wall's shadow, cleaving to it, on the road, or a shadow-coloured stain running alongside it.

At night, he hears the crying of a child again, followed, shockingly, by the muffled sounds of a couple quarrelling. All kinds of tumultuous thoughts go through his head: has Salim informed the authorities? Are they already on his tail? Are they biding their time, waiting for the perfect moment to catch him? Is he being watched by some of the people who live in this complex? Has the crooked priest shopped him, out of spite because he moved his act elsewhere, depriving him of his cut? How will he ever find Ramlal? Is he alive? Everything is curdling.

In the morning, he and Raju go to the school. There is no music over a loudspeaker today. The number of itinerant vendors has halved. Inside, there are men dismantling the stage – the bright-orange cloth that was its outer skin has already been removed, exposing the skeleton of bamboos and planks. Chairs are stacked in discrete piles all over the dusty ground that is the school's playing field. There are no girls, no teachers, no guardians, only the silence of their absence.

– It's closed today. The school's closed today. Nothing for you here – the tea-stall owner tells him.

He makes his way with Raju to the temple, anxiously, reluctantly. A thin drizzle begins, more fine spray than rain. The purohit ignores him. Lakshman has no energy to do his usual prelude to drum up business, no interest in making Raju dance. He hopes that the sight of the bear tied to the tree will be enough indication to passers-by to gather.

The spray becomes more substantial, a proper drizzle. The tamarind tree, in resplendent leaf from the killing summer sun, offers them a comforting circle of protection. He notices the trunk of the tree for the first time: there is a strange pattern of huge eyes, much like Shiva's on the slope of Nanda Devi, on the bark, eye above eye above eye. The trunk is watching him with dozens of those eyes. His world cants around him. After an hour, or two, or three – Lakshman loses track of the unmoving mass of time – he has made only ten rupees, and his clothes and hair are damp. When the priest pokes his head out of the temple chamber and hollers – You bring bad luck, you look like a jackal – he knows that it's time to go. Everything is curdling.

And, as if in confirmation, the skies really do open this time and the rain comes down in lashing sheets with such force that the drops seem to perforate the ground on which they fall. Before he knows it, he's soaked. Raju looks shrunken, with his dripping wet pelt. He lets out a set of low squeaks and grunts and keeps opening his jaws wide, as if yawning, and shaking his head repeatedly. The road turns into a swift-flowing stream in no time, and the earth margins dissolve and flow into it. The trees offer little shelter from the strafing; in any case, the movement towards home, from one tree to another, gets them so drenched that it becomes pointless to seek shelter any more.

At the housing complex, Lakshman cannot decide whether to bring Raju inside or leave him out in the rain all night. Maybe it'll stop, he thinks, and leaves the bear tied to his tree outside.

All night it rains. The sound of it, first loud, then musical, ultimately monotonous, keeps Lakshman awake. Then he hears the drips inside, over that unchanging background of water pounding everything in its way with steady, focused obstinacy. Rain is coming into the flat through unseen cracks and holes, a few of them seemingly quite near him. He lights the candle to investigate. At first, nothing, except the sound of two sets of drips, out of step with each other. Lakshman discovers them after some strenuous searching – one at the threshold, from the top of where the door-frame had been, and one from the ceiling, a few inches away from where Lakshman sleeps, but near his feet. He goes out to bring Raju in – the animal is a sodden hulk, which keeps shaking itself vigorously and spraying huge quantities of water around him – and while rushing back, soaked himself now, he notices the lights at exactly the same windows where he has seen them on previous occasions. Who are the people behind those windows? Why has he never seen them outside? Do they know he is here? Have they noticed Raju? He wants to scream into the pouring night and ask them to come out and show their faces.

In the morning, he catches a split-second's glint on one of the walls in the front room where Raju is. It's on that stretch of dark slime, explaining its presence – water is thinly and steadily seeping down the wall. He looks up at the rust-coloured stain on the ceiling: could that be the point of entry? But that means that the water could be penetrating through the floor of the flat above and, in this manner, all the way up to the roof of the building. When will it all cave in? While they are here? On him and Raju?

It is raining relentlessly, his world now trapped between mud at his feet and unbroken grey above. From now on, there will be no hope of regular work. He'll have to take his chance in the gaps, if any, between downpours, and it will be the most difficult thing in the world to set up, solicit, get a crowd in this weather, because it is against the vital thing his trade needs – time.

Over the next seven days Lakshman and Raju manage two shows; or, rather, one, because it starts raining one-third of the way through the second gig and what few people there are run off to find shelter without paying. He spends the last of his ready money buying tea, samosas and sweets at a shack inside which he waits for the rain to let up. The woman behind the huge kadai does not allow the bear to come inside. Lakshman goes out to share his food with Raju. He comes outside and stands beside him, holding his leash, in the sliver of mud under the narrowest of awnings formed by the jutting tin roof. It offers almost no protection from the pelting rain. The runnel of dirty dishwater at his feet swells with the steady, generous run-off from the roof until the sliver of mud on which he is standing begins to be swallowed by the drain. He will have to break into his savings under Raju's collar band if they are to survive. The thought of nibbling away at the packet, which he has been meaning to send home, does not bother him as much as he thought it would. Different sorts of calculations go through his head, such as how much he would save if he were to buy a chulha, a pot, rice and dal, and cook for himself in the room that used to be the kitchen in his flat. He would have to check how much money he has saved. The thoughts of housekeeping instantly summon up, as if they are words of magic, the presence of his old friend – that invisible boulder, lately absent from his life, presses down on him. It's that familiar feeling of being buried alive, of light and air all around him being squeezed out inexorably. Would it have been better without Raju if, for whatever reason, he had been sheltering in these ghost-haunted ruins on his own? He knows the answer, but denies it in the argument he is having with himself – Raju is not a burden to him even though being chained to an animal, who is his responsibility, is burdensome on a day-to-day basis. Instead, it's the only freedom he has ever known.

It's dark and still pouring when he and Raju return home. He strips off all his clothes, wrings them and hangs them out to dry. He will need to buy another pair of trousers and a shirt, maybe a large sheet for lying on or covering himself with.

Raju tries to get away from the small puddle that has dripped off him, but four feet of rope will only allow him so much manoeuvring space. Lakshman ties him to a different spot and loosens his wet collar band to take out all his money. What comes out on his fingers are wet shreds, almost a pulp. Incredulous, he takes off the band entirely – Raju is free of his leash for the first time since he was found by humans. Lakshman runs his hand first along the inside of the collar, then along Raju's neck. The paper money has disintegrated into wet confetti. Even the notes that seem to be whole come apart in his hands the moment he tries to lift them out of the soggy mass. The band lies on the dark floor, knotted to a length of rope, which is tied to a metal bar on the window. Raju sits beside it obediently, not yet aware that he can move around at will. Lakshman shifts through the chyme of paper – how meagre it seems now – looking for something, anything, to salvage; even a ten-rupee note will do. No, nothing.

If he doesn't sit down, he feels that he will be blown away, out of the barred window, like a mote of dust or a feather. He holds his hands to the sides of his head and sits on the floor. Then he howls. Unmindful of who may be listening, whom he awakes, what unwelcome attention he may be attracting, he screams. He screams not from his throat but from his lungs, his navel – the sound comes from somewhere deeper than where the voice is. He screams and screams and screams until there is no sound left in him. It is only when Raju, chattering lowly, comes up to him with hesitant steps and tries to take his head between his paws that Lakshman comes out of himself to realise that Raju is free.

Through the murk inside him a single thought rises to the surface – what does the animal think?

IV

I: *Axe*

The first image that came to her when she thought of that day was the way the blood had arced and sprayed as they threw her brother's right hand into the surrounding bushes. Her eyes had followed the flying curve of the drops of blood as the severed hand flew into the bushes and disappeared. What else did she notice? That blood on green leaves in the shadow was not red but black. And even on the green that had the sun on it, the blood was also black until you looked carefully, very carefully, and then it would appear to be red, but only if you already knew that it was blood and, therefore, red, not black. Milly remembered all this.

This was when she was little, before she was called Milly, before the conversion. She was still called Manglu then, because she was born on a Tuesday. And her eldest brother, the one whose hand they cut off, was born on a Wednesday and so called Budhuwa. They had come into their hut and dragged him out. There were six of them and it was winter, their faces covered in shawls and woollen hats. Budhuwa didn't shout or cry. They took an axe from the corner where all the farming implements and tools were kept – the sickles, the ploughshares, the tangi, the chherkha. The lohar had visited recently and sharpened the tools of all the families in their tiny village. He had sat outside in the courtyard around which all the homes were built – he was not allowed to enter any of them – and sharpened scores of these tools and knives on a whetting stone and on the pedal-driven sharpener that was ingeniously connected to his rusty bicycle. The more furiously he pedalled, the more generous the spray of orange sparks from the sharpening edge against which he held each tool. The children all gathered round to watch the fireworks; so exciting they had been. The lohar brought his own glass for water and a plate for his food. Someone gave him roti and pickles for lunch, all of which he ate quickly, wiping his plate clean. Milly, transfixed, like all the other children, by the presence of this magician who could send such short-lived flowers of fire flying at will, remembered that he had sharpened their family's axe right after he had finished his food.

This was the axe that the men grabbed that afternoon. Four of them came in and got hold of Budhuwa and pulled him out. There were two more outside. They must have already been to the rice fields to look for him and knew that he was at home. It was terror that had silenced Budhuwa, she understood now, not courage. The only person crying was their mother, crying and falling at the feet of each of the men, saying over and over and over, 'Please let him go, he's my son, please, I'm falling at your feet, please spare him, let him go.' Their father, too drunk, even at this hour, to plead, had tottered around the place, barely able to keep his eyes open, or to string intelligible words free of slurring. There was a crowd in the courtyard – people had come out of the surrounding huts to see what was going to happen. Even the children were there. Two women chased their little ones inside, lifting the crawling babies on to their hips. Milly's mother didn't have the presence of mind to do that, and neither did their father, so Milly and her six siblings witnessed everything.

Two men held down Budhuwa's neck, one his feet, while the man wielding the axe said, 'If you don't hold out your right hand, I'm going to let you have it in the neck.' Budhuwa held out his right hand – the fingers were trembling, Milly could see even from far away, where she was standing, almost hidden behind the legs of one of their neighbours stationed at the edge, near the bushes – then withdrew it immediately. She couldn't see her brother's face. The axe-wielding man shouted, 'You choose, then, is it going to be your head or your feet? If you can't hold out your hand straight and still, you choose.' Budhuwa held out his hand, still shaking. Milly thought, was this going to be like the time she saw the slaughter of the cockerels for Sarhul, the head of the red one, meant for Luthum Haram and Luthum Buria, chopped off in one blow, the thin jet of blood first sprinkling the pahan's face, as he had turned his head away, then his clothes, and the headless torso of the bird spinning and spinning and spinning around on the ground, getting blood everywhere. Why could he not have held it down and cut it into pieces?

The axe came down, Milly didn't remember if she saw that, only the flinging of the hand, which flew past her into the bushes, and her head followed that arc and her eyes got fixed on the brief agitation and parting of the leaves and branches and the blackness of the blood on the green. She couldn't turn her head back to the source of the terrible sound: her brother. Something had frozen her neck. Or her eyes. After a long time the howling changed to whimpering and she could turn her head. The first thing she saw was the axe, which they had left behind. The sparse amount of blood clinging to the edge of the blade was out of proportion to the cries that she had just heard.

2: *Friend*

The youngest daughter of the woman from behind whose legs
Milly had watched the mutilation of Budhuwa was her dearest
friend. The girl's name was Soni and she and her family lived in
the same village. The girls played in the dust together, ran along
the narrow aars of the rice fields, chasing each other, sat under
mango trees to shelter from the rain and made up songs about the
way raindrops or downpour sounded on the leaves. 'Jhim jhim
jhim, it goes,' Milly said. 'No, jhum jhum jhum,' said Soni. They
climbed trees and made reeds out of the long leaves of palms.
They discovered that the stem of the papaya tree was hollow; they
dipped it in soapy water and blew bubbles. They saved tamarind
stones after eating the ripe fruit off the trees in the summer, or
tamarind pickle at other times during the year, cleaned them and
put them to use in invented games. They lay on the ground, balanced a stone each on their foreheads, exactly between their eyes,
and a garland of the brown seeds around their necks, and kept
very still so that the stones didn't fall off, and pretended that they
were both brides, decked out on their wedding day. The girl from

whose neck a stone slid off first would be the first to get married. There were no shop-bought toys or dolls, but they made do with painted clay birds that someone in the village made – they had dried palm leaves for tails and ears – and little carts made of sticks and dried sal leaves, and garishly painted carved sal-wood or bamboo creatures: humans, animals, once even a bus with wheels. They had to be told what it was because they had never seen a bus before. They played with leaves and stones, arranging them in pretty patterns, sometimes strewing flower petals around them and singing the songs from Ba-parab: *'Rupa lekan ba chandu setera kana / Sona lekan ba chandu mulua kana'*.

They sat next to each other in the local school, which was three miles away, and a few metres off a tar-metalled road, in the middle of open land with nothing around it except a long, low knoll on the horizon to the east, a few trees dotting the red earth, and some bushes, scrub and other vegetation. Children from all the villages within a radius of ten or twelve miles had to walk to, and back from, this school, the only one in this particular block of the district. They didn't mind; it didn't occur to them that something such as minding existed; this was the way things were and they knew nothing else. Sometimes the long journey in all seasons meant that they missed class, but this was infrequent. There was certainly a lot less absenteeism among students than among the teachers.

The school was painted pink and had two large rooms, a blue 'kitchen shed', where the students' midday meal was cooked, and an outhouse, which was the latrine and had a wooden door that did not reach all the way to the floor. It had to be shut with a hook lock, which had begun to rust. This toilet was a new thing for all the children because their homes didn't have any – everyone did his business in the open – and they had to be taught by the teacher how to use it. Much embarrassed giggling had accompanied these demonstrations. Milly and Soni had been the most helplessly tittering of the lot.

Everyone between the ages of seven and eleven sat in one classroom, and the older children in the other. They sat on the floor, cross-legged, facing the teacher and the blackboard. There weren't enough chataïs for all of them – anywhere between thirty and forty-five – so some had to sit on the bare concrete. Sometimes as often as fifteen or twenty days a month the children walked to the school and the teacher didn't show up; or she did and left around noon. Over time, this had the effect of thinning student numbers, too – who would want to walk so far, especially during the merciless summer and monsoon, to sit in a room, waiting, waiting, until it was time to walk back again? And when they tenaciously continued to come regularly, it wasn't because of the lessons – there weren't many – but for other reasons: a close friend or two; an escape from being sent to the fields to work; or simply a way of keeping at bay the weight of endless days of nothing. And the biggest reason of all, the one square meal they got in school, regardless of whether the teacher was present or absent.

But Milly's case was slightly different. She had her best friend not very far away in the village; there was no need to do a round trip of over two hours every day to be with her. True, the midday meal was a big attraction but there was something bigger than this. Milly was on fire to study, to learn to read and write, to go to a bigger school where she would get to wear a uniform and carry a pile of books in her hand or in a bag, books she would be able to read easily from cover to cover and retain in her head everything they contained.

But after barely two years at this school, Milly, at the age of eight, was taken out and sent by her mother to work as a housemaid in distant Dumri, eight hours by bus from her village. The family desperately needed the money, and her mother, who tried to hold everything together, couldn't see how they were to hold off starvation if Milly wasn't sent away. She was going to need every paisa from those extra two hundred rupees a month that were going to be Milly's wages. Her mother had nine mouths to feed – herself, seven children and a drunkard of a husband, who instead of earning money was a drain on what little they could pool together. They struggled to raise the bus fare, which was one hundred and twenty-five rupees. The money necessary for a return ticket for her father or one of her older brothers to accompany Milly was beyond their means, so they had to wait until someone else was travelling to Dumri. Arrangements were made for Milly to be met when she got off the bus. This was all done without her knowledge; not because her mother thought that the girl would be upset, but because the idea of consulting a daughter on a decision already reached by her mother was unimaginable.

Milly was told two days before she was scheduled to go. At first, she thought she was going to see a town far, far away, a different world altogether, so there was some excitement mingled with the fear that she felt, excitement especially about travelling by bus, which she had never done before.

'How long will it take to get there?' she asked.

'Six, seven, eight hours,' her mother said.

Milly did not have any notion of time to understand what this actually meant, she only knew that it was a very long time.

'Oh, that's very far. When will I come back? After how many hours?'

'You won't come back, you will stay there,' her mother said.

'Stay? Stay where? Many days?' Milly was baffled.

Even after the situation was explained to her – that she was going to be living in the home of a couple in that far-away town – and a consolatory lie, that she was going to come home every month, added to the mix, it only dawned on Milly by slow degrees that she was being sent away to work. She looked at the healed stump of Budhuwa's arm, its end gathered together in a tiny knot-like pucker like the kind she had once seen at the end of an inflated balloon, and realised that it would look a little bit different when she saw it next time; and something went in a sweeping movement inside her child's chest, emptying it.

'And school?' she asked in a small voice. 'Studying?'

'Nothing doing,' her mother replied impatiently. 'Studying. What good is that for a girl? You'll be more useful bringing in some money. Now shut up.'

The pictures in her school book, with the words written large under them – ainak (glasses), kachauri (stuffed pastry), titlin (butterfly), aurat (woman), gilhari (squirrel) – went through her head. There would be no more books, no more pictures. She looked at the faces of her brothers and sisters; Budhuwa's was turned away. Three of them were too little to understand what was going on. The faces of the other two looked small. Or so it appeared in the shadow-casting flame of the sooty hurricane lamp. Then a different thought struck her: Soni.

When Milly said that she was going to a different country to earn money, and that she was going to come back every month in a bus, bearing gifts of tinsel, sweets, pictures, and red, blue, green and yellow ribbons, all things she considered beautiful and desirable, it wasn't at all clear that Soni understood the full implication of what her friend was saying. There were no goodbyes, no promises or expectations to see each other soon, because there was no understanding of absence and not having each other's company. There was no wrench, no exchange of tokens or mementoes. The day's play ended as it did on any other ordinary day.

The next day, when boarding the bus, Milly was eager to sit at a window because Budhuwa had told her that she could see the world, the trees, the houses, the fields, all moving past her in the opposite direction when the bus was in motion. She sat at the window and looked out. The bus was stationary, still boarding. She looked out at Budhuwa standing beside her mother, who had a toddler on her hip and one of the younger brothers holding on to her hand. Milly saw her father with his crumpled face. Someone was selling bananas. Budhuwa bought one, reached his hand in and gave it to Milly. The bus was beginning to fill up rapidly. Something shifted and she began to cry, not as a child cries, with its innocent and skinless complaint against the world, but as an adult, silently, trying to keep it all in, only just beginning to understand the weight of the world.

3: *Friend, part II*

Soni was the one who first noticed it. She said to her mother, 'What do you have in your mouth?'

'What do you mean? Nothing,' her mother said.

'You do. Open your mouth. Show, show.'

'Here, haaaaaa.' The jaws opened. Nothing in there. The jaws shut. 'See, nothing. I told you.'

'No, you're hiding it. See, here, here', and Soni touched the slight protrusion on her right jaw, low down, almost under the ear. It was as if she had tucked in a morsel of a treat, a sweetie maybe, and had stowed it far back in her mouth to savour it slowly. 'No, no, show again,' the girl demanded.

Soni's mother obliged. Soni stuck a finger inside and poked around. Teeth, wet flesh, but no hidden sweet. Her mother gently caught hold her wrist and moved her ferreting hand away.

'You're very naughty,' she said.

Yet that lump persisted: Soni could see it clearly the moment her mother shut her mouth again. Then she forgot about it.

Until her elder sister, older than her by seven years, noticed it too and pointed it out in front of the others.

Soni piped up, 'Yes, there are sweets she's hiding in there.'

Their mother, rushed off her feet, snapped back, 'Sweets, sweets! Where do you see sweets? Why have sweets got into your head? Where are we going to get sweets from, you mad girl?'

There was no mirror in their hut, so Soni's mother couldn't check for herself. She felt along her right jaw, pressing at and around the point her daughters indicated. Yes, there did seem to be some kind of swelling, but she didn't feel anything out of the ordinary. She thought of asking her husband but forgot about it. Then someone else, her neighbour, mentioned it as they were picking sal leaves and dead branches in the forest one afternoon. The two women walked back to the village to verify the matter in her neighbour's hand-mirror, a rectangular one framed in green plastic, which was so small that it showed only segments of the face, not the whole thing, if held too close. It took Soni's mother a few tries to get the distance between mirror and reflection right so that she could see her entire face in perspective.

Yes, there it was, exactly as her daughter, Soni, had said; it was as if she was sucking on a lump the size of a sparrow's egg. She opened wide and shut her jaws a few times to see if she could feel the thing. Nothing, except a few clicks. Anyway, it didn't hurt, so it was nothing.

That nothing became something. At first, the pain was a dull ache, sometimes flicking over to a throbbing, then returning to the steady state of ache. The monsoons had tricked them that year by not arriving and the rice in the fields had died to a brown waste. The only thing the villagers could salvage was bundles of hay and straw from the dried plants. Soni's mother had fallen over, face down in the sharp stubble, while tying a bundle she had harvested earlier in the day. An egret, watching the ground intently, strutted a couple of steps and flew off. The pain seemed to have come alive:

it was moving its hundreds of fingers up into her ear, her neck, the back of her head, her right eye, her throat. The sparrow's egg had given birth to an animal that was struggling to get out.

She gurned and drooled. The pain wouldn't allow her to speak. They gave her tribal remedies: a hot poultice of quicklime and turmeric on the growth; a paste of jumuri leaves; dried red berries of the ajarini infused in hot water. These did nothing to abate the pain. Soni watched her mother let out the screams of a woman possessed at night, when she said the thing in her jaw was moving. At other times she saw her writhe and thrash on the floor, once beating her head against the mud wall so hard that a small crack appeared on it. Soni's own heart thrashed inside her little chest. Why couldn't they take her mother's pain away?

The nearest doctor's clinic was three hours' walk away. She was never going to be able to do it, not now. Soni's father rode his wife pillion on a borrowed bicycle and took her to the doctor, worrying not so much about the reduced person he was pedalling into town as the doctor's fees. He only had thirty rupees with him. How would he pay for the medicines on top of the fees? The doctor waived his fee, wrote out a prescription and said, 'This tablet, number one here, give two to her every four hours. Then you need to take her to the hospital. This needs to be removed. She'll need an operation. Quickly. I'll give you a letter, show it to the people in the hospital.'

With the money he had, Soni's father could only buy fourteen tablets. He watched the young man in the dispensary cut out four tablets with a pair of scissors from a blister-pack of ten to add to the one full pack. The pills were gone in two days. The pain, which hadn't disappeared but had somewhat lessened, came roaring back, as if punishing her for daring to use something to battle it. Soni saw her mother return to becoming a wraith again, and her heart felt like it was rice being threshed. Her older sister stopped going to school to take over the duties their mother could no longer perform.

They went picking kendu leaves in the forest together. For every hundred leaves, they would get twenty-five paise. One afternoon they were late coming back: dusk had already begun to settle and soon it would shade into dark. Soni's sister led through a wider path, away from the denser jungle. They heard a vehicle not far away: forest officials on duty. The sound came nearer and nearer and, with it, the two beams of the headlights. Without exactly knowing why, the two girls tried instinctively to hide, but a beam caught Soni's sister as they were attempting to scurry into the interior. The Jeep came closer and stopped. Two men jumped out. The girls could hear voices.

'Who's there? We're forest officers. We've seen you. Show yourself,' one of them shouted to the trees.

The girls might have stayed undiscovered, but someone shone a powerful torch and the light caught Soni's sister straight on her face. Later, Soni would think, they could have run into the cover of the jungle; they would never have been found.

Now, Soni watched her sister transformed to stone. The men came nearer.

'What are you doing here?' one of them demanded. 'Why are you trying to run away?'

'Come here, move closer,' the other man commanded. They were holding lathis. 'What, you've swallowed your tongue?' he barked. 'What were you doing in the dark in the forest? Do you not know, it's not a good place for girls to be?' His voice changed with the last sentence; something else had crept into his tone, something slow and lazy.

The other man laughed. 'Yes, tell us, what were you doing?' he asked. 'What are you holding?' He extended his right hand and took the bundle of leaves that Soni's sister had collected.

'Aha, kendu. Do you have a licence to collect leaves? Don't you know it's illegal otherwise?'

Licence? Illegal? Everyone in the village had been doing it for as long as the girls had been conscious, and their parents and grandparents and ancestors before them. But Soni's sister was too cowed to answer them. What if there really was a new rule they didn't know about? Every day the government people made some rule that made their lives more and more impossible. They kept hearing talk about how they would have to leave their village and the forest and move far away because big companies wanted the land. Where would they go? What would they do?

'You have to come with us,' the man said, and grabbed Soni's sister's wrist. She seemed to have become stone, yet that stone was trembling, a tremor that was transmitting itself through the narrow gap of air to Soni standing by her side.

The man nearer the Jeep added his voice to this. 'Yes, you need to come with us. We'll see what we can do with you.' And then a laugh like a crow manically cawing its death.

Soni could feel her sister trembling. Why wasn't Didi speaking? Where were they going to take her? What were they going to do?

'Let's take the younger one too,' he said. 'There are two of us, and two of them.' That carrion laugh again, like audible gusts of rot.

Didi let out a cry – 'No!' So clogged, from the depths of a dream, it seemed. Then that stone-like inertia broke and everything happened so fast that it outran thought. Soni's sister reached out a hand towards her, pushed her away and said, 'Run! Run back home' in a ferocious whisper. She tried to wiggle herself away from the man who was still holding her wrist. The grip tightened. One beat, two beats. Then Soni moved sideways, turned her back to the men and her sister and started to run. She heard rustling, a cry go up from the men, heard one of them shouting and beginning to run after her. She was nine, light, fleet-footed, powered by fear; and she knew the forest, where she could slip into a brake or take cover behind a close-packed sentry of trees. And the light was going fast, particularly near the ground, up the trunks of trees now almost to the height of an adult. She ran like a spirit escaping the case of its body at the moment of death. All she knew was the particular small clearing, at the junction of two thin, almost invisible trails, that she had to get to before the dark devoured everything. If she couldn't, she would be lost for the night and eaten alive by a leopard or a bear. She looked back only once. What light was left was like ash. Through the screen of the tree-crowd, she saw, or imagined she saw, one of the men, visible only because of his white shirt, huddled on the ground as if weeping over a dead loved one. Or an animal eating its prey. The darkness, and the swiftness of her backward gaze, made it impossible to see what he was hunched over. The forest seemed to stick in her throat.

They sent a search party into the forest at first light the next morning. They couldn't find her. They came back to the village at dusk, in total silence. When Soni and her father entered their hut they found her sitting with her back against a wall, her face in the shadow. Their mother was crying, but to Soni's ears and eyes it was a different kind of crying, a different sound, not of pain but what she could only think of as anger. Didi was a stone again. Her knees and elbows were scabbed, her legs cut in places. In the darkness inside, Soni couldn't see what she would discover over the next few days – bruises everywhere, a slow, pained walk as if everything inside her sister had been broken. She remembered her mother saying only one thing when they returned from their search: 'She crawled back, she couldn't walk.'

Over time, Didi learned how to walk normally again. Yet something felt lacking – sometimes she bared her teeth in a kind of simulation of a smile but, lacking the corresponding illumination in her eyes, it couldn't be called that; it was a perpetually failing, half-hearted rehearsal for it.

Even as Soni's mother's body came to resemble a scarecrow's – she could barely eat anything – her face seemed to be sucking up all the matter in her body and storing it in that bulging angle. Her face changed shape: it was a small, empty, shrivelled sack from which someone had forgotten to take something out from a hidden corner. Her eyes were distant and out of focus all the time, as if they had become strangers to the head to which they felt they didn't belong any longer.

There were two trips to the nearest public hospital, a four-hour journey on a bus. The seventy-five rupees for the bus ticket for each passenger were out of their reach. Soni's father borrowed the fare and an amount he guessed he would need for medicines; the total came to five hundred rupees. He was told that he would have to pay six hundred rupees if he repaid after one month, seven hundred and twenty-five after two months, eight hundred and fifty after three, and so on. But he couldn't think ahead to the time of repayment or the reality of the incremental sums involved; they meant nothing to him; now was the only thing that mattered.

The hospital – how was he going to negotiate that? Who was he supposed to talk to? Who was going to guide him to the right person? He should have brought someone from the village, someone educated, someone who could speak, someone who would know whom to speak to. This place was going to crush him. Wherever he looked there were sick people, people with bandages or casts, the bandages sometimes with a visible blot of blood underneath, dark at the centre, fading towards the peripheries, people walking very slowly with the help of sticks, people lying flat on the floor and in the entranceway, people lying absolutely motionless, eyes wide open, in some cases, staring at nothing, people groaning, coughing, wheezing, people with missing hands or legs, with open sores and grisly protuberances. A man was sitting, back to a wall, the left side of his face a bulging hive of tightly clustered black berries. Soni's father's stomach heaved. He couldn't read a single sign, he didn't know how to. How stupid was it to have come without anyone to help him? This place was going to crush him.

He went from person to person, the doctor's letter clutched in his hand, asking for guidance, some kind of direction. The only word he thought could help him was 'operation'; the doctor had said she needed an operation. Someone said, 'Go to that table there, they can help you.' When he went to the table, he was told he had to go somewhere else. At a counter, the press of people clamouring to be heard, reaching forward pieces of paper, elbowing and jostling, defeated him. How was he ever going to get to the front? When he did get there, after an hour, he was told he had come to the wrong place. He had to go upstairs. They couldn't help him here, this was the ... then some unintelligible words. He went up two flights of stairs to the next floor. People rushing about, waiting, sitting, standing. Who was he going to ask for help? He fixed on a woman he thought looked like a doctor; she had that listening rope around her neck. She told him he had come to the wrong place. He had to go downstairs and ask at the main counter. He went downstairs again. He was a tiny piece of straw in the wind. When he jostled his way to the counter downstairs, he was told to go upstairs again. This time he said that he had already been, but had been sent back down. The man said there was nothing he could do, and could he move aside – he couldn't spend the entire day talking to just one person, there were others waiting behind him.

Soni's father turned away, came outside and sat down on the steps. Against his will, his mouth twisted, like a child's; he couldn't make it hold its shape; he failed to make his crying resemble a dignified adult's. His wife tried to comfort him. What a strange world, he thought; she comforting him when it should be the other way around. He was utterly defeated. People around them probably thought he was crying because some near one had died in the hospital and he had just received the news. What were they thinking? He had never felt so ashamed in his life.

An elderly woman, hobbling on her stick, came up to him to commiserate; it was all up to him, uparwalla, she said, and looked up at the sky. It was she who accompanied him to the main desk of the surgery section, on the other side of the building. Here the collection of people waiting to be seen was even grislier. Some of them hardly looked human any more. There were dogs sniffing at sores and winding their way in and out among the humans. No one seemed to have the energy to chase them away. It was the elderly woman who spoke to the man in charge, who filled out the forms for him and who conveyed to him the most important information: the people here had been waiting for operations for days because there were no doctors to do them. They would have to return the following day, but there was no guarantee that a doctor was going to be present to look at Soni's mother. They would have to keep trying until they got lucky one day; how long that was going to take, no one knew.

Soni didn't get to hear the details of what happened on her parents' first outing to the hospital, but only gathered a sense of how reduced they were afterwards, like husk, without weight, without any consequence.

They went again, after two months. Soni's father borrowed money again, while the previous loan remained unpaid, accruing interest. He could no longer bear to see his wife thrashing about like a cow in labour. He felt his insides had become the floor on which the thrashing happened. He had to save her and he had to save himself. This time he asked the Christian man, Joseph, to accompany him to the hospital. The fear, which had paralysed him, of dealing with that huge, crushing, opaque world was mitigated when Joseph agreed.

Joseph's presence certainly cut out the time wasted in the previous visit going around in circles. Soni's father let him do all the running while he followed him like a faithful dog. That same crowd of afflicted people again, that same assortment of maimedness and leprous sores and growths, skin like crust, arms and legs no longer arms and legs but leaking barrels, withering branches, spongy sacks. And everyone waiting, some for days, months, who knew how long, waiting to be relieved of pain. Illness was a luxury for the rich. Illness had reduced everyone here to a beggar.

Joseph returned with news that there were no doctors in this ward who could perform an operation. Everyone was still waiting – there was a huge list – and no one knew when a doctor would show up; there hadn't been one for weeks. The last doctor in attendance, many days ago, came and did four operations: one of the patients had died, the other three had had to come back with aggravated problems. This information came not from the staff but from the assembled people, awaiting treatment, and their relatives.

There was nothing to do but go back.

Ten days after this, Soni's mother hanged herself. It was Joseph who discovered her; the tamarind tree from which he found her hanging by her saree was in the woods behind the clearing at the back of the church. It was only after they brought her down that he recognised who she was. She had tried to cut out the tumour at the back of her jaw, almost under her ear, with something sharp. They couldn't find the instrument.

4: *Paper*

The only thing Milly took with her on the eight-hour bus journey to her new life was her school textbook and some sheets of dirty, blank paper which she had saved from a small sheaf distributed in school earlier in the year. She knew that the book was called *Pratham Kiran,* although she couldn't yet read the first word, only the second. The clothes she had were what she was wearing: a pair of old drawstring pyjamas frayed at the bottom edge, the string replaced by her mother for the purpose of travel and held together by a safety-pin; and a shift, which was once white with a bold red paan-leaf pattern on it, but now looked like a greyish-brownish swabbing cloth. The rubber flip-flops on her feet had mismatched straps and were of slightly different sizes for each foot because they had been found in that state.

The people who employed her belonged to the same tribe: Munda. The man, Lewis, and his wife, Pendo, both Christian converts, like Milly, had moved from a remote village to Dumri because Lewis had bagged that ultimate prize – a government job. He worked as a clerk in an offshoot of the state government's Forest Department.

Milly's parents knew them, and the grandparents of both families had lived in the same village many years ago. This was how the job had come about. Lewis and Pendo wanted a Munda Christian girl and Milly's mother had put her daughter forward.

These connections were vital: while they did not treat her as one of their own – she was the servant-girl, after all – there was some fundamental commonality that linked them, a sort of tribal bond. Milly was fortunate; it could so easily have gone in the other direction: the hatred of the successful for the less lucky of the same group. Maybe it was this tribal sympathy which made them notice that Milly's sole possession was her school textbook and some cheap paper from an exercise copy, yet not treat her with contempt or cruelty.

While cleaning one morning after Vinti, the nine-year-old daughter of Lewis and Pendo, had left for school, Milly found herself alone and dared to reach out for the other girl's small pile of books by a chaupai on the floor. She thought of the possible consequences of touching what was not hers but the temptation was too great. She laid down the broom, picked the biggest book and opened it. A forest of words and pictures emerged, beckoning her in. Not a single word made any sense – none of them was in Hindi, the only alphabet she knew.

A shout from Pendo, 'Milly, Mill-ee-ee, what's taking you so long?'

Startled, she dropped the book, then replaced it hurriedly. 'Coming,' she called out, afraid that she had somehow been seen and was now being summoned to be punished.

For the following two days she cleaned around the books in a frenzied hurry, willing herself not to touch them, and ran out of the room. But in the evenings, when she was engaged in her duties – making roti, filling the buckets in the bathroom, helping Pendo with the preparation of dinner – half her mind was in the room in which Vinti was busy with her homework. On days when Vinti read aloud from one of her books, whether in Hindi or in their own play language, Milly felt an odd emotion tightening her chest – a mixture of restlessness, lightness and anger. She wanted to spit in the dough. The rotis were rolled unevenly and came out singed. On more than one occasion, a roti caught fire as she was holding it with a pair of tongs over the coals on the chulha. Pendo scolded her roundly.

One day Pendo discovered Milly poring over one of Vinti's books, rapt, her entire being elsewhere, softly mouthing something that sounded like nonsense to Pendo, but on close listening was deciphered as repetitions of certain words – ainak, aurat, titlin, gilhari – that made even less sense to her.

Pendo revealed herself. 'What rubbish are you up to?' she said. Milly looked stricken. Softening her tone, Pendo said, 'Do you know that speaking to yourself is a sign of madness? Do we want a mad girl on our hands? What are you doing with Vinti's book? You don't know how to read.'

Milly, who was on the verge of bursting into tears, felt proud of the little literacy she had and decided to defend herself. She said, 'Yes, I do. I can read from my book, and a few words in Vinti-didi's.' The avidity on her face was like a glow.

Pendo couldn't be much bothered with her maidservant's breathlessness about her incipient education – she had two small children to look after – so she let the matter pass. Milly, fearful of being caught browsing Vinti-didi's books, took to leafing through, again, the latter half of her own tattered book, the sections she couldn't read because she had been taken out of school before they reached them. She looked at them in the afternoon, when everyone had a nap and she had a free hour or two, then again at night, just before getting into her bed, which was a couple of thick sheets, folded over, on the kitchen floor, another bundled-up sheet for a pillow and an old, greasy mosquito net, the four corner strings of which had to be tied to a window bar, the tap in the sink and two nails on the wall opposite, to erect it. She sat outside this dented, misshapen parallelogram and looked at her book in the light from the naked bulb on the ceiling and wished her mother would fall face down on the burning chulha one evening, or get lost in the forest while gathering kindling or mahua flowers fallen on the ground and get eaten by a jackal or bitten by a snake, or have her arms and legs cut off by the men who had come for Budhuwa, the men (and women) who came to the village every night and had to be fed and given places to sleep. She looked at the opaque words on the pages and ripped them out, one by one, and scrunched them up and put them inside her mouth, chewing slowly and carefully, using lots of saliva so that the ink which created the words dissolved thoroughly and dispersed as a thin stream of disassembled words through her insides. In the morning she knew she would wake up knowing the words that had withheld themselves so far.

A week or so after this she was caught by Vinti, eating the balled-up pieces of paper that she had discarded from the fair copy of her school homework.

'Ma, ma,' Vinti shouted, thrilled and slightly appalled. 'Milly's eating paper, come quickly.'

Milly's mouth was full. She could neither swallow nor spit out in front of Pendo and Vinti – either would be an unacceptable thing to do right under the noses of the people in whose home she was a servant-girl. Her eyes filled with tears of shame and fear.

Pendo, stunned for a few minutes, found her voice. 'Why are you eating paper? It's a disgusting thing to do, you savage girl. Are you hungry? Don't you get enough to eat here?'

Milly nodded to indicate that she did. The bolus felt larger than her head. It was consuming her. Vinti looked at her as if she were something floating on a particularly toxic open drain.

Pendo said, 'You're not in your village any more. These kinds of junglee things are not done here. Is that understood?'

Milly, her cheeks swollen with the matter inside her mouth, nodded again. She had been caught in her magic ritual; now she was never going to learn the words that Vinti-didi had written and rejected.

A few days later, a moment of inspiration. Vinti, in Class III of Birsa Munda Girls' School (a private school, despite the name), was going through a phase of wanting to be a schoolteacher. It suddenly came to Pendo that, in Milly, her daughter could have the perfect companion to play games of Student – Teacher; Vinti could truly teach Milly the elements of reading, writing and arithmetic, not only in play.

Milly's first experience of two meals a day – two-and-a-half, if the morning tea and stale chapatti were counted – was at the home of Pendo and Lewis and Vinti-didi and the little one, Suraj. In the village, on lucky days, they had one meal, which was usually bajra ki roti and til chutney. A two-meal day was a rare gift; also a great struggle. There were days when they went hungry. Milly remembered those by the absence of smoke and its particular smell because her mother didn't light the chulha to cook – there was nothing to put on the fire. Even into adulthood, the smell of a chulha being fanned to get the flames to catch filled her with a simple joy, a sense of security. On smokeless days, Milly remembered her mother sometimes berating her father, drunk and stretched out in a stupor in a corner or outside, in the courtyard, but the more frequent scenario was of her mother crying silently and bitterly, her lip torn and bleeding, her face livid, one eye bruising up, from the thrashing she had just received from her drunken husband. On one of these evenings, with the smell of violence still hanging in the air, Milly had watched, with a kind of horrified fascination, the blood, snot, tears and saliva from her mother's face all mingle while she had cried out, twice, words etched indelibly in Milly's memory – 'The pangs of hunger are great pangs, it's a burning. God gave us stomachs to punish us.'

Still, this was the way things were, and Milly and her brothers and sisters, not knowing a regular or even occasional alternative where meals were numerous over long uninterrupted stretches, did not know to complain – this was the way their world was; there was no other. The glimpse of the alternative, village feasts and festivals, was not seen as such because, by their very nature, they were exceptions to the ordinary run of their days. A cow or a couple of goats were slaughtered, and all the families in the village paid for the meat, which was then distributed among the households according to how much each had paid. A meal of rice and beef was what they imagined heaven to be like. Even if what they got on their plates was gristle, tendon, a pucker of skin or fat, it was still flesh. Communal feasts were cooked and distributed centrally. These offered a higher chance of getting actual meat, not just a nub of bone and the translucent fat that clung to sockets. Milly sucked out the marrow from sections of the shinbone, if she ever got one, and was sorry to have to throw the cleaned and picked bone to the dogs roaming through the eating area, alert for scraps.

At the conversion ceremony, the church paid for the feast following the entry of eight families – fifty-five members in total – into the fold. Milly was too young at the time to have had much understanding of why their mother had decided one day to christen all the little children. She had asked, many years later, what impelled her to do it.

Her mother had said, 'They promised a big sack of rice. It was food for a month. I had reached the limit with not having enough to feed you lot. They also said all of you could go free to school in the big town, which would mean government jobs for the little boys when they grew up ...'

Then it had dawned upon her that school was a touchy subject between her and Milly and she had stopped and looked away.

The christening feast involved the sacrifice of two cows and a big fat pig: it felt as if the days of plenty had arrived. The feast lasted two days. Then, over time, there were the four days of Easter and Christmas Day, all of which included communal feasting. To a lot of people that was inducement enough to convert, although non-Christians were welcomed to these feasts, and sat down, side by side, with the Christians, ate their food, tried to sing their hymns. They could even go into the church, but not during service.

Here in Dumri, Milly was given lunch after the family had finished eating. In other words, she ate whatever was left over, which often meant that if the family had, say, a dal and two kinds of sabzi, she would get rice or roti, some dal and whichever vegetable dish had not been eaten entirely by Lewis, Pendo and Vinti, and Suraj, when he grew up a little. This rule of priority applied particularly to fish, egg and meat dishes: by an unspoken rule, Milly was not allowed to eat – or not given – these special things, the leftovers being saved for the children and Lewis and Pendo, in that order. If anything remained after they had had a meat dish several times, Milly was given the final residue, which often consisted only of potatoes and gravy with tiny shreds of meat here and there, or an inferior piece, all bone, gristle, fat and membrane, which no one wanted to eat, or when Pendo thought the dish was on the turn and couldn't be given to the family any longer. Milly didn't mind, didn't even notice most of the time. She had plenty to eat – plenty of rice, which was such a luxury back home and, crucially, a reliably regular supply of two full meals every day. She no longer went to bed, after writing out the difficult words from her one page of reading every night, wondering whether she was going to eat the following day.

A child breaks things. Milly was eight, going on nine, when she started working in Dumri. Her child's hands could not carry large, heavy objects, get a saving grip on a soapy saucer or cup intent on slipping from her grasp. They did not have enough span to arrest something from falling and breaking while she was doing the cleaning. Such accidents were not frequent; they were usually limited to dropped knick-knacks. The plates, glasses and bowls were all stainless steel at Pendo's, so there was no danger of breaking them. A set of four china cups and saucers arrived once. They sat in a cupboard and were taken out for very special guests, not so much to honour them as to advertise Pendo and Lewis's upward mobility. After one of these outings, Milly broke the handle of a cup while doing the washing-up. It was such a delicate little toy-ear-like thing, it simply came off in her hands. Pendo scolded her – 'Look what you've done, you clumsy pagal! My set is ruined for ever' – and Milly felt afraid for a day or two, then it all blew over. The lame set sat in the darkness of the cupboard and was forgotten.

The reprimands were, predictably enough, in direct proportion to the cost of the object broken. There were few expensive things in Pendo's home; usually the value was of emotion or attachment. Milly broke a terracotta doll belonging to Vinti once; Vinti brought the house down. Again, Milly was told off, but this time she felt that Pendo's words and tone had something of the performance about them, as if she felt she had to be seen by her daughter to be punishing the servant who had broken her toy. On this occasion, Milly felt far worse – and far more fearful – than the time she broke the handle on the cup: her lessons were dependent entirely on keeping Vinti-didi happy. This storm, too, passed; it was a children's quarrel, temporary and trivial, although clouded by the element of class.

Nearly four years after she started at Pendo and Lewis's, Milly was taken out of their home by her mother and sent to a Bengali couple in Jamshedpur, an even bigger town. By now she could read Hindi effortlessly, write slowly and haltingly but clearly, and do basic addition and subtraction. She knew the English alphabet and could read small words – 'cat', bat', 'car'. She read the word 'bus' one evening and smiled at her younger self, which had not known what a bus was, until the moment of the journey to Dumri.

5: *Fate*

Soni had known them to visit their village frequently; in fact, a few of the group were familiar faces. She was sure that she had seen the woman in the blue sari with the medicine van on the two occasions it had visited their village. The new water tank, behind the school, had been built by some of them. They gathered in front of the school, or on the neat green in front of the church, or the raised square platform under the circle of the eight giant trees by the river where the gram sabha sat. 'Samaj sewi', social workers, she thought they were called. She had heard them give speeches, long, fiery ones, and had tuned out; everyone who wanted to win elections gave speeches. Those men during election time came from big towns or cities, promised big things, smiled, bowed, then left. Everything carried on as before. But the social workers were different. She could tell by looking at them that they belonged here, were people like her and her neighbours. Word went round that they were putting on a play.

What was a play? She had only the haziest notion. She joined the crowd assembling near the well. She stood next to her sister, intent on watching her face during the play – maybe this could make her smile again? Would it have singing? Yes, it did. They were words she didn't understand. What language were they singing in? Would the play be incomprehensible too?

The song was over. The group disbanded and moved to the sides. Two women returned to the centre. They pretended to be picking kendu leaves. Or was it kindling? They spoke about how the forest was their home and protector, how it provided them with everything they needed. But the government wanted to move them out and give the forest to rich people, big companies, who wanted to cut the trees, sell the wood, dig up the land for the riches under it ... The water of the rivers and streams would turn red from green and would no longer be fit for any use. They would lose everything, their homes, the forest, the air, the water, their freedom, and would be made to work as slaves on the land, no longer theirs but someone else's. Soni watched, unblinking.

They talked of adhikaar, haq, izzat: 'The government does not give us those things, rights and respect. We have nothing except the rights to jal, jameen and jangal. They're going to take our water, land and forest away from us.'

Then they shifted to talking about how much they were paid for every kilo of tamarind collected, or every pile of hundred kendu leaves, and how much the tamarind or kendu was then sold for. They said the difference could pay for a doctor's clinic at the village, or a month's supply of rice and lentils.

'Why have we been poor and hungry for decades? Why do we always hear of vikas, of crores of rupees given by the Centre for development, and never see a paisa of it? Where does the money go? Why has our situation not changed?' There was a lot of talk. Sometimes Soni couldn't understand what was going on.

Things perked up. Two men joined the women. The women announced, in loud, frightened whispers, that one was a forest official and the other a contractor. Why had they shown up? The two men started harassing the women. Did they have permission to pick leaves? Where was the piece of paper that gave them permission? How much had they collected? Did they know they would be fined for the illegal picking of leaves? Everything in the forest was government property. The women would have to come with them and pay a big fine, and if they couldn't ... here the men began to laugh. They caught hold of the women's arms and started dragging them away. The women cried for help. One of the men pulled at the clothes of the woman he was holding by the wrist. Soni felt a tremor passing through the skin of her arm where it touched her sister's. She looked sideways. How could anybody sitting so still – Didi's eyes were not blinking, she didn't seem to be breathing even – generate such a steady, low hum of trembling? Soni turned back to look at the actors. They were gone, but the audience could still hear the women screaming and crying, the men laughing. The sound held. She sensed an ultimatum in the play that she was seeing.

Two of the samaj sewi came onstage, a man and a woman, and asked how long the people here were going to put up with such humiliation, such indignities? Were they not humans, too, or were their lives as nothing to the big people?

She noticed that her sister's trembling had transmitted itself – it was she, Soni, who was now the core of the tremor. She was approaching the realisation of something fateful in herself. Something her sister had said after she had come back, something Soni thought she had forgotten, now inserted itself in her head – just a few words: 'I didn't put up a fight because they would have killed me otherwise.'

The meeting happened by chance. Soni and her sister had gone to wash clothes by the river when they saw a group of people appear out of the forest, on the other bank, and begin to wade across the water towards the village. It was winter and the river was a narrow green channel running through a wide expanse of sand and black-and-grey-and-white rocks that were now exposed. As they came nearer, Soni could recognise most of them. She was now better informed and thought of them as 'the Party people', not samaj sewis. They were the ones who organised the meetings and plays, the ones who had recently started visiting the village in a truck, with doctors who spoke to anyone who was ill, with injections for babies, medicines for fever and pain and stomach trouble, bandages for burns and bites.

They seemed to know who her sister was and what had happened to her. The woman who was always part of the medicine-van group spoke first. She said her name was Bela. She squatted at the edge of the water to be level with the girls, then she put both her hands on Soni's sister's shoulders. She looked at Soni and asked her to leave them alone. Three days after this, Soni's sister left home to join the Party.

Soni waited for a few years until she had finished with Class 8. Their school was now being used as a base by the Army to flush out guerrillas who had taken over the forests. She could wait for months, years, before the school was returned to its proper use. But it was too late for all that. She knew to whom to talk, now that she had seized – by both hands, it felt – the decision that she had made years ago. It felt like acknowledging someone familiar, someone destined, who had been within her sight for so long.

The Maoist activists operated in the surrounding forest and often held meetings in the bordering villages. They found a sympathetic audience in the villagers whose lives of unchanging poverty and misery and hopelessness needed a radically new kind of hope, which the militants provided. The Party, as the Communist Party of India (Maoists) – CPI(M) – was called, had two guerrilla wings; the group Soni joined was the People's Liberation Guerrilla Army.

She couldn't join the group her sister was in because there were strict rules against having family members and relations within one squad. 'Liberation' was a loaded word around these parts – all areas of forest in this state under the control of Maoist guerrillas were called 'liberated territories'. Their village meetings were well attended and one of their chief purposes, recruitment of young men and women, was often successful. Some were inspired to join because they wanted change, improvement to their lives of hunger and squalor. Others joined because they had no prospects – low education, no jobs, no possibility of changing their lives for the better. Still others, because the guerrillas paid money to the new recruits: an upfront payment of fifteen hundred rupees, then the promise of a monthly payment thereafter; besides, they would be fed and clothed and even given further education at no cost. And who wouldn't want to leave the dirt and mess of the villages, the open drains and sewers, the lack of sanitation, the river polluted by a mining factory upstream, its green water now the colour of the dark-orange soil? Soni certainly felt this new experience, of waking up in the forest and being the first to breathe in the air that smelled of dew and trees and leaves, as a wonderful thing in her life.

First, the new recruits had to undergo a year-long training session. Soni, along with her new comrades, got up at four in the morning and ran up and down the hills, did sit-ups and push-ups and presses. The squad commander drove each recruit to better his or her performance over the months, expecting him or her – there were nearly as many women who joined the guerrillas as men – to shave time off their personal best. She learned to crawl through jungle floors and was marked on, among other things, how noiseless she could be during the exercise. She was given increasingly intricate lessons on camouflage and that most vital of all talents: how to appear silently and disappear with the swiftness of a snake bringing its head down to strike. She was taught target practice and given lessons in using explosives. She learned how to make IEDs – Improvised Explosive Devices – that could be set off using basic, easily available and seemingly innocuous things such as catapults made out of twigs and rubber bands, flashbulbs in cameras, hypodermic syringes, water pistols, even battery-operated children's toys.

In that first year of training she went to a school run by Maoists; there were several such schools, mobile or permanent, in the base area. There she was taught English, mathematics, science, geography and Communism. She learned about capitalism, labour, exploitation, about the bourgeois and the petit bourgeois, about false consciousness and the dictatorship of the proletariat.

The recruits got training in how to set up their bunker and, equally important, how to dismantle it quickly and move on without leaving a trace. Bunker meant no more than a plastic sheet or thatch spread over four bamboo posts. Soni's squad had five women and six men. The women got extra rations of food, particularly eggs, and if eggs were not available, groundnuts. Life on the move, in the open air, was tough. Sometimes it felt that they were little more than wild pack-animals, carrying loads on their backs and heads, sacks of rice and grain, heavy kitbags, moving from one village to another through the jungle. The guerrillas' main – often only – source of sustenance was the food levy they imposed on the surrounding villages: they took five kilos of rice and lentils from the thirty kilos that every villager who held a ration card was entitled to, from the public distribution system. Not infrequently they would have to collect the food from villages which had missed the ration day, because they were so far away from the distribution hub, so there was either nothing the guerrillas could be given, in the worst situation, or they had to do with very little, with food that could barely be called food: rice that was more stones than rice, lentils that had gone maggoty. There were days when they subsisted on this stony rice and tamarind paste or a fiery chutney made with ants, salt, tamarind and dried red chillies. On such days they looked upon every animal they glimpsed in the jungle – a bird, a scurrying rodent in the undergrowth, a crashing boar, a snake – with hunger, wanting only to bring it down, roast it over a fire and fall upon it. Weakness and exhaustion slouched and pressed against them.

The guerrillas slept outdoors in the winter months, with nothing but a thin blanket to cover them. They learned how to harness nature for their purposes: which trees were best to hide behind because their trunks could withstand or absorb bullets; how to read the forest so that they knew how to navigate, where to walk, where to go, where to hide, even though there were no visible paths; how to create traps with trees or in the undergrowth without any sign to betray their existence; what kind of formation to follow while spreading out in the forest to surround the paramilitary forces sent to hunt them out, so that the soldiers did not know from which direction they were going to be attacked.

There were speeches on most evenings to remind everyone what and who they were fighting, to keep them fervid, their anger shiny and whetted. Her blood ran swifter, hotter, when she listened to the leaders. Theirs was a different approach – no longer the old lies of 'If you vote for me, I promise to bring about this and that change', but the direct action of taking power in your own hands. 'If you kill, we kill too. If you have guns, we have guns,' as one comrade had put it so simply. Here was a kind of equality, at last.

6: *Jamshedpur*

Milly's mother considered the new position in Jamshedpur a move up because Milly's salary increased. The increment was only by a hundred and fifty rupees, but to her this meant a week's worth of staples. The young Bengali couple at whose home Milly began work – Debdulal, a railway engineer, and Pratima, his wife – did not mistreat her in any egregious way, but worked her hard and grudged her any leisure or resting time. 'Standing at the window again?' Pratima would scold her. 'Don't you have work to do? Is the rice picked? Did you hang out the washing?'

Once Milly made the mistake of responding. 'I've done all that,' she said meekly.

'How dare you answer back?' Pratima shouted. 'Idling away all day! Go soak the bedcover and wash it, then make the bed in our room. Why is this table here? I have told you to move it to that corner so many times that my mouth is foaming. Why are you standing here, staring at the floor?'

Pratima was particularly incensed if she caught Milly napping in the afternoon, even if there was no work to be done. She invented tasks to prevent this – an errand to run in the blood-drying heat of the afternoon, spice pastes to grind, various forms of spring-cleaning. She gave Milly two square meals a day, generous portions, heavy on the rice, but Milly felt the food discrimination here more than she had at Dumri. If Pratima's nagging, scolding and surveillance hadn't existed, Milly wouldn't have noticed, but one kind of ungenerosity sensitised her to another.

There was one incident that lodged like an arrowhead inside her. Pratima discovered Milly with a book, one of several of Vinti's from her earlier school years.

Pratima had laughed with open derision and said, 'Turned into quite the educated lady, huh? Shouldn't you be doing something more suitable? Have you kneaded the flour for tonight's rotis?'

Much later it occurred to Milly, as she was picking the scabs of this wound, that she was far better at Hindi than her Bengali employers were: they always got their hota and hoti, karta and karti wrong.

The thing she learned in Jamshedpur, however, was how to cook Bengali food. Like most Bengali people, Debdulal and Pratima wanted to eat their own food all the time and looked upon what they called non-Bengali cuisines with a degree of contempt and suspicion. Milly was taught how to cook egg curry and, when Pratima was in a more economising mood, omelette in a thin gravy with diced potatoes. She learned about the use of the Bengali spice mixture, panchphoron, and various ways of cooking cabbage and cauliflower and peas in the winter months.

Milly had a plate (stainless steel) and bowl (aluminium, enamelled, chipped and dented) for her food, and a small stainless-steel beaker for her water. These were separate from the crockery which Pratima and Debdulal used; she wasn't allowed to eat off those. Her things had to be kept in a different cupboard, the one that held the gas cylinder for their cooker. The rule was set on the very first day she started work. But to Milly, it was the availability of regular food that mattered, not the plates and bowls from which she ate it. She never gave the business of separate plates a thought.

There were other, subtler rules, made known to her by some process that eluded her, leaving only the strictures in her mind. She had to make the bed but she wasn't allowed to sit, let alone lie, on it. On the occasions she could only reach a tricky corner to tuck in a sheet tightly or smooth a crease by lying partially or by supporting a part of her body – say, knees or upper half or haunch – on the surface of the bed, she used the special broom to beat, extra-hard, the areas her body had touched. This rule did not need to be spelled out simply because no servant would ever have thought of the possibility of sleeping on their master's or mistress's bed. And although Milly had never broken this cardinal rule – in fact there was no rule holding her back, since the act was unthinkable and had, therefore, never occurred to her – she was once reprimanded by Pratima after she discovered the imprint of Milly's palm indenting the soft surface of the bed. She had needed to press her hand down in order to shift a corner of the mattress, but from that day she had taken great care to erase all traces of her touch.

She wasn't allowed to sit on the sofas and chairs. She could watch television when Pratima turned it on, but she had to either stand or sit on the floor to watch it. Again, she didn't mind; she knew the rules. But when she was alone in their home, she sometimes sat on all the chairs, armchairs, sofas and divans in turn, just to see what it felt like. She was also very careful to remove any traces of her sitting on sofas and armchairs: she dusted them again, and used the special broom for the bed to beat the seats and fluff them up. After a while, she lost interest in sitting on the forbidden furniture when she was alone.

One evening, hypnotised by *Kyoon Ki Saas Bhi Kabhi Bahu Thi*, Milly was told by Pratima, 'Don't lean back, your spine will become crooked.' Milly, sitting on the floor, was supporting her back against the edge of an empty armchair. She straightened her back but it still touched the chair.

'Move forward a little bit more,' Pratima said.

Milly obeyed. She still didn't get it.

After ten minutes, Milly, lost in the world of television, heard Didi again, her words a little bit more commanding this time, 'How many times have I told you not to lean against that chair? Sit up.'

The following evening, before the television was turned on, Pratima reminded Milly, 'Don't lean back against the furniture.'

Milly nodded. There was no melodrama unfolding in front of her eyes to dilute the message this time.

Watching television was a flexible activity that sometimes depended on Pratima's mood. Generally speaking, it was allowed if Milly had finished all her chores and didn't neglect her duties. She was mostly undiscriminating about programmes – she was so fascinated by audiovisual entertainment at the flick of a switch that she could joyously sit through anything that involved moving, speaking figures far removed from her life. But slowly distinctions began to open up: she preferred serials to the news, films to talk shows, programmes that featured a suite of songs from different films. She quickly picked up the times of the day and the days of the week when her favourite shows went out, but whether she got to watch every one of them was up to Pratima's whim. Pratima strongly believed that servants 'sat on your head' if you indulged them by letting them watch television or allowing them anything they appeared to enjoy. Whenever she got a whiff of any such activity from which Milly derived pleasure – and watching serials was an obviously readable one – she clamped down on it by inventing extra, unnecessary chores. If Milly did them swiftly enough to leave her some time in front of the television, Pratima invoked the mistress's prerogative: a curt 'Don't sit here and watch TV, go to the kitchen.' Milly had never been able to detect any rhyme or reason behind Pratima's conflicting signals on this matter, unlike the clear directive about sitting on the furniture, for example. Still, orders were orders; she couldn't question them. What the fickleness left

Milly with was an escalating tension in the evenings: would she be able to watch *Nukkad*? Or would a mood swing see her banished to the kitchen from where she could hear every line of dialogue, every note of the billowing music, but not see any of the action?

It was in Jamshedpur that the matter of accidentally broken or damaged household items became an unpleasant issue. Pratima used some of the vast reserves of time on her hands to form strong attachments to objects. She had what she called a 'showcase', a wooden cupboard, about six feet high, glass-fronted, with shelves inside. It housed objects precious to her – porcelain plates and cups and saucers, a few framed photographs, glass and terracotta decorative bric-a-brac; in short, things she thought of as suitably indicative of her status as the wife of a man who had a government job. The crockery inside the showcase was never taken out and used, not even for guests Pratima and Debdulal were trying to ingratiate themselves with – it was for display purposes only. The moot question was who the showcasing was for, the couple themselves or for their infrequent visitors. Milly was not allowed to touch the contents of this display cabinet, which was kept locked anyway. This did not hold back Pratima from complaining how dusty and untidy everything inside looked and blaming Milly for it. By this time Milly had learned that she was not to answer back. If that china was ever used, she would have to clean it, handling it with all the care and delicacy extended to a newborn's head; the very prospect filled her with terror.

So when she was asked to clean the interior of the showcase – 'Take out every single thing, I don't want to find dust hiding behind and between things, understood?' – Milly thought she had avoided great danger: it was, after all, the safer job of cleaning the cupboard, not the dangerous task of handling the fragile contents. She took out the china very carefully, set it on newspapers laid down on the floor and did the same again with everything inside. Pratima sat on a stool, watching her and repeating, 'Be careful, very careful.

I don't want a single thing broken.' By the time Milly finished dusting and cleaning the inside, and putting everything back, intact, her hands were shaking and she felt that she hadn't exhaled since the task began. Then she turned and thought she saw something on a piece of newspaper that she had forgotten to put back in – it was nothing, just a large picture on the paper that had caught the corner of her eye – but in her tense state, nervous that she was going to step on something fragile, she overcompensated her correcting movement, lost her balance and hit the showcase with her shoulder and side. A neat crack went through the pane that she collided against. Pratima was speechless for what to Milly felt like aeons, before she exploded. It was a relief to be slapped by her, and shouted at, after the build-up to the inevitable.

'I'll deduct it from your wages, you just wait and see,' she screamed. 'Everything you break, big or small, will come off your wages. That'll teach you to break things you won't be able to afford in your lifetime.'

It was not an empty threat, made in the heat of the moment; Pratima deducted money for every article that Milly broke during her time in Jamshedpur.

7: *A change of place and a meeting*

Just when she had begun to think that the low hum of unhappiness in Jamshedpur would last for ever, Milly went back to her village on her annual leave and was told that she wouldn't be returning to Debdulal and Pratima's, but instead going to Mumbai, for five times the pay. It had come about through Sabina, a Christian woman from the village, who worked as a domestic maid in Mumbai; Milly barely knew her. When Sabina had returned home for a month's holiday after her first year in Mumbai, she had told everyone how there was this endless demand for housemaids in the city. Word reached Joseph, a local clergyman, who was always on the lookout for ways to make the hopeless lives of his poor flock a tiny bit better, whether through using what little influence he had to get them small jobs, 'loose-change work', as they called it, or through acts of charity. What he managed to acquire for them was, in the long run, trivial – a week's work as replacement labour in a bottling factory, slightly higher margins on sales of basketloads of tamarind or mangoes or mahua flower, getting an NGO based in Patna to give some kind of vocational training, such as machine wool-weaving classes, to women – but this business of going away to big towns and cities, especially Mumbai, to work in people's homes, struck him as a somewhat bigger opportunity. Besides, there was nothing to do, especially for girls, in this village; gathering kindling, grazing cows, helping in the fields ... that was the extent of it. And now some of them had started joining the guerrilla squads in the surrounding forests, a course of action that could only end in one thing. A Mumbai salary could mean significant money sent back home to the families; the girls would, after all, be living and eating in the homes they worked in, therefore saving the larger part of their wages. His head buzzing with hope and ideas, Joseph went to see Sabina.

It took Sabina a few phone calls to find a home for Milly; what helped was the fact of Milly's work experience. Sabina, about to return to her job in Borivili, was taking two girls from the next village for whom she had found jobs as housemaids, also in Mumbai. Milly's appointment was to the home of a Sindhi family in Lower Parel, the Vachanis. The biggest city she and people in her village had ever heard of, unimaginably big with an unimaginably large number of people living in it, everyone making money, living a life of ease, of four meals a day, a brick house with two or three rooms, a world of opportunity and plenty, a world very far from their own ... the excitement, stoked by stories Sabina had to tell, was so palpable that even Milly, who was slowly being gripped by an escalating fear at the prospect of going to such a big place, occasionally felt its touch. Sabina wore a wristwatch with a golden metal strap on her right hand. Her sandals, a tiny red flower at the junction where the two side-straps met the toe-peg, had big city written all over them. She spoke more Hindi now than Sadri.

Budhuwa's first reaction to Milly's new job was a laconic, 'You'll find it more difficult to come back here on holidays.' Ever since Milly had returned home from Jamshedpur, she had struggled with watching Budhuwa go about his daily life with his one, left hand. He was much better, of course. He had learned to do most things with one hand, even his work unweaving the large plastic sacks, separating out each cord and then tying it on to a spool. He could now do it with a degree of deftness; the money he earned was calculated by the number of spools finished and Budhuwa could often manage to do up to four or five bobbins a day, depending on how many sacks had come his way. In the months after the attack, he had found it impossible even to take apart the sacks, holding them down with his foot and using a pair of pliers to pick out the threads: an entire day would go and he would have disassembled about one-third of a sheet, the frayed, untied ends sticking up like the unruly hay at the extremities of a bundle. Now, however, he had a rhythm, and a fleet one, too, and an ability, his own peculiar, imperfect way of getting things done.

Milly watched him at work and said, 'You've become quick at this.'

Budhuwa looked up at her, turned his head back down to his plastic cords and said nothing. After a while, noting that she hadn't gone, he said, 'Yes. Doing the same thing every day for hours ...'

Pause.

'Not that I'm good at anything else,' he added as an afterthought, or maybe a negation.

Milly gave a wan smile which he didn't see. She could not say why witnessing him in this state, when he had managed to rise above what had been inflicted on him, should overcome her so – this feeling of disintegration was so much more powerful than when she had watched him struggle and lose, struggle and lose, time and time again, to trivial, powerless inanimate objects such as sacks and pliers and cord and wooden spool. It was all he could do; it was everything. The knowledge slayed her.

Nearly nine years had passed since Milly had left her home village for her first job as a live-in domestic servant in Dumri. During this time, Milly visited her home only four times on annual leave from work: three times while she was at Dumri and once after she began working in Jamshedpur. She saw Soni the first couple of times but missed all that befell her family while she was away at Debdulal and Pratima's. Milly's memories of Soni had not exactly faded but had slowly become unvisited, tangential, irrelevant. Childhood friendships were often like that – intense in presence and in the present tense, remote and unreachable in absence. But coming back home again after so long gave sharper outlines and brighter colours to those memories, and Milly found herself curious to know how her childhood friend had turned out. Did Soni get married to a man who had a government job? She was the one who had managed to stay still the longest, despite the annoyances caused by red ants or mosquitoes, to keep the tamarind stones balanced on her forehead and neck. Asking about her now revealed more than Milly had reckoned: the death of Soni's mother, all the business with her sister, came out tersely from Budhuwa and their mother. All Milly could do was ask if Soni was still living here or had she, like Milly, moved far away from home.

'No, she's still here. She is a member of the Party now,' Milly's mother said. Her face was unreadable.

'Party?' asked Milly, shocked. It was the Party that had been responsible for Budhuwa's hand. Milly knew about the death of Soni's mother but not much else besides.

'Yes, she has become a samaj sewi,' Budhuwa said, but Milly couldn't quite judge if he used the term with anger. In these villages people who joined the Party were seen both as extremists and as 'social workers'. Many looked on the guerrillas as 'our boys and girls', as 'one of us'.

'She lives in the forests now,' Milly's mother said. 'They come to the villages in the dead of the night for food, then they go back before sunrise. They carry guns.'

Milly was too stunned to say anything.

Her brother said, 'She's joined the liberators, that's what they call themselves. Two months ago these liberators blew up the school building, the school she and you went to, because the CRPF men were using it as a base.'

Milly, eyes now round as plums, said, 'You saw?'

'No. What's there to see? They went around telling people they did it. Some others saw, they said it was the guerrilla group she had joined.'

The pressure of the unsaid became so intense that Milly couldn't bear it any longer. She began to ask Budhuwa, 'The same group ... the same group that ... that ...' but couldn't proceed any further.

Budhuwa helped her out; it was all one to him now; he wasn't going to get his hand back. 'No, she joined the other group, but there's no difference between them, not really. They are all part of the same Naxalbadi party.'

The bitterness in his voice was now another presence in the small, dark room. Milly looked down at the floor. Their mother was trying to light the LPG gas cooker she had bought with money that Milly sent home.

In the end it was Soni who came to her first. A weak hammering of fists on the door very late at night, around one or two o'clock, sent fear running through the whole family, but it was soon quelled by a young woman's voice, 'Milly, ei Milly, is Milly there? This is Soni.' She was trying to balance waking up Milly with keeping her voice down; it was the rattling of the chain on the door that awakened everyone.

In the moonlight, with the shadows so accentuated, and with the changes wrought on her by time, it could have been someone impersonating Soni. They stood facing each other and they had nothing to say.

'It's very late, no?' were Milly's first words.

Soni had nothing to return to this except an obvious 'yes'. They stood looking away from each other, at the shadows, heard the taut, watchful silence of Milly's family behind her, all of them waiting for something to happen. Milly imagined she heard objects being moved very stealthily, objects that could be used as weapons. The awkwardness between the girls continued to tick; time had made them strangers.

Soni gave a little laugh and said, 'I can't tell in this dark what you look like now.'

That laugh hadn't changed. Milly was, in the blink of an eye, back to the age of six.

'I can't see you properly, either.'

'I have to go soon. You'll come to me tomorrow? On the other side of the river? Not the village side, but across the water. Stand exactly opposite where the gram sabha sits. You'll come?'

Milly hesitated.

'Don't be afraid. Nothing will happen to you, you're with me.'

Much later, Milly thought that it was this reassurance, unprompted by anything she had said or done, as if Soni had read the silence, that made her keep the rendezvous the following day.

At four o'clock on an April afternoon it was impossible to stand anywhere except in full shade. The river, Baniya, was green; one could cross it at its thinnest spot partly by stepping over the stones that had come out of their underwater hiding during the run of dry months and partly by wading across. On the other side lay what looked like the border of a jungle, but there were narrow paths through it and one could walk down them to the edge of another village. Right now, the mahua trees were in bloom, the red soil decorated here and there with small rugs of fallen cream flowers. Milly was surprised that they hadn't already been picked by the villagers to make mahua, or eaten by deer and langurs.

Beyond that was the larger surprise of not being able to fit the seventeen-year-old Soni to the image Milly had of an eight-year-old girl. That old image was not sharp, but she would never have thought the new reality in front of her as a development from that faded memory.

'What are you staring at?' Soni asked, laughing. That sound again, like cool, green water flowing over rocks.

Was there something of the girl she had known in that smile, that laugh? Would Milly have recognised her in a crowded street of a different town? Was Soni thinking the same things about her: that Milly, too, would be unrecognisable to her?

As if she had looked inside Milly's head, Soni said, 'You know, you've changed a lot, I wouldn't have recognised you if I bumped into you somewhere else, somewhere far away from here.'

Yes, that flowing chatter, that complete ease with everything, that's not left her, Milly thought. She said, 'I was thinking the same about you.'

'They tell me you live in big cities now, Ranchi, Jamshedpur. You've moved up in the world. You earn lots of money? Have you married someone from the city?' Her eyes were dancing with excitement.

Milly felt shy and turned her head away. They were still strangers to each other and she didn't know if their shared past was going to be like a change of weather they could easily slip into as they walked the red paths through the trees, shafts of sunlight falling on them wherever there was an opening in the canopy. She noticed that there weren't one or two people from the village in here, collecting firewood or kendu leaves. Budhuwa occasionally picked kendu leaves from the forest floor now, to supplement his income from the plastic-thread-making, but he complained that he was not too good at it, not sufficiently nimble. Besides, Budhuwa had said, the traders, to whom the villagers sold their bundles of leaves, had to pay a tax to the Party people, which they resented, so they were wary of taking on new, unfamiliar collectors, whom they suspected were in cahoots with the Party. Milly looked at the thick, fissured bark of the kendu tree, a regular grid of rectangles, like cracked earth during drought. It didn't seem so benign any more. She had learned in her childhood that spirits lived in some of these large old trees, Burubonga and Ikirbonga and Chandibonga and many others, not all of them benevolent. Lutkum Haram and Lutkum Buria had their very own sal tree. She had always wanted to see the bonga in his or her tree but when she had asked, her mother had waved a hand in the general direction of the forest and said that they could be found there. Father Joseph had tried to discourage them from believing in such things, but Milly had left the village before either system of belief could take hold.

She breathed in that familiar vegetal smell, the smell of sun and the sun-baked bright earth. A dazzling butterfly flitted past. Did she miss this in Dumri and Jamshedpur? Did she prefer to live in a town which had none of these things? Yes, she did. Sabina was going to send her to Mumbai. She wanted to be in Mumbai rather than stuck here with forests and rivers; you can miss something without wanting to be reunited with it, without wanting the other things that necessarily came with the thing you missed.

'Why have you become quiet? There *must* be a man. Tell me quickly,' Soni was laughing again.

Milly laughed, too, and said, 'No, no man anywhere. But I hear you're carrying guns nowadays. You joined the Party? How come?'

The one question that was like a fishbone in her throat was one that she couldn't bring herself to ask.

Soni didn't reply.

Milly asked her again, thinking she hadn't heard.

Soni said, 'You haven't lived here for a long time, you don't know how bad things have become. You can't fight them with votes. How can you fight a lion with toy bows and arrows made for children to play with?' The words seemed dragged out of her.

There were cloud-islands of insects, a dense patch for a few inches, hovering in the middle air, then clear light-and-shade-and-heat again. On a low bush, a spider's web was teeming with scores and scores of tiny baby spiders.

'Do you understand? Elections are not going to improve our lot,' she said. That ease, that familiar laughter, all had disappeared. In their place was a focused avidity in her face. If the red soil of the place, and the April heat, had a face, Soni's, now, would be that.

'But why did you join?' Milly asked. 'I thought you wanted to get married and move away from here.'

'I told you, I started to go to their meetings. Then I thought, we are women, we are killed over dowry, and our parents cry and say, oh we lost a girl, and then they forget about us. We are forgotten. We'll all die, but why not do something in the short time that we have, so that people remember us? If I die tomorrow, my father won't cry and say, oh we lost our girl, he'll cry and say, she fought for the people, she laid down her life for the people, she died fighting for adhikaar, for the rights of our people, and they won't forget me. My comrades will build a monument to my name, keep it alive.'

Milly was silent, absorbing the torrent of feelings that had gushed out of Soni. Eventually, she said, 'You fight too? You know how to fire a gun?'

'Yes, of course I do.' Soni proceeded to explain their training, their life of drills and exercises; of muzzle-loading rifles and country-made revolvers, learning how to shoot, target practice, raiding police armouries, lifting guns off policemen killed in encounters; of the art of hiding and running away, of the greater art of surrounding and disappearing. She left out the recurring bouts of malaria and diarrhoea, the exhaustion like a second skin over them, the slow erosion of the body that was the gift of living in the open, like animals.

It seemed to Milly that they were talking about children's games, hide-and-seek in the forest, jumping around with sticks and leaping on each other in a game of ambush. All this military training, guns and bunkers and guerrilla warfare seemed unreal to her, and to Soni, too – she talked about it so casually, so laughingly, that Milly, hearing her, could not invest it with either seriousness or menace. Yet she wanted to: she had witnessed, as a little girl, that these matters were not play-acting and could blast lives, but what she couldn't do was draw a strong, legible line between that childhood memory and what she heard now from a friend who was still associated with days of play, of innocence and stippled sunshine under tamarind trees, of dolls made with bamboo and leaves. How did guns appear in the picture?

Then all that she had been holding in came hurtling out against her will.

'Your people cut off my brother's hand,' she said.

Soni looked puzzled; she didn't know what Milly was talking about. But when she worked it out, she was stunned, as if Milly had slapped her.

'How can that be? It cannot be,' Soni said, shaking her head.

'Yes, the Party did it. Everyone knows that.'

'But how can it be? There was no squad until four, five years ago. And your brother, that was when? Much before that. We were small then ...'

It was Milly's turn to fall silent with confusion. She could only repeat stubbornly, 'Haan, it was the Party that did it. Everyone says that.'

They walked on in silence for a long while. The setting sun had turned all the sunlit patches in the forest a glowing golden-red. Occasionally their faces encountered strands of invisible webs. Previously, this would have made Soni laugh and gently curse the spiders but that ease had vanished. Milly couldn't read the darkness that had settled on Soni's face; the light under the areas of dense canopy was fading.

Breaking the crust of uneasy silence that had settled over them, Soni said, 'Let me walk you back to the river. It's getting dark, you should go home.'

'Are you going back to your ... your place in the forest? How will you get there in the dark? How far is it?'

'I will stay in the village with you. We are taking food to the camp with us tomorrow night, so I'll need to be in the village with some comrades tonight.'

The birds were headed homewards. Milly thought she could even discern one or two early bats.

Suddenly Soni said, 'Do you live in a big house in the city? How many rooms?'

'Yes, a big house. Three rooms – two for sleeping, one for sitting. And another room for the kitchen.'

'There are separate rooms for sleeping and sitting?'

It struck Milly that besides wonder, there was something else in Soni's voice, some wistfulness, a longing for what she had never experienced and her friend had, perhaps even the slightest touch of envy. It made it easy for Milly to bridge some of the distance between them.

'And cars? There are many cars in the city? You've been in one?'

'Haan, hundreds and hundreds of cars, but I've never ridden one.'

'They pay you a lot of money? What do you do with it?' The question made Milly coy, but Soni was now saying: 'They are exploiting you. If you are providing labour and those punjipati are paying you wages, they are exploiting labour. This is one of the reasons why we have started our deerghkaleen ladai, our protracted battle. Kranti is the only way forward.'

She continued, driven by some opaque reason to narrate. Her lines of thought became jumpy and disjointed, moving erratically between lifeless political jargon and the animated account of her daily life in all its density and details. Her face had become flushed with the passion of the telling. All those big, new words that Soni brandished – burjawa, punjipati – were incomprehensible to Milly. She found herself deeply uncomfortable with this kind of talk. The long words felt so odd, so *wrong*, coming out of Soni's mouth. Ten years ago Milly had sung the hymns she had been taught in church – 'God's love is so wonderful', 'Praise Him for He comes to save us' – without understanding a single word, learning them instead by memorising and repeating the sounds and the intervals. When she had sung them to Soni, she had asked Milly, 'What does the song say? What do the words mean?' Rather than confess to ignorance, Milly had given her version of what little she had understood of Father Joseph's preaching and stories and added her own colour to them.

Soni now continued, 'You don't feel scattered, a little bit of your life here, a little bit of your life there? A broken life, in bits and pieces.'

Milly tried to change the subject. 'Aren't you afraid? All this kranti, explosives, guns, sentry posts, the police hunting for you . . . Don't you feel fear?' she asked.

The revolutionary's mask still intact on her face, Soni repeated her earlier words, 'What's to fear? We'll all die, anyway. This death is more honourable. I'll be immortal, written about in the Party's letters and papers for other comrades to read. The lives of people like us are nothing. But you can make something of *your* life, stop being nothing.'

The mosquitoes had come out in force; the girls knew they were nearing the river. Suddenly, Soni's mask slipped and she said, in a completely different tone, 'Yes, this will take my life. If I go outside the jungle, I'll be killed. I can only get out after the revolution.'

Something sounded extinguished inside her. Milly couldn't see her face in the dark.

The brief river-crossing turned them into little girls again: squealing over the possibility of falling into the water, mock-fear about not being able to discern the stepping stones in the dark. But it was only playing at being children; that time was over.

Later that night, Budhuwa said to Milly, 'Careful. They often force people to join them.' For a few moments, Milly had no idea to what he was referring. Before she could react, Budhuwa asked, 'Did she persuade you?'

'No! You must be mad to think that.'

'You shouldn't stay here, in this village, much longer. It's good that you're going away to Mumbai. Now that young people have started moving to the towns and cities for jobs, they are finding it hard to recruit guerrillas. We heard that they are holding some young boy who was visiting his family from his school hostel in Rourkela. They are holding him in the forest and teaching him about revolution and not letting him go, either back to his father's village or to the hostel. Once they get their claws into you ...'

Milly countered meekly, 'No, it was nothing like that ... We haven't seen each other for so long, she was asking me about my life, and telling me about hers.'

'Did she say anything about police informers?'

'What?'

'If you were seen chatting to her in the forests today, the police would be after you very soon and they would keep harassing you.'

'How would the police see? Soni said that they are so afraid of the Party that they dare not step out of their new buildings.'

'No, not the police, but someone from the village might have seen the two of you and informed them.'

Milly was confused. 'But ... but the villagers are on the side of the Party people, I thought. You told me so. So did Soni.'

'It's too complicated. The villagers are caught between the police and the Party. They play both. It's a risky game but they – we – have to survive too, na? If we are seen to be permanently for one side, without any change, then we'll suffer when the other side has all the power. Do you see?'

Milly felt dizzy.

'Don't think about it,' he added, as if in consolation. 'It's good that you're getting out soon. Good for you and good for us. Bad times are coming.'

Something in his voice discouraged Milly from prying. In less than a week's time she left for a new world and a new life in Mumbai.

8: *Imprisoned*

Milly's first train journey. To get to Ranchi, from where she would catch the Hatia Nagpur Special to Mumbai, there was a series of bus journeys: anything between an hour to two hours from her village to Manika, then over an hour's wait for another bus, which took three and a half hours to get to Hatia station in Ranchi. She had a send-off party of one: Budhuwa. They were joined by Sabina and the two girls. They had all set out at five in the morning to join the crowd for the unreserved general compartment early.

It seemed to Milly that uncountable numbers of people were waiting to board. She had a ticket but how was she ever going to find a place? Yet it was not this particular anxiety, or the seethe of people, that was at the forefront of her mind. It was the sight of Budhuwa trying to jostle, and bring tea, holding three hot glasses in one hand, needing to go back for more, that broke her anew. She had to hide her face, but not before Sabina had taken note of the welling eyes and the quivering mouth hastily covered with the dupatta.

'No need to be afraid,' she said. 'You're going to a better life. You'll be able to send money back home regularly, quite a lot of money.'

Budhuwa's face was intense with effort. He sweated easily now, Milly noticed. Was it because small things were more laborious for him to execute? At the same time his face had become more and more impassive, withdrawn, she felt, as if in some kind of protective measure against the contempt or pity instantly visible on the face of the world when it encountered a man with a missing limb.

The face got tighter and tighter as her departure time approached; some mechanism inside him, connected to the skin of his face, was being screwed slowly and surely. The chaos and density of people on the platform and even inside the narrow corridor of the compartment were smothering; and dangerous, she was sure – any minute now someone could be crushed, or trampled underfoot, or dragged by the more able, the stronger, and hurled away and dashed against something like a thin clay pot. But the fears were not for herself, they were for Budhuwa – how would he, with only one hand, be able to secure a firm standing point at her window, watching her as the train pulled out? Would he get pushed on to the tracks? How would he be able to withstand the wave of people and prevent himself from being swept away, pushed under the wheels?

In the end it was she who couldn't get to the window because so many of the passengers were pressed against the metal rods, saying goodbye to the people who had come to see them off, that you could hardly tell they were windows – the blocking out of any chink of outside light was total.

The train started to move with a giant judder and a high-pitched creak; an enormous sleeping beast waking up. Was Budhuwa running on the platform, trying to keep pace with her moving window in the hope of catching a glimpse of her face? Was he going to collide with someone and fall as he ran with dozens, scores of others? She was seized with such a desire to run out and throw herself on to the platform from the slowly inching-forward train that she put her hand to her mouth and bit the fleshy bit at the base on the inside as hard as she could bear, and then a little bit more. A woman sitting opposite her was unknotting a bundle which, it was revealed, contained stacks of rotis. Later, Milly thought it was just as well that she hadn't caught a glimpse of her brother's face on the platform – how would she ever have coped with the sight of that tense impassivity, that skin wet with sweat, that mouth slightly open with a mild breathlessness?

In the foetid general compartment for women, with people packed in like puffed rice in a sack, and some staking out their sliver of sleeping space on the floor – the bunks had long been taken – by stretching themselves out or spreading a bit of cloth, Milly was forced into companionship with the two other girls and with Sabina. After the first six or eight hours, it didn't feel strenuous, instead companionable, even welcome. How would she have survived this long journey, pressed on all sides by strangers, without the help of Sabina? Sabina was doughty, street-smart, a seasoned traveller – she knew at which stations the train stopped for half an hour; she knew to get out of the train and buy tea and poori-aloo and samosa; she led the girls to the ladies' toilet in the station. Without her, Milly would have been lost; or worse, if it was discovered that a young woman was travelling alone.

When she got her turn at the window, she saw, speeding past on the other side of the iron bars, a brick factory with piles of bright red-brown bricks stacked around it like unfinished walls and tall, thin chimneys spewing out blue-white plumes of smoke; scrub; endless stretches of fields and dry earth; a tin shed in the middle of immense empty land; deserted temples, some, it seemed, no bigger than a doll's house; a scarecrow, arms akimbo, its figure tilted to one side, the rags covering it flapping in the hot breeze ... there was too much place in the world and it made her afraid.

At one major station one of the girls asked, 'Where have we stopped?'

Milly looked out of the window, peered a bit and said, 'Bilaspur Junction.'

'How do you know?'

'The name of the station is written on that yellow board.'

The girl turned to her with a changed expression. 'You know how to read?'

Milly looked down and didn't answer.

The girl persisted. 'How come you're coming with us to work as a servant if you can read?'

Within minutes, the other girl knew this amazing piece of information. Milly refrained from telling them that she could read the names of the stations not only in Hindi but also in English.

Huddled on the floor at night, pressed tight between the bodies of two girls, she was lulled into a kind of hypnosis by the regular jhikki-jhikki-jhik-jhikki-jhik racket of the wheels, right under the floor. Right under her! Soon, she thought they were saying something, a mantra, unvaryingly repeated. They caught a half-line from a snatch of song inside her head and fished it out, set it to their relentless music and made it their own. Now the wheels only chanted those truncated song lyrics until she fell asleep. Or maybe it was the gentle rock-and-sway motion of the carriage that brought on sleep, for she kept waking up whenever the train halted at a station for any length of time.

There was the spontaneous camaraderie of their fellow travellers: the Bihari woman sharing her last littis with strangers; the elderly Vaishnav woman who occasionally broke into Krishna-bhajans; a middle-aged woman, on her way to visit her son in Mumbai, chattering away, spouting stories about everything and anything – a big temple, shaped like a chariot, in Puri; the crush at Gangasagar Mela on Sankranti; her little grandson's amusing mangling of words he was beginning to learn; miracles at some shrine in Gaya; people she said she knew who had been affected by consuming adulterated palm oil sold in a ration shop in Rourkela ...

The whole world was fitted by magic into the tiny confinement of the train carriage, so that when they got off at Lokmanya Tilak Terminus in Kurla, Milly could at least give a name to the sensation that swallowed her. It was drowning.

The Vachanis lived on the first floor of a high-rise apartment block on Ganpatrao Kadam Marg in Lower Parel. Milly, who had never seen large, multi-storeyed apartment blocks, not even in Jamshedpur, certainly not in this density, felt awe and fear. The building had a name: 'Sukh Niwas'. It had a cage-like machine that carried you upstairs and downstairs. Milly was to learn later the name of this machine that made the staircase unnecessary – 'lift'.

The flat was laid out in a way not dissimilar to the one in Jamshedpur. There were two bedrooms, each with a bathroom attached to it, a big room which was used as a sitting room at one end and had a dining table and four chairs to the side nearer the kitchen. The kitchen was narrow, a standard size. It doubled as Milly's bedroom at night. For her food, she had the use of two plates, both identical melamine ones, white with a green rim and green circles all over the surface, the white background of which had discoloured with time and the turmeric in the food. She had a plastic beaker for her water and an old, chipped mug for her tea. As in Jamshedpur, she had to keep her things separate from the family's, although here she was allowed to stack her dishes, after washing up, right at the end of the hanging draining rack above the sink, but, crucially, leaving a gap of anything between three to six 'slots' between their plates and hers.

Her toilet and bathroom were on the ground floor, which had no flats but served as a car park for the residents of the building. The guards sat in the pillared open space next to the entrance hallway housing the letter boxes, staircase and lift. The bathroom and toilet cubicles were at the far end of the car park, at the back of the building, away from the entrance and the guards' gathering place.

Milly learned, very early on, on her second or third day, how to avoid the guards' gaze as she went to use the public conveniences meant for the servants, drivers and security guards who worked in the building. The experience of going downstairs to use the facilities was a mixed one for her – on one hand, there was the ever-present anxiety that she would be seen by one of the guards; on the other hand, there was the undiminishing joy of using the lift to go down and come up, even if it was for the elevation of only two flights of stairs.

Jayant and Hemali Vachani appeared elderly to Milly's eyes – she learnt soon that they had two grown-up daughters and a brood of little grandchildren – although she could not have put an approximate age to them. Her division of people's ages was broadly descriptive: very young, young, a middle stage of neither young nor old, then old.

The outlines of Milly's tasks were explained to her over the course of days. Besides the usual duties of cleaning, sweeping, dusting, doing the laundry, the washing-up, it emerged that she was also expected to cook. She would be trained by Hemali Vachani to cook Sindhi food – sai bhaji, elaichi gosht, sata bhajyun, toori chanadal.

Although her salary in Mumbai was nearly five times what she got in Jamshedpur, she discovered later that she was being paid only one salary, the live-in housemaid's, when she should have been given twice that sum, since she was saving them the wages they would have had to pay a cook. There was no way she herself could bring up the matter of a double salary. She called Sabina's mobile to see if it couldn't be sorted out.

'They're giving you a place to stay and food to eat, saving you rent and food money,' Sabina said. 'Stop complaining. Who has been putting such ideas in your head? You've been here for three months, four months, and you've already started to get so greedy?'

Milly felt chastised. The Vachanis had set up a bank account for her. They had helped her to negotiate how to send, every month, most of her salary back home. How could she ask them to pay her more money? Where would she go if they took umbrage and fired her? Where would she live?

But over the four months that she had been in 'Sukh Niwas', something more worrying emerged: she wasn't allowed to leave the building. Her only forays outside the flat were to the bathroom downstairs. The stricture hadn't been announced to her from the very outset, but was rather something that she came to understand in slow degrees. It didn't strike her as odd, at first, that rather than sending her out for a small item that had been forgotten, or run out of – say, milk – they would go without milk in their tea. An entire dish at dinner would be foregone if an ingredient, one that required a small walk to a corner shop, was missing; Milly wouldn't be sent out to fetch it.

Without noticing that this was the deliberate order of things, Milly said one day, 'I can go out and get laundry soap. Just tell me where to go and what brand of soap you want.'

Hemali gave her a look and said curtly, 'No need. We'll send the driver out tomorrow morning.'

Milly, who was at once curious about and frightened of the world outside the gated compound of 'Sukh Niwas' but had not seen anything of it, except the large segment of road on which the building stood, felt an increasing impatience to venture out. She lingered over the dusting and cleaning of the windows facing the street and, when she realised that an excuse was no longer necessary, she simply stood gazing out. Two big trees framed the view; she didn't know their names. People passed by, and cars, autos, Tempos, cycles, taxis. A clutch of vendors set up their makeshift stalls on the far side – they sold snacks, cucumber, vada pao and pao bhaji, starfruit, peanuts, and Milly wanted to run out and taste all of them and feel the traffic fumes and the warm, humid outside air on her skin. The whole world was caught up in movement; only she was still and rooted to one spot. She began to identify a few people who regularly, and at more or less set hours, passed up or down the road. There was the woman with stainless-steel utensils balanced in a wide basket on her head who came every Sunday morning. She had a long, thin, unintelligible cry to announce her presence. There was the ironing man, who collected clothes from people in the apartment blocks, and carried off a huge bundle tied in a large bed sheet on the back of his bicycle. He visited the Vacanis to take in their ironing too, four times a week. There were the snack vendors, of course, but they were too far away for her to make out their faces. There was a young man who walked towards the right at five o'clock every afternoon. She knew this because he had looked up at her once and their eyes had met for the briefest of moments before she had looked away. She wouldn't have given it another thought, or even remembered it, had the same thing not happened a week or ten days later, then again on the consecutive day. Three times amounted to meaning. Every time he looked up, Milly turned her gaze away almost instantaneously, although she allowed herself – and perhaps him, too – the luxury of what could only be called waiting, waiting for him to walk past and look up when he was exactly opposite her window.

The first indication Milly had that she was strictly forbidden to step outside the two heavy iron gates of 'Sukh Niwas' was when she decided that she would go for a little walk to see what lay beyond the margins of her view from the window. The Vachanis were away and there was no one to stop her. She walked to the iron gate and started opening it – it was heavy and she first had to slide the bolt out of its socket. Before she had even begun, one of the guards came running.

'What are you doing, what are you doing?' he barked. 'Get away from the gate, you can't go out.'

Already daunted by having a man, and a stranger at that, speak to her in such an aggressive way, Milly was even more cowed by the spectacle of his companions, a loose gaggle of guards and some of the drivers who were on duty, all standing up and watching the spectacle that was unfolding. She felt naked.

She asked weakly, all prepared to flee upstairs, 'But why?'

'Your masters' – he used the words 'malik' and 'malkin' – 'have given us orders: no maidservants can leave the building.'

Disbelief silenced her. A dozen questions struggled to come out, but the weight of the words 'masters' and 'orders' were too powerful. Besides, the awareness that all these men were gulping her in with their eyes, enjoying watching her get into trouble, was even more powerful. She turned tail and walked up to the lift, feeling the air behind her back turning to something hot and crackling.

Most likely the guards were bullying her, she thought; how could it be possible that she wasn't allowed to go out for even a few minutes?

After the Vachanis returned, she asked Didi, 'The guard downstairs wouldn't allow me to go out.'

'You wanted to go out?' Hemali asked.

'Yes, just to walk and see what's outside, I haven't been out once since I came here.'

Hemali's face hardened. In a voice that could cut stone she said, 'There's no call for you to go outside. Young girls going outside on their own – it only leads to trouble. And others have to pick up the pieces afterwards. You stay where you are.'

The tone of her voice denied any possibility of a rejoinder from Milly. Besides, she was a servant, she couldn't question or argue or oppose. When she found a sliver of time away from Didi – not an easy thing to do; it took days – she called Sabina to complain, and also to ask for an explanation, a reason for the existence of this strange rule. Sabina could shed no light on the matter but she added, 'They're just being cautious. You've come from a village far away, and Mumbai is a very big city. They're afraid you'll get lost, or ... or something worse. I'm sure they'll let you go out soon.'

Milly wasn't convinced but she tried to draw hope from Sabina's words. But something tenacious and easy-growing had lodged inside her head and it let its presence be known, only occasionally at the beginning, then with such increasing frequency that it became everything.

First, she noticed the collapsible iron gates on all the windows, including the ones at the back of the flat, but this was not unusual in any city – she had seen such security in Jamshedpur, too. What was unusual perhaps was that they were kept locked all the time. She had never seen a key, or seen the gates ever opened, even by Dada or Didi. Then the business of not being sent on errands took on a different meaning. As did several other seemingly innocuous things: the fact that the front door to the flat was padlocked from the inside every night; that the kitchen windows had nets on them (although she knew well that this was to prevent birds and insects from flying in); that she was never told, or never discovered for herself, where the key to the night padlock was ...

Slowly, she became unable to think about anything else. It was not that she needed to go out – where would, could, she go, in this endless city, without knowing anyone? – but something so fundamental denied is that thing made disproportionately enormous, consuming, and she began to think of herself as a caged bird, defined by the fact of nothing except its imprisonment. The Vachanis didn't treat her badly – they didn't hit her, or deny her food and clothing, or shout at her, at least not too much or too regularly (there was, of course, the usual chiding when Milly got something wrong, accidentally broke a glass or a plate, or when Didi, in a magnification of her persistently nagging mode, found fault in everything Milly did, but these instances, while upsetting her temporarily, she had learned to accept as part of her job). But there were times when she thought that she would happily put up with crueller behaviour if this one overarching cruelty could be removed. What was a slap or two, angry shouting, compared with this?

She experienced a new feeling, at night, of the kitchen walls inching forward slowly from all four sides to crush her, lying in the middle. Their hut in the village had been tiny and eight of them had to sleep together, huddled, but she had never thought of that as small. Besides, there was always the great open outside – fields, forests, groves, river bank. The idea of space as something small or big, something that could be reduced, had never occurred to her, not even on the train, in the general compartment so dense with people that the air had sometimes felt too thick to breathe, not even in that battery-cage had the thought ever crossed her mind that 'this is too small'. Now, in a Mumbai flat bigger than any house she had ever known, she felt trapped and squeezed. She called up Sabina again to complain tearfully. And everything that Sabina had to say in response – 'You are getting things wrong, how can they lock you in? You are not telling me something; you don't know the full story yourself; they may have their reasons' – Milly felt was worse than unsupportive: Sabina was defending the Vachanis.

Things continued in this vein for a while. During one of Milly's plaintive phone calls, Sabina said with considerable irritation, 'Whinge, whinge, whinge! Do you know how good you have it out there? Thank Jesus that you weren't the ten-year-old boy working for this Marwari woman in Kolkata. Do you know what happened to him? She picked him up and threw him down the hole through which the lift goes up and down. You know what a lift is? And you know how high up she lived in the building? Eight floors. The boy was thrown down eight storeys. You think not being allowed to go out to walk and look at the people and the shops or whatever is comparable? You should be grateful for what you have – things are far worse out there.'

Milly knew then that she wasn't going to get any help from this particular quarter, but before this understanding had settled inside her head she had blurted out the words, 'What happened to the boy?'

'Oh, he survived. He went to hospital with many broken bones. The woman and her husband are rich and powerful people – the police came but nothing happened. She said he fell down because he was playing with the lift and didn't know how to work it, when he should open the door to get in. It was their word against the boy's. Who would believe an illiterate boy from nowhere over a city-woman dripping with jewels? You think anyone would believe you if you whined about not being let out?'

Milly's blood froze when she heard the story, but later she wondered about how exercised Sabina had got in the telling of it, practically screaming, as if the boy's situation had caused her great anger and pain. So why was she so unsympathetic to her, Milly, and on the side of the Vachanis? A feeling of intense loneliness swept through her – she felt she was going to be blown away by it. She realised that she could not rely on the only person she knew in this city, the only link between her new life here and the old life back in the village. She had been untethered, set free, when all she wanted was the security of being fixed to one place, the safety and comfort of not being alone.

The sense of desolation broke her. It was as if the feeling made the fact of her imprisonment final and irreversible, whereas before her last phone call with Sabina, Milly had hopes that it was a mistake, or temporary, or some simple thing she was failing to understand. Her reaction to this hopelessness spanned a whole spectrum. She cried in private a lot, and sometimes in front of Dada and Didi, unable to escape that weighed-down feeling even for the short duration when it was required of her to put on a public face. The constant crying annoyed Hemali so much that her manner towards Milly changed from one of cool and indifferent lordliness, the hauteur of a mistress towards her maidservant, to one of active, angry dislike. She shouted at her a few times, 'Stop snivelling! Someone's died or what, that you're like Water Supply Corporation all the time, eh? You think I'm the kind who yields to tears?' When this seemed to have no effect, she lost all restraint one evening and slapped Milly across the face. Milly dropped the teapot she was holding. It shattered into fragments of all sizes; the tea splashed all over the floor and caught a large corner of the rug. Hemali lashed out with her fists and hands with abandon. Shocked, and busy with cowering to avoid the blows, Milly forgot to cry.

That night, in the dark kitchen, with the whispery rustle of cockroaches emerging from their daytime hiding places, Milly felt the cold, metallic taste of fear and it froze her tears. From now on, all her thoughts and energies were concentrated on one thing only – an escape plan. But surely they must know that she, or anyone in her position, sooner or later into their stay here, would plot to run away and, consequently, had put in place all kinds of measures to prevent such a thing? Where, where could she find a crack, an opening? How could she slip out? She checked, and checked again, the solidity of the doors and windows of the flat. When no one was watching, she tried to slip an arm or a leg through the collapsible iron shutters on the windows to see how much of herself she could get through. She got stuck one day when she managed to get one leg out up to the thigh – there was no way she could fit in both, or her hip – but then couldn't pull it back in. She tore her shalwar to get the few extra millimetres or two of leverage, but her leg was held fast. A pincer movement of panic began to crush her: what if her masters walked in right now, and what if someone outside, a neighbour at a window, someone passing in the car park downstairs or, worse, one of the guards, saw her like this? She peed with fear and anxiety and felt even more ashamed; much better to yank the leg out of its socket than risk being seen like this. She pulled and stretched and twisted; the skin on her thighs broke; the pain was irrelevant, she wanted to make it far worse if it could have been the price for freedom. Her mind whirled – if only she could reach for some soap or oil, if only there was the thigh equivalent for sucking in one's stomach, if only she could summon someone reliable and trustworthy for help, if only she had a knife to slice off bits of her flesh ... and, then, suddenly, with another pull, and not a ferocious one, she was free. She toppled over and fell awkwardly on the floor, hitting her head on the corner of the bed.

Desperation gnawed away at her until she felt she was losing her mind. She woke up at two or three in the morning and looked for cracks and fissures in the corners of the kitchen she could use as the point to begin digging a hole secretly. The thought of digging would then send her looking for suitable implements. Would the biggest knife do? What about the smaller ones, with sharper points? She tried one on a small area next to the fridge where there was an indentation on the floor, close to the wall where the electrical switchboard was, and broke the blade in one clean snap. Did Didi count the number of knives she possessed? Would Milly have to pretend to break it while cutting something tomorrow? Would she be slapped for it? She looked at the huge rake of tines the collapsible window had left on her thigh and thought how pain could be ignored. Every time an action defeated her, such as digging a hole through the wall – either through the sheer impossibility of executing it, or being brought up short by the immovable barrier that was the iron gate of 'Sukh Niwas' and its guards – she inflicted some damage on herself out of frustration, knowing that the lash of pain would allow her mind to get away, if only for a moment, from battling the thing that was eating it. She bit her arms, sinking her teeth in; cut her fingers under a cold running tap; tore out clumps of her hair ... and had the idea that if she could maim herself, or catch an illness so severe that it would necessitate a visit to the hospital, she could make a run for it. For a while she would soar on the wings of this fantasy, until one question brought her down crashing: where would she go? From that one question a maze in hell emerged: could she go to the railway station and buy a ticket to return to her village? All on her own? She would first need to go to the bank to withdraw money, but her passbook was with Didi. How would she ever retrieve it? Even if she could, how would she negotiate all the bank business? How long would it take between running away from the hospital and getting herself to the railway station? And again: all this on her own? She didn't have any money with her ... She felt she was drowning; the whole world was empty and it was just herself on an endless stretch of water and she knew that it was going to swallow her.

Prodded not so much by guilt as pity, the kind that made people throw one-rupee coins to beggars from the hastily rolled-down windows of their air-conditioned cars, Hemali Vachani had not only allowed Milly to watch whatever television she desired, but had also taught her how to turn it on and operate the remote control. The television was a lifeline, especially when Dada and Didi were away and she could forget the great burden of her imprisonment for a few hours, watching the joys and sorrows of other people's lives; her own felt thin, colourless, flat.

Nearly a year passed until Milly, now resigned and fatalistic, had another idea – what if she performed her duties so badly that they had to let her go? She began subtly, then escalated in gradual steps. First, oversalting the food, burning the rice and rotis, putting salt in tea and heaped tablespoonfuls of sugar in the savoury food at lunch and dinner. Hemali complained about the first couple of instances, then scolded severely, finally resorting to hitting Milly, who seemed to have become inured to corporal punishment. This fanned the flames of Hemali's rage. She forced Milly to eat all the ruined food in one sitting, shoving her fist full of food into Milly's mouth when she could no longer ingest anything.

'I'll punish you so badly that you will be screaming for help,' Hemali shouted, 'and there won't be a soul on earth who will lift a finger to help you. Next time you think of such tricks, remember, I'll brand your face with a hot iron, you'll be marked for life. How would that feel?'

Flat 10, 'Sukh Niwas', Lower Parel, had become a circus.

Then one day, a real possibility of walking out of the building and never returning presented itself. Sabina called to tell Milly that her father had died. Before she felt the loss, she was lifted up with hope and joy – they must let her go to her village now, they must, how could they not?

'Will you call them and ask them to let me go?' she said to Sabina.

'You ask them first, see what they say.'

'She'll say no, I'm sure of that. If you speak to them, they may agree.'

'Ask first, na.'

So Milly did, reluctantly, unhopefully, and it was while uttering the words 'My father has died' that she was overthrown. The tears that welled out were simple tears, uncomplicated, pure in origin, out of an altogether different source from her tears over the last year.

Hemali grimaced and said, 'You're lying. It's a ruse you've cooked up.'

'No, I'm not lying. Ask Sabina. She called me to give the news.'

'Then the two of you are in cahoots.'

Milly fell on her knees and pleaded. Stone idols were more responsive.

For the first time in who knows how long, Milly's mind moved away from its usual obsession. She felt she was being lashed by a different kind of anguish now. Under the greasy mosquito net, a sleepless Milly thought of one of the earliest memories she had of her father: herself trying to run away, giddy with delight, as her father, pretending to be a tiger, chased her, but kept top-pling over every time he stood up, something that sent her into gales of squealing laughter. She had understood years later that the instability on his feet had not been part of his attempt to entertain her but because he was drunk. She felt something being wrung inside her and she howled noiselessly, her fist in her mouth. She would never see his crumpled face again. They were certain to have cremated him by the time Sabina had called. Milly didn't know how long they would keep his bones until they were buried under the sasandiri at the jangtopa. Had she been back home, the church people would probably have forbid-den her from going to the ceremony, but they were not rigid in enforcing their rules and were easily dealt with. She wouldn't even have the luxury of rebelling against Father Joseph because she would be stuck here.

Would she ever be able to leave 'Sukh Niwas' any time before Dada and Didi died? Would she be passed on to one of their daugh-ters after their deaths and continue imprisoned in another house until she herself became old and died? Wasn't that what happened to birds in cages? Did that shambling, drunken man, who beat his wife, and was useless at any job, did that man ever think that his daughter would be in a situation like this? Would he be as helpless at rescuing her as he had been when his son's hand was chopped off? The thought of her father's habitual feebleness rinsed her insides again with pity. She wanted to protect him but he was gone beyond all that now.

In the end, Milly wasn't allowed to go back home, not even for the jangtopa. Hemali Vachani told Sabina on the phone that, if she didn't like the current state of affairs, she was welcome to go to the police. This provoked Sabina to come over to Milly's side; no doubt, Milly reasoned, because Sabina was afraid of the damage it would do to her reputation back home, if people found out what kind of life some of the girls from the villages had entered in the big cities with her help.

Two days after she was rebuffed, Sabina called to say, 'I'm trying to find a place somewhere else in Mumbai where they could take you in.'

The conversation went aimlessly in eddies, and Milly had no energy to sustain chatter that consisted of Sabina's suggestions and ideas for escape, which Milly had already been over hundreds of times. And then, in all that well-ploughed soil, an unexpected gem – Sabina said, 'Be careful not to give them your mobile if they ask for it.'

Milly became alert. 'How come?' she asked. It was a rhetorical question: neither she nor the Vachanis had considered her phone as something that could be used as a tool of escape. She didn't know how yet, but here was something to think about. It was just as well that Sabina had taken care of topping up her pre-paid Air Tel account.

Was it quite by chance that she spotted him again or had he been walking past every day, looking up faithfully, sometimes seeing her, distracted, unhappy, not noticing him, and at other times glancing up but not spotting her at the window at the usual hour? A weak memory of distant familiarity – no, not even that, just a whisper of recognition – stirred in her mind; it was a different life, perhaps one that had still held the promise, or hope, of freedom. She did not remember. This time, however, she fell into the routine of looking out for him, waiting for the moment in the day when their eyes would lock and she would turn her face away in shyness. She began to take longer to avert her eyes, until one day she forgot to do it. He smiled; a shy, tentative smile. And one day she returned his smile.

Shortly after this he was emboldened to ask her to come down. She shook her head and moved back into the darkness of the interior. She watched him from the shadows, unseen herself, as he waited for a long time for her to re-emerge. This delicate equilibrium, of looks exchanged, followed by watching in hiding on her part and waiting on his, lasted a good while until he took his courage in his hands and mimed the urgency of her necessity to come down and talk to him. The gestures were all extemporised, so she took some time to read them correctly, but she signalled back, with a heightened version of a stricken look on her face, that she wasn't allowed to go out ever. Again, this short act of the silent drama was repeated over several days until she showed him her phone, then provided her number, one numeral at a time, with the correct number of fingers held up and displayed. He called her while she was still at the window, holding her phone, but the moment she answered, she looked out at him, staring at her and smiling, and disappeared into the inner gloom while continuing with the call.

Shyness affected both sides. Milly didn't utter a word after her first 'haan' unless she was asked a direct question.

'What's your name?' he asked. She noted that he had used the politest form of 'you' to address her.

She could barely bring herself to reply and, when she did, he had to ask her to repeat the name several times before it was audible. A long pause descended. She was clearly not going to ask his name.

'Binay,' he said. 'My name is Binay.'

She offered nothing but her silence.

'Did you hear? My name is Binay.'

This time she whispered a 'haan'.

He asked, 'Come outside? Just for a few minutes?'

Long pause.

'Will you come?' he pleaded.

Pause, then a faint, 'They don't let me go outside.'

'Can you not make up an excuse and come out? On an errand?'

Perhaps this was what Milly was waiting for, an expression of interest from the world outside, a door opening to another, bigger place, that would allow the echo-chamber in her head to become a story that could be told. That story started spilling out, but halfway through she heard the front door open. She whispered a panicked, 'They've arrived, they've arrived, don't call me', and hung up.

It took her over a week to give him the whole account. At the end of the story, he surprised her by remarking that the problem was not so much her masters as the guards: her masters went out of their home often, leaving Milly on her own, an interim when she could have done anything, including escape, but they relied on the guards to prevent any such mishap. It was the guards that they – no, he – needed to think about.

Ten days after the last instalment of the phone conversation, the doorbell rang. She opened the door and there he was, hardly the distance of two hands from her, standing with two large paper boxes in a plastic bag, his face a picture of sweaty nervousness, one of the 'Sukh Niwas' guards at his side. They had planned this meticulously – when the Vachanis would be away, how he would say to the guards that he was the delivery man from a shop, how she would corroborate when the guard accompanying him to Flat 10 rang the bell – but no amount of rehearsal ever took the dread away from the first night of the performance. As soon as Milly had confirmed that something had been ordered by her malkin, the guard went downstairs to resume his game of cards.

She kept her head down throughout, refusing to make eye-contact or speak to Binay directly, choosing instead to address the doorframe, the threshold, the white-grey-and-black tiled floor of the landing. When she had to look up, her eyes focused on the red swastika on the lintel of the door to Flat 11, behind his head, and on the tiny glass Ganesh perched on top of that, right in the centre. She had never seen it before, never having paid such attention to the front door of the opposite flat.

'Take,' he said, handing her the plastic bag.

She didn't take it, but asked, 'What's in it?'

'Food.'

'What food?'

'I work in a restaurant. It's food from there.'

A pause as she absorbed this.

'I had to have something in my hands to convince the guards that I had come to deliver,' he said, almost injured that she shouldn't accept the food, although it was only a prop in a somewhat elaborate game.

'What food?' she asked again.

'Chow mein and chilli chicken,' he said.

She didn't understand a single word; her mind was elsewhere. 'If they see the food, what am I going to say to them?' she asked. 'I'll get into trouble.'

'You can eat it now.'

She smiled, then said, 'So much?', and went back to looking anxious.

He knew it was dangerous for him to linger, and unwise of him to force the food upon her, but he wanted to eke out the moment – who knew when he would be able to come next? Above all, he wanted to hear her speak the words she had said on the phone, but face-to-face, looking into his eyes: 'You'll rescue me from this place, na?'

They moved with the stealth of stalking predators. Binay knew that making friends with the guards and depending on their connivance, or even sympathy, to smuggle Milly out was not a reasonable option. They planned on the phone, in conversations snatched hastily during the rare moments of privacy that Milly had when the Vachanis were out of their home. She had little to contribute to the plans except to convey her fears – fear of the plan failing, fear of being found out before it was executed, fear of the hundred and one things that could – would – go wrong, fear of repercussions, fear of the guards being sent after her ... The world was one giant pitfall.

The greatest of the insurmountables was the question of the police. 'What if we are found out?' Milly would chant her mantra.

'In that case we can call the police, if they force you to go back,' Binay would reassure her.

'The police won't bother to listen to people like us.'

Binay knew this was true, but he didn't want to be appear to be daunted. He said with bravado, 'The world has changed, the police can't get away with everything. This is a big city, not a village. There are crores of people here. We can make a big havoc with the people in the streets.' He didn't have a clear idea of the hue and cry that he said he was going to raise, but it sounded good and it seemed to calm her temporarily. But at night, when Milly was alone with the indefatigable choir inside her head, the questions would come out of hiding again, like the cockroaches, stealthy but unignorable. What if they sent the police to find her and bring her back after she managed to escape? They were the police, they were in the business of knowing how to find people hiding from them. Binay's words about how in the city the two of them would be like two grain-sized pieces of stone in a granary packed with rice sounded hollow at this hour. Didi could easily bribe the police. And who knew if they didn't already know of this racket? The thought of that Marwari woman in Kolkata resurfaced, as if in illustration of her fears. Milly curled up like a foetus. She didn't think she had it in her to go through with the plan. Then it struck her – what would happen to her bank passbook? Would she be able to get her hands on her money without it? Would they send the police to the bank and wait for her to show up? Even if that were not the case, the bank people could easily inform on her when she went in to take out or deposit money ... Various scenarios played out in her head until, exhausted, she thought: perhaps it was better to stay put and see it to the end of her days in this cage. Some of the possibilities that could follow, if the plan was put into action, could be far worse than what she had in this house. Why not shut up and put up with the present state of affairs? Look at Soni – what was she doing with her freedom? Running around in jungles, wielding guns, living under the sky, barely getting two proper meals a day; she was a marked woman who would have to remain in hiding for the rest of her life – that was a kind of imprisonment too, wasn't it? Especially that life? Wasn't she, Milly, better off? She thought of Soni's words, 'The lives of people like us are nothing.' Yes, her life may be nothing to others, but to her? Wasn't it something to her? Everything?

It had to be on the day the Vachanis went to the Siddhi Vinayak Temple for the big festival of Ganesh Chaturthi. Didi talked about it for days beforehand and Milly remembered that temple visits often took three to four hours; a good, clean window for her and Binay. Their plan seemed more and more absurd, unworkable, as the hour approached. She found herself thinking of ways to sabotage it, just to have the inevitable consequences happen early and put her out of her misery. What if the guards didn't let Binay in? That wouldn't be such a bad thing; to have the plan ruined at such an early stage meant that at least she would not be implicated.

No such mercy. She watched the iron gates downstairs open to let in two cars, then close again. A woman, clearly someone who worked in one of the other flats in the building, clanged on the gate and was let in. Milly's heart was a rattle in the hands of a child. A guard opened one of the two panels that comprised the gate to chat to someone – she couldn't see who it was; she felt faint. He closed the gate again. Was it Binay? Had he not been allowed in? How could that be? There seemed to be a hollow where her chest and stomach used to be. There was another short banging on the gate. A guard walked up and opened it a crack. Brief exchange. Then he lifted up the bolt that fitted into a hole on the ground and opened both doors wide. A huge wooden cupboard was carried in, held aslant by Binay and another man, both of them dwarfed and angled sideways and slightly backwards, by the effort of wielding it. Before she could assimilate this sight, there was a rapping on the front door of the flat.

A guard stood outside. He said, 'Almirah delivery. There are two men downstairs. Shall I send them up?'

'Haan,' she said, but she couldn't hear herself above the roaring of her blood.

The cupboard had to come inside the flat horizontally. The door was shut. As planned, Milly walked into the wooden box – there was room inside for at least two of her. Beyond her own weight, Milly didn't have much to make the cupboard any heavier. She had very little to take with her: two shalwar-kurta sets, her Hindi textbooks, a book of elementary English words, a toothbrush, a comb, a small hand-mirror, her mobile, her little purse, which held next to nothing, and the most important thing, her ration card. This was the card that she had to show to the bank to prove that her account was hers. This was the card that Sabina had said she must hide from Didi, and guard with her life and never, ever give up if Didi asked for it.

Binay and his friend tested the thing on which everything turned – whether the bolt could slip and the doors fling open while carrying her out. They had even come prepared for this eventuality: a lock they could attach on the outside, securing the bolt in its place. It was roomy inside, and the cupboard was made of wood, not cheap plywood boards, so she imagined it must be very heavy. The men lifted. She felt the whole world, or what little there was of it in the confined scrap of pitch-darkness, tilt around her. She gave a little scream. They set down the cupboard gently.

She heard Binay's voice, muffled, 'Everything all right?'

'Haan.'

'What?'

'Haan,' she repeated, louder.

'Listen. We'll lift the almirah and lean it forward, so that you are pressed against the door. Do you understand? Put your entire body on the door, don't resist, don't rest against the back wall. Understood?'

'Haan.' She didn't, not quite, but she wanted to get this over with as quickly as possible.

Again, that lift and cant, that brief feeling of weightlessness followed by the tiny, dark space going topsy-turvy. Then an awkward jerk brought her sharply in collision with the door. It held. They rehearsed this three more times. Milly could hear the exertions of the men, their grunts and huff-puffing, even smell their sweat. She felt like a ball in a game of catch-catch between giants. She summoned all her courage and asked meekly, 'Can I come out for a minute?'

Outside, the world was full of light – blinding – and air. Standing on the tiled floor of the living room felt so solid, so good; she had never thought she would consider any part of this flat, however fleetingly, as offering a feeling of liberation. The smell of the men's sweat was ranker now. Their foreheads were wet.

Binay said, 'We have to be quick. Is it too bad in there? Give us a glass of water and then we'll get out of this place. You're sure you aren't leaving anything important behind?'

Milly said, 'Why don't you put the almirah – with me inside it – in the lift? It'll save you having to take this down the stairs.'

Out on the landing, Milly showed them how to operate the lift. 'Make sure you close both the doors tight shut. Like this. And press this button after that, the one with the zero on it, do you see?'

They went back into the flat and Milly entered the cupboard, which Binay locked from the outside. They were ready at last.

In her dark, moving cabin, Milly heard her own pounding heart, that betraying beast, and was certain that the guards outside could hear it, too: the wooden walls of the almirah were fairly pulsating to the beats. The world outside came to her in the form of muffled sounds – traffic, perhaps the aimless conversation of the guards? – and that needle-thin line of light where the doors joined. Would she be able to see thin segments of the world if she pressed her eye to it? Here she was, in a rocking boat, like the one she had read in her Hindi book: 'The fishermen go out to sea in boats. The sea is full of waves. The waves rock the boats and the boats sway. The fishermen, too, sway in their boats.' Here she was, borne aloft in a locked box from one life to another, swayed not by waves but by the imperfect strength of those delivering her and the cumbersome nature of the delivery. She heard fragments of conversation: '... taking away the old one ...' in Binay's voice, then something she couldn't make out in another, unfamiliar voice. She held her breath. She had put her trust in one man, a man she didn't know at all, with whom she had only had a number of phone calls, she was putting her whole life in the hands of this man. The air in the cupboard was suddenly not enough. She put her nose to the hairline of light and tried to breathe in. It did not improve matters. Were they out of the building compound? She did not remember hearing the sound of the iron gates opening and closing. If they were outside, why weren't the street noises louder?

Suddenly she felt elevated higher, as if Binay and his friend had lifted the box up above their heads, their arms fully stretched vertically. It was not possible. Just as suddenly, she was lowered with a thud: the cupboard had been put down on some surface but on its side; she was in the sleeping position now. Voices, again, but speaking unintelligible words; sound of slamming vehicle doors, metal on metal, a metal door or gate being bolted. The long, thin crack of light had disappeared. She could not breathe, she was going to be choked to death. The sound of a vehicle starting up. She understood then that her almirah was in the back of a truck or Tempo and that it was moving. She let out a trial scream, but who would be able to hear her above the incarnation of noise that was Mumbai? So she screamed and screamed and pounded on the door with her fists, but in that cramped space she couldn't get enough leverage to strike with full force ... But who could hear her weak cries, dampened by the coffin enveloping her on all sides, and swallowed by the roar of life's unimpeded flow outside?

She stood on the open deck of the Tempo, clutching one of the metal bars behind the driver-and-passenger capsule. Binay sat on the floor next to her, holding on to the side. The almirah lay open, still on its side; inside, two plastic bags containing Milly's worldly possessions. She breathed in huge lungfuls of the heat and dust and traffic fumes and was silent. Her eyes were wide open to take in everything. She felt small yet infinitely alive, like a tiny baby sparrow in the middle of a huge human palm. When she spoke, it was almost to herself, in just above a whisper.

'So big? We'll get lost here.'

Binay, who couldn't hear her, who didn't even know that she had spoken, said, 'We're coming into Bandra soon.'

She sat down and held the side of the Tempo with both hands. So many cars. So many people.

Binay said, 'Look, the sea. Have you seen the sea before?'

That, the sea? Like a huge pond whose other side you couldn't see?

9: *Home*

It was Sabina who found Milly a new position in under a fortnight of her escaping from the Vachanis. Binay had to keep reassuring Milly that her former employers couldn't come after her, since no one knew who he was, where he lived, what his role in the escapade was. They married the week after she started her job on Mount Mary Road, a ten-minute walk uphill from her new home in the seaside jhopri between a luxurious hotel, Taj Land's End, and Bandra Band Stand. The job, in a seventh-floor apartment in a high-rise called 'Sea Crest', was not a live-in one: she had to turn up early, just after 6 a.m., to make breakfast for the family of four (a couple and their two children). The man left for work around seven-thirty, taking the children with him to drop off at their school on the way to his office. Milly stayed for another hour and did the dusting, cleaning, washing-up, laundry, and even ran a few errands. By eight-thirty she was done. Binay, who worked evenings in a restaurant in Pali Hill nearby, would still be asleep by the time she got back home.

She thought of her village as home, too, but she used the word gaon for it, never ghar; the jhopri in Bandra was home now. Three narrow alleys traversed the slum, each wide enough to fit one person of average height, fully stretched out, with some wiggle room at the extremities. She knew exactly because she saw, on numerous occasions, drunken men lying at full stretch, barring the way.

The homes – a room for each family – were ranged along these lanes, packed tightly and joined. The sizes of the rooms varied, as did the number of people living in them; some of the rooms housed as many as twelve members of a family. The walls were brick, most of them painted, some in eye-piercing blue or pink or green, while others were simply whitewashed. The tight, dense cluster of rooms built alongside and behind each other meant that access to a lot of homes was through the patchwork of even narrower side-alleys, down which it was impossible for two adults to walk abreast, and through back yards or even part of the living quarters of some of the dwellings. These spider-web alleys turned into overflowing drains during the monsoon.

It was a watery world in other ways, too – the western side of the slum, bordered by the sea, was built almost flush along the water's edge and separated from it by a raised-stone, compacted-mud and brick walkway, crooked and cracking in places, of a width that allowed people to walk on it only in single file. Water lapped against one side of this path permanently. On the other side, two feet from the water, were the backs of the rooms that formed the western extremity of the slum. During low tide the walkway stood about four or five feet above the surface of the sea, and at high tide about less than half that height. For the three months of monsoon, this path, which was also a boundary wall, remained submerged under water and those homes backing on to it regularly and continuously flooded. When the rains were extremely heavy, the entire slum got inundated, parts of it swallowed by the rising sea, and the inhabitants had to be evacuated by the police and the fire brigade. Milly and Binay's home was towards the eastern side, nearer the road that connected Band Stand to Land's

End, so they were spared these contingencies, although flooding caused by heavy rains turning the interior alleys and lanes into temporary waterways and overflowing drains was something they still had to contend with.

Each of the alleys had a runnel along one side – in one case, on both sides – which was the drain, a channel for general liquid filth and sometimes solids too. In the monsoon the drains brimmed over, turning the alleyways into tributaries of mud and effluent; veins of liquid the colour of milky tea, with small islands of waste, running through a close huddle of dirty, dark organs in the innards of an unknown animal. These tributaries spilled their borders and the liquid oozed into the homes, even into those that stood on stretches raised a couple of feet above the lanes, not level with them. Still, these minor annoyances brought out the innate resourcefulness of some inhabitants, much as the toasting of spices releases their aromatic essence. Someone had the bright thought of putting several sealed bags of cement – stolen from a building site – just outside the front door of his home, the idea being that the cement, like sponge, would absorb all the water and if not keep the front powder-dry, then at least prevent water from entering the room, especially through the unsealable space under the front door. The bags of cement were not enough for the volume of water that the monsoons unleashed. Absorb water they did, but the sacks got super-saturated quickly and were drowned intermittently for three months, sometimes lying submerged, at other times showing their swollen grey backs like some stranded dolphins. Three or four months after the end of the rainy season, they had hardened into concrete boulders, forming a set of disorderly giant beads in an unfinished amateur-crafted necklace discarded permanently outside the front of the home. Sand would have been better, several residents with the gift of hindsight advised; we told them so many times: get sand instead of cement, they said. No one pointed out that sand was not saturation-proof.

Toilets were communal. A set of nine cubicles – four for women, separated by the width of the slum from the five for men, serving the twelve hundred or so residents – stood on the northern edge, beyond which there was a strip of black rocks giving way to the placid sea. The women's toilets were built of brick, had rusting tin doors, which had to be tied with a piece of coir or plastic rope into a metal hoop hammered to the inside wall in order to be locked, and the most common kind of roof in this slum, not brick or concrete but an improvised thing made of beaten cane boards, bamboo, plastic and wire. Black plastic sheets on top were meant to keep the toilet waterproof. There were no windows or ventilation, save for two postcard-sized squares punched on the top of each back wall. Since there was no electricity connection in the cubicles, these holes served as the only portals for letting in light during the day, although the light was so ineffectual in the enclosed darkness that some women joked they couldn't tell if it was a stationary rat or a pile of shit that hadn't been sluiced out, the latter an all-too-common occurrence since the toilets – or the entire slum, for that matter – did not have a water connection and the small plastic mug, canister or bottle of water that most of the users carried into the toilet all went towards cleaning themselves, leaving nothing for flushing, which, in any case, was not a priority.

There was no running water in the jhopri and the residents said, not entirely unseriously, that they valued water above gold: the neighbour two doors down from Milly and Binay maintained that his son's dowry would be a home with a twenty-four-hour legal water connection. Taps, not jewellery, he said. The wish was not far-fetched. Each home had a small army of containers – cans, buckets, drums, jerrycans, canisters, ewers, empty litre- or two-litre plastic bottles – occupying a significant proportion of the indoor space; indoors because thefts of water were not uncommon. There were fixed hours when the municipal corporation turned on the water supply at designated spigots dotted through the city. The slum-dwellers had to queue at these taps with their empty containers, fill them up and carry them back home. If you didn't make it to the tap on time to join the line, you had no water for the next twenty-four hours. The queues at this spigot were long and intensely competitive and bad-tempered: this was the only tap within convenient distance of the slum. The supply was activated for such a limited time that it was vital to be at a point in the line that would ensure filling up; too far back and the connection was turned off before you got to the front and you were left to return empty-handed. As a result, the number of containers each person brought to the tap was ruthlessly monitored, with the vision of vultures, by fellow residents.

Milly had always been the person responsible for fetching water. She had done it when she was a child, back in her home village, and she did it now in Bandra, not only because it was mostly the work of women and children but also because she was free in the evenings, when the spigot was turned on, while Binay's job in the restaurant meant that he was away during those hours. She now had two jobs, both nearby, the second one from around nine in the morning to noon, which left her free for the rest of the day.

Their water came free of charge but the electricity did not, although this was not because they paid electricity bills sent by a power company. The power in the slum was illegal, siphoned off from the supply by tapping into power lines. A slumlord paid the man who did the technical work, and in return the slum residents paid the slumlord. In the case of Milly's jhopri, the man in charge of providing stolen electricity also owned a number of rooms, which he rented out. Milly and Binay paid three thousand rupees a month in rent, and an additional charge for cable television and electricity connections.

Besides a television mounted on a wooden trunk, their ten-feet-by-fourteen-feet room had a bed, the rank of water containers, a single-burner stove connected to a five-kilo LPG cylinder, and a cheap metal almirah that could be locked. Their two plates, one pot, one pan and one tawaa were kept on the floor, beside the gas stove. There was a chaupai on which Milly sat while she cooked. A rope was suspended in one corner, held in place at either end by two iron nails hammered into the walls; this was used to hang clothes. A naked light bulb was suspended from the ceiling. A laminated picture of Christ, halo behind his head radiating rays in all directions, white robe bared at the chest to show the sacred red heart, auburn locks cascading down to his shoulders, was pinned to the wall beside the television; in fact, he looked a little bit like Salman Khan. Milly had bought it from one of the vendors who sat outside St Mary's Church, selling candles in the shapes of hands, legs, arms, all looking like waxworks of amputated limbs, and other things deemed necessary for devotional purposes – prayer books, posters, pictures, matches, incense, ordinary candles, oil, holy water.

Over time, Milly and Binay acquired other domestic necessities: a table fan; a second bed, made of coir rope and wood, that was left upright, leaning against a wall, with one of its narrow sides on the floor, and only put down at night; two steel bowls; two big tins, one for rice, the other for dal. The battle in this matter was a three-way one, between space, money and need, and need almost always lost.

Milly held on to the two jobs in Bandra until late into her first pregnancy. They liked her at 'Sea Crest' and 'Baseraa' well enough to have her back when her daughter, Mallika, was three months old; better still, she was allowed to bring her child with her. She had to juggle the hours a bit, and was anxious about the baby crying and annoying her employers. In the event, the people at both places were indifferent to the occasional mewling and squalling. What nearly did for Milly were the sleepless nights, especially when the baby was teething. During this period she often went to her first job at the Chandmals in 'Sea Crest', at seven in the morning, having been awake from three or four. There were days when she knew that if she didn't keep moving – sweeping the floor, cleaning the windows, washing the heavy sheets by hand – she would fall asleep at work, and that would be not only embarrassing but perhaps reasonable grounds for being told off or even dismissed. None of these fears came to fruition. Her employers were not unkind and as long as they felt that their lives and routines were not inconvenienced by their bai's new motherhood, they were mostly helpful, the Didi at 'Sea Crest', who was a mother herself, even going so far as offering Milly advice, giving her a cot and rocking-horse and her two boys' baby clothes, which she hadn't had the heart to throw away.

In gratitude, Milly cooked Sindhi dishes as surprises for the family at 'Sea Crest'. The Chandmals were Gujarati and vegetarian; her sai bhaji, learned in Lower Parel, was a big hit. Her trick was to use the obligatory dill in the dish not as a herb, but as another vegetable, similar to the spinach that was also included. And it required hardly any cooking: she soaked chana dal overnight, chopped generous amounts of spinach and dill, a small handful of sorrel and a bunch of fenugreek leaves, diced a couple of onions, a potato, an aubergine, an okra, half an arbi. In a pressure cooker, she heated oil and sautéed the vegetables and onions for five to seven minutes, added all the greens, the drained chana dal, some slit green chillies, salt, half a teaspoon of turmeric, some ginger paste and a heaped teaspoon of coriander powder, a little bit of water, then gave it a good stir, locked the lid and counted seven to eight 'whistles'. She opened the lid when it was safe to do so, added more dill, and coarsely mashed the contents until it was a thick, jungle-green swamp.

When Mallika grew up a bit, Milly began to leave her at home with Binay. Binay earned seven thousand rupees a month in his job as a cook. He used to send fifteen hundred to his home in Lalthekar – ageing parents, three brothers, two sisters, both of them unmarried, money that disappeared the minute it arrived, like a pot of water on a parched, fissured field – but with Milly earning eight thousand rupees from her two jobs, he decided to increase the amount of money he sent to his village. His parents needed all they could get, particularly now that the expensive business of marrying the sisters was upon them and had to be seen through in the next two to three years. So Binay's entire salary was swallowed up in paying the rent and sending money back home, and Milly's money became the fund for household expenses.

But bringing up a child was an expensive business and the only solution that they could come up with was for Milly to take on another job. Binay could look for a different restaurant kitchen to work in but his salary wouldn't be much higher, nor would he have more flexibility with his hours, since any restaurant would need him for the entire duration of the evening shift. Milly did not find it easy to come by a third job: most people wanted a bai to come in the mornings and Milly was not free until just after noon. Mallika was four and Milly just pregnant with her second child when she got the cleaning job at the Sens' in Band Stand.

On her second week at the new place, she saw a vaguely familiar face leaving the Sens' flat just as she was arriving. She searched her head to pin down where she had seen the woman, but it kept eluding her until the new Didi, making conversation with Milly as she went about her duties, told her that the woman she had seen leaving was Renu, their cook. She came for an hour in the morning, then at around eleven in the morning and left around one, then again in the evening to cook dinner. She lived in the same jhopri as Milly – had she never seen her around?

Yes, of course, Milly thought: that was who she was, the woman she had noticed a few times in the queue for water.

The new Didi, Tulika Sen, was a kind, generous person; also gratuitously helpful and not circumscribed by the unspoken laws that governed the mutual taking and giving in a servant – mistress relationship. She tried to engage Milly in conversation and find out about her life back in her village, her life in the city now, about Binay and his job, about Mallika. Milly, wary from her experiences in Jamshedpur and her first job in Mumbai, gave monosyllabic replies as far as she could; she had no idea that this could be seen as discouraging or insolent. It was not Milly's intention to be cold to the new Didi, only self-protective. But Didi persisted; her warmth and interest were genuine and penetrated through the protective shell to the person beneath. Milly was surprised, because she didn't think her life could be of interest to anyone else; it wasn't to her; she only lived it because that's what one did. She started giving more expansive answers to Didi's questions but some things – Budhuwa, Soni – she felt she couldn't bring herself to speak about. She told Didi about Debdulal and Pratima and the Vachanis and, as an aside to those stories, all her desire to finish Class 12, still burning but now buried under the ash of days, was uncovered.

Tulika Sen looked after Milly. When she found out that Milly was pregnant with her second child, Mrs Sen began to give her a huge lunch every day. There was maximum democracy with food here, the greatest Milly had come across so far. In the beginning, Didi had taken portions of leftovers from the fridge and microwaved them for her around two o'clock. Over time, after Milly had learned how to work the microwave, Didi put out the bowls and Tupperware containing the food that she wanted Milly to have, asking her to help herself; and later still, she pointed them out in the fridge and let Milly do the rest. Milly ate what Didi and her husband ate – dal, rice, roti, sabzi, fish, meat. She was given everything, and not only when they were stale or about to go off.

The Sens ate well, although it was Milly's understanding that their cook, Renu, had been trained by Didi to cook the kind of food they wanted. It appeared that when their son, who lived abroad, came to visit once a year, he gave instructions every morning to Renu on the menu for lunch and dinner and, frequently, the recipes for the different dishes. One day, when Didi was away, he served Milly her meal; in slightly uneasy Hindi he explained what everything was – chana dal with coconut and raisins; chicken in white poppyseed gravy (he used the Hindi word, khus khus, and asked her hesitantly if he wasn't getting it wrong; she looked away and murmured, to the wall, that she knew what he meant); fish-fry; cauliflower with potatoes and peas ... Milly knew that the luxurious food was because his parents wanted to shower their mostly-absent son with love. She knew how affections and feelings spoke through food; and often need, too. Sometimes, when she was given something at Didi's home that she knew her daughter Mallika had never tasted, did not even know the name of, she set aside a little bit and took it away in a plastic bag to bring it to the girl back home. Binay frequently brought back food from the restaurant – chow mein, chilli chicken, fried rice, chop suey, chicken manchuri – new food, new tastes for their tongues, new words for their mouths. Milly ate with gusto, after the first few seconds of hesitation in front of the unfamiliar dissipated into nothing; hunger, or greed, was so much more powerful.

A small corner of Milly's mind was always busy calculating how much household expense was saved when Binay bought home food from his workplace.

'You have to pay for the food you bring home?' she had asked him once. 'Do they take it off your wages?'

'No, nothing like that. There are leftovers of the staples, chow mein, fried rice, almost every day. Sometimes we serve it the next day if we think it's not going to spoil, but some days we just share it out among the staff.'

Silently, she savoured this novelty of excess food, of food being given away for free. A knot deep inside her began its long, slow untwisting, but even then she felt it was never going to go away for good. She felt a sort of mingling of fear and shame and anxiety when she bagged the food given to her by Sen Didi for her children, as if she was stealing. A small question, asking Didi's permission, could easily have sorted it out, but she was too shy, too afraid, to say the words, until one day Didi came into the kitchen and caught her in the middle of spooning crab curry into a plastic bag she had taken out of the cupboard under the worktop, where all the reusable wrapping and containers were stored.

'Aren't you eating that? Don't you eat crab?' Didi asked.

Milly, her back to Didi, let the option of lying flash through her head for the briefest of moments, but the words that came out of her mouth, while she still had her back turned, were, 'No, I'm taking it for my daughter.' Then she stopped, wishing the earth would swallow her.

Didi, however, did not react the way Milly had expected her to. She said, 'Why are you using a plastic bag? All the gravy will leak ... Use one of the tiffin boxes and bring it back tomorrow.' And two days later, 'Milly, if you want to take any food home for your children, just take it. You don't need to divide your own portion and eat less.'

Milly bent her head sideways to acknowledge the permission, but did not turn round from her washing-up to face Didi. It wasn't until much later, after Milly had learned to notice and read the generosity and kindness in this family, things she never looked for or even secretly sought, that she realised what she had been given was a kind of freedom. It took her time to relax into it. Recalling her time in Jamshedpur, Milly thought that the bigger the city, the greater the penal strictures about errors and accidents, so when she broke a teapot at Sen Didi's, she confessed to it right away and asked for her wages to be cut.

Didi laughed. 'It's only a teapot, it doesn't matter,' she said. 'It didn't cost me a lot, don't worry about it.'

Tulika Sen increased Milly's salary but in slow instalments, always adding on some extra tasks or an extra quarter- or half-hour so that Milly wouldn't think it was charity. It was she who told Milly of an adult-education night-school in St Mary's Church, the church Milly attended every Sunday morning, and gently nudged her to attend; you can even take Mallika with you, she said. Shortly after her boy, Amit, was born, Milly's salary at the Sens' went up to five thousand rupees. Following Mumbai custom, she was paid a bonus – one month's salary – every Diwali, at each home she worked for. This money, amounting to twelve thousand rupees and increasing to fourteen thousand by the time Amit turned one, Milly deposited entirely in a savings account.

She had found that the current account she had had, the one in which Hemali Vachani had deposited her salary every month, had not been frozen by the bank, on the instructions of the Vachanis, or its money cleared out by them. When the people at 'Sea Crest' had paid her in cash at the end of her first month there, she had told them about her fears for that account and all that money. Milly had not imagined that it would be so easily sorted out. But Mrs Chandmal at 'Sea Crest' had asked her to bring her ration card with her and had taken her to the Bandra branch of the bank. It was here that Milly learned there was nothing called a 'passbook' any longer; everything was on a machine. They printed out a summary statement for her. She worked out later that day that her money was safe; no one but she could touch it. In a week's time she had what she had presumably been shown as a 'passbook' by Hemali Didi – a new cheque book for deposits.

Over and above her bonus and Binay's, she squirrelled away into the savings account what she could from her net monthly salaries – sometimes a thousand rupees a month, sometimes a little bit more, or less. She sent money home to Budhuwa and her mother every month without fail. After all these outgoings, there was not a great deal left for food, clothes, phone plan, Mallika's school uniform, books, stationery.

Mallika went to the local Catholic school, St Catherine of Siena: a small charitable institution, in terms of resources and achievement, but it had big grounds and took in street-children and children from poor and lower-middle-class families. This last factor, that so many children were from lower backgrounds, was both an advantage and a disadvantage, but people in Milly and Binay's position did not have a wide array of choices: it was either an extremely rudimentary state set-up, teaching only Marathi and Hindi, or no school, which was the commonest state of affairs for children in this jhopri. Who had the vision, will or fearlessness to send children to a private school, even a charitable one? Besides, children were required to bring money in, not be a drain on resources – they had to start work as early as they could, to help out their families. Milly's religion put them in a fortunate position because St Catherine's gave preferential treatment to Catholic children. The school's greatest attraction was the fact that the medium of instruction was English.

Milly's own efforts to attend night-classes for adults at St Mary's were sporadic; the working day, followed by looking after the children, devoured all her time. It was one thing to take a five- or six-year-old girl to a class and make her sit quietly for an hour, perhaps even encouraging her to do her homework, but bringing two children, one of whom was a toddler, was impossible.

As her daughter grew, Milly had to start thinking of a secondary school for Mallika, since the highest level in the current school was only up to Class 4, until the age of ten, although, in reality, the class level was no indication of the ages of the students in it – Mallika was a rare instance of a student in St Catherine's whose age and class-grade coincided. There was no way of sending her to a bigger, better school without having to pay more, much more, and that, in turn, was not a possibility without Milly taking on a fourth job. The school she had in mind was Carmel on Hill Road, a girls' school where the monthly fee would be two thousand rupees. Milly had already found out that the fee was only a rough indication of how much they would have to spend: there would be more expenditure for uniform, books and the huge initial admission cost of nearly ten thousand rupees.

When she broached the subject to Binay, he was sceptical. 'What will she do, studying, going to school? We can't afford it.'

'I can take on work at one more home.'

'But she's a girl, what's the point of educating her to such a high level? There's the boy to think of now.'

'They'll both go to school.'

'But it's beyond our means to send two children to high school,' he repeated. 'She knows how to read and write. By the time she finishes in this one, that'll be enough education.'

'No', Milly was adamant. 'She's going to go to school.'

'But look at you, you didn't go to school, you earn fourteen to fifteen thousand every month ... If you are going to take on another home, save that money for Amit's school.'

Milly had, without knowing it consciously, become resigned to the fact that she herself was never going to go up to Class 12, even through the more informal channel of night-school, and sit board exams. With the necessity of a fourth job looming, she now acknowledged it.

All the enveloping noise of the slum that they always heard but were never disturbed or bothered by – it was the very medium of their lives, like air, and who singles out air for attention? – suddenly took on a singular clarity for Milly, each outlined in its sharp auditory shape. More than one television was blaring out the theme song from the opening credits of *Balika Vadhu*, the little girl's voice clear as a bell, '*Chhoti si umar, par nai re babosa ...*' The woman next door was shrieking at her husband, drunk again, 'Churail! She's a churail! I'll blind her with my own hands, we'll see if I'm the daughter of one father or not.' Then: the sound of a crash and breaking glass, followed by sobbing. A group of boys walked past their door, trailing behind them the song playing on one of their mobiles: 'Why this kolavery kolavery di?' The song faded slowly as the boys moved further and further away. Mallika's head was bowed over her homework. Milly couldn't see her face, only the head of thick dark hair, which was shining, almost blue in its blackness, in the light from the bulb overhead. How could she see her books if her head was obstructing the light? There seemed to be an invisible wall around the girl, something to hold the world at bay.

Milly said, 'She is going to school to the very end, until she's eighteen and has taken her board exams.'

II: *An epilogue*

It's Budhuwa who calls her. This is surprising because she is the one who always phones him. Her first thought is that there is bad news. The timing is not encouraging: it's seven in the evening on a Wednesday, and she is on her way back home after picking up Mallika from school, because on Wednesdays her daughter does three hours of computer lessons offered by the school to interested students from Class 7 and higher. Milly has to pay an extra five hundred rupees a month for this. Before she can disengage her right hand from her daughter's left and hit the green button, he has rung off; maybe he meant to give her a missed call as a way of signalling to her to call back. The thought of bad news deepens. She phones him immediately.

'What?' she asks.

He plunges in straight away. 'Soni's died.'

It takes her a second or two to work out who he is talking about; the life here is a great distance from the one she has left behind.

'What? How?' she whispers when the meaning hits her.

'No one knows. The paramilitary have started to come again, lots and lots of them. It could have been them, or it could have been her own people. There are lots of stories buzzing around. Some say she had become a police informer and her people found out and killed her. Some are saying she was caught trying to escape her squad – otherwise why would her body be found just outside the village?'

'Where did they find ... it?' She has to say something; this is the only thing she can manage. Without looking in her daughter's direction, she searches for Mallika's hand with her free one and laces her fingers through hers.

'The big mango tree after the turn-off from the road.'

She cannot bring herself to ask the next question, not in Mallika's hearing, but Budhuwa seems to have guessed it.

'Bullets, not machete,' he says. Then he adds, 'I didn't see the body.'

She flinches. She doesn't want Mallika to get wind of what they're talking about but she doesn't want to let go of her, either.

Budhuwa keeps talking: 'The soldiers' clothes that she had on her, everyone's saying that it's CRPF uniform. Apparently the guerrillas bought it as a job-lot in some market somewhere.'

She wants to ask so many things but cannot in her daughter's presence. She says she'll call him later.

All the things that Soni had said to her on that walk in the forest tumble through her head. So many questions ... Before she has fully finished thinking one, her mind jumps to another. Something Soni had said suddenly appears, like a light she didn't know existed around a corner: 'Your life is in bits and pieces – a little bit here, a little bit there. One year in Dumri, another year somewhere else, then another year yet somewhere else again ...' Milly disagrees silently, vociferously. Her life is not fragmented. To her, it has unity and coherence. *She* gives it those qualities. How can movement from one place to another break you? Are you a terracotta doll, easily broken in transit? But she can no longer give Soni the answer, which has occurred to her so many years later.

V

Someone whose name he has now forgotten one of their lot maybe or a foreman from another site tells them a story one night while they are drinking their adhaa or pauwa of Toofan whichever size each can afford someone tells them you see that Taj Mahal the great Mughal emperor Shah Jahan built it for his dead wife hundreds of workers in construction like us lot thousands of us it took years and years to build and when it was done the emperor saw it was so beautiful that he did not want anyone who might want to rival this gem to copy it not even a single part so he cut off the thumb of the right hand of each of those mazdoors just imagine you're building this big hotel and at the end of it you go back home without your right thumb buss khel khatam you'll never work again and you will have to beg and your life will end with dogs eating your flesh

but before the dogs something else is eating his flesh the flesh on the inside of his chest because when the coughing comes it feels like the insides are turning into the kind of cloudy wool-like dust which emerged when he was once asked to remove yards and yards of a corrugated grey roof by breaking it up into manage-able chunks manageable for the women working on the site to carry them away on their heads except the transference of that dust inside him is the human flesh version so he imagines a kind of red foamy wool where his chest is and it was all fine it began slowly just a little cold a cough and when it grew from little he went to a dawakhana and got a red mixture in a bottle marked with white squares standing on their corners in a long strip show-ing how much he should take every day but that didn't cure it so he paid more money in a bigger dawakhana the one with angrezi medicines and got a small bottle of thick green stuff which did nothing either except perhaps send him to sleep until another mazdoor pointed out that the combination of the green medicine and Shokeen or Toofan gave a nice depth to the buzz from the alcohol all he got from it was the feeling of being a stone and a sleep like drowning impossible to rise to the surface in the morning to go wait in the line of mazdoors to be picked for a day's work and sometimes he didn't bother to get up or couldn't bring himself to become human again from stone on time and just let the day's work go laziness and ache like a vast snake that has got him in its coils and will not let go until it has squeezed out the last drop of breath from him and then he will be husk and where would he be then floating away in the breeze

but the green medicine didn't work and someone told him that it only soothed the throat and his coughs were coming from deeper down from his centre and now there is the fever a chhip-chhup bukhar as they used to say never so high as to fell you never so low as to make you feel that nothing's the matter with you it doesn't burn you up but rumbles on a bubbling drain under the surface of your skin and some lafanga mazdoor sleeping alongside him on the pavement near the big chowk so that they can be in the queue the moment they wake up instead of having to walk with a pounding head its shattering weight feeling odd sitting atop the slightly shaking weightlessness of the rest of him this lafanga says with that face of yours when you cough you're like a barking fox this isn't new at least two mistrys have laughed at him asking him if he's come out of a human and one of them refused to take him on because foxes brought bad luck to a building site he said this is a cremation ground or what that foxes should roam around in human form he said

he thought he could escape the shame of his looks by leaving his home far behind but no his face is everywhere he is but no that was not why he left not seriously although when he was a child he had often thought of leaving just because of that and when he grew up more pressing reasons pushed down that child's anger or maybe the rage became something else like a seed becomes a tree bearing fruits that contain the seed from which will grow the same tree but the original parent tree he thinks the one that produced the first seed of rage is always one thing money and lack of work to make any money and how long could he and his brother till a scrap of land the size of a raees admi's garden land that could barely provide one square meal a day throughout the year to two men their wives and children let alone produce any surplus that could be sold to get money for all the things apart from just food one needs money for and sometimes often for food too because that patch produced nothing for three months of winter and money to produce money as their father said when they were little money makes money like cats and dogs have kittens and puppies which grow up and go on to have more kittens and more puppies but you need to start some-where and his father wanted to start with a government job until the fire swallowed him the whole forest in flames and the strange sound of birds in the dead of the night over the hum and crackle of fire and he watching his twin's face aglow as if the fire was light-ing him up from the inside but he wasn't going to go down the road his father had attempted to take he wanted to leave his village because there was nothing there nothing everything was in the cit-ies in construction in building which someone said always needed people endless supply of people like feeding a fire as his father and his forest had fed a fire and he could make so much money that he would be able to send money home and save and then one day he would have enough punji to start a business and punji is what one needed if one wanted money to bear money-children and money-grandchildren like cats and dogs

and look what happened how many years in big cities two three four he has lost count how many years digging breaking rocks stone bricks digging carrying rubble and sand and stones and cement and sacks on his head on his back digging and lashing two or three ladders together with rope and tying the tall bamboos for the scaffolding verticals and horizontals in a giant criss-cross and the long training to get it right putting together the bamboo the planks the cloths and securing them to the outside of the building in a way that no one could fall or nothing could dislodge and land on another mazdoor working below how the bamboo had a gentle rocking give swaying him ever so slightly when he was on that skeleton of wood a lulling comforting movement almost one that could soothe him and make him forget almost forget the world below it made his head spin to look down better to lean forward and keep himself connected to the wall inches in front of him with his fingers and paint or scrape or hammer that almost imperceptible rocking flipping between comfort and terror the gingerly sideways movement that hint of elasticity in the bamboo like sitting on the pliable branch of a tree is this what birds feel like that temporary bit of solidity between air below and air above or do they feel like husk too and maybe when he was lucky he could put brick upon brick upon brick with the slather of wet concrete between each be indoors to whitewash a wall surface a floor make it smooth

all of this better no comparison really than days sitting on the road in a bazaar or a chowk waiting waiting to be picked sometimes you are and sometimes you aren't sometimes there is need for only so many and he is not among those needed in the end it's not despair that kills you but hope at other times when he is chosen the work can be for a day or three days or weeks then there are days when there is nothing only waiting only time and hunger in the end it's not despair that kills you but hope in the beginning he was lured in with the promise of hundred and twenty-five rupees a day but got only seventy-five and when he asked timidly he was told he could leave if he didn't like what he was getting there was always someone else to do it so he settled for seventy-five for ten hours of hauling twenty-kilo sacks of cement on his back and carrying wet concrete on his head up three four seven floors and breaking stone every day the same repeating the same actions yet every day singular the destination the fellow workers even the work changing ever so slightly while remaining the same and digging in the sun for eight ten hours when stepping out in that heat could evaporate your blood and make you a different kind of husk seventy-five rupees was something

yes something to put away in the triple-inside-pocket that he had had sewn on the inside of his one shirt on the advice of some other mazdoors who were also getting it done because money was safe nowhere someone had his shoes stolen off his feet as he was sleeping the sleep of the dead because that's the sleep you sleep after mazdoori work then the friendly embrace of Toofan and in his case the additional caress of the sickly sweet green medicine you could have your head taken off you and you wouldn't notice but what kind of cast-iron protection was it you could have your shirt torn off you or cut skilfully with a knife and you wouldn't know you would be sleeping the sleep of the dead and he keeps it in the plastic pouch that houses his ration card folded into quarters to keep it from damage from moisture rain and his own sweat the money in that bluish plastic pouch too and in the beginning when he felt the ties of home and the faces of his wife and children and brother floated up in his mind when he was still hopeful about saving for punji and sending money back home simultaneously looks laughable to him now but then he was hopeful and it's hope that kills you in the end he sent back god knows how much how long ago it was three or four times maybe thousand rupees in total nothing really a baby's piss he had to live after all how to live on seventy-five to hundred rupees a day when that income was random and uncertain the thought of saving makes him laugh like he is barking someone will call him a fox again the only thing to save is himself and how is he going to do that

when his earliest dream for himself all he wanted to be was the pampered son of a rich man who rode in cars and looked out at the world from behind a pane of glass which could be lifted up or down depending on how much of the world you wanted it could be turned on or off like a tap he would like that world to be able to turn it on or off whenever he wanted he saw a boy like that in his village they must have been the same age and the boy in the car had looked at him and his twin and a few of their school friends standing by the side of the narrow road doing nothing staring at the car watching it halted and trying to start up again to negotiate a hairpin bend up to the big new house in which the boy and his father came up for the summer months the boy had looked at them and their eyes had locked and he had said something to his father then the window had come down and the boy had stuck out his hand and given them all tangerines from a bag inside the car no words had been exchanged he and his twin and the boys had moved closer to the car and taken the tangerines then the window had gone up again as they sat on a stone peeling the fruit they both discovered that there were little cloves chhora hiding near the bottom in between the bigger ones and someone told him and his twin that they were for motherless boys they had been secretly put into the fruit by their dead mother's soul for her children for them how did he know how did that boy know that they didn't have a mother and now a father swallowed by fire the boy was not from here

he doesn't know whether he dates his obsession with that boy from that day he never saw him again but he wanted to be him to be inside a car with his father on their way to a big new house distributing tangerines to children on the roadside and the boy's face floated up too unbidden at strange times so many years later and even now even now he can picture that face the big eyes looking at him the shape of the tangerines in his hand and their dull yellow-green glow oh to be born in the next life as a boy in a car sitting beside his father

where was all that time if he got it all back and he was that age again would he be here at this point again a mazdoor on the streets or would he could he walk along a different path and end up being that boy then he smiles and thinks he cannot be the boy at the end of that path because the boy has grown up like he has but could he be what the boy is now and what was he not a mazdoor on the streets certainly but he didn't have to try his father had a car in which he rode with the rest of life outside and that was all that mattered you had to be born into the life inside

for without that you are nothing as he is nothing to the great world outside spread out below him the trees so many trees from up here they look like a colony of green animals hulking in the form of huge smudges and sometimes it looks like an interrupted green river foaming up here and there among the scatter of buildings like a toy town and the cars like toys moving in a line but more often a narrow snake of dozens of them stuck outside in a jam some waiting to let the ones ahead go into the hotel so that they can move forward to their destinations he has always noticed this sometimes still sometimes sluggishly inching snake of cars outside the big hotel and wondered if one of those cars is carrying a boy and his father to the hotel like a gigantic palace storey above storey above storey what does it look like inside what are the rooms like built by someone like him who'll never get to see what it's really like someone once said to him one hundred times the number of people in his village could fit easily into a single floor of such a building he never gets to see what it's like once it's finished with people living in there people not like him yet it is he or mazdoors like him who built it not they if he turns his head a little he knows it is going to look like a box of stone and glass some giant bird dropped on its flight and he thinks if anyone standing at one of the hundreds of windows can see him what does he look like to them can they even see him an ant on the side of a huge hill

while he can look at the air-lashed world only from the corner of his eye otherwise he feels that strange funnelling feeling that begins in his rectum and moves up how is he ever going to move along the ledge hardly wide enough for a bird to perch on to fix the bamboo and cloth rigging around the corner because it cannot be reached by any other way and then paint the outside of the window frames how is he ever going to do that moving on the pliable bamboo ribs inch by inch on his bare feet the world spread out far below and so much air between him and the world how is he ever going to do that he has heard that in buildings this high it is required by law that the mazdoors work on planks built as wide platforms outside the facade on each level and there are machines to take you up and down and you wear a helmet but where is all this he has never seen any where are the laws and who thinks of laws when the mazdoors are nothing their lives less than nothing

he is not going to look down he is not

he stands there shivering the sun is on the other side he cannot tell if it's the fever again he has to finish it no one else is going to do it and they've promised him two hundred rupees today his fingers against the wall and behind and below him air those cloths flapping what were they doing he inches sideways the bamboo sways the next his fingers can get a grip is a foot away maybe two he cannot tell his head is so close to the wall he has to reach that point is he shivering with fear he cannot think that two hundred rupees if he can do five days of this being a bird then that's a thousand he can send half of it home then that effervescing inside him again no he cannot he cannot not before he reaches that point one or two feet away but there's no stopping maybe if he lets one cough out it'll appease the rising creature inside the one who eats the inside of his chest which has become like keema he can feel it one cough he has to there's no choice he lets out one cough and his chest explodes

in one breath all of his life in one breath because everything is air everything pouring up around the rushing arrow that he cuts through the unimpeded air its short embrace he is husk of course he is at last

Acknowledgements

This book could not have been written without a five-week residency at the MacDowell Colony. To that 'haven-heaven' (Maureen McLane's words), I am profoundly grateful.

Alexander Cappelen and Bertil Tungodden arranged for a three-week stint in beautiful Bergen, where I did the final stretch of writing. I would like to thank them for their generosity and kindness.

Jean Drèze, *sine qua non.*

Devashri Mukherjee.

Poppy Hampson, Penny Hoare.

Clara Farmer, Peter Straus.

Ellen Barry, Rohini Pande.

Kartick Satyanarayan & Geeta Seshamani at Wildlife SOS India, Lis Key at International Animal Rescue.

Jill Bialosky, Meru Gokhale, Mandy Greenfield, Dominic Leggett, Vestal McIntyre, Fran Owen, Mrinal Pande, Aakar Patel, Tushita Patel, Sharmila Sen, Tarini Uppal, Edmund White, Anumeha Yadav, Mari Yamazaki.

For giving me a home-away-from-home, again: Arpita Bhattacharjee & Archishman Chakraborty, Devashri & Udayan Mukherjee, Mrinal & Arvind Pande, Matthew Rabin.

Suzanne Dean.

M. John Harrison and Sjón, for showing how it is done.

Matt Phillips, for his beautiful paintings.

Renu Jena, Mili Kerketta.

Without Matthew Rabin, this book could not have been finished. I am grateful to him for many things, but mostly for cleverly getting me to do all his modelling for the last ten years.